MW01381356

RUINS

Book One

Corpses in Armor

Complete in One Volume

G. D. Giles

First published YouWriteOn.com, England, UK 2009
First American Edition Nouveau Classic Imprints, Virginia, USA 2022

First American Edition

Library of Congress Control Number: 2022911218

ISBN 978-1958658-00-0| 978-1958658-02-4| 978-1958658-03-1 (hc)
ISBN 978-1958658-01-7| 978-1958658-04-8| 978-1958658-05-5 (pb)
ISBN 978-1958658 -06-2| 978-1958658- 07-9 (ebook)

Book cover design and logo by Cat Noir

An imprint of Nouveau Classic Imprints, LLC
Brookneal Virginia USA
nouveauclassicimprints.com

To Billy:

Wanted to be as good as you are, wanted to be as unique, and I wish you were here so I could ask you what you think. Wish you were here so I could ask 'cause yes, you were right when you said, "*All the world's a stage*". But, Billy, whatever do you do when you find out you've got stage fright?

RUINS

Memories of an Old Man

A Foreword

Excerpt from the Life and Times of
Major Evelyn Archibald Lee, R.F.
(1865-1953)

Compiled and organized by
Colonel, Sir Justin Henry Charles, Bt, R.A.F., R.A., O.B.E.,
and Jonathan Michael Palmer

March 8, 1932
A motorway north of London

Liz's quizzical and unconcerned comment, "How odd" had occurred about ten minutes into a lull in the general and unremarkable conversations of the car's occupants. Justin Charles would need more than his Black Box to confirm the object of Lady Charles's attention had been a black sedan she could have sworn had passed them only a few minutes before. In short then, the scenario Justin embraced of what happened was largely speculative even though no one was saying there wasn't another car out there on the road that cold silent day. There very well could have been.

The same as everyone was certain if something in particular had struck Liz's fancy, so would it have struck Henry's as he sat in the rear with Liz and Katy, his hand comfortably around his pipe.

As anything out of the ordinary would have caught Bob's attention as he sat in the driver's seat, the dowager Martha beside him.

The matter of fact neither Henry nor Bob were the sort to go off half-cocked supported Justin's conviction the continuing minutes of silence following Liz's remark were provocative. Even Justin's critics agreed with that. Confident the men's initial response would have taken the form of exchanging silent looks rather than unduly alarm the ladies. The only trouble with any of it was it was just theory. No rhyme, reason, or evidence to explain the apparent excessive rate of speed Bob was traveling when he went into a skid he could not pull out from, inspiring the next surviving recorded comment to be one of Martha's. A simple and chastising "Robert" moments before Bob spoke his quiet and chilling words of finality "We're lost".

Henry's intentions of shooting someone, possibly Liz out of mercy, dying with him as the town car plunged a hundred yards down a ravine, exploding before, after, or upon impact. By the time the local Constable's office arrived on the scene, there were about seven people standing around, most noticeably a rather shaken young woman of about twenty.

"Miss Maple Clarke." One of the footmen on the scene identified the visibly shaken young lady whose passport indicated she was just twenty.

"Mabel Clarke, perhaps?" the Chief Constable accepted the passport without so much a glance.

"Could be." The bobby was interested, young, though well trained, and not about to argue with his superiors. "They're both locals, sir. On their way to book passage for their honeymoon ... Heard the commotion, saw the car ..."

"And, of course, ran to see what they could do to help, which was nothing," the Chief swallowed a tablet of aspirin, dry. "Allergies."

"Wicked this time of year, sir," the bobby nodded. "You're right about that ... That's her fiancé with her ..." He called up a rather stunned looking young man identified as one John MacEnroe of the Chief's jurisdiction. His face and voice clearly Irish, the Chief never heard of or seen him before.

"McCoy," MacEnroe informed the Chief, correcting his name, and accepting his second-class citizenship without too much lip. "And it is Maple like the tree. Maple Clarke."

"Charmed." The Chief couldn't have been less interested though certain the girl's parents probably were about the sort of company she kept. "What's all this about a commotion?"

"Explosion, sir," his studious deputy assured. "Petrol ignited, is my guess. You can see the trail where they went over the edge ..."

John McCoy was frowning, of a different opinion apparently, or not quite sure either way?

"No?" the Chief waited impatiently. "Yes?"

"Yes ... Well, no, actually," McCoy acknowledged, changing his mind again immediately. "Perhaps."

The Chief would hate to be hanging waiting for this one to decide.

"What I mean is ..." McCoy attempted to clarify. "We saw the car explode, yes. But it was the first ... well, *sound,*" he debated what to call it and couldn't think of anything else. "It certainly was loud enough ..."

"Hit a tree, sir," the public's attentive servant lent a helpful hand. "Took half the front ... Sheared it right off ..."

"As it went over the edge," the Chief nodded. "Couldn't have happened on the way down."

It was a statement, not a question, catching the bobby off guard and confusing him. "Beg your pardon?"

"What's Clarke have to say?" the Chief asked, dropping another tablet of aspirin, dry.

"Oh, just something about the fellow's hand. Thinks she saw it move."

As it protruded from under the crushed hood, blackened and fairly charred to the bone? The Chief glanced over their witness perspiring in his tweeds. "MacEnroe?"

"McCoy," the gent sighed, wanting his name at least right should he end up having to take credit for something he either did, or did not do. "John McCoy. You have to understand, she has had quite a fright—"

"Could it have moved?" the Chief interrupted, looking around for the verdict from someone with a badge.

"Wouldn't think so." He was answered. "It's a sight down there. Need a stomach. Why?"

"Let's have a look." The Chief headed down the ravine, the

ground crisp and frosty as the wind, the sky gray and trees barren.

"Service issue, sir." The Copper in charge produced a pistol dangling off the end of a pencil.

"So?"

"Found it on the ground," he explained with assurance in his tone. "Bullet's in the chamber. Looks to me like it might have jammed."

The Chief glanced back up the ravine, his assistant nodding and feeling sorry for the misguided lass, pretty little piece that she was, tear-streaked and chewing on her nails. "I'm sure she is just shaken, sir ... Interesting though, gun like that on the ground."

"Call in the number plate."

"This one?" the Copper's excitement heightened, apparently believing it was the guilty who always lost, in this case, died, rather than hang about posing and passing themselves off as witnesses to the unfortunate end.

The Chief was actually a fair man under all that stuffing. He tried to be. "Both."

"Right, sir." He got on it immediately with a jump for the hillside, careful of the evidence. Like there wasn't enough of it strewn around. Bits and pieces everywhere, black as the dirt and the shell of a car with much of its human remains still trapped inside. "There's a farm not too far. That's where they rang from. I'll send one of us on..."

"Do that." The Chief moved on to join the fellows working over the scene, the smell of cooked flesh souring the air.

"Yes?" A fair-haired man of above average height and apparent breeding opened the door to a crew of Macs from CID. Their boss, an Inspector, and therefore of presumed intelligence and experience, put the fellow's age at about thirty.

Or so. The fellow looked somewhat understated excepting his height, and the Inspector couldn't help wondering briefly how much the gent might be worth, while naturally wondering who he was. Country bloke, the Inspector settled on, rather than some visiting schoolmaster or priest, and worth plenty by the quality of his herringbone tweeds.

Actually, Joseph Lee was a schoolmaster, worth quite a bit more than what he looked, understated though he might be as his tweeds. Currently on sabbatical to reconsider his calling, that was neither here nor there. On his way out and running late for the day's planned affairs, it just by chance Joe happened to be there at all. That would never happen again. A few hours from now Justin would be making a note to make sure it never happened again. Joe, like the rest of them, would find himself locked behind those doors, a veritable army of technology and men surrounding and protecting the lot of them. Civil liberties lost to peace of mind gained.

To the point Justin could ensure it, anyway. No guarantees, of course, but Justin was a gambler at heart. Knew the odds. Born and raised to know and beat them, and worked hard to do just that. Today was no different from any other, just a little closer to home than most.

That it was. "Sorry to trouble you, sir," one of the plain-coats tipped a hat and flashed an identification tag, while the others looked the obvious gent over in surprise, "but would the Major Evelyn Lee happen to be at home?"

"An accident?" Joe repeated when told, his unblemished complexion twisting slightly in his effort to understand what it was they were saying. He was a peaceful man, pleasant, exactly as he seemed, comfortable and quiet as his surroundings, misleadingly at ease.

"Quite, sir," the Inspector nodded. "Car accident. Rather a bad one, I'm afraid. Vehicle has the Major's number plate. One of those newish Bentleys. Would you be familiar? Lend it out possibly to someone?"

"Yes, actually," Joe agreed tentatively, though certainly knowing how he ought not to say anything, least of all to strangers. It was just one of those odd situations where you are not quite sure what to do. "That would be Robert Lee, the Major's son."

"Concerned it might be something like that," the Inspector apologized. "You would be again?"

"Joseph Lee," Joe answered. "Major—Major Robert Lee that is," he clarified, "is my father. Evelyn would be his. My grandfather."

"Haven't had the privilege, sir," the Inspector smiled however slightly. "Sorry it had to be today. Never easy, but that car accident of your father's would be fatal, I'm afraid."

"I'll ring the Major," Joe stepped clear of the door. "Come in, please."

"Thank you, sir." The Inspector accepted the invitation, one, or two of his cronies following him inside to stand in a foyer larger than the collection of huts the lot of them owned. Sparse though, it was, serene and empty. A heavy flight of stairs, walls and closed doors of dark oak and mahogany, a simple table with a telephone resting on it, that was all. No furniture, draperies, or hangings of any sort, let alone a manservant or mistress in sight.

"Just moving in, sir," the Inspector agreed being he did not believe he knew these folks any more than he knew the couple they had down at the station. "Let her for the coming season?"

"No," Joe said.

"Out then," the Inspector nodded in understanding of the times and troubles some of the upper class were facing, though in thinking of it, he couldn't say he even knew this house was out here, never mind any tenants, established though it was on its foundation. A rambling, and respectable country estate parked rather firmly in a hilly glade of pastures and gardens, undoubtedly green and flowering in the springtime with a small stream in the background completing the scene. Picture perfect. A little, too.

"Fairytale she is at that, sir," he supported the notion. "You'll find your buyer."

"Yes, well, neither," Joe said.

"Right," the Inspector cleared his throat, returning to the facts and reason for his call. "Before you do that though, actually?" he stepped quickly, his hand down on the telephone.

"Yes?" Joe looked at him with a fair mixture of expectation and surprise.

"Any idea, sir," the Inspector verified, "who may have been with your father? There have been no survivors, I am sorry to say."

"And this was on the coach road?" Joe considered, thinking perhaps of somewhere else? Expecting them to be in London, or town? The car was heading north, the Mick MacEnroe and his fiancée Clarke claimed. The city well behind them, Cambridge still miles off.

"North of London," the Inspector assured. "On their way here possibly?"

"My mother Kathryn." Joe stared at the telephone. "The Major's wife Martha."

"Right." The Inspector had an idea this might be more than just the usual unpleasant call.

"And Sir Henry," Joe picked up the phone.

"Beg your pardon?" the three Macs startled.

"Sir Henry Charles," Joe replied. "I would think his wife. Elizabeth is her name. Excuse me."

"Not at all," the Inspector quickly stepped out of the way. "You said Sir Henry? MP?"

"Yes." Joe rang his grandfather's mill, a family hobby for a couple or so hundred years keeping them wealthy, legitimate, and sane. "The Major, please. Fairly urgent."

"I'll be there for tea," Evelyn promised Martha faithfully as he took her ring.

"No, it's Joseph," Joe confused him. "There's been an accident. Robert. Out on the coach road."

"Robert?" Joe could hear his grandfather frown. *"On the coach road?"*

"Fairly bad one, I'm afraid."

"Yes, yes, all right," Evelyn was nodding brusquely on his end. *"Who's there? Where's the car?"*

"CID, I think," Joe glanced at the Inspector. "Where's the car?"

"Still at the scene." The point of the question eluded the Inspector. "Would that be the Major you're speaking with?"

"Still at the scene," Joe repeated to the old man. "He wants to speak with you."

"CID?" Evelyn sputtered. *"The devil why?"*

"Bob's dead," Joe apologized. "Mum. Martha. All of them. Henry and Elizabeth I gather as well."

"Yes, well, there would be six of them to be all of them." Evelyn was reaching for a chair. *"Joseph, are you listening to me? Tell that Inspector—or whomever it is you have there—there were six people in*

that car. Henry. Elizabeth. And that daughter of Liz's, Joanna."

"Joanna?" Joe stared at the Inspector who hadn't mentioned anything about a child.

"Do it," Evelyn instructed. *"And do not go anywhere near that house. Understand me? Joanna's fine, yes, of course she is. But we want her to stay that way, don't we? Bastards find out they missed one they'll go after the one they missed. Doesn't matter it's a child, doesn't matter who it is. You're to stay away from that house of Henry's. You hear me?"*

"I understand," Joe felt cold under his shirt and jacket, prickly little shocks tickling his skin.

"Good," Evelyn approved, certain Joe did understand even better than he wanted to. *"Soon as you get off this telephone with me, you're going to get Mike up there with you. I don't care what you tell him ... tell him Claudia's had a change of heart. I want Mike there, and I want you to keep him there if you have to lock him in a cupboard. Claudia should just about be on her way ..."*

"Yes, well, actually, I ..." Joe started to explain how he had been on his way to fetch Claudia in some mood or another about something.

"I'll take care of Claudia," Evelyn assured, *"and I'll take care of Justin—And, well, all right,"* he reconsidered against his will, *"put that Inspector fellow you have there on the phone."*

"Knox, sir." The fellow sounded somewhat flustered to Evelyn on his end. "Inspector Knox."

"Yes, well, Knox," Evelyn assured the bastard, flustered or not, *"I know a Knox. Though I would rather think if the two of you were related, you wouldn't be standing there in my hall. In the meantime, however, since you are apparently, you should know you're going to have a few of my boys there in a short while—not in the damn hallway, there at the car. Wherever it is."*

"On the coach road, sir," the Inspector peered at the telephone.

"Understand that," Evelyn was called the Old Man because he was old, not stupid. *"Of course the damn road's a hundred miles long, but regardless, they'll be there—you say you traced Bob through the number plate on my car? They're there now. And I would appreciate*

any assistance you can give them, any information ...

"*And then I would appreciate it,*" he fumed, "*if you would get and stay the hell out of the way. Understand? Hear any of this on the wire before I want to hear it, I'll know it came from you, and it'll be the damn mistake of your career—Care about your career?*"

"Course, sir," the Inspector stared at the telephone.

"*Yes, well, we'll see, won't we?*" Evelyn agreed. "*Off you myself if I have to, don't you think I won't. In the meantime, my son Robert had a heart. Got that? Robert had a heart. I believe you'll find he suffered an attack, lost control, and end of story. Unfortunate, but it happens.*"

"A heart attack," the Inspector repeated.

"*A heart attack,*" Evelyn assured and hung up to ring Justin, Henry's son, off in Ireland of all God forsaken places. More trouble Evelyn believed than the damn place was even worth.

"Palmer?"

"Aye, right here." Evelyn's man John appeared, Irish himself by blood and personality, though he kept the politics to himself and that was all that mattered.

"About time," Evelyn nodded. "Martha's dead. Bob. Katy. All of them. Get a crew out to Joe, and another to Teddy's for Claudia before I lose any more of them—and get someone over to that damn town house of Henry's," he insisted. "The child's not supposed to be with them, don't know if she was or not. One way to find out."

"Right," John took an unconscious step forward.

"No, I'm all right," Evelyn believed. After all, seen his first wife die, watched her. The look of pain spike across her face as that uterus of hers burst, drowning the sheets and his newborn son in blood. Now couldn't be any worse than that, just felt that way. "Not so sure about Joe, not exactly his cup of tea. But if he's a Lee ... and, well, he is a Lee and so that settles that. It's Mike I'm worried about. He takes that Italian blood of his to heart. Bit hotheaded, he is ...

"So he is ..." His fingers drummed on the table waiting for someone to pick up the damn telephone. They did. Ten minutes too long and he was finally talking to whom he wanted to talk to, someone who mattered. "Graham? This is Lee. Justin about? Need him. Yes, I need him. Not here, need him at home. Now. While you're at it, there's an Inspector Knox. Whitehall. Scotland Yard. Something like that. CID. Someone's giving out my damn home address. Take care of it. Have enough trouble for one day—yes, there's trouble. No there's nothing you can do. Nothing anyone can do, unfortunately."

"Nothing that will bring any of them back," Evelyn ruminated as he sat in a car near the spot where he lost better than half his family and two of his dearest friends, reading Joe's hastily scrawled press release of an ill-fated automobile trip on a country motorway outside London, north to Cambridge. Paid to have a teacher in the family, it did. Joe's statement was short and to the grisly point. Sir Henry Charles, honorable Member of Parliament, was dead at fifty-one. Cause of death, an automobile accident attributed to black ice, his body burned beyond recognition.

That brought a cluck of disapproval. "What the devil does that mean? We know it's Henry."

"Forensic." Justin answered, speaking the first word he had spoken in over an hour, and it was cold, sullen. Justin was angry, looked it, pipe clenched in five years growth of a woolly black beard. Scare the devil right about now with his fixed owl stare. Pupils as black as the beard and hair crowning his long thin frame. Dangerous in his air force fatigues, poised and wanting to kill, probably planning it as he stood there. Yes, he likely was. Do the deed himself that he would, too.

. "Reads like a coroner's report," Evelyn grunted, continuing to screen what would be London's account of the death of Henry Charles and his thirty-one year old wife of six months, Lady Elizabeth Edwards Charles, and Liz's nine year old daughter Joanna by her previous marriage to Sir John Edwards.

"Another bright and upcoming politician," Evelyn evaluated Edwards who had met his own, rather untimely death two years earlier in the wilds of the Australian outback. "But it happens. It happens. Doesn't mean a thing."

He forewent qualifying what he meant. Fair to presume most would assume money, position, and power precluded bad luck.

"And, of course, most, as usual, would be wrong," Evelyn eyed Justin, Henry's son by his first marriage to a young and beautiful woman by the name of Phoebe Jones dead herself fifteen or so years.

"Flu epidemic, 1918," Evelyn recalled what took Phoebe's life, Justin glancing up from trying to read the damn tea leaves, or whatever it was he was doing, standing there like a statue, cup more or less frozen in his hand. "Not that that's either here or there. Other than it happened. Yes, like Henry happened. Liz—if I'd thought fast enough I would have told them you were in that automobile, not only Joanna. Didn't think though, and I apologize. Change it, if I could, but I can't. No more than I can change Henry. Liz. Martha."

Evelyn thought about Martha Douglas Lee for a little while, also dead, burned beyond recognition in the ill-fated automobile. Age sixty-one, beloved wife of veteran RF Major Evelyn Lee alive at sixty-seven, a former Cavalry officer and founding member of the Royal Air Corps, now with close ties to the Foreign Office.

"Foreign Office," Evelyn snorted, casting Joe's account aside. "Well, I suppose they have to call it something—for that matter, me something. I'm a damn spy, is what I am. Same as my father before me, and his father before him ... Same as you," he reminded Justin, lest Justin forget his own cloak and dagger lineage. "Your father and his father before him—four centuries. The Charleses, Lees, and Drakes—doesn't mean a thing."

It hadn't at the beginning of his rumination, and twenty minutes later, it still didn't.

"Bob would agree with that," Evelyn assured Justin, knowing full well Justin believed otherwise and would proceed to the ends of the earth to prove it. "That is if Bob were alive to agree."

Which, no, Bob wasn't alive. RA Major Robert Lee, forty-eight, son of Evelyn Lee and the late Eleanor Lee likewise perished in the same automobile crash along with his lovely and beautiful wife Kathryn Allyn Lee, also forty-eight.

"Almost got us all," Evelyn reached to retrieve Joe's hard work and give it a second, fairer look.

"Didn't, but almost did. A little too close for comfort, is that what you're thinking? Could have been a bomb. That's true. Could have been the Irish, Shiites—Henry was heavily involved in the India situation. Always was and probably always would have been—"

"Irish," Justin interjected. Second word he'd spoken in over an hour, cold and lifeless as the first.

"Same as you with those damn Micks," Evelyn agreed. "What's that *box* of yours tell you? Or whatever the devil it is you call it."

"Flight recorder," Justin replied, though admittedly, the gadget had made its home in the dashboard of Evelyn's car rather than a cockpit of an airplane. But the principle and purpose were still the same: information. Speed, function, and those all-important voices. However, rather like the trouble encountered when a plane went down not too much of the recorder had survived the car crash. Justin gave up deciphering his tea, aiming for the Scotch Palmer had been thoughtful enough to pack.

"Well, it should have something to say, oughtn't it?" Evelyn ignored him other than to tell him that. "What's the sense of having one if it can't? Henry knew the damn thing was there, didn't he? Knew its purpose. Pretty damn stupid time to keep his mouth shut, wasn't it?"

"Quite."

"Quite is right," Evelyn was back to reading about the two young witnesses, neither of whom seemed to fit or figure in a world of espionage. "Same as Bob did. And neither of them said a damn word because there was nothing to say. So there you have it. Robert lost it plain and simple, for whatever reason—speed, more than likely. Car shot off that cliff like it was shot out of a cannon. From there the petrol exploded, is my guess. I don't care what those two young ones think they heard and saw. Sight and sound has a way of playing tricks, you should know that. Liz had to be thrown fifty feet."

"Fits nicely with your cannon theory," Justin agreed.

Evelyn eyed him, tempered, since the lad had just lost his father. "It's still a damn sight better than yours. Now that I've said that, there's a bit of a difference between shooting your wife so she doesn't suffer—know what it's like to have your skin burnt off your body?

"Yes, well, neither do I," he assured Justin looking at him. "Though I came close once and I can tell you it wasn't pleasant, not even the thought. That's the point. Bit of a difference between shooting your wife out of mercy and helping her out the damn door while you're rolling ass over teakettle down a damn cliff. It was an accident, my boy, an accident. Never convince you, or believe it myself, but it is what it was. Robert had that back of his, don't forget."

"And a heart," Justin reminded.

Evelyn chuckled, surprised he had one in him, for that matter any left. "Quite. And a heart. Good a reason as any. Thought fast enough I would have told them you were in the car, not only Joanna, and that would have taken care of ... well, most anyway ..." He eyed some young upstart bucking for a promotion. "What?"

"Ready to take you on to the morgue, sir."

"Bully for you," Evelyn retorted, but then this fellow hadn't lost anyone whereupon he had. He had lost his wife. His son. His daughter-in-law of almost thirty years who he loved as if she was his own blood and he was here to see where his family died.

"If that's all right with you," Evelyn slowly shifted his ponderous frame up from the seat of the car to its still towering height and reasonably secure stand despite the wooden pin he wore in place of his lower right leg. He was a large man, tall and large, fat and muscle resting on his waistband. Powerful in his younger days, strong. Still was that, too. Mean. Kill you quick as look at you, as they say. Slit your throat and cut his own damn leg off, if he had to, and so he had, because he had to, rather than die of certain gangrene. Hacked off what was left of it—snapped off, actually, since there wasn't much left of it. Wrapped up the stump and made it back to talk about it, the details softened, of course, if there were ladies around.

"If it breaks, it breaks," he assured the bloke glancing down on the handicap that had grounded one of England's first airborne sons. For fun before the Great War, for fun and business during and now after it. "About time I had a new one anyway, one with a foot. I'm single don't forget. Might want to go dancing—where's that damn shillelagh of mine?" He looked around, Justin handing it to him without comment.

"Smart boy," Evelyn approved, heaving himself forward, Justin's long limbs falling into their meandering lurch beside him. "Never lock horns with a bull. I should know, I'm a bull, the same as you are. So, what are you going to do—mind you, going to do, not want to do about those two 'witnesses'? They're either involved, or they aren't. You're right if you're thinking no one will ever find their bodies out here, because they won't. I'll back you one hundred percent whatever it is you decide to do, just make sure you know what you want to do. Blood's a little harder to wash off when it's innocent, but it's not impossible. Take it from me ..."

He looked around for Palmer, right there, flask in one hand, cup of tea in the other. "True or false? Talking about those two young ones who claim they happened by. Want their necks if they're guilty, not sure I care if they're not."

"I can understand that," John gave the tea a healthy dose or two, holding it out with a wink at the old man. "Do your soul some good."

"Might at that," Evelyn accepted the offer. "It's the Irish who drink to get the edge on, English drink to take the edge off."

"Oh? Now, who says that?" John's wink eased into a salty grin.

"I do," Evelyn downed his tea and resumed drilling his peg into the dirt. "One sniff of a cork—I've never met a Mick who wasn't philosophical or suicidal and reaching for his gun either way. Justin, in the meantime, thinks a couple of your Catholic friends may want to take credit for this."

"Well, now if that's true," John reassured, sincere about it, too, "they better make themselves scarce, and that's the God's honest truth. The lads are one thing, the ladies quite another."

"My sentiment," Evelyn profoundly agreed. "Comes with the territory. Henry and Bob both knew that."

"Did," Justin paused to light his pipe and see what he could do about burning the rest of the forest down with a careless toss of the match that lay there flickering before it died.

"So does the ego," Evelyn roused himself from watching the match to remind Justin, "and I hate to be the one to deflate yours, but you're wrong. Henry was the target, not you. That's why it was Henry. The same as if the target were me, it would have been me. Robert's too far in the background to be given the time of day—or he was." His peg bore deep as he stopped at the edge of where Martha and Bob left this life for a better one, Justin and Palmer exchanging one of those silent glances.

"How old's my damn grandson, anyway?" Evelyn changed the subject, peering down on Joe trying his hand at playing detective—or Merlin. Not quite sure which, or what Joseph thought the trees could tell him, other than they, too, had surrendered without much of a fight.

"Oh ... twenty-six? Twenty-seven?" John was handy with the family affairs, not necessarily its bible.

"Never know it." Bitter cold March wind, two university degrees, one from Cambridge, the other from the Academy, and Joe was out there cavorting around in a pair of trousers and a shirt.

Of course, the fact Justin was standing there showing off half of everything he owned from the waist up with his shirt unbuttoned and chest bare, was beside the point. Evelyn never met a Charles with the slightest sense of public decency, except for possibly Henry, and that was only because his mother insisted on the social benefits of good manners and hygiene. Lord knows Henry didn't come by it naturally, not by way of his father Scotty, Evelyn's mentor when he was once a young cadet. Oliver Barnard Scot Charles was a devil of a man. A giant in Evelyn's memory, seven feet tall, and almost as tall in life, hair and eyes black as midnight. Scotty looked like a savage, dressed like a savage, and could be savage if someone got on his wrong side, and Justin was not only his grandfather incarnate, he was beginning to look like his grandfather more and more every day.

"Where's your jacket?" Evelyn lambasted Joe hiking his way back up to them. "Catch your death out here, and I think we've had enough of that for one day, don't you?"

To Joe's credit, he had enough of his own upbringing to accept the dressing down. "Quite. Sorry. Didn't think."

Evelyn softened, of course he did. Lad had just lost both his parents, and that was a lot to take, even at twenty-seven. "Yes, well, there's not thinking and then there's not thinking ... and, well," he admitted with a glance down the ravine, "probably should apply that rule to myself. Anything down there I need to see?"

"Well ..." Joe eyed the wreckage and gave it his best. "I guess if they used just enough powder to blow a tire ... or the door ... that could explain Bob losing control ...?

"I don't know. It's just an educated guess." His supporting smile was humble and apologetic. "I don't see anything out of the ordinary, but it's not exactly my cup of tea."

"You're allowed," Evelyn assured.

"Aye and it's a good guess. Done it myself," John added his

support, offering the lad the flask. "Go on, takes the edge off."

"Right. Thanks," Joe borrowed Justin's teacup. "What do you think?" he asked him. "Can you prove it wasn't an accident?"

Yes, well, if Joe was going to be a stickler for proof, "Doubt it," Justin replied and Joe nodded, "Just an educated guess."

"That's about the size of it," Justin relit his pipe, turning his back on the ravine to ogle the roadway cleared now except for theirs and them. "Rifle, maybe. Take out one of the tires. Less chance of leaving any evidence. Toss the casing over the side. Never find it."

"Have to be a damn good shot," Joe frowned.

"Mike could do it."

"So could you."

"Probably," Justin imagined, turning his sights on Evelyn.

"Anything about this mortuary business I should know?" Evelyn beat him to it. "Realize Martha's burned, they're all burned, asking if there's anything else."

"Went through the windscreen?" Justin shrugged.

Evelyn had the picture. "Use your imagination from there. And, well, all right. I'm sure I've seen worse—in fact, I know I have." With that, he turned away but stopped, because quite frankly he could not do it. No, he could not. "Sorry, but I can't." He did not apologize, no reason to. He was the one who was going to have to forgive himself, no one else. "I've seen too much. Never gave me a turn. Never would, unless it was one of my own. I've seen Eleanor die, Teddy, Scotty, and Robert through those back surgeries of his and that was bad enough. I'd like to remember Martha the way I remember her. Not some charred hunk of ... well, mutton."

"I'll take care of it." Joe had his youth on his side to protect him and Evelyn was grateful for that.

"Thank you. Sure it's a violation of some protocol ... but, well, I've never been much for protocol and I'm not about to start now ... you?"

Justin just looked at him and Evelyn nodded again. "Understand Henry's funeral will have to be some sort of State affair, but I'd like to keep the rest of them private."

"Will," Justin agreed.

"Henry's, too, if you had your druthers. In the meantime, there's that child of Elizabeth's who has to be taken care of—"

"Joanna," Joe seemed particularly concerned, probably the schoolteacher in him.

"Quite. Joanna. Must have been found by now ..."

"Oh, yes, she's up at the house with Mike," Joe assured, "and Claudia. I've been thinking Claudia ..."

"Smart thinking." Joe did not have to explain any further. Claudia had nothing but time on her hands, anyway, even with that little Andrea of her own, and if she could be talked out of this divorce business with Michael, Liz's daughter would be all set. New mother, new father, and even a baby sister to play with. It all sounded good to Evelyn and he doubted if anyone had any better ideas, if they had any idea at all.

He knew one who didn't. "She's not about to end up in a work house," Evelyn directed that point to Justin, in this up to his neck whether he wanted to be or not. "Never live with myself if I let that happen. Realize she's no blood to anyone, and that none of us really even know her from Adam, but that's hardly the child's fault. We'll help you all we can you have my word on that. But your father married that little girl's mother. She's your sister. Stepsister, I'll grant you, she's still your moral responsibility, and be prepared or not, my boy, considering that child's age, I believe you've just had yourself a daughter."

With that, he did turn away, aiming himself for the car before Justin fell over the precipice to his own death, never mind anyone else. Ridiculous though, when you come to think of it, after all, spies, though they might be, instead of business men, bankers, or thieves, that had nothing do with sex or marriage or propagating the ranks by virtue of marriage or otherwise, the same as everyone else in the damn world. Evelyn should know. He had walked that path himself a few times; twice once, he would wink when asked, to the same damn woman. The same as every Lee, Drake, and Charles had for the last four centuries. Married, that is. Respectably and legitimately contributing to their family trees. Granted there weren't many of them, but that had more to do with the nature of their business and its limited life expectancy rather than it did with some physical or psychological failing.

"That is except for Justin," Evelyn confided to Palmer.

"Aye, you've got yourself a hard sell," John had his own ideas about that one.

"Yes, well, something short of Nancy boy, one would hope," Evelyn snorted. "Justin's no more one of them, than I am, any more than he's some sort of monk. He's self-centered, is what he is, a little too. He's got Scotty's arrogance, if you want to be kind. A snob, if you don't. And don't think they don't know it when he looks down on them because they do."

John supposed they did. It did not matter. John wasn't thinking anything about Justin other than him suddenly having a tot on his hands. It would never happen. Michael did not have a monopoly on shying away from that sort of responsibility.

"Think it may have been better if you stopped with reminding our boy Justin he had a sister," John proposed wisely. "Never met a fellow who ran at the idea of his mother having a child. Met plenty who'd run at the idea of someone giving them one."

"As well as plenty who'd drop him in his damn tracks unless he assumed his responsibility," was Evelyn's answer to that social problem.

"Oh, no, now you can't do that," John dissuaded him from any hasty action. "Not but, what? Twenty-five years old himself? He'll come around. Just not time yet. What's he going to do with a wife and family at his age? Nothing but drive himself and her crazy."

"So he's a man's man," Evelyn stopped to sputter about what had to be one of the most ridiculous things. "What the devil does that mean? Fear of women? Never heard of such a thing. Can someone explain it to me?"

If someone could it wasn't John.

"Didn't think so," Evelyn snorted again. "No one can. Just one of those things. Like fear of needles, or something. Yes, that's what it is, like fear of needles. Lord help me—and that child, while he's at it," he clucked sadly. "Yes, Lord help that little girl. Doubt if she woke up this morning expecting to lose her family, never mind me."

"Well, now, that other idea of yours," John could help all he could with that. "The one about Michael and my darling lady Claudia taking her in as one of their own?" he reminded. "Can't do much better than that. Like you said, they're already married, a child of their own. And Michael's not been in any hurry to leave since Henry's wedding, not that I can see ..."

"No, that's true," Evelyn considered, "that's true."

"Is," John promised, however tactfully, since Michael's sudden interest in staying around no doubt could be traced to the unexpected sight and scent of the lovely Elizabeth Charles rather than any renewed interest in his own wife. John wondered briefly if anyone had bothered to check Claudia's whereabouts at the time of the deed before settling on blaming the local Mick. Be a rather spicy twist to the tragic state of affairs if it were true. It wasn't, he was sure, and he dismissed the thought of a woman's revenge to focus on the here and now. "Little of the right sort of encouragement and I'm inclined to agree with you. Don't believe anyone's going to have to be concerned about a divorce between those two any time soon."

"That, and Claudia's Roman," Evelyn agreed. "Yes, she is. Converted to marry Mike. First Roman in the family to my knowledge—certainly the first Yank. Surprised Teddy didn't turn over in his grave, yes I am surprised that did not happen. If that didn't beat all."

"Talk to me about it when one of you brings home a Mick," John got the door, helping the old fellow load himself back inside as comfortably as possible. "That's what I want to be there to see."

"Oh, well, now, that will never happen," Evelyn was close to laughing to the point he had tears in his eyes. "Never happen. Every damn ancestor there ever was would be in an uproar. The closest any of us ever got to crossing that line was that smidgen of Scot Scotty had in him. Not enough so that it counted—it was on his mother's side in the first place. Just enough to make him a contrary son-of-a-bitch. I should know. I'm a contrary bastard myself. Word to the wise, word to the wise, don't let my jovial nature fool you. I am an evil old man ...

"Yes, I am an evil old man," Evelyn patted his shillelagh with a shake of his head. "Same as my father before me, and my son aft, and one of these days I'm going to have to figure out how the devil I ended up with a schoolteacher for a grandson. Love him dearly, don't get me wrong, I just have no idea where he came from ... must be

from his mother's side. Yes, it must. Devil knows it's not from mine."
"Was Henry the target?" Joe watched the old man hulk away.

"Doubt it," Justin highly doubted it, also doubting if Joe really wanted to know the reason why he thought that.

"You're right," Joe cast a short, sunny smile around the gloomy hillside, "I don't. Sometimes I almost wish I did, but then I'm glad I don't—no disrespect intended, old chap," he cast his smile briefly over Justin. "You might be a bit barmy, but who isn't? And we'd be lost without you, just the same."

"Yes, well ..." In Justin's opinion, Mike was the one who was barmy, but he supposed Joe had his point. "At least my sister will have a good education."

Joe had to laugh a little at that. "The best. Take's care of my needing to find a new position as well, fancy that."

"Yes, well ..." Justin didn't have much to say about that.

"No," Joe didn't expect he would and let it drop there. "Well, you have my word, the old man's, too. As far as Claudia ..."

"Claudia can do what she's damn well told to do," Justin fell into his gangly lurch for the car. "That goes double for Mike. Stuff and nonsense, the two of them; Evelyn's right. Not to say a workhouse probably wouldn't be the fairer choice, because it probably would be. Were she a few years younger, it definitely would be. She's not though and so, quite, Claudia and Mike are it, like it or lump it, or there'll be two more bodies out here no one will ever find."

"Cold, Charles, cold," Joe paused in his own easygoing gait, a touch surprised by the venom. He looked up to Justin, fair to say. Not meaning in the sense of a pun considering Justin's rather extraordinary height, but looked up to the man himself. Though Joe was the elder of the two, Justin was the sage, old as Evelyn in his own way, at not but twenty-five. "She's a Drake, is all I was going to say, Teddy's daughter. Evelyn's cohort in crime ..."

The light dimmed briefly in Joe's eyes as he thought of the freakish way Teddy had died. A hunting accident, weekend outing. There was more to that story Joe was sure, the same as there was more to this one, though he doubted if one would find the answer to this one in the family stables.

"Your point, Lee?" Justin requested.

"Right," Joe roused himself. "Just Claudia, that's all. Fairly confident she'll go along without the need for your thumbscrews, or whatever it is you use. She knows enough to accept what she doesn't understand. The same as me." He looked around again, lost in thought for another moment or two. "Sorry. It's just me. I shouldn't even be here. But I couldn't just sit there. Not the sort of thing to just sit there."

"Yes, well, does that include a dead child quite alive and having free run of the parlor?"

"Sorry?" Joe looked at him.

"Claudia," Justin lit his pipe. "Somewhat less confident in Claudia than you are ... somewhat less confident in her than I am in Mike," he admitted. "Bit of a hag when she wants to be."

Joe smiled, "If you mean as far as the idea of a child having free run of Claudia's parlor. You're right. It will never happen."

"Yes, well, good," Justin said, because she certainly wouldn't have the run of his, and he didn't have the time or patience to train her.

"Oh, quite," Joe's gasp was contrived as Justin dug into the back seat for a jacket that out of spite turned out to be his. "That's what's really getting to you. With Henry gone, you have responsibilities. A house. A home. Furniture—"

Joe had the RAF eagle whammed into his chest.

"Chicken?" Justin drawled, as Joe looked the jacket over.

"About frostbitten," Joe admitted, and therefore would survive. He slipped the jacket on, the leather cold and well worn. "Wouldn't happen to have a cigarette hidden away in the glove box—or a pocket somewhere—that and a flask—"

"Yes, well ..." A flask and a match Justin had. The cigarettes he had to pinch from a subordinate strolling past.

"Thanks," Joe exhaled, unmindful of the fact they could have been to Killarney and back by now. "It's this mortuary business. You said Martha went through the windscreen?"

"Decapitated," Justin yanked the throttle and sat there revving the engine.

"Right," Joe's voice was tight. "No, the Old Man wouldn't have been able to take that. Still, Liz had to bear the brunt of it, didn't she, dashed on the rocks like that?"

"Did," Justin lied.

"Good," Joe exhaled that time in relief. "Sorry, but its Katy. Bob's one thing, but Katy? I realize she's my mother, not my wife ..."

"Yes, well ..." Justin realized Henry was his father, not his wife. Liz was one thing to him, Henry quite another. Not saying he did not like Liz, because he hardly knew her well enough to like or dislike her. Their relationship, had one evolved, would likely have been more of a respectful relative rather than some stepmother had Henry's and her marriage endured, which it had not. Unfortunately not because Henry had decided to come to his fifty-one year old senses.

"Do you remember Phoebe very much at all?" Joe was just curious, though knowing Justin had to remember his mother. Justin was young when she died, desperately sick himself, but certainly at eleven old enough to remember her quite vividly. And so did Justin remember, Joe supposed he was wondering, not her, but what it was like to have her, and then lose her so suddenly? Justin so difficult to know sometimes, what touched him and what did not.

"I remember my cot." Justin threw the car into gear and tore out of there like a bat out of hell, wrenched the steering, spun her around and hit the curve at forty, taking it clean.

"Brilliant!" Joe gasped when they came to a halt. "What's her top speed?"

"About eighty," Justin lit his pipe.

"The devil it is."

"The devil it's not," Justin took off again without any further shenanigans. "Mercedes invented the damn SS supercharge in '26."

"That's true," Joe admitted. "Rival Royce, if you can believe that."

Justin could. He nodded ruefully. "De Valera isn't the only rotten fish in the sea, there's Mosley and his gang and that bolshie Hitler."

"Of course," Joe sighed. "Mosley. Forgot about him. So what's next? If it's not the IRA responsible for this, you and the Old Man set your sights on the Blackshirts? Honestly, Charles, what a wretched life we lead, really. Thought the need for any of this would be over by now ... for that matter," he fingered the jacket, "thought you fellows were about disbanded."

Yes, well, if Joe meant grounded, he was right. Disbanded, was another thing. Not quite. But then flying wasn't all there was to it. Justin should know. Flying not exactly his cup of tea. Not because he did not have the skill, because he did. But more because he was more valuable on the ground—that and at six-foot five and a half, he could just about fit inside a damn cockpit, at least the modern ones, at least not comfortably. "It's De Valera," Justin assured.

Joe nodded. "And it's not over. Well, one step ahead of them is the best any of us could hope for, I guess. Two more bodies, you said, I mean when we were talking about Claudia and Mike. Two more bodies out here, you said as if there were already two. I take it, it's less important if those two witnesses are saints or sinners than simply not worth the risk."

"Quite," Justin said.

"War is hell," Joe sighed.

For some, Justin supposed. Personally, right about now it had the potential of being quite satisfying. "They're not going to get away with it, Lee." In the meantime, he did top it out at eighty along the road to London, just to prove it could be done, despite the damn black ice.

"That's an odd couple." Evelyn noted as Justin tore out of there like his tail was on fire after proving his point to himself. "Yes, that's an odd couple—trio, not to exclude Mike. But then, well, so were Teddy, Scotty, and I. That we were. That we were."

"Been a while," John agreed.

"Thirty years," Evelyn nodded. Thirty years since any of them died in the line of duty. That would be Scotty in the Boer War. Teddy's demise, quite, was a family affair. "Overdue, is that what you're saying?"

"No," John said. "Just that it's been a while."

So it had been. It was eight years later, almost nine, before the black wreath hung on the door again. That time for RAF pilot Joseph Lee who died in service to his country on or about the 20th of December 1940, age thirty-five. But then it came with the territory, yes, it did, whether it was the Irish, the Shiite, Dutch, and so forth and so on.

“So forth and so on.” Evelyn Lee puffed on his pipe, putting aside the faded photographs of Teddy, Scotty, Robert, all of them. Joe now added to the chronicles. His young widow left behind. Joanna.

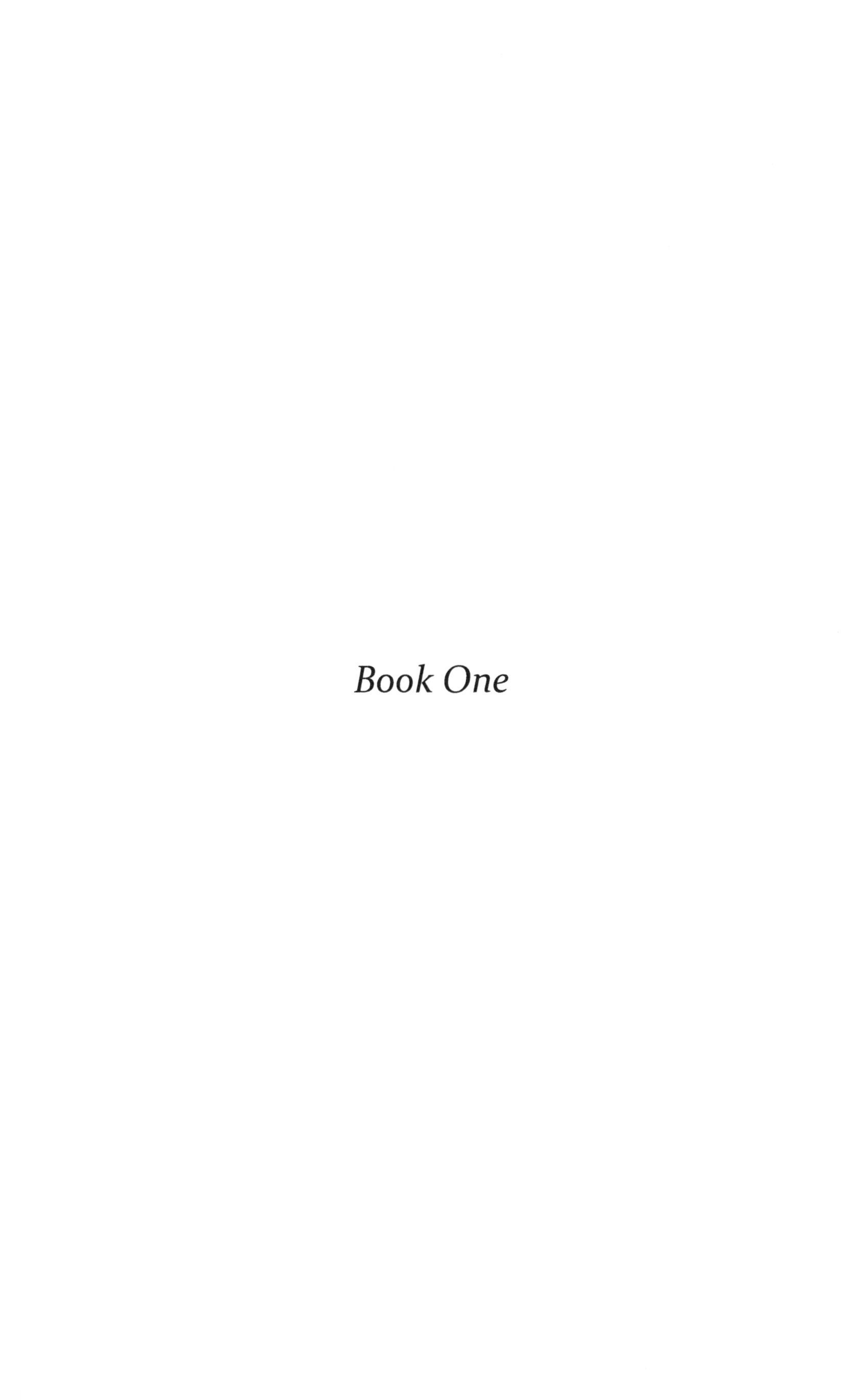

Book One

Prologue

The Fezzan,
Territorio Militare, Libya
Sunday, March 8, 1942

Thirty-two year old Hauptmann Dieter Reineke raised his field glasses and scanned the surrounding sand dunes. It was so hot. Emaciated stalks of a benign species of plant life made no attempt to hide their shame beneath the scrutinizing eyes of his powerful lens. They would not want to. Gifts from nature, their mockery was intentional, and they grew as thorns along the sands that tried to strangle them. He believed them to be spurge flax, one of this desert's annuals. If he was in error, it was irrelevant because he wanted from those withered yellow shrubs an answer, that was all, an answer—

Answer me!

But the plants were sleeping, and the sand just stared, stubbornly refusing to disclose its secrets; and it was so very hot.

His glasses lowered. Tiny droplets of moisture momentarily blurring his piercing glare were blinked away and slid along the mask of stone that held the palest of blue eyes—and those eyes could not, would never accept the emptiness as a confirmation the silence was all there was to see ....

Answer me!

Narrower still, his eyes repeated their demand; lips parched and split tightening against his face frozen and silent. No throes of emotion evident, he lay in peace with only a vague reference to inner turmoil—

And it was a coverlet typical of births native to the month of September! Except he had been born in August. Such a hot day in August. So hot. So yellow. Rather like today ...

Answer me!

Yellow shrubs in barren pockets of dead yellow seas, it was not August. On fire, the sun flamed yellow in the sky, though it was not August. But it could have been. It could have been. Such a hot day in August, such a hot day today, it could have been the 23rd of August 1909—

And it WAS August. He could feel it in his chest. He could see it in the heat rising from the blistered sands around him, and he could hear the fossils moan, August. August ...

ANSWER ME!

That silent scream was a howl, damning the quiet for he knew it lied. The unruffled sands claiming there was nothing to see for miles, lied, and the fire burning in the blue depths of his eyes brightened, becoming white. For as of late, as of the past few months, it had become increasingly difficult to contain the volatile thoughts beginning to metastasize to the muscles straining against flesh, cords that tightened and twisted in his throat, and sweating palms clenching into fists—

"ANSWER ME!" Reineke broke the unnerving silence. His scream so loud, demonic in its fierceness, it echoed—

(And two hundred meters in the distance, Oberleutnant Heinrich Thiele stood up in the rear seat of the wagen.)

But the desert took notice of the cry simply for pity's sake. The drowsy vegetation repeated its answer the silence was all to see today, *Madman.* That was all.

"Liar!" Reineke challenged the sand, and turned around to walk away, but it must have been the fossils, for the shiver started at the back of his neck, and slid along his spine. Its terrifying fingers spreading out across his back, and he heard them moan, *August.*

August.

And though it was March, it could have been August, and he had been born in August.

Born in the Rhineland, the Feast of Vulcanous, heir to its river, castles, and trees. *Living link*! to the fables and lore, Frederick the First greatest of all, surviving soul of his Prince dead some two centuries and immortal in its fetus Dieter Reineke. A reticent child, reclusive man, preferring the company of servants to friends ...

At fourteen, Reineke deposed his father. The fierceness of his hatred erupting during a fencing lesson and his father's foolish attempt to cut his son's cheek marking Reineke as the man he claimed Reineke would never be. Reineke was a man, his father's throat held at the mercy of his sword until the father bowed his head to the son who would not bend, retreating defeated and disgraced.

And later, after having humiliating his father, Reineke watched his reflection in a mirror, repeating his arrogant challenge a second time, "I am a man."

A flawless face of near-perfect symmetry, the flesh hugging his marvelous cheekbones needed no scars to entice the moist, approving glances of anyone feminine. For some time now, women twice his age had warmed themselves on the smoothness of his skin. And in the mirror, his smile changed to a rare grin, pleased in the knowledge of how sex also did not necessarily make anyone a man. "Mirror, mirror," his head cocked teasing, watching himself in the glass, waiting for his grandfather's call, the beloved giant passing nine years later, shrunken and old. His title and sacred Prince's Cross passed to Dieter Reineke, his grandson, not the beast sired by his loins.

At twenty-three Baron Dieter Reineke walked from the cemetery, master of his fate and empire. The allies long gone from his homeland, the French, the Rhineland Palatinate free and secure, it was winter, late fall, 1932, and more and more people were talking. He ate dinner at home alone that night. Sometime later, the younger of his two sisters, Alexia, decided to join him, explaining her interruption by confessing to a bad dream.

"Why a bad one?" Reineke inquired with a smile. She was a glorious child, Alexia, pure and gentle, so unlike the hated Helena who stole his face and longed to steal his throne.

"I don't know," she shrugged her shoulders, and if she did not know, he did.

"It is your birthday a few hours from now," he mentioned, and she looked up at him slyly from under her lashes.

"Is it too terribly callous of me?" she asked, what with her grandfather only just buried, she should be mourning, not thinking of jewels and pearls and cosmetic creams.

"No more than it is of me," Reineke agreed. "Only if either of us were to forget—which is inconceivable!" he set her down on the sofa next to him with a laugh.

"So what did you get me?" she asked as they studied the Baron's cognac together, admitting they would both rather drink poison, even the smell was just so vile.

"A house," Reineke shrugged.

"A house?" Alexia blinked. "I'm only nine."

"Ten, in a few hours," he reminded, though still not quite ready to marry her off just yet. "A house in Switzerland. A chalet. You like to ski, right?"

"I can ski here," she assured, "with you."

That was true. Though not as dangerously as either of them liked, not as extreme.

"What about the river?" she asked, viewing him suspiciously. "You made me promise we would never leave the river."

"It is right there," he assured. "Right outside the windows. Just like this."

"The same one?" she remained skeptical.

"The only one," he laughed again. "Indeed, the Rhine. So, what do you think? Is it acceptable or do I have to drive myself crazy trying to think of something else?"

"I'm considering it," Alexia waved away the smoke from his cigarette so she could rest her head comfortably and toy with his cross. "Why isn't there a princess's cross? I think there should be a princess's cross."

"No." It was the only thing he ever refused her. Death from an attempted suicide in 1939 did not count, Alexia mercifully surviving her ordeal, and he went on with his army to France.

"But I am the Baroness," she said.

"This is very true," he agreed, "and I am the Baron."

"I do not see where there's a difference," she shook her golden head, its color so much darker than his, the strands long and curly. "Is it big, my new house?"

"Very big," he promised.

"High on a hill?"

"Very high," he assured, "extremely; on a cliff. So, is it acceptable, or am I going to have to find some other Baroness to give it to for her birthday?"

"It's acceptable," she agreed, only teasing it might not be. She settled down, happy enough to fall asleep. "What did the Baron mean when he talked of unification?"

Reunification and it meant different things to different people, many of them afraid. "A newspaper story," Reineke sipped his wine. "A silly one. The Rhine is German and Germany. No one can ever change that. Not any man or any map."

"Do you think they will come back?"

"The outlanders? No." The Siegfried line of defense built four years from now would take care of any chance of that.

"And that there are no Nordics on the Rhine?" she smiled up at him.

Reineke had no idea. He was Nordic, the chancellor and champion of Aryan superiority without having to be taught or told. His family on the Rhine a thousand years, his manor built as a summer home for the prince in 1604 and never fallen. Alexia retired to Switzerland in 1936, the chalet her fortress against the mandatory conscription of beautiful young girls. He continued not to care about Helena, whom she married, or where she went. Death from a glass of cyanide waiting should she ever decide to return and avenge their father. She never did, afraid beneath her cold arrogance, possibly more afraid of Alexia than she was of him since he was not there.

He had no idea why he joined their party. It was a business decision, of course, little else. One he made to secure his family legacy, fortune, and home. He was an aristocrat, Lutheran, by 1936 few, if any of them left, their lives and lands gone, confiscated and consumed as the Nazi peaked in popularity and strength. A dethroned and treacherous father hovering in the background alongside his comrades with their rantings of the rights and ideals of the common life he knew nothing about. The son's existence, a flagrant example of everything so right and so wrong ...

And Reineke would be lying to say he did not believe in a truth beneath the rhetoric, the state of Germany critical, punished for a war they did not start and failed to win.

Lying, if he said he did not believe in a divine right, ultimate power, and new Reich, stronger than the Second, enduring as the First.

Lying to suggest if after three years of service in Germany's new uniformed army he understood or cared anything about politics, struggles, or strife, which he did not, familiar only with the name. Hitler. Some Austrian implant who seemed to think he knew what was best for his German cousins even if they did not, and who knew if they did. Exalted as a redeemer, the people's hero was a puppet for the party's headliners of bourgeois wealth with their own aristocratic dreams, and Reineke had no need or desire to mingle with the crowds drowning in the halls of their temple Berlin ...

Such arrogance or ignorance clearly chosen and contrived, he was an intelligent man, trained and skilled in the interests and excesses of his position and wealth. Sophisticated, successful, and perpetually bored. Few serious ventures extending beyond the cloistered existence of his estate. But four years spent at the universities of England and Germany, the degrees earned in architecture and engineering remained virginal. They were only whims anyway, interesting ways to stay the boredom. As was this army an adventure, a quest, opportunity to display his prowess at games and sport ...

But games can become tedious, and nerves ragged, watching the insanity multiply and there is no culmination, no relief, or satisfaction obtained ...

On September 1, 1939, they invaded Poland. In two days, war was declared between England and Germany, and on September 30, 1939, a new Polish government was formed in Paris while *Deutschland über Alles*! was sung to a country laid to ruin ...

Ruins.

Thirty-two year old Hauptmann Dieter Reineke stared at the sand listening to the fossils cry. In months, they rocked the foundations of Europe with Holland, with Norway, with France. To fight in the fields of France had been a game, indeed. Revenge for the near annihilation of his people lost in history and a hundred years of war. But revenge left a bitter taste, and he had been glad to leave France behind and come here.

Beneath the scornful eye of Nature, the shoulders of a still-young man bowed, hunching deeper into a shirt encrusted with layers of dirt and oil. The thin cotton, the bland color of this world, blended well with his skin turned yellow from sweat and creams protecting his body from the sun and heat. Gently, Reineke raked a fingernail over his arm, lifting a layer of the congealed creams clogging his pores.

"Paint me a picture," he murmured to the scum with its consistency of cheese. Posters and voices foretelling palm trees and salted breezes sweeping cliffs along such a beautiful, beautiful Mediterranean.

Liars.

He had not believed them, but they were liars still.

"Liars!" he snarled and wiped his hand clean. He could indeed taste the salt even buried this deep in the bowels of Libya, for you ate it with the sand. It burned your throat and seared your lungs as you ate it with the sand. Not in breezes, but in the sudden winds called *ghibli*.

Reineke shut his eyes, perspiration creeping out from under the band of his cap. The winds. The silence could be a foretelling of the winds, warn the rodents to run and hide.

"*Khamsin*," he whispered into the air, praying the desert might answer. It was the Englishman's word for the winds.

"*Khamsin*," he chanted to conjure an image the desert could not refuse to answer, the god himself, the Holy Man, master of the sand.

"Pierre?" Reineke opened his eyes because he thought he heard a sound. "Pierre?" he whispered. "Answer me."

But it was not ready yet, not yet—

"ANSWER ME!" Reineke screamed. "Pierre, answer me!"

But the desert refused to answer, and it was not fair! He knew the words, learned the words, used the words Pierre had taught him, and Pierre would know. It could be the winds. The silence a prophecy of the wind. It was SO quiet.

"PIERRE!" Reineke shouted and started to run. "ANSWER ME, PIERRE! ANSWER ME!"

(And two hundred meters in the distance, Oberleutnant Heinrich Thiele vaulted over the side of the wagen.)

But against the yellow Reineke had little chance, the shrubs springing to the defense of their desert, catching him, tripping him, and he watched himself crumble, such a helpless fledgling sobbing in fright.

He went down on one knee. One sharp branch had gouged his boot.

But not his boots! In dismay, Reineke touched the wound. Such a proud peacock, determined to flaunt his regal tail he wore the black leather accessories, not the brown, never the brown, and the black would never blend into this desert, never!

"Never!" he damned the sands. "Never!" Strong fingers digging deep, he tore at the roots. "Damn the devil, never!"

Madman! The fossils laughed. *Madman*!

"Devil!" Reineke cursed. "Devil—ANSWER ME!"

That scream pierced the yellow, and he stopped. Still shaking, he stopped. It was so hot. So quiet.

TOO quiet.

"Madman?" Reineke whispered, questioning the sand's condemnation, and started to smile.

Madman. The sand affirmed, though not with certainty.

"Indeed," Reineke whispered. "Answer me. In all your silence, answer me!"

But it could not. The desert could not. It was *too* quiet.

"Thank you!" Reineke said, and perfect white teeth flashed lethal in his smile. Madman or not, his mind was keen. Remember, he had wanted to come here. They needed peacocks. Proud, independent peacocks, adept at strategy, elusive foes, and he was one. SO adept that of the five installations he was the closest to the embattled coast road.

SO adept that of the five Hauptmanns he was first. As always first! Arriving with the first at Tripoli, and since coming here, his plots, his tricks, his games eluded the Allies—

From the background yet!

And he wanted to be in the background, to come this far south to perfect those tricks and games, never caring if his importance, or their importance, ever reached beyond the few of his sect.

And he wanted to stay in the background, safe from the blurry circle of ignoble defeat and victory, if only to bury with him the secret their existence was bound to be lost in the sand, the eternity of the sand ...

So hot ...

So yellow ... *August.*

The trance was threatening to return, but Reineke did not care. He had his answer. The desert answered. It was TOO quiet.

And through the yellow heat of August, the eyes of a handsome young man narrowed, fashioning into slits burning from a face made hideous from so much hatred.

And he knew he was right, because he felt the ground shudder, the long dead skeletons writhe in their tombs, and he heard the fossils resume their chant, *August.*

August.

And though it was March, it would soon be August, and before the heat of August, this desert would remember Dieter Reineke and admit he had won.

It would go down on its knees and bow its head, and remember Dieter Reineke.

"Indeed!" Reineke answered their quail, and started to laugh, loud. His head snapped back, eyes bright and burning as he continued to laugh, and in his insanity, he was up on his feet.

And the desert cowered, for in his triumph he started to mock, legs bounding forward, black boots swinging in glee as they ruptured the sand, and he started to sing, "You will remember me! You will remember me! You will remember the madman!"

"*Hauptmann*!" It was a voice. An actual voice that nearly shattered his daydream. Reineke turned around. Oberleutnant Heinrich Thiele stood less than two meters away. And Reineke was tempted to explain about the heat, about the fossils, but Thiele's face was saying, *Madman,* and he decided to explain nothing. Nothing.

For You

Corpses in Armor

In December 1941, five German officers, each equipped with a squad of men, ventured deep into the Sahara to establish a lifeline of munitions complexes in defiance of the idiosyncratic management of Berlin that threatened Rommel's North Afrikan Campaign.

In February, the British forces in chaos, near ruin, German victory seemingly on the brink, Rommel unexpectedly ended his major offensive at Gazala, west of the British stronghold in Tobruk, Libya, his army, and supplies equally spent.

But while General Rommel sat through those weeks in February and months to come, the idea of the complexes began to take shape and grow under the noses of the Allies, Italians, and Berlin alike ...

For a while, anyway, for a little while.

This is the story of one of those five officers, Baron Hauptmann Dieter Reineke. It is the story of what he found, and what he did, and the Englishman Charles who waited one step ahead.

Ruins, Book One

Corpses in Armor

The Axis

Chapter One

The Fezzan
March 8

Reineke wondered if Thiele knew what he looked like, never mind him, out here in the dust of man and mankind glittering like gold in the noon sun. He eyed him. The young lieutenant's flushed face frightened and confused. Reineke wasn't quite sure why. The twenty-seven year old son of a shopkeeper claimed to know his Captain well, understand him without difficulty, wealth, or university degrees. The Hauptmann, privileged and talented, infused with ego and eccentricities, was spoiled. By self and circumstances, deranged.

"Indeed," Reineke smiled, a superman long before the theories of Aryan purity proven in the unclean hybrids of carnations and pigs. Birthed, and bred from the loins of Nordic Kings.

"Indeed," Reineke smiled, an exotic being, beautiful, beguiling, powerful, and strong. A divine, god-like creature, fluid and flawless, near painful to behold ...

"Indeed," Reineke said, exhausted and worn, little more than a Frankenstein, manufactured son of his father, cousin to himself. The untainted pool of genetic matter tired, stagnant, and drained, crippling its offspring with emotions and ills far too unstable to survive in a world outside the pleasures of his estate. Grandeur and grace crumbling under the pressures of mortality and men, tortured and tormented, radiant on the outside, but hollow within; or so Reineke suggested, today, pretended to be, today. Embraced. Tomorrow, of course, would be different. An hour from now it would be different. Thiele was not any of those things, and never different, but always the same.

"Indeed," Reineke continued to eye Thiele, comfortable with himself, and with this Thiele, who was an asset beyond his flustered appearance and tempered impatience for the naughty Nordic royal who should know better but refused to.

"It is too quiet, Thiele," he suggested wryly as a reason for his overheated fit, but Thiele was not amused. In this heat, as tired as Thiele was, his massive chest still heaving from his maddened dash across the sand, his darker, rounder blue eyes studious and intelligent behind their sturdy wire frames were not appreciative of the coquettish flutter of the Hauptmann's lashes. The tolerance in Reineke's voice with its amusement directed at him, Thiele. Suitably shorter than the striking Captain an impressive 1.92 meters in height, the abundant muscles of Thiele's typically broad physique did not have him particularly skilled in acrobatics. Two hundred plus pounds, no matter how firmly packed, Thiele was not graceful or attractive in flight. But powerful biceps and equally powerful forearms carried hands quite capable of snapping any neck, never mind one as delicate as ...

"Waterholes," Reineke interjected, and Thiele frowned, "*Was*?"

The Hauptmann smiled, and Thiele eyed him, the androgynous figure before him who looked less like a man than an engaging woman except for that imposing height.

Thiele eyed him. The boned, porcelain features and brushed straight bang, the hair so blond it was white. The Hauptmann was almost albino, nearly invisible in the bright desert light, but he was still a man, not a god, or angel, or whatever he pretended to be. The superior Nordic race matured later than Thiele's common Western stock, and this one had yet to mature at all. "Herr Hauptmann," he replied with the look and tone of a parent scolding its child, "we are thirty kilometers from the ridge your men are waiting for you."

Down went Reineke's head, debating as he conducted his silent appraisal of ...? Of what? Thiele stared at him, not completely at ease for all he claimed to understand.

"It is too quiet, Thiele," Reineke decided finally and he was back to smiling coyly at the wary Oberleutnant with the grim face. "Find me a caravan, hm? Between here and the ridge? One full of natives? Their bodies as hot, tired, and dusty as ..." his gaze flickered over

Thiele, a swollen pumpkin in his uniform with his knotted tie strangling his throat, even in this heat formal and dignified. Reineke's tie was home somewhere at his compound, his stiff shirt collar limp and open. "We are Thiele. Their bodies as hot, and tired, and dusty as we are."

"A caravan?" Thiele gaped at the suggestion that could only mean danger, trouble for the small convoy of soldiers, certainly not something they should intentionally seek out. "We are only thirty kilometers from home."

"So you have said," Reineke agreed, "so you have said." And back down went his head as he walked a few meters away to stand with his back to Thiele who could not feign being amused.

"Herr Hauptmann ..." Thiele began again, restrained.

"Waterholes." Reineke turned around.

Thiele paused. "Waterholes?" he repeated. "The waterholes? What about them?"

"Yes," Reineke said simply. "You found them, did you not?"

Found them? Thiele had not found anything. They knew where the waterholes were already. It was what they were doing out there, inventorying the waterholes. The quality and quantity of the nature-made wells for comparison to the original reconnaissance a short three months ago. Thiele looked around though as if expecting to find a new one rising, bubbling up out of the sand. He didn't, and there wasn't.

"Hauptmann ..." he said with his frown and a tip of his sandy-blond head.

"Yes," Reineke was well aware of what they were doing out there. They were his squad, after all, following his orders, for that matter, and by claim, his waterholes.

"And they were full, Thiele, still full. Well done, Thiele, well done," he congratulated the efficiency of the man.

Thiele was going to say, "What?" His mouth opened, he knew he was gaping again, and damn you, he would not say—"*Was*?" his face twisted comically in frustration.

"Waterholes," Reineke smiled. "The waterholes. Is it me, or is it you? I think it is you."

Damn you! Thiele flushed. "Herr Hauptmann ..."

"No," Reineke shook his head. "No, it is very hot, Thiele. And it is quiet, *too* quiet," he whispered not to disturb the silence. "Find me a caravan between here and the ridge? One more? I want one."

And he was gone, off in the opposite direction of the wagens, Thiele shouting after him, "Hauptmann!"

"No, Thiele," Reineke refused, gaily bouncing away, "I want another caravan. We have seen only three caravans in four times as many days, and it is early ..."

He whirled back around, amusement gone from his face, "And it is quiet—*too* quiet. I want another caravan between here and the ridge. Order it!" he insisted. "Order it now!"

Order it. As if Thiele could. "Where are you going?" he questioned sullenly, Reineke walking away from him again.

"For a walk, Thiele. Pick me up on your way."

Single file, the kübelwagens bounced over the sand. Their idling engines springing to life, the column rolling as Thiele assumed his seat with a wave of his hand. He did not verbally direct the driver to secure Reineke. A snap of his fingers and the soldier understood, the motorcade purring along to reclaim its commander.

He did not repeat Reineke's orders. He said nothing and it would not have mattered if he had. Ten pairs of vacant, staring eyes, half-hidden beneath canvas helmets, would not have found anything peculiar with the Hauptmann's request.

Request! Thiele snorted, violently shuffling the maps. Reineke was, after all, the Hauptmann, their Hauptmann, and Reineke would not tolerate anything less than vacant, staring eyes.

Marionettes! Thiele labeled the soldiers lounging in various positions on the seats of the four kübelwagens. With painted smiles, and starry eyes they danced to the whims of the Hauptmann.

But Thiele was not a puppet, his meaty hand strangling the map as he clutched it, recalling a day not too long in the past.

Tunis, Tunisia
December 1941
"*Herein lies the strength of the German Army, Oberleutnant Heinrich Thiele.*" had been Reineke's introduction of his squad to his newly

appointed First Officer Heinrich Thiele. "Mindless creatures, each and every one. Zombies."

The startled lieutenant disagreed, finding the comparison insulting, his posture stiffening in defense.

"Indeed. You think otherwise?" Reineke noted the defiance.

Thiele did. But the Hauptmann was right to question. It was not Thiele's place to think, and certainly not to say. He stood down immediately with apologies. "Order is necessary, Hauptmann," he agreed. "I believe I understand what you mean."

"Indeed," Reineke walked away from him to stand, looking at the picture of the Führer on the cool, stone wall. "You are different than what I anticipated," he said finally.

"In what way, Hauptmann?" Thiele asked.

"Order is strength," Reineke suggested.

"It is," Thiele said.

"It wears glasses," Reineke assured. He turned around. "You wear glasses, Oberleutnant," he pointed out with a dismissive wave of his hand, aborting any need for Thiele to explain or defend his imperfection. "It is all right. However distracting and unattractive, they are apparently necessary. I understand ... Indeed," he assured, "I understand completely. I know who you are, Heinrich Thiele. I know why you are here. You are my watchdog ... Yes, watchdog ..." he briefly considered the reasons why he needed a chaperon. "Tell me, watchdog, Thiele, what did Herr Oberst, our Colonel, tell you? What!" he gestured dramatically, "concerning I, did he have to say? That I am mad? Egotistical? Insane?"

He took a step closer like a movement in some dance. "Did he say, 'Watch my Hauptmann Reineke, for he is all that and more? Though he is good at what he does, you can never be too careful or too sure'? And what is it that I do, eh, Heinrich Thiele?" he requested. "What could he be talking about? What could he mean?"

Murder. Herr Colonel Schönfeld was talking about murder, the timely and coincidental deaths of those who had offended or defied Reineke. There had been three. Thiele knew of one. "I am aware of Oberleutnant Goetz," he acknowledged the unanticipated demise of his predecessor found shot to death at the tip of Reineke's prized and polished boots. A crime, whose evidence Thiele did not believe, any more than their Colonel who did not believe in anything except his Hauptmann Reineke who enjoyed his moments of notoriety.

"I killed him," Reineke assured, lest there be any lingering doubt to his guilty plea. "They say I did. They may say I killed you."

"They may," Thiele agreed with a shrug.

"Indeed," Reineke straightened up, intrigued. "We are not a suicidal race. That would be the Japanese."

A culture of barbarians Thiele knew little about, leaving its concerns to his superiors the way it should be. Still, he was not quite sure if Reineke was making a joke or what it was he was doing. Thiele studied him. What he thought he could see behind the bright pastel eyes a transparent blue-grey like a fading sea, large and curved like a sphinx or stone cat. There was a distinct hint of an animal in the Hauptmann's features with the stark, bold cheekbones and cut, firm jaw. A suggestion of seduction in his stance, seriousness in his tone and ordinance *we take no prisoners*, be they the enemy or his own.

"What we are is capable," Thiele replied, it seeming a fair compromise, a safe one. They were Rear Services after all, Transport and Supply, their ranks hardworking, occasionally undisciplined, and generally bored, hardly the knights of legend or lore.

"Capable." That was a bold claim. Reineke looked over his shoulder at the picture of Hitler on the wall. "Indeed. You are capable, Heinrich Thiele. I have your file. You are quite capable. Intelligent. Versatile. Why is this? How can it be? You are common, your people slaves to their factories, farms, and mills. What right do you have to rise in the ranks alongside someone such as myself ...

"Indeed, I question your capability!" his head snapped back with a hiss. "It simply cannot be. You are stupid, you have to be. How is it you are not? Why is it? Is it possible we are all truly equal after all? Answer the question!"

"What is the question?" Thiele verified.

"Do you ever dare to imagine," Reineke stretched forward across his desk, "that a man's background is not necessarily an accurate measure of his capability? Eh, my watchdog Heinrich Thiele? Do you ever dare to question what you have been taught, what you have been told? Is the East as great as the West as great as the Phalic, as great as I, the Nordic man?"

"No," Thiele replied without having to consider his answer. The truth indisputable in what he had been taught and told.

"Indeed," Reineke inclined his head. "You have a great deal to learn from me, Heinrich Thiele. I demand your loyalty."

"You have it," Thiele promised.

"Good." Reineke smiled. "Because I will kill you if I find out I do not. A *distinct* capability of mine."

The Fezzan
March 8
Reineke was also capable as a commander, despite his whims and moods. Extraordinarily overqualified to stock his complex of munitions and supplies and therefore, yes, bored. Thiele dismissed the memories of Tunis for here and now. The maps lay at his feet and were useless, anyway. Orders or wishes could not produce a caravan. He did not understand the sudden importance of finding some caravan when they had seen caravans that were not important at all. Because he could not understand it, he did not like it. He glanced forward at Reineke standing upright in the front seat of the wagen, arms draped leisurely over the windshield as they bounced along, and it was Thiele's turn to shiver despite the heat.

"My reputation precedes me, Oberleutnant. I am well aware of that. It is, after all, my reputation."

Madman. His sanity in question, Reineke was not insane. Calculating, manipulative, devious, and deliberate, he was above all, "Lucky!" Thiele whispered. "You are lucky!" But only because Reineke always somehow managed to get away with it whatever 'it' was, other than no act.

Deep in thought, Reineke shifted his weight as they rode. His high black boots, dramatic in appearance were not comfortable. The hard leather hot and heavy in this heat, he was contemplating sitting down for a while. This recent trip into the desert surrounding his compound had been uneventful, and as Thiele correctly surmised, like his squad, Reineke had spent the majority of his time bored. The dormant bulk of the German army lay far to the north, silent as the enemy on their side of the Gazala line. Here, two thousand kilometers south, contact and conflict with the Allies or French was distinctly nonexistent, and though they had wandered over quite an area, not to contradict the sand, the waterholes were also devoid of life.

And he had assumed there would be life. Locating a cigarette in the pocket of his shirt Reineke surrendered to his feet, folding his legs and easing himself down onto the seat of the wagen, the wheels busily devouring the last few kilometers to the oasis and home.

Home here in Libya was his compound. A magnificent ten thousand acre oasis, remnant of an ancient world uncharted on current maps, and artfully concealed in the sea of dunes. Wakes and waves of the sand rising and falling off the end of the earth, pouring down into a great hole of marble and limestone, alive and flourishing with vegetation and water, natives, and of course, sand. *Eden.* Eden in the middle of the great Sahara of nothing and nowhere.

A thousand feet below the desert, ringed by the scarred steep cliffs of an ancient dried riverbed, the oasis lay impenetrable to even an army of men. A working quarry at the time of Egyptian reign, wind, and sand seeded the rock, trees erupting from an old womb creating parcels of land ranging in size from mats to the ruins of a Roman city built upon the Pharaohs' past glory, and subject to the same decay wrought by time.

Three thousand years of conquest and civilization, now two thousand years forgotten and lost, and only briefly reborn to the Ottoman Empire in the late 16th century, until Turkish hold on the North Afrikan region weakened to pirates and the lore of the Barbary Coast. The oasis failed again, surrendering itself back to the sand, Egyptian and Roman triumph, and the Moor restoration overrun with desert nomads, most recently fleeing the Italian-Libyan war. At the time of Reineke's arrival, a league of pagan tribes populated the oasis, particularly along the northern court with its surviving Emperor's villa and labyrinth of lifeless stone gardens. Laying his claim to the oasis, Reineke did not expel them. Instead, the nomads' retreat to the ancient Roman ruins decorating the western sector of the oasis was an agreement. Their few hundred bodies providing an ideal facade for any curious French or Allied reconnaissance and were allowed, to a degree, the freedom to wander—

Reineke snapped to attention. It was *TOO* quiet. Warn the rodents to run and hide.

Even now, the emptiness reverberated, and he whirled around to Thiele. "How far are we?"

Was? Thiele bolted free of his daydream of the taming of Hell, Egypt, and his impetuous commander Reineke.

"How far are we?" Reineke demanded.

"Twenty kilometers?" Thiele guessed. "Wait!"

Except Reineke was not going to wait. He snatched the papers away from Thiele, glaring at the maps.

Twenty kilometers, and the civilization beyond remained anonymous, hidden.

Twenty kilometers, and his native facade allowed the freedom to wander was nowhere around. Not so ideal.

Of the five munitions installations, his was closest in proximity to the front, the first in line.

Reineke stared at Thiele. Only Thiele was not aware of any natives wandering, their movements disciplined and monitored or not. And only twenty kilometers ...

Yes! *Yes*! The swollen radiators agreed. Only twenty kilometers to the compound et al!

Nineteen! The squealing wheels corrected, gobbling the glassy sand.

"Verdammt!" Reineke hissed, and was off his seat, and out of the wagen, running to break his fall as his feet hit the ground.

Chapter Two

"Halt!" Thiele shouted. Hand up to stop the procession he grabbed the door for balance and support as the wagen's suspension groaned under the circle spun tightly in the sand.

Reineke had found them. Meters away, he glared through his binoculars and summoned, "Thiele!"

Field glasses in hand, Thiele could make out what appeared to be tracks drawn in the sand, but he waited for the wagen to stop rolling before heaving himself over the side and he was there, stooping to touch the ground, running his finger through the impression to calculate its depth. "A truck," he interpreted the first of the two sets. "Wide base—possibly a supply truck."

"Indeed," Reineke crouched beside him, poking at the second.

"Staff car," Thiele was convinced. "The tread is narrow."

"Indeed," Reineke said, and Thiele winced, "Their treads are narrow."

"How long ago?" Reineke was already standing, watching his collected clump of sand trickle down.

Thiele blinked. "That is impossible to know."

"Is it," Reineke said.

"It is not possible to know," Thiele insisted. "Their freshness could be deceiving—"

Reineke scoffed, discarding his handful of sand and walking away, hands on his hips, staring out over the silent, arid canvas.

"Hauptmann," Thiele persisted behind him, "there is no breeze to disturb them. Without a breeze ..."

But Reineke was not listening, and rising to his feet Thiele tried again. "It is longer than an hour ..."

"No dust." Reineke understood the rules of science as well as he understood his gift of the sixth sense. "I knew something was wrong,

Thiele, I knew it. Out there in the sand, I knew it." Even though he could not see it, touch it. He turned around. "Knowledge, Thiele. Not hallucination or guess. Knowledge."

"Yes," Thiele agreed after a moment. "But it still could be hours ago. Two. Three. Even four—"

"German," Reineke considered, a somber and annoying thought.

"The vehicles?" Thiele blinked. "Of course."

"Their occupants hopefully German as well," Reineke nodded. "Either way I will not have my caravan after all, will I? A convoy in the area and any natives would quickly make themselves quite unavailable ... to the Germans," he looked Thiele in his worried and wondering eyes. "You think so, Thiele?"

"Yes," Thiele thought so with confidence, but then he was German and the desert Arab was little more than a rat scurrying in and out of its hole.

"Indeed," Reineke said. "We are two thousand kilometers from the front lines."

"Yes," Thiele said.

"Still, this far to the south, is there something else I would like?" Reineke coldly agreed.

"Like?" Thiele repeated.

"Prefer, Thiele," Reineke clarified. "Would I prefer our visitors to be someone other than us? Indeed. If it were to be something I preferred, you are quite correct, it would not be a German convoy—of two, Thiele. Of two."

The emphasis on the number of suspected vehicles was unnecessary. Thiele thoughtfully studied the tracks. "The tire pressure is uneven," he observed, "the truck may be empty."

Empty or full was irrelevant. "A single truck is not a convoy, Thiele," Reineke assured. "Not of supplies or of men."

"No," Thiele agreed. "You are right. Something is wrong. I do not understand."

"Reconnaissance, perhaps?" Reineke suggested.

"Reconnaissance?" Thiele's warrior flared.

"German reconnaissance," Reineke assured. "We are an equally safe distance from the French as we are from the Coast Road. Indeed, I have no idea why anyone would be out here, Thiele—including us."

He returned to staring around the windless sea. "Neither am I pleased to have to be thinking of one now."

"No." Neither was Thiele. "Under the circumstances ..."

Yes. It was probably a good idea for them to get out of there. Reineke followed Thiele's glance back to the kübelwagens and the men, and the light weapons their squad carried. The small arms and number put them at an obvious disadvantage to anything larger than rats. Ironically that had been a complaint of Thiele's when they started out, now proven valid. "One of the kübelwagens," Reineke decided.

"What?" Thiele's scowl turned on him, apparently under the impression a good idea was the only idea.

"Two of the men," Reineke was nodding, "and you."

"To follow the tracks?" Thiele hissed. "*One* kübelwagen?"

"And I," Reineke volunteered. "The rest stay here."

"You?" Thiele choked.

"Order it."

"It might be a truck," Thiele reminded. "It might not be empty!"

"Order it," Reineke repeated. "I wish to find out what it is and who."

"They might not be German," Thiele screeched. "We are guessing!"

"Order it!" Reineke barked, and Thiele sputtered, "Damn you!" and bolted, shouting the orders as he ran.

"Du sau," Reineke pivoted, glaring down on the tracks running roughly parallel to those of his column, and would, the same as his column, in less than nineteen kilometers, come to an abrupt halt at the ridge unless the visitors had changed course, which he doubted they had. "Du sau!" he swore, and it was an oath.

"Du sau," Thiele also swore, though quietly when Reineke's long strides deposited him on the running board of the kübelwagen where he chose to remain. Standing there like a target in Thiele's opinion, not a king. Such grandstanding was not worth the risk.

Thiele was wrong. Reineke rode along on the running board not to impress but to ensure recognition by the unseen nomad he knew was out there. It was already almost certain he was a target, or they were, or could be, until the visitors were identified and perhaps even then. It remained to be seen. In the meantime, the reasons for the show were Reineke's, not something Thiele understood. More of what Thiele did not know, and distinctly present and pressing on both of their minds.

The demarcation point Reineke referred to as *the ridge* was the summit of a deep gorge, a savage rip in the earth's crust, where the desert fell into a valley of stone. Eden? Oberleutnant Heinrich Thiele moaned. Eden was little more than the skeletal remains of some ancient lake, or riverbed buried by Nature and unearthed from its tomb by man. A thousand years, two, or five, Thiele had no idea how long the quarry had actually been there, only that too much stone had been removed threatening the stability of the crumbling walls. Twice, in the three months they had occupied the oasis, portions of the ridge in the west had collapsed revealing an ambitious honeycomb of caves and tunnels supported by petrified wooden shoring. A mountain balancing on stilts, Thiele awaited the day when the dried, riddled props would surrender, bringing the desert crashing down around them.

Reineke would laugh. Never sound, the ridge had withstood ten thousand years of torment and would survive a few more. The tropical island below camouflaged by a canopy of date palms only appeared inaccessible. There had to be a way in. The task was to find it, which they did. At first, only an artery of what appeared to be steps fractured by wind, sand, and avalanches of rock, and then the Egyptian goat path impassable as the steps, and finally the smooth wonder of Roman engineers: a road. Built for their two horse carts, the narrow, harrowing twisting passage through the mountainside was wide enough for modern day trucks, and most importantly, intact.

And in the beginning, Reineke had initiated an effort to re-shore the mineshafts, for the deterioration in the west was acute, until suddenly he halted the work. It was not necessary. They did not use the land in the west. There was no reliable road to the west, and he confined their camp to the renovated north where man and Nature had been kinder to the mountain towering above the courtyard, its majesty glittering diamond white in the sunlight and ghostly sallow at night.

Thiele was not satisfied, steadfast in his refusal to believe man, ancient or modern, had also not sabotaged the northern wall that carried the weight of the road, and if the land were to shrug? If it were to shrug?

Hauptmann Dieter Reineke, riding atop his wagen's running board like a king, enjoyed Thiele's fear. If he ever were to admit to the possibility he might be wrong, and that the land beneath the road had been tunneled through so that every truck was in danger of causing the land to shrug, then let it shrug. When the time came there would be no way of stopping it, and until that eventuality, Reineke would forever be in awe of the frenzied and fantastic imagination of Nature and man who fought to control and use the great stone pit. A feat of engineering likewise embraced in the construction of the villa, for the ridge was not the only monstrosity balancing on stilts.

Oh, yes, Hauptmann Dieter Reineke would always enjoy the return trip home ...

Always?

It was Thiele's turn. Barricaded in the rear seat of the lone kübelwagen, Thiele knew the oasis really was an excellent location for their complex. It had water—an abundant supply of water, particularly in the west. It had more than ample space for storage, and you could search the area for hours and never find the road.

Thiele groaned. They had found the road only by accident, after a storm, though it would not have mattered. So in love was Reineke with the possibilities the oasis offered, he would have built a road, as narrow, winding, deceptive, a terrifying, confusing passage down the mountainside, barely wide enough to allow a single line of trucks. Only one road, and only in the north, no other road was ever found, just countless crumbling steps vanishing and reappearing in a mindless, pointless arrangement.

It was not mindless or pointless. It was a labyrinth constructed on the backs of Egyptian slaves as Rome flourished, and Egypt failed. Markings of an ancient prayer walk of some divine oracle where recessed stations provided the perfect camouflage for Reineke's sentries. Men, who could, from their posts, see for kilometers in every direction. In turn, inform the villa of any trespassers. Whereupon the villa with its conspicuous lack of uniformed patrols could, from the villa's twin towers, observe the road, the one road.

The only road up, and the same road down.

And anyone approaching along that dusty route was well within sight and range of the deadly 88 mm guns housed within those towers. Oberleutnant Heinrich Thiele, riding in the rear seat of the lone wagen, squelched the panic he felt.

Reineke stepped off the running board at the rim of his canyon to greet the tracks that had not turned off in another direction, but continued to run parallel to his column, stopping where he stopped, at the ridge, approximately thirty meters west of their position.

"Three o'clock and all is well, eh, Thiele?" he remarked softly to Thiele stealing up behind him. "We shall see."

Mute, disapproving, Thiele followed him back to the wagen, Reineke snapping his fingers in a brisk signal for the soldiers to disembark. "Take the men, Thiele. I will meet you at the gate."

Thiele's crawl changed quickly to a trot. "Hauptmann, it is foolish—"

"Now, Thiele." Reineke's knuckles rapped sharply against the armor plate of the wagen putting his reluctant driver on notice to hurry up and get out of the way, "You, too. Out."

"But, Hauptmann, your pistol is inadequate," Thiele insisted. "The rifles are inadequate at such a range—distance! It is useless," he swallowed, confidence waning under Reineke's lofty gaze. "It would be foolish?" he concluded, "To endanger yourself? I will go instead."

Particularly since it was far more likely simply foolish rather than potentially dangerous at all? Thiele had no knack for hiding his thoughts, saving Reineke the trouble of having to read his mind. "I said now, Thiele," he replied.

Thiele's eyes dropped, the driver sliding out from behind the steering wheel, wary as Thiele, but obediently relinquishing his seat to the Hauptmann. "I will meet you, Thiele?" Reineke verified. "At the gate?"

"Yes, Herr Hauptmann," Thiele acknowledged Reineke's foot burying the accelerator, the gears screaming from reverse to first as he sped away.

"But," Thiele whispered through the stinging cloud of sand kicked up by the wheels, "we would see." Regardless of who could or could not see them, did or did not see them, one lonely, even carelessly tossed grenade and they would know if their visitors were German, or the enemy instead as a thousand tons of ammunition erupted in flames. The volcanic explosions deafening and visible for miles instead of quiet like it was. So quiet. The broiling air silent, eerily still.

Thiele looked around. An uncomfortable sense of something out there mocking them, a feeling of being watched and not alone was difficult to ignore, but he ignored it. Tried to. "Move!" he turned angrily on the men waiting, but then he knew there had been no call over the radio to warn or advise them of anything whether the operator was desperate, concerned, or simply confused. That was wrong. If everything else was all right, that was wrong. Something was wrong.

Reineke drove as he had run, crazed and maddened, the air gasping with sand. Thiele quickly lost sight of him except for the billowing cloud of yellow dust. The cloud was intentional. Not wearing his goggles for protection was not. Reineke forgot about them and remembered them quickly when the stinging rain of sand stung his eyes. He needed the jolt perhaps. He had to focus, remain focused. Stopping, he strapped them on. This close, the nomads, if they were out there, could see him clearly. There would be no mistake, or mistaken identity insofar as who he was. He stopped again fifteen minutes later, in a private place, invisible against the peaceful scenery where no one watching from the towers could see. Adjusting his binoculars, he found Thiele. A smile briefly coated his tight lips as he watched Thiele and the men attempting to navigate the savage rock two hundred meters above the canyon floor. It would take Thiele an hour, perhaps more.

"They are German, Thiele," Reineke nodded, confident. "Indeed, our visitors are German, Thiele," he assured. But there was still a little time. Waiting for the intentional blinding cloud of sand to settle, Reineke still had a little time before he had to leave. The arc of his field glasses moved west, away from the northern face and the compound for the ruins of Rome and the nomad settlement, the broken white columns of marble marking the end of his territory, and the entranceway to theirs, coming into view.

"Talk to me," he encouraged his hidden audience he knew had to be watching him. But there was nothing to see, no sound, no one. The natives remained barricaded in their settlement, their spies, silent as the air, and the binoculars thudded against his breastbone when he dropped them in disgust. His little time was running out quickly. Thiele would think he stopped to check the perimeter. Thiele would watch the cloud of sand kicked up by the wagen, and too much time passing and Thiele would think that something was wrong. Reineke rolled his eyes. Thiele's concern for his safety however founded on the rules of engagement and war was nevertheless unwarranted. He was safe. Of them all, he was safe.

"Our visitors are most definitely German, Thiele," Reineke scowled. "Warn the rodents to run and hide, and so they have."

But he should perhaps still check. He should perhaps drive a bit further just to be sure. His annoyed return to his wagen, slowed. His hand stretching to retrieve his discarded pistol closed over the steel with reluctance. It was perhaps a wise idea to make sure.

It is always a wise idea to make sure. The haunting presence of the natives surrounding him agreed.

"Indeed." Reineke disarmed, emptying the ammunition from his gun into the sand and tossed the unloaded pistol into the back seat with his hat and holster. There would be no stinging clouds of sand this time. Carefully, Reineke eased the wagen down along the second treacherous road hidden in the mountain's side.

Hiking their way down the road was out of the question; it would take too long. Thiele aimed for the nearest cutback of steps, from there, straight for the bottom, skidding and sliding, his boots desperately seeking any foothold along the slippery rock. If this was some actual operation, instead of simply temperament, Thiele would have studied and planned the descent. It wasn't, and Thiele just wanted to get down to the bottom without killing himself. That would be a victory unto itself. Field maneuvers were not something at which Thiele excelled or enjoyed. A decorated marksman, deadly accurate, his skills were useless and laughable when his rifle was currently much more valuable to him as a crutch or brake to stop his body from falling. He had to slow down, plan what he did not want to spend time planning and that was where to put his feet. It was infuriating. He did not believe the intruders were the enemy. He knew they were not. Reineke was simply angry at the surprise appearance of guests and so they were denounced as the enemy, regardless of who they were, unmindful the probability of some French or Allied invasion was as thin as the air surrounding them.

"As thin, mein Hauptmann," Thiele muttered, successfully managing to twist his neck around and fix an irritated glare on the cloud of dust from Reineke's speeding wagen. Except it was gone. The air was clear. Thiele blinked, briefly uncertain in his conviction that the visitors were German. But then he rejected the idea of enemy infiltration as fiercely as he rejected this exercise in suicide. It was just more of the same nonsense. The cloud was a diversion, diverting the attention of the enemy's fists tightening around the handles of the cannons below away from Thiele and the men on the wall to Reineke. It would be the Hauptmann who died first. A martyr to the cause, sacrifice to his compound, hero to his men subsequently buried themselves in the ensuing avalanche of rock as a bombardment of anti-aircraft shells pounded into the mountain, the ridge disintegrating into rubble beneath them.

"Du sau!" Thiele seized his field glasses, his neck craning forward, searching for the road through the canopy of trees, imagining what the perplexed soldiers must be thinking watching their insane Hauptmann speed toward them, and the Oberleutnant who staggered down the canyon steps before plunging to his death.

"Du sau!" Thiele cursed the guards in the towers he knew had fallen laughing to the floor. Guards who could not hear Thiele's words, but could see a gesture, and gesture Thiele did, as obscenely as his precarious position would allow him.

And he was thinking. He was seriously thinking about demonstrating his opinion to the Hauptmann when the hot, sour breath of one of the men mumbled in his ear: "There are two vehicles parked just inside the gate, Oberleutnant."

Thiele's head twisted back around. "What?" he said, but did not really mean it.

"There are two," the soldier nodded with a point in the direction of the courtyard.

"TCH!" Thiele yanked his field glasses into place. There were two. One staff car, and one supply truck, both unmistakably German, their swastikas proudly displayed on their flags and painted sides, a small group of four equally distinctive guards posting watch over them.

"SS," the soldier offered his sympathy.

"I can see!" Thiele snapped, conscious how his fingers were suddenly cold, rigid.

"I can see," he whispered, his fingers gripping the binoculars, staring back over his shoulder, desperately searching for the Hauptmann and his wagen. But the cloud of dust was gone. It had been gone awhile. That made no sense. If Reineke hugged the side of the cliffs and crawled, eyes thoroughly trained would still see something.

Ears no longer dulled by civilization would still hear something.

And if Thiele closed his eyes and concentrated, he would hear the distant hum of the wagen's engine. When he opened his eyes, he would see the grains of sand floating through the air.

But it was clear and quiet. Thiele's chill spread along his arms. The Hauptmann did not like surprises. To the contrary, Reineke not only coveted his privacy, he insisted upon it, and trespassers into his domain were likely not to be treated politely.

"But they are German," Thiele begged, refusing to remember how the suggestion had seemed to annoy Reineke as much as any thought of Allies or French.

"You are German," Thiele reminded, as if he should have to. He stared through the field glasses at the SS. Wishing for one insane moment of his own the visitors were not German, but the enemy instead who could be dealt with swiftly without having to explain why. He turned back around, his glasses desperately searching the mountain for any sign of Reineke. But he turned the wrong way.

Inadvertently to the west, and there was nothing in the west. The road did not go to the west. Yet Thiele stood for one other moment just gazing at the horizon, the western horizon, and his thoroughly trained eyes, tired as they were, did not fail to notice the thin cloud of dust floating through the air. "Gott im Himmel," he muttered, swallowing the words and no one heard him.

"Go," he ordered the men, surprised his voice was steady. "GO!" And he went first, his ponderous thighs suddenly agile, the boulders no more threatening than the gravel under his feet.

Reineke was angry, sitting stiffly in the passenger seat of the wagen waiting for Thiele beneath the gateway to the complex. Thiele shook his head. It was no more a *gateway* than the oasis was *Eden*. The Hauptmann elevated everything around him to some fantastic level of importance for reasons known only to him. What *gateway*? After three months, it was today Thiele wanted to ask, if he had never wanted to ask before. The gateway was two broken Corinthian columns of pitted and chipped pink marble missing their capitals and cornice, standing like headless sentries, ten meters tall, frozen in the sand. That was it, nothing more. No barrier, or blockade of wire or men. Two worthless pieces of rock that when the Hauptmann was not angry the men did not dare drive around them, but through them as they should whether they were ever a gateway, part of a gateway, or what they were, the ripples of the cream sand sea eventually bleeding into a courtyard of crushed limestone, bedrock for the Emperor's villa. The ancient monstrosity towering and top-heavy as the great wall with its massive arcade protruding like a pregnant belly over a supporting colonnade where the sun struggled to shine, and its marble skin turned from comfortably cool to icy cold in the desert night. Quite unlike the courtyard where the sun shone without mercy and a man could die between dawn and dusk.

That was an idea. Thiele was not above violent thoughts, and briefly considered all options available to them. They could just leave their visitors alone, standing there. If the remaining four or five hours of sun was not enough, or the frigid night insufficient, another ten hours of sun, would definitely suffice. They would be dead by this time tomorrow. When it was over, Reineke could issue the order to pry their cooked boots from their station, burying the carrion in unmarked graves if it wasn't for one simple fact. "SS," Thiele noted quietly as he approached the wagen.

"Get in." Reineke's reply was terse, the sharp nod cold, but contained.

That should make Thiele feel better. Give him hope Reineke could be reasonable. It did not. Angry or subdued, Reineke was a man balancing on a fine wire. A high wire. Thin and tight.

Thiele attempted to keep his attention focused and straight ahead on their guests who weren't merely German, but SS. There was an unpleasant difference between the Wehrmacht and the SS, even in Thiele's mind. The SS were there for a reason. That was also on Thiele's mind. Their munitions complex however top secret it might be was a secret not only from the Allies and Free French, but also from the German bureaucratic machine that knew as much about fighting a war as Thiele knew about the Emperor Hadrian who had built this resort. The compounds were an act of desperation, some might say defiance, initiated by Rommel, and carried out by a small group of Afrika Korps officers, determined to supply the starving troops. In that way then, and only that way, they were all renegades, rebels, not only Reineke. Stealing their German munitions back from the well-fed Italians, and stockpiling them for support of Rommel's renewed push across North Afrika. And so yes, in that way also, Reineke wasn't necessarily extraordinarily overqualified to command his desert supply complex, no more than Thiele was, or any of them, but perhaps instead perfect.

Thiele's scrutiny returned to Reineke stiff and silent beside him. Perfect, Reineke would have radioed the compound when they discovered the tracks to advise and confirm any reports of unscheduled movement in the area before he issued any order.

Perfect, he would have alerted the compound of the danger he believed the movement represented whether he ultimately decided to break or close ranks, or whatever he decided to do. Including some ridiculous exercise that proved nothing, except perhaps that it took Thiele twice as long to climb down the walls into the compound than it took Reineke to drive a road that did not exist.

Thiele eyed the SS. A second road was possibly how the SS had gained access without prior announcement. The posted sentries along the wall could not possibly see everything, everywhere, not if a road also came from the west.

The same as the existence of a second road did not necessarily have to be a case of deception on Reineke's part. It could be Reineke followed the visitors' tracks, and in doing so found a second passage none of them knew anything about.

Thiele wanted to believe that more than he wanted to believe anything. He did not believe it. Reineke did not leave his men to circle the perimeter in hopes of identifying their guests. Unchallenged by his soldiers, the visitors were obviously German.

He did not leave his men to examine the perimeter and determine how and where the visitors had gained entry when there was only one way in—which apparently there wasn't. Reineke knew about the second passage, that was why he left. He not only knew about it, he obviously knew it well since he was sitting there in the wagen, waiting for Thiele to arrive. Six spent cigarettes on the ground marking how much time he had sat waiting, which had been quite a while.

Thiele drove silently through the gate of the pillars. Not around them, or into them, as he might want to do, but through them toward their visitors, only meters away. The SS making their appearance at this time was unfortunate. Thiele was a firm believer in their project, confident of success and equally confident success would stay any need for explanation to Berlin. Six months to establish the compounds and fill their bins was the plan. What could Berlin say when Rommel marched triumphantly into Cairo with the same lightning speed that first brought him to the brink of victory before he ran out of supplies? No?

No, Berlin could not say no. It could say nothing except thank you to its desert commander Rommel for his success and loyalty. Thiele looked over the throng of soldiers roused from their preoccupation with the SS and on the run for the Hauptmann approaching them. It had only been three months, the eve of December to the first week of March. An army grown from a squad of twenty to over two hundred in three short months with close to half of them in the courtyard circling the SS like hungry wolves.

Thiele glanced again at Reineke, the Hauptmann's expression unemotional and unchanged. *Your front lawn abounds with military apparatus and uniformed personnel, mein Hauptmann.* Thiele agreed silently with what he knew Reineke had to be thinking above all. *The anonymity of your compound has been compromised, not only by the SS, but also by your own men in clear violation of your strict regulations. This is why you are angry, isn't it? Isn't it?*

It added to Reineke's anger, yes. Along with the SS invasion, his men's disregard of his orders was a blow to his authority, neither of which Reineke would tolerate. Careful and diligent in shielding the depot from the invisible enemy out there in the sand Reineke's sentries patrolled the courtyard dressed as Arabs from the native camp. Thiele could see only three men in Arab robes in the foreground of the swarming, angry mob pressing forward. As they pulled closer, he spotted three more hovering uncertainly in the distance by the low walls of the dead marble gardens. That made six sentries. It should be eight. Thiele would find them. Deal with them, as he would deal with all of them, later, after the situation with the SS was resolved.

However it would be resolved. Thiele scowled, in favor of reason not kowtowing. The SS were certainly smug for men outnumbered more than fifty to one. Casually at attention, a burning cigarette in the hand of one of them, unimpressed by the jeering catcalls of the men guaranteeing the reprisal they had only threatened before as the Hauptmann's wagen rolled in and halted in front of them. Reineke rose from his seat with ease, his hands slipping behind his back, resting comfortably on his tailbone as he just looked at the four SS guards.

"Not too far," Thiele cautioned quietly. It was not worth it, and something yes, they would work out.

"Not too far," he barely whispered aloud as he alighted to hold the door open for Reineke.

"SS," Reineke commented, something disturbing in his voice, his attention on the skull and cross bone badges of the capped blond heads.

Thiele felt the hot metal of the door handle begin to scorch his fingers.

"Relieve these men of their weapons and post," Reineke instructed his waiting squad, the threat of eruption distinct, inevitable.

"Not too far!" Thiele moaned. His hand was going to stick to the metal if he did not let go, but he couldn't.

"Kill whoever refuses," Reineke ordered and the door handle turned to ice.

But they are SS! Thiele did not say as Reineke stepped down from his perch to disappear into the mansion. Behind him, Thiele heard the single satisfied click of the rifles locked and pointed. *They are SS*! He stared at the assembled firing squad, but the soldiers did not care, they were smiling. And it was out of Thiele's hands. He knew he released the door because he saw his knee come up, and he started to run, but it was already completely out of control.

Chapter Three

"Where is Erich?" Reineke demanded the appearance of his Staff Sergeant clearly not at his post. The broad stone steps of the villa disappearing two at a time under his boots, he was inside, pounding across the polished marble foyer, gilded and gaudy in its sparkling pink brilliance and fading colors of the Eastern Empire. Recognizable as an atrium, common to Rome and its territories, the once open walls and ceiling had been closed to the sky for four centuries, changing the villa's purpose from pleasure to defense, its god from Jove to Allah, waxy pillar candles caged in copper chandeliers providing an illusion of air and light. Reineke headed for the grand staircase, a lazy flow of worn marble lava that would carry him to the mezzanine and his office.

"He is in the wine cellar, Hauptmann!" tried the Korporal who rushed to meet him at the door and was roughly pushed aside.

"Get him!" Reineke ordered.

"He is!" the Korporal said.

"Get him!" Reineke insisted.

"With the prisoner!" the Korporal finished, and Reineke came to an abrupt halt.

"Prisoner?" his back arched. Everything he had been trying not to think flooding into his mind. His reign was over, finished, done, his world, his life. He knew that before he raced to the nomads' settlement. He knew it now. The visitors might be German, but the guns would be French and they would be there before morning. Two-hundred men slaughtered. Two-hundred German suicides.

"Indeed," Reineke said, and it was hardly in surrender to the French or the SS.

"Yes!" the Korporal leapt to explain, foolishly joining him on the stairs.

"Prisoner?" Reineke accused, the dangling binoculars around his neck swinging madly as he whirled.

"Yes, Hauptmann ..." the soldier startled with a step back, flushed with freckles and giddy fear.

"From where?" Reineke loomed above him.

"From?" the Korporal repeated, confused.

"Where? From where?" Reineke pounded back down to him, wrenching his bobbing glasses free, their cord catching his hat, sending it on ahead to the frightened youth, quick enough to catch it before it hit the stairs.

"From the truck, Herr Hauptmann," the Korporal stammered, "the SS!"

"Liar!" Reineke accused. He saw a car, not a truck. *One* car, not ten, and *four* guards castrating a courtyard of two hundred men!

"No, Hauptmann, I swear!" the Korporal said.

"Liar!" Reineke's hand struck his hat, knocking it from the juggler's grasp.

"Hauptmann!" Thiele appeared, bolting through the door with a jump for the stairs, pushing the Korporal out of the way.

"Verdammt!" Reineke shoved Thiele instead. "SS!" he insisted. "SS!" he fired his binoculars like a missile cutting through the air. They crashed into the wall, skidding across the floor.

Yes. Thiele caught his balance to stare at him.

"Herr Hauptmann, it was the Leutnant ..." the Korporal dared to move forward, but Reineke turned on him and he retreated.

"A prisoner!" Reineke hissed at Thiele, and he was gone. Down the stairs and off down the hall for the cellar, his heels clicking on the wood as he ran.

"What Leutnant?" Thiele seized the Korporal by the arm, propelling him toward the door.

"Faust," the soldier hastily defined. "And a Major Weiheber—SS, Herr Oberleutnant. They are SS."

"Yes!" Thiele had eyes, two of them.

"Gestapo!" the young man cried. "They are demanding the Hauptmann's arrest."

"What?" Thiele stared at him. They were heroes not traitors or anarchists. "What are you talking about? How do you know this?" he insisted. "Who even admitted them—who?" he demanded. "Where is Erich? Why isn't he here? What is this about the cellar?"

"Sergeant Erich admitted them, Herr Oberleutnant."

Thiele dropped his arm. "Erich?" he repeated. "Sergeant Erich is SS?"

"Yes," the Korporal nodded. "He was expecting them this morning, when he was expecting you—"

"Never mind!" Thiele silenced him, the details irrelevant, the facts, fact, Erich's betrayal of the operation to the SS apparently one of them. "Find them, I don't care where. Find them and bring them here—and have the courtyard cleared!" he reached for the door to fling the man outside. "Do as I tell you. Move!" he barked, and did an about face, heading for the cellar, cursing Erich. "Fool! Fool! FOOL!"

If the fool had any brains at all, he would be gone.

Except fools, do not have brains. That is why they are fools, and there were four fools in all. SS spies or agents, or simply opportunists, the ranks were riddled with them and that fact apparently applied here regardless of how scrubbed clean. They were also drunk, or drinking in premature victory. Thiele clamored down the steps of the cellar to find Reineke waiting in the doorway of the subterranean vault that like all cellars lacked the luster of its upstairs palace and was instead simply old, the air damp and stale. Silent, the Hauptmann appeared almost relaxed, comfortable in his misleading posture, his hands calm and clasped behind his back.

So, I look like the ridiculous one. Thiele bit his tongue, damming his mad dash to catch him. Erich and three other soldiers who Thiele recognized as belonging to them were on the left, near the dusty racks of wine. Absorbed in their conversation they did not notice Reineke. His words muffled in wine, Erich said something Thiele could not quite hear, but had the men laughing.

"Sergeant?" Reineke responded to the joke, announcing his presence with a single step forward.

And the private celebration died. The slurred voices silent, the full, wet lips of Staff Sergeant Erich paused in molesting his bottle of wine.

"An explanation," Reineke took a second step deeper into the intoxicating smell of machinery and fruit, "Sergeant?"

Erich glance down at his boot tops before he looked up, an insolent smile on his face. "You are late, Hauptmann," he said. "I should have been advised of your return."

"So I see," Reineke inclined his head toward the others, but they averted their eyes, less confident in their betrayal than their leader was in his.

"I see," Reineke repeated, and stepped past them into the alleyway lined with racks of wine. Bits of green glass littered the dirt floor, glittered like emeralds under the naked bulb of light powered by the generator slowly leaking gasoline. Bending down, he retrieved the discarded bottle. It was broken, severed in half, and as he rolled the neck between his fingers, the air around him seemed to grow thick, heavy. But, then, the pungent aroma of the wine was rather thick, heavy, and so it was possible the bottle had been dropped?

Indeed. The racks pressed close. The fractured body of the bottle was ragged and sharp, as if someone had intentionally struck it against something and ...

He rounded the corner, a sour sickness quickly rising in his throat. It was not what he expected. The prisoner was white, a young girl, perhaps fourteen. The blood he expected, there was blood on his men—but so much! Everywhere he looked he saw blood. The walls, the floor stained in the crying red rain. It was not what he expected, and he thought he heard a sound rather like that of a wire snapping.

"English." Thiele's voice spoke behind him. His middle class upbringing surprised by the carnage, but emotionally flat.

"Indeed," Reineke replied. At first glance, he had been unable to distinguish her from a bag of trash, least of all identify her race and political affiliation. Thiele a better soldier than him apparently, cool, and detached under pressure. Reineke stared down on the bare, bruised legs protruding from the lightweight wool skirt a filthy and bloody gray-green. She had been beaten, undoubtedly raped, and possibly dragged by the telltale friction burns on her arms and legs, a broken coil of wire still wound tightly around one of her ankles.

"No jacket," Thiele continued with his observation, and so he was guessing. Without her jacket he couldn't possibly tell what she was other than someone's child.

Reineke stared at the long twisted red braid of hair as she lay face down in the mud in an odd, deformed position, her wrists lashed with the same wire binding her ankle. "Untie her," he said, feeling Thiele's eyes shift in his direction.

"She is alive?" Thiele countered, it of some relevance apparently.

It was not. "Untie her," Reineke repeated, "or I will kill them here, now, the SS as well. Choose. The choice is yours. It is not a war against women and children."

Or old men. So Thiele had been told. He knelt, feeling her throat for a pulse. "She is alive," he announced, but Reineke was silent and Thiele obediently slid his knife from his belt to pry the wire loose.

"Indeed," Reineke said when Thiele turned her over to lay her flat. Hair clung to her battered face. Filthy strands held fast by the drying blood. Her eyes open, staring and dilated, Thiele was acutely conscious of the Hauptmann's stare bearing down.

"Call the sentries," Reineke instructed, and Thiele's head jerked up.

"Sentries?" he repeated. "For the woman?"

Reineke's stare bore into him.

"For the men?" Thiele stared back. "They are your men!"

"Now," Reineke said.

"The woman is alive!"

"Now," Reineke said, the broken bottle he held in his hand suddenly ominous, very important.

"Hauptmann ..." Thiele said.

"*Now,*" Reineke whispered, and Thiele obeyed. Hurrying away to hurry back with two sentries to find Reineke where he had left him, his hands and trousers bloody from where he had tried to wipe them clean. Thiele glanced at the prisoner. Her blouse was closed covering her naked breast, hair no longer clinging to her face.

"Pick her up," Reineke directed. One sentry shouldered his rifle pausing as Thiele's hand shot out, stopping him.

They are here for your arrest. Thiele stared silently at Reineke staring back at him. *Arrest. Do not give them a reason.* It was however a worthless argument not merely unspoken, so Thiele lost. Thwarted by the very rulebook he waggled in Reineke's face, held in check by the first commandment: The leader is always right. Reineke was the leader, not Thiele.

"Do it," Thiele muttered as if he had a say. He lowered his hand and the sentry stepped forward to lift the prisoner from the floor.

Reineke nodded satisfied. "Bring her upstairs."

"You," Thiele directed the second guard, "go with him."

"No," Reineke stopped him. "Thiele, dismiss the men."

"Hauptmann ..." Thiele said.

"*Now,*" Reineke whispered. "Do it now." And Thiele walked out from the racks with a scowl.

Staff Sergeant Erich was a large man, tall, Reineke's height, and Thiele's muscular build. A Phalic by race, driving force, even-tempered and reliable, his mental abilities second only to the leadership of Reineke's high-strung Nordic man, or so the truth read.

The truth was true. Erich had apparently forgotten that. He was second to Reineke who was first and second to no one.

"Oberleutnant?" Erich reacted slightly at the dismissive wave Thiele gave to all but him. The soldiers nearly tripping each other in their haste to get out of there, and though they ran now, they would not run far. Reineke carefully selected a bottle from the racks.

"Oberleutnant?" Erich repeated.

"Shut up," Thiele muttered. "Just shut up. Keep still. Don't be an idiot, don't say a word."

"What?" Erich's frown shifted to the racks and Reineke emerging, one foot in front the other, his left hand behind his back, the bottle dangling in his right.

"Hauptmann ..." Thiele sighed, though he did not really believe Reineke would do it, anything.

"Indeed." To the contrary, Reineke's attention was on Erich who knew he would. "Sergeant?" he asked, a question that wanted no answer. Not what Erich was thinking, or why the betrayal. Reineke did not care. Erich studied the bottle in Reineke's hand. Seconds passed, twenty, then thirty, Thiele could hear the ticking of his watch, the volume seeming to increase as the time wore on.

"Hauptmann ..." Erich smiled finally, bored with the drama and

Reineke snapped violently to attention. Rage inspiring strength, Reineke was a strong man. The body, muscles of an athlete, acrobat, dancer, and Erich despite his size was driven back against the stone wall, Reineke's arm across his larynx that for all Erich tried he could not move, the bottle threatening his gut, Reineke's leg slammed between his promising to crush his pelvis and groin.

"Will I?" Reineke's head tipped in the slow, erotic movement of a snake. Taunting and teasing, watching the pulsating throb of the Erich's jugular vein, the sweat Erich tried to ignore, beading on his forehead, tickling the tip of his nose, it was not hot in there, it was cool, almost cold. "Indeed," Reineke assured, "a man would."

"Hauptmann ..." Erich said.

"Beg!" The bottle smashed into the wall, Erich's eyes straining in their sockets to stare at the jagged glass. "Like she did," Reineke encouraged. "Say, *don't. Please.*"

"Do it!" Thiele insisted behind him. "Do what he says!"

"Don't ..." Erich agreed, but the words were lost, his gasp sharp and unbelieving as the glass slashed his cheek, blood bubbling out from the torn flap of meat.

Reineke released the bottle. It fell, shattering into pieces at Erich's feet. "Sixteen," he advised Erich down on his knees, searching for the bottle with a confused grope.

"*Six*-teen," Reineke stressed, promoting the woman from a fourteen year old child to a young woman based solely on the development of her naked breast, like two small buds he could cradle or crush with his hand. She was half his size, half his age, and helpless under the brooding power of his Sergeant Erich.

"You are dead," Reineke promised Erich, and was gone.

"Leave him alone," Thiele threatened the sentry taking a step toward Erich. "Get out of here. Leave!" he ordered, and the soldier gratefully obeyed.

"Idiot," Thiele cursed Erich. "Sergeant!" he scattered the glass with a determined kick, and Erich's head snapped up.

"You are a fool," Thiele assured him. "Fool! Radio for our patrol to return and put yourself on report." And he was gone, after Reineke.

Chapter Four

Reineke stalked across the foyer. "Find the Holy Man!" He ordered the small army of men crowded in the front hall to search the complex for the toddling old priest. "If he is not with the children, send one of the women—" Reineke's attack abruptly changed direction, noticing the girl deposited awkwardly on a wooden bench meant as a decoration, not to be used as a litter for the dead.

"I said to pick her up," he charged the sentry. "Bring her upstairs, not fling her in a corner!"

"Yes, Herr Hauptmann!" the soldier jumped to snatch up the prisoner and stand there trying to decide exactly where the Hauptmann meant by upstairs.

"And, I said," Reineke turned back on the others, "to find the Holy Man. Do it!"

"But he is here, Hauptmann," he was told. "Already in the compound."

"Then get him," Reineke insisted, not sure why, or when, it had become necessary to repeat himself. "Get him!"

"But he is!"

"GET HIM!" Reineke screamed and the soldiers fled, Reineke sputtering after them, "Misfits!"

No. No, they were not misfits. They were startled perhaps by the arrival of the SS, worried as to what it meant, confused in what to do without their leader, so, tell them. Thiele stood at Reineke's elbow. Give them orders, not temperament. "Hauptmann ..." he said.

"Bring the girl to the library," Reineke ignored Thiele for the sentry apparently still struggling with confusion.

"Hauptmann!" Thiele's request immediately flared to a warning.

"Indeed. She belongs where I put her," Reineke corrected.

"Not in your office!"

His office. His library. Sanctuary. A magnificent gallery, largest of the vault arcades, the finest the villa had to offer, spanning almost the entire width of the northern façade it was the villa's pregnant belly as Thiele called it. Reineke's ability to walk on air. Perhaps. It was a porch, a portico atop the colonnade, whose purpose was more than likely a private shrine for the owner's convenience. Originally open on three sides, it too, like the atrium, had been enclosed. Clay walls and heavy wooden doors divided its interior into three compartments. Paned glass French windows installed along its front and sides opened onto an exterior balcony where the hand and footprints of the Emperor Hadrian lay on its original rail and floor. The other two compartments his quarters, and a small apartment kept maintained for guests. It seemed perfectly reasonable to Reineke to order the prisoner remanded to the gallery's vacant apartment. She was their guest.

"My office, Thiele," he agreed, where he, like the Italian dictator Mussolini, could pretend to be Hadrian, Lord and ruler of this withered and once-auspicious retreat. "If it will help you, look upon her as yet another ornament for my office."

With that, Thiele expected him to turn with a flourish for the grand stairs, on the heels of his clumsy sentry, but he didn't. He walked to the front door to stand, impatiently glaring outside.

"Hauptmann ..." Thiele was again at his side.

Reineke sighed, heavily and tired. "Indeed, if I had a gun, Thiele, I would shoot you."

If? Thiele's eyes dropped to Reineke's belt missing its pistol and holster, Reineke waiting when he looked up.

"I threw it away, Thiele," he agreed. "I had my reasons."

"What reasons?" Thiele demanded.

That would depend, Reineke supposed, if he were as concerned for the nomads as he claimed to be, or only for himself. It was both. His concern naturally extended from the vulnerable natives to his munitions and men, something to do with being German and not being a traitor, merely schizophrenic. Yes, that was what he was, schizophrenic. Reineke knew this, realized, and decided it. And since he had now decided, he knew it was hopeless. He was hopeless.

whether or not Thiele continued to believe he could somehow be miraculously cured by this desert vacation. "Pick a reason that satisfies you, Thiele," he offered, "and go away. You are dismissed."

Thiele had no intentions of leaving. "Hauptmann—"

"The penalty is the same for insubordination as it is for treason," Reineke reminded him. "That is not only my rule."

No, it was the law. "They are here for your arrest," Thiele snapped. "Their reasons I can only guess!"

Reineke looked at him. They were here because of the munitions compound, even Reineke in his insanity, knew that. "Arrest," he scoffed. "Indeed. Who is here for *our* arrest, Thiele? The SS? Do as I say. Today is no different than any other."

It could not be more different. "Hauptmann, I think ..." Thiele nodded.

"Do not!" Reineke stopped him, his hand raised calling halt. "All right? Do not. I do not want you to think. There is nothing for you to think about."

"It is you who is not thinking," Thiele insisted, "and you have to. Listen to me!" he grabbed Reineke's arm. "There are two SS officers here. Gestapo. Berlin has sent them. They must have sent them. You have to think, Hauptmann. Think!"

"Indeed." Reineke shrugged free, reaching in his pocket for a cigarette. "I do not care—"

"Are you out of your mind?" Thiele was in his face, snatching the cigarette out of his hand.

"Not about Berlin!" Reineke angrily shoved him away. "Anything it thinks or wants, least of all its SS! You are dismissed. Do not make me tell you again!"

Except Thiele did not want to leave. He wanted Reineke to leave, come away from the door and his vigil for the Holy Man, but Reineke was staring again outside, impatiently waiting for the priest to appear, and Thiele pushed past him for the shaded heat of the porch.

The courtyard was clear and quiet, the vehicles and uniformed soldiers gone, order restored. The security of the villa returned to Reineke's costumed Arabs, two of them were on patrol now, high-powered rifles easily accessible under their loose robes, heads and faces wrapped in layers of white gauze, protection from the sun and recognition as Reineke was unwilling to risk healthy tans and patent black hair as being sufficient in passing inspection even at a distance. This close it did not matter. Any unauthorized person would already be dead.

Or those were the orders. To date they had not yet needed to enforce the orders, not even today. The SS, while unexpected, were not unauthorized. There was another Arab-soldier on the porch. More alert than his comrades and rising from his slump against one of the columns in response to Thiele's presence. Thiele's response was crisp, a nod, and roll of his eyes. He disagreed with the need for the masquerade, finding it more of a game than a trick to fool or deceive anyone. A form of entertainment concocted by the Hauptmann to amuse the troops, rejection of the boredom they all struggled with aboard the lonely oasis so deep within the Sahara seas.

This particular soldier was good however, taking his role seriously, imitating the sly slink of the Arab ferret to perfection as he moved away from Thiele for the end of the porch.

"Du ..." Thiele called him, only interested in ordering the patrols halted for now. The SS were likely sufficiently entertained for one day. If not, Thiele was.

The soldier had a different idea. He took off, straight for the banister with a vaulting leap over it.

"Halt!" Thiele recovered with a shout and rush for the stairs to give chase.

"Thiele!" Reineke's harsh bark interjected and Thiele whipped around.

"Dismissed?" he hissed. "Dismiss them! What is the matter with you? Get them out of here!"

"That is enough," Reineke warned.

"Enough?" Thiele spat, and was up and down the steps, spinning in his tirade. "That was an Arab, and you are telling me, enough? You call for your Holy Man, and you are telling me, enough? I saw you!" he assured, only he did not have a chance to say where. A crack across his face from the back of Reineke's hand sent his head reeling.

"Enough!" Reineke seized Thiele by his jacket lapels, catching him as he stumbled, struggled to keep from toppling backwards down the stairs, and when Thiele looked up the Hauptmann looked possessed, eyes on fire in his face. Thiele had never seen him so crazed. "Leave now or I will kill you, do you understand. Kill, not reprimand!"

The hall clock chimed the half hour. It was four-thirty. The Hauptmann remained outside, positioned on the steps, waiting and watching for the Holy Man. Thiele's chin was wiped clean of the light trickle of blood, his shirt neatly straightened, having sacrificed only one button, his hat set securely back on his head. Reineke's hat lay on the floor, its proud eagle at an odd angle.

Thiele studied the hat, ignoring the sentry who, for some suicidal reason of his own, was back downstairs with the prisoner sprawled back on the bench. Perhaps they had never left. Thiele vaguely remembered they had, but he could be wrong.

"Herr Oberleutnant ..." the sentry petitioned for Thiele's attention.

"So you are a misfit," Thiele agreed, retrieving Reineke's hat to revive its crumbled peak, laying it to rest on the newel post. "You have your orders."

"Yes, but the doors are open."

"Doors?" Thiele said absently.

"The library doors, Herr Oberleutnant," the sentry whined. "They are open."

Instead of locked and under guard. "SS?" Thiele guessed.

"Yes," the sentry assured.

"Of course." Thiele remembered his orders to have the SS officers located and brought there for the audience they seemed to want so badly they came there to have it. Two of them, Thiele understood. Two officers, four men, six SS in total. Six was not enough. There had to be more of them out there, a platoon at least under the Leutnant's command, and who knew how many under Herr Major, possibly a hundred or more. There were certainly more than that north in the Italian stronghold Sebha. But Thiele was not thinking as far north as Sebha. He was thinking of a small village, not too far from the complex, only a few hours no more. Their village where their Colonel Schönfeld was scheduled to arrive from Algiers to supervise the first major shipment between compounds, theirs, and the struggling next in line. A village Reineke controlled, a second compound he wanted just as he wanted Sebha, not only for her munitions she could give him, but her power, position, and size. It would never happen. It did not work that way in the modern world where the SS controlled the cities and towns worth having, either openly, or through their puppeteers. They were under siege. The SS was not there to punish. They were there to take. The Hauptmann should be flattered how after three short months his compound could be so valuable as to be stolen from him.

Back outside the dreaded Holy Man was still not yet in sight.

"Have the girl placed in the apartment," Reineke clarified his earlier instructions, his office no more appropriate as a morgue than the hall. Thiele did not take the ring of keys offered. The prisoner could not go into the apartment and neither could the Holy Man. They would have to pass through the library, and the SS blocked their way.

"Do as I tell you," Reineke snapped.

But, "SS," was all Thiele said, and he stepped aside, allowing Reineke to run.

For the moment, Reineke's temper was confined to the pounding of his boots claiming the stairs. Enraged, he still remembered to collect his hat, and the pounding came to an abrupt halt when he reached the library doors.

Parade rest. Thiele watched Reineke assume his pose of confidence and control, feet spaced and hands behind his back. One SS officer was in the library, a Leutnant, Thiele's age, standing at the helm of Reineke's compound, loitering at Reineke's desk stationed on the raised landing, in front of the wall of French windows.

Faust. Thiele recalled the Korporal mentioning the name. He was ugly, SS Leutnant Faust, fat and fleshy, with thick lips and a broad face squatting on a short fat neck. Thiele thought of a turtle first and then a python. A turtle wanting to be a python was probably closest. Thiele was not intimidated, his own confidence intact.

"Ah, Hauptmann Reineke," the turtle closed the book he was reading with a crisp slap, his smile contrived and misleading. "I am

SS Leutnant Günther Faust. My colleague and I thought perhaps you and I should meet first ... *Sooooo ...*" he swayed toward them, down the short steps of the landing. "I have been waiting to do that."

"Waiting," Thiele sneered; he could not help it. The SS was not *waiting* for anyone. Faust had been brought there, ordered to appear. Thiele knew this. He had ordered it. He caught himself though with a quick look at Reineke whose anger appeared briefly displaced by his amusement for Thiele's bold display of ill temper. The Leutnant Faust did not share in Reineke's pleasure, but was shocked by the affront. Thiele shrugged. He wasn't necessarily brash, he was just truthful, and no more a fan of the SS than any of them.

Especially this one, Thiele eyed Faust, some fat man with some ridiculous order for the Hauptmann's arrest. For what? The compound? What compound? Thiele could play games, too. He also outranked this Leutnant, whether Thiele was merely Wehrmacht, and this one elite SS. "You have orders," Thiele took a step forward, hand outstretched. "I want to see those orders ..."

"Open the apartment, Thiele." Reineke interrupted, pressing his ring of keys into Thiele's hand.

"Hauptmann ..." Thiele stared at them.

"Do it now," Reineke advised, Faust's eyes following Thiele's sharp steps across the room before revolving back to Reineke with a smile.

"You have an excellent library here, Herr Hauptmann," he congratulated.

A meaningless observation, irrelevant. He had questions, this Faust, but no evidence to support them. If he had evidence, he would not have the courage to be there. Lies, he had whatever courage he thought he needed. Reineke smiled under his deadpan expression. The SS knew nothing and were afraid, struggling to regain ground, ill prepared for the resistance by his men even in his absence.

"There are some old—some very rare manuscripts."

The SS worked hard at showing its ignorance in its effort to show culture and class. Reineke had a library that rivaled Alexandria, the secrets of mankind fragile as silk and turning to dust on their shelves. *BANG!* The lacquered brass handle of the apartment door interrupted that time, striking the plastered clay wall, disturbing the fresco buried underneath. A sound like something scurrying as a few chips crumbled and fell. Thiele did not apologize. Wrenching the key from the lock, he retired against the molding his arms folded and face sullen.

"Oberleutnant," Faust acknowledged before returning again to Reineke. "But then we are not here to discuss books, are we?" his porous, fleshy hand extended in greeting went ignored.

"I see," Faust said, concerned by such behavior, and certainly most perplexed. "Yes, well, very well then, may I?" he waved at an available side chair, its baroque design as oddly out of place as the French windows. "Yes? No?

"Very well then, Hauptmann," he sighed when Reineke did not answer, "obviously, there are far more important matters to discuss than your squandering seditious literature ...

"Munitions, for one," his smile broadened, teeth flat and white in his pudgy face. "It would make matters much simpler if you would see to cooperate. Once these tiresome matters are finished, we are then free to discuss your position on any issue of your choosing ...

"Unless you would rather begin, Hauptmann?" he wondered. "Yes? No? Hauptmann," he sighed again, "am I boring you?"

"Boring me, Leutnant?" Reineke replied, and Thiele's hands tightened their hold on his jacket, the fat of Leutnant Faust beginning to redden under the Hauptmann's unwavering gaze. "Indeed." Reineke called for his sentry who responded, carrying in the prisoner, and Leutnant Faust stopped turning red. "One of your tiresome matters," Reineke agreed as the girl was paraded across the library, disappearing through the apartment door.

"Yes," Faust said, "so I see."

"Good," Reineke approved. "It is my position."

Was it? Faust looked at him. "Is it?" he said. "Really, that is most interesting, Hauptmann ..."

"Which this conversation is not," Reineke assured. "Leave my complex now. Get out."

"Out?" the abundant flesh of Faust's cheeks pinched tightly. "Hauptmann, you fail to understand—"

No, he did not. Reineke failed at nothing, including suicide. The idea of it, the risk, already having crossed his mind, he rejected it until he was ready to accept it. When he did, it would be his choice, not the SS. He called out again, that time for the guards, two more sentries quickly responding, standing on either side of him. "Remove this ..." Reineke looked Faust up and down, the uniform of the elite snug across his girdled belly. "Remove this swine from my office. If he refuses, kill him."

"Kill?" The ring of keys slipped from Thiele's hand, clattering to the floor.

"Kill?" Faust sputtered, not quite managing to take a step, the butt of a sentry's rifle responding, burying itself in his abdomen, sending him crashing to the floor.

"But he is SS!" Thiele bridged the distance to Reineke in two steps.

"Indeed," Reineke said, thoroughly unimpressed.

"You cannot do this," Thiele insisted. "Tell them to let him up or I will. I will!"

Reineke looked at him, the silence between them long. Faust's eyes closed under the sights of the sentries' guns, waiting for the click of the triggers.

"I said to let him up!" Thiele turned on the soldier nearest him, wrenching the gun painfully from his hands.

"Let him up!" Thiele insisted and a powerful kick with his boot would have dislocated a knee, except the second soldier spun, his rifle presented at Thiele's chest. Thiele stared at it.

"So that is enough, eh, Thiele?" Reineke's soft voice brought the rifle down. "Enough."

But, no. Oh, no. "No, I do not think so." A new voice entered the scene, and with the grace of a mechanical toy, Thiele turned around to the SS Major breezing through the library doors.

Chapter Five

He was fifty, Herr Major, thin and tall as the Hauptmann, but dark. *Sudetendeutscher.* Thiele guessed. A Czechoslovakian cousin of the Nordic race. This one of Hungarian or Romanian descent, the face foreign and sharply angular, creased with power and age, the hair black beneath his blue cap. Thiele stared from the cap to the uniform resplendent with medals and field gray. The medals inappropriate, the color, and uniform itself an unusual choice for the region where the khaki standard of the Afrika Korps provided comfort but also camouflage; the last thing apparently on Herr Major's mind. Thiele bit the inside of his cheek. Well dressed, the SS were from the north. Tripoli or Tunis perhaps, Berlin even, as claimed, and they were here for conquest definitely. The business attire of Herr Major complete with dangling party sword.

"We would have been introduced earlier, Hauptmann," the Major assured, his finger extended like a pointer as he strode across the floor, unmindful of the sentries quick to fix themselves to his hip pockets. "Except your men thought it best to postpone our meeting—a commendable attitude, I might add. We are second to no one in our appreciation of the soldier who knows his duty, performing it without question or complaint," he smiled, so terribly pleased with the little joke.

Thiele's teeth clamped tighter, his eyes traveling back to the breast of the jacket with its dozen medals—

No, nine. Thiele counted them quickly. The Knight's Cross with oak leaf clusters was coveted and rare, restricted to the most exceptional circumstances and men, and still nowhere near as impressive as his wound badges. Gold wound badges, two of them. Five or more wounds each, they boasted, *each.* Herr Major had been wounded in duty at least ten times, probably in two different wars.

The inside of Thiele's mouth was going to bleed, and he released the tortured flesh, staring at the man who was either extremely lucky or careless, or insane.

He was left-handed. The packaging blinded Thiele. Reineke observed the man, and he would not have expected anything less from this illegitimate peasant calling himself SS. The sword was on the wrong side. The hand he held out, the wrong one. An insult Thiele should have noticed having been born with the same affliction, and only awkwardly cured.

"Hauptmann?" Herr Major retracted his finger stained by nicotine, ending the temporary pause. His eyes bright under the influence of his drug, the face pitted with the pox of disease and age, the shoes were worn beneath their polish, the tailored wool suit with its inappropriate display, three years out of date. They had no place for him in his new Reich once established, not even in the elite SS. He was saying something about intrusion, moving past Reineke for the steps of the landing, apologizing and understanding how their unexpected appearance could account for any unorthodox behavior, the words overflowing his tongue ...

And then his foot touched the first of the three steps, the sentries separating to stand in front of him, block his way, and he hesitated for the first time, one foot up and one foot down, stood there posing in his fading finery with its pretty little pins soaked in blood.

"Oh, no, shhh, Oberleutnant," he smiled at Thiele for some reason, stepping back down. "Please do not say 'Hauptmann'. We know who he is, as we know who I am."

"Herr SS Major Hanse Weiheber of Berlin," one of the sentries provided to Reineke.

"Yes," Weiheber chuckled softly, "yes," shifting his attention to the rotund figure on the floor. "Ah, Faust," he noted. "Ah, yes, Faust." His SS Leutnant Günther Faust.

"We both have reputations, Hauptmann," Weiheber agreed with an accompanying amused shake of his head, "and neither of us, I am certain, wish to waste any more time flexing our ... celebrity ..." he paused with a savoring, fluttering look over the fine Nordic specimen. Such poise Reineke had. Beauty. A flawless figure and face.

"Mythical, really," he teased. "Man or angel, Hauptmann?" he wondered equally amused by the Oberleutnant Thiele's startled blink when surely the lieutenant must have thought it himself at some point, some time.

"Man or angel," Weiheber mused, producing a pair of rimless spectacles, perching them on the bridge of his nose for a closer, clearer look.

"Michael, Hauptmann?" he smiled. "Or is it the Archangel Gabriele you prefer?"

Neither. Thiele knew. It was Lucifer. The most beautiful of all. Those were not the eyes of an angel watching Herr Major. "Hauptmann ..." he attempted to claim Reineke's attention, but was ignored.

"Either way you have succeeded in your humiliation, Hauptmann," Weiheber assured Reineke, "of my ... well, somewhat *wanting* specimen," he agreed. "Won't you now take pity on him and allow him to get up? After all, he can't *go,* Hauptmann," he reminded, "unless you let him. He can't leave and let the men talk."

Never. Thiele knew, and he blushed in embarrassment for the Leutnant, a frightened turtle on his back.

"Up, Faust," Weiheber encouraged. "Get up, Faust," he waggled his finger, waved his hand.

"Hauptmann ..." Thiele tried again and was ignored.

Weiheber sighed. "Now, we can't all be heroes, Hauptmann, can we?" he said. "Try as we might, as much as we may want to. There is only one Göring, one Richthofen. One *Rommel,*" his tongue brushed his lip.

And one king. "Get up," Reineke instructed Faust.

"Thank you," Weiheber beamed. "Really, thank you very much, Hauptmann. You see how easy that was?"

"And get out," Reineke directed Weiheber.

Weiheber chuckled again at the sentries with their rifles, one of them tapping his arm. "How possessive you are of your little sandbox," he agreed. "I was told I would find you possessive. As a matter of fact, Hauptmann," he winked, "I have been told a great many things—"

"Fire," Reineke ordered, and the guards obeyed. Two-dozen

bullets hammered into the ceiling over the Major's head, showering him and the room with chips of plaster and white dust as they penetrated the mosaic panels, ricocheting off the marble arches, scoring angry black furrows across the face of the dome, and six more sentries armed with machine guns barreled into the library. Reineke stood in front of the dumbfounded SS, his steel-toed boot toeing the powder until he found a chunk to his liking. Retrieving it, he held it out. "A piece of my sandbox," he offered. "Now get out, or they will cut you in half."

"Swine!" Weiheber lunged faster than Thiele could stop him. It was only the second time in his life Reineke had ever struck anything with his bare hand; Thiele had been the first, outside on the steps. Weiheber he hit with his fist. It was unsatisfying and hurt, angering him more. His knuckles immediately bruised and swelling, cut by the defiant eyeglasses as he caught Weiheber's face flush, and Weiheber was down on his back in the dust, his spectacles shattered, Reineke reaching to rip the cross from his throat, the silk ribbon unraveling as he tore it free.

"Filth!" Reineke spit and flung the medal in the dust.

"Swine!" Weiheber screamed. "Insolent swine!"

"Drop it!" Thiele barked. His pistol drawn and pointed before Weiheber could finish groping for his. "You are not a fool," Thiele warned, the sentries looming threateningly behind him. "Drop it or die!"

"I see!" Weiheber said.

"Do you?" Thiele doubted it. He yanked Weiheber's pistol away, emptying the clip. "He is letting you leave, can you see that? They want to kill you, can you see that?" Thiele could. It was in their eyes. The puppets laughing, happy, unmistakably proud.

"Now, get out of here," Thiele tossed the gun back to Weiheber, "or I will give the order. Get out of here!" he screamed. "Leave!" They did.

Thiele intended to keep watch from the library balcony overlooking the courtyard until the last of the Major's dust settled onto the road. The arrival of the Holy Man changed that, the dwarfed brown figure appearing on a toddling run across the blistering stones for the villa.

"Du sau!" Thiele angrily released his watch over the SS to meet the priest on the grand staircase.

The door of the villa whisked open by the Korporal, the sentries stood at stiff, respectful attention for the Algerian Jesuit priest whom Reineke had cried out for in the desert as if invoking some god.

He was no god. His fat body crippled and dwarfed from birth and age. His misshapen brown face flushed and perspiring, he cursed Thiele in words Thiele could not understand, daring the German lieutenant to block his way, try to stop him, as he boldly hoisted himself up the stairs.

Thiele did not stop him, not because he did not dare because he did dare, and would suffer Reineke's wrath for having dared. It was just oddly, for a moment as Thiele stood on the stairs the priest sputtering in his French, "Out of my way, pig! Out! Go!" he wanted the Holy Man there. Someone, something to bring the Hauptmann under control, a potion, a spell, Thiele did not care. Then the priest could return to his village and children, and they could return to their munitions and war.

Chapter Six

Reineke was in the apartment, the smallest of the three suites of the arcaded gallery, overlooking the eastern courtyard from its wall of installed French windows and narrow stone balcony. Reserved for visiting officers or guests of distinction, there had never been any, and was only on loan now. His sentries he sent to help in the search for the missing Holy Man and a basin of water. They were going to need water.

The prisoner lay prone on the bed, mangled, but still alive, her eyes unchanged from the cellar, wide, open, and unseeing. Her chest was moving though, unevenly as she gasped and strangled on her breath, and so she would die soon, choked on the blood covering her. Reineke studied her irritably, curious whose face lay beneath the beating she took. She was extremely young, barely sixteen, and so unless the Allies also engaged their youth in military service, he failed to see what possible threat she could be to anyone. It did not make sense, none of this. He needed to relax and think. Relax so he could think and it would make sense. Think until it did make sense. Her clothes were from the north like the SS pigs who brought her there. She was possibly new to the North Afrikan arena with her woolen suit. A recent transplant or implant with no intention of staying long.

Either that or her luggage had been lost. Such an idiotic thought to cross his mind. It was the heat of the room. The sudden silence around him for which he should be thankful, but was not.

Who are you? He bore down on the bed, looming over her. The helpless, almost peaceful expression she wore, ridiculing his silent interrogation. A fleeting chill of embarrassment passed over him. Why? He was uncertain, and pushed it away. His interest was natural. To be expected. This deep in the desert? Three hundred kilometers from the nearest hint of European civilization, and even then it was Italian, not Allied. *Who are your people*? He persisted, annoyed by her clothing that did resemble a uniform. Without its jacket, though, he could not be certain if the issue was English or French. This could be traced to the Holy Man. It was absolutely the work of the Holy Man. Some hapless band of gypsies with some sad story—yet another band of gypsies with the same sad story the Holy Man never tired of telling. *Where are your people*? He demanded, as if he did not know. Lost in the desert, as she was lost. Lost, and probably dead. *What are you doing here*?

He stepped back from her in disgust, her smell so much worse in the heat of the room. This close to her, she made him nauseous, her body reeking of urine, teeth thick with bile. "Mademoiselle?" he attempted to penetrate those ragged last breaths she took, looking for information and trying French first, and then English. "Mademoiselle, can you hear me?"

She could in fact. With a snap, her eyes turned on him, their swollen pupils staring up at him. She said something, possibly a word, but he could not understand her, not even what language.

"Mademoiselle?" he requested impatiently. "Try to speak slowly. You have been injured, severely. There is a priest on the way for you to make peace with God."

She said something again in a hoarse dry whisper, moving as if she was trying to sit up, and so he stepped closer, leaned over her to hear her and she attacked him. So fast, she was up, clawing at his shirt, knocking his hat from his head and pulling at his hair, her heels digging into the bed, trying to run, the sting of her broken nails slicing across his cheek as he struggled to untangle himself without hurting her more.

"No!" she hissed, her words English and perfectly clear. "No!" She was going to vomit. He watched her start to heave, the heaves bringing up bile and that he did not want to see. His only intention was to stop her. In her fright, she was going to fall off the bed. But those claws came at him again, and he hesitated, her hair the easiest thing to grab. That filthy knotted braid of dark red hair ...

There was a *pop* as he snatched it. A neat *POP* like a cork released from a bottle. In midair, she stopped, dropping to her knees and Reineke brought his hand away sticky with blood.

"Mademoiselle?" he said, quite perplexed.

Death tried again to take her. A series of violent, spastic convulsions attacked her that she attempted to fight and failed. Her eyes rolling up into her head, she fell over backwards, a thin trickle of blood slowly seeping out from the back of her head staining the sheets as she lay there gasping. Shocked, Reineke yanked her practically back to her feet, desperate to find the wound he had caused, but the blood suddenly gushed, and he panicked, almost dropping her on the floor as he clamped his hand over the gash to staunch the flow, her body dangling over his arm like some bizarre rag doll.

"Mon Dieu!" the Holy Man Pierre exclaimed horrified from the doorway. "Raise her head, mon capitaine, not her feet! Quickly!"

Pierre pushed his way into the room, Thiele catching a pointed elbow in his side as the priest shoved past him to snatch the towel away from the sentry returning with the basin of water.

"Sit down, mon capitaine, sit down," Pierre's arthritic claw fastened itself around Reineke's wrist. "It is all right. You do not have to let her go, just sit down!"

Reineke stared at him. His eyes wide like a frightened child himself. "Are you deaf?" Pierre insisted with a sharp crack on his arm, rousing him awake. "Sit down!"

Reineke obeyed, the girl securely cradled on his lap.

"Good!" Pierre approved, surveying the situation quickly. "We will need water. Very hot water, very cold, and these, more of these," he bounced the towel in Thiele's face. Thiele ignored him, and Pierre angrily turned on Reineke for help. "Tell him what to do," he insisted. "Do not just sit there. What is one towel, eh, idiot?"

"Do as he says." Reineke snapped in German at Thiele, annoyed, the black eyes of the Holy Man brightening happy with the support. "He wants towels. Bring him towels, cloth, anything. You can see the girl is bleeding!"

"Thank you, mon capitaine," Pierre beamed, not forgetting to curse Thiele. "The stupid German Lieutenant listens only to the German capitaine, even though he knows what I ask, is what mon capitaine wants. And!" he shook his crooked finger in Reineke's face, "what you want is many things. Pay attention so you can tell those clowns out there what we need."

Thiele did not stay to hear the orders rapidly translated from French to German. He left it to the sentries crowding the doorway. Moving across the library, he was in Reineke's chambers and back out with more towels, though he was too late to prevent the last of the guards from leaving.

Arschloch! Thiele damned the wily Algerian priest condemned to spending eternity in Hell for some crime against the Holy Empire of Rome. Outspoken in his hatred of Mussolini and the German occupation he was lucky either of them did not kill him.

Rather than indulge him, which the Hauptmann did. Thiele glared at Reineke, talking to the Algerian in his French. Thiele did not speak or understand French, and so he was also condemned, reduced to interpreting the priest's gesturing hands and anxious excitement he could see in Reineke's face.

It was not excitement. Reineke did not know what he felt, only that it was not excitement. The appearance of the Holy Man startled him as much as the prisoner had, especially since he had expected to find the Holy Man dead, the host of his orphan flock along with him, Diana, the village matriarch, dangling beside her sons in the courtyard, not this. He continued not to expect this. Some child alone and on her own hundreds of kilometers from any European settlement? How could he be expected to expect this? *Relax!* Reineke ordered himself sternly. The explanation was reasonable. It was war. The explanation lay with the Holy Man. Reineke knew it if he knew nothing else.

"You see, mon capitaine?" Pierre explained as Reineke sat on the bed, clutching the girl to his chest, the towel clamped tightly to her head. "The blood is stopping already. Pressure, oui, pressure, that is the answer. Head up, feet down."

"That is what I was trying to do," Reineke insisted. "I have no idea what happened, none. She slipped. That is what happened. She slipped."

"Of course," Pierre had no doubt of the good intentions behind the circus act. "I did not think you were trying to dance."

Dance. This priest would be in Hell before him. "Watch how you joke," Reineke suggested coldly. "She is dead."

"Possibly, oui, probably," Pierre agreed. "If not now, very soon. She has been poisoned, drugged. Henbane, nightshade. An overdose. Her heart is very erratic."

"Drugged?" Reineke said.

"Truth serum," Pierre nodded. "It dilates the eyes."

"Indeed," Reineke stared down on the child in his lap. "Who could she possibly be that the SS would drug her?"

"Or bring her here," Pierre pointed out, and Reineke's head jerked up to eye him. "I do not know, do you?"

"Yes, " Reineke assured. "This is not me, it is you."

"No, it is not," Pierre denied. "A few more minutes and I will wipe her face so we can perhaps see for ourselves who she is, no?"

"Yes," Reineke said. "Of course, yes—indeed, why do you think I sent for you?" he snapped. "This is why. She is why. Why are you even asking me?" he demanded. "Just do what you do and be done."

"I am," Pierre handed him a fresh towel to hold in place while he quickly rinsed the first in the basin. "The head bleeds very much, mon capitaine. That is not always bad, it can be good, a natural way of cleansing."

Good? Reineke stared at the water bleaching the towel pale pink, a slick of blood sticking to the sides of the basin. His stomach turned, sick as he had felt in the cellar. "I did not do this," he repeated. "Good, or bad, I had nothing to do with any of this."

"Oui, Pontius Pilate," Pierre agreed. "You do not have to explain to me."

Reineke glared at him. "I am innocent," he assured. "I tried to help her. Certainly not hurt her in anyway. She was going to fall. I pulled her hair to stop her from falling, but the braid was stuck like glue." He stared at the saturated bed sheets. "Glue." And just like glue, it gave way.

"Oui, I know," Pierre vigorously attacked the woman's face. "An accident. For a ballerina, mon capitaine is such a klutz—"

"Gently!" Reineke slapped his hand away. "What is wrong with you? You are not polishing some boot!"

"She is dead," Pierre reminded, "soon to be."

"Gently!" Reineke insisted.

"All right, gently," Pierre shrugged. "You worry about your reputation at the oddest times, mon capitaine, in the oddest ways. Gently, it will not come clean, but, you are the master, I am only the slave, have it your way."

His way? Indeed. Reineke should be so lucky and the Holy Man so inclined. He had no control over this priest, none. Try as he might, as much as he might want to, he was not the master and the Holy Man hardly some slave. "Indeed," Reineke said coldly. "My reputation is above reproach."

"For this sort of thing," Pierre agreed, "oui."

"For all things," Reineke assured, "in all ways, every way."

"It is an all right one," Pierre granted, "yes."

All right. It would be better if he wore a different uniform, such as Allied, or best of all, French, instead of the one he did wear.

"Not French," Pierre said.

"What?" Reineke said aloud.

"She is not French," Pierre said.

No, she was English according to Thiele. Reineke studied her skirt.

"Is she German?" Pierre asked.

German? Of course, she was not German. Reineke could not actually know that, any more than Thiele could know who she was, but he did know it. "She is injured," Reineke replied. "She has been injured—enough, I would think, regardless of who she is."

"Oui, mon capitaine is a patron saint of kindness," Pierre agreed. "He does not have to defend himself. It is good, because she is lucky. Oui, very lucky," he acknowledged, sympathetically. "The man with her not so lucky, no, his ears filled with blood."

Man? Reineke had not heard anything about any man. "What man? Indeed," he was incredulous. "You attended to some man first?"

"I did not attend to any man," Pierre corrected, "I buried him. It was his head, like Mademoiselle, but much worse. The skull crushed. Bones like spikes sticking out through the flesh—"

"All right!" Reineke silenced him. Accounts and lectures on

German pigs could wait. "The man can wait. We will discuss the man later. Tend to this one now. Focus your energies on this one—and do not!" he grabbed that deadly paw, "scour her. Wash her. If it takes ten minutes, it takes ten minutes. Your spies can wait to give you their report!"

"Are you sure?" Pierre asked and Reineke sighed. No. No, of course he was not sure, not of anything. Clearly, obviously, he was unsure of everything, including the reasons for the apparent murders of some man and child on his doorstep, only that once the SS were done with her, they threw her like a bone to his dogs.

"What happened?" Reineke insisted. "What went wrong? Where are the rest of them? Her family? People?" This priest could not tell him there were only two of them. There were never only two of them. By this point, if Reineke counted them, they had to outnumber his men. "Be assured she has told the SS whatever they wanted to hear. You must tell me now what happened. I cannot help you, if you do not tell me!"

Pierre scoffed. "Mon capitaine, we can talk about whatever you want, now or later, and it will change nothing. This has nothing to do with Pierre. The SS would be dead if it did, and they are not. You think not, think again. Pierre is as afraid of the SS as he is of you, and he is not afraid of either. Think about that."

Think. Where had Reineke heard that before? Though they were on different sides in this war Thiele and the Holy Man had more in common then they realized. "Indeed," Reineke closed his eyes. "I have not had time to think."

"So think now. Does mon capitaine really think if I had known about this child, I would have waited?"

No. No, of course, he did not think that. He just did not know where the priest was. He could not understand why he was not there. "Where were you?" Reineke insisted. "You were not in the village, and you were not here, where were you? I went to the village," he assured before the priest could lie, "and no one was there. The people were alone."

"Did you go to the children?" Pierre asked. "No, of course you did not," he agreed as Reineke reacted. "Mon capitaine would never frighten them more than they are frightened already. And that is where they were," he said, "that is where they are. To protect them, of course. Reassure them for when the SS walked among them—which, of course they did not," he assured. "Mon capitaine's men are not too smart, but they are not stupid. The SS went nowhere except here, the villa. If they tried, the men lined up," he gestured, "stopped them."

"You were not at the children," Reineke said. "I sent the men to the children to find you."

"No, I was in the gardens," Pierre agreed, "because I knew nothing about her. You, on the other hand, can wait until the crack of doom. How would I know she is why you called for me?"

"Why did you not know?" Reineke asked.

"Pardon?" Pierre said.

"Why did you not know anything about her?" Reineke repeated. "Why do you not?"

"Because I do not," Pierre said simply. "I know nothing about this at all. Not who they are or why, and I was too busy burying the first victim of your police to find out for you."

That was not an answer. A flimsy excuse for a priest who knew everything, *claimed*, to know everything, and now when it was under his nose? "They are not my police," Reineke corrected. "I have nothing to do with the police—indeed!" he snapped, temper rising. "You know *that*. When have I ever had anything to do with the police? Do not be insane."

"Mon capitaine, I have known you three months," Pierre reminded. "Hitler has been here a year, Mussolini, twenty. You could be them, or you could be you. In time we will see."

"Never," Reineke insisted. "Never."

"I know," Pierre grinned. "Because they are pigs, dogs. You believe that, and so I believe you. I just like to hear you say it."

"Indeed," Reineke shook his head. Dizzy, he felt no less than dizzy whenever he was around this priest, nothing to do with some prisoner, the heat, or the smell, but simply the priest alone. "Talk to me about this man you buried," he requested, a safer subject far more important.

"So soon?" the priest laughed, his eyes wicked and sly, sliding to the side and the hovering presence of Thiele, remembering him even if Reineke had forgotten. "Later comes quickly even for you. Less than a breath, what is no, is suddenly yes. Something perhaps though you have forgotten about?"

Reineke had forgotten nothing, least of all about Thiele. It was simply ridiculous to suggest his interest in the affair did not extend beyond the melodrama of some child dead or dying on his lap. "Yes, now," he said. "*Now.* Talk to me. A white one? Mufti, as they call them?"

"Mufti is not what they call them," Pierre said. "Mufti is civilian clothes, not a civilian man. The word you are looking for is wog. Their word for Arab is wog, yes, wog."

"Just tell me!" Reineke demanded. "Their skin white or brown? And their clothes, what about their clothes? Could you recognize them?"

"White," Pierre shrugged, "and only one. One man and this child. I do not know anything about their clothes. They are similar, I guess, but not the same, no, definitely not. So, who she is? Who knows? There is a belief the man could be American. Oui, an officer," he nodded and Thiele's unfortunate scuff of his boot as he bristled at the one word *Américain* that he could understand had Reineke quickly on the alert.

"Army, I think," Pierre agreed. "Oui, army, I am almost positive this is what was said."

"Later," Reineke silenced him.

"Pardon?" Pierre said.

"Later!" Reineke insisted.

"All right, later," Pierre shrugged. "Now, later, make up your mind."

Reineke had. "Go and start a fire in the stove," he directed Thiele, leaving him to scowl as he left, hating the Holy Man. "Not here, my quarters. We will need fresh kettles of hot water. Bring them when they are ready. Indeed." Reineke stared at the enemy in his lap. "A master understands what it is to be a master," he told the Holy Man smiling so shrewdly at him. "I am a master. This is the work of hoodlums, filth."

"I understand that, mon capitaine," Pierre agreed.

"So do I!" Reineke assured. "So do I."

Chapter Seven

"She is very young, mon capitaine, you are right." Tongue clicking in dismay, Pierre gently patted the girl's face dry.

Yes, she was young, and not dead. This was absurd, some sort of trick. Ten minutes, twenty, and she still was not dead. Reineke's body might be hostage to the prisoner making her bed on his chest and lap, but his mind was not and his thoughts continued to race, unable to settle, focus on one thing at a time. He returned to scrutinizing the girl, cruel bruises and a freckled suntan emerging from under the washed blood, the thin marks of a chain pulled from her neck. He briefly wondered what the chain could have been, its purpose, but then decided he did not want to know. The less he knew, the more he could decide what he wanted to be the truth rather than the Holy Man deciding with his glib tongue and honest heart. Politician, philosopher, caretaker, priest, the Holy Man could be any and was all of them. Thiele was not the only one who did not trust the deceptive brown beggar neither did Reineke. If he ever had, he did not now he could not now, not with the SS, Allies, and whoever else roaming around, alive, dead, or somewhere in between.

"Indeed, this is ridiculous," he accused finally. "How long can it possibly take to bathe some child and give her your last rites?"

Pierre looked up, but Reineke was already ordering him to silence. "Never mind. Just do what you are doing. Continue," he waved, "doing what you are doing."

Pierre disobeyed of course, speaking even though he had been warned. "Would it be easier for mon capitaine to talk about the man again?"

What did that even mean *would it be easier*? What Reineke might find *easier* was not the point. The point was it was taking too long. "Thiele will be back any moment," Reineke reminded. "I ask you again, if this has anything to do with the village, you must tell me now."

"What village is this?" Pierre requested.

What village did he *think*? The Arab, the native, the nomad, the settlement where Reineke had remanded the civilian population and even that was not far enough, not then and certainly not now—obviously not now. He was too generous, too reasonable, compassion teetering on the brink of treason and giving aid and shelter to the enemy. Thiele was right. And where had it brought him, what had it gotten him, other than this? "Your native village," he assured. "Or is that too fantastic to even think?"

"It is paranoia, possibly," Pierre agreed. "I do not know about fantastic, but paranoia, oui, perhaps. You are as annoying as a fly, mon capitaine. Six times, I have told you it has nothing to do with Pierre, but still you insist. So, paranoia, oui. You are paranoid."

Paranoid. Paranoia was unreasonable panic or fear, imaginary persecution from imaginary persons or things. The village was neither, but far too real, much like its priest. Strength in his bent posture, gifted with intelligence, blessed with education, and training, cursed and defrocked, crippled from age, birth, or beatings to whittle away his sins and other earthly delights, the limbs twisted and broken and healed as they were, but still a master. Once master of the desert oasis, father to countless orphans from babies to adolescents, one quarter of the oasis's population, half of Reineke's native façade as young as or younger than the girl on his lap.

"Indeed," Reineke said. The answer had to be the village. There was no other reasonable or even plausible explanation. The first weeks of Reineke's occupation had been a constant battle between him and the Holy Man. The comical Algerian spitting his resistance loudly to the all mighty German with his demands, refusing to surrender what Reineke called the villa and Pierre called the children's home. The random adult population, the Holy Man had insisted were unaffiliated with his orphanage. A scattered band of nomads simply visiting the oasis for its water before moving on—which they would continue to do whether the Holy Man had the power to stop them or not, which he also refused to do.

"And as far as you!" the unyielding priest had assured, picking

up a glass paperweight from off the desk where he had once sat reading stories to his illiterate brood, heaving it at Reineke, striking him in the chest. "The next is a bullet!" he promised if Reineke insisted upon staying even the night, the German Captain, nor his troop, alive to leave in the morning.

Reineke had stayed, unafraid of some priest fearful for his children. The screaming group of them gathered up with their priest and the nomads and marched to the desolate western sector of the oasis and its tomb of ruins, and in the morning, despite the heavy ring of guards, the heads of two goats hung in the courtyard, their bloody carcasses thrown on the steps of the portico in warning. Reineke ordered the heads cut down, the carcasses cleaned and cooked for dinner, and come the second morning there were two more goat heads hung in the courtyard, but no carcasses; the children had to eat, too.

Reineke was convinced the natives would consume the whole of their livestock by the end of the week if the nonsense did not stop. He tried reason. Threats of punishment and even death when reason failed, vowing to kill them all, which he did not, but instead, agreed to a compromise and it was Thiele's turn to explode. You do not compromise with the enemy!

But Reineke refused to listen, severing the children from the nomad tribe and returning them and their priest to the main ground, remanded to a private area of their own. The nomads remained in the west, the borders of the oasis the boundary of their prison, and Reineke would know if they attempted to stray, because he would count them if necessary. It was settled and it worked, for two weeks. Thiele was not surprised when the arguments started again, only this time he was excluded, first by the language, no longer in French and explained in German, but in French and not explained at all. Then suddenly, the feud moved away from the villa, out of Thiele's sight and hearing all together. But he knew the fight continued, until one day, as before, some agreement was reached, a pact made, the terms of the contract known only by its two authors. Confounded, Thiele had no choice but to watch, eventually, begrudgingly, admitting to the treaty's success as the Hauptmann emerged from the drama focused and concentrating on the complex, the rapid and thorough organization helping much to soothe the concerns of his uncertain First Officer.

Impressed, Thiele's apprehensions faded, convincing himself, he was capable of balancing Reineke's high-pitched emotions with logic and cooler heads, and the two officers were becoming ...

Friends?

The Holy Man did not leave. Not the villa or the main grounds but was as free as Reineke to wander where he wanted, walk where he wished. Thiele attempted to overlook the relationship, ignoring it at first, but it was becoming difficult as the two opposing authority figures also continued to talk. The private conversations now quiet, increasing in frequency and length as the days and weeks passed on. The bond between the Hauptmann and the Holy Man was not something Thiele could understand, least of all solve, and manacled him with its strength. The Jesuit monk was a private possession and at the top of Reineke's strict list of rules and regulations was Rule One: No one interfered with the Holy Man.

Not even you? Thiele stood in the doorway in the minutes before Reineke ordered him to leave, watching the meek and submissive Hauptmann obediently sitting in his enemy's blood, the prisoner cradled on his lap. It was disturbing to see, disturbing to think how the hands controlling the puppet strings might not necessarily be Reineke's.

What did he offer you? *What did he promise*? *Eternal life*? *Divinity*? Thiele was at a loss. Reineke was not even Catholic, he was Lutheran. A heretic by the monk's Roman measure, child of the demon Beëlzebub, spawn of the anti-Christ, Lucifer ...

Who was leaving, they were leaving finally. The Hauptmann shifted in his seat and Thiele's tight lips parted, a cool breath of relief escaping to be cut short. Thiele stiffened, bristling when he realized they were not leaving. In disbelief, he watched the Holy Man tip the woman's head away from Reineke to allow him to adjust to a more comfortable position before he took her back into his arms.

"Go and start a fire in the stove, Thiele," Reineke directed him. "Not here, my quarters. We will need fresh kettles of hot water. Bring them to us when they are ready."

“Mon capitaine?” Pierre’s voice roused Reineke from his thoughts.

Yes, he was listening. Paranoia, indeed. That was the taunt of the sibyl Diana. Her harsh threats and promises of annihilation issued in concert with the Holy Man’s schemes of redemption. Reineke had yet to decide which of the two of them was worse, which of the two he could trust least, knew best, but he had a good idea. “I saw two in the courtyard,” he assured, hardly paranoid, simply not blind. “Thiele saw them. Hanuk on the steps—”

“The dentist and the lawyer,” Pierre interrupted, “yes.”

The dentist and the lawyer. Somewhere, somehow, if only in his mind, Reineke held the belief he was the commander of a munitions complex, and in control. That this was a munitions complex—a *German* munitions complex despite appearances to the contrary, of which he was at least partially to blame.

“Indeed,” Reineke said. He was not responsible. Perhaps in some small way that did not count, such as the inspired scheme of an Arab façade, but that was the extent of it. That was the limit. The dentist and the lawyer, he did not know. Not which was which or who was who. The doctor among them, yes, the doctor among them he knew. The doctor he dealt with when needing to deal with things, occasionally talked to on subjects other than the neuroses of Diana or the Holy Man they conspired to apply to him. And the doctor among them would never have been so ... what? Stupid? Brazen? Bold? The doctor among them was clearly not there, but elsewhere, leaving the dentist and lawyer to fend for themselves however inept they were, which apparently they were.

“Defense, of course, mon capitaine,” Pierre was claiming as the reason behind the native infiltration of his camp. “Interest, and, yes, defense.”

“Suicide,” Reineke assured.

“Not really,” Pierre denied, “there were only a few SS. Six, I heard, six, I saw. Four men and some fat lieutenant, and uglier Major with the syphilis face and the Devil’s hand—you have seen him?” he verified. “When you see him, you will understand.”

Reineke had seen him, and his face and hand were irrelevant. Six SS did not travel the desert alone. There were more of them. “Suicide,” Reineke assured. “If their interest was defense, they would have killed the SS in the desert before they arrived." He failed to understand why they did not kill them, only that the dentist and the lawyer were not the only ones who were inept when his own squad also let them live. "They wanted the prisoners the SS brought. They are from the village, stop lying."

"If they wanted the prisoners, mon capitaine," Pierre countered, "they could have taken them in the desert and killed the SS."

That was Reineke's argument. That was what he was saying. "Why then?" Reineke insisted since they agreed. "Why come and look and do nothing?"

"I do not know," Pierre said. "Perhaps to see who they were? Understand why they are here?"

"Why?" Reineke maintained.

"Why do you want to know?" Pierre smiled.

He did not. Were he to tell the truth, he did not care. Not why or who they were, but he would have killed them in the desert without question, without a doubt, the SS, and the strangers they brought with them.

Or perhaps not the strangers they brought with them. Reineke glanced down on the girl in his lap. He would not have killed them until he was certain, unless he was sure. Unsure, he probably would have called for counsel with the Holy Man, Diana and her sons, the dentist and the lawyer and the doctor among them.

"Talk to me about the SS," Reineke instructed. "Did you see them arrive? I know you did, and if this is some sort of trick to auction me to regain control—"

"Has mon capitaine lost control?" Pierre asked surprised.

Only of his mind. But that was so long ago Reineke had not only forgotten when, he had forgotten why. "Talk to me," he warned, "or I will destroy the village and bury what is left of it in the sand like the Romans did Carthage."

"Salt," Pierre corrected him, a threat, not just a history lesson behind his words, a promise, reminder, portent. "Carthage was buried in salt and the sand was born, a curse upon anyone who attempted to rebuild her."

Reineke looked at him.

Pierre shrugged. "I, as a priest, of course, do not believe it such things. Curses, sand, salt, it does not matter, Carthage survives, and you will never live to bury anyone. Two hundred men, two thousand, many more have tried, all have failed and so will you."

"Did you see the SS arrive?" Reineke repeated his question.

Of course, Pierre had seen them. Knowing something was wrong before he had seen them when he had first noticed Erich and the two sentries who should be in the gun towers arguing outside. "You always tell me who are where," he reminded unnecessarily, "so I know because I do not speak German." Or so he claimed. No more than Thiele, or any of Reineke's men, spoke French. Those who had were gone, less so they could not speak to the Holy Man but so he could not speak to them.

"From the hill I saw them." Pierre reported in detail how he climbed the mountain despite his crooked, bowed legs to watch them arrive, his head swaying sadly for the murdered child in Reineke's lap. "It is my fault, for when I see how they are SS, I went to the village, oui, naturally, and it is hours before I am here. Had I not done this? It would never be like this, no, never. This is terrible, mon capitaine, terrible. She is not of the village, I swear. Nothing to do with the village, or anywhere for hundreds of miles, I would know. A white woman like this? I would know."

"She could be Scandinavian," Reineke agreed absently, eyeing her and thinking of the lawyer so blond like him, a ghostly white in his sea of brown brothers. "Polish even perhaps."

"Pardon?" Pierre said.

"Nothing," Reineke shook his head. "A thought, that is all. She is clearly European." He touched her stained auburn hair wondering what color it was when it was clean, the texture coarse or soft. Her skin was freckled from the sun, or just from chance.

"Like Martin, yes," Pierre smiled. "I did not realize you knew."

That the lawyer was Polish? Or that he was Martin? Of course, Reineke knew. He knew everything. John was the dentist, a burly man, darker hair like his mother, with stone-blue eyes. "You were saying something about Erich. Sergeant Erich," Reineke reminded.

Only that Erich had been outside, and that he knew. "Oui, mon capitaine, he knew." Pierre told him. "You know this for yourself by now. He is the traitor, the betrayer, not Pierre and his children. Had

I not come down the long way, the American might not have died until later like this one, or perhaps not at all. It is hard to know," he admitted. "Only that if they lived, it is possible we might know more."

Such as who? If not why? And therefore from where? Instead, it all died with him, there on the ground in the middle of the compound. "What?" Reineke said.

"His head, mon capitaine," Pierre said. "The butt of a gun, sometimes it kills, not only the bullets. Boots, perhaps, but I do not think so. Too severe, too much. His head was crushed, beaten until his brains lay in the dust."

"Of the courtyard?" Reineke hissed. "He died in the courtyard?"

"I saw him, and so I know," Pierre nodded. "I buried him, and so I know. He was dead. The blood fresh and red."

And his men did nothing. The SS killed some man in the middle of the courtyard and his men did nothing.

"They were angry, mon capitaine," Pierre offered as if reading his mind. "If that is what you mean."

Angry. Reineke could hear the catcalls in the courtyard when he arrived, two hundred cowards in men's dress, peasants hurtling angry barbs at the king SS, but daring to do nothing.

"They sent for your sergent," Pierre nodded, "the small one who watches your supplies?"

"Linke," Reineke replied. "Sergeant Linke."

"And he was extremely angry," Pierre assured. "Arguing and fighting with your Erich and his SS, because he knows how the people could riot—which they will not, mon capitaine," he quickly promised. "I swear. There will be no trouble in the village. I will talk to the people. They already know it is not you."

It was not him and he would talk to the people himself. He did not need the Holy Man, or Linke. He waved Linke and his loyalty aside. "You should have sent for me; *you* knew I was en route. The dentist or the lawyer come for me, not Sergeant Linke!"

"I did," Pierre said. "I told John 'check that fancy watch of yours and see where mon capitaine is. He could be dead himself'. I did not see Hanuk and so I thought they had sent him to meet you on the sea." He hesitated.

"What?" Reineke insisted. "*What?*"

"Nothing. I was thinking perhaps there was another person." Pierre shook his head at the remnants of clothes the prisoner wore, discolored and stiff as her hair. "Oui, I am positive, at least one more. This is too much blood, much too much and too long. It was the same with the man. She has been in these clothes for days. This much blood from either of them and both would be dead before now, and so another person, at least one more, at some time before."

And from some other place other than there.

"A grave perhaps." Pierre offered, able to see bodies lying in some mass grave. "But why bring two here?"

Reineke had no idea. "An airplane," he said suddenly.

"Pardon?" Pierre said.

"Indeed, airplane," Reineke assured. "They went down in an airplane. They could have been there for days. There could be more bodies at the crash site. A plane!" he stressed.

"Oui," Pierre nodded, "I understand. That is very good, mon capitaine. Very possible. But what about the SS? Where were they? Just there? Just found them?"

Possibly. "Indeed," Reineke said. Erich's betrayal was far reaching if the Allied were around, and it would be Erich, not some Allied prisoner, who swung from a rope in the courtyard. Trouble or no trouble in the nomad village, Reineke would turn his dogs loose on Erich in a second. "I will take care of the SS."

"Oui," Pierre grinned. "It is why I like you. You know how to be the boss. That is good because unlike you, Diana does not threaten, but kills. Turn her dogs loose, you can be sure, and that includes, mon capitaine, on you."

They would have to catch him first and like the SS, probably not like the taste very much if they did.

"If Diana were here," Pierre was continuing. "She is not. Too bad because Pierre is a priest, not a doctor, but we will see what we can do. Will you stay, mon capitaine, will you help?"

Stay? Reineke looked up.

"It is deep," Pierre nodded. "I will need to close it."

Close it? Reineke stared at the assembled stack of medical supplies; he had not heard the soldiers return, Thiele in the doorway with his basin and steaming kettle of water. "Stay?" he repeated. And do what? What was this priest talking about? He could not stay!

"Mon capitaine?" Pierre said.

"Dismissed," Reineke released the guard, Thiele setting his kettle down and leaving with them. Surgical needles and thread in the ready hands of a priest not something he wanted to understand.

"Mon capitaine?" Sometime later, the Holy Man Pierre stopped Reineke before he left. "It will be all right," he believed, optimistic about the prisoner's chance for survival. "She is young, but she is strong. The young are always strong."

That was not good news.

"Mon capitaine?" the priest said curiously, when Reineke did not respond.

"It is nothing," Reineke replied. "Continue."

"Thank you." Pierre smiled, and Reineke stepped into his office, glad to breathe the fresh air of the library.

Thiele was waiting, and would demand to talk. Reineke did not want to talk. Thiele was too honest, applying pressure without diplomacy and flattery. He fumbled in his breast pocket, searching for a cigarette, but the pack was blood soaked; there would be no way to avoid the confrontation and he laughed. A short, hollow laugh as he walked toward Thiele tossing him a fresh pack. The long awaited nicotine satisfied only his lungs and he laughed lightly again, watching his bloodied hand as it moved back and forth in front of his face.

"Your men need a lesson in discipline, Thiele," he proposed with an eerie smile.

Discipline? Thiele preferred to pretend he had no idea what Reineke meant.

Reineke nodded. "Would I, or would I not?" he agreed. "Slit Erich's throat, or merely cut his cheek? Which were you thinking? What? A man would have killed him."

He was brooding about the SS Major, remembering what was said. The teasing, the taunt implying he was something different than a man, something less. He wasn't, and right now Thiele couldn't care less. “A sane man would have done neither,” he retorted.

“Which I am not,” Reineke agreed. “I think ...” he watched his hand. “Yes,” he decided. “I think I will bathe, Thiele.” He walked away.

“Hauptmann!” Thiele came alive and Reineke stopped.

“Yes, Thiele?” he said as if he did not know.

“The woman cannot stay where she is.”

Indeed. The woman was a child, not a woman. Perhaps slightly older than sixteen as the Holy Man had proposed, and simply small, extremely small, *la petite mademoiselle,* Reineke believed the Holy Man had said if once, six times, like it was a name. And *la petite mademoiselle* was, and remained a child, in Reineke's opinion whether she was sixteen or what she was, if only because her persecutors could not have been any better a judge of her age than he was, any less interested in her age than he was.

“Indeed,” Reineke said. “The girl is currently occupying the apartment, not my office. I would have thought that would have been of some consolation to you.”

“The woman is a prisoner,” Thiele reminded harshly, hardly consoled, and Reineke turned around to him.

“You are observant, Thiele,” he agreed, waiting expectantly.

“A prisoner of the SS,” Thiele assured.

“Indeed.” Reineke mocked, not to be disappointed, and two small patches of color brightened on Thiele's cheeks.

“They are the SS,” he insisted.

“So you have said,” Reineke tossed his cigarette to the floor, grinding it under his boot, “repeatedly.”

“For all it has mattered to you!” Thiele snapped as Reineke turned his back on him again.

Mattered to him? Why? Because they were SS? Reineke fell into a thoughtful pose, studying the scorched ceiling above his head. His father was SS, a Colonel living lavishly in Berlin, the cancers eating away at him as stubborn and ruthless as he was, refusing to die.

“I suspect my father may have something to do with our predicament, Thiele,” he replied. “Though, admittedly, by this time, I would have expected him to be too tired, too old, and too dead, to trouble me.”

"What?" Thiele said.

A reasonable challenge. Reineke's father could have nothing to do with any of this. That was fantasy, infantile and thoroughly unrealistic. It was the munitions, of course, what else? Not only him, their entire effort had been betrayed by Erich to the SS.

"Indeed," Reineke's head came down from his observation of the ceiling. "This is a munitions compound, Thiele," he reminded coldly, "not a Stalag. It is my compound. I have a thousand tons of ammunition. That is what matters to me. Not the SS and not some child."

"And what are you going to do with her?" Thiele insisted.

Do with her? Reineke could not answer that question. He stared at the cracks in the worn marble floor smeared with the soot of his cigarette. He had absolutely no idea what he was going to do with her. Hopefully, she would die. Quietly, though, in the middle of the night, and everything would take care of itself. He did not take prisoners, ever. The implications of that rule unnerved him for the first time. *Never*. The word hung suspended, deadly, a thousand voices alive inside his head, their curses, and screams so loud he knew even if he screamed he could never drown them out.

But there were reasons! He tried anyway. *Legitimate reasons*! Prisoners brought problems, questions, the obvious complications of unwanted guests. He could not risk either. He had no desire to extend a welcome to either. It remained, as always, so much simpler just to ...

His stomach turned, his mouth dry and tasting foul. The Holy Man said she would live; he wanted her to die. "The Holy Man could be wrong, Thiele," he wished, though he doubted it. "He still could be wrong." He had been wrong, was wrong about the Amerikaner. The man would have indeed died.

But, quietly, though! Reineke insisted to the floor. *Not in the compound. In the middle of the compound, MY compound*!

But this is different? It whispered back. *Is this different*?

Of course, it was different. "I do not know, Thiele," Reineke charged him, "but perhaps you can enlighten me. Do you think Allied scouts take their children along with them on their missions, or perhaps you think she is a scout herself?"

Thiele had no idea.

No, of course he did not. Thiele had so far managed to avoid fighting his war, satisfied to quote its rules he knew so well. "What would you like me to do, Thiele?" Reineke insisted. "What do your rules say? Hang her in the courtyard? Would you like her to die in the courtyard? In the middle of the courtyard like the American?"

"What American???" Thiele jumped, wanting to know.

"Indeed!" Reineke said.

"What American?" Thiele insisted.

"It is a fact, Thiele," Reineke said coldly. "The only fact you need to know."

Was it? "And can your Holy Man also tell you why the SS are here?" Thiele demanded. "The reason, *cause* for your arrest?"

He was talking about the village. That was ridiculous. After considering the nomads initially himself as the source of interest, Reineke had since decided it was ridiculous, at least from the perspective of the SS. The SS were there for the complex, to claim it and take it for themselves. No one knew about the village. His men barely remembered it was there.

"Indeed," Reineke said. Thiele was worried about the Holy Man, the children, complaining as usual, as in the past, and now this new one with the English skirt and torn blouse and what was left of her at only sixteen years of age. "I do not care why the SS is here," Reineke snapped. "Paris is occupied, are all her citizens dead? Are we traitors because we do not kill everyone who crosses our path?"

Thiele did not believe him. He considered Reineke wanton, his displays of compassion, kindness and diplomacy misplaced, indicative of weakness, not strength. "Hauptmann ..." Thiele said, prepared to offer him what? A pill to cure whatever ailed him?

"No!" Reineke silenced him. "There is no difference between here and Paris, Oslo or Warsaw. They have their ghettoes, I have mine. They have their whores, conscripted servants, I have mine. I care to bathe, Thiele, that is what I care to do. You may join your SS, or whatever it is you care to do!"

He stalked away. Thiele screaming, "Hauptmann!" after him like a rabid dog.

Chapter Eight

Reineke was in his quarters. His suite of two rooms and a bath, similar to the apartment with its high mosaic ceilings, towering stone columns and painted marble walls, though much larger, German under its Arab décor. Less congested by furnishings and flourishes, stark and grand, just the way he liked it.

"Indeed," he resented the reminder of how imperfect, rejecting it. He was not responsible for the world.

"Indeed, I do not care," he repeated to the haggard exhausted face waiting for him in the bathroom mirror. His flesh pinched and drawn; scratched with anger, frustration, and some frightened child's fingernails. He touched his wounded cheek, the injury cosmetic and annoying. She assaulted his vanity, insulting it, her blood soaked through his shirt to his chest, the pattern of her head outlined on his skin. The heavy, dangling gold chain and Prince's cross he had worn since he was fourteen, stained and wet as he was with her impending death.

He did not particularly want to bathe. Finding he had no pressing desire to sit in a tub of water and watch it change colors from clear to cloudy rust.

But you have already started the fire. The stove behind him reminded, the heat from the burning wood beginning to dance over his back.

"So I have." Reineke could see the little cast iron stove in the corner of the mirror. It was going to be very hot in here, very soon. Steam would cover the mirror and he would not be able to see himself anymore.

That might be nice. Reineke moved as far out of sight of the face in the mirror as he could until the fog rose to cover him. But the bath was too small for him to escape entirely.

"Indeed," Reineke cursed his marble prison with its gleaming tub, toilet, and sink, and a little ornate cast iron stove for heating the cool desert water. "Ingenious," he mocked. His predecessors as determined as he was to bring a sense of civility to their insufferable world. There were five such stoves in the massive building, all of them designed for their companion baths ...

"No," he shook his head. No, that was not true. There were only four stoves. One was not missing, merely relocated, given to the Holy Man for his children. There were no stoves in the smaller, outer buildings to heat their water, and he did not think it was right.

"But, I made a mistake," he admitted, confessing to the steam. He had told Thiele what he planned to do, and, oh, what an argument they had. Reineke treated to a dizzying deluge of facts and fears of the natives taking advantage. "Of whom, Thiele?" he wondered. "Whom?" Him? The complex put at risk of attack by stones and spears?

"It is a stove, Thiele," he nodded. "Over a stove, Thiele." A furnace for heating Nature's caldron so brutally cold at night. Yet Thiele was the realist, and he a dreamer.

"Or fatalist," Reineke shrugged. It amazed him how he could be both, but apparently, he was. Still, dreamer or fatalist, he did it anyway, despite Thiele's lengthy list of reasons why he should not. Just him and the Holy Man, in the middle of the night inspected the limited selection before deciding, and come morning, Thiele found his stove gone—*poof!* like magic.

And the unexpected labor of hard work. Reineke did not know much about disassembling and reassembling century-old stoves. But the Holy Man did. The Holy Man knew many things. Sixteen years he had lived in Libya, in this house with his children. It was for them he learned his things. Survival, he called it, and Reineke could not argue with him there. One would have to learn many things if they wished to survive here.

"Including how to best to survive with the occupying forces parked on your doorstep, eh, Holy Man?" he suggested. "Indeed."

He stared in the mirror, the fog uncooperative in covering the glass. Diana, matriarch of the nomads living among the ruins, was an occupying force all her own, her marble statue intact and high on its pedestal, stretching three meters tall. One hand to the heavens, one hand blessed her flock, a smile on her face, her dogs positioned and poised. But then Reineke had warned the Holy Man he would check on the settlement camp, conduct a census to ensure all remained present and accounted for, and so he had.

The Fezzan
January 1942
"*She looks like you.*" It occurred to him as they stood there and so he said it, the sun high and hot above the brilliance of her Temple. He meant her strength possibly, her two thousand years of survival and torment, or perhaps he just felt like being fresh.

He was fresh, and just so handsome. An air of humor about him among all his other airs and sins, surprisingly poised and dignified with a devil behind those blue eyes as they say, threatening to distract her for all her years of wisdom and worldly ways. It was a good thing she knew them for what they were. Her daughter's soul beside her in case she forgot.

"*Does she*?" the crone looked up at the goddess with a laugh.

"*No*," he assured.

"*You are right*," she agreed, old, and soiled, and fat, her rifle automatic and pointed at his head. "*My husbands should be so lucky.*"

"*Husbands*?" he said and she shrugged.

Indeed. "*Where did you get that*?" he inquired instead into the gun holding him hostage.

"*It's standard issue*," she teased.

"*It is French*," he said.

"*You have better*?" she said.

Of course. "*How long have you been here*?" he asked.

"*Five thousand years*," she assured and his eyes rolled.

"*I meant ...*" he said, speaking less of her Moses having taken some wrong turn than he was speaking of her personally.

"*Oh, you mean this time around.*" She understood. "*Long enough. Two, three years. Since they closed the gates to Eden. Why*?"

"*You speak German like a native*," he said simply.

"*So do you*," she slyly agreed. "*And so if I kill you now, how many more will come*?"

"None," he shrugged. Alone and on his own apparently, for the first time in his life, not just at night, but during the day.

"Really?" she said. *"The bishop seems to think there are thousands."*

Bishop? *"What bishop is this?"* he frowned.

"Pierre," she said. *"You didn't know he was a bishop?"*

"I thought he was a monk."

"No, he's a bishop," she said. *"With a son your age, a little younger. They're like that. Catholics."* She shrugged. *"Latins. Men. What are you going to do?"* She took his cigarettes, lighting two and offering him one. *"Where are you from? Berlin? Do I know you? Should I?"* She eyed him. He was so German like any good officer should be. He didn't work for a living, the hands were too soft, and unless her senses deceived her, smelled almost spicy, fragrant, of incense and lilacs. *"Come on. It's not a difficult question, not even important. I just want to know."*

He hesitated. *"The Rhine."*

"That's it?" she said. *"The river?* The water? *Funny, you don't look like a fish to me."*

"I am Hauptmann Dieter Reineke," he said. *"You do not know me."*

"You're right," she agreed. *"I don't. I've never heard of you."* And that put them on equal footing if nothing else could. She lowered her rifle, cradling it in her arms like an infant, but still he did not chance it. She looked too serious, adept, and so she was in many ways. *"I am Anna who knew Albert. You may call me Diana since you think I look so much like her."*

"Albert." He considered the Alberts he knew. There were a few. He eyed her.

"Einstein." She blew a thin stream of smoke from her lungs. *"You know if you were young and handsome, Hauptmann, I might consider having sex with you."* And she laughed again as his eyes flew wide, a reassuring tap of her steel on his arm. *"It's all right mein Liebchen, we'll think of something else."*

And so they did.

March 8

Reineke stared at the water pump, her voice in his head. "*Prison's not so bad, Hauptmann,*" she promised whether she could support her words or not. "*You'll see. Especially since you get to live in a big beautiful house when all we have is this.*"

Outrageous, utterly absurd, he was not a prisoner he was a king. Whether or not he was a king here, should be a king, ever belonged being a king here, he was still a king. "Indeed," Reineke touched the pump. He was giving himself a headache. He needed to think about something else, anything else.

"*And the children*?" He had questioned the crone about them first, and then the priest, one of them more boastful than the other, one of them less cooperative and shy.

"*Pardon*?" the monk said from his seat where he had been ordered to appear and sat like his arms were strapped to the side; would probably claim they had been strapped to its sides.

"*The children*," the German repeated. The band of creatures the monk claimed as his.

"*What about them*?" the monk said.

"Nothing," Reineke assured aloud. He was thinking about the pump, remembering when he had questioned the Holy Man as to how there could be such a pump in the middle of a desert he received an unwanted lesson in geography. The few existing rivers were not perennial, rarely even above ground. But under the desert, were many rivers, springs that fed the waterholes and like the Roman before them with their baths, the Arab had cleared the rubble and tapped a spring.

"*Though that is not to say*," Pierre had also strongly advised, "*there will always be water.*" In the summer, it only trickled. And many times since he had lived there, it had not run at all. "*But!*" he assured. Beyond the villa were the wells in the west, and the baths in the east, and so he could foresee no immediate or acute problems.

"Oh, yes," Reineke nodded, talking to the pump, "no immediate or acute problems." Simply mutiny, SS, Allied prisoners alive and dead, and a thousand tons of ammunition to shield and protect. One thousand tons. Fortunately, the Holy Man who knew so many things did not know about that.

Or he pretended not to know. For now. For as long as it remained convenient for him and his children, the Holy Ghost of the unholy trinity, Pierre, Diana, and him.

"Indeed." Reineke stared at the kettle of boiling water, its mist spiraling up around the chimney. It was probably not a good idea to have two fires lit at one time. Dual columns of smoke might attract the attention of whoever else was out there.

"Such as the survivors of your mass Allied grave, Holy Man." Reineke's gaze followed the riveted stovepipe up to the ceiling. "Precautions. One should always take precautions." An excellent excuse for delaying his bath, the heat making him sick. He picked up the ladle, the flames howling as he tossed the water over them, but they lost in the end, and the ladle splashed into the kettle to stay.

"I will use you tonight," he forewarned the dry tub, sitting down on its edge. No one would see the smoke in the night.

"A great many things," he joked at the drain, his heels kicking against the side, "go unnoticed in the night—Indeed," he stood up. The dampness of the rim of the tub reminding him the seat of his pants was also wet with the prisoner's blood. He really should bathe. He looked from the kettle to the small sink with her deep inviting bowl. "Sufficient," he shrugged. The water pump belched as he grasped it, her ancient plumbing angry at being disturbed twice in such a short time, but the air abated, the water gurgling into the bowl. The scratches on his cheek stung when he touched them, and he pouted, attacking the water. The marks would be there for weeks, could be there for months, infected within days from her dirty, broken nails. He did not want scars. He had one scar on his leg and it was enough, the flesh thick and still raised after two years, a flaw where he had been flawless.

"Indeed," Reineke wiped the moisture from the mirrored glass, studying his face, wondering what the Holy Man might have in his bag of tricks to help him. He had already given him a lotion of berries and zinc to protect him from the sun, and though he was tanned, darker than he had ever been, his skin no longer cracked and bled, sucked dry by the vicious climate. If the Holy Man could manage a remedy for the sun, it was possible he could concoct a medicinal compound that would soothe, instead of irritate. Even if Thiele persisted in criticizing him, for the heady olive salve made him shine, it was still worth it. He had the skin of a woman. It seemed only fair he should be entitled to the same vanity.

"Indeed!" Laughing, Reineke dunked the cloth. The cool water felt good and he remembered his body with a glance at the tub. A cold bath? It sounded inviting. Smiling, he grasped the handle of the pump. If it proved too cold he could always get out, though he did not think he would, no, he did not think he would.

Reineke emerged from his frigid bath forty minutes later to paw roughly through his closet, searching for the perfect uniform. The elaborate style of the SS Major, frayed and out of place for the region had not impressed or escaped him. He, too, owned beautiful custom uniforms and he might decide to wear one. Two dandies entrenched in a duel? It would have made for an interesting evening had Herr Major insisted upon staying. He had not, and Reineke was almost sorry he had not for he enjoyed a good fight, the excitement and victory.

"Indeed," he assured Thiele's ever-hovering ghost hovering somewhere. "A duel to the death, Thiele. Not simply a prick of the cheek like some child's game, or scolding."

Herr Major would understand and appreciate the difference. One of those scars on his face had come from the point of a sword. Reineke should know, having seen them often enough. His father had one, a telltale cut below the apple of his cheek. It made him a man, and was the motive for their argument so many years ago when Reineke refused to stand for the same baptism of blood. At times, Reineke preferred to think he rousted his father in defense of Alexia whom the father hated, so desperate for another son to replace the one he did not like. Both reasons were probably true if Reineke needed another reason besides the simple one of hate.

"Do you know my father, Herr Major?" he wondered. Herr Oberst Reineke of the SS? A violent, sadistic man, abusive of his wife and infant daughter, cursed with fits and epileptic seizures, and a son stronger than he could ever be.

"You should know my father, Herr Major," he agreed, and would be surprised if the two had never met.

"Indeed." Reineke stared down on his uniform laid out on the bed, envisioning the Major's chest aglitter with its trinkets of gold and silver and blood. "I do not have nine medals," he admitted, though he did have a Knight's Cross, proudly worn on its narrow silk ribbon. He earned it, together with his promotion, in *France* ...

The memory started with a whisper. He did not like to think about France. He died in France, becoming some man he still did not know whether homicidal or suicidal, and either way he could not feel sorry for *France* ...

Reineke let his body fall backwards onto the bed, watching the mosaic panels of his vaulted ceiling as if watching some film. It was from France he had borrowed the idea of keeping the nomads as cover for the compound. They were being harassed, continuously harassed by an irritating band of French raiders. But his Captain did not care for they were advancing, eternally pushing onward. Oberleutnant Dieter Reineke did care, and backtracked with the squad of men under him, finding the irritating band of Frenchmen in a village not too far away. The successful nighttime raid might still have ended in a reprimand, except Reineke went in to make sure. He wanted them all ...

They took that village apart stone by stone, and what they found was not a sleepy country parish after all but a well-stocked resistance cell filled with equipment, supplies ... land mines ...

Reineke touched his thigh. There were few actual villagers, perhaps thirty, mostly children, all dead. He shut his eyes. There were children here, but no land mines. You could not have land mines with children, children ran around ...

They leveled the village as a warning, and when Reineke left the hospital, completely recuperated from the mine that had killed the soldier with him, he was a Captain with his own command and a Knight's Cross. A hero, all because he cared, and his Captain had not.

Reineke opened his eyes, the film speeding along faster. He did not like officers who did not care about their men. He cared a great deal. And now he was in North Afrika still fighting under the famed General Rommel who continued to care as much as he did.

He sat back up. Reineke held a great admiration for the General Rommel. Self-made men impressed him. Men of nothing who became men of power and dreams, usually they impressed him. Some he paid little attention to at all, still others he scorned. "You boast German supremacy, *mein Führer*?" he called out to the ugly little man whose picture disrupted the beauty of his library wall. "Rommel is your German supremacy. Not those creatures skulking around the courtyard—*MY* courtyard," he assured just so there would be no misunderstanding between them either.

"Indeed," he glanced down on the rumpled uniform he had clutched thinking it was his torn leg. He did not wear wrinkled clothing. Back in the wardrobe, he flipped over his formal suits. Some were field gray, all of them tailor-made of the finest linen, soft as cashmere. "Not wool, Thiele, not wool," he advised. "No one wears wool in this heat, not even the English." He touched his parade dress, so similar in color to the girl's skirt in the other room. She had to be from the north where it was still cool, perhaps from one of its convents or schools. He could not imagine why, or what had brought her here except an airplane. Unless the Holy Man was lying and she did belong to the village, her family dead in their mass grave.

"Indeed," Reineke chose one, its crisp white jacket and luxurious gray pants so perfect for a summer evening and a chat with the crone. "No, I do not have your medals, Herr Major," he agreed in the mirror, fastening the perfectly creased trousers, "but I have a great many reprimands. Would you like me to pin them on my chest? Hm? Are you going to threaten me with another? Have me deposed from my command not only my compound? Arrested or shot for protecting instead of killing the enemy regardless of affinity or age? Indeed!" he laughed.

The laughter was brief. His hand stopped buttoning his blouse.

He might know. The mirror nodded sympathetically.

"He cannot know!" Reineke threatened the glass with his hand. There was no way. No way! The prisoner was unrelated to the village, merely a coincidence as the Holy Man claimed.

"Stupid!" he cursed and spun around, hands jammed in his trouser pockets. It was his own fault. The Holy Man had said he would understand when he saw him. He had seen him, and he did understand. Herr Major was not at all like him. Herr Major was not stupid.

Like you. The jacket whispered from the bed.

"Indeed!" Reineke seized it, sending it sailing through the air. "Who are they?" he turned on the mirror. "Why are they here? From where?" he insisted. "Where?" But the mirror refused to tell him, it was not a crystal ball, besides he already knew. Whether from the village or the north they were undoubtedly the Allied. "Fool!" Reineke sputtered, damming himself. "Thiele is right, I am a fool."

Arrogant. The mirror corrected.

"Ha!" Reineke said. "I am a king. And you are nothing," he assured the jacket crumbled in the corner like the SS crying for its life, "filth!"

And? The jacket prodded from the corner.

"And?" Reineke stared back at it. "And what?"

But the jacket only shrugged.

"Games," Reineke marched back to his wardrobe. "Indeed. I do not have time for this."

Games. His uniforms agreed.

Reineke paused. "What?"

Games. They assured.

"Indeed," Reineke studied them, thinking. "Do you like games, Herr Major?" he eventually turned back to the jacket. "I do."

He was very good at games, playing and winning, he made sure of that.

"You should know, Herr Major," he warned, "murder is not difficult for me. To the contrary, I find it simple and easy, and satisfying. There are few vices some investigation of me would reveal, simply murder and—

"Women?" Reineke blinked. "Indeed." That was interesting. He turned on the mirror. "What are you saying? The prisoner is not a woman. She is the village, a child. There is no difference, they are the same. I did not *take a woman away* from him, I took a woman *away from him*—never mind," he shook his head. "I know what I am saying, and it is different—and, *IF!*" he promised the jacket, "you bring another woman here in the condition you brought that one, I will take her away from you, too.

"If you bring a dog," he assured, "in that condition, I will take it away from you. That is what some 'investigation' of me will reveal."

And? The jacket waited, holding its breath.

"And I will not kill you," Reineke scooped up the jacket to toss it in the laundry pile, "not yet."

But in the end, he would, because he had to.

For the children. The mirror understood. *The children*.

"Indeed." Reineke resumed his search for the perfect uniform.

"I think this one," Hanuk's hand appeared beside his, his head tipped and midnight eyes teasing in his handsome face. The hood of his robes flung back and collar open, exposing the leather strap of an arrow quiver slung over his strong shoulders.

Chapter Nine

How long Hanuk had been there in his quarters, Reineke could only guess. Long enough and the Baron's arguments with the inanimate fixtures around him were nothing new or particularly alarming to Hanuk. It made Reineke seem somehow more human, not less, distinctly fascinating and intense, not crazed, lonely, or lost. Still, one or the other should be embarrassed, Reineke for himself, Hanuk for him. Neither of them was. Hanuk, bemused and sly, Reineke in control and in command, disapproving, tolerant, adult, suddenly Thiele, though calmer, much calmer, composed and self-possessed.

"Angry with me?" Hanuk laughed at Reineke's vexed expression for the tall young man forced by circumstances into being much older than his seventeen years, though Hanuk was still only seventeen, boyish and brash, and disarmingly charming. A lover in another world and life, a killer in this one, deadly and calculating as the savage he pretended to be.

"No, you are not angry with me." He patted Reineke on the shoulder, wandering away toward the glass windows and wandering back. "Anne sent me to tell you to come to us and we can tell you what you want to know, which we can't," he shrugged, more realistic about such things than his little sister. "Not really anything. It's just Anne being Anne, but we can probably help you find out. Today, tonight, tomorrow, just come," he requested. "You know Anne. She'll kick and scream and call me a coward and come here herself—cigarette?" he offered with a clever smile, picking Reineke's pack up off the bed.

"Indeed," Reineke surrendered, accepting the cigarette with a critical nod for the burnished chest of muscle sporting its courage and weapon of choice. "A bow and arrows? Are we cowboys and

Indians now?"

"It's quieter than a rifle," Hanuk assured. "Besides, I'm good. Very."

"Really," Reineke said. "I have a Luger on the floor of my wagen outside. If you were as good as you think you are you would not only know that, you would have it."

"Who says I don't?"

"I do. There is another in the chest," Reineke pointed, returning to the bureau to change into his uniform. "Take it and keep it. It is much better than your French ones. I will send more tonight, rifles, too, as many as I can. The men may arm, but they are not to do anything. You understand?"

"I do."

"Good. The Holy Man is in the apartment with the SS prisoner, a young girl, your age. When she is feeling better, and if you are polite, perhaps I will introduce you." he winked at Hanuk in the mirror. "Right now, I do not want you to disturb them. Understand me?"

Completely. What he said, and what he meant, but then Hanuk was German under his stained mulatto skin and sable black hair, at least half, a native of Poland and Berlin society, a distinct however distant memory. "Is she pretty?" he teased.

Not at the moment. Reineke stared at the mirror. "Small," he replied, attempting to be polite. "Anne's size. Perhaps a little larger, I do not know," he agreed briskly, wanting to change the subject. "She is a small woman, yes, young—*la petite mademoiselle.* That is what she is. You speak French. How do you communicate with the Holy Man if you do not?"

"Latin," Hanuk shrugged.

"Latin?" Reineke paused.

"And French," Hanuk laughed. "Enough to know she's no taller in French than she is in German."

Reineke ignored him, eying himself critically, the uniform standard, and nondescript, principally identical to the one he just took off. "Well, there is room for improvement, particularly if you are planning to make a career as a fashion consultant ... are you sure this one? I do not agree. I wish to make an impression."

"On whom?" Hanuk wondered.

"The world," Reineke laughed with a flick of his head for Hanuk's exotic robes worthy of a sheik. "Look who is talking, a young stallion in a sea of kindergarteners. It is all right, though," he nodded, collecting his boots and belt. "I would probably do the same; definitely. I want you to stay here. Those are your orders. Here, until I return and tell you it is safe to go."

"I can do that," Hanuk returned to the expansive stretch of French windows. "I like this room. It reminds me of home."

"Home?" Reineke stood up. "The opulence, I would understand you to mean, rather than the scenery. Or you are from a very different Berlin than the one I know."

"It would be a very different Berlin than anyone knows," Hanuk assured. "I was born in Berlin, but we lived in Khartoum, in the Sudan until I was ten. My father, like Abe's, was mixed. Sudanese, Indian, Turk. Call them anything but what they were—*English,"* he laughed. "Yet another noble officer in the British crown. After my parents' divorce, we moved home to Berlin for a short time until my mother married Hermann and we moved to Czestochowa. Poland."

He turned around, but Reineke was busy in the mirror, refusing the opportunity to comment on what he knew of his tenants' plight, the presumed death of Hanuk's mother Hannah among them. Hanuk had a feeling he would refrain. He nodded. "And then back to the Sudan, and then to here. Summers, yes," he said, "before the war, were usually split between my grandmother in Berlin, and my father's family in Kent, until my grandmother decided Berlin had become very different than the one she knew, and she called grandpa khalif for help in opening the gates of Hell for the Promised Land." He smiled. "He couldn't. He tried, or he didn't. I say he did. My grandmother says that's why she divorced him forty years ago because he was pretty but not much else, kissing the boots of the English and drinking their tea, wanting to be one of them."

"A very interesting life." Reineke agreed. "Still," he combed his hair, watching Hanuk in the mirror, "why are we having this conversation? What are you waiting for me to say?"

"Nothing in particular," Hanuk shrugged. "I'm sure you've wondered about the brown skin."

"Not really," Reineke denied. "When you say mixed, I think of your grandmother, Bohemia, and that the sun here is very hot."

"Yes," Hanuk laughed again. "Conveniently so, if not why we make such good Arabs." He winked. "Better than the ones you have out there."

"Yes," Reineke said. "Who else is here with you? I saw two in the courtyard, before I saw you."

"John and Martin," Hanuk acknowledged. "The intent was to blend in with the guards. I just wanted to get a little closer than they were willing."

"Yes," Reineke agreed. "Thiele saw them, and you. But you know that, right? Of course you do. That is why you ran, smart and foolish at the same time. The SS know Arabs, and they know German guards. You think they would not know you?"

"There are enough of us," Hanuk assured. "Yes, enough of us—why?" he teased. "You want to know specifics?"

Not necessarily. "Stay here." Reineke tossed him the pistol from the chest.

"Promise," Hanuk caught it, tucking it in the sash around his waist. "It's why I'm here. To stay and make sure everything's all right; with you," he grinned again. "Pierre, I know can take care of himself."

"And do not ..." Reineke reminded.

"Disturb them," Hanuk shook his head. "I won't. It's all right, though, I've already seen her so you don't have to worry about protecting me."

"Embarrassment," Reineke corrected diplomatically. "It is not a question of fear, or protection. I do not wish to embarrass you, or her. Since you have seen her, you understand what I am saying."

"I guess so," Hanuk shrugged with the callousness of his youth. "She's not much larger than Anne, you're right."

"Indeed," Reineke did not wish to think about it. "You said you saw her, the Holy Man says he did not."

"He didn't," Hanuk agreed. "He and Uncle John had taken the body away. I stayed behind with Uncle Martin. She was still in the truck—until they took her out, and then I saw her." He smiled. "I practically had to sit on Martin to keep him under control. It's probably a good thing Pierre did not see her."

"And the man, did you see him?" Reineke asked. "Was it an American who the SS killed in the courtyard?"

"I think so," Hanuk frowned, not thoroughly convinced. "My English is worse than my French. It said US Army on the jacket, easy enough even for me to read. But I didn't recognize the uniform. None of us did. It had a lot of patches on it, odd ones with symbols. John's the expert and his best guess has him some sort of engineer—*Army Corp of Engineers.* Something like that. Martin, as naturally, has his own ideas. Insisting it's too early for them to have any organized outfit of their own, especially out here." He winked again. "Perhaps a special detachment, like you. Rommel's no monopoly on hunger or thirst."

"Something else of value to learn," Reineke sidestepped the topic of his complex, "English. English is business, money, a language of the financial world. And money," he said, "as you know, is power; opportunity and ability. I can think of no greater assets a man can have or miss should he lose either of them."

"It's the end that matters," Hanuk echoed the mantra of the SS. "How you get there, doesn't."

"Yes," Reineke said. "I will be rich whoever wins this war. That is not greed. It is good business and common sense."

"And a Swiss bank account or two," Hanuk nodded.

Reineke laughed. "Indeed. A few Swiss bank accounts yes, of course, right next to your grandmother's."

"Well, I'm working on it," Hanuk assured. "English, and Arabic, too, though only so I can swear at them in their own language, no offense." His grin flashed.

"I am not offended," Reineke assured. "If you want to swear, swear. Refugees ... and, yes, prisoners," he granted, "are a casualty of war, not only the dead or wounded. They should be respected, assisted, whatever is the need, not ignored or mistreated ..." Even before he finished he knew he sounded like he was talking to a five year old. How, even Anne at her age would find him patronizing. He smiled. "You know what I am saying. The SS changes nothing. You know that also, or you would not be here." He nodded again at the burnished naked chest of courage and muscle. "To protect or to kill me. Anything else? Or are we finished?"

"I don't know," Hanuk said. "Are we?"

"I am thinking," Reineke agreed. "A curiosity, perhaps, but one I cannot seem to resist. Since you are the smartest—"

"No, Abe's the smartest," Hanuk assured. "As John says, the rest of us can only try."

"Since you are so willing to try," Reineke granted, "as I asked the Holy Man, is there a particular reason one of you did not first attempt to find me, before coming here?"

"You can say it," Hanuk nodded.

"What is this?" Reineke requested. "What can I say?"

"Their names," Hanuk assured. "John, Martin, Pierre. You have no trouble with Anne's or mine. It only hurts a little, and only the first time."

No. Names were personal. Acknowledgement something was personal. He called them what he called them, the dentist, the lawyer, the Holy Man. As with Thiele, and all others, he called them who they were, what they were. Not to keep them apart, or distant, himself aloof or dignified, he was naturally aloof, and as naturally dignified. They were not friends they were acquaintances, faces, and bodies in a particular point in time.

"Want to know what they call you?" Hanuk asked.

Reineke knew what they called him. Dieter, if they were young or the doctor Abraham appointed ambassador from their camp to him. Dieter, if they were Diana, though usually only to scold, otherwise it was King David to annoy him, le Metapel to entice him, the others, most frequently, the Baron, not the Hauptmann, never Herr Hauptmann that would be too painful and impossible to ask of them. *Mon capitaine,* the closest any of them dared, and that was only the Holy Man.

Reineke smiled. "What I know is that you apparently left your manners not only your silk handkerchiefs and ties when you left Berlin, spending too much time in the Sudan. You forget your position, as much as you conspire for me to forget mine, as I said, so smart and foolish at the same time."

"It is the end that matters," Hanuk's hand clapped his shoulder again in a gesture of assured friendship and trust. "If you're curious about Erich, he is in Thiele's office waiting for him. When you need me, let me know. The arrow is quick, quiet, and native," he hinted. "We can always find some bandits for you to execute should the local authorities insist upon it."

"I will keep it in mind," Reineke promised.

"Good," Hanuk said. "As far as you, you, I missed catching by this much," he demonstrated how little. "I got there as you broke away from the convoy with Thiele. But I knew you were on your way here, so I came back. Why risk frightening someone and end up getting shot?"

"And Thiele?" Reineke asked amused. "Where is Thiele?"

It was Thiele who skulked about the courtyard. The tale of Reineke versus the SS reaching the barracks of the men before Thiele did, the outcome fell short of the mob's expectations that wanted and expected more blood than some trickle from Erich's cheek. They looked forward to the show, spectators at an arena where the gladiators failed to appear. Disappointed, they settled for keeping the truck and casting the SS adrift on the sand sea without water or gasoline where they would die in sacrifice to the Hauptmann. Revenge, all they cared about; a sudden and mass outbreak of amnesia befalling them, closing ranks with Thiele firmly on the outside when Thiele pressed for information on the prisoners. Annoyed, Thiele moved on for the depot, Sergeant Linke, and the commandeered SS truck.

Idiots. Thiele denounced the group of them, unable to appreciate what they thought they would accomplish, hoped to gain by declaring war on the SS. Thiele hopped up onto the back of the truck, and pulled the canvas drapes aside. Someone had died. The rank odor of rotting flesh assaulted Thiele's nostrils as he looked over the interior painted with blood. The severed hand he found in a corner belonged to a man. Three of its fingers still attached, the missing two were probably there somewhere or long gone. He settled for the evidence of the hand, climbing down out of the truck with a signal for one of the mechanics working nearby.

"Yes, Oberleutnant?" the man asked, wiping his hands clean as he walked over.

"Now, where is the American?" Thiele waved his gruesome find in support.

The soldier paused.

"Well?" Thiele demanded.

"I believe he is dead, Oberleutnant," the soldier said.

"You believe," Thiele said. "Who knows?"

He still was not going to tell him. None of them were. All work had stopped, the men watching him in silence.

"Wash this truck down and move it out of the sun!" Thiele flung the severed hand at the Korporal in retort.

"Sergeant Linke is the one you should speak with, Oberleutnant." A second soldier stepped forward in defense.

"Get him!" Thiele said.

"Yes, Oberleutnant!" he exited to a chorus of jeers.

"Dismissed! Back to work!" Thiele sounded like Reineke with the barking, clipped orders, only the Korporal would never have dared bang the truck's gears as he drove away.

Thiele impatiently waited for Linke. The soldiers stubbornly slow in moving on as ordered confirmed for Thiele his suspicions of the Holy Man's involvement. Thiele's dislike of Reineke's Algerian mascot was not a secret it was unimportant. The Holy Man belonged to the Hauptmann. That alone was sufficient in ensuring no interference or comment from the men.

"Sufficient." Thiele moved to the corner of the truck yard where he could see the villa, the outline of its roof through the trees. He glanced at his watch. The thin tail of smoke rising from the chimney of Reineke's stove had dissipated into the air nearly an hour ago, and yet Reineke remained closeted inside. Disinterested apparently as his men in pursuing the issue of the SS. Satisfied the crisis was over, finished, when the SS left, leaving things to return to normal.

"How normal?" Thiele insisted. "What normal?" Things were hardly normal nor would they be. He stopped short of saying *ever again* because they would be eventually. They just were not now, or yet.

"Oberleutnant?" Sergeant Linke was behind Thiele. A small square man in his forties, Linke was another Western commoner, ordinary, a city laborer, rail yard worker, tough with a hardened liver and weatherworn skin, not a secretary like the Oberleutnant Thiele with the clean fingernails and smooth soft hands. Linke liked Thiele though, continued to like him. That had not changed. Linke just also disagreed with the Oberleutnant wanting to pursue what was over with the SS leaving and Erich's arrest. It was the SS, Erich, not the Hauptmann, or his Holy Man who needed to be stopped and so they had stopped them. It was Linke's idea to set the SS free without hope, keeping their gasoline and water. They would make it, if they were lucky, perhaps sixty, seventy kilometers, no more, and probably less. A simple order simply offered to the SS: "Leave, and die later, or stay and die now", and so the SS left, the six of them piled into the one staff car. The truck was too precious and Linke would never have let it go.

And so, they kept it, adding it to their supply. Enjoying the looks on the SS faces, the registering disbelief, apprehension in the men, cocky confidence of Herr Major, and stunned shock of his fat Leutnant, Linke wasn't sure why. They had told them, tried to tell them, warn them for several hours until the Hauptmann returned to tell them for himself. So now, they knew. And not one man there saw any SS, heard of any SS. A small squad, who, if they even existed, clearly must have died en route before reaching their destination, whatever that destination might have been, and therefore, what prisoners? Allied, American, or French, not one man there saw, or heard of any prisoners. Linke had no idea what Thiele was concerned with, or even talking about.

"All right!" Thiele interrupted Linke's creative bullshit. Linke's opinion of the SS was just that, opinion. Thiele was interested in fact. But it was the facts that were remarkably clear to Linke. Sergeant Erich had conspired with the SS to betray the Hauptmann and them. That was unacceptable and unforgivable, It was treason.

"Treason?" Thiele repeated. Could this man hear himself? They were tantamount to treason, their very existence. Coupled with the murders, yes, murders of the SS? They were not the heroes they aspired to be. Erich was the hero with his clear and indisputable loyalty. The bad made good, and the good made bad. "I do not suppose the idea of compromise occurred to you, Sergeant, once it was realized they were SS?"

"Compromise?" Linke followed orders, as did the men, and

compromise was out of the question. They did not heed Erich and would not heed Thiele now. Reineke was the Hauptmann.

"Yes ..." Thiele admitted to Linke's drawn cheeks. Reineke was the Hauptmann, Thiele his First Office, and Sergeant Linke was out of line.

"I doubt if you would find the SS interested in compromise, Oberleutnant," Linke suggested. "They were here to take or destroy not thank us."

"I think I am aware of the role of the SS," Thiele snapped, "including why they are here. That is my point. No, don't *give* them the compound. But, yes, show them around. Compromise, Sergeant. *Compromise.*"

"Show them around?" Linke frowned.

"Yes, around, Sergeant, around," Thiele said sourly. What was wrong with this man? Show them around the compound. They had nothing to hide, and everything to prove. To hell with *orders,* Thiele was talking about common sense. The SS was there, and Linke could not just snap his fingers and expect them to disappear.

"They were here for the Hauptmann's arrest," Linke assured.

That was ridiculous. Something that had happened, *because* of the men's resistance and behavior, Thiele was sure of that. "Why didn't you radio the Hauptmann?" he charged. "Killing the SS are not your *orders,* Sergeant," he assured. "Defying the SS does not *protect* us, are you mad? This *is* a munitions compound, exactly what they came to see, so show them. From one end of the oasis to the other, if that was what they wanted, who cares?" They had all been from one end of the oasis to the other ...

A shadow crossed over the sun, and Thiele shivered despite the heat. He had been from one end of the oasis to the other, but the soldiers who came after the first squad had never been, and the original men had never gone back.

The cloud moved on, and the heat beat down. Thiele removed his hat, wiping the sweat from his forehead.

"Oberleutnant," Linke suggested wisely, "don't worry about it. They're lucky all we did was take their truck. A small troop like that out in the desert?" he smiled, an unappetizing sly smile of teeth and nicotine. "Anything could happen. No one will know who or where."

"I know," Thiele corrected. "I know."

"And you'll get over it," Linke promised. "So will the SS. No radio, no water, no food."

"And three cigarettes." Someone in the background laughed, a group of them placing bets the fat one would be the first to lose his life.

"And no map," Linke assured. "They might make it to the waterholes before the water boils out if one of them has the memory of a camel, and the others can see in the dark. After that?" he was open to suggestions from the audience, but the stage was his. "They could kill and eat the fat one but at some point even he will rot. The wagen cannot run on urine, and if they decide to walk, walk where? Back here? That brave, they would have stayed.

"So, don't worry about it, Oberleutnant," he advised. "Not the munitions, the SS, Erich, or anything. It is over."

"You are relieved," Thiele retorted. "You are relieved!" he insisted, and Linke shrugged. Relieving him wasn't going to change anything, except perhaps delay the scheduled shipment they had planned for later this week. Linke was a camel, able to see in the dark, knowing the procedures and caravan routes blindfolded, and Thiele could not afford to relieve Linke of his duties. He knew this. Linke knew this.

"You are dismissed." Thiele relented, revoking the order to report and Linke smiled again with that toothy mouth of his.

"Don't," Thiele suggested. "Don't." he warned, cursing the retreating back of the sergeant, blind, deaf, as the rest of them, so self-confident and smug because of some unbroken chain of luck. *But a chain can break*! Thiele warned. And when had it even been tested? It hadn't. More time spent on collecting equipment than supplies. But now they were ready, and come Thursday they would be heading north to intercept and seize a major shipment slated for Sebha, turning it south to feed them and ultimately the fifth complex in line struggling in the southern plateaus of Algeria. It was that big, that grand. And what if they failed? It was four-hundred kilometers to Sebha, another hundred to position. Linke should be reviewing his strategies, preparing to leave, not playing games ...

No. If they failed, it would not be Linke's or the Hauptmann's fault, but Erich's, the SS whose appearance threatened the safety, security, and secret of their munitions compound—

"Damn!" Thiele hit himself in the head with the heel of his hand, remembering what he had forgotten to ask Linke. The prisoners. "Sergeant!" he broke into a trot after Linke.

"Yes, Oberleutnant?" Linke turned around.

"Where is the body of the American?" Thiele insisted. "And do not tell me you do not know what I am talking about."

Linke wasn't going to tell him that. "The Holy Man buried it in one of the gardens."

"What?" Thiele said. "Buried it?" he repeated. "You did not stop him?"

"Stop him, Oberleutnant?" Linke was puzzled.

"Yes, stop him," Thiele said sourly. "Stop him, Sergeant. Stop him." Stop him from taking the prisoner from the SS as Thiele had tried to stop Reineke and failed to the marked amusement of the SS.

"No," Linke said, and Thiele hung his head staring at the dusty toes of his boots.

"Oberleutnant ..." Linke said kindly, an older man to a young one.

"No!" Thiele's head snapped up. "No, everything is not all right. The Allied came from somewhere. Or are you prepared to tell me the SS brought them with them—from Berlin?" he barked.

Linke laughed and Thiele stared at him. "What?" Thiele insisted. "What?"

"We are all rascals, Oberleutnant," Linke assured, "even you."

"No." Thiele said finally and walked away dismayed to learn Linke's talents did not include common sense.

It was five degrees hotter inside. "Where is the Hauptmann?" Thiele asked with little enthusiasm when he returned to the villa.

"He is in your office, Oberleutnant," the Korporal reported gleefully. "He said for you to come."

Thiele was already on his way. Erich was in his office, also.

Erich was not in his office any longer. The room a pantry by comparison to the luxury of the library, cramped and crowded with a desk and innumerable wires to run the necessary assortment of telephones and radios, Reineke used the convenience of the opened drawer of a filing cabinet for a tabletop as he stood there, reading one of the personnel folders. Several others he had pulled out and discarded on the floor, the dangling ash from his cigarette threatening to ignite them. Thiele looked hesitantly around the disarray, worse than usual but that was all. "Where is Erich?" he asked.

Reineke did not look up. "In the guardhouse with the others—the wine cellar," he clarified when Thiele was silent. They did not have a guardhouse, Reineke finding them unnecessary until now, *expecting* them to be unnecessary, as he expected them to be unnecessary again.

Under the ground or above? Thiele was wondering. Buried in the dirt or simply lying on top of it? He glanced at the scraped knuckles of Reineke's hand, but they looked the same. He nodded. "There are a few areas we can use ... for a guardhouse," he clarified as Reineke slapped the folder down on his desk.

"They are to be transferred," Reineke assured. "Until they are, the wine cellar is sufficient since they seem to like it so much—we will need a new Staff Sergeant," he tossed the files on Thiele's desk. "Choose a suitable candidate, at least two. We will discuss them."

Thiele nodded again. "The body of the American is buried in one of the gardens."

"I know," Reineke said.

Of course he did. Thiele sat down to tackle the transfers first. There were five. The fifth was the Korporal from the truck yard. "Hauptmann!" he leapt up, file in hand. Reineke hadn't gone far. Thiele found him on the mezzanine, leaning over the rail watching the ashes from his cigarette trickle down to the floor below.

"The American and the English are Allies," Reineke said. "I do not think you will find the association any more mysterious than that."

"What?" Thiele said.

"You seemed to think the girl was English," Reineke prompted.

"A guess?" Thiele tried to remember when this had occurred.

"Reasonable," Reineke drew heavily on his cigarette, eying the personnel folder in Thiele's hand. "Or is that not what you wanted?"

Hardly. "Hauptmann, this soldier ..." Thiele waved the file like a cardboard flag.

"What about this soldier, Thiele?" Reineke took the file to look it over and hand it back. "I do not tolerate insubordination. I am surprised to hear you do. He is to be transferred with the others."

"Insubordination?" Thiele repeated.

"Precisely," Reineke walked away.

"Hauptmann," Thiele followed him. "It is Sergeant Linke who is insubordinate."

"Sergeant Linke was following my orders," Reineke corrected. "There is a difference."

"How do you even know any of this?" Thiele insisted.

He knew. That was the point. "You require respect and obedience from the men. I not only expect, I demand this."

"Respect?" Thiele challenged. "Sergeant Linke refused to obey superior officers, abandoning men to the desert and certain death. Members!" he gasped, "of the SS!"

"If you consider that to be a reason," Reineke surrendered, "be sure and include yourself in the transfers."

He turned for his office.

"And yourself!" Thiele bulled after him. They collided in the doorway. The Holy Man was in the library, sitting in the Hauptmann's chair, books stacked four high on the Hauptmann's desk.

Chapter Ten

"Mon capitaine," Pierre stood up, book in hand. Seeing Thiele he put the book down, apologizing for his intrusion with a quick bend of his head looking to slip away. "I am sorry, mon capitaine, I will come back."

"No," Reineke stepped past Thiele with a glance at the apartment door. "What is it you need?"

"Nothing," Pierre assured, "you are busy. I will come back."

"You will stay," Reineke corrected, an edge to his tone, "and tell me what you need."

"Mon capitaine," Pierre looked down at the desk. "Mon capitaine," he looked back up, "I need to check something that is all."

"What?" Reineke glanced at the books. "What do you need to check?"

"It does not matter," Pierre assured, "it is not here. I thought it was, but I was wrong, and so, I will need to go."

"Where?" Reineke said. "Go where?"

"Mon capitaine," Pierre sighed, but Reineke had already snatched up the book. It was one of Diana's, an anthology of medical journals from twenty years ago. But it was obviously something she had considered valuable enough to keep at one point, and informative enough to give to the Holy Man, the priest struggling through the Germanic language he claimed not to be able to read and could, but only to a limited degree.

"The girl," Reineke flipped through the pages. "What has happened to the girl that you thought you would find in here?"

"Nothing," Pierre denied. "Mademoiselle is fine."

"You are lying," Reineke slapped the book shut. "Tell me and I will find the articles for you. Read them to you if I have to."

"No," Pierre said. "It is just that I do not know everything, and there are some things I do not know well at all."

"What things?" Reineke said. "What are the some things, the nothings you need to check?"

"Mon capitaine, please," Pierre requested.

"What things?" Reineke insisted.

"Fine," Pierre held up his hand. "Mademoiselle has been assaulted. This is not something beyond Pierre's experience. It is something I do need to check. Collect a few additional supplies you do not have here."

"Assaulted," Reineke said. "You mean the rape?"

"Yes, of course, I mean rape," Pierre took the book away from him with a huff. "There is no reason to be indelicate. These are pigs, and we know what pigs do, to her, to whomever they please. Venereal disease is epidemic in the desert, no one is immune, and few are clean. I need the recipe to ensure she is properly washed. I had it, but I cannot find it. There has been no need for a long time. May I go now, please?"

"Go," Reineke waved. "Go!" he stopped him from wasting time collecting the books. "Just, go."

"Thank you, mon capitaine." Head bent, he scurried past Thiele and out of the library.

Reineke clutched the books tightly, convinced they would take flight around him if he were to let them go. He was so hot, sweating, and then cold. The books crashed in a heap on the floor. He sat down and reached for the telephone, ordering a patrol sent after the SS.

Thiele was on top of the desk in seconds, ripping the receiver out of his hands, wrestling him for the cord. The telephone came apart, falling to the floor, its bell ringing on impact. Reineke stopped, his head tipping in curiosity as he stared at it, covered his mouth with his hand, and started to laugh.

"You are out of your mind." Thiele picked up the phone, slamming it back on the desk.

"Am I, Thiele?" he whispered. "Am I?" Was he quite, quite, insane?

"Yes!" Thiele gave up trying to put the phone back together, flinging the receiver aside. "If the prisoner is dead, there is nothing you can do about it."

"Dead?" Reineke perked up. "Indeed. What makes you think the girl is dead, Thiele? What makes you think," he could not wait to hear, "something has happened to the girl at all?"

"No?" Thiele said. "Fine! So then nothing should be the matter with you."

The matter with him? "I?" Reineke said.

"You!" Thiele assured. "Why do you want a patrol? What did he tell you? What is he telling you?" he insisted.

"The matter," Reineke said, "with me?"

They were in the sand, so hot, quiet, and the desert refused to answer him. He stood on the rocks overlooking the village, on the floor, above the dirt of the cellar, and he heard them laugh. He heard the soldiers laugh.

"The matter with me?" Reineke's fingernails dug deep into the polished wood of his desk as he straightened up. "Indeed!" he exploded, and the telephone went flying. "A child has been assaulted, raped. Here, by them, and you are asking, what is the matter with me?"

Thiele groaned, bending to retrieve the telephone.

"Leave it alone!" Reineke ordered.

"Hauptmann ..." Thiele said.

"I said to leave it!" Reineke's foot slammed into his chair sending it spinning into the French windows, crashing through the etched, beveled glass. "I am waiting for you to answer me, Thiele. I am waiting to hear something other than '*Hauptmann*' and '*SS.*' come out of your mouth."

Thiele juggled the broken cradle of the receiver, and then placed it down on the desk.

"Well?" Reineke demanded.

Thiele looked away, remembering the cool stubbornness of Linke in the truck yard; he looked back. "Linke said ..."

"I am not talking about Sergeant Linke," Reineke snapped.

Neither was Thiele, just something Linke said. "We are all rascals," Thiele nodded, "even I. And, no," he said. "I am not. I am not Linke. I cannot be Linke, or you."

"And I can?" Reineke said. "I can be any man. Sergeant Linke.

Heinrich Thiele. Whomever," he said, "they tell me to be."

"Hauptmann ..." Thiele weighed his words in his mouth.

"What?" Reineke said. "I tell you a girl has been raped and you tell me you cannot be Linke. What does that mean?"

"You fight everything," Thiele nodded. Something Thiele did not do. That was what he meant. Thiele chose his battles usually carefully, sometimes choosing not to fight but compromise, yes, instead. Reineke fought. No matter who, no matter what. If it was not his idea, his thought, will, or whim, he fought. "You rebel to rebel. This is a war—"

"A war," Reineke said.

"Yes!" Thiele snapped. "And I would assume—"

"Assume?" Reineke accused.

"Yes!" Thiele insisted. "I would assume, I would expect, I would think you would be capable of realizing—"

"How these things happen." Reineke nodded like he was quoting from some book. "That these things happen."

"Yes!" Thiele said. "It is a war, not one of your stupid games. Damn you! How long must it take for you to realize the game they play is a war out there?"

"Out there," Reineke agreed, "not here. Your things do not happen here. A child is not assaulted here, beaten, raped!"

"You don't know that it was here," Thiele stared at him. "You only know what that priest tells you!"

"There was blood on those men!"

"There was blood all over you. You!" Thiele slapped the desk disgusted. "And you just closed her blouse. You!"

"Indeed," Reineke straightened up. "Child's blouse, Thiele. *Child's* blouse."

That was a matter of opinion. She did not look particularly like a child to Thiele. He did not know what she looked like, other than the enemy. That was what she looked like. That was what he saw. "Hauptmann, I think ..." his hand ran tiredly through his hair.

"Assume, yes," Reineke mocked. "Indeed, expect."

Thiele looked at him. "Shut up," he suggested. "Just, shut-up."

"Condone," Reineke had no intentions of shutting up.

"Condone?" Thiele echoed. "I am not condoning anything. I am telling you, your soldiers are men. She is a prisoner!"

"She is a child," Reineke insisted. "And they will be punished!"

"Punished?" Thiele said. "They are your men. She is the enemy, not them!"

"They are filth!"

"Hauptmann ..." Thiele said.

"Filth!" Reineke grabbed up the broken telephone determined to hammer it back into working order.

"Hauptmann!" Thiele insisted, and Reineke grabbed him, shoving him away. Thiele hit the chair, landing on it, bringing it over on top of himself as he hit the floor.

"Get up," Reineke ordered. "Get up!"

Thiele got up slowly. "That is twice," he said. "There will not be a third time." He walked to the door as if he were thinking of walking out.

"Where are you going?" Reineke insisted.

"I am leaving," Thiele assured, only his hand never reached the latch. The smooth glass paperweight found its way into Reineke's grasp and he flung it. The weighty ball whizzed over Thiele's shoulder, smashing into the door, narrowly missing his head.

"You are going nowhere," Reineke assured as Thiele stood there silently studying the chipped wood. "You are going to stay here until you learn—"

"I am leaving," Thiele interrupted. "You can call for your sentries, all two hundred of them, if you like. They can hear your outrage in the courtyard and attribute it to another one of your fits. They think you are mad, but I know you are afraid." He turned around. "You were afraid out there, and you are afraid in here. But whatever it is, you are afraid of, mein Hauptmann, take it and get rid of it out there, not here. There is a war to fight here."

"Indeed," Reineke said.

"Yes," Thiele nodded. "Yes."

"Delay the rendezvous with the convoy shipment," Reineke replied, and it was enough to rock Thiele's newly discovered strength.

"What?" Thiele said.

"Do it," Reineke instructed. "And issue a notice of radio silence.

The idea of the Kufra intrigues me."

"The Kufra?" Thiele marched back to him. "The French are in control of the Kufra."

"A reason why it intrigues me," Reineke agreed. "Perhaps the girl is French, not English or American. Perhaps a survivor of an air transport or courier off course and downed in the heat. It is irrelevant. The Kufra intrigues me. It is two weeks minimum to supply the Coast Road under the most ideal circumstances. What we gain with the depots, we lose in time. That is unacceptable."

"What are you talking about?" Thiele insisted. "We have no time for the Kufra. The convoy will be in port in a week. That's it. Our one chance to take what we can, at the docks, there is no other. After that the cargo will be on the supply trains and it will be too late. It must be the docks, the trucks must leave immediately for Sebha, and *we* must leave to meet them on the supply route, as scheduled, as *planned.* Unless you think they are going to hold the convoy, the trains, the trucks for you, timing is critical."

"I think," Reineke said, "an airstrip at the Kufra is ideal for our cause—"

"The airstrip was destroyed!" Thiele snapped.

"By the French," Reineke agreed, "one year ago. It is time to reevaluate the area and determine if the French have decided to keep her, share her with the English, or abandon her ..." He collected his chair to sit at his desk, hastily scrawling a message. "Dispatch a courier to Schönfeld ..."

"Herr Oberst is in Algiers." Thiele snatched up the note, not bothering to read it. "For that you need the radio! By the time this reaches him, he will be here—wondering why you have not left and the munitions on schedule for Sebha instead of en route here!"

"Dispatch a courier to meet him," Reineke said. "We are at radio silence. The cargo is to be intercepted as planned, at the docks. The trucks can simply camp and wait, yes, for me."

"Camp where?" Thiele insisted. "Wait where? Once they leave the coast, they are on the supply road to Sebha. An open target until they do, unless they do, and even then. They must keep moving. There is no place to camp or wait—except Sebha. If we are not there to meet it, they will destroy the convoy. Those are their orders, *your* orders. Linke must be there to meet them en route, or this is some useless exercise. *You* are the one who refused to give them the route here!"

"*You* are dismissed," Reineke said, "When I am ready to tell you more, you will know more, until that time consider it your punishment. Indeed," his eyes narrowed. "If you are fortunate, your only punishment. I am hardly afraid, Thiele, of anything. Now, get out."

Unfortunately, I am unable to accept your invitation and attend the celebration. My regards to your family and friends. Hauptmann Reineke.

Outside in the hall Thiele read the message and read it a second time. The only *celebration* he knew about was the interceptions of major shipments to the Italian forces planned for the next few months. Reineke couldn't be anticipating a delay of all of them. All of them? Thiele turned back for the library, twisting the latch open. Reineke sat on the floor in front of the French windows, the glass paperweight at his feet, his head buried, resting in the crook of his arm, one thumb absently chipping away at the peeling paint.

"Get out, Thiele," he said, knowing who it was without needing to look up.

Thiele's steel-blue eyes bore into the apartment door, cursing the prisoner, whoever she was, English, American, or Free French. "Die," he whispered, "Die!" and headed for the radio room with the order to fall silent.

Chapter Eleven

It was very late when the Holy Man returned to the library. Reineke sat in his chair at his desk, his fingers tapping his mouth, studying the small brown figure seated across from him. His throat felt dry, sour and he kept trying without success to moisten his lips with his tongue. The monk knew that. He knew everything. Did he? "I thought it was you," Reineke said finally, quietly. "I had thought the SS prisoner was you, not some child."

"I, mon capitaine?" Pierre's voice echoed in the darkness. "No, not I, mon capitaine, never. Never."

Of course not. The Holy Man was far too clever to fall prey to the SS. But when the prisoner turned out not to be the Holy Man, instead of being relieved, Reineke had no idea what to do. He rose to study the stars through the French windows. "I had to choose," he explained. "It seems I continue having to choose who the enemy is, and who it is not. You cannot know how that feels."

Of course, Pierre could know, having made such a choice himself three short months ago. But that was not important right now. "Mon capitaine ..." He moved forward on his seat of velvet cushions worn and fraying in spots, and dry. Everything in this desert was so dry, everything in the room. "You are very upset. Let me give you something."

No. His body, like his skin, was highly sensitive, easily upset, and irritated. It was not only his emotions or his moods. It was not worth the risk. "The wine will do." He returned to his desk, his tongue still feeling foreign as he drank and he tried wetting his lips again.

"As you wish," Pierre sat carefully back in his chair, watching.

"I am angry," Reineke assured, "not ill. Indeed," he studied his glass, the deep blood color of the wine, full and rich, regal, like his, "if I am ill, I have been ill since the time of my mother's womb."

"Melancholia," Pierre agreed, "not battle fatigue."

"Civilized," Reineke downed the wine. "I am civilized." He could feel his uniform pressing against his flesh, the color of his flesh, part of it, seamless. The flattering lines soft and smooth as the material, inseparable, the two of them, rather than a misfit. He was not a lost man, simply misplaced. This was not his life, his world. The monk should understand such things.

Pierre did, tried. "Nordic," he said, as if reading Reineke's mind, "not Nazi. Mon capitaine is a being, not a political ambition."

"Civilized," Reineke said with a reach for the bottle to refill his glass. "This is unacceptable to me, what has happened, the girl, the prisoners, even the American with the bones sticking out like spikes in his head. I would think it would be unacceptable to anyone. It is inconceivable to me it would not be. It is inconceivable to me," he said, "it would not be to you."

"Unacceptable, mon capitaine?" Pierre said. "Oui, of course it is. Inconceivable? Non," he shook his head. "It is not inconceivable to me."

"This is war," Reineke quoted Thiele.

"Oui," Pierre agreed. "It is war. What war looks like, what war is."

"Thiele said that," Reineke nodded with a sip of his wine.

"He is right," Pierre apologized.

"No," Reineke said. "No, he is not. War is a fight, a battle, offense, defense. In war men do not have time—"

"To rape?" Pierre injected, and Reineke looked at him over his wine. "What men are these? Of course they do. You are angry, mon capitaine, not naïve. In war, men have time to do whatever they want to do. Fight their battles the way they want to in any manner they wish."

"This is not Russia, indeed, we are not Russians," Reineke insisted harshly, having heard the tales from both sides. "I expect a soldier to conduct himself with honor. I demand a soldier conduct himself with honor."

"Nor is it Warsaw, Oslo, France," Pierre agreed, having heard those tales as well. "Whose soldiers are these you expect so much of?"

Indeed. Reineke stared into his glass. France was a fact, not a confession. He could not feel sorry about France; he would never feel sorry for France. "Indeed." The crystal cracked in his hand, blood running down like wine. He was on the balcony, the smoke from his cigarette burning his eyes, the heels of his hands pressing tightly into their watering sockets, trying to catch his breath.

He caught it and he was not at the windows, but still at his desk, staring into the unbroken glass of wine, everything else in his mind. "We are not all monsters," he repeated. "I refuse to accept we are all monsters. I refuse to accept those who are. The men responsible will be punished."

"Punished?" Pierre asked visions of a spanking in his head. "How mon capitaine?"

Executed. Shot, hanged; Reineke did not care which. He rose for the cabinet and a bottle of wine that looked less like blood. "You and Thiele are so obsessed with my weakness for compassion you forget how easy it is for me to kill."

"The men responsible are partners with the SS, mon capitaine," Pierre replied. "Do you have the authority to execute the SS?"

His authority was limitless. "Do you have a better idea?"

"I have no idea," Pierre assured. "I have concerns the SS will return, that more will come and take your complex from you and all will die. You, your men, the children, everything we have strived to protect."

"Diana's reasons for not taking care of them," Reineke nodded.

There was a pause before Pierre answered, brief, but long enough. "Is it?" he said. "That does not sound like her."

That was what he had said, but apparently, he was wrong. "I meant before," Reineke said. "The reason why she let them come, instead of killing them on the sea."

"Oh," Pierre said. "Oui, yes, of course. She would want answers, mon capitaine, just like you. Assessment of her exposure could not be gained from dead men."

No, it could not. Reineke returned to his desk with a doubtful bottle of Bordeaux. "And I am talking about the men here who are responsible, Erich, the others. I will have answers, and they will be punished. The SS are banished to the desert without water or fuel, map, or any means of contact. They will die walking in circles. That should be enough to satisfy her. If not, tell her to send the dentist and lawyer to kill them as she should have done before."

"Be assured, mon capitaine," Pierre nodded at the scarred and blackened ceiling, "what you have done is enough."

Indeed. He had already ordered the ceiling repaired, the broken glass panes of the French windows replaced, the bruised and dented wood of the library's door smoothed. The glass paperweight he could do nothing about except order it polished, which it was, and back on his desk, an interesting pattern of tiny fractures deep within. The ashtray however was filled and overflowing with ashes and cigarettes. It seemed incapable of looking any other way. He seemed incapable of not having it look that way. "It was worth it," he assured.

"Pardon?" Pierre's head tipped.

Worth it. *Worth it*. The looks on the faces of the SS who thought he was too pretty to mean what he said. More than one had made that mistake before, more than one would probably make that same mistake again. "Worth it," he assured. The cork snapped off in his hand, dry from age and improper storage. The next bottle was much more cooperative and satisfying, the cork slipping out like it had been greased. Reineke returned to his desk for the third time, finding room in the ashtray for his cigarette before he lit another. "The men responsible here will be removed, transferred and tried for failing in their orders." And therefore executed, shot. He should be satisfied; he was not. Like the SS condemned to death in the desert, mere execution was insufficient. He wanted them to know who killed them and why.

"Not a bad idea," Pierre shrugged, a demon under his pious cloak. "There are children here."

"I am thinking of the children," Reineke assured, and he was. The children, as always, were on his mind. He drank his wine.

"I know," Pierre smiled.

"And what to do," Reineke acknowledged, "should the SS return. Indeed."

"Return?" Pierre dismissed. "No, they will not return. Die in the desert as you said."

As Linke calculated. Far enough away from the complex, and far short of their encampment, wherever it was. At least a hundred kilometers, it had to be. He should have followed the tracks back to see where they were from, not forward to where he knew they were going. "The rest of them," Reineke assured. "There are not only six SS, as there are not only two Allied out there."

"What Allied is this?" Pierre verified.

The ones who did not exist. American, English, or French. The ones who came from nowhere and somehow managed to end up there. It had to be by airplane. An engineer suggested perhaps the Suez Canal. The only thing he could think of except for the Kufra. Flying in or flying out, off course and downed in the heat, extremely off course. "You are to stay here," Reineke nodded. "Here, at the villa until the girl lives or dies, then you may go."

"Of course," Pierre agreed, surprised. "Naturally, I will stay."

"I will make certain," Reineke said, "you have anything you need."

"Nothing," Pierre assured. "I need nothing. What I need I have with me."

His hands. He called them hands. Reineke knew they were wands, magic wands, moving as wands, thin as wands. "How is she?" he asked. A remarkably rude inquiry when he knew the answer he wanted to hear. "Do you know yet?"

"Still sleeping?" Pierre shrugged. "I think tomorrow she will probably wake up—alive, mon capitaine," he assured. "If she survives the drugs, she will live. The injury to her head is old, days, perhaps even weeks. Since she has lived, I think she will continue to live, the other injuries are not life threatening."

That was not the answer he wanted to hear. Dead, was the answer, continued to be the answer he wanted. She had to die, saving him the responsibility of executing her. "You said something about drugs before." Reineke sipped his wine, an image coming to mind of him trying to sneak into the apartment while the Holy Man slept and suffocating the prisoner with her pillow, laying her death to the drugs. He would never get away with it. Probably take too long to decide which pillow was appropriate for the act and by then he would be caught.

"I said something about drugs because I believe she has been drugged," Pierre agreed.

Henbane. Nightshade. "The ether could not have helped her situation." Reineke suggested, fooling no one with the proposed innocence of his remark. The Holy Man opened his mouth as if he intended to retort, but then did not. It was all right. Reineke knew what he was going to say. "I did not say I wanted to kill her," Reineke assured irritably. "I am simply saying it would be far less complicated if she died."

"Less complicated for whom, mon capitaine?"

"Us," Reineke insisted. "You, the children, and I."

"Then it is complicated," Pierre agreed, "because she may not."

Apparently. Reineke rose for the French windows and the cool night air. "Why would they drug her?" he asked. "Who could she possibly be? What could she possibly tell them, a child her age? The SS might use a child, yes, of course. But to rely on them would be foolish."

"We have children here," Pierre said.

Yes. A sea of kindergarteners armed with guns, bows and arrows, and knives. "I am not saying a child cannot know things," Reineke assured. "But what a child knows they cannot fully comprehend or is even necessarily true."

Pierre shrugged. "To keep her quiet perhaps?"

Quiet? Why? Because she was screaming? Reineke stared through the French windows.

"Who knows?" Pierre said behind him. "Why would they do anything to her other than they are soldiers, she is a woman, and this is war? It is all right though, I think ..." he looked away as he thought; Reineke could see him reflected in the glass, a frown between his black pig eyes replaced by confidence when he looked back. "Oui, I am positive the blood is not all from her. There were others."

At least one. "The American you buried in the gardens," Reineke nodded, "under the nose of the SS."

"A good guess," Pierre agreed. "They cut off his hands. I did not tell you this before, but I tell you now. They cut off his hands. They are butchers. Mademoiselle is lucky to be in one piece, not simply alive."

"The SS have been condemned," Reineke reminded. "I said I would take care of the men responsible here."

"Good," Pierre shrugged. "And I will not pray for their souls, not even to burn in Hell. Hell is too good for them. There is no place for them. Hell is for you and me, where we will live together as we do here, in harmony."

It was time to change the subject. "Who will stay with the children while you are here?" Reineke moved on to the Holy Man's assignment as nurse. "You cannot leave such a responsibility to Anne—or Hanuk," he made a point. "Obviously still a child himself. Thiele could have shot him, or any one of them. Indeed," he heard himself say, "the adults are as bad as the children they swear to protect—"

"Mon capitaine!" Pierre requested as Reineke spun around, panic on his face, realizing what he was saying, who he had to be talking about.

"No!" Reineke insisted. "What is she doing in camp, are you insane? She can see who they are—indeed!" he seethed. "Regardless of what you say, none of you can defend why the SS were even allowed to penetrate the perimeter. Why I did not find their bodies alongside their tracks! What did Diana think? I had decided the guards should pose as SS instead of Arabs to deceive your French?"

"The woman Sotma," Pierre nodded. "It is the woman Sotma who is with the children."

"I do not care what she calls herself!" Reineke insisted. "I have a thousand tons of supplies—"

"And men," Pierre agreed. "A thousand tons of supplies and men; fine," he said. "I will stay here with Mademoiselle. You can go sleep in the village to make sure your men and supplies will be here in the morning when you wake up."

Reineke looked at him.

Pierre grinned. "Keep your storm troopers quiet, eh, mon capitaine? Diana will keep hers. That is what she is doing here, of course. An assessment of her exposure. And destroy you as quickly as she could the SS. But, it is all right," he promised with a wave, "no big deal, the dentist says. A bargain you have, a bargain Diana will keep, and, oui, Pierre will keep his, too."

"I have no bargain with Diana," Reineke assured. "Any bargain she believes we have is all in her head."

"Yes, you do," Pierre nodded. "Oui, you do."

No, he did not. His bargain was with this priest, some crippled old man, and his army of orphaned children, their families long missing or dead.

January 1942
The Fezzan

"The children," the German repeated one last time. "I want to know about the children."

"Pardon?" the Algerian said. "I know nothing about the children. I do not know what you mean."

Yes he did. "The children," the German started to pace. "I want to know how many there are, exactly how many there are, and why there appears to be more since they were remanded to the settlement camp." He finished triumphantly, his fists down on his desk.

"Fifty-two," the Algerian smiled. "All Catholic."

Fifty-two. Fifty-two was the number revealed by the census, a staggering number that shocked him. However, there were at least two more. The pair with the crone who had held him captive for hours he had never seen before. One of them admittedly was not a child but a young man of perhaps eighteen. The girl was definitely a child of approximately ten. "Catholic?" If his tone sounded tired or irritable, it was at the idea of a roving band of desert Catholics.

The Algerian's smile widened until he was grinning like some clown. "Libya is a very different country, you should know. It is not like everywhere or anywhere else. There are Catholics, and there are stone men who live in caves."

"Caves?" the German echoed.

"There are caves beneath the wall," the Algerian reminded what the German had already discovered for himself.

"Those are tunnels, mine shafts and tunnels," the German huffed. Accosted by some crazed witch he was in no mood to learn of a band of desert trolls.

"Mines?" the Algerian smiled. "No, you are wrong. They are graves. This is the temple Diana of the Emperor Hadrian. The wall her citadel now holding back the sea as the sand fights to consume her. The desert it like that, it rises and spreads, and will eventually consume her, yes. Like the Great Sphinx, buried to its neck. When you get to Egypt, you will see."

The German looked at him, continued looking at him until the Algerian shrugged. "Mine, graves. Who says a grave cannot be a mine, or a mine a grave—"

"How many are there?" the German interrupted. The crone claimed hundreds, he was guessing that was not true, and was still lucky to get out of there alive. He remained uncertain as to why he had been released alive, only that it bolstered her confidence, supported her claim she was as powerful, if not more powerful than he.

"I have no idea what you are talking about," the Algerian insisted. "Some trick of the sun."

It was no trick of the sun. The sun was not armed with French guns. The pool of water, yes, he thought it was a mirage himself at first. A shimmering lake in the distance, struck by how real it looked, incredulous to find it was authentic as he approached. Clearly an imperial garden had stood here once, so peaceful and calm in her surviving beauty amidst the graveyard of marble stone. One lone goddess standing proudly in the background of the empty pedestals and ring of columns surrounding the ancient pond, one hand raised to the heavens ... in the other a gun, the steel barrel approaching his head reflected in the water cool, and crystal clear.

"*Mon capitaine*?" in the distance the Holy Man's voice attempted to penetrate from the present day, but Reineke could barely hear it.

"Dangerous?" the German sarcastically answered the Algerian's claim of the native settlement being too dangerous for the children to live. It was obviously much more dangerous than it should be, and nowhere near as dangerous as it could be if he did not get the cooperation he sought. "Talk to me," he encouraged. "Now is your chance. There is no reason for these games. I do not believe in witches, and I do not believe in trolls. What do you want from me? Tell me, and I will see what I can do."

"I can prove it," the Algerian smiled.

"Prove it?" the German said. "Prove what? How?" More dead goats hung in the courtyard? Or simply the gift of some blackened necrotic hoof waiting when Reineke woke to find the Algerian standing at the side of his bed.

"Foot, not hoof, foot," the Algerian explained as the German leapt from the sheets, gagging on the stench. "See? Here is where the toes would be ... it is all right," he reassured the German recoiling from him. "It cannot hurt you, it is dead."

"And the rest of it?" the German said hoarsely, the smell still burning and vomit aspirated into his lungs.

"Rest of it?" the Algerian sat on the rim of the tub, offering him a towel to wipe his face. "It is all right, take your time. There is no rest of it. Eaten away."

"Body," the German snapped. "Where is the body? Where have you hidden it?"

"Oh, the body is fine." The Algerian laughed, amused by the German afraid to do what? Open his cupboard? Climb back into his bed? "She is fine. The foot, no."

He stuffed the rotted limb so casually back in its sack. "The temple is too dangerous as I told you for the children to run or play. It is very beautiful, yes, but too dangerous, unsafe."

"She," the German stared at the sack.

"Oui, she," the Algerian watched him. "A little girl."

"Girl?" the German looked up. "There was a girl with the crone. This could not have happened in a day, not a day."

"Anne," the Algerian said finally with his smile on his face. "No, this is not Anne, this is Adva." he patted the sack, his smile softening a little. "Palestinian," he offered after another pause, in afterthought. "But, what does is matter, eh?" he shrugged. "It does not. There are seventy-five children here, some Catholic, some Arab."

Seventy-five. That was twenty-three more than the census had revealed, an entire third of their population unaccounted for. It did not seem possible. Where were they?

"What is wrong with you?" the Algerian inquired, a dangerous question, but he was asking it anyway with that smile on his face, thinking of the look on the face of the German, the vomit erupting from his throat when he saw the amputated limb. "What happened? Who did you think this was?" he held the sack out. "Who did she remind you of?"

"Where is Czestochowa?" the German answered finally. "I have never heard of it."

"Poland," the Algerian nodded. "A slaughter in Poland. There has been none worse some claim."

"I was in France." Was the German's defense, forgetting perhaps the man he was talking to was French.

"Recently?" the brow of the Algerian cocked in tune with his consideration.

Of course, recently, if not a thousand times before, what did this priest expect him to say? That he went shopping, leaving the invasion to someone else? He did go shopping, check on his friends upon his arrival, Maxim turned from couture to whore. She hit him when she saw him, but then gave him a hug. He urged her to go to Vichy and she laughed, reminding him this was Paris. And who leaves Paris? No one leaves Paris, any more than they ever leave the Rhine.

"Did you tell her that?" the Algerian asked.

What? The German watched him. Tell who, what? That he spent his recuperation in Paris where the whores made him feel better about his torn leg?

"Diana," the Algerian assured. "Moses she called herself when she first came here, but agrees how Diana is much better suited for her. Did you tell her you never heard of Czestochowa? She would believe you if you did." his smile deepened for the German continuing to frown. "That you know nothing of Czestochowa. Too stupid a question for you to ask if it was not true, too stupid a lie to tell. It had to be true."

"Moses," the German repeated.

"It is the same thing," the Algerian shrugged, his voice sounding louder for some reason, outside Reineke, not inside him. Reineke roused himself. It was today, not three months ago, and he was outside on the balcony where the air did not help.

March 9

"The woman Sotma?" Reineke answered sourly.

"Oui," Pierre grinned. "Pretty good, eh? I like it."

"Indeed," Reineke said. "Any bargain *the woman Sotma* believes we have she violated when she sent her sons into my camp."

"That was for your own protection, mon capitaine," Pierre assured and Reineke scoffed. A moment ago, it was in the spirit of annihilation, his and his men, along with the SS.

"The SS came here without the roads," Pierre reminded. "Roads they cannot know, and yet they came here anyway."

"My Colonel knows the road." Reineke walked back inside for his wine.

"Is he SS?" Pierre asked and Reineke's eyes rolled.

"No," he assured. "I am saying the caravan routes are not necessarily the secret you believe they are. Indeed, perhaps two-thousand years ago, but not now." He drank his wine.

"That is because you gave them to him," Pierre nodded.

"Of course I gave them to him," Reineke snapped. "Yes, naturally I gave some to him. Indeed," he said caustically, "something to do with the bargain between him and me."

"Mon capitaine has too many bosses," Pierre advised. "He should pick one and then we would not have problems like this."

Gods, he meant, gods, not bosses, with this priest wanting his to be the only one. "What *problems*?" Reineke insisted. "Indeed, this is the first *problem* we have had in three months."

"And it is a big one." Pierre assured, disputing what the dentist had called 'no big deal', whatever that meant. Like Reineke, he preferred speaking with the doctor whose French he could understand. "You have a spy in your organization who reports to the SS," he made his point about the roads. "It is the only way."

"Erich," Reineke walked the length of the room. "We know that, and he has been confined. Diana's involvement is not only foolish, it is unnecessary—"

"The woman Sotma," Pierre interrupted. "The woman Sotma is with the children."

Reineke looked at him, and Pierre shrugged. "You were saying?"

Nothing. He was saying nothing, and the Holy Man would not listen if he did. He gave up, returning to the topic of the prisoner that for some reason seemed more pleasant. "Tomorrow you are to begin exercising the girl in the gardens. I will order a guard."

"Pardon?" Pierre startled.

"Exercise," Reineke sat down at his desk. "You are to begin her exercise. You said she was fine."

"Not dead, yes," Pierre agreed. "But not tomorrow, mon capitaine, a few days perhaps."

"Tomorrow," Reineke assured. "I have ordered us on radio silence—"

"Is that wise?" Pierre interrupted again.

He had no idea what was wise. He was trying to think of something wise, making it up as he went along. "Indeed," Reineke downed his wine. "We are four days from the Kufra. The oasis can be the only logical explanation for the Allied."

"French," Pierre said. "Kufra belongs to Leclerc, no one else. No English has ever seen her, no American even heard of her."

"According to you," Reineke made a face.

Pierre laughed. "According to Mussolini the Italians are in control of the Fezzan. One of us is right."

Reineke did not have the time to decide which. "In any event, not German," he assured. "I have supplies coming in a few days that must be able to reach us."

"So soon again?" Pierre replied quietly.

"Food supplies," Reineke said impatiently. "Indeed, food supplies. We eat, too. You may take whatever you need."

"Thank you, mon capitaine," Pierre's head tipped.

"And you are to begin the girl's exercise in the morning," Reineke instructed. "There can be no delay. She is to be ready to return with the convoy for more suitable quarters. This is a supply depot, not a Stalag. I do not have the facilities to house prisoners of war."

"Camps," Pierre corrected. "What you have are camps not facilities, prisons where you would not send a dog to. It would kinder of you to leave Mademoiselle on the sea with the SS."

"There are no camps!" the wine bottle banged down on his desk. "Indeed, you tell me *facts* no one else has ever heard about, least of all seen!"

"That is not true," Pierre shook his head. "Two-thirds of the population of Libya interned by Mussolini in his Italian War, one-third killed, slaughtered, and the League of Nations did nothing,

nothing. One million people, nothing, and they look away again now. Oui," he assured, "continue to look away, just like you do."

No, he did not. He did not look away, and he did not look at things that were not there. Germany fought to restore its position and dignity, regain territories and lands stolen from her. Occupation of opposing governments was a necessary act to ensure cooperation, expand the borders of protection against Russia who thought it could just sweep in—what did that have to do with camps? There were no camps. "Indeed," Reineke felt the gold of the Prince's cross beneath the breast of his uniform, cool against his chest warm and perspiring. "The girl is to be ready to leave with the trucks. I am not Mussolini. This is not the Italian War."

"If you insist," Pierre shrugged.

"I do!" Reineke said.

"Fine," Pierre rose to his crippled legs. "Mademoiselle will begin her exercise in the morning, and she will be ready to leave in a few days. This will never happen," he predicted, "but that is all right, too. It gives mon capitaine a few more days to think."

He was finished thinking.

"You have a sister?" Pierre smiled.

What? Reineke eyed him. He had two sisters, the priest knew that. One whom he hated, one whom he loved. Alexia he loved. The eagerness in her fingers and fascination she had for balls, brightly colored balls, when she was just a little baby, and he was a child of fourteen, his father's brain rotted from the gases in the trenches, poised to take the Baron's throne. "You know I have a sister," Reineke assured. "Why?"

"I do," Pierre agreed. "Would you send your sister to this camp where Pierre would not send his dog?" He walked away, for the door.

"Holy Man," Reineke said.

"Yes, mon capitaine?" Pierre immediately turned around.

"You understand what I do, I do for the children," Reineke said. "You must trust and believe the decisions I make are for the best."

"We are all children, mon capitaine," he replied.

No, they were not. Children were innocent. "The girl is to be ready to leave with the trucks," Reineke repeated. "She is not Arab or French, otherwise I would consider keeping her here. Remanding her to you, not only now, but permanently. But that is not possible. The SS did not choose us by random. It would be naïve to think I could somehow trace them back to my father's wrath."

"That would be something more than naïve, mon capitaine," Pierre agreed.

Insanity, yes. Paranoia, heat stroke. Unfortunately, he simply had a headache and upset stomach from too much wine. "If the SS came from the north, the south, east, or west, they did not come without a reason or without a map. If they are here, they are everywhere, the Allied obviously as well. Indeed," Reineke said, "would you sacrifice your children in this girl's stead, sending them to this camp where you would not send your dog? Because that is what will happen and is what I will prevent—if you let me. Please let me."

"I understand your reasoning," Pierre stopped him there. "Good night, mon capitaine, sleep well."

That was unlikely, Reineke knew, and gave up on the wine before he could not sleep at all.

Chapter Twelve

The Fezzan
March 8

Joanna Lee was nineteen years old. Neither English nor American, as she lay sleeping on a strange, foreign bed. She wasn't even Joanna Lee yet. Not in her dream. In her dream she was Joanna Edwards and she was nine years old. She remembered it well that afternoon in the parlor of Grandfather's home in Cambridge. She hadn't been peeking or anything of that sort. She hadn't been doing anything in particular for that matter, except pressing her nose tightly against the window pane and drawing pictures with her breath when the auto drove up.

At first, she thought it was her mother and stepfather Henry coming home, but then the door opened and the people got out and she could see it wasn't her mother and Henry after all, but Michael with Grandfather and her stepbrother Justin, which was surprising because Justin was not supposed to be there, not that she recalled.

She would have met them at the door, but she needed to find her shoes. Claudia would scold if she did not have her shoes. She didn't seem to understand how Joanna hated them, but Joanna still took them off anyway, every chance she got. Shoes were boring. You couldn't feel anything with shoes.

No one heard her coming down. The stairs were thickly carpeted and she was barefooted, not having been able to find her shoes after all, but she really didn't think Claudia would say anything, not with Michael there to protect her and she brought along one of the dolls Michael had given her, just to make sure.

The door to Grandfather's study was almost closed, the voices coming from inside very soft, but she must have known before she even went in—children do that sometimes, they just sort of know—because she stepped ever so quietly, and, yes, that was proof she knew something because Joanna was anything but quiet.

No one heard her come in, they were all so busy with their conversation, and it did not take her long to realize how her mother and Henry would not be coming home, ever.

Never.

Her eyes were wet. In her dream, Joanna shook her head trying to shake away the tears, but she kept bumping up against something ... a pillow. Some stupid oversized pillow, soft and damp. How odd. She didn't seem to remember her eyes being wet, or any pillow.

"In fact!" Joanna snarled, she distinctly remembered hanging onto her doll as she listened, refusing to allow her eyes to be wet.

"But it was so hard!" she whispered, the pillow beginning to fade. "So very hard." They were all so upset. Poor Justin. Joanna looked at her stepbrother standing with her friend Michael asking him so many questions. Michael wanted Justin to tell her. But, Justin couldn't. Henry was his father too, and he had been a father to Justin a great deal longer than he had to her. To her he was still brand new.

So Joanna understood. The grown-up person inside of her understood about fathers, because in the dream she remembered something else. She remembered how her mother had come to tell her when she was only about seven, how her father had gone away and would not be coming back. Ever. Now they were all gone. All of them.

Joanna believed it was then her doll developed its permanent lump of stuffing as the little person she was, tried to decide if she should just back away and let them come and find her, or what she should do. She would never know because Claudia looked up from her handkerchief and saw her and the men turned around to stare at the little girl, who could only say, "Hello," in such a child's voice. Justin turned away, and Claudia ran out. No one said a word for the longest time until Michael dashed across the room, swooping her high up in the air, laughing. Only this time she didn't laugh back, which was something she always did, and Michael set her down, his handsome face pinched, and Joanna felt sorry for him, she really did, but she had to know. So, she asked him—not fresh, just curious—if she could stay, anyway? If it was all right anyway, if she stayed? And they were all there. Hugging her, patting her, reassuring ...

No, that was wrong. They were not all there. Certainly not Justin. But there was someone there she could not quite see. In her dream, Joanna's head moved around, trying to shoo the clouds away. It was all so confusing. They were beginning to talk so loud. Michael was saying, and kept saying, "*Mademoiselle*?" And that was wrong. Michael hadn't said, "*Mademoiselle*?" There hadn't been a pillow. Her eyes had not been wet, but they were. "Michael?" she whispered.

"Try to speak slowly," he answered in a voice she could barely understand, "You have been injured, severely."

Injured? Whatever did he mean? She hadn't been injured. Never in her life had she ever been injured, though people around her certainly had been killed, first her parents and then Joe.

"Joe," Joanna whispered. That was who she couldn't quite see. Of course, Joe was there. She remembered it now quite clearly. Joe had come into the house with Michael, Grandfather, and her stepbrother Justin. Really, how wrong of her not to have remembered Joe from the beginning. Claudia would never approve. Joe was her husband. She married Joe. Scolding herself severely, Joanna settled back into her dream. Her marriage to Joe was a long way off. She was still a child in her dream, and she wanted to think about Michael.

"*Michael.*" The young woman lying on the bed smiled and the dream took on a rosy glow. Michael was wonderful. So absolutely, wonderful. So much better looking than Gable, a hundred times more exciting than Flynn.

Michael had been born in the States. The isle of Brooklyn. The balls and backbone of the United States and New York, the greatest city in the world.

Michael had the most God-awful voice, and with those grating adenoid-suffering sounds, he slew all her dragons, gorged her on fairytales, and pranced his way into her heart forever.

"Oh, God, Michael," Joanna muttered, and her sweat soaked body twitched. She needed Michael now to ward off the nightmares. It always worked before. He was always there before. Even after, yes, even after they had shuttled her off to live with Grandfather, he came as often as he could.

Even when, yes, even when the war came Michael was still there.

And especially when, yes, especially when the war took Joe away.

"Oh, God, Joe!" Joanna cried, a host of demons appearing to surround her. It was unfair. So terribly unfair. They had no right!

"Go away! Go away!" she screamed, but they refused to listen, their heads starting to bob, twist, and spin. *"Noooo ... !"* she echoed as they swarmed over her, pushing her down, and they would come again, and again, even in the dream, even though it was her dream, her dream ...

"My dream!" Joanna was gasping. "My dream. It's mine. Mine. Mine, MINE!" and she tightened her grip on her doll until she strangled the life from it.

Her eyes were wet, but she didn't care, and she made a promise to fight. "I'll kill you!" she told the last of the demon faces, glad to see it was bleeding.

"I'll kill you!" she hissed, clutching at its arm, trying to fend it off, and it stopped. For one moment it stopped surprised and Joanna reached for the pillow, but it was so far away. She lunged for the pillow, but the floor was too soft, tugging at her ankles, and the demon cheated, catching her when her back was turned. It raised its hand and grabbed her hair, trying to take her head away.

The Allied

Chapter Thirteen

Cairo, Egypt
March 9, 1942

Dr. Michael Delegianis MD, PhD, Abc, xyz, etc., ditched his duffel bag and hopped sprightly from the jeep. Cairo. In ten years, it was as common, sultry, steamy, as he remembered it.

"What about you, Red?" he almost looked over his shoulder and asked Red, but did not. Red was not there. He had promised her once, a decade or so ago, give or take a month or two, but it never came to be. He took her just about everywhere else though. Six weeks after the car crash that killed her mother and stepfather Henry, Michael booked the trains, boats, and bicycles, and they were off; around the world in eighty days. Swear to God. From London to Paris to Timbuktu, she in her polka dots and patent leather, he in his white bucks and Panama hat, a couple of hefty side arms strapped under his jacket. The 14-karat cheaters he wore necessary only so he could see his hand in front of his face never mind the Eiffel Tower.

He wasn't half bad though, still wasn't at thirty-seven. Still had the movie star good looks, Einstein IQ, and Jimmy Cagney swagger. Still dressed the same way, wore the same gold frames, carried the same two guns.

He wasn't much bigger than Cagney, shared the same birthright, the USA, though Michael's stork set down in Brooklyn, not Manhattan's lower east side, *"Kiss this"* his motto on St. Paddy's Day. Because when it came to rough? As in tough? As in doing a tap dance on someone's face? Dr. Michael Delegianis *Jr,* only son and progeny of Brooklyn's Mick-the-Prick rubbed out in Harlem in '38 (they were picking up his forensic evidence for a week) Mikey, as some of Michael's friends sometimes called him, would give you three guesses who'd win hands down? He had an edge, Michael, what you call an attitude. Came by it naturally. Thirteen bullets his father took to the chest, count them, thirteen. "*A baker's dozen*" the tabloids read.

"'*Rumor has it my mutter done it.*'" Justin quoted the sub-caption blazon underneath, losing a lot in the translation and like Michael *knew* what he said would be repeated when he wasn't even there, not even stateside at the time but home in England in jail, or it felt like jail. Thirty-three years old and if it wasn't his wife, it was everyone else still telling him what to do.

London, England
A hotel room, 1938

"'*Answered the mobster's son when asked,*'" Justin continued flapping his gums. His beard still black and hair practically gone, you remember Justin, unforgettable that he was, tall thin guy son of Henry begat by Scotty, it was Michael you haven't met. Hotshot, hot-blooded Italian-American with the golden yellow curls and killer blue eyes, husband to Claudia daughter of Drake buddy to the old guy now called Gramps the father of Robert father to Joe, and so forth and so on. "'*The notable Dr. Delegianis, Rhodes Scholar and Nobel laureate.*'"

"Yeah, well, I'm not a Nobel laureate," Michael assured. Not to say he couldn't be, for that matter one day might be despite a chronic battle with booze. By '38, a creeping alcoholic stiffness to that Jimmy Cagney swagger. "Shows you how much they know."

"Still wasn't too bright, Mike," Justin tossed the rag on the bed.

"Yeah, yeah." Michael also wasn't the one with the secret handshakes and decoder ring. He was just a *guy*.

Actually, Michael was a physicist, an impressive and elitist profession, respected by his peers and barkeeps alike, but that was beside the point. With or without Michael to keep him on his toes, Justin was a spy, protection of the family paramount and still weighing heavily after six years and the car accident that damn near wiped out the lot of them. The fortress Justin built in response to the IRA come calling wasn't only there for Evelyn and Joe, or the surviving tot Joanna now fifteen, but also for Michael and his growing brood what with Claudia's connection to the secret society via her old man.

"See you got a promotion," Michael nodded at England's newly commissioned Squadron Leader whether or not Justin had to curl into a fetal position to fit inside a cockpit. "Only took you what? Ten fucking years? Is that what this is about? What's the matter? Afraid I might ruin something for you?" he took a drink, but only to clear his head. "What the fuck time is it anyway?"

"Noon," Justin said. "Down to business. Want to do something about this or not? Your father, I mean."

Michael looked at him; he couldn't be serious. "You serious?"

"No," Justin assured. "Asking if you are."

"Nah," Michael said after a while. "His racket, not mine, never in the racket. Just talk, you know that, small talk." He found his coat and hat. "Come on, let's ditch this place, I've got a funeral to get to."

Justin and Joe went with him because that's what friends do whether one of them was a spy, another a schoolteacher, and the other a louse, which Michael admittedly was. But he still felt bad about his father getting nailed on some street just like Justin felt about the passing of his old man, and Joe felt about his, until Joe kicked the can himself leaving Joanna once again in Michael's hands.

Cairo
March 9

"To the left as you go in ... a few doors down ... you can't miss it," claimed the friendly tour guide with the Groucho Marx eyebrows and yesterday's lunch fermenting on the dashboard of his cab, interrupting Michael's personal and private heartache of misplacing the pint-sized kid he nicknamed Red. He refused to acknowledge Joanna was *lost*. He refused to admit she was *dead*.

"That easy?" Michael cocked a brow beneath his sunshades protecting his hangover from the sun.

"Easy as pie," the Brit assured.

"Righto," Michael dug in his pockets. "Ta-ta, toodle-oo, whoop-de-do, va fa'n cul—what's the damage? Can you handle a fin?"

"Sure can," the cabbie laughed, and drove away with Michael's change.

“Fuck you, too,” Michael flipped him the one-finger salute and lifted his duffel, toting it up the steps, stopping at the sign that promised “Joint Divisional Headquarters” **TEMPORARY** stamped through it in glossy black.

“Ya got that right,” Michael assured, now that *Over There* was right here, not that you’d know it by the sign.

“‘XIII Corps’” Michael read.

“‘XXX Corps’” OK, he was getting the drift.

“‘New Zealand Division, Second New Zealand Division’, Charge of the frigging Light Brigade,” Michael nodded. “Yeah, OK, whoever you can think of, except for us.” But he went on inside anyway because why the hell not?

“I’ll tell you why not,” Michael figured out presently when to the left and a few doors down said MEN on a slip of cardboard instead of Office of Squadron Leader Justin Charles.

“Yeah, well, why the hell not?” he shrugged, gave Justin the bird, wherever he might be, “Here’s looking at you,” and went inside to do his duty, straighten his tie, and give his suit a wipe. He changed glasses while he was in there, too, from dark to light, only it failed to make the place look any cleaner.

“You know, I’ve seen subways better than this,” Michael swaggered back out, scraping a host of pathological specimens from the sole of his shoe. “Hey, buddy!” he called for what appeared to be a Redcoat on the horizon. “Yeah, you. Wait up!

“Wait!” he hollered. “Yeah, screw you, too,” he thumbed his nose at the soldier who gave him a blank look and kept on going where he was going, which was exactly the way Michael just came.

“I mean,” Michael said, “what the hell gives here, anyway?

“I mean,” Michael said, “who won the frigging war, anyway?” He just wanted to know. “The Big One. The one back in ... what the heck was it?” he scratched his frontal lobe. “1783? Yeah, that’s the one.

“And!” Michael said, “Who won the fucking rematch after that? 1812, if you follow my drift?”

Which if anyone did, or did not, it did not matter since there wasn’t anyone around to care. On the third swing past the toilets, Michael’s duffel bag ended up against the wall with Michael’s head on it and his legs stretched out across the floor. For a large building, it was largely empty, but there were a number of doors all over the place, and odds were someone was going to have to go in or come out of one of them sooner or later. Hard of hearing, failing eyesight, it wasn't as if they could lose Michael in the woodwork. But if they failed to notice the great White Hunter sleeping off a good one in the middle of the hall, they'd notice him soon enough when he tripped them and they fell down—

"Hello!" Michael said to the pair of knees carefully stepping over his. There was no way he'd trip that. He scrambled to his feet, pushing his hat up and off to the back of his head so she would be sure and get a load of just how lucky her day was.

"Your lucky day, sweetheart," he growled. "Your lucky day."

"Yes?" she said, not that she was necessarily agreeing with him, merely acknowledging the whistle blown up her skirt.

Oh, yes, yes, yes, yes! Michael perused her up and down. "I'm looking for Major Charles—Major Justin Charles—Seen him lately, around?"

"I'm sorry?" she said, which made sense if one knew Justin like Michael knew Justin, which Michael did.

In the meantime.

Oh, no, don't be sorry. Don't EVER be sorry. Michael quickly vetoed that idea, because if someone had something to be sorry for, this lady did not. We're talking Jean Harlow, Veronica Lake, and Mrs. Clark Gable, Carole Lombard, all rolled into one sweet perky package sealed with pencil-thin brows, cherry-bomb lips, blue eyes, and bottled blonde hair, but that was all right. What worked, worked, and this kid, from the tip of her stacked heels to the top shelf of her padded brassiere, worked.

"Squadron Leader," Michael apologized with a lick of his lips, "keep forgetting where I am. But, look, strike that, OK? Forget Chuckles. I'm Michael Delegianis—*Dr.* Michael Delegianis," he wowed her in her tracks and had her hand, "Alumnus of Oxford, Cambridge, Johns Hopkins, and Yale."

"How do you do?" she agreed, though unaware she was scheduled for a physical.

Michael did just fine. So did she apparently from the feel of that pulse. “Eighty,” he congratulated her, “on the nose. I’ll bet there’s nothing wrong with those lungs either, can tell from here.”

“Yes, thank you,” she appreciated the information however aware the last thing he was ogling about her chest was her lung capacity. “Doctor,” she smiled politely while carefully measuring the distance between her knee and his degree.

“Michael,” Michael offered, really an informal sort of guy.

“I’m sorry?” she paused.

“Michael,” Michael nodded. “My friends call me Michael. Just Michael—the ones registering an IQ that is,” he tipped her off. “The rest of them are meatballs, but there’s no reason to get into that. Especially,” he crossed his heart and hoped to spend the night, “since my past is behind me, swear, two, three feet at least.”

“I see,” she said.

“That’s a start,” Michael approved, because so could he. There was nothing wrong with his eyes, positively nothing wrong with them to the power 10, which was the approximate magnification of his baby-blues on her side of his Coke-bottle lenses.

“Yes ...” she said, for some reason thinking of Carroll’s Cheshire cat rather than Kipling’s white anything despite her being British and his dusty white safari suit that at least suggested he might consider himself some great hunter. “However, Squadron Leader Charles ...” she turned to point him back across the Atlantic where he quite obviously belonged.

“Who?” Michael said.

“Squadron Leader Charles?” she offered. “Your friend?”

“My friend?” Michael said, and she nodded. “Oh, yeah, sure!” he remembered. “Justin. Hell of a guy. Know him?”

“No,” she hadn’t had the privilege or the pain.

“That’s good,” Michael assured. “Save yourself a bundle on aspirin.”

“I’m sorry?” she said.

“Not important,” Michael promised. “Sure you’ve got better things to do.”

“Oh, yes,” she agreed with a polite tap of his wrist. “So, if you wouldn’t mind, please?”

“What?” Michael said. “Oh,” he noticed.

"Yes," so did she. "So, really, if you wouldn't mind, please?"

"Yeah, hey, sorry, about that," he gave her back her hand.

"Quite all right. However, Squadron Leader Charles ..." she turned to point him back to Mars, if she could somehow manage it.

"But, you see," Michael said, interrupted, actually, "you are terribly attractive."

"I'm sorry?" she paused again.

"Positively, terribly attractive," he nodded.

"Thank you," she smiled. "However, Squadron Leader Charles ..."

"Who?" Michael said.

"Squadron Leader Charles," she said, a little firmer that time. "I'm sorry, Doctor, but what did you say your name was again?"

"Mike," Michael nodded. "Short for Michael. But, it's OK. I got it; figured it out. You're talking about Justin, right?"

"Actually ..." she believed he was the one talking about someone named Justin.

"Known each other since diapers," Michael disclosed. "Odds are he still wears them, but hey, who cares?"

No one she knew.

"So back to the low down," Michael said. "Fifty bucks says I can talk you into dinner before lunch."

"Fifty bucks," she repeated, though not because she thought the price was extraordinarily high or low.

"Make it pounds," Michael helped her out.

"I see," she said. "Well, yes, actually, Doctor ..." she found she found herself between the proverbial rock and his hard place where no doubt dozens had found themselves before, "you really are quite handsome yourself."

"Oh, yeah?" Michael said.

"Oh, yes, positively, awfully handsome," she nodded.

"Yeah?" Michael said.

"Positively awful," she assured.

"Right," Michael pointed, getting her drift. "Back to Justin."

"Yes, please. You will find Squadron Leader Charles upstairs."

"What?" Michael said.

"The office of Squadron Leader Charles is upstairs," she nodded.

"Upstairs?" Michael looked around. "What stairs?"

"These stairs," she pointed down at the steps they were standing on.

"Oh!" Michael said, "*these* stairs."

"Yes," she nodded.

"Yeah, well, you see," Michael confided, "I'm lost."

"I beg your pardon?" she startled, being as they were only fifty feet from the front door.

"What I mean is," Michael said, "I was lost. Several times. Look, let me tell you something, kid, in case you haven't noticed, there are an awful lot of doors around here, all over the place."

"There are more upstairs," she imagined.

"I'm sure there are," Michael agreed. "Probably hundreds. So, I don't suppose you would be willing to drop whatever you're doing and help me out? Screw King and country, I am definitely something you owe yourself."

"No," she assured.

Funny, she didn't look like a nun. But hey, win some, lose some, break even every so often when you've been at it as long as he had, and he'd been at it a long, long time. "Yeah, well, thanks anyway," he said. "It's been very nice chatting with you, Miss ... ah, Miss?"

"Assistant Section Officer, WAAF," she smiled, just in case he missed the RAF eagle stiffly pinned to that padded brassiere.

"Yeah, right, *sieg heil* to you, too," Michael forwent the curtsy and stuck with the salute. "It's still been what you call nice ..."

"Not at all. Upstairs, and to the left," she pointed right. "You'll have no trouble."

"Excuse me?" Michael said.

"To the left," she nodded. "The office of Squadron Leader Charles is upstairs and to the left, just a few doors down."

"Of course it is," Michael agreed. "Right next to the can."

"I beg your pardon?" she said.

"The toilet," Michael assured. "Look, honey, I've been in there six times, and if Chuck has his own stall, I didn't see it."

"Oh," she said. "Yes, well ..."

"Not worth the wrinkle cream," Michael stopped her. "I'll figure it out."

"Oh, yes," she was certain he would.

"Good-bye then," he tipped his hat.

"Good day," she said, and beat it out of there as fast as she could in her heels.

Oh, yes! Michael grinned, watching the knees wiggle away. *Oh, yes, yes, yes ...*

Wrong. Upstairs and to the right, then left, was a desk.

Oh, no! Michael stared at the sergeant who stood up and kept going. *Oh, no, no, no, no, no.*

"Why, hi, I'm Dr. Delegianis!" Michael explained brightly to one of the nipples eyeing him from the naked breast of meat coated with a copper-colored carpet of fuzz. "Dr. Michael Delegianis. I'm here to see Major Charles. Major Justin Charles of the RAF. I have with me letters of introduction ... official letters ..." he fumbled in his jacket pocket, pulling out a stick of gum. "All official—would you like them?"

"That I would," the you-ain't-never-seen-a-fellow-quite-the-likes-of-me-before assured with a Belfast drawl.

That's what you think! Michael corrected the seven-foot primate with the wiry orange pipe curls hanging down past his shoulders like some mutant Tarzan of the Apes. *I've been to the zoo.*

Out loud he said, "Say no more!" slapping an envelope down and deciding to throw in for some stupid reason, "Hey, you're Irish!" as the big guy took the papers, and Michael looked down at the desk plate that read *John James Joseph Neil Reynolds* in Kelly green. "I thought you guys were neutral. I'm Italian. American, of course."

"Of course," the freak agreed like he even knew the world was round.

"Oh?" Michael looked him up, up, and back down. "Well, then, hey, can I?"

"No." He was flatly told.

"No?" Michael said.

"No," the eighth wonder of the world shook his curls, causing a down draft that nearly blew Michael's hat off his head.

Now, see here. Michael glared at the envelope stuffed back in his hand. "Hey!" he sputtered. "See here!"

"Now, what would you be wantin' with Charlie, anyway, Doc?"

Johnny James Jack Joe Jim chuckled with a slobber, bending his back and replanting the whole of his entire arse on that one little chair. "Can you tell ol' Nellie that?"

"Can I—can I—what?" Michael said. "Huh?"

"Charlie," Nellie cooed, like just being ugly wasn't enough.

Charlie? Michael wrinkled his nose and screwed up his eyes trying to figure out who in the name of Darwin was Charlie. "Who the hell is Charlie?" Two hundred and twenty-plus IQ, Mikey didn't have a clue.

"You tell me," the fossil smiled.

He was trying to. *Justin*? Dr. Michael Delegianis stared at Mighty Neil Joe Young. Now, Michael had known Justin thirty years, and there was no way in hell anyone would ever call Justin, Charlie. "Look!" Michael said, diplomatically. "Fuck you and the mammoth you rode in on. The papers say I've got a right to speak with Justin ... and, I've not only got a right," Michael leaned over the desk, looking the bastard dead in the eye, easy enough to do when he was sitting down. "I'm gonna do it. Read 'em and weep, OK?" he shoved the envelope forward. "Read 'em and weep. They're signed, you seedless cantaloupe, by the goddamn fucking President of the United States, as in Franklin DR."

"Now, Nellie can't tell you what they say, Doc," Nellie advised.

"Excuse me?" Michael said.

"That he can't." Nellie did not lie, but left it up to Michael's imagination just what it was he meant.

Try common sense. "You can't read?" Michael said. "What the hell are you saying, you can't fucking read? Fine!" he picked up the phone, cramming it under the hairball's nose. "Then raise your leg and fart three times and get somebody out here who can, or do I have to split an atom to get some attention around here?"

"Charlie is busy," Nellie was comfortable right where he sat.

"Well, tell him to get fucking unbusy," Michael nodded. "Mikey's been here over an hour. Got it? Get on the horn and tell him Mikey is hot, he's bothered, and Chuckles will find out if that's a pistol in my pocket the hard way unless he's out here on the count of one. Got that? On the count of one."

"Aw, now, easy, Doc," Nellie said. "Didn't anyone say we

wouldn't be telling him about you. Didn't none of us say we wouldn't be doing that."

"We?" Michael snarled. "We, who? The only apparition I see here is you."

"We," Nellie nodded, and Michael grabbed the desk as the floorboards rolled and quaked under his feet, peaking at around a 3.6 magnitude.

"Oh, hello!" Michael said to Tweedledum or Tweedledee appearing to belly his way down the hall and block Michael's path.

"Bobby," Nellie mentioned as Michael stared at the monstrous navel holding him at bay, "Doc here is wantin' to see Charlie."

"Is he now?" the whale of a Welshman drawled from deep inside a herniated testicle, and that did it.

"Oh, for—look, pie face," Michael barked at Nellie, "just show him the fucking papers, OK? Just show him the goddamn fucking papers!"

"Easy now, Doc," Nellie continued to smile as the one named Bobby took Michael's papers to have a look over them himself, "we will be telling him, we will ..." he looked to Bobby for verification of what the papers did say.

"Let him pass, Nel," Bobby folded the envelope neatly between the fat of his forefingers and thumbs.

"You don't say?" Nellie smiled.

"Yeah, he do say," Michael nodded, "he do say."

"Well, now, then, find Nellie's boy for him, won't you?" Nellie requested. "And tell him we've got a guest."

"Yeah, fetch him," Michael nodded after the medicine ball rolling away, "fetch him!"

"Aye, he will, Bobby will," Nellie grew once more from the seat of his chair. "If you, Doc, would come this way ... right this way ..."

"You got it!" Michael did his strut down the hall.

"This way, Doc," Nellie directed. "Right this way ..."

"You know it!" Michael assured, and got the door himself.

Now, you know Justin had always been a man of simple tastes, but that room had one lousy piece of furniture in it, one lousy piece, a lousy fucking chair.

"Oh, hello, again!" Michael said to the fat guy as Nellie gave him a hand slamming him inside.

"Hello!" Michael said to a third freak with a pasty face and skeletal paw leaning over to help him off with his jacket with a wink of his ice-blue eye.

"Bend over, and say, ah!"

"Huh?" Michael said.

"Do what the lieutenant says, Doc," Bobby nodded, while Nellie folded those red hairy arms of his and said, "Drop 'em."

"You got it!" Dr. Michael Delegianis ditched his trousers while meanwhile ...

The Fezzan
March 9
Hand over hand they dissected the goose, fingers ripping its flesh from the bone. The wine spilled, drunk in huge satisfying gulps.

"*You are so very attractive,*" Reineke whispered to the woman seated across from him at the table, enjoying her cool lips devouring the fruit.

"*Do that to me,*" he requested, and she smiled. "*Do that to me,*" he implored, and could feel himself fill.

She ignored him, blonde after blonde, dripping gold gowns, cajoled flooding the room. The candles burned and the flowers bloomed. He stood up to cross to the table, but the floor was crowded and two gunners blocked his way.

"*But, you are so very attractive,*" he protested to the woman, watching himself take off his shirt and sit down.

"*Do that to me,*" he coaxed as she eased around the table, bringing her peach with her.

"*Do that to me,*" he spread his legs and touched her thigh.

Someone laughed and she crushed the fruit on his chest. He was surprised, but she whispered, "*You want it anyway,*" as she smeared the pulp over his breast, up his neck and down, its juice becoming butter, its oils teasing, but then glass, mutilating, and she whispered as he touched the blood, "*But, you want it anyway. Won't you want it, anyway?*"

"*Indeed!*" he grasped her.

"*Oh, no, mon capitaine!*" Pierre sat in the middle of the table. "*It is too dangerous! Please, mon capitaine, please, I beg you!"*

"*But I want,*" he pouted, looking for the woman who was gone, so far away.

"*I want!*" he insisted, and back she came, back across the floor she walked, so small, thin, then fat, and she was bleeding.

"*No, mon capitaine,*" Pierre pleaded "*No!*"

"*Indeed, I want!*" Reineke said, staring at her face, she was older, but then so was he.

"*Remember?*" she whispered and had a new peach. "*Do you remember?*"

"*Nine,*" he said the number and she tipped a smile.

"*But you want it, anyway,*" she bit the fruit, chewing tiny bites. "Won't you want it, anyway?"

"*Indeed. Do that to me!*" he tore the gown from her shoulders.

"*Do that to me,*" he moaned, her teeth sinking into his throat as he had her on the table, ignoring Pierre vomiting blood, his stomach exploding as he died. "*Promise! Promise!*"

"*I promise,*" she whispered, matching his violent thrusts, her nails shredding his back, the blood mingling with the wine.

"Hauptmann."

Reineke woke up with a jump, the sheets damp with sweat. The last thing he remembered he had been falling and someone called his name.

"Hauptmann?" The Korporal was bedside, coffee ready. It was 6:30, a mistake to go to sleep even for such a short time.

"I will need a uniform," Reineke answered, not bothering to sit up. "The smallest one you can find."

"Yes, Herr Hauptmann," he nodded and disappeared, leaving the coffee behind.

Reineke stared from the cup to the French windows and daylight almost an hour old. Deciding to ignore it, he rolled over onto his stomach, rearranging his pillows, wondering how long it would take them to realize the Hauptmann had decided to retire—

The photographs were still in the bed. Hanuk's gift waiting for him under the sheet.

"Damn you," he muttered at the soiled faces captured in terror, and could smell the fire behind them, burning.

"*Mon capitaine it is not necessary*!" He heard Pierre say so many times, but Pierre was wrong, and Reineke was dressed and gone, the pictures locked in his hand.

Chapter Fourteen

An arid cemetery of gardens surrounded the villa. A marble wasteland of the erotic and exotic reduced to barren basins of dust and stone broiling in the sun, lifeless as the ghostly tomb markers of past aristocrats and slaves. The truck yard and supply bins occupying the eastern range, to the south and west, a maze of walls threaded their way undisturbed across stone plains bordered by an orchard of cypress, palm, and olive trees strangling each other in their quest for survival. It was the line between the two worlds of the German Reineke and the Holy Man Pierre. A barrier of snarled tree limbs reinforced with fences strung with barbed wire, flimsy in many ways as the verbal agreement between them. But still, no one from either side would think to enter the tangled grove. The children had no reason, any soldier shot on sight. Even the Holy Man never came along the gardens, though he continued to walk them from time to time during his visits.

As had Reineke spent time inspecting them, particularly in the early days. Intrigued by the variety of tomb markers and the opportunity for private thought, he walked them less often now, preferring to disappear completely, sometimes for hours at a time. The unnecessary and useless fences of twisted barbed wire he had ordered built to satisfy Thiele. No secret passage or pathway in and out of the woods, the dense overgrowth was much too difficult for the aged Holy Man before the installation of the German's blockade. Reineke tried it once just to see how hard it really would be. It wasn't difficult, not for him, if he didn't mind the scrapes and scratches from the unforgiving and unyielding olive trees, cruel as the wire. He did mind them, common sense and vanity colliding and equal for once.

Virtually inaccessible then via the gardens to all but an

advancing army eager to display its might, the children's area was reasonably accessible from the northern courtyard, through the gateway, across the sand, a laborious walk in the sun, perhaps five minutes by wagen. Reineke took one of the wagens, calling out for Anne as he arrived in the market square, center of the children's world. The protected area nearly as large as the compound, it was more tropical and lively. Remnants of the town's forum still evident with its surviving rows of shops, comfortable and safe in the crumbling foothills of several large buildings, the apartments and houses had all but collapsed. Their remains choking the avenues and streets, there was no egress in or out of the forum except from the direction of the Emperor's villa.

"Dieter!" the thin, young girl with dusty brown skin, looked up from her seat on the edge of the well with the approach of the wagen. Her long raven hair flying like great black wings as she raced to greet him, the sturdy ankle-high boots she wore were heavy and large for her eleven year old legs bare and free under the ragged hem of her skirt. The little general of the crowd of babies and school children, Anne was not the romance of her brother Hanuk, but an odd mixture of awkwardness, strength, and dirt. Reineke her hero in a world she could not possibly understand at her age. "Did Hanuk give you my message?" she verified excitedly, wanting it to be true, but also wanting Reineke to have come to them on his own without having to be told.

"Indeed. What do you know about these?" Reineke withdrew the photographs from his pocket. "No, they are not for you," he stopped her from taking them or even seeing them. "If you know what they are, you do not have to look at them, correct? If you do not know, you just say 'Dieter, I have no idea what you are talking about.'"

She did know, of course, there with her uncles when the pictures were taken. "They're Diana's." Anne pushed her hair out from her eyes, tucking it behind her ears with a sigh. "From her to you. Some silly reminder, I guess, I don't know. I do know Hanuk is such a coward to listen to her. It's all right, just ignore them, I'll talk to her."

"Where is she?" Reineke asked. "I know she is here. Tell me."

"The temple," Anne nodded. "She said she would be back, in

hospital at nine for rounds." Nine was too long. "Come." Reineke took her by the hand, escorting her to his wagen. "You will be my agent."

"Aren't I always?" she laughed, hopping up to stand in the seat.

"Yes." Reineke pulled her down to sit like the proper young lady she was rather than the boy she pretended to be. "And as always, you are to sit. How many times do I have to tell you this?"

"Oh, please!" she stole his hat, scrambling to stand back up on the seat, and hang over the windshield. "We'll just pretend I'm you."

He returned from the temple at eleven o'clock without Anne. By eleven-thirty he stood over the opened grave of what had once been an American Army Colonel of advancing years, mutilated prior to being killed by a crushing blow to the head as the Holy Man had reported, the hands severed for some reason, and brains exposed. Making note of the patches identifying the officer as an engineer, and the significant amount of blood that seemed to support the Holy Man's proposal of at least a third person, Reineke's examination of the corpse was otherwise unrevealing. No nausea or guilt like he had experienced when finding the girl, this had been a man, a willing participant in his game of war. He turned to Linke. "Where is the hand Thiele found? Unless it is one of his, there is another body somewhere."

"No other body, Hauptmann." Linke presented him with a burlap sack he ordered dug from its hole two meters away.

It was that of a young adult male, white. Reineke examined the hand but could tell nothing more than that from it, other than the cut severing it was clean like those of the Colonel's suggesting a sharp, quick, force such as Herr Major's sword.

"Arabs," Linke proposed and Reineke looked at him. The sergeant shrugged. "That's what most would think."

"Yes," Reineke agreed. If they were oblivious to the involvement of the SS and just happened to find the grave, which no one would. "Burn it. Everything." He dropped the hand back in its sack and left the gravesite for the villa, arriving in time to hear the screams coming from the opened French windows above, and he flew to answer the Holy Man's howls for help.

"Michael," Joanna whispered.

"Shhh, Mademoiselle, c'est tout exact," Pierre promised how everything would be fine, soothing her florid swollen face with a cool wet cloth as she tossed and turned, threatening to wake up.

Joanna could feel a cloth on her face like when she was a child. Michael determined to wipe the fever away before she suffered a brain hemorrhage or seizure, or something equally lurid and frightening. She would eventually wake up at noon, a harsh coughing spell rousing her to a state of semi-consciousness, the room stifling hot and out of focus.

"*Shhh,* vous êtes en sécurité, *Mademoiselle,*" Michael reassured from somewhere close by, repeating his promise of safety with a gentle stroke of her head.

French? Joanna struggled to understand the words in the gloom surrounding her. Why on earth was Michael talking in French? She tried to ask him, but could barely see him, little more than a shadow leaning over her, her throat burning when she tried to talk. "Don't," she said. "No, don't touch my head."

"*Oui,*" he agreed sympathetically with her flinch of pain. "*Mais il passera. Dans tandis que votre tête se dégagera et ne blessera pas tellement.*"

No, it would not be fine. Joanna didn't know why he seemed to think her head would be fine when it hurt so much. "Don't," she repeated, "Michael, please don't touch my head," she insisted, sensing his silent huff of impatience, feeling his hands firmly push her back down, something soft laying on top of her that quickly seemed to wind itself around her legs as she tried to sit up.

"*Ici, Mademoiselle, laissez-moi vous aider,*" Pierre offered to help, eager to assist her, and Joanna felt hands again as they grasped her, strong and tight around her shoulders and arms, but it was his hood that frightened her. This enormous dark brown hood floating down to envelop her, swallow her up inside. She screamed, her hand striking the edge of something hard, a bottle falling over; she heard a bottle fall over and saw the bright, white bundles of what looked like table linens, fluffy white table linens stacked neatly in a row.

"*Je suis Monsignor Pierre Beausoleil. Vous êtes tout fait en sécurité, Mademoiselle, n'ayez pas peur.*"

Michael introduced himself as a Monsignor, saying again how she was safe as Joanna stared at the bandages trying to figure out what they were. She frowned. A Monsignor was a priest, something like a priest. She gave up studying the bandages to eye the hood. It wasn't Michael, but a fat brown face with wrinkles appearing from inside to peer back at her. So old, so horribly and hideously old, he did not look much like a priest either, his long clawed hand coming toward her gnarled and twisted like the roots of some old tree. She hit him, her fist catching him on the chin, fighting and screaming as he tried to stop her and she tried to kick her way free of whatever it was that had wrapped itself around her legs.

"Mon Dieu," Pierre grunted in pain as her foot found his stomach. He shouted for the guards he did not want to call, and who did not want the responsibility of answering the uproar they could not pretend they did not hear. Wrong if they did answer, wrong if they did not, it was not always easy to forecast the Hauptmann's position and this was the Holy Man. They answered, and their sudden appearance in the apartment made the situation even worse. It was Reineke who bolted in from the library to subdue the riot, untangle the screaming naked prisoner caught and twisted in the sheets, the Holy Man too old and fat to do much more than try and keep her from falling on the floor.

"Mon capitaine!" Pierre breathed gratefully righting himself, fumbling to straighten the bandage she had tried to rip from her head as Reineke grabbed Joanna, forcing her down, holding her tightly.

"Fix it later!" Reineke insisted, the girl staring up at him in terror, damming him over and over until Pierre's needle put her back to sleep.

"Well?" Reineke turned around from studying the courtyard through the French windows with Pierre's appearance in the library.

"She is a fighter," Pierre was shattered and apologetic. "I am sorry, I did not know. I did not realize she would be so upset."

"That is not sufficient," Reineke assured, "when it is your duty to know." He marched out onto the balcony where he managed to smoke almost an entire cigarette before the Holy Man interrupted.

"Mon capitaine!" Pierre announced his arrival with a pointing finger, "it is exactly as I told you. I did not realize Mademoiselle would be so excited. Forgive, please, but Pierre, unlike you, is not God. Oui, I understand your embarrassment ..."

Embarrassment? What was there for him to be embarrassed about? "Indeed," Reineke snapped, "What are you talking about?"

Pierre thought about it. "I do not know," he shrugged. "But it is still your fault. You come in—and do not think I do not thank you for this, because I do," he assured. "Mademoiselle is a little mademoiselle, but she is a mighty one, and I thank you for the rescue.

"But!" he reprimanded, "Mademoiselle is also awake today, and when she sees you she is going to scream. She is going to fight, cry, spit—"

"She was already screaming," Reineke said, "which is why I came in there!"

"Oh," Pierre said. "Oui, this is true, isn't it?" he frowned, thinking about that, too. "Well," he decided, "it is still your fault."

Of course it was.

"Hopeless, mon capitaine, hopeless," Pierre stalked back into the library where Reineke found him, slumped in a chair, exhausted with despair.

"What is hopeless?" Reineke asked coldly. "Other than I am German, and you are French?"

"Everything," Pierre nodded. "Her room is her sanctuary. I her friend, savior from whatever devils she does or does not remember—that would be you," he pointed, "and this," he gestured around the room "I did not want Mademoiselle to know anything about this or you, until she is much stronger."

"And it is my fault she does," Reineke said coldly.

""Well, it is not my fault," Pierre assured. "I did not do any of this to her."

Neither did he. "If you cannot control the prisoner," Reineke sat down at his desk, "I will find someone who can."

Pierre sneered. "Such as who? Your Thiele, perhaps? Or maybe your Gestapo to finish their job? Ach, poo, I spit on all of them!" he spit on the floor. "Live for them to die."

Reineke was not impressed. "Such as Diana," he assured. The Holy Man should know how her suggestions of what to do with the girl were as cold and unfeeling as Reineke's. It must be the German in them, as she so often said. The two of them finding themselves in agreement with each other more often than one might think, or possibly prefer.

"Her, too," Pierre waved Diana and her threats aside, too. "If I want to protect Mademoiselle from the knowledge of you, I certainly want her to know nothing of Diana."

"That would be wise," Reineke agreed.

"Ach, wise," Pierre dismissed, "you give yourself too much credit, the two of you. You are extraneous, meaningless. And, so we try again," he nodded. "We do, and, in a few weeks, you will see. Pierre and Mademoiselle will be best friends. I her salvation, her life raft. She will reach for it, cling to it, and yes, survive because she has to, because she wants to. It is how the mind works," he smiled at Reineke. "You know this, yes?"

He knew more than that. "The girl is leaving with the trucks.

"That is what you think," Pierre said.

That was what he knew. "What she trusts, believes in, or clings to, is irrelevant."

"Again what you think," Pierre agreed, "but it is all right. Mon capitaine has many more important things to concern himself with. Mademoiselle is English, as he has suspected."

"Indeed." Reineke sat up straight, the threat of the Kufra looming. "How do you know this?"

"How?" Pierre said. "Simple. Her voice. You did not hear it?"

"I heard her scream," Reineke agreed, "little else."

"The dead can hear her scream," Pierre assured. "So you will leave her treatment to Pierre and stay away. One nightmare is enough. You do not need to frighten her anymore."

"How do you know she is British?" Reineke insisted.

"English," Pierre corrected. "I said English. But British could be more accurate, you could be right. I am right when I say when she speaks, it is in English whether she is of Britannia, or from one of her colonies since this is Africa and she is here."

"Indeed. *Amerika* is one of her colonies." Reineke was on his feet, at the French windows, the smell of smoke in the air from the fire out in the truck yard. "The man with her was an American."

"If you say he was," Pierre shrugged. "Mon capitaine, to exhume a body from its sacred ground is against God's law, blasphemy. And it is God you will answer to for your actions, not Pierre."

"My answer would be the same," Reineke lit a cigarette, "we cannot have it here. Particularly since you are right, there was at least one other person, also a man. Thiele found a severed hand in the truck. It did not belong to the American. There is another body somewhere."

"Which Mon capitaine can find, as he could find six more," Pierre agreed. "Perhaps this is something he should do. Track them down and burn them all if he thinks that will somehow relieve him of their significance and stench."

"Significance?" Reineke said.

Pierre smiled. "Perhaps. Perhaps not. Perhaps, mon capitaine," he proposed, withdrawing a thin silver chain from the deep folds of his robes, "the SS are not as clever as they think they are whether they are trying to be clever, or are just stupid as I think.

"I question which it is," he nodded as Reineke took the chain, "yes, naturally. I question who lost this and why? For what purpose?"

"Where did you get this?" Reineke fingered the tarnished chain with its two metal identification tags, identical to each other and unfamiliar other than knowing they were not British.

"The pocket of her skirt," Pierre said, his answer suspect in that it was so simple. To tell the truth would be to tell how Hanuk found the chain in the sand outside, apprehension in the eyes of his uncles when he showed it to them, or perhaps it was just surprise. Pierre was unsure which, but took the chain away from them anyway to bury it with her. Immune to his interrogation, the sons of Diana were not immune to him, but lived because he lived, safe in the bowels of the Arab world alongside their German benefactor. "I believe they are what the American calls the 'dog tag', no?"

"I do not know," Reineke absently circled Pierre's chair. "You would have to ask Diana. The American had no identification. But this is an identification tag, clearly, yes, of some form." He was almost afraid to look, but did and the girl's name had no particular celebrity of which he was aware. It was simple like the tin chain she had worn around her neck. "Jo*h*anna Lee." He pronounced it wrong, inserting an *h* where there was none. It was not intentional, just Germanic like he.

"Oui," the priest said in his French. "And the rank mon capitaine reads is one commonly of a nurse. See?" he pointed out, in case Reineke had missed it. "'Lee, Joanna Lieutenant'. A nurse. Oui, mon capitaine, a neutral."

"Neutrality is not a guarantee," Reineke threw the chain at him. "She is too young to be a nurse. Some clerk perhaps, some intern—or some lie," he loomed over him. "Indeed. You claim you found them in the pocket of her skirt. How do I know that is true, or that it is even hers?"

"You don't," Pierre did not lie then. "And Mademoiselle is possibly more or less important than her dog tags ... that are not dog tags," he dangled the chain temptingly with a sly smile. "Identification tags with no identification number? Mon capitaine is either tired, or he is blind."

Reineke snatched the chain back to finger its thin metal tags not quite as flexible as they should be. "Silver," he nodded slowly. A jeweler by trade perhaps, or just rich and familiar with the precious metals, their oils, their touch, feel, now that he was giving them the attention they deserved.

"Oui," Pierre said. "And this is odd, no? Who would give such a strange piece of jewelry to a young woman?"

"Interesting," Reineke had to admit.

"Dangerous," Pierre corrected, and Reineke treated him with a thoughtful eye.

"Why?" Reineke asked.

Pierre shrugged again. "She is a woman, mon capitaine. A woman in North Africa and she is not a nurse? Perhaps a driver then? But it is the native who drives the officers here. To bring the English would be unlikely."

"She was with the American," Reineke reminded. "You claim these are their tags."

"Perhaps," Pierre admitted. "I know very little about them."

Only that they called their identification tags, dog tags. Reineke did not know much more, if he knew that. Until today, he was probably less interested in knowing anything about them than the Holy Man was. "I am no fan of the American," Reineke assured, "whatever you are conspiring."

Pierre blinked. "They are your enemy, mon capitaine, as much as the English. What could I be conspiring?"

Reineke ignored him, studying the tags, cautious about making any final decision. "A school girl, perhaps. Student of some sort. She was in uniform."

"Remnants of a uniform," Pierre agreed, "oui. A mess."

Yes. "Perhaps you are right in that she lives here." Reineke sat back in his chair. "Algeria. Cairo. There are Europeans."

"Oui, I am European," Pierre said.

So was he. "A family member," Reineke dangled the chain, still studying it. "The man was not young."

"No," Pierre said. "But?"

"It still does not explain," Reineke assured, "why they were brought here unless they were close by. There is nothing for hundreds of kilometers of which we are aware. If there is no Allied encampment, it had to be a plane crash and the SS just there, in the vicinity, perhaps even shot them down. The American would intrigue them. They would interrogate him. Bring them here, why not since they were coming here." He smiled thinly. "You see I can think, and that much of the mystery is really not too mysterious at all."

Pierre nodded. "It also does not stop someone from looking for her. The daughter of someone, the sister, lover, friend, it does not matter. She is a woman, and they will come looking for her. A woman, mon capitaine, always belongs to someone."

Unless they were dead also.

"What did Diana say?" Pierre asked, more than mere curiosity for his reason.

Diana? The same that she said about the SS. Leave it alone. Wait and see, lay low, play dead. "Do nothing," Reineke replied, "and send the girl away with the trucks if she survives."

"That does not sound like Diana," Pierre shook his head.

No. No, lying in wait would be much more accurate as she had laid in wait for him. Three weeks, it was three weeks before he had even known of her existence, nine weeks since he had. "Never mind about Diana," Reineke said. "What do you want to do?"

"I?" the priest feigned surprise. "I thought it had been decided. Mademoiselle is to be moved with the trucks."

From her obvious condition that would be weeks from now, the Holy Man had also been right about that. "I am talking about her people," Reineke said, "collectively, as a whole."

"Yes, of course," Pierre said. "This Allied encampment mon capitaine believes is out there alongside his SS. I do not know. Perhaps mon capitaine should consider checking with his sources to confirm what he already believes is true."

"You are my source," Reineke whispered unintentionally, it just coming out that way.

"Oui," Pierre agreed. "And with time, I can find anything."

Of that, Reineke had little doubt.

"Good," Pierre smiled. "Is that what you want?"

He should say yes. At the very least, it would be a test of the Holy Man's claimed power over this desert and its inhabitants, friend or foe. "I have to think," Reineke replied. "There is a little time as you suggest. The girl is far too ill to be moved yet. Perhaps the next delivery."

"As you wish," Pierre inclined his head, biting back the smirk Reineke could see on his lips.

"Stop laughing," Reineke suggested. "I am not kind or weak. It has nothing to do with compassion. If there are more of them out there I want to know. I will know," he assured. "Indeed. You are right. A woman always belongs to someone, especially one as young as that."

Chapter Fifteen

Cambridge
1940

Joanna Lee belonged to Justin Charles, Evelyn Lee, and Michael Delegianis in precisely that order. At sixteen years Justin's junior, as his stepsister, Joanna had been Justin's legal ward since the death of her mother and his father a decade ago. Her arranged marriage at seventeen to Joseph Lee, twice her age at the time, was a practice steeped in antiquity, still widely accepted by the xenophobic upper classes. A convenient and practical solution for Justin serving his interests and the families of continued safety and security. Joe, with his conciliatory nature, and limited involvement in the spy game, was the natural choice of predecessor to Evelyn, Joanna's current principal caregiver. Justin and Joe had known each other all their lives, united in their friendship, and their families' historical ties. Evelyn, Joe's grandfather and surviving patriarch of the collective family born out of grief and need following the fatal car accident was getting on.

Born Christmas Day, 1864, Evelyn was sixty-seven years old at the time of the accident. Eight years later, with few signs of slowing down, Evelyn had thus far managed to shoulder much of Joanna's actual daily care. Claudia, initially interested in extending herself for Henry's orphaned stepdaughter, ended up having several more children of her own and with that understandably little time. Justin, normally not one to shirk from responsibility, was nevertheless far too busy making his mark a hemisphere away in South Africa, his cold reserve not untouched by the tragedy that befell the families already too small to survive many more generations. To the contrary, Evelyn knew Justin as he had known Justin's father Henry, and his grandfather Scotty before him, and the wound was deep and raw. Justin blaming himself for what happened as much as he blamed the Irish, convinced the culprits were Irish, Henry's death just a point to be made to him. In his own way, seeking to ensure it never would happen again. Justin's way was to separate, move halfway around the world, except for financial support of his stepsister, only a rare visit with the family once a year or so.

Evelyn's way was to become involved. He didn't give a damn about the money. He had money, plenty of it. They had a tot on their hands. Uprooted from her own world, Australia, more than halfway across the planet, and dropped down in their laps at not but nine years of age. She didn't need a pocketbook; she needed love, a family. That left Evelyn, old, and fresh out of family himself, except for Joe, and with Mike there for entertainment, Joe to take care of the formal aspects of her education, Evelyn was free to collect and give the love he had too often held in reserve. Surprising no one more so than himself with how much love he had. She was his granddaughter. He anointed her that, and declared her that long before she married his grandson Joe. As much a part of him as if he'd given birth to her himself, and was she a hellcat, not some timid little mouse as one might first think or suspect given the size of her, but a tornado, with a backbone and spirit stronger than his. She brought life to the house, noise to its too-quiet hallways, always involved in some mischief or another, wild and untamed as that country of hers. She made Evelyn young, think young, be young, realize what he had missed with Robert, and again with Joe, understand what he had been afraid of all his life, and that was life, to live life rather than just try to own and rule it. So, quite, while she might belong to Justin in the legal sense, whom she actually belonged to was Evelyn and he'd dare anyone, including Justin, to suggest otherwise.

Justin was not about to. Certainly not go toe-to-toe with the old man over something so trivial particularly when Evelyn's involvement with Joanna was also the ideal solution in what to do with Evelyn. How to provide for him, satisfy, occupy, and pacify him in his waning years, give him something to do. Regardless though of Evelyn or his good intentions, of which Justin had no doubts or complaints, there remained the fact that Joanna's care and protection would extend beyond her childhood, and Evelyn was not going to live forever. Irresponsible, Michael was out of the question for anything but entertainment—Justin quickly stepped back from the initial Claudia as surrogate mother notion once he thought it over. That left only Joe to pick up the reins in Justin's absence, offering the solid, stable influence Justin believed Joanna needed beyond the luxury and attention piled on her by the old man.

Spoiled her silly, is what Evelyn did, unmindful of what might be good for her. A burgeoning felon at nine, headstrong, careless, and carefree, Joanna was a veritable anarchist at seventeen, one of Michael's *Dead End Kids,* all boy. Which was fine, except not only was Joanna not raised in a New York tenement, she was not a boy. A boy, Justin could not only knock the chip off his shoulder, he could knock his head off, if the need arose, with one swift sock to the chin. If Joe and Evelyn had their hands full, which from time to time they did, Justin's usual even and reserved temperament would be no match for her, had he been around, and so it was probably a good thing he wasn't. However, Justin's remedy of moving Joe forward in rank with Evelyn's advancing years was destined to be almost as short-lived as Henry's marriage when Joe and his plane exploded into a fireball over London in December 1940. The papers said the North Sea. They were also off by a day or two, but that was not only all right, it was intentional. Justin did not like facts down on paper for others to read. Lest anyone forget, public record also listed Joanna as long dead, killed in the car accident alongside her parents. It might have been kinder had it been true. At only age eighteen, orphan Joanna Lee found herself a widow, back with Evelyn. Claudia there to offer advice, Michael parked on the doorstep to rescue her from the two of them, because let's face it, for all Joanna belonged to Justin and the old man Lee, Joanna did not belong to anyone except to Michael.

Cambridge

1940

Joanna really did not need rescuing from Grandfather, what they all called Evelyn, except for Justin and Claudia, and even Michael who shortened Grandfather to Gramps. Claudia on the other hand? Oh, yes, Joanna definitely could stand being rescued from Claudia.

Without ever knowing why, or with any interest in ever knowing why, Joanna did know she and Claudia did not get on together very well. That was something Michael could relate to. He and Claudia did not get on together very well, either. Claudia Delegianis, nee Drake, was a shrew, a rigid and demanding woman under her bridge socials and afternoon teas, a saintly witch with soft hands and razor tongue, discriminating and discriminatory. Michael was not sure why he married her in the first place and did not divorce her when he had the chance and only one kid instead of four—or was it five by then? All girls. Michael lost count of how many kids he had after a while. The same as it did not matter after a while. Michael's way, like Justin's, was to separate, move away from what he did not like, go out for some air and make his way back eventually to check in on how life was going with Red, what he called Joanna and no one else did.

But then she was his kid. The one he wanted. Whether or not Michael ever wanted any kid for that matter, which if he did, it would be Joanna with her freckled face and electric red hair. A pint-sized package of what Gramps called spirit and Justin looked down on as criminal. Michael had the same sort of spirit. He just did not have it in him to live up to Justin's idea of self-discipline or even consider a reason why he should. Even though back in the days when Michael was a child he already had more brains than anyone knew what to do with. There was nothing he could not do, nothing too hard, or impossible. He was a real-life progeny, Renaissance man, with an inflated IQ and ego to match. So maybe that was the reason Michael seemed to make a career out of misbehavior, nowhere to go except down.

Or maybe he was just a drunk. A monkey on his back. Talents and gifts second to alcohol. Whichever, Michael was happy being Michael, and that would never change. The fact that Michael could afford to be Michael probably made him worse, a fist full of dollars in his pockets, at his fingertips, with plenty more of it in the bank. However ill gotten, Michael could never spend what he was worth in the six lifetimes he tried to crowd into one. Independently wealthy and set for life, all thanks to his father who made a killing during Prohibition like a few other respectable American millionaires.

Not that respectability was something Michael's father ever quite achieved. No, he was a villain 'till the day he died. An Italian stone mason with a fourth grade education, few prospects, and a wife and son underfoot. A dead-end street, dead-end kid except times and things change. On the flipside of life, Michael's side, the increasing popularity of the Anti-Saloon League offered a boon to the underworld in the pre-Prohibition era. From there the rest was American and Michael's history. Not quite ten years old himself when he set sail the wrong way past the Statue of Liberty, shipped home to Europe and the best in education. A brief stint on the continent proper, by spring, Michael was in England, the first of several schools behind him, two wide-eyed chumps by the names of Justin and Joseph hanging onto his shirttails and every word. From prep boys to frat brothers, the three of them thick as thieves, Michael their ticket to adventure, Justin and Joe, Michael's ticket into the annals of society that had eluded his father. Who cared that it was British? Not Michael, not then. Married Claudia Drake when he was twenty even though she was ten years older than he was, she was pretty and classy and looked good on his arm. Two schools and three years later they had a kid, Andrea. Might have worked out better between Claudia and him over the long haul had Andrea been a boy, but she wasn't, and it didn't, and who knew really. Michael settled for Andrea instead of Andy, calling her Annie after one of his early mentors, Dr. Anna Kassim Haas. A physicist and pioneer in radiation and modern cancer therapy, one hag of a dowager, face like a mule, tough as nails under her diamonds and furs, with a brain and ego big and bright as his.

Oh, Michael liked Annie, and she liked him, even though he was about as far removed from being another Schweitzer, and she was banging the old guy Lee behind wife Martha's back. Michael was close with a few of Anna's sons, too, John, in particular. Michael went to Yale with John, stayed in touch over the years, though not recently. The last Michael knew, around the time everyone was leaving, John decided to go home to Germany. Probably not the brightest thing he ever did considering he was a Jew, and since Michael had not heard from John that probably more of less settled that.

Four years after Andrea was born, Michael filed for a legal

separation from Claudia, the first of his medical degrees hanging by where it still hung, rather lopsided somewhere in a corner of the old man's home in Cambridge. Justin put the kibosh on the filing and read Michael the riot act for taking things public and Michael blew town. Six months on the prowl Michael was back home in England for Henry and Elizabeth's wedding where he met the love of his life. Rumor in the servants' quarters and the looks across the dinner table hinted it was Elizabeth, Joanna's mother, a perky little piece from down under, practically half Henry's age. Rumor was wrong. Joanna intoxicated Michael. Six months later her parents were dead and they had been inseparable ever since. He was her best friend, her sidekick, her confidante. His idea of getting her involved with the ATS, England's *Auxiliary Territorial Services a* week after Joe died, and Justin finished barking orders from his side of the globe, was harmless enough, Evelyn supposed. He couldn't help though being a bit concerned about the London part of the equation and the shock it might hold for Joanna who, contrary to Justin's concerns and Michael's influence, had led an extremely sheltered life.

Cambridge

1941

"I'll put her in a bunker," Michael promised with fingers and knees crossed. "I'll build one around her, like this place, tailor made." Every frigging gizmo known to man tucked behind those oaken walls, including an escape hatch and tunnel to Never-Ever Land. Hard to believe Justin, a man who still believed in the rack and chastity belts, also believed in things like television and rockets to the moon. Justin was Justin, or Chuck, as Michael called him, though only to break his stones, and Michael had given up on trying to "understand" Justin around the same time Justin had given up on trying to "understand" him. Gramps, on the other hand, was just Gramps, inclined with Michael, as he was with Justin, and had been with Joe, to let them have their fun. They were boys, after all, or by that point, men.

Maybe Michael was. Justin, Michael maintained was some sort of cross between the missing link and an autocrat, and Joe? That was a whole other story Michael did not like to talk about. Joe though was dead, Justin, his usual elsewhere, and Michael, who probably could put a rocket on the moon, was averse to the sort of plumbing hidden behind Evelyn's walls.

Michael was averse to living his life surrounded by listening devices, cameras, and plain-clothes dicks who followed him everywhere. Even the cook Maria was in on it, a DP from the Franco War. Michael wondered how often she had to sit on the old guy's lap to keep that visa of hers current. "Are we cleared for takeoff, or do you want to run this around the block a few more times?"

Evelyn chuckled as he always chuckled about Michael, yes, he did. The first of his stray cats, as Justin called Mike, not maliciously, just a matter-of-fact. It wasn't Michael's intentions, or his devotion, for that matter, sworn protection of Joanna, Evelyn doubted, not in the least. He knew Michael. Knew him well. Appreciated and understood him. He was a Yank, in the first place, an American. Couldn't be expected to think the same thoughts, abide by the same rules as the rest of them. But he was a goodhearted lad underneath it all. He tried to hide it, of course, but he was a decent man, yes, Evelyn did believe that. "Yes, well, believe that's my point," Evelyn assured. "London's ground zero in England's war."

"She'll be with me," Michael insisted, that much true anyway. "I'll stay for the goddamn duration. Fucking enlist, if you want me to."

Evelyn chuckled harder, so hard one would think he was Santa Claus instead of some old cold-hearted dick. "Enlist, my boy? Think more than a few people might have something to say about that," he winked. After all, Michael wasn't a doctor, not really, now was he? Not the kind who took temperatures, delivered babies, or set broken arms. No, Michael was a physicist, an atomic scientist theorizing about the relativity of bombs. "So, we'll see," Evelyn nodded, "yes, we'll see."

"Yeah, we will," Michael promised, and tried to take Joanna out of the house that very same night. Fell and broke his ankle under the blind of the spotlights as the two of them climbed out over the roof, of all things. Spent three months in a plaster cast, another six months lobbying his cause before Evelyn finally gave in. But only because Evelyn doubted if Joanna would take well to finding herself confined in some office once the novelty of London wore off. Evelyn gave it a week, and two months later, much to his surprise, she was still there, beginning to blossom even, develop a little poise and self-confidence. Something she has always been a little shy about, same as Mike, and just like Mike, exactly like him, hid her light under a barrel, covering it up with bravado. Evelyn knew that, he did. Born before the days of electricity, Christmas Day, 1864, by seventy-seven and 1941, Evelyn Lee knew a lot.

London
1941
Except that, Joanna wasn't hunkered down in a bunker below the streets of London. She started out in one, but as the old man predicted, she was quickly bored and threatening suicide if Michael did not show her all the exciting times he had promised her. The constant threat of bombings wasn't exciting enough apparently, or the idea of spending the night in the tube. Both were, of course, but something, anything had to be better than spending every day cooped up in a steel box staring at filing drawers.

"Filing," Michael corrected, looking fairly silly with toilet paper stuck on his chin. "You're supposed to be doing something with them, Red, not just staring at them. You know, like A-B-C?"

"Well, I want to do something else," Joanna absently ran her finger through her name she drew with his shaving cream.

"Such as?" Michael couldn't wait to hear.

"Well, I don't know," Joanna said, "maybe I could be an air raid warden."

"Uh, huh," Michael said. "Maybe I could slit my throat."

"I'm serious, Michael," she said.

So was he, at least about the chance of it happening. "Fine. We'll make it simple. No. That's N.O., nada, nano, incorrectamundo, nein. I don't care if they land here in droves. It's nix on the idea of you walking around with a bullhorn. Give me a break, kid. My head aches enough. Think of something else."

"But I can't," Joanna groaned.

"Yeah, you can. Come on." He threw on his jacket and shirt, in the correct order, he might add. "Give me a ride over to the office and we'll figure something out."

“A what?” Joanna said.

“A ride.” He stuffed her behind the steering wheel of his car. “Drive. Make it the station. Westminster. I think it’s still there.”

“Oh, but I can’t,” Joanna panicked at the very thought never mind the part about how she could barely reach the pedals.

“Sure you can. Go up here and take a left.”

“No, I mean the car,” Joanna nodded. “I can’t drive the car, Michael. I don’t know how.”

“Well, imagine that,” Michael whistled with a wicked, evil laugh. “I think we might have thought of something already.”

“Think of something else,” Joanna nodded. “Really, Michael, think of something else.”

“Drive.” Michael pulled the throttle and cranked the key, and so she drove. Propped up on the cushion of his wadded up raincoat so her feet could reach the pedals, she lurched her way down the street, for the most part managing not to hit anything too important. Michael promising as they finally pulled up to the curb Joanna swore she’d never reach they would try it again as soon as her knees stopped shaking and he stopped praying, and so they did. Again and again, every day, until the time Michael had to return unexpectedly to the States.

London
December 1941

“Well, that’s it,” Michael snapped the paper open. “That’s what the ruckus is all about. They just sunk the *Arizona*, kid. We’re in it now.”

“What?” Joanna said.

“Not the state, the ship,” Michael nodded. “Pearl Harbor. The Japanese bombed Pearl Harbor. We were there, remember?”

“Arizona?” Joanna frowned over his shoulder like she couldn’t see the headline from the moon.

“Hawaii,” Michael assured. “You don’t remember, do you?”

“Oh,” Joanna said. “Well, yes. Of course I remember.”

“We were there a week,” Michael said.

“Michael, I remember,” she assured.

“Yeah, I know,” he said, “you were nine. Well, now you’re nineteen, and it’s a date when I get back. Screw the Japs. They can have Fresno … yeah, Fresno," he moved on to the funny papers. "Ever tell you about the week I spent in Fresno?"

"Back?" Joanna bellowed in his ear.

"New York," Michael promised once his head cleared. "I'd take you with me but it's not only the Pacific where the sailing's kind of rough. It's OK. Couple three weeks will go by just like that. I'll be back before you know I was gone."

"But, Michael!" she whined.

"Wanna go home to Gramps?" he threatened. Which, of course Joanna did not want to go home. Once having gotten her feet wet she rather liked it outside in the real world.

"But what do I do?" Joanna insisted. "Honestly, Michael, what do I do? I'm all alone."

"Easy enough," Michael assured, easy enough for him to say. For her, she was back inside, hunkered down below the streets of London with only the files to keep her company. Worse, because she not only had to stay there during the day, but at night, living and sleeping in a small windowless room with two other people she barely knew. Michael told her to pretend it was college or camp. Joanna could pretend it was the moon and she wouldn't be any less depressed.

"You're in the army now, kid," Michael straightened her up from her slump. "Chin up, shoulders back, chest covered, and legs crossed."

"ATS," Joanna corrected. "I'm in the ATS. I'm not a child, Michael."

Tell him about it. She was a pretty girl. Woman, he hated to admit, and it was starting to give him the creeps. "Look, Red," he reminded, "there's a lot of creeps out there. I should know. I'm the king of them. El duce. Capisce?"

"Michael …" Joanna sighed.

"The answer is yes," he threatened.

"Fine," Joanna said. "Yes. What about Hawaii?"

"Huh?" Michael said.

"You said you'd take me to Hawaii."

"I said that?"

"Yes," she assured.

"Well, I don't know when I said that," Michael shook his head.

"But you've seen the news the same as I have, Hawaii's been attacked. *Nnnnroooow! Rata-ta-tat, ack-ack-ack!* Probably should give it awhile, at least until the smoke clears."

"Yesterday," Joanna assured. "You said it yesterday when you were reading the paper."

Yesterday. He barely remembered breakfast. "If you say," he shrugged.

"I do," Joanna assured, "and I want to go to Hawaii to see the *Lusitania* or I am not going in there."

"What?" Michael said.

"You promised!" she stomped her foot.

"How the fuck old was that newspaper?" Michael frowned. "The *Lusitania* was thirty years ago, kid, Ireland."

"Michael!" she said.

"OK, fine!" he swore. "We'll go to Hawaii and see the *Lusitania*. Might be a little tough to work out, but not to worry, I'll figure something out."

"Thank you!" she said.

"Don't mention it. Or this," he reminded, "to anyone. Gramps will have my scalp."

"I'll remember," Joanna assured.

"Good," he smiled with a comforting pat of her shoulder. "Couple three weeks, Red, I swear. I'll be back before you know I'm gone."

Joanna knew it the first night. By the end of the week, she was even considering calling Grandfather to come and bail her out. Definitely, something Michael would find extremely disappointing when she had faithfully promised him she would never tell Grandfather how he had left her, for which Grandfather would surely kill him.

Grandfather wouldn't kill him. Joanna knew that. That was just Michael being Michael. But it didn't make it any easier knowing that, particularly since who might kill Michael, of course, was Justin. Her stepbrother Justin. Ol' eagle-eyed, owl-eyed Justin, there, whether he was ever there or not, which he seldom was, thank God.

Joanna had no foundation for her belief or fear of Justin. In fact, she remembered Grandfather scolding Michael for telling her Justin's secret identity as the boogeyman. She was apprehensive around Justin though for some reason, uncomfortable and self-conscious as if she had been caught in some dastardly unforgivable lie.

She decided to find Michael, call him, speak to him, just to hear his voice. In one way, it did not work out because she was quickly (if not mysteriously, if she thought about it, which she did not), hauled into her manager's office for a severe dressing down and harsh reminder to remember her place. Her place? Joanna knew her place quite well because for all her manager's caterwauling in another way it worked out fine because Michael called her. Full of apologies for his unavoidable and unexpected delay he had Joanna paroled from the filing room and she started driving again for a friend of Michael's, an American engineer by the name and rank of Colonel Mahlon McDowell on assignment to London from Michael's States. It wasn't perfect, the Colonel wasn't Michael, but it was all right, particularly since she was no longer inside. Joanna enjoyed driving and she drove the Colonel all over England until nearing the end of February when he needed to go to Cairo and decided to take her with him.

Joanna fell in love before the plane finished landing. This was Michael's Cairo, Michael's Egypt, Michael's pyramids, and Michael's desert Nile. It was en route to Justin's Tobruk where the accident occurred just outside the Siwa Oasis at the border of Libya. It really was her fault. She was driving too fast for the road, and when the tires skidded onto the rough shoulder, she couldn't bring the jeep back under control. The tires exploded and the world flipped upside down.

Siwa Oasis, Egypt
February 1942
It wasn't the road that ruptured the softened rubber tires of the jeep. The explosion happened first, the crack of a bullet from a sniper's rifle. Joanna remembers waking up among a great many rocks, the jeep on its side, the wheels spinning crazily. She could see the Colonel standing not too far away, but the pain racking her head danced in the sunlight, whisking him out of sight, and so she tried to move to find him, but today the rocks moved with her and she saw they all had guns.

She could understand only part of the speech. Vaguely familiar with German, the voice of the man doing most of the talking seemed different somehow, and the Colonel's aide Paul was lying so close to her, he was distracting.

"Paul?" Joanna shook his arm, trying to wake him. "Paul?"

"Hierher!" The man talking reaching down and Paul's head bounced over to her, landing in her lap. She has no clear recollection of what happened after that, remembering only at some point they all left, she and the Colonel and the men. The last she saw of Paul he was sitting in the driver's seat of the jeep. His arms lashed to the steering wheel to keep him propped up straight, his head bobbing in the wind like some bizarre pedestrian crossing as it hung suspended from the antenna wire, his blue eyes watching her as she walked toward a truck and climbed inside.

Chapter Sixteen

Cairo
March 9, 1942

There was nothing palatial or even neat about the office of England's Squadron Leader Justin Charles. Housed in an oversized government building built sixty-odd years ago in the flavor of Islam, the room was large and overcrowded with weary steel boxes and card board files. In compliment to the plaster walls papered with maps, a discolored series of Venetian blinds hung on the windows facing the street, bright sunlight and heat filling the room with a soiled yellow glow.

The dirt, blinds, and decorative stains of age and seeping lime were there in December when Justin arrived from South Africa by way of Tobruk. The boxes were an accumulation of new and ones he had brought with him, dropping them down in a heap, and dropping himself at a desk to begin to work. He was working now, contrary apparently to a few of his staff.

"Nel!" Justin flung the report he was reading aside, pushed away from his desk and stalked across the floor. "Find that stupid Mick and tell him to get in here now!" he yanked the door open with a bellow at his startled secretary, a moment ago polishing her nails without a care in the world.

"Aye, sir!" she jumped up, ran her stocking, came close to breaking her neck on the regulation stilts she was wearing, and gave up attempting to screw the cap back on her cuticle varnish, or whatever the devil it was she had in her hand.

Justin peered at her, his hard black eyes piercing and round like a cruel fierce owl's in his sun-blackened face—or a wolf, actually. He looked more like a wolf. A skull and face straight from Hell with large sunken eye-sockets and skin stretched tightly over his pronounced features, the apples of his cheeks two hard lumps, shining and ruddy beneath his blackened tan.

A bearded wolf, actually. She eyed the heavy black bush of oily curls blanketing his jaw and chin in striking contrast to his massive dome head glistening with sweat and fairly bald. The few hairs left, black as the beard, though straighter except for the curl at their ends, not a hint of grey in their shining soiled strands. She grimaced. He wasn't old despite his leathery appearance. The hairs that had fallen out had just given up early, burnt, more than likely, to a crisp, given the ebony color of him.

Definitely, a wolf, she decided. Foul and savage, his breath reeking as he loomed over her, the only thing missing was the chest hair. She flushed, embarrassed to even be thinking about such things, but she was if only because she was staring dead at it. Not some burly bush of unkempt curls as one might rightfully expect him to have given the hefty beard and hint of a highland burr behind his slow gentleman's speech. But, no, more like his head, his chest was also nearly bald. Just a thin strip of hair, like a black line slicing straight down the middle, parting him in half. Her flushed deepened. He looked like a wolf, all right, thin and starving as one with his concave abdomen and boned breast ribbed with sinewy muscle. Two tiny teats, round, hard, cold, and black as his eyes, another pair of eyes staring at her. Daresay if she stared back at them, or him, long enough she'd see the veritable outline of his heart, thin as he was. She did not stare, not any longer than she could help it. In all, it was really much more than she needed to know, and certainly far more obvious than it ought to be, but only because he didn't button his shirt. He never buttoned his shirt. Any more than he wore too much of anything when it came to clothes other than some unsightly pair of groin-high shorts that for the sake of common decency, and her certain relief, while they might not be any cleaner than his unclean shirt, their buttons, quite unlike his shirt, were at least closed.

Oh, she disliked this man, really she did, immensely, finding him crude, coarse, and outlandish, to say the least. Embarrassed for him even if he seemed to be quite comfortable and detached, most of all from any reaction he might cause appearing near-naked in public. Never in her life had she found herself confronted with the option of either ogling a man's groin, or desperately trying to ignore it. Both virtually near impossible not to do considering his height, for that matter the length of his long naked legs, and the fact she was sitting down, or had been moments before his assault. The rumpled, threadbare crotch of his shorts appearing quite literally eye level in front of her shouting at her to get off her duff, or something to that effect. In all, sufficient to say, the reason why she got up off her duff, immediately jumped up, and if it wasn't for his astounding height and despite the fact, she did wear heels, rather high ones even though she wasn't a short woman, but average in height, damn near slammed her head off his chin. Fortunately, at six–foot five and a half inches tall before the thick soles of his over-sized boots, his chin remained quite safely out of reach and harm's way.

Oh, she loathed this man, really she did, despised him, utterly, most of the time, anyway. For some reason some of the time, he seemed to want to fascinate her. Not intentionally on his part, of course, but solely and inexplicably on hers despite the fact he was oblivious to her. Quite oblivious. Quite.

"Yes, well, who the devil are you?" Justin demanded, unable to see for himself under all her paint and hair dye, and actually expecting to find Joe sitting there. A different Joe than his deceased friend Joseph Lee, but a fellow named Joe just the same. One who practically lived there, didn't he?

At least recently. Justin eyed the blonde who damned near killed herself and him while she was at it, springing up in front of him like some grinning Jack-in-the-box. A blousy piece of common goods more so even than the last one who had sat there on her starched behind before he ordered her tossed out. He was surprised possibly though, just a touch, rare as an occasion as that might be, but only by the fact there seemed to be no end in sight to them. In three months there had to be at least nine of them he had ordered on their way and out of his. Needing some personal assistant like he needed ... well, buttons on his shirt. This was the RAF, after all, SIS, for that matter MI6, the grandfather, godfather, of them all.

"Cain, sir," she nodded hastily with her bobbing blonde head.

"Assistant Section Officer Laura Cain. Your ... well, secretary," she acknowledged as she had upon occasion. Not that it meant anything to him, which it obviously did not if after nearly three months he was still asking her who she was. And, no, she wouldn't say Joe *lived* there. She lived there, or rather sat there at her desk.

"Yes, well," Justin tore her bottle of glue out of her hand for some reason. She really had no idea why he did that, proceeding to fling it in the dustbin, "explains the typing."

"Yes, well ..." Actually, Laura could explain her rather limited typing skills as she studied her dustbin. It was simply that she hated typing. She had no interest in typing, any more than she had any interest in being a nurse. Unfortunately, those were the two positions usually available to her as a female officer of the RAF being as the male officers had yet to allow their female constituents to fly their stupid airplanes, which was her interest.

This, of course, she did not say. Any more than she commented on his personal hygiene, or lack thereof, or inquired into when he last had a square meal. He really was so thin. So rugged and weather-beaten thin. She could count every rib, map the outline of his beating heart ... which, of course, she didn't. She straightened up, briskly. He was her Commanding Officer, after all, and beyond that, he was a man. An ardent, if not career, she suspected, daresay goose-stepping member of his boys-only club who did things like tear bottles of glue from their secretary's unsuspecting hands for reasons known only to them.

"Yes, well, go on," Justin waved, now that the amenities were out of the way.

"Yes, well ..." Laura also did not ask him how he would like her to "go on" in what direction, through him, over her desk, or over her typewriter? No, she just stood there with glue on her hands, a run in her stocking and scrape on her knee where she had slammed it into the desk, saying things like, "Yes, well," and having no idea where to go on from there.

"Yes, well, you know who he is, don't you?" Justin insisted, confident she must have a brain somewhere under that bleached cloud surrounding her head. If not a list in the mess she called a desk, explaining who was who, and who was not.

"Oh, yes." Yes, Laura knew who "Nel" was. Rather the same as she knew her desk was spotless. But then that probably had something to do with her spending much more time in the canteen than at her assigned post, but only because she wasn't allowed to sit, stay, or do any work whatsoever, certainly not there. To the contrary, he was correct in his belief he had relieved her of her duties and post at least a dozen times in the last two and a half months, for whatever reason. Rather like the glue, she suspected.

As for Sergeant Reynolds, or Nel, as the group called him. A man, who, yes, apart from being truly gargantuan in height and size, it was rather hard not to know who Sergeant Reynolds was. He was a Mick, the same as she was. Only to where Sergeant Reynolds was Protestant and ardently loyal to the Crown, she was Catholic and reasonably loyal to the Crown. Even though at the moment she was seriously contemplating tendering her resignation and joining the IRA as an assassin. Interestingly enough, and by sheer coincidence, the chosen career of two or more of her six brothers.

"Yes, well, he's around here somewhere." Justin withdrew his head back into his shell and slammed his office door shut, leaving her free to breathe a sigh of relief.

It was more annoyance than relief. "Oh, for goodness sake," Laura glared down on her torn stocking. Such luxuries were frightfully difficult to come by and now utterly destroyed, the ladder quickly spreading down her leg to her ankle as she stepped carefully, testing the stability of her shoe. "What a horrible man." Really, what a thoroughly despicable and vulgar man, she had to say, thinking of another vulgar man she had only just recently met. A doctor. An American doctor who claimed, no less, to be a friend of this one, Squadron Leader Justin Charles. Something Laura no longer doubted, if she had ever doubted it, but believed ardently they were best friends. Mates, as her kind would say, chums.

"Sergeant!" Laura did breathe a little in relief a few moments later, but only because she had forgotten completely about Sergeant Nel until connecting with him not too far down the hall. It was at the water cooler where she pranced to wet the corner of her handkerchief and wipe the smear of blood staining her knee as best she could. She looked up and there he was, his massive presence and frame filling the hall.

"Not to worry, little lady," Nellie winked his wink, smiled his smile, sauntering on down the hall and inside Charlie's office to see what all the fuss was about.

"Well, of course, I'm not worried," Laura assured, hardly worried, or even aware of what there might be to be worried about, other than the war. But even there she was extremely limited, if not outright restricted from worrying too much about it, and certainly barred, as mentioned, in doing anything personally about it.

Shortly after Sergeant Nellie Reynolds came and left, *Joe,* or rather, Private Joe DeSapio also happened by to announce he was "Just going in to see the Maj," with an apologetic look down on her knee as she sat there practicing her typing on a blank piece of paper set rather crooked in the carriage of her machine.

"Here, let me get that for you," Joe offered, handy with all of that kind of stuff.

"Squadron Leader," Laura smiled while Joe straightened her paper. For that matter, straightened up her desk to make sure she had enough room should some actual work ever be forthcoming, and finishing with a short instruction course on how to work the levers so the paper wouldn't get stuck the next time. Something Laura already knew. But she liked Joe, she did. She liked most of them. Joe, in particular, Bobby, the older, heavyset man, definitely. Even the disconcerting Sergeant Nellie who frequently came around, most recently with a young lieutenant whose name she did not know, and did not trouble her, as in not cause her any sort of personal alarm.

Joe was a bit odd, but then, quite honestly, they were all odd. Eccentric, Laura preferred to consider the lot of them somewhat more kindly, and certainly none of them more odd or eccentric, or outright bizarre than their Squadron Leader Justin Charles, who was not only vulgar, but a snob. Oh, yes, she knew that as well as she knew her own name, disdainful, disapproving, and disagreeable. The paper jammed. "Quite," Laura said harshly, aloud.

"Huh?" Joe said.

"Nothing," Laura assured. "Nothing at all." Back to Joe who was a Yank quite unlike the rest of the small group who passed through the corridor doors to visit Squadron Leader Charles on a frequent daily basis, but that did not matter. The significance of Joe being a Yank was limited perhaps to explaining why he said things 0586526158like "Maj" or "Major" rather than "Squad" or "Squad Le" in a shortened form of "Squadron Leader", both of which would be utterly absurd. It was a different language, American English. Not simply a dialect, but a different language entirely, and here to think how she had always presumed being English it was therefore the same one.

"Yeah, well, I think we've got it now," Joe assured as he popped the typewriter carriage back in.

"Yes," Laura agreed while he moved on to confirm the working status of the rest of her equipment to ensure she hadn't accidentally done something like dismantle her telephone in her confused female state. He was saying something along those lines now. Not about English, but about the ease or simplicity of "Maj" or "Major" versus "Squadron Leader", citing a few German ranks in example of what he meant, as well as his own name. A grin flashing through his handsome face, that was quite handsome, strikingly so with strong lines and chiseled cheekbones, a thick blue-black crop of wavy hair complementing his rugged and muscular American physique. At twenty-six, Joe was the same age she was, though oddly, as odd as anything else when it came to gender or sex, twenty-six somehow seemed so much younger on a man than it did on a woman. At twenty-six, Laura could be, or should be what, Joe's mother? To where at twenty-six Joe could be who, her younger brother? Tall, zestful, and robust, Joe was really extremely handsome in a primal, near animal sort of way, regrettably not at all her type.

"Rank," Laura pleasantly corrected Joe's use of the word "term". "It really is a rank, not a term."

"Yeah, I know it's a rank," Joe said. "That's what I'm saying ...

"I mean ..." he said, drawing it out long and thinking about it. "OK, like Sarge," he nodded, meaning Nellie. Nellie was Sarge, Bobby just Bobby, and that other freak they hired, just some freak. "I could see myself out in the field, yelling 'Yo, *Unterfeldwebel!*'" he let out a yell. "Hey, yo, *Unterfeldwebel!*" he hollered with a wave. "I mean, if I was German," Joe explained. "And instead of, you know, Sarge."

"No, I understand," Laura nodded.

"Yeah," Joe said, certain she did. "I'd end up with half my head blown off before I even got his rank out ...

"Or, um ..." Joe said backtracking fast from the gruesome details. Not sure why he felt like he had to throw them in there other than to scare her half to death, which he wasn't trying to do. "My name, OK?" he settled on. "Like my name," he nodded. "It's Joe, or it's Guiseppe—which is what it really is," he assured with a laugh. "Honest. Swear to God. We're talking first generation American. I'm first generation American. I remember the boat," he nodded, remembering it. "I do. I remember the boat ...

"So, um ..." he wrapped it up, because after all he had to get in there before the Maj came out here and grabbed him ... Joe didn't know, by the belt or something. His hair maybe since he didn't wear a shirt buttoned or unbuttoned. Nah, he didn't bother. In the first place, it was hot. Real hot. Like 106 degrees or something in there and that was with the fans, the hair on his chest heavy and hot enough to wear without adding another layer on top of it. In the second place? He didn't bother, nah, didn't feel like it.

"Which is easier?" he asked, talking about his name. "Joe or Guiseppe? You tell me."

"Joe," Laura nodded.

"It sure is." Joe laughed honestly, rising to give her back her seat with a point down on her wounded knee. "I can get you whatever you need, seriously, however many you want."

"How much?" Laura hesitated, slightly surprised by the offer, though not to suggest she wasn't grateful, or short on funds, for that matter that she found his naked sweating chest disconcerting or particularly attractive, which she did not, and it was not, either. To the contrary, for such a noticeably attractive young man, Joe's chest was possibly the least attractive, most noticeable aspect about him. The curly black hair wet, almost slick, and bronzed skin decorated with some of the most amazing and unattractive tattoos of snakes and hearts carved neatly with a razor blade or knife and painted India blue.

"Um ... you mean like dollars?" Joe verified, aware of the subtle differences in their language.

"Or pounds," Laura nodded. "Yes, I suppose I mean that."

"Whatever." Joe considered a fair asking price, though not seriously. "I don't know," he grinned. "Free sound OK?"

Free. "How much?" Laura repeated a little more firmly than the first time. Not to suggest she didn't believe him, or to clarify what he meant exactly by free, which she highly doubted if he meant anything in particular at all, other than what he said, but just to ask.

There was a pause before he answered, or at least a moment of silence before his grin spread again followed by another genuine laugh. "Nah, that ain't my style," he assured, catching her drift, which, of course, he would catch it. I mean, she was a dame, and he was a guy, and he could mean a lot, we're talking *a lot* by free.

Still, he found it a little disappointing she didn't know it wasn't his style. Not that she knew him all that much, but she knew him well enough to know while he might not be a rocket scientist like some of the guys around there, he wasn't stupid, nah, far from it. The same as it wasn't like she was out of his league or something, because she wasn't, but she was out of his reach, definitely. He didn't stand a chance. Everybody knew that—him and Bobby at least. The Sarge probably didn't, but the Sarge was a different kind of guy, and who the hell knew or cared what the rest of the freaks had to say. He and Bobby knew that was the point. The same as he knew, this lady, if she had eyes for anyone, never mind who might have eyes for her, which was plenty, she had eyes for one guy only, and that was the Maj. Written all over her face, like they say. This lady was in love, we're talking *in love* with the Maj. To the point she was walking into walls, and falling over chairs, the proof right there in her wrecked stockings with the run down to her ankle and creeping up toward her thigh.

Oh, yeah. Joe eyed those legs that were sturdy and healthy like the rest of her. She definitely had it for the Maj. With the high heeled shoes and short skirt that was really short and equally tight, molding her rear like the padded brassiere molded her chest into a high proud shelf crowned by her cocky little hat atop her perfectly coiffed blonde hair. All proof the lady did not have a life beyond this place, but spent her nights working on ways to get the Maj to notice her, and *that* not only made the Maj particularly thoughtless and unkind since he didn't notice anything, it also made him pretty damn blind.

Or a fag, Joe shrugged. Yeah, maybe he was a fag. It didn't matter to Joe if the Major was because he liked the guy, would, still, and did like the guy the same as the rest of them did, a lot.

"What I will tell you is this," he pointed with his grin while Laura stood there paralyzed, almost too afraid to move. Though Joe would bet she was a lot less frightened of him making some kind of pass at her, than she was scared to death of the Maj unexpectedly walking out and thinking what? Exactly that. Oh, yeah, exactly that. "As much as you need them," which she did need them, what was she going to wear, socks in her high-heeled shoes? "With legs like that, you deserve them."

"I'll take that as a compliment," Laura nodded.

"Good," Joe approved.

"And ... I don't know," Laura said, "two? Two pair?"

"Two?" Joe's face screwed up into a frown. Can you imagine prostituting yourself for two pairs of silk stockings? He didn't think so.

"I don't know, six?" Laura said, really wanting to get back to her desk, even if she only sat at it.

"Make it an even dozen." Joe left it and her there, the door closing on the Major's mumble and his explanation, "Yeah, I'm here, just making sure everything's off ..."

"Oh, for goodness' sake," Laura sat down at her desk. A short time passing before she realized exactly what Joe had meant by everything being off, but only because it crossed her mind as she sat at her typewriter, the carriage and paper immediately binding, almost as if deliberately. She stared at it, and the more she stared ...

"Everything's off ..." Joe's words seemed to echo as Laura's glance strayed to the intercom not quite daring to touch it to find out if it was working, more out of fear of finding out it wasn't ...

"Oh, for goodness sake," Laura said annoyed, flipping the intercom on, boldly snatching up the telephone. It was disconnected. No response when she clicked it, just dead.

"Or off," she repeated what Joe had said. "*'Just making sure everything's off.'* Well now." Laura sat at her desk as she had often sat there over the last near three months, wondering what to do. Since discharging her hadn't worked, her dear and good friend Colonel Jim Peterson having taken care of that, there was nothing else for them to do except break everything around her, Joe, her friend, who was apparently not her friend at all, in on the game as well.

Laura did not mention it though when Joe came out after not being in there very long and left with a reassuring wave he would not forget, meant what he said about the twelve pairs of silk stockings.

"Oh, yes," Laura smiled. Meaning what she said, or thought, about grown men resorting to such childish pranks as sabotaging her typewriter and telephone simply because they did not want her there, and had to accept her being there if only because those higher up than them, put her there.

The American doctor from downstairs came by next, recognizing her as she recognized him, he with a scowl on his face, she as thoroughly disinterested as she had been before. Bobby was with him but only as far as the door, a brief pleasant nod for her as he left, "How's it going, luv?"

"Oh, fine," Laura replied, "just fine." Shortly thereafter, however it wasn't fine at all, far from it. But she was getting ahead of herself, far too far ahead of herself. Before the arrival of the doctor and the mayhem that quickly followed, there had been Joe who went in and out, and before him, Sergeant Nellie Reynolds.

Chapter Seventeen

"What the devil is this?" Justin turned around from his wall of maps with a wave of Nellie's latest field report.

"What it says," Nellie replied easily, confident Joe had accurately written down what he told him.

"It says the damn depot has disappeared," Justin assured. "We've spent a month to come away empty handed."

"Does it now?" Nellie chuckled, not remembering putting it exactly that way, but if Joe said that's what he said, it must be.

"Is it there?" Justin cut to the bottom line.

"No," Nellie shook his head, "it ain't. It was, but it isn't, and, so, disappeared? Aye." he guessed that was true since it was gone, like the other one before it.

It wasn't there to begin with. No more than the one reported last month had been there. Not there now and not there before. One month. An entire month wasted. Justin tossed the report on his desk and lit his pipe, the stench quickly adding to the flavor of the room.

Nellie waited, continuing with his easy smile, his hands folded on his tight stomach, unperturbed. Charlie's tantrums were always brief, his blood rising only when he thought he was wrong, and at thirty-five, Justin was seldom wrong. Seasoned and hardened, he was exactly what he looked like. Tough, rough, menacing, cold and calculating, power supported by education, background, and twenty years training and experience in England's elite SIS largely spent in the field whether it was a jungle, Belfast, or the concrete suburbs of Johannesburg, South Africa. He had his fair share of critics and an equal number of fans. Neither meant anything to him. With few failures and an impressive list of successes, Justin enjoyed what did mean something to him. Respect for him and his family name. He was a man who followed through, and most importantly, came through. Criticisms usually only having to do with his methods, which could be brutal, appear brutal and unnecessary to the ignorant, innocent, or ill informed. The lot of them apparently forgetting that by the veritable nature of his profession he was always involved in some conflict or another, this latest one, otherwise known as a world war. His specialty was coups. *"French for terrorism,"* he once said. Accurate in that he was a licensed killer, terrorizing groups, countries, and men, his passions poker and getting the job done, a league of experts on his private roll call to help him do that.

Justin ogled Nellie his Red Ace for thirteen of those twenty years. He relied on Nellie to do more than guard the gates of Hell and keep the occasional dissident in place. Fearsome and fearless, the giant Irishman was crafty, intuitive, and lethal as he looked. Up for any job, Justin passed his way. Except this one, apparently, when it counted most. Justin did not buy it. By the smug look on Nellie's granite face, Nel didn't buy it either. Something else was wrong, and it had nothing to do with Nellie. Something more than a reliable report of two depots on the far side of Libya's map, both now as reliably reported to have disappeared. Who then? What? Justin's gut told him he was not going to like the answer even if he did not know it yet. He would. He had the means, the power, and the men.

A few men anyway. Justin straightened up out of his temper to make a note. He had a handful of men who could spend a little more time figuring out what was wrong, since ferreting out depots wasn't the only thing on the agenda. No, that would be the war. Currently, a desperate situation inflamed by the Pacific and the increasing strain it was putting on the British forces already overburdened. If that wasn't enough, the sudden entry of the Yanks into the mix proved sufficient in coaxing the enigmatic Charles out from protecting England's interests in the south, for the north in December '41. British interests in Cairo deciding Justin could do his directing better from behind a desk in an office instead of a tent, handing him a command that included a division of the army's Long Range Desert Troops. They must have gotten him confused with some other fellow. Justin might be a director, but he was no desk officer. King Charles to his peers, he was *sir* to his men whether they called him *Maj, Boss, or Bwana,* or whatever they called him, code name *Charlie* to the current list of bastards trying to shut him down. No one ever had, and neither would Rommel and his crew.

Immunity assured, with authorization to use his own methods, Justin packed his boxes, taking Nellie and the equally irreplaceable Bobby Roberts with him to Egypt. En route, he stopped by Tobruk, Libya, the last of England's Saharan strongholds, to pick up Peter O'Brannigan alighting from his airplane with an IRA twinkle in his eye and Eire's Coat of Arms on his beret. His consecutive life sentences commuted once again to life with Justin Charles.

North Africa
December 1941

"Oh, now, have faith, lad, have faith," Pete cajoled Justin's somber expression, pressing a bottle of his special rum into Justin's hand as a personal and holiday greeting. "If I ain't going to give my Emerald Isle to you, I sure as hell ain't going to give it to no Jerry. We'll work it out, lad, we will. Win, is what I'm saying. You have Peter's word and support on that." And just to prove it, Pete got the car door for him. "Where to?"

Cairo. Midnight, Christmas Eve, 1941. The needed African foothold a coup, brazen in its simplicity of surrounding the palace with tanks and telling the Fascist Prime Minister to get out, the flag of Britannia quickly straightened neat and tidy overhead.

"Interested?" Justin asked. "Now that the job's been done?"

"Oh, the job isn't done, lad," Pete disputed. "The job, you might say, has just begun."

"Get in." Justin took the driver's side for himself, still a maniac behind the wheel, still trying to prove how his father's death could not have happened the way everyone but him knew it had, and that was by accident. But Pete was Irish, a firm believer in the little people who he counted on to get him to Cairo alive. Bobby was old and accustomed to Justin, and knew they'd make it, and as far as Nel?

Pete looked over the vision of all that was wrong and yet to be right in the United Kingdom of English rule with that orange hair of Nel's the crown and color of his wretched protestant soul. Larger than life, the fellow was, physically and by deeds in a world wanting and needing its heroes. He was no hero, though, that ol' Nellie fellow of Justin's. He was some freak of nature, morally wanting and reprehensible and damn ugly at almost seven-feet and three-hundred pounds. Even his head was two times the size of Pete's, with his eyes small and crystalline green and too close together, the skull sloped, and brain compressed, pressed tightly into some abnormal shape crushed down into the bridge of his nose.

"You still alive, lad?" Pete gave Nellie a different smile than the one he had given Justin. "Thought for sure one of those natives would have gone and eaten you by now." His tongue touched his lip like he might want to, but Nellie was too stupid to think of something clever to say back. Nellie was too stupid to do most anything except what Justin told him to do, and that was usually kill, and who couldn't do that? Pete had more notches on his belt than Nellie could ever hope to have. Peter O'Brannigan was a mass murderer, that's what they told him, tried, found, and convicted him of being criminally insane, had to be close to twenty years ago. All sorts of innocent men, women, and children, Pete, and the likes of him, had maimed and slaughtered over some six-hundred years of misbehavior otherwise known as the Irish-English dispute. England's infamous Broadmoor prison his home in between times hanging with Justin.

Maybe so. Pete would be the first one to admit that, and move right on to doing it again however much trouble he found himself in. Incorrigible, that's what he was. A career insurgent, ardent anarchist, worst of the criminal element, making his bed and somehow managing to live long enough to lie in it.

"Aye, and you, too," Pete gave up trying to get a rise out of Nellie to riddle Bobby. "Feed a damn village with the belly you have on you." He turned around to behave himself after that, sticking to business, which was what he was there for, not to make enemies or go away friends. It was war, after all, not some popularity, or beauty contest. Pete's eye flitted over Justin. Looked the same, he did, Henry's little boy Justinian with his saturnine features. Been a few years since they'd seen each other, but Justin looked the same, sun-burnt to a crisp with an expression that could either be exhaustion or surprise with those big, penetrating black eyes overwhelming his face. Be a doll if he somehow managed to be cute, too. He wasn't, and so he was more or less stuck with being a prick. Mean and tough as Pete for all his fine upbringing, not fooling anybody with his gentleman's drawl, least of all Pete. "Must be something if they called you up," he agreed, hunting for specific information.

"War," Justin assured.

"Oh, right," Pete scoffed. "Got yourself on some one's list, sounds like it to me if they stuck you out here. Don't no one give a damn what happens here, rightfully so." He looked around. Bleak, it was. Bleak and empty, and hotter than hell, he seemed to recall. "Got to head home if you're looking for a war, mate. Less action here than your local."

"Volunteered, actually," Justin said.

"Well, that I believe," Pete agreed. "You're a bastard, aren't you? Not going to find anyone out here but bastards." he looked around again. "Couldn't have picked a worse damn place on the earth to make a stand, could they now? Must know something we don't."

"Oil," Justin said.

"Suez, you mean," Pete nodded. "Aye. Heard the rumor. Take the Suez, you can forget about those oil fields, is right."

"Yes, well, it's no rumor," Justin grunted. "Take the Suez, you can forget about most things. It's the supply route."

"Still ours?" Pete checked.

"For now," Justin agreed.

Pete nodded. "Heard another rumor you might find interesting. Our girl Jewels is back inside. Two years solid for violating her probation, and not but a call away from you getting her out."

"Oh?" Justin said. "What do I need her for?"

Pete looked at him, a lot said in the look, but that was all right because Justin just looked back at Pete, a lot said in his look as well.

"She's a pilot, lad." Pete kept the conversation clean and polite, smiling his discolored smile of a life of poverty and crime, the wall of his winking right eye slightly weakened by one too many fights, but handsome just the same in his manly Irish way. He looked like he lived, saucy and sassy, and worldly-wise, tall, but not too tall, strong, but lanky, his eyes blue and hair a true red. A man. That's what Pete looked like, a man. His features kind of craggy with a few lines, some deeper than others especially around the eyes. "Don't have too many of those lollygagging around with nothing to do, and so she might come in handy, experienced as she is."

"Might at that," Justin considered, and put a call into Kenya as soon as they pulled in to set up shop in the shadows of the great pyramids and Sphinx, deep in the belly of what had to be one of the filthiest cities in the world. Big, and loud, and unimaginably overcrowded, dangerous even during the day. Her alleys and causeways permeated with the smells of intrigue, sex, and double-dealings flourishing beneath her celebrated Egyptian glory commingled with the modern. Even had a Metro movie theater, faded posters of Gable and Crawford immortalized in soiled peeling layers of celluloid skin.

"Yes, well, think that would be more the citadel," Justin commented on Pete's colorful take on the neighborhood.

"Casbah," Pete corrected. A strange world it was. Evil. Bad Mojo like some of those sub-Saharan tribes. Roof dwellers scurrying like monkeys overhead. Come out of there alive, come out of anywhere. "Remember that?" he sighed fondly. "Had ourselves a time there, didn't we?"

"Yes, well, a Casbah is a citadel." Justin had the last word as he was rightfully entitled and accustomed to, and got the office door for himself, only to stop dead still in disbelief, possibly for the first time in his life.

Cairo
December 1941

"Yes, well, who the devil are you?" Justin insisted, quick to notice the dyed stacked blonde racing him to his throne, but only because of his observational skills and training.

"Your secretary, sir," she smiled prettily, her face as Irish as Pete's under all her modern plucking and cosmetics, "Assistant Section Officer Laura Cain."

Oh, well, now, Pete noted to himself how unless his eyes and memory deceived him, to be more honest and accurate it would have to be Assistant Section Office Laura *McShane* Cain whether or not she considered scrubbing her face morally clean. Of the McShane Cains, most notably Ian, eldest of a rough band of illegitimate half-breeds born of Ireland's soulful Mary Margaret, and England's sweet-talking Johnny Cain with the holes in his pockets and big ideas. Ian, who shunned him and his father's name, slated to go down in municipal history as the fellow who killed Justin's distinguished daddy and got away with it. No more evidence to hang Ian McShane or any of his brothers than what already existed in the chronicles of the English-Irish dispute, no matter how hard Justin pushed the issue, which he didn't after the first round or two. Out of respect, responsibility, and duty to the Crown, and a few other reasons, not exactly publicly known such as there being as much evidence to suggest the assassination of Sir Henry Charles, MP, had been an insider job by a group of disgruntled Fascists annoyed at the prospect of being exposed.

Still, it was an interesting quirk of fate, born of fate or some malevolent sprite that found the sister of the man accused of killing the father of another together in the same room. A reasonable explanation sure to be forthcoming, Pete settled for the sprite that drew McShane's baby sister all grown up and not half bad, to that very room, and the tumultuous childhood that pinned the prideful RAF emblem on the spit-and-polish jacket of the fine upstanding young lass. The pin as bright and shining as she was, brand spanking new.

A bit of a surprise, the uniform, yes, it was. To Hell with Justin, Pete couldn't have been more surprised to see Cain's sister dressed in England's finery than he was to see her. Justin, on the other hand, had apparently stopped his investigation with Ian and three of his score of brothers old enough to be taken seriously at the time, never moving on to meet the rest of the family, or he was just better at deadpan than Pete would have guessed.

It was the latter, Pete decided. Justin didn't have the faintest idea who this bird was any more than she had any idea about him. No one was that good at keeping their reserve not even a Brit, and definitely not a Mick, half though she might be on her mother's side.

"Yes, well ..." Justin mumbled something unpleasant for such a well-brought up gent, while the lass busied herself apologizing for the sorry state of the office a few of the boys had likewise seen to overthrowing on their way to taking the palace back.

"I'm sorry?" Laura requested, not quite catching what it was the Squadron Leader said, and rightfully, as noted, for the sake of her Catholic upbringing, she should not have.

"Out, luv," Bobby translated for her, catching her up gently by the arm to show her the door.

"Out?" Laura repeated, still not quite sure what was meant.

"Out," Bobby clarified, handing her, her shoulder bag along with her cards, passing her off to be escorted down the hall and out of the war.

"Right ..." Pete eyed the attractive bint leaving in a confused fluster, but he refrained from saying anything about her heritage or family tree. It would eventually come to light without any help from him. He did know and believe that. Not much else to look at though now that she was gone, his attention returned to the small group that counting him currently totaled four, and would soon become five with the promised release and arrival of the earthy and lovely Julia Jones.

Right now though, they were only four and close to two hundred years' experience among them. With Justin the youngest, though one would never know it by his balding double-dome, Pete was next at forty-five, grey starting to work its way through his shaved strawberry curls. After that came Nellie at just over fifty, and Bobby Roberts, Justin's lifelong mentor and guru, no less than sixty-five, the brains Nellie didn't have, slow moving and morbidly obese, his breath shallow and frequent in the dry desert heat that would kill him likely. Make him miserable if it didn't. Succeed, where in sixty-five years all else and all others had failed, but Bobby insisted on being a part, postponing his coming and due retirement to help the lad out one last time. Stupid, in Pete's opinion, who knew demolition as well as the son of a Welsh miner, the world Bobby had been born into. Pete knew no fear, the same as Nellie, the African continent like the back of his hand. Pete knew a lot, except his place, a long-standing point of contention between him and Justin who otherwise got along fairly well despite their marked political differences.

Pete's place this go-round would be the same as every other, in the field. Number Two to Justin's Nellie, and Number Three to his Bobby Roberts.

Nellie would also spend half his time or so in the field. Bobby, no. Bobby's place was at Justin's side when Justin needed him, down in the dungeon when Justin did not, playing with his guns. Pete did not care either way what either of them did. He was his own man, had his own mind, excusing himself when Justin handed out the commissions of sergeant to Bobby and Nellie to find the whisky, since he also knew where it was.

The same as he knew who the drinker was in the crowd, and the one not above indulging in a little India hemp every now and then. It brought a personal sense of satisfaction to Pete to be so close to who should be his enemy. To be privy to the man and what some might consider his dark side, potentially damaging to Justin's public and personal reputation.

Justin and Pete were neither enemies nor friends, in the strict sense of the words. What they were, should Justin ever think about it long enough to label it or them, which he did not, was probably closest to associates. Something Justin was with most people, certainly his men, except for Bobby. Bobby Roberts was probably closest to being a friend of Justin's, and Bobby Roberts, never mind Justin, could tell Pete a thing or two about Justin regardless of what Pete might believe or think he understood or knew. Including Pete must be thinking of some other fellow insofar as Justin being the sort to wonder or worry about what society's reaction might be to the revelation of his occasional indulgences. Bobby did not think so. To the devil with Pete, Justin was a man, and men do what men do. Pete's gassy jabber and his declining to play along by not accepting an appointment of rank put Bobby on the alert. An early reminder of Pete's potential for misbehavior.

Bobby was right, of course, about Pete's potential, but he was also wrong where it counted most. While it might seem odd to some, sending a lifer, confirmed and committed IRA to boot, into the field, Justin was not about to worry about it, above all, second guess himself. Pete was not going to stage a jailbreak, escape for parts or plains unknown. The ties that bound Pete and Justin, and hence the earth, were neatly encapsulated in Pete's opening words, *"If I ain't going to give my Emerald Isle to you, I sure as hell ain't going to give it to no Jerry."* Ditto when it came to England who, might one day eventually lose Ireland to Ireland, but Justin would be damned if he'd lose it or any part of the British Isles to Germany. That was not only a fact it was a simple matter of world politics and history. Pro-German sentiment, vogue among England's young, bored, or elite in the 20's and 30's, with the war, vanished with any remnants driven deep underground.

In neutral Ireland, however, it not only thrived, but also openly succeeded in driving an irremediable wedge between the Irish rebels already divided since before the 20's. Pete was Old IRA, pro-treaty, and fiercely anti-Blueshirts, positions that within the extraordinarily muddied Irish situation, found Pete and Justin at each other's side. Squared off against mutual opponents, they were equals in Pete's mind, partners, if they never quite achieved the distinction of friends. So, no, Pete wasn't going anywhere, least of all back to jail. Might indulge in a little sass every now and then, succumb to the irresistible temptation to occasionally stick it to them, seduced by the desire and intent of being and remaining his own man, but he was not about to go back to jail until he had to.

"Wouldn't be a war without you," Pete raised his glass rather than bow his head, chance offending the patron saints of the *Dáil Éireann* by accepting Justin's RAF pin.

"Yes, well," Justin grunted, so it wouldn't be. Something goes balls-up though, even once, and Pete was out, or rather back in. Justin did not care why. He had fifty pounds that said none of them, himself included, was going to get out of this go-round alive. Fifty pounds more salary a month for each month they did. Didn't matter who they were, what their rank was whether real or otherwise.

Neither Nellie nor Bobby was commissioned in any branch of service, or convicts, though Nellie, in a civilized world, was certainly a candidate for Broadmoor. Pete was wrong about the assignment of rank being window dressing in an attempt to fit in with the regular crowd that ruled Cairo. The point and purpose was to install an order of hierarchy for the field personnel soon to follow. If there was an unusual choice or action in Justin's future, it would probably be the addition of a Yank. Giuseppe "Joe" DeSapio. A truck mechanic and avid short-wave radio hobbyist who was a convict, or criminal, of a particularly elite status. A cop-killer from the streets of Brooklyn, at large, and on the run, and who apparently thought he'd beat the gallows by enlisting in the army.

Fair to say Joe wouldn't have made the first cut if it wasn't for Pete's intervention, what with Justin akin to being a copper himself, simply for the world. Pete liked Joe and his story immediately, finding the concept of volunteering for Uncle Sam to escape the electric chair interesting whether or not Joe's theory of self-rehabilitation and redemption worked, which it did not, not even close. No more than his attempted jumping ship worked. Wanted dead or alive, Joe landed alive in Cairo, just not again where he wanted, jail. Two hours away from being shipped out permanently when Pete happened upon him after thumbing through the assortment of resumes passed his way.

"What about this one?" Pete handed Justin the report, the folder thin but wicked as they come what with the fellow widowing some decent and hardworking policeman's wife.

"Yes, well, decent and hardworking sounds like a pipe dream." Justin concurred with the notion finding a municipal foot soldier who wasn't on someone's payroll alongside the one he was supposed to be on was unlikely. As far as the civic-minded killer: "What about him?" Justin took the bait.

"Dead man walking," Pete winked. "Personally, I find they're usually the most cooperative, myself a shining example."

"Yes, well, I'm looking for more than ghoulies." Justin scanned the sheet that placed the enlistee's story among the top ten stupidest he had ever read. "He's a damn Yank."

"He's got skills." Pete played defense council for the wayward American colonist, understanding how their little revolution might have come about. "Says right there he was an automobile mechanic before he took to a life of murder and crime."

"Yes, well, actually it says," Justin read, interested now that he did, but only because he was a gambler at heart, "that motor shop was a cover for a betting operation he ran over his short wave."

Pete smiled. "Say that like it was illegal."

"Apparently so there," Justin handed the log back. "All right. See what he's got, and we'll take it from there."

"Ain't you the charitable one," Pete praised. "Go straight to Heaven, surely you will. Be there alone, but you'll go there."

"Doubt it," Justin neglected to clarify which, the part about going to Heaven, or the part about being there alone.

A month after picking Joe for his first radio and gizmo extraordinaire, Justin wasn't any closer to finding whom he referred to as his second "gun". That would be a fellow to complement Pete. An invaluable asset to any man's army or squad, and not that they weren't out there, because they were. They just weren't going to waste them by bringing them here. Pete seemed apparently right about that. Those who hadn't already written off North Africa apparently seemed hard put to remember it was there. Justin kept looking though believing in the inevitable as well as patience paying off. Another month and his crew had expanded to close to a hundred with most of them answering to Nellie before answering to him. Something else that didn't set well with Pete, as Justin continued not to care what did or didn't set well with anyone. His interest was solely the North African war, no less than winning it despite the odds. Pete would have his chance at stardom at some point, some time, particularly since Justin still couldn't find his coveted "gun". Until told otherwise, however, the primary duty of Justin's private task force was to assist in the collection of information, rather than doing some actual job themselves.

That is, all but one. Jean Paul Dumont. For the first time in his thirteen-year history with Charlie, Nellie found himself sharing the position of Justin's right hand not with Bobby, or Pete, but with the French. The reason Nellie found himself in that position was because Justin was not about to share his position as King. Intimately involved with the Free French long before Justin's arrival in Cairo, Jean Paul Dumont lived in Algeria, the pulse of French resistance. A twenty-one year old corporal left without an army with the fall of France, the entrepreneurial Dumont founded his own intelligence organization with associates numbering into the thousands.

A particularly useful contact for Justin keenly interested in keeping a close eye on Vichy, Jean Paul maintained sole power and control over his side of the line, including deciding what and when to hit, or if there should be a hit at all.

Justin did not like that part of the arrangement any better than Nellie did. Jean Paul's "side of the line" arguably stretched from the western border of Libya, deep into the Great and small Atlas mountains of Algeria, north to Tunisia, and south to the ancient Tamanrasset region where Jean Paul left the protection of the southern Sahara to the fabled forces of Leclerc.

General Leclerc, whether Jean Paul actually knew him, or was just blowing smoke, was no fable. To where de Gaulle fought the war from the comfort of London radio, Leclerc's arse was on the line. Few knew his real name, or his background, for reasons as many as they were irrelevant. Leclerc's commitment to the fight in North Africa and from there the liberation of Paris was indisputable and unsurpassed. His mistrust of the British to a degree innate, to another acquired, nevertheless set aside for the greater good, rather like Pete and his Irish Nationalism. England should be so lucky as to come up with her own version of Leclerc, particularly since Germany had come up with its Rommel.

Despite Leclerc or de Gaulle, French and British relations in North Africa were not good, barely civil. Justin was there to make use of what he could, not strain them further by dismissing one of France's loyal and hardworking sons, at least openly. Privately, valuable though Jean Paul might be, he was not immune from Justin, or his scrutiny.

Around the end of January, Justin finally managed to come up with the linguistic expert he was also looking for, Lieutenant Jeff Mulrooney, British Army. A young fellow, about Joe's age who spoke something like thirty different dialects and languages—Pete didn't know—including the big three: French, German, and Italian, what got Mulrooney his commission, Pete believed that, because it sure wasn't for any other reason, not that Pete could see. When Mulrooney finally showed up about a month later, Pete did not like him and did not want him, whether or not he could read and write hieroglyphics. Mulrooney was nervous, chewed his nails, and "liked it the Catholic way" as Pete called it, referring, with all due respect, to the time-honored method of birth control among the heterosexual faithful. Specific to Mulrooney, Pete meant he was a sodomite, homosexual. Pete, who had spent at least half of the last twenty years in jail, objected to men who "liked it the Catholic way" versus those who made do.

Justin probably objected too on the basis of some moral principle should he take moral principles into consideration, which he did not. Mulrooney, when he finally showed up, was a fair, somewhat nervous young man, who, yes, had a tendency to bite his thumbnail, at least park it between his lower teeth during moments of thoughtful consideration before responding with hopefully the right answer to the questions put to him by the intimidating Squadron Leader Charles.

And so, Mulrooney had a tell. Joe had a tell. A tendency to swipe his hand across the back of his neck when trying not to say something he wanted to say. There was nothing unusual about that. A lot of people had tells, certainly most men. It meant something, of course, always did. Stood for something. Compensated. Occasionally for nerves or some other failing.

"Yes, well, we can't all be perfect." Justin sat back in his chair and lit his pipe, getting down to what he was inclined to consider. Such as field experience, which Mulrooney unabashedly had none. In fact, he was almost entirely inexperienced, six months at best, which, yes, might set someone to wondering what in hell he had been doing the first two years of the war.

"Trying to grow a beard," Bobby muttered something to that effect, in reference to how Mulrooney looked even younger than he was. Justin checked the top sheet. He was twenty-four and unmarried.

Twenty-four was probably older than most fellows on the front lines regardless of how "young" it was. His age was fine and went in the *For* column opposite the lack of experience in the *Against*. Not married was mandatory, non-negotiable, whether or not Mulrooney could read and translate the Rosetta Stone or whatever it was Pete had said. Justin less considerate of widowing some poor week-old bride than the simple reality his casualty figures for first time recruits was somewhere in the neighborhood of 93-94 percent. The fellow wasn't coming back, in other words, hadn't a chance. And, so, yes, Justin supposed if he cared to acknowledge it, consideration of some widowed bride did figure into the equation.

So did experience. With two checks in the *For* column, not having any was a life-sized handicap to overcome. Some sort of Cabaret spiritualist who talked to the dead in a plethora of tongues, one look at Mulrooney explained his lack of experience despite being two years deep into the war. He hadn't made the cut, whether he had tried or not. He had, according to his sheet, and promptly failed. Spent time like the rest of his artistic crowd entertaining the troops until someone in the audience realized the "act" included a fellow who could speak in tongues, and the rules changed.

The army's rules perhaps, but not necessarily Justin's. Shy of Pete's exaggeration of thirty languages or dialects, Mulrooney did speak two Arabic dialects, and six languages fluently including the big three. Arabic, admittedly was interesting, useful since Justin's tongue was limited and five years rusty, almost as bad as Pete's.

What figured more was Mulrooney failing the army's physical, and therefore stood about a cat's chance in Hell in measuring up to Justin's strict requirements, which were the desert's requirements, survival for something more than an hour. Meeting the height well enough at six-feet, Mulrooney had to be two stone shy of the minimum weight and just too damn white. The desert would consume him first time out.

Had damn near consumed him his first time in. Justin considered the sunburned face sitting at attention in front of him, the pasty pale skin red, blistered, and painfully raw.

"Aye, well, he's a decent shot," Bobby shifted in his fat, adding that to the *For* vote likely only because he wanted to see how long it would take Pete to vomit outright.

"Which Peter is about to," Pete assured. "God love me, the only damn company's he's toured with is the bloody burlesque crowd. He's an entertainer—pardon me, *artiste!*" his finger jammed down on the file. "It says so right there. *Troupe performer.* It doesn't say that? *Troupe performer?*"

"Yes, well, I believe they meant troop performer," Justin said, "as in performing for the troops. Quite all right, same thing. And, all right," he decided, "we'll give it a go. See how it goes. Can always put him with Nel, I suppose, if too many of the fellows take offense."

Bobby eyed him. "You sure?"

"How the devil do I know?" Justin said. "Ask Pete. He's the one insisting he's a sodomite."

"He is," Pete assured.

"Then it ought to be all right," Justin agreed since so was Nel.

"All right, I'll get on it," Bobby hoisted himself to his feet to begin their check on the fellow's background. "Got a few things he can do in the meantime, not too much harm to anybody."

"Got quite a lot he can do," Justin assured, "for that matter, eat. While you're at it get a bit more information on why he failed his physical. According to this he should have passed. Damn near did pass," he grunted, meaning theirs. "Nothing here three squares a day can't cure."

"Aye, well, that's not why he failed, lad," Bobby hinted, apparently secretly agreeing with Pete, though he'd never let it be known.

"Yes, well, believe we took care of that," Justin handed the file off to Bobby.

"I don't want him," Pete said.

"Be a few weeks before you have him," Justin assured. "If he's that good, I might keep him here."

"Your prerogative," Pete supported.

"Yes," Justin said.

Joe was the one who nicknamed Jeff, Hollywood. Nel, who abbreviated it to Holly, though usually called him, *boy,* as he did with most others. Pete had the dubious honor of being right, Bobby, the dubious honor of being wrong, at least in finding nothing remarkable in Jeff's background, at least not right off. As far as Jeff? Yes, well, Jeff was not only as good with languages as his file claimed, he had the distinct honor of being the first mistake Justin had made in years—or was he?

"Bobby," Justin said after Pete had left, "Make sure you get a bit more on this knack he apparently has with languages. Won't go as far as saying it's unheard of, but it is unusual."

"He's a knack," Bobby shrugged.

"Yes." Justin read that.

"Uses it in his act," Bobby said. "You know, talking to the dead."

"Yes." Why Justin stopped reading. "Didn't make the infantry, but it's a guaranteed ticket to Bletchley and the lot of us. Think it's possible we've got ourselves a mole. Make sure you find the connection."

Bobby scoffed. "Oh, right, lad, who doesn't know that? Got Jerry written all over him."

"Just find it, if it's there," Justin said.

"Will," Bobby promised. "Will at that."

That was the lot of them, except Jean Paul also employed personal bodyguards, which Justin did not do. The Germans and presiding Vichy government had known of Jean Paul a long time, and Jean Paul was not sitting in an office in Cairo, the Eighth Army surrounding him, he was sitting in a hut somewhere in the Algerian Atlas Mountains.

Chapter Eighteen

Cairo
March 6

"Where?" Thirty-seven year old SS Hauptmann Eric Danzig of the Propaganda Ministry sat up straight in his disguise to turn around and stare thoughtfully at his wall full of maps. A large, gregarious man with a misleadingly glib style Eric looked and felt somewhat ridiculous in his Arab robes complete with sandaled feet, but what worked, worked, and for some reason dressing like an overweight Lawrence worked. "Really ..." Eric nodded along. "You don't say ..."

Oh, but, twenty-four year old Lieutenant Jeff Mulrooney aka Hollywood aka SS Oberleutnant Peter Reiss did say with a bat of his baby blues and tip of his tow-blond head, a line of raggedy teeth fixed in a pasty smile.

Horse manure. And they would get to that, yes. Right now though: "Yes, well, I suppose we'll have to find out more about this, won't we?" Eric picked up the telephone at his side to discuss with his superiors, so they could discuss with their superiors, this rumored link between something called the British Long Range Desert Troops and some French Resistance Group headed by a man code name Charlies? Eric was lost already, and disinterested either way, none of this having anything to do with him as far as he could see.

"Charlie!" the lieutenant stopped filing his nails to snap. "And it is not rumor. Charles commands an array of forces, an array."

Big even. Impressive, if it extended from Algeria to the Western Desert and Cairo, Eric would go along with that. "Beg your pardon," Eric begged his superior's pardon with a wave at the lieutenant to keep his thin-lipped trap shut, "make that Char*ly*. Yes, of course I understand ..." And, of course, Eric did understand how the identity of Charlie took precedence over the already identified Jean Paul Dumont.

"Who?" Eric frowned, but continued along, agreeing with complete and utter confidence, a contorted expression, and a shrug. "Oh, yes. I am thoroughly confident photographs can and will be quickly secured of this ... one moment ..." he grabbed a piece of paper and a pen, hastily scribbling down, "Major Justin Charles ... Believed to be potential candidate ...

"Well," Eric straightened up, beaming into the telephone, "I rather doubt if we didn't believe Charles to be a potential candidate we would be wasting our time trying to take a picture of him—I'll get a picture of him!" Eric promised faithfully, extending the receiver to arm's length, and even that wasn't far enough, "if I have to take it myself." With that, he hung up the telephone to sit back and stare somewhat blindly at the almanac of photographs and facts presented to him by this Peter Reiss, a Russian, no less. A Russian operant engaged as a spy for the German SS while spying on the English, and of course the French. It was a complicated world, extremely. Occasionally too complex.

"I have photographs of Charles," the Russian's squeaky and irritating little voice penetrated Eric's heavy masculine thoughts.

"I know that," Eric assured being as he was currently looking at them right?

"Right," Eric massaged the aching temples of his tired brow with his thumbs. He did not like the Russians, as most of his kind did not. There was no reason why he should like them. He especially did not like this one sitting impatiently across the table from him. A man, Eric dared to call Jeff, wrapped up in his long girly figure and fine artistic hands, fixed in self-absorption. Disconcerting for a less confident man than himself Eric would suspect, there was a reason why these he-she types were not only discouraged by the new Reich, but openly shunned and shot.

Eric straightened up again (not really but at least he didn't appear to be falling asleep), acknowledging the Russian's intolerant expression with his own counterfeit smile, alluding to how underneath it all he might be as contemptible as this grappling wannabe, striving for a world that wasn't his. Wealth and riches, Eric would personally settle for, and after that, wine, women, and song. Eric was exactly who this Russian was underneath it all. They all were. Liars, if they said they weren't.

"Let me try putting it this way, Lieutenant Mulrooney ..." Eric nodded, a haughty opening statement, timeless and well worn.

"Reiss. Peter Reiss." Jeff interrupted coldly, not particularly liking his employers, the Allied, or the Axis, any more than they liked him, especially this one. Danzig. Eric Danzig. An arrogant German who thought he was more than what he was, which was nothing. Jeff eyed Eric, hunger in his thoughts. He was there for a reason. Desperation some might say, anxious to regain property stolen from him by these Germans, or just revenge. He could taste the pleasure of death in his mouth, and he would get Eric Danzig, the same as he would get the thieves, after he was done with him, after there was no need. His head cocked, not like a girl's, more like a serpent or snake waiting to spring. Danzig seemed to be oblivious to his fate, more interested in his own voice.

Eric was interested in only his own voice for reasons other than he was German, and the lieutenant was not. Eric could barely understand the Russian Reiss calling himself Jeff today. Barely follow him, when he could understand him. Reiss's syntax, while better than most, remained inevitably punctuated with awkwardness, struggling through the nuances of his adopted language of his adopted land that separated the native-born from the imposter.

Eric smiled. He smiled when he couldn't understand Jeff, and he smiled when he could. He smiled because he always smiled. The same as he never meant his smile, certainly not now. Why would he? His difficulty with the Russian's speech, his overall disinterest in being treated to a lecture on British intelligence efforts to rout out and trample Germans where and when they found them, taking a back seat to being simply agog at this Russian who seemed to think Eric should be interested enough to be willing to pay for the information.

"Or whatever your name is," Eric agreed. "Let me see if I have this right. I wouldn't be here, you wouldn't be here, if it wasn't for the fact ..." Eric checked the wordy and rambling report, searching for *the* name among all the names listed, certain there had to be someone in particular responsible for his detour other than this Russian with his high hopes and pipe dreams.

"Weiheber," the Russian informed him with a sneer. Herr SS Major Hanse Weiheber, big and bad and stereotypical as they came, even his skin was unclean. The flesh, dark, pitted and taunt in a Goebbels-like way. But then they made them that way if they weren't, didn't they? *Picked* them on occasion apparently with this Weiheber who appeared to be some sort of Czech implant, one of Himmler's clowns. Eric was of the Ministry, and therefore one of Goebbels'.

Now, *that* could prove to be a problem, yes, it could. Prophetic even and certainly as good a reason as any as to why Eric's immediate and direct superiors felt an hour or two dialoguing with some Russian comrade could not hurt. They did not get along Herr Goebbels of the Ministry, and Herr Himmler of the SS. Something far less publically known than Hitler's invasion of Russia ...

Well, perhaps something *somewhat* less publically known, Eric acknowledged. At the very least, something not talked about. Loudly, anyway. Whichever, and so what? So, Herr Goebbels and Herr Himmler did not get along, but were instead entrenched and preoccupied with stealing each other's thunder, with Goebbels currently odd man out of Hitler's divine favor. This was *news?* To whom was this news? Certainly not to Eric who knew regardless of who might be in or out now that would soon, if not surely change.

Oh, yes, *that* Eric knew for a fact, regardless of who else knew what, or thought they did, including some Major Weiheber. Eric had never heard of Weiheber. He had no idea who Weiheber was, or thought he might be, other than by way of his dossier. A sizable packet handed to Eric when he stepped off his plane, reasonably expecting to step onto another, only to be ushered away and eventually here to meet with some *Russian,* and buy, of all things, *buy* whatever the little Soviet seemed to think he had to sell. "And he is not my Major, he is my contact, like you," the Russian was saying whether true or false. "Old, and still much to prove."

Eric looked up. He didn't do anything. He just looked at the prickly little twig he could snap in two with a flick of his broad meaty hand.

"Well?" Jeff said impatiently.

"He has something to prove, you mean. To Berlin," Eric smiled. "Yes," Eric had spotted it finally, two or three paragraphs down. SS Major Hanse Weiheber lately of Berlin, and Eric was no more, and couldn't be any less interested now than he was before, so therefore, remember it? Probably not. But then Eric was *the* Berlin connection to the five top-secret German munitions complexes buried in the bowels of the Sahara and elsewhere. Algeria, Eric believed. Three were reportedly in Algeria, two in Libya, the closest almost two thousand kilometers from the front lines. That sounded like a lot to Eric, but he had been reassured how it wasn't in the grand scheme of things, and they were—the complexes—*extremely* interesting to Herr Goebbels screw Himmler and his boys.

"It's called politics, Lieutenant," Eric enlightened Jeff to Weiheber's scheme. "Let's, for the moment, anyway, forget politics, and try to stick to the facts."

And Eric's fact-finding mission to rout out the facts surrounding the five secret munitions complexes—*unauthorized* would probably be a better description since munitions complexes were seldom secret for very long, their munitions complexes, or anyone else's, though they were usually authorized, which these five were not. No, they were tantamount to a rebellion, possibly even treason, sedition at the very least, if one wanted to be hardnosed about it, which the Ministry did not, not necessarily. An unusual situation, admittedly, and time, of course, would ultimately tell, and time for the moment, was on Eric's side. His assignment, much like the installations, was also secret, if not extraordinarily sensitive. Early reports suggested the instigator could very well turn out to be General Rommel. Field Marshal-to-be Erwin Rommel, his name appearing (however invisibly) on the bottom line. His fingerprints smeared over every page. And Rommel, in case this Russian was unaware, was something of a National Institution to Germany, and therefore sensitive? Oh, ha, ha, *sensitive,* Eric supposed could be the operative word for his mission and subsequent how-best-to-handle the rebellious going's on within the ranks of the German rear services of North Afrika and keep the proverbial egg off the faces of the Axis, not the Allied, who, right now, Eric personally didn't give two pfennig about.

The SS was how, and not some random blitzkrieging outfit to go in boots kicking and guns blazing, but the Propaganda Ministry historically proven in its ability to sell anything to anyone, including itself.

Case in point. Eric looked around the sweating room, a veritable oven, veritable. It escaped him, truly, what conquering this place, for that matter Siberia, had to do with ruling the world. "How did you say all of this was connected again, Lieutenant?" he verified, still having trouble with Jeff's speech whether he could understand what he said or not. "I mean, other than the war?

"I mean, Lieutenant," he turned back with his smile for Jeff, "specifically connected, specifically to me aka Germany. Talk. Make it quick and keep it short."

"It isn't, wasn't," Jeff assured, alluding to how it might be now? "You have your Major Weiheber to thank for that."

Meaningless, utterly, the Russian was clearly playing some game. Eric nodded. "Is that English accent for real?" he wondered, a natural question, but Jeff just looked at him, and Eric continued to smile back. "Make that short, quick, and to the point."

"Fine," Jeff shrugged. "I give Charles to you or you to Charles. Which is it?"

"Which," Eric glanced down on the paper mountain sprawled in front of him. "Well, that," he agreed, "is elementary. However, Lieutenant, I believe you need to understand irrespective of the Ministry having no intentions of being sold to the Allies it's not to be construed as an offer to *buy* anything from you regardless of what some ... *Major Weiheber*, may have led you to believe. Is that clear, Lieutenant?" he smiled, "Or would you like me to repeat it? Clarify perhaps?

"I mean, Lieutenant," he continued to smile, "hypothetically, of course, but, if for example, you were to die from a sudden bullet hole, I would have all of this, the Ministry would be safe, and you would have nothing. Unless I'm missing something. Am I missing something, Lieutenant? What am I missing?" he asked.

"*Weiheber,"* Jeff assured.

"Weiheber," Eric digested. "Are you saying, Lieutenant ..." he inquired when it just sort of lay there undigested, "Himmler—

pardon me, *Weiheber,* is poised to sell the Ministry to the Allies? That is absurd, Lieutenant, utterly absurd, politics aside."

Jeff shrugged.

"Fine," Eric agreed, "have it your way—not forgetting, of course," he said, "hypothetically, I could always torture you to make you talk."

"Weiheber is there," Jeff leaned forward—loomed, actually, leered, suddenly, with a lick of his lips either literally or he just seemed to lick his lips. Eric almost recoiled, but did not. The Russian was good, he'd give him that much. A real confidence artist, sizing up his audience identifying their weaknesses and playing on them, using them to his advantage. "At your complex."

"What complex?" Eric didn't move a muscle, didn't flinch, but pitched the ball right back at him.

Jeff's head tipped. "Fine," he said, "let him destroy them, it doesn't matter to me, that's up to you. I was employed to secure something for him. He took it, and I want it back. I want you to get it for me, or, yes," he promised, "I will give your complexes to the Allies."

"Funny," Eric smiled, "to think I thought you were going to say something more like how you tried to sell him something he either took without paying, or didn't take, and in either case you're looking to sell me something. You're an information specialist, Lieutenant, let's be honest with one another. You buy and sell information. Is that closer, Lieutenant?" he asked, sure that it was. Particularly since he wasn't sure there was such a thing as a quadruple agent. That would seem a bit overdone.

"Weiheber is Gestapo," Jeff sneered. *"Gestapo."* A dated term, defunct. Apparently these Russians were not only behind the 8-ball, they were a few years behind the times. "He isn't just anyone, he is Gestapo."

Eric smiled. "I trust you mean SS, Lieutenant, SA, SD. We are one, after all. All for one, and naturally, one for all ..." he fingered the paper mountain, not for any particular reason, only because it was there. "Not good enough, Lieutenant. I want to know what you wanted to sell Weiheber. What he took, or didn't take, whichever the case may be."

"Better idea," Jeff countered, "you worry about what he wants—*Rommel*. Now," he said, "do we have a deal? Or would you like me to clarify it for *you*, Hauptmann? You give me what I want, I give you what you want ... and Weiheber?" he dismissed. "He's yours. Free of charge."

Eric smiled. "The crux of my point, Lieutenant—*Rommel,*" he clarified. "Forgetting how astounded I might be that you seem to think we would acknowledge the existence of some *rumored* complex, General Rommel is precisely what separates Herr Goebbels from the pack."

"Oh?" Jeff said.

"Definitely," Eric assured. "Setting aside General Rommel's celebrity status among the general populous, if the whole truth be known, he actually isn't well liked by most of the *General* population who consider him to be something of an upstart. Interestingly enough, and certainly, under the circumstances you propose, quite apropos. A rogue in hero's clothing," he smiled, "independent. You seem shocked, Lieutenant, I don't know why. Surely, it stands to reason if Herr Himmler has heard these rumors of complexes, if Herr Goebbels is who Herr Goebbels is, and I can assure you he is, the Ministry has no doubt heard the rumors as well.

"It doesn't mean they're true," Eric shook his head, "No, it does not mean that at all. What it does do is illustrate the basic difference between your Herr Himmler, and mein Herr Goebbels who understands exactly what your Herr Himmler has apparently chosen to forget—and that would be a sincere appreciation of who likes General Rommel most of all—Hitler," he promised. "So enough with the idle threats, Lieutenant, about—"

"Charles," Jeff interjected.

"Yes, well, definitely enough of that," Eric's eyes rolled. "Really, Lieutenant, you and what army are going to get anywhere near—"

"Your complexes," Jeff assured.

"The nearest shithole!" Eric snapped. "You're not only suicidal, Lieutenant, you're nuts if you really think the Ministry is about to back off for fear of you handing anyone over to anyone whether it's Himmler, some Weiheber—or this man!" he snatched up one of the photographs of the so-called Charles. "Or this one!" he snatched up one of the shots of someone named Nellie. “Or any other of your Allied chums!”

“No,” Jeff said.

“No,” Eric agreed. “because you can’t, Lieutenant. Not because you wouldn’t, or naturally shouldn’t since you’re not working for them, but are working for me ...” he ogled the picture of the serious and emaciated Charles with the receding hairline and bulging eyes. “Consumption?” Eric hazarded what was a reasonable guess. “Cancer? Death?”

Jeff sneered. “Are you a doctor?”

“Car salesman,” Eric grinned. “Used cars. The Propaganda Ministry a simple matter of evolution ... and since we’re on the subject ...” he poured himself a bourbon from the bottle on the desk, “I should take a moment to clarify the Ministry’s position on any threat of Allied ... well, Allied threat,” he waved. “Call it what you like. We don’t care. No, we don’t,” he downed the bourbon with a shake of his head. “They’re supposed to try and find us. Hound, harass, rout out and destroy us, and we are supposed to do exactly the same thing to them. It’s the name of the game, and the game is war.

“On the other hand,” Eric said, “you can be assured, Lieutenant, as well as assure anyone you care to, the Ministry does care very much about the suggestion our army would have the audacity to steal and keep our munitions for ourselves rather than give them all away to the Italians as we have been instructed to do. The Italians are our allies. They are our friends.

“They are stupid, incompetent oafs,” Eric shrugged, knowing that as well, “who will never win this war I don’t care what new Caesar sits on their throne.

“But, regardless, Lieutenant,” he nodded at Jeff, “we are to supply them. Nurture, spoon-feed, and diaper them throughout their fight, which is our fight—though only Hitler knows how that happened,” he admitted. “Whether or not we have enough for ourselves is irrelevant.”

“And that order doesn’t come from me, Lieutenant,” he continued to nod emphatically at Jeff, “it comes from Berlin. We are to win this war Berlin’s way, even if we lose. To dare to do anything else is treason, and the traitors will pay with their lives.”

"Oberleutnant," Jeff stuck in, crossing and uncrossing his legs in an expression of boredom, "Herr SS Oberleutnant Peter Reiss. Lieutenant Mulrooney is dead. I know. I killed him. I needed his papers, and I needed his name."

"Painfully," Eric smiled, thinking of his Luger tucked safely under his robes, the warm sweating leather of its holster tickling the saturated hairs of his barrel chest. He was not a violent man by nature, but he could learn to be, yes, he could. The choice was there, the choice just that, a choice, and it was all his. Fortunately, for the Russian, it not only seemed a waste of a precious bullet, it also seemed a waste of time. Eric returned to the subject of the compounds. "Unless, of course it is determined Rommel is behind this novel idea of keeping a bullet or two," he said. "No, we won't hang General Rommel," he shook his head in certainty, "I can assure you. We'll kiss his ass as we always do, and wish him Godspeed ... And, that, Lieutenant," he winked, "is no propaganda.

"Now ..." he folded his hands across the almanac of facts and faces, the moist celluloid immediately gluing itself to his sticky wet arms, proving what he said about the Propaganda Ministry's ability to sell anything, even this place. "Unless you have something significant, or even relevant to add, which clearly you don't, I suggest you leave the way you came in, considering this to be your lucky day. Arrivederci, auf wiedersehen, adieu."

"Herr Major Weiheber is at your complex," Jeff replied. "You may not want him to be there, you can *deny* anything you please. He is there to destroy them and he has something that belongs to me. If he does not return it, I will do what I need to do, including giving your complexes to Charles. It is up to you."

"Lucky as in you get to live," Eric smiled back. "You're going to have to do better than that. Proof would go a long way, evidence. So far I've heard and seen none."

"Yes," Jeff knew. He was something like a minute or two away from being shot. "You have a great deal of faith in these walls, Captain. Personally, I wouldn't chance it. Why don't you break my neck instead?"

"I wouldn't say it's faith in the walls, Lieutenant." Eric rose to check his reflection in the soiled window panes of this average two-story mud building sandwiched between dozens of others not far from the hub of commerce, high-life, and intrigue, to see what he could do about his appearance that was about as believable as the B-films they cranked out by the hundreds. But then this was also a very naïve world, pathetically so, not just suddenly so extraordinarily complex. He smiled. "More faith in the neighborhood. The clock is ticking, Lieutenant, you either give it up—all of it, or get out while you still can—leaving, of course, Charles," Eric nodded. "Yes, you can leave the binder behind. I wouldn't want to appear unappreciative of all your hard work."

"He has the daughter of an Italian nuclear physicist with him," Jeff said, and Eric quite literally almost put his own eye out as he repaired his sweat-soggy grease paint. "If she dies, I would think the chances of finding the physicist would be more difficult than they already are.

"But then," he smiled as Eric stared at him, "I also wouldn't want the Ministry to think I lack appreciation of the interest in developing atomic power—before the Allies," he said, "and, yes," he shrugged, "before Russia, if you insist. But only if we have a deal." he assured. "So, I don't know, " he said as Eric stumbled back to the table, "do we?"

Eric did not stumble, he walked. Poured another bourbon and was perfectly fine now that his eye had stopped watering and the feeling had returned to his fingers and toes. "Ah!" he even extolled happily after downing his drink. "So for all my bluster I'm actually intrigued."

"It's a one-time opportunity," Jeff forewarned him. "Here while I am here, gone when I am gone."

"Just get on with it," Eric suggested.

"Fine," Jeff shrugged. "Charles is Charlie. Some sort of code for his fingerprints. You know this already. Your superiors confirmed it for you."

So they had. "Not Charles. The hell with Charles. That I can read." He wouldn't, but that was beside the point. He would keep the almanac and give it to someone else to read, someone much better with those sorts of details than he was. "And cut to the point, Lieutenant," he sat down with a wave for the mess littering his desk.

"What would you consider proof?" Jeff confirmed.

"Oh, I don't know," Eric said. "I'll know it when I hear it, how's that?" he tapped his watch. "Time, Lieutenant. One-two-three-*Go*."

Jeff shrugged again. "The American intrigued Weiheber—I knew the American would," he assured. "I needed the girl to get to Charles. He took the girl even though he knew that." He sat back. "The girl is the daughter of the physicist."

"Yes," Eric agreed, "you said that."

Jeff sat forward again. "Weiheber does not know what he has."

"Six to one, half a dozen to the other," Eric cautioned. "It's entirely possible he does know—or why he took her."

"No," Jeff shook his head. "No. Weiheber is a cocaine addict. A drunken old man," he indicated Eric's bourbon with his chin. "He appeared obsessed only with the complexes instead of what he was there for. *I* tracked the girl from Europe to Africa. Her itinerary Tobruk, and then Gibraltar to the United States—"

"Of America," Eric interjected. "Explains the American engineer. Interesting ... and, continue, please," he encouraged Jeff who had stopped. "Continue."

"Their contact was Charles, some British Intelligence officer named Charles."

"Who you promised Weiheber," Eric nodded, "as you promised him ... this *American* ..."

"Gave," Jeff assured. "I gave Weiheber the American. I needed the girl to get Charles. To find him."

"You have Charles," Eric indicated his desk.

"Now," Jeff agreed. "Not then. I had to find another way to get to him and I did. Mulrooney. So, do we have a deal, Hauptmann?"

"For me to assist you in securing an atomic scientist for Stalin—which apparently no one has regardless of who else they may or may not have?" Eric checked. "Well, I don't know, Lieutenant, let me think about that." He stood up and started collecting up the Russian's collection of faces and facts.

"What are you doing?" Jeff scowled.

"Me?" Eric smiled. "I'm leaving."

"Are you crazy?" Jeff leapt to his feet, his fist striking the desk.

Crazy? No. Eric smoked, drank, and ate a bit more than he

should upon occasion, but, no, he wasn't crazy. "Lieutenant ..." he said. "Well, Lieutenant ..." he said, picking up the particularly unflattering black and white glossy of the unsavory looking Charles. "In the first place, British, I'll grant you, and therefore enemy, as in foe, but honestly, Lieutenant," he whipped the picture around for Jeff to see, "if this is the picture of an intelligence officer, then boy is the Axis in for one hell of a surprise."

"What?" Jeff said.

"A joke, Lieutenant," Eric assured, his tongue firmly planted in his cheek. "He's ugly, Lieutenant," he helped Jeff out. "Extremely. Physically defective. It's elementary the spiritual, moral, and intellectual abilities therefore are, and must be, equally flawed ... Herr Goebbels, of course," he dropped the photograph down, "an exception to the rule. Herr Goebbels is an artist, and, well, we all know how artists are ..."

"You're missing the point!" Jeff insisted.

No, Eric wasn't. "You want Weiheber ... or rather this girl with him ..."

"*Daughter,*" Jeff assured. "Daughter of an atomic scientist. Yes, I want her. She is the hostage to secure the physicist. Either that or you pay for the physicist now. I have not done all of this work for nothing."

"Now we're getting to the crux of things," Eric smiled. "To do that you need my help as Weiheber is apparently at these ... *complexes*," he waved, "you think we have."

"You do," Jeff assured.

"Perhaps," Eric smiled. "In exchange I get to keep our complexes, and also Charles as a booby-prize. Do I have that right?"

"If you believe in National heroes," Jeff agreed. "That they are heroes, not upstarts, yes, you have it right."

"The Rommel card," Eric pointed.

"The Rommel card," Jeff assured.

"What if I want it all, Lieutenant?" Eric wondered. "What's to stop me? Especially since I appear to already have it all. The complexes, Weiheber, the girl ... even Charles whom you just gave me. I'll just ship the girl to Berlin. No doubt there are a few experts there who can coax her father out of hiding. What do I need you for?"

"Charles thinks the French can tell him about your depots," Jeff said.

"The French?" Eric said.

"Jean Paul Dumont," Jeff nodded at the telephone.

"Oh," Eric said. "Right ... *Dumont*." And here to think he was just about to say: "What the hell are you talking about?" Instead, he smiled, "Oh, well, they can't tell him."

"Are you so sure about that?" Jeff challenged with a cocky swish of his head.

"I'm positive," Eric grinned. "But then the Germans can't tell me about my munitions depots. They're a secret even from us. Now, if you will excuse me," he picked the binder up with a friendly pat. "I have a plane to catch."

"Yes," Jeff sneered, "for your complexes and your national heroes. You should know, Captain, he killed his First Officer six months ago, two others before him. He has a lifetime of defying authority, including his father's, who he deposed at fourteen. I wouldn't expect an honor guard to greet you, if I were you."

"Weiheber?" Eric guessed, though not to suggest he was impressed.

"You tell me," Jeff smiled, a soulless satanic leer.

"Weiheber," Eric nodded. "Sounds demonic, you're right. Definitely not something anyone would ever associate with the SS. We will have to set him straight."

Always it was something funny. Jeff eyed the comedian. "Are you sure you're SS?"

"Oh, yes," Eric crossed his cold though beating heart. "Are you sure you are?"

"Yes," Jeff assured.

"Bullshit," Eric whispered. "You're nothing, and you will always be nothing, I don't care whose clothes you wear. But that's all right," Eric nodded, "yes, it is. You say you have my 16th Army surrounded at Staraya, and it will only be a matter of time, one million-five casualties the first six months of the war. I say, in your Siberian dreams. By summer, your mother Russia will be utterly destroyed."

"According to you," Jeff said. "We'll see which one of us is right. Personally, I think the one with the scientist stands a better chance than the one with the daughter." He turned to walk out, Eric's foot catching him sharply on the sole of his behind as he turned, knocking him flat.

"I mean, Lieutenant," Eric crouched down so Jeff could see him eye to eye, his Luger out and pointed at Jeff's chest, "you do not seriously think anyone is going to buy into your single-handed ability to make or break one of the greatest heroes Germany has ever known unless we see things your way? Do you? Do you really? Because let me repeat, you and what army, Lieutenant? You and what army?"

"The 8th," Jeff smiled. "Who will win the war London's way even if they lose. So far they haven't. The offer is Charles, Captain. Charles for Weiheber. Before you say no again, remember your complexes and whose signature appears on the bottom line."

Eric was remembering the complexes. "What Himmler calls impertinence on the part of the Afrika Korps, the Ministry is quite prepared to call ingenious—providing of course, it is Rommel," he clarified, "and this plan to ensure sufficient supplies for his annual march across the desert for the gates of Alexandria works, which we sincerely hope it does. After all, it will be his second try. And if Napoleon could do it, Alexander, quite obviously, and a Caesar or two without the advantages of empty guns and cardboard tanks, then we really don't have much of an excuse for our failure, now, do we?"

"I don't know," Jeff said. "Do you?"

"That would be ingenious, as in ingenuity, Lieutenant," Eric explained, though not to suggest Stalin knew anything about that. "Strength, superiority, and last but not least, balls. We have them. Trust me when I say there are none larger. Now, tell me again how Weiheber doesn't know what he has in the girl, and how much Charles knows about the scientist ... and, yes, of course, these complexes while you're at it."

"Oh?" Jeff countered smartly, "What happened to no deal?

"I'm the one with the gun," Eric reminded.

"Yes," Jeff said, "and I'm the one offering you the opportunity to take a scientist home to Berlin, not simply ship his daughter. Fame, Captain. You like fame. I can see it in your eyes. You lust for it, after it. You're Weiheber twenty years ago. You want to be Weiheber now when you're fifty, or do you want to be Herr Goebbels?"

"Did I forget to say tell me now?" Eric checked.

"Weiheber knows nothing," Jeff assured. "He thinks he has an American spy. The girl merely his PA—personal assistant," he explained.

"Secretary," Eric nodded, "yes, I have it. And Charles?"

"He shouldn't have wanted her," Jeff insisted, "Weiheber. He shouldn't have cared. He should have listened when I said I could use her to get to the American's British partner Charles. But he didn't listen because he's an idiot. Seeing spies, spies, everywhere."

"And Charles?" Eric encouraged.

"About the scientist?" Jeff said. "Nothing. He knows nothing. The American Colonel was the connection. Acting on behalf of the United States. They gave him introduction papers and sent him to secure assistance from Charles in getting the girl out of Europe to the United States. They never arrived in Tobruk, so, no, Charles knows nothing, not yet. Who knows if the United States will even tell him, They probably won't."

"How elating," Eric beamed. "And, of course," he said, "explains why we, not he, are called Superman ... Or at least, I am," he agreed. "Dare I ask are you sure about this, Lieutenant? You wouldn't be trying to pull a fast one on me, would you?"

"I'm positive," Jeff assured. "He knows nothing. It was all a mess. Charles wasn't even in Tobruk, he's in Cairo, and not waiting for the American Colonel or some daughter or anyone. They are a piece of paper in a file about a lost American envoy, stamped received three weeks ago."

"But you're sure the scientist is out there," Eric said.

"He is or he will be," Jeff promised. "The itinerary was Cairo to Tobruk, Gibraltar, to the United States, as I told you. The American Colonel is an engineer, Malcolm McDowell. He was traveling from Cairo to Tobruk with his aide, Paul Reid, and his driver—that's the girl. The aide is dead; I know. I'm the aide and I killed him."

"I thought it was Mulrooney you killed," Eric smiled and Jeff paused. "Continue."

"I'm Mulrooney." Jeff said.

"Ah!" Eric said. "Continue."

"The girl's papers are false. The scientist is Italian."

"And your name? I mean, his name?" Eric asked.

"I don't know," Jeff assured. "The recognition code is her assumed name: *Joanna Lee.* Remember it. *Joanna Lee.* Tobruk and Charles were dead-ends. They're out there, Hauptmann," he assured. "The contacts, and the scientist. We need the girl to find them."

"Or a girl," Eric smiled, "But we'll worry about that later. How many men does this Weiheber have with him?"

"Six or seven," Jeff shrugged. "And an officer, SS Leutnant Günther Faust.

Eric's eyes rolled. "In total, Lieutenant. He must at least have a platoon."

"Then he has a platoon," Jeff agreed. "Fine. Have it your way. I don't know. He is an envoy from Berlin out of Tunis where they all are—where *we* all are. He was supposed to be my contact. He came but he was not interested. Only in the complexes. When I could tell him nothing about them, he took the girl."

"Ah!" Eric said. "So he took what he could get."

"Do we have a deal or not, Hauptmann?" Jeff asked. "Such opportunities only come around once in a lifetime."

Eric was thinking about it, considering his Luger, and settling for a sprinkling of coins as he stood up. "Keep the change. In the meantime, Lieutenant," he said as Jeff glared, "I want you to find out precisely ... and I mean *precisely* what this *Charles* knows about the compounds. *IF* he knows anything at all, and report to me. Do you understand? *Me.* Not Russia, Mussolini, *Japan,* or anyone else who may enter your head, but *me* alone."

"And the scientist?" Jeff said.

Eric smiled, "Well, obviously if you come upon any information relative to the scientist, be sure *not* to include it in your written report. After all, we wouldn't want information like that falling into the wrong hands, now would we, Lieutenant? I'm sure you realize this "girl" could be dead, if this Weiheber is really oblivious to her value, and even then ... presuming any of this is even true. There's one way to find out—and don't worry, we will be in touch either way. True or false, Lieutenant, your story true or false, we will be in touch. In the meantime, not a word, Lieutenant, not *one* word," he stressed, "to anyone. I'm sure you understand that as well."

"Asshole," Jeff picked himself up off the floor as the door closed behind Danzig, moving on to get back to the allied side of town before Nellie started wondering where he was.

Chapter Nineteen

Cairo
March 9

Justin studied Nellie sitting there in a WWI doughboy helmet for some damn reason or another.

"What's the matter, Charlie?" Nellie drawled, his Irish brogue distorted by ten years of South African dialect having to confuse the hell out of the Yanks from Tennessee. "Can you tell ol' Nellie?"

The matter was a munitions depot Nel had reported in western Libya, south of the Tunisian border, south of the Coast Road, damn bang on the dividing line between Justin's and Jean Paul's territory. The supposed site spitting distance from Gadames, a dazzling mythical city bathed in marble on the Algerian-Libyan border few even knew was there. "If they brought them in at Bone, or Phillipeville ..." Justin began slowly, watching Nellie's smile spread with the implication of Algeria.

"Quite," Justin said, "it could be Algeria, or it could be Tunis. Out of Sicily, into dock, from there, fairly straight shot to the Coast Road, straight as any."

"This ain't along the Coast, Charlie," Nellie reminded.

No, it wasn't. It was inland, and dry as a bone.

"It's not Algeria," Justin assured. "Not worth it."

"Oh, well, now," Nellie chuckled, "it's not Algeria because that's Johnnie's territory, and Johnnie would know if someone were using him as a pipeline."

Jean Paul would know that went without saying. It wasn't Algeria because it wasn't worth it whether Jerry decided to cross into Tunisia for Tunis, or just head south. South, they'd hit the mountains and the Erg. It would take them a month and they would still never make it. Crossing north from the Algerian seaports into Tunisia also wasn't worth it. More mountains and time, losing whatever they hoped to gain by taking the long way around and down to the Coast Road.

"You still got Tripoli," Nellie reminded.

Yes. Or rather Mussolini had Tripoli, shared Tripoli with Rommel, yet to lose it even once in this war that had both sides moving forward as often as they fell into retreat. After a year, they were almost back to square one with Jerry on one side and England on the other of the Gazala Line, neither moving, both fair to say recuperating, long on troops and short on ammunition and supplies, England with the added burden of what was quickly becoming a round-robin of Generals. If Rommel struck now, he'd win. For some reason he was quiet. Justin, somewhat less interested in knowing why Rommel was quiet, than in making sure he stayed that way.

He ogled Nellie through a haze of pipe smoke, pensive and undecided. If the port at Tripoli made the most sense, some depot four hundred miles west of her did not when Rommel sat hungry and waiting eight hundred miles to her east. Justin had a few threads to follow, but no pattern yet. Uncertain if there even was a pattern. Currently he had two reliable reports of depots in almost random locations, and then both of them confirmed gone, vanished, from his own men, stationed in the west to keep an eye on things. Conclusion: there were no depots. Early reports were wrong. That made Jean Paul right who insisted there were no depots, and Justin's men wrong, who insisted there were. Justin had to presume his men were right. So, where did the depots come from, why were they there, and where did they go? Justin had insufficient information to answer any of those questions and only enough information to conclude something was wrong.

"Something's wrong, Nel," Justin said.

"Not this time, Charlie," Nellie smiled easily.

Not twice, he meant. No two depots there and then suddenly both gone. "Sounds more like transfer stations than depots," Justin lit his pipe. "Large enough apparently for the fellows to think they might be looking at a depot, but ultimately since they're both gone, the installations weren't fixed, but only temporary."

"Awful lot of supplies, Charlie," Nellie said.

"Yes," Justin agreed. A transfer station of that reported size implied troop movement, of which there was none at the front lines, let alone a thousand miles to its rear. "More of those facts. There's also been no damn convoy in here in months if you care to add that to the pot. So, quite. Where the hell did they come from and where did they go?" Justin sloshed an early Scotch into his teacup and rose for his maps, his pipe clenched in his teeth.

"Algeria," Justin pinned the map at the Algeria-Libya border. Jerries moving into Algeria under Jean Paul's nose.

"Sebha," Justin pinned the map at the location of the reported Italian stronghold in central Libya. "Any deeper and they would be treading into Leclerc's territory and there's been no reports out of there, so, quite. Up from Sebha if they came out of it, down south to Sebha if they went in. There's no other choice. Let's say up for the moment and then where, since they didn't come this way ..." he scanned the map. "Algeria," he nodded. "You're right. They'd have to move into Libya to circumvent the Erg. Out of Algeria, down to Sebha, or up from Sebha into Algeria. Still doesn't explain why or where, but we'll figure it out. Jean Paul's been sloppy, that's the point, or he's covering for someone who's been sloppy or worse. Won't have it, can't. Source isn't worth it unless it's reliable, too risky otherwise, too much depending upon it, too many."

"Something's wrong, Charlie," Nellie agreed, "I can feel it in my bones."

"Then let's get back out there and find out what it is," Justin relit his pipe, sitting back down at his desk, "before Rommel renews his push for Tobruk, Cairo ... and," he nodded, "the world. Someone's out there moving supplies around we need to know the details. Jean Paul's probably been trying to rout them, clearly with limited success. We'll consider that to the situation, unless you come back to me with something different. Got that?"

"Aye," Nellie said.

"Good," Justin said. "Take Holly with you. He can use the experience, and you can use the help with the lingo. I'll let you know when everything's been set up, where you and Jean Paul will meet, and when. In the meantime, you and Holly will have a few days to check things out before I let Jean Paul in on it, so get on it now, the two of you. The usual place. Frank's not here, so he can't bring you out, but it will be Frank who picks you and Holly up."

"Aye," Nellie rose with a stretch.

"Oh, and Nel?" Justin said with a point of his pipe stem at Nellie's outdated steel bonnet. "Take that damn tin cap off your head. It's a Yank's in the first place, and the wrong damn war."

"Oh, well, now I know that, I do," Nellie's eyes raised, surveying his helmet with a chuckle. "But, you see, it's my halo. Holly gave it to me. Said without it, it was hard not to mistake me for the devil."

"Yes, well, you are the devil, Nel," Justin assured, "so take it off. The fellows already think we're nutter, no need to rub it in."

"If you say," Nellie sighed, compliant about it either way.

"Thank you," Justin said and made a note to have Bobby pull Mulrooney's file for review now of whatever Bobby had been able to come up with to date. Mulrooney was hard core if he was a mole, out of line, if he wasn't. Fraternization within the ranks was not allowed under the rulebook, and Justin, in general, ignored those who broke the rule as long as it didn't spill over into the work. His reward for his leniency was it seldom did. All of them dabbled from time to time, himself included, with the usual number of a few more serious players, Joe being one of them. It wasn't unusual for Nel to participate, more often than not, easier to handle whenever he had a boy to pal around with. Mulrooney was the current boy. Somewhat more flagrant than Justin had anticipated with his self-conscious stammer and nervous stares, Mulrooney had so far managed to keep all but the most ardent hecklers at arm's length, Nel, in the background more or less guaranteeing his success. This was flagrant though, and Justin wasn't about to jeopardize Nellie's position with the men for some fop undercover or in heat.

"Oh, and, Charlie?" Nellie mentioned as his hand touched the door. "Bobby wanted me to be sure and tell you, not to be adding to your troubles, but there's a boy by the name of Michael who's been waiting to see you. Doc Michael, he says he is, and Bobby says to tell you he can't speak for his papers, but the fingerprints do match."

Justin had stopped being surprised years ago at anything Michael might do. That apparently included showing up in Cairo in the middle of the war. He already had a note to the fact Mike had. A memo handed to him by his secretary when he walked in. Justin underscored the note he had already written on the memo. “Thank you,” Justin said. “Joe will set you and Holly up with a decent pack radio. Stay close to it. Holly’s all right as second radio, but I rather it was you.”

“Aye,” Nellie assured, and left.

“Ruddy bastard,” Justin picked up the phone for Bobby.

“*Got my message*?” Bobby answered no humor in his voice or question.

“Got it,” Justin said. “Pull Mulrooney’s file and we’ll look over what you’ve got. Seen the helmet, I take it. Out of character for Nel, completely. Fellow’s a tease apparently, not quite as shy with Nel as he appears around others, a flatterer for some reason, likely his own, possibly for any number of reasons including Mata Hari. Want to know now.”

“*Aye, I’ve got it,*” Bobby assured. “*Anything else*?”

He meant Mike. “Yes,” Justin said, “see what’s out on the wire, and then we’ll talk. Might be something out there of interest we should know about first.”

“*On it,*” Bobby said. “*The Doc what have you wondering about Mata Hari*?”

“Yes, well, Mulrooney’s the wrong kind of blond to get anywhere near Mike,” Justin said, “so no. That secretary’s more his type. Told Joe earlier for you to get rid of her. Now, do it. Get her out of here,” he crumbled the note into a ball. “Drown her in the damn Nile. I don’t care what you do. We’ll have Joe cover the room and see what Mike has to say, if anything, before we shut things down.”

“*All right*.”

“Let me know if you find anything or not before sending Mike up.”

“*Aye,*” Bobby said.

“Sons of bitches. “ Justin hung up and lit his pipe, setting the damn memo ablaze while he was at it, and that took care of that.

Michael looked nervous, trying hard not to be when he walked in. That was a little surprising alongside everything else that was routine. The silk white suit, straw hat, his penchant for alcohol showing a little more on his face, tanned, with lines around his eyes, Mike was two years older than Justin, always managing to look ten years younger, not any more. Mike looked his age, yet to act it though. It had been two years or more, since they had seen each other. Justin hadn't made Joe's memorial, something to do with the war. Mike made it, of course. Flew in from Cuba, claimed to have, and probably had, so what was putting in an appearance in Cairo by comparison to making it through the bombardment of Britain? Not much. Nothing was much with Michael. Not even the war. Least of all the war until it suited his fancy, which it apparently had a month or so ago per Bobby's preliminary report, until the bottle took over.

America, Mike's home town, slow to enter the fight until Japan hadn't been quite as relaxed in coaxing its limited number of physicists back from foreign shores for the green hills of home. Two years and counting since Washington first made the call to gather 'round the flag, with Mike one of the last holdouts. But that would change. Six months at best, was Justin's guess, and Michael would be looking at becoming official government property whether he wanted to or not.

"Yeah, well, who the fuck are you supposed to be?" Michael got down to basics in his assessment of Justin. One look over Rip Van Chuckles sitting there in black face, shorts up his ass, and not much else, was all it took. "It ain't Christmas, so it's got to be Halloween."

"Yes, well, could ask the same of you ... *Rocky*," Justin read over Michael's "official" letters of introduction signed by *MGM*.

"'*Angels with Dirty Faces*'," Michael pointed. "One of the best damn films Cagney's made. And try fucking *Warner Brothers*, OK? Jack and the others, what's-their-names, can never think of the other ones' names."

"Wouldn't know." Justin tossed the papers in the general direction of the rest of Michael's belongings surrounding him. "No offense to you or your Mr. Cagney."

"Hey," Michael said. "You think I don't have more? I've got more."

"Yes." No doubt, introducing Michael as *Bugs Bunny*. Another of his favorite characters, if Justin remembered correctly.

"Uh, huh," Michael said. "You mean kinda like you and Mr. Hyde?"

"Yes," Justin gave a nod toward a chair parked not too far to the right. "It's all right, Mike, have a seat. Long way to come just to say hi. Sure you're here for a reason, so let's have it. Word on the street is you're looking at twenty years to life in Leavenworth this time if they don't hang you. Something to do with the Manhattan Project being rather big to think you can just walk off."

"Yeah, well, the word is wrong," Michael kicked the chair up a little closer, but did not sit down. "I didn't walk, I ran. First, unless you consider four guys sitting around scratching their asses a project, it ain't a project, nor will it be for some time. Second, it's got about as much to do with New York as you do, and third, they're looking to make bombs, Chuck, not a better bubble gum. If I screw up and drop one of those, no one will have to tell you, you'll hear it from here."

"Yes, well, there's a way around that," Justin lit his pipe and leaned back. "Get back on the wagon."

"Wrong again," Michael eyed the pile of his stuff that looked remarkably like the stuff he had packed in his duffel bag before someone took it all out. "First I've got to be on the wagon to fall off. Second ..."

"You don't want to," Justin retrieved the Scotch and a glass from his desk, setting it down. "Ten minutes, Mike, and then it's my turn. I'm on a clock, you know."

Hey, Michael could leave now. He wasn't chained. Not to anybody or anything, not there. "That it?" he indicated the rot-gut.

"That's it," Justin said.

"You always were a cheap son-of-a-bitch," Michael dug in his pocket for a cigarette. "I suppose there's a water shortage here as well."

"Is," Justin said.

"Explains the smell," Michael poured himself a double dose though something told him he could drink the bottle and it wouldn't make life any better, or easier. "Not for nothing, but there was a river around here the last time I was in town, pretty big one. Push comes to shove, you take what you can get, know what I mean?"

"Maybe tomorrow," Justin checked his watch.

“Explains why she keeps the door shut,” Michael ignored the time check, downing his Scotch with a flick of his head toward the blonde bombshell who sat outside looking suspiciously like the celluloid doll he had met downstairs. “That’s a looker, by the way. Don’t know how the hell you managed it, and something tells me I’ll up, Chuck, if you tell me, so don’t.”

“Five minutes left, Mike,” Justin nodded.

“Fuck you,” Michael poured himself another with an eye on his duffle. “I sat around fucking nine hours waiting for you.”

“Three maybe,” Justin agreed. “Just about zero-nine, now. Nellie said you came in around six.”

“Nellie,” Michael said. “That the big one with the red hair?”

“Is,” Justin acknowledged.

“Outdid yourself with him,” Michael assured. “A turnip’s got a bigger frontal lobe.”

“Yes, well, you trawl the pubs, Mike, I trawl the jails,” Justin reached for the Scotch to put it away. “Some of the fellows can be pretty rough at first. Need a crew boss, not a shoulder to cry on—”

“Cry this!” Michael drained half his drink, firing the rest at Justin followed by a pair of underwear. “Those are my fucking shorts!”

“That they are,” Justin calmly plucked them from his shoulder, opting to wipe his face with one of Michael’s shirts instead.

“Yeah, well, who the fuck are you to tell some geek to clean my ass with his nails?” Michael insisted. “What the hell did you think I would be carrying in there?”

“I don’t know, Mike,” Justin agreed, “what were you carrying in there?”

“Shit!” Michael assured. “And I should have fucking given it to him.”

“Yes, well ... ” Justin relit his pipe with a nod for the door where the secretary sat outside waiting to be relieved as soon as Bobby got off his duff and took care of it. “Think you could tone it down a little?”

“Tone this!” Michael grabbed his groin. “Fuck her along with you. How would you like someone’s fingers rammed up your ass? You’re a piece of work, Chuck, you know that? A real piece of work.” He sat down with a snatch for the Scotch.

“Said cool it, Mike,” Justin picked up the phone to ring Joe who answered with a laugh, knowing what the Maj wanted and it was for Bobby to get his ass upstairs and get rid of the dame.

The phone on Joe's end was a radio console, a behemoth, the size of one of the walls down in the dungeon of the building, the heart of Justin's command. Deep below ground where the air was cool, moist, and loud with the sound of jackhammers drilling into the building's granite footprint and frame, extending the bunker a hundred yards out under the street, and what would eventually be quarters for Justin and his staff when completed. A series of cell-like rooms, comfortably sized. Right now, they all lived together dormitory style in the main area about half the size of a football field. Joe was luckier than most in that he got to spend at least half of his time with his radio, walled off from the construction by a haphazard collection of doors, sound panels, and blankets when they ran out of anything else, to protect the sensitive equipment.

The dirt, dust, and noise still managed to find its way in however, as dirt, dust, and noise does, but Joe just wore a full headset so he could hear, and maintain an acceptable level of confidentiality by not having to scream. If someone wanted him, they could always call him on the radio or tap him on the shoulder. Usually it was Bobby quick to move his workshop of gadgets and guns into Joe's space. They got along fine though. Joe, happy for the company as long as he had room for his pinups and barbells, Bobby, able to tune out Joe's "need to unload" that could have Joe going on for hours before he took a breath.

Joe felt the need somewhat more frequently than Bobby might secretly appreciate, but they still got along fine. Even Justin occasionally wandered down from his office to visit their homey little setup to eye the pinups and the barbells, poke over Bobby's workbench, and share a beer, which Joe usually managed to have handy. When Joe couldn't, it was because he was down to his last dime with three weeks to go because he had gambled it all away, or spent it on other necessities such as dancing and girls. Justin and Bobby were generous however, kicking in with their fair share, and in return, living vicariously through Joe enjoying his exploits as much as he enjoyed them.

"Just cost one of us half a buck," Joe's hearty laugh cackled in answer to Justin's call before Justin had a chance to say anything. That was all right because Justin wasn't anticipating on having to say much. Joe was covering the room as instructed, listening to every word, the tape running, his feet propped up on the console of the radio, a bottle of water in his hand. "Figured you'd be hollering for help before long, but Bobby says, nah ..." he winked at Bobby keeping him company, poking through his assortment of toys like an old elf, looking for something to do now that Jeff had left the roost on his first overnight outing. "You just remembered Laur and want her out of here."

"That's right, lad," Bobby nodded. "That's what I said, and it's unchanged from what I said before. He can do it himself, too, if he wants it done. Nothing wrong with that lass. Just doing her job. Should leave her alone and let her do it. Tell him I said that. Go on, tell him."

"Yes, well," Justin replied in Joe's ear, keeping it simple, and presuming *Laur* was the latest secretary, *"that sounds about right."*

"Yeah, OK, we're on it," Joe assured with a wave at Bobby to keep it down before the Maj heard him. "Or at least Bobby is. She's out of here. On his way. Five minutes tops. Consider it done."

"Aye, I'm on it," Bobby promised in chorus, not moving much, for that matter, not moving at all, just sitting there, ignoring the inevitable for as long as he could.

"So, um ..." Joe grinned into the hand receiver trying to picture Justin all stiff-lipped and dignified trying not to shrink from every other *fuck* thrown at him by some guy named Doc. "Doing OK there otherwise? Need a hand with anything else?"

"*Yes, well,*" Justin said, "*no.*"

"Suit yourself," Joe clicked off with a reminder for Bobby. "Says he wants Laur out of here."

"I know what he said," Bobby assured. "And that's four bits, please. Told you that was what he wanted, and he did. He's getting better at checking up, too. Lass didn't even make three hours today. Pretty soon he'll be meeting her at the door with a damn gun since he knows neither of us will be; he's wise to us, lad, wise to us."

"Yeah, well, don't hurry on my account," Joe tossed him the change and straightened up, sending the Maj's office to the speakers while he checked a few other channels to see what else might be going on in the world. "I'm in no hurry to see her leave. Just saying that's twice he's told you."

"Aye, and he can tell me twice more, too," Bobby groaned at Michael's colorful nasal rant filling the room at some ear-splitting decibel worse than any jackhammer. "Don't think so, lad. Shut it down. That's confidential."

"Nice try," Joe tried not to laugh as Bobby clicked off the speakers. "But you cleared the place out, remember? Nobody here but us chickens, so don't worry about it. I'm on a schedule here, too, you know. Got work to do."

"Got more work if I break it," Bobby threatened. "Sorry, lad, but what you've got to do is to sit there and listen for however long it takes. Nothing else you have to do you can't do later."

"You mean like getting rid of Laur?" Joe grinned.

"I'll escort the lass out of here when I get around to it," Bobby assured. "Not my arse or me you have to worry about. Fifty laps, I'm telling you for that crack about lending him a hand with the Doc. Four bits says you're looking at fifty laps, and then only if he's feeling generous."

"Nah, twenty-five," Joe said, "maybe, at most. He's got a sense of humor, and besides, it's hot out there."

"Aye, well, you keep dreaming," Bobby said.

"Yeah, he is a pistol, isn't he?" Joe agreed.

"Who?" Bobby said. "The Doc? Right. Pistol," he sputtered. "More like a pain in the arse is what he is. Always has been."

"Oh, yeah?" Joe said. "Why? You know him?"

"No," Bobby was happy to say, and could have lived without meeting him now. "Of him, of course. And right about him, I can tell you, Justin is."

"Nah, he's harmless," Joe promised. "Grew up with guys like that, you know? Six to every street corner. Oh, yeah," if he closed his eyes right now between the dust and the smells and the Doc in the background he couldn't tell he wasn't home. "Just kind of surprising the Maj knows him."

"Oh?" Bobby said. "Why so?"

"I don't know," Joe shrugged. "Just kind of surprising that's all."

"Well, he knows us, lad," Bobby nodded, "remember that. He's not some snob, if that's what you're saying."

"No," Joe said. "Saying it's kind of surprising. Guys like that, kind of low on class—what?" he asked. "You saying we don't have class?"

"No, I'm saying," Bobby tapped on the console, "pay attention to what you're supposed to be doing. Fellow's not harmless, capable of anything."

"Yeah, well, school's out," Joe nodded, "remember? And I passed, long ago. Been covering the room—what, like a month, right? Got to be a month, at least. Listening to some jerk for an hour as some sort of final exam isn't going to change that. Because ... yeah, OK, the guy's a jerk," he agreed, "calling himself *Bugs Bunny,* and, yeah, yakking about bombs like a show off. He's a big mouth. Thinks he should be bigger than he is. I'm telling you," he said, "I know these guys, grew up with them. Wouldn't want to be in a bar with him, heck no, apt to find myself in trouble, picking up daisies because he decided to mouth off to the wrong guy." He settled back in his seat listening and paying attention like he was told to do. "The Maj is a big boy, he can handle him. If he can't, well then, heck, probably I should be in there with him, right? Instead of sitting here listening, keeping an *ear* on things." Joe was quiet for a few seconds. "Yeah, OK," he said finally, "I surrender, what is this crap about bombs? He serious?"

"No," Bobby passed it off. "Just checking the boundaries. See how far he can go. It's all right. Justin can take care of himself, you're right. What he can't do, is pick his family. No one can."

"Huh?" Joe said.

"That's his family, lad. Doesn't share it with many. Doesn't share it at all," Bobby acknowledged. "Be stupid if he did. Still likes an ear kept on things, though. Usually it's me sitting there ... Aye, always it's me," he agreed. "Right now it's you, though, and it's about as confidential as it can get. Remember that, lad. Don't remember, and he will kill you. Trust me, he will kill you."

"Get out of town," Joe stared at the console. "That's his family?"

"Aye," Bobby chuckled slightly at Joe sitting there at a loss for words for a change, possibly for the first time in his life. "Well, don't take it to heart, lad," he said. "Relax. Clearly, he trusts you. That's the point. I'm getting old, lad, can't sit there like I used to—especially through that ballyhoo," his eyes rolled. "Needs someone who can, when he needs them. Not often, I can assure you. Once in a blue moon, if that—lad," he clouted Joe's arm. "You still with us? Not going to have to talk with him about it, if that's what you're worried about. He doesn't talk to anyone save for me, if there's something he feels he needs to talk about, rare unto itself."

"Huh?" Joe's head turned to him.

Bobby smiled. "Saying you're not going to have to talk with Justin, lad."

"What?" Joe said. "No," he shook his head, "I wasn't thinking that—I mean, heck, guy wants to talk, let him talk. I'm just saying—wow," he whistled at the console, "the Maj's family. Wouldn't have thought that."

"Oh?" Bobby said.

"Well, no," Joe said. "I don't know."

"Not what you expected," Bobby nodded.

"Heck no."

"Aye," Bobby nodded. "It's all right. That's it, though."

"No kidding," Joe said. "What is he? I mean," he said as Bobby looked at him. "He sounds like ... I don't know, *me*? You know, American."

"Oh," Bobby said. "Well, aye, he is. Italian, I believe. Like you."

"Yeah, well, that figures," Joe scoffed with a laugh. "Christ, I probably did see him on a street corner. What's he look like?"

"What?" Bobby was frowning slightly, stretching for the second headset. "Oh, I don't know what he looks like, lad. Looks like what he sounds like ..."

"No, that's OK, I got it," Joe got the headset for him. "I'm cool though, don't worry about it. Mum's the word."

"No, I know that, lad, I know," Bobby agreed. "Just a little curious myself, have to admit. Hope nothing's happened to any of them," he frowned again slightly as the Doc came in clear.

"Oh, yeah?" Joe grinned. "You mean there's more of them?"

"Well, not of him," Bobby assured. "God help me. Only one of him. But there's a few of them, aye, a few ..." he was still frowning. "Old fellow is whom I'm thinking about. Got to be ... oh, I don't know, seventy? Eighty? Not his old man," he advised. "No, Justin's old man is dead. Mother as well. They'll get into that, aye," he nodded. "You'll here that. The Doc'll be bringing that up before long if he hasn't already."

"Um ... no," Joe said. "No, I don't think so."

"Aye, well, pay attention, lad," Bobby reminded. "That's even more the point."

"Yeah, I am. I am. I got it. It's OK. Go on. Get Laur out of here. I'll probably still be here when you get back; oh, yeah," he grinned at the Doc going on and on. "Definitely will be here. I need help, I'll holler, and if the Maj needs me, well, I'll hear him."

"I'm going, I'm going," Bobby said. "Justin can take care of that, too, if he really wanted to. Get that Peterson on the blower and tell him right out instead of leaving you and me to do his dirty work. Lad's a coward. You should know that if you haven't figured it out. Damn coward when it comes to the ladies. Like they're going to bite him or something. Take his head off and hand it back to him ..." The Doc was talking about something now that sounded like trouble, definitely sounded like trouble.

Chapter Twenty

"It's called security, Mike." Justin hung up the phone after saying a fat lot of nothing, which meant either the place was wired, or he liked to pretend it was. "Some of us care about that. Bobby and Nel don't know you—or *Rocky Sullivan,*" he granted, "from Adam."

"Bobby, huh?" Michael would bet his mother's uncle he was being broadcasted live and in stereo over a loud speaker somewhere. "That the fat one with the same first and last name?"

"Yes," Justin said between puffs on his pipe-load of camel manure. "And, quite, I outdid myself with Bobby, also."

"Wrong," Michael said. "You outdid yourself with the blue-haired fairy."

Justin glanced at the door, seeming to remember Peterson's latest Mistress of Public Relations was a blonde.

"Fairy," Michael helped him out, "being the operative word."

"Oh," Justin said. "Yes. Jeff. Yes, well, Jeff ..." he said.

"Is a fucking faggot," Michael assured. "He's a fucking faggot."

Meaning a homosexual, not a ball of meat. Justin understood without having to ring Joe for a translation. "Your point?" he asked, but only because Joseph Lee had been homosexual. Though that hadn't stopped Joe from giving his life for his country, any more than it had precluded him from being Justin's or Michael's friend for thirty years, though Justin suspected it was occasionally to Michael's chagrin.

"Nothing," Michael's nervousness seemed to increase, lighting a cigarette with the one he was smoking. "Got a few of them where I come from, too."

"Yes, well, if that's it ..." Justin reached for the Scotch, on the alert that time, but Michael's glass was dry. "Your ten minutes are up, Mike."

"No, that's not it!" Michael was up with a snap and a grab for the bottle, slamming it down on the desk. "Keep your fucking shirt on!" He got up to walk around a while, critique the joint while he smoked his cigarette. He didn't like the place, of course, any more than he liked the fellows. Justin let Michael go on another ten minutes or so of a lot of jabber and not much else, until he had to call it quits.

"Mike ... " Justin said.

"Look!" Michael turned around. "I've got a headline that reads a friend of mine's been missing for a couple of days ..."

"*Whoa.*" Down in the dungeon Joe blinked at Bobby. "Think we've got something here?"

"Aye ... maybe," Bobby nodded, "maybe ..." listening intently like you couldn't hear the Doc across the room through the headphones. "Put one of those corks you're always talking about in your mouth, and get me that report."

"Um ... report ..." Joe looked around.

"The one I pulled on him, lad," Bobby said. "Third file, top drawer, it's right there; *Michael Delegianis.* Dr. Michael Delegianis."

"Um ... yup, got it!" Joe was already up and rummaging through the drawers, finding it under *A*, rather than *D*, since Bobby being Bobby just stuck it in the front where he could find it. "A for asshole!"

"Just give it to me," Bobby insisted.

"Ya got it!" Joe shoved it in his hand, leaning over his shoulder, helping him dissect it. "But there's nothing here, unless you're going to tell me it's in code or something."

"Said cork it, lad," Bobby reminded, trying to read three pages in Olympic time. "If someone else has gone missing from that project of his we'd know."

"Project?" Joe said.

"Project," Bobby was up and heading for the Telex faster than Joe had ever seen him move. "That Manhattan business's no joke, lad, no joke, wish it was."

"Huh?" Joe said. "Oh, yeah, right, got it, got it," he remembered what the Doc had said. "And, I didn't think it was a joke ..." Joe snatched up his headset because, wow, *hello*! One of them really should be listening. "Thought it was ... don't know ... like a dame, or something. Him just trying to be clever. You know, 'Manhattan project'? Heck, was thinking of using it myself ..."

"Atomic bombs," Bobby nodded, typing away. "What, he's talking about, lad, atomic-powered bombs," he assured Joe suddenly gone quiet again. "It's what he is. A physicist."

"Yeah, I got it," Joe assured, his headset clapped to his ear. "Talking about some Colonel ... fuck!" he snapped his fingers in excitement, dropped the headset, hit the speakers so they could listen, and headed back to the cabinets. "I know where that is!"

"Lad!" Bobby reminded as Michael blared out into the room.

"It's OK," Joe assured, "there's no one here remember ... there's a report. I saw the frigging report, a couple of weeks ago ... fuck!" he kicked the drawer closed, yanking open another, as Bobby glanced at the console. "Goddamn Jeff ..."

"Jeff?" Bobby's head snapped up.

"Yeah, I had him helping me ..." Joe nodded.

"Who says?" Bobby demanded.

"I sez," Joe assured. "It's OK, don't sweat it. Nothing important. Just the routine crap that comes in—Christ!" he slammed that drawer closed, too, hunting through a third. "If the Maj just let Laur do her goddamn job ... if I explained the goddamn system to Jeff a hundred times ..."

"Lad!" Bobby insisted.

"I got it, I got it!" Joe yanked it out. "Siwa, February 21st ... what I fucking tell you, huh?" he said, handing it over. "What I fucking tell you?"

"Eighteenth, actually," Bobby scanned it, and it was pretty basic, though he wouldn't go as far as calling it routine. It still wasn't much though, save for them being Americans. "On or about."

"Yeah," Joe nodded, "yeah. So, um ... what's this about bombs?" he took a breath. Christ, he was so hepped up, he was almost gasping. "You on the level?"

"Don't know what you mean, 'on the level'," Bobby started typing again. "No bomb out there, if that's what you're worried about."

"No, I know that," Joe assured. "Hell, yeah, heck I know that. I'm just saying what's going on? What do you think is going on?"

“Seeing if we can find out,” Bobby nodded. “What’s that fellow’s name again?”

“Um ... McDowell,” Joe read. “Yeah, McDowell. Two *L*’s. Want me to do that?”

“I got it,” Bobby assured. “I got it.”

“Not that that means anything to you,” Michael drank his drink.

“Should it?” Justin sat back easily in his chair waiting for the bomb to drop, hopefully not on them.

Michael ignored him, staring into space. “I mean it’s like I was sitting in Manhattan, see ...”

New York USA
February 1942

“Mike ...” Lucky Seven pried himself away from the lady in the blue dress to answer the telephone before it tolled its final bell. “Mike!” he hollered like the neighborhood he was raised in instead of the uptown Park Avenue digs he was living in now with the linen shades and white deco charm.

“Keep your shirt on.” Michael emerged from the can. A place he always seemed to be going into or coming out of at a crucial moment in his life. “I’m trying to take a fucking leak. Can’t a guy take a fucking leak without someone yelling fire?”

“It’s England,” Lucky extended the phone.

“England?” Michael stared at the receiver. “New or old?” Though he knew, yeah, he knew which it was. The same as he knew who and why, and, Jesus fucking Christ what had she gotten herself into now?

“I don’t know,” Lucky shrugged, which was why he was called *Lucky* since he didn’t have a brain in his head.

“Give me the frigging phone,” Michael grabbed it. “And get her the hell out of here, what do you think this is? A motel?”

“We’re going to dinner,” Lucky reminded.

“Yeah, *we’re* going to dinner,” Michael nodded. “Nix on the Queen of Washington Heights—hello?” he answered the call.

“Oh, well, now, not trying to rain on anyone’s parade,” the old man Gramps chuckled in between bites of static and Michael’s heart sank.

"Nah, it's not raining," Michael dragged the phone over to the bar, looking for a little fortification, his brain working overtime on what to say, what not to say, how to get out of this one with his hide. "Kind of late for you though, isn't it?" he checked his watch that appeared to have stopped in sync with his heart. "Like two o'clock?"

"*About*," Evelyn agreed. "*Yes, just about.*"

"Yeah, well, before you read me the riot act for being here and not there," Michael decided to go for broke, but only because he was caught without a prayer. "I can explain ..."

"*Oh, no.*" Evelyn laughed so hard Michael thought the old guy would pop a vessel, convinced Gramps had popped one with the next breath he took. "*No, not necessary, not at all. I understand, yes, that I do. I understand completely. Called, as a matter-of-fact, to tell you that. Did. That I did.*"

"Oh, yeah?" Michael stopped beating the daylights out of his martini to check under the bar for a pipe bomb complete with fuse. "What, have you been hitting the sauce? Got the place wired to explode? Or have you figured out we're at war?" Not personally, of course, but Gramps knew what he meant.

Did. That Evelyn did. "*Well, now that's the point, isn't it*?" he agreed. "*And that's all right, is. Not going to say I told you so. No, not going to say that.*"

"Um ... " Michael wiped his chin. "Yeah, OK, what's the point? Said like three things. Sauce, bomb, war. Which is the point? You listening, Gramps? We've got kind of a bad connection on this end, or you do. I'm not following you."

"*You just give Joanna my love*," Evelyn suggested, "*and go out to that dinner of yours. After all*," he said, "*that is the point, now, isn't it? Yes, that it is*," he assured. "*Get out. Test her wings, live a little. And*," he said, while Michael tried to figure out just what the hell he was talking about, "*coming up on a rather ... well, don't want to say special*," he clarified. "*Nothing special about it. But, it is an anniversary, call it what you will. Ten years. Yes, that it is, ten years.*"

"Huh?" Michael said.

"*So you and Joanna just go to that dinner of yours*," Evelyn said again, and that time it registered, at least what he said. "*Don't let me keep you.*"

"Joanna?" Michael stared at the telephone.

"*She there*?" Evelyn asked a touch wistfully, missing her, of course he did, especially now that she was six-thousand miles away, not just off in London where if he missed her too much he could just get in the car and drive to see her for himself. The States? Yes, well, the States was something else entirely, even for him, what with the war. Hard enough to get a damn call through, yes, that it was, difficult enough.

"Joanna?" Michael repeated, his heart—fuck pound, it was hammering like a snare drum in his chest. "What? You forget you dialed zero or something? I'm in New York, Gramps."

"*Yes, well, you be sure to tell her everything's fine, it's fine*," Evelyn said, nodded actually, on his end.

"Yeah, it's great," Michael agreed impatiently. "Whoa. Talk to me, Gramps, I'm losing you over here. Where ... wow," he cleared his head, untying his tongue while he was at it. "Where the fuck else would she be?"

"*Exactly*," Evelyn chuckled and Michael almost passed out, he did, almost collapsed, his elbow missing the edge of the bar as he sat down, the telephone more or less frozen in his hand.

"*And I would have rung sooner* ..." the old man was saying, "*But, well, not easy even for me nowadays and I didn't want to be a bother, after all, she is with you* ..."

"She's in the can," Michael shook his head not quite sure why he said that or where he even came up with it. "She went downstairs for ice cream, we're having a fucking heat wave. I mean ... whoa," he didn't know what he meant, or even where to begin.

"*So see you*?" Evelyn checked in his own way, subtly, just when she might be coming back? "*In a few more weeks*?"

"Why?" Michael said, barely. "Why, how long has it—FUCK!" he caught himself, trying again evenly. "How the fuck long has it been since we've seen you? An hour? Couple of days? A week? A fucking month of Sundays? Gramps!" he said, trying to wrack his brains and figure out when the last time it was he had talked to Joanna—yesterday. He was sure it had been yesterday. Maybe the day before.

"*You just go to that dinner of yours*," Evelyn reassured one last time, and Ma Bell took care of the rest.

"Fuck," Michael sat there with the telephone dangling in his hand. "I mean, fuck!" he slammed it down to pick it up dial furiously and slam it down again.

That was two weeks ago, count them, almost three and Michael could still see Lucky and his round-eyed broad staring at him like nobody ever misplaced a kid before in their life. Like nobody ever got up in the morning and didn't have somebody they had when they went to bed the night before.

Cairo
March 9
"Mahlon," Michael said dully to Justin almost three weeks later in Cairo after combing the goddamn planet for Joanna and coming up short every time. "You have the fucking report, Chuck," he reminded.

"Did you read the goddamn report?" he asked. "Mahlon McDowell. Colonel. USA."

"Yes ..." Justin recalled hearing something about a Yank Colonel now that Michael filled in a few details. "That's a couple of weeks ago, Mike, at least. Doubt if he's MIA. They brought his driver in."

"Aide," Michael said. "Paul Reid was his aide."

"Wouldn't know," Justin apologized. "Sorry, didn't realize you knew him."

"Kind of," Michael said. "Sort of. He's an engineer."

"Yes," Justin assumed he'd be something like that, though one shouldn't ever assume. Weren't many Yanks here yet who weren't engineers or geologists, swelling the ranks of those already looking for the oil everyone knew had to be out there. "Bit out of your line of work, isn't it?"

"League," Michael said. "Bit out of my league. Career. Big time. Like you."

"Heavy water then," Justin agreed. Those experiments also pretty much standard nowadays, too, North Africa no exception to the rule. "Still, if what you're doing out here is looking for answers, I can see what I can find out, though I suspect you'll find it's pretty cut and dried—"

"Red's missing," Michael interjected, and downstairs Joe's head snapped up from reading the Telex. "Red. You know, Joanna? Your sister? She was with him. I'm pretty sure she was with him ..." he frowned while Justin just sat there his eyes set, concentrating.

"*Holy fucking shit* ..." down in the dungeon Joe broke with a whistle and was gone, just gone, across the room and gone before Bobby could bark at him to get on it, he was yelling, "I'm on it! I'm on it!" Screw the elevator, he was up the stairs, all of them, breaking the quarter mile record as he rounded the corner to grab Scarecrow by his collar, bust through the doors, skid for Laura and get her the hell out of there before someone said something they shouldn't say, and she overheard them. He wasn't in time entirely, but he tried, gave it his best.

"Christ, Chuck," Michael stared bleary-eyed back at Justin. "I don't fucking know. She was supposed to be with him. I've been killing myself for, yeah, weeks, trying to find out if she was still with him. Hoping to God she wasn't or that she's not ...

"But, you see," he squinted through the tears starting to burn, "it's kind of like this. If she's not with him, I don't know where the hell she is because I can't find her. I cannot find her. I do not have a clue."

Chapter Twenty-One

The Fezzan
March 9

SS Major Hanse Weiheber sat comfortably cool in his inappropriate desert attire. His fingers curled around the first of his remaining three cigarettes, his men huddled together for warmth, Faust's wet face smeared with evidence of his gluttony having consumed enough water for the six of them. They reached the first of the waterholes by starlight. Twice as long as it should have taken them if they knew the way, the petrol exhausted three hundred meters short. The mirage of a sparkling lake in the near distance, while not a lake, but a lonely puddle, also wasn't an illusion. It had water. Wet, cool, water. They fell to fate, divine intervention, an example of the enduring strength and destiny of the Reich—they got lucky, gambled, and guessed, finding their earlier tracks and retracing them slowly as they faded, swept away by the light breeze turning stiff and frigid, threatening to bury the abandoned car by dawn as the sun set.

"It makes no sense, Faust, it makes none," Weiheber gazed up into the romantic celestial lights known as *Bernice's Hair.* Three weeks ago, he was in Tunis, gazing down on her dull grey streets, watching a sleek black staff car snake its way along the cobbled stones to turn and park leisurely at the curb. Someone was in town. Someone he did not know, not then. By now, he had his file. Danzig. SS Hauptmann Eric Danzig of the Propaganda Ministry, and Weiheber couldn't be any more interested in Hauptmann Danzig than he was, extremely interested, Hauptmann Danzig second to only a few.

"What is this, Herr Major?" Faust requested.

"What?" Weiheber looked at him. "Did you say what, Faust?" What did Faust think made no sense? Who?

"Hauptmann Reineke, of course, Hauptmann Reineke. Indeed," Weiheber smiled coyly. The enigmatic Hauptmann Reineke, pretty to look at, difficult to control. Weiheber hadn't noticed too much more than that ... and yet? "There has to be, Faust," he nodded, "there has to be much more to Hauptmann Reineke."

Weiheber was a predator, an animal stalking its prey. The bungled Russian plot to lure some frightened Italian physicist from his hiding place brought Weiheber into Afrika to secure the scientist for the Reich. It was his chance for another pin for his cushion of medals, perhaps the brightest of all. His name elevated to that of Heydrich's, Himmler's prized pet.

There was no scientist, only some *child* in his place. The agent Reiss hired to infiltrate the Russians reported the operation had been so poorly managed as to allow the scientist to escape, leaving his daughter to make her way to Gibraltar with his friends.

Siwa
February 1942

"Daughter," Weiheber grasped the girl's dangling head by the chin. She was unconscious or perhaps simply pretending. Maybe or maybe not. "Really. Does this look like a daughter to you, Faust?"

"That is the report, Herr Major," Faust nodded efficiently.

"Report?" Weiheber asked amused. "Whose report, Faust? Whose report?"

The English aide was as dead as the girl pretended to be, killed as the jeep unexpectedly overturned, much to the surprise and annoyance of the Russian Reiss who muttered *"Shit,"* between his clenched teeth. Herr Colonel, an American Weiheber understood him to be, bleeding to death, trying not to, from the stump of his severed hand.

"Herr Oberleutnant," Faust glanced apprehensively at the impatient Reiss.

"Really," Weiheber smiled at Reiss. "She is English."

"So what?" Reiss retorted. "So she is English. The scientist will come whether his daughter is English, or what she is—Hierher!" he bent down and severed the aide's head, tossing it to her. "Now, talk," he threatened, grasping her hair tightly as she tried to attack him and missed to Weiheber's continued amusement. "Where is your father? Who are your contacts? Where are they?"

"Spies," Weiheber confidently assured Faust. "Spies."

"Spies, Herr Major?" Faust hesitated.

"Of course," Weiheber looked at him surprised to learn Faust could not see this for himself. "What else, Faust, what else?"

"Spies," Faust glanced at Reiss.

"Well, it is either that," Weiheber chuckled, "or the Russian's story of a scientist at hand is true. Do you see a scientist, Faust?"

"Well, no, Herr Major ..." Faust agreed.

"Perhaps both," Weiheber patted him consolingly. "Perhaps these are the contacts, Reiss seeks, eh? Have you thought of that? He follows them here while the scientist flees. A brilliant plan if it works, Faust, a brilliant plan if it works." Which, apparently it had.

"Of course," Faust sighed relieved. "Yes. That is brilliant of you, Herr Major ... but ..." he hesitated again, "Do you think the scientist will come, Herr Major, as Reiss maintains?"

For his heartwarming reunion with his *daughter* at some later place, some later date, and the last of their exodus to America? "Who knows, Faust," Weiheber shrugged. "Who knows. That is what we have Reiss for. Let him find out."

"Reiss ..." Faust glanced apprehensively again at the agent. "He is Russian, Herr Major ..." he reminded needlessly. "I do not think it is wise to leave him alone ..."

"No, but he thinks we have the daughter," Weiheber nodded. "Faust, he thinks."

"And we don't," Faust eyed him. "We really don't."

"No," Weiheber chuckled. "No. We have his contacts, Faust, perhaps, we have his spies. But, it is all right. It is all right," he reassured him consolingly again, "we will take the *daughter* with us so if Reiss strays, he won't stray far, as he works to find ... to find ..." he snapped his fingers trying to remember what it was Reiss claimed he needed to find.

"The scientist?" Faust said.

"Yes, Faust. But, no, the contacts, Faust. The contacts."

"Of course, Herr Major," Faust beamed. "Excellent. We will return to Tripoli immediately."

"Tripoli?" Weiheber looked at him.

"And wait, Herr Major," Faust nodded. "We will wait for ... *Reiss,"* he sneered at Jeff, "to finish his job."

"We will wait, Faust," Weiheber agreed, "but not in Tripoli."

"Berlin," Faust understood. "Very important," he tried not to stress too hard, "if the spies have information on the scientist, as we believe."

"Know, Faust," Weiheber nodded, "as we know."

"Yes," Faust beamed.

"And we will wait, Faust," Weiheber agreed, "in the Fezzan."

"The Fezzan?" Faust blinked. "Sebha?"

"One would think," Weiheber chuckled. "Yes, one would think that, wouldn't one?" he agreed. "But we know differently, don't we, Faust?"

The Fezzan
March 9

"Don't we?" Weiheber looked out into the frozen heat of the desert, Reiss gone, retreating to Cairo to ingratiate himself with the English Allied the American engineer had insisted were instrumental in the scientist's flight.

The same American who insisted the scientist would be there as soon as he found out his daughter was not. Reiss believed him. Weiheber did not, any more than he believed they had some *daughter* in their possession, rather than only the scientist's contacts. But it was a good enough reason, an excellent opportunity to wait, amused by the file on Danzig that arrived to help pass the time, and then not so amused the deeper Weiheber read.

It was an exaggeration perhaps to suggest Himmler had a file on everyone. Or perhaps just easier to believe it had to be an exaggeration. Either or, Herr Himmler did have files on many. From the smallest, to the greatest, and the Ministry's entrance into Afrika on the coattails of Himmler's SS, interestingly had nothing to do with some *scientist*, but with Herr General Rommel, and the reports of insurgency otherwise known as five munitions depots.

A recent conversation with a comrade in Berlin was purely coincidental. Many a luncheon had been spent with Herr SS Oberst Hans Reineke discussing the exploits of some flamboyant son long estranged. Deposed from his rightful position as Lord and heir to a vast family fortune by a plot of his own father and only son, Colonel Reineke was an embittered, angry man, ill-tempered, and in ill health. Steadfast in wishing his son's demise, he remained steadfast in denying and defying the death that would ultimately consume him as it had consumed his father.

"It is such a romantic story, Faust," Weiheber chuckled. The gas poisoned so many of them, destroying the lungs, and the brain. The latest round of seizures bringing on a stroke, leaving Herr Reineke with a paralyzed and useless right hand at only fifty-one. Politically, however, while so many of the old found themselves replaced by the new quickly on the rise, Colonel Reineke lingered on the threshold between power and extinction, feared, if never quite respected. Known to those not familiar enough, or inclined to be afraid.

His son would qualify as one of the latter. Colonel Reineke gazed at his lost empire from afar. His overbearing father long dead, the abused and terrorized wife a prisoner of her mind, and hated son currently stationed several thousand kilometers away, while he remained sentenced to his exile and Berlin, daring only to complain.

"Interesting, don't you think, Faust?" Weiheber nodded. "Interesting." He looked up this Baron Dieter Reineke whose power extended beyond ballrooms, across continents, oceans and sand, and as Reineke would later promise, he did not like what he found. Expecting the spoils and excess so typical of wealth, Baron Reineke was a decorated Panzer Captain. The 6th Army in France, the 1st Panzer Division in North Afrika. However, in less than a year after his triumphant arrival in Tripoli, Hauptmann Reineke was relieved of his command. Something to do with battle fatigue. A complete and irreversible mental breakdown, menace to himself and his men, prone to violence and bouts of amnesia, utterly insane.

Except madmen do not break down, and Reineke was a madman with three dead officers to attest to his uninhibited violence and emotional instability. The last, his First Officer, a week before Reineke was relieved and subsequently vanished, transferred to Rear

Services and oblivion. A seemingly harsh curtain call when on all three occasions Reineke had been completely absolved of the crime, the accusations an obvious conspiracy by jealous associates. Weiheber was not so sure about that. The idea of some conspiracy tried and failed three times was as foolish as Reineke thinking he could get away with a trio of murders. Weiheber discarded Danzig's file for the biography of Baron Hauptmann Dieter Reineke, studying it. The reported disagreement with the Oberleutnant Goetz was a petty contest of wills, inappropriate on Goetz's part, and unlikely to result in murder on Reineke's, particularly since as the commander Reineke was the final authority. A madman gone insane? Weiheber looked around, beyond Africa, back into the past, and such unrestrained aggression fit well with a similar portrait of Reineke painted two years earlier in France. Of a man whose hatred of the French shone in his repeated bombardment of a village long after any return fire had quieted and of his march to plant a flag.

A very frightened soldier would tell the story of the tall, blond man who could have been one of Germany's finest sons. Of the light that stayed in Reineke's eyes, though shrapnel from an exploding land mine tore an eight-inch gash in his leg. Of the laughter it triggered because his limb remained intact while the enemies lay scattered around him. The devil himself must have chosen the arm Reineke picked up from its resting place across the torso of another. It was a child. The body whole, the head nearly severed and face destroyed. He was so small, perhaps eight or nine years old. The light in Reineke's eyes died, the laughter stopped, his hands fumbling to reconnect the pieces, make it live, and the soldier would tell how Reineke started to cry when it would not. Of a German officer rocking the mutilated corpse, telling it stories while his men collected the villagers' bodies, burying them in separate graves, markers on each, and though Oberleutnant Dieter Reineke eventually fainted from the loss of blood, his men did not dare stop before finishing their task.

Weiheber closed that chapter of Reineke's journal with fingers tapping. Danzig's file was helpful in identifying his contacts in Afrika, specifically an agent Erich, successfully installed at one of the compounds. To date, Erich's diligence had proven helpful in identifying a Colonel Alfred Schönfeld as the ranking officer in charge of the project, locally. As well as five Hauptmanns under Schönfeld's command, one of whom was Erich's commanding officer, Baron Hauptmann Dieter Reineke rising like the Phoenix, up from the ashes of oblivion and the ranks of the undead, a new First Officer at his right hand, Heinrich Thiele. Oberleutnant Thiele was an officer whose otherwise spotless record should have cast him above reproach, a hero in his own right, highly decorated marksman, one of the best. Clearly, the malignancy of these anarchists had spread deeper and faster than anyone knew, their contamination and crimes far exceeding mere mutiny. Reports from the agent Erich stationed at Reineke's compound also contained an intriguing footnote about the presence of children living freely within the top secret complex. As many as seventy-five children, and one other particularly unusual and interesting individual a French priest. Hauptmann Reineke was indefensibly and undeniably a traitor. Guilty of high treason. Giving aid, and comfort to the enemies of his country and who knew what else. Weiheber intended to find out.

"Simply a question of how, Faust," Weiheber nodded. "How." This little trip south to inspect these compounds had quickly evolved into a mission, a quest with Reineke's dramatic and defiant display of temperament. The matter of some atomic scientist relegated to the background.

"What is this?" Faust was only half-listening, his voracious appetite wetted by the water but little else, leaving him starving in his fat.

"Hauptmann Reineke, Faust," Weiheber assured, "how best to approach Hauptmann Reineke. He cannot go unchallenged. It is unthinkable."

Was it? Faust scanned the lonely world of Hell, finding it colder without food or even Mussolini's ass to console him, the salty, canned meat supplement sounding delicious right about this time. "We will prevail, Herr Major," he obediently agreed, rousing himself from the pain and rumblings of his hollow stomach, denying the madness waiting to overtake them, the water simply delaying the inevitable starvation and heat. "Hauptmann Reineke's interference with the Allied spy is temporary and meaningless. We will replace her with an agent, and when the scientist comes, he will be ours."

"You should eat something, Faust," Weiheber turned to smile into the sounds and shadows of the desert, the ghostly song of the wind moaning softly in the distance. "However irritable, Hauptmann Reineke is not a man to squander his opportunities, and neither should we. There is no scientist, Faust, as there was no daughter. Spies, yes, like Hauptmann Reineke's efforts to trap us, but instead we have trapped him."

"Eat something?" Faust frowned suddenly alert to what could not possibly be the wind in the background of the darkened desert sand unless it was attached to a motor. "What is that? Who is that?" he insisted, up on his hot, tender feet, the men also rising from the shelter of their huddled mass, angry over their death sentence and willing to fight their executioners with their bare hands.

"That?" Weiheber smiled as the lazy, drifting shadows were also suddenly awake, scurrying away from hazy orbs of light piercing the blackness, bobbing and dancing two, perhaps three feet off the ground. "Propaganda Ministry," he agreed easily as what was clearly a staff car come into view. Simply not a black one as it had been in Tunis, but desert beige with a canvas top, a standard transport vehicle carrying six men traveling alongside.

"Propaganda Ministry?" Faust gaped. "What would they be doing out here?"

"I do not know, Faust," Weiheber said. "What would they be doing anywhere ... other than their job." He raised his hands in polite surrender to the approaching victors. "Do it, Faust," he encouraged Faust to strike the traditional pose of defeat while their men stood poised in a ridiculous looking line of defense, admittedly confused themselves. "Do it, or die. For if you think he is not out there, you are wrong."

"He?" Faust raised his hands.

"Hauptmann Reineke," Weiheber assured as the car stopped, the large smiling face of an unfamiliar Korps officer filling the side window frame in friendly greeting. "Of course, Faust. Who else?"

Chapter Twenty-Two

"Ah!" Eric concurred with his driver's startled *"What the!"* as the orphaned group of Himmler's henchmen loomed suddenly in the beams of the headlights. "What *have* we here?"

"SS," the driver nodded, apparently a man with his own droll sense of humor, recognizing the stained, dusty uniforms.

"Yes, one can see that, can't one?" Eric agreed with what one could see without too much difficulty. The tried and true blue suit of the apparent ranking banana a dead giveaway to more than just its wearer's affiliation, but also his state of mind, questionable, yes, it was, right off the bat. A *lu-lu*-lulu standing like a flag out in the middle of the sand, either that or a man who was extremely, *extremely* lost. Those were the only two choices in Eric's opinion, apart from the one of who the lunatic had to be. A name crossed his mind. Weiheber. A man on his way to investigate compounds. Herr SS Major Hanse Weiheber. Eric put two and two together and came up with zero. Apparently, the Russian Reiss had told something of the truth after all, about the man's drug use or his mental state, or perhaps both.

"But that's all right," Eric beamed, though not in a manner of condoning mental illness or drug use among the elite. His gilded fatness Herr Goering, the obvious exception to those two rules as Goebbels and Hitler were to the rules of Aryan good looks.

"That's quite all right," Eric nodded, definitely in the manner of condoning the SS in general and as a whole. "After all," he smiled at his driver, "we're SS." Their telltale and random tattoos (it would be an exaggeration to suggest all SS sported a tattoo) neatly tucked and hidden away beneath their underwear. Their Wehrmacht costumes just that, costumes, as Eric's Arab garb of a few days ago had been, deceptively authentic and comfortably thin. During the day, that is, not at night. In the night, wrapped up in goat hair or some greatcoat of cotton duck, Eric froze, as he was freezing now. So the blue-suited clown perhaps had the remnants of a brain after all. Much more so than what might be apparent at first glance, particularly since during the heat of the day he could always take the jacket off.

"Shall I stop?" Eric's driver asked.

"Versus what?" Eric wondered back. "Mowing them down or passing them by?"

"Fine," the driver sighed.

"Thank you," Eric presumed his chauffeur understood which course of action was fine. "After all, it would be the courteous thing to do."

They stopped, and Eric grit his teeth, smiling into the wind and the extraordinarily cooperative group of Supermen posed in surrender, their faces as unfamiliar to him, as his was to them.

"How long have you been out here?" Eric inquired gaily, seeing no vehicle or otherwise obvious mode of transportation, for that matter any Allies, French or otherwise, and poo-pooing the idea of Weiheber and his troop having to prostrate themselves for mercy with a wave.

"Eight hours," the fat Leutnant sighed like it was a lifetime, but took Eric at his word he was friend, not foe, lowering his pudgy white hands.

Au contraire, it was apparently equivalent to a lifetime for one. "Kill them now or die yourself." Herr Blue Suit with strudel for brains jammed his mealy, scarred face in Eric's window frame, his breath thick with cigarettes, his eyes glittering, definitely in need of a fix. The aforementioned "them" the dope fiend referred to, Eric assumed as he regrouped from the assault and stench, the apparently valueless squad currently staring at their commander like Weiheber had three heads instead of none. "It would be his orders."

"Whose orders?" Eric replied more out of reflex than interest.

"Hauptmann Reineke," the Leutnant sighed again.

"Oh," Eric said. The identification meaningless and not worth pursuing, he smiled. "Well, I am Hauptmann Danzig, and these are my men—who take orders from me," he assured with a sigh himself and reach for the blue-suited arm. "Just get in the car," he encouraged roughly, before he hauled Herr Fruitcake through the window. Something Eric possibly would have done, not simply could have done, if it wasn't for the Leutnant's quick thinking grab for the door.

"Good God, man, it's freezing out there," Eric nodded. "There's more than enough room for everyone. If not, we'll—*make some!*" Eric barked at his men not exactly shoving each other out of the way to make room for their brothers piling into and on the kübelwagen and staff car without having to be asked twice. All eventually seeing their way to cutting out the comedy routine and cooperating, and Eric settled back satisfied.

"There, now isn't that better?" he proposed as Herr Major's dutiful servant carefully propped his master up on the cushioned leather seat next to Eric. "And all without having to kill even one."

"Do you have petrol?" the Leutnant asked as he climbed into the front seat to hang over the back of it like an anxious child.

"Ah ... yes ... yes ..." Eric believed they must have; they were moving, right? Right. "Enough," he agreed. "*Just* enough," he assured, "for ourselves. So let's not even bother with that."

"That?" the Leutnant said.

"The attempted hijacking of a Wehrmacht vehicle," Eric assured, "Italian though it may be. Before you even think about it, let me take a moment to clarify that would be *SS* Hauptmann Eric Danzig. As in I would be, *SS* Hauptmann Eric Danzig," Eric clarified to the numbed nut sitting aside him. "Don't let my uniform, or my style ..." his smile slid over his tongue, "mislead you ...

"As far as your squad," Eric waved. "The one I am not inclined to shoot ..." he eyed Weiheber's uniform, noticeably dirtier than the others and certainly appearing that he had recently butchered someone or something. Possibly explaining those missing two or three men (the Russian had said about six or seven and there were only four), possibly in battle, possibly for lunch. Either way, it appeared someone or something had fought back, attempted to anyway, since one of Weiheber's eyes looked blackened beneath its stain of dust and sweat. His cheek swollen and lip definitely cracked. *C'est la vie.* Eric shrugged since he also noticed there appeared to be no evidence, or should Eric say remnants, of any American or child.

“Do I really think what is widespread, Faust?” the wasted addict interrupted his euphoria and Eric to ask (or answer) a question that had not been asked by anyone. “The political independence among the leaders and troops of North Afrika? I think ...” he rested his head prepared to elaborate, or fall asleep.

“Clearly?” Eric countered with a grin, and Herr Poppy’s head snapped up to eye him. “Herr ... ?” Eric inquired, though honestly wondering less about Weiheber personally than wondering where he had come from, out here in the middle of nowhere. What had happened to his car or camel or plane, unless he had walked? Eric really did not think Weiheber walked, but that was just his opinion.

“SS Major Hanse Weiheber,” the Leutnant disclosed, identifying himself as SS Leutnant Günther Faust.

“Ah,” Eric smiled. “Who else? Else, indeed?”

“Really,” the Leutnant was fat but quick. “Do we know you?”

“Not at all. Just acknowledging the introduction, that’s all,” Eric assured.

Weiheber nodded, breathing after a few moments of necessary silence to remember not only who but where he was, and he was close, in the ballpark more or less. “Hauptmann Reineke is a decorated officer. A bright, however brief shining star ...” he eyed the notebook at Eric’s side, good for light reading, what could Eric say? “You know,” he waved for Eric’s understanding. “One of those thousands who came out of France. You have read the report?”

“Ah ... this?” Eric touched the binder. “No, I’m sorry. This is a report on someone else ... the life, times, and history of someone else, I should say. Somewhat dense and lengthy.”

“He’s very good.” Weiheber’s attempted wave tired quickly, waggling his fingers, calling the binder to him.

“Hauptmann Reineke?” Eric held onto the almanac. “In what regard?”

“Reiss. The notebook, Hauptmann, give me the notebook.

“Oh,” Eric said. “Oh, yes, of course,” he smiled. “I was just thinking that myself, actually ...” he said, naturally thinking nothing of the sort, while definitely thinking of taking the Russian up on his offer to exchange Weiheber for Charles.

“You know him?” Weiheber asked.

“Who?” Eric said.

“Reiss,” Faust huffed, fussy little thing under all that blubber wasn’t he? “SS Oberleutnant Reiss.”

“Oh,” Eric smiled. “Well ...” he said with a gesture for the notebook, “indirectly, through his work.”

“Mine, Hauptmann,” Weiheber nodded, “Mine.” he fell back again, exhausted.

“Of course it is,” Eric grinned. “I mean ... well, how could some *Russian* possibly manage to be that good? On his own? Clearly, he not only had to have substantial help, but also realistically had to have acquired it from someone such as yourself ...

“No, I understand,” Eric nodded, lying of course, but confident so was Weiheber. “Where it came from, and even what it is,” he smiled at Weiheber frowning. “Yes?”

“Hauptmann ...?” Weiheber was all the way back there, trying to place, or possibly remember Eric’s name.

“Danzig,” Eric assured. “SS Hauptmann Eric Danzig, born in Hamburg, late of Berlin, wife Ingrid, parents Otto and Emilie, both deceased.”

Weiheber nodded. “Reiss is mine, Hauptmann,” he closed the notebook. “I do not know what that is. Some book. Faust, give him back his book. Foolish to waste your time reading, Hauptmann, when there is so much work to be done.”

“Very foolish,” Faust chimed in, stretching to take the almanac and hand it to Eric. “Few men are given a second chance. You should know this, Hauptmann.”

“Ah ... ?” Eric said.

“It is all right,” Weiheber dismissed with another sleepy waggle of his wrist. “It is all right, Faust. When Hauptmann Danzig fails in locating Herr Oberst Schönfeld ...”

“Alfred?” Eric blinked, not that there couldn’t possibly be another one.

“You know him?” Faust gaped.

“Ah ... yes,” Eric nodded. “Yes, I do. If it’s the same one. Including where he is,” he grinned, though not with any desire to show Faust or his superior Weiheber up. No, the latter already a has-been, Eric had quickly deduced, rather than a never-was what with that gilded breast of company dues matted with someone's hair and skin. A physically large man himself once, perhaps, not only tall. Foreign, Eric noticed, possibly a true Hun, with his dark complexion and almond eyes. It was interesting to Eric how as time went by the elite Waffen SS became increasingly foreign—twenty-six, twenty-seven percent? Dutch. Flemish. Norwegian. Even American and French, and certainly Soviet.

"Let's cut to the chase ..." Eric offered a cigarette as a substitute pacifier to cocaine, himself more of a confirmed and old-fashioned drunkard, and so personally he wouldn't know.

"Yes, thank you," Faust snatched hungrily at the pack. "You are sure of this?"

"Well, if I'm not, it's too late now," Eric agreed with a flick of his head for the match Faust struck against the heel of his boot. "Or did you mean Alfred's hideaway ... pardon me, command?" he smiled at Weiheber. "Yes, I'm quite sure I know where Alfred is. About a hundred kilometers ... or roughly a liter and a half," Eric reached with a sigh for his bourbon he had tucked under the seat.

"Of petrol?" Faust expressed concern.

"Of alcohol," Eric qualified. "It's late, I'm tired, and we all have our vices ... and limits," he rubbed his stiff and aching neck, raw from the sun, flies, and heat, and it hadn't even been a week. "This is not a road. I don't care if we call it a road, it is not a road by the stretch of even our imagination."

"The siphoning of the petrol was more than deliberate, Hauptmann," Weiheber assured, though again what he meant exactly by that, Eric could not guess. "Presuming the command post to be in a different direction than the water, he knew the choice would be the water, assuming an impossible walk."

"Ah," Eric said, "I believe I get it—part of it, anyway. So you do, or you did have a car. Which explains, yes," he acknowledged to Faust, "you inquiring into my petrol supply. Interesting."

"Interesting?" Weiheber cocked an ear.

"Elementary," Eric shrugged. "After all, you did have to come from somewhere by some means. Sebha would make the most sense, a plane. There's so few of you ... or is it possibly so few of you left?" Eric eyed Weiheber. That breast again. Bloody and emblazoned with all those medals. "Did something happen, Herr Major? Is there possibly something of which I and my men should be made aware? Something out there with guns or big teeth?"

"Hauptmann Reineke," Weiheber nodded.

Right. "Back to Alfred," Eric proposed.

"Yes," Faust agreed. "What is your report?"

"Ah ... report?" Eric said.

Faust huffed. "You said you have identified him, the location of his command."

"Something like that," Eric agreed. "Yes, I said something like that."

"And?" Faust insisted.

"And what?" Eric said.

"Is this some sort of game, Hauptmann?" Faust snapped. "You will take us there immediately."

"Or what?" Eric smiled. "You will give me to Charles instead of giving him to me? Sorry, but you should know, I turned that invitation down the first time."

They both looked at him, Weiheber raising a brow to study him. "It's all right," Eric waved them back to their respective corners. "I didn't believe it then, and I don't believe it now.

"No, gentlemen," he shook his head, "I have my own *theory* if one will, on the point, purpose, and *truth* of your charade, never mind mine. Your Reiss is a detour. Whose job the same as yours, is to locate and track Alfred—not some *Charles,* or some dissident band of French," he waved at the notebook, "but Herr Colonel Alfred Schönfeld. You set Reiss in place, hoping to delay the Ministry's arrival with all that prattle about English, French, and I don't know who else, that some of us swallowed, yes," he agreed, "or at least considered worth checking into. *I* not being one of them." He inclined forward with a serious nod. "How am I doing so far?"

"What did I tell you, eh, Faust," Weiheber returned amused. "What did I tell you? However irritable our Hauptmann Reineke may be—"

"Danzig," Eric corrected. "Herr SS Hauptmann Eric Danzig of the Propaganda Ministry—of Berlin," he clarified lest in his haze Weiheber confuse it with some other. "The Propaganda Ministry of

Berlin. I'm a spy. For our side," he assured, "on our side. But then someone has to make sure we maintain a clean and orderly house, now, don't we? We do, gentlemen," he nodded at Weiheber's breast, "that we do. Your map of Bohemia reeks Heydrich, Major, I must say. *The* Heydrich. Protec*tor*." There was someone who sang soprano with his high-pitched voice and questionable pelvic region.

"That makes a little more sense than Himmler sticking his neck out quite this far," Eric agreed. "Not that it matters. I'll raise you your Heydrich or Himmler one Goebbels, and even better one *Rommel*. The invincible, undeniable Erwin J ... or is it *S*?" Eric briefly frowned. "*A*? Does he even have one? A middle name," he clarified for Weiheber, "not a party affiliation. That we know he doesn't have. Little matter, we'll keep him just the same. It's not merely a matter of privilege and therefore *known* innocence that you will find General Rommel is not involved in any of this. It is by decree he is not involved in any of this. So, hands off, and the Ministry will even spring for the ride home."

"Threats," Faust scoffed. "Do you realize who you are speaking to, Hauptmann? Do you?"

"No," Eric smiled back. "No, actually, I don't. I do know it doesn't matter. My orders come directly from Berlin. So, we can either do this the friendly way, or you can get out of the car. You wish to consider that a threat, take it up with Berlin—when you get there, Leutnant, when you get there."

"What Faust means, Hauptmann ..." Weiheber yawned, "is we find it an interesting premise the Ministry endorses these pirates and their munitions complexes, promoting them as loyalists rather than what they are. Traitors, Hauptmann. Traitors and mutineers."

"Pirates," Eric considered, as such was his job to consider such things. "Yes, that is an interesting premise, isn't it?" he agreed. "I get it though. Pirates. Sahara seas. A little obscure, but clever, useful possibly even." He scribbled it on the cover of Reiss's overblown crap.

"It confounds me," Faust shook his head.

"Well, that is only because you are not of the Propaganda Ministry," Eric assured, "where tanks are made of cardboard and bullets, jellybeans. Marketing, in other words, Leutnant, marketing. It's all in the marketing, in which truth has no role ... decidedly has no role," he popped his pencil back in his pocket and rubbed his sore and tired neck again. "Quite all right, quite unlike the ranks, I will be leaving this *Paradise* soon."

"Then you are saying the Ministry supports and agrees with these ... these ..." Weiheber sputtered.

"Pirates?" Eric offered. "I'm saying ..." his head tipped back.

"Anarchists, Hauptmann," Weiheber insisted. "Anarchists, all of them!"

"My call," Eric's head returned forward with his grin. "That's my call. Perhaps I haven't made myself clear. My orders are from Berlin. There will be a sacrificial lamb, yes, naturally, to pay for all of this. Possibly Alfred, probably Alfred," he agreed. "High enough in rank to be believable ... obscure enough not to matter, or be missed ..." he smiled again at Weiheber's breast. "You're a Czech, aren't you? That's not exactly Russian, but it's also not German, now, is it?

"No, it isn't," he assured as Faust sputtered something and Weiheber just stared at him. "Admittedly curious, though, I admit, are you completely out of your mind or merely colorblind with that sky-blue suit? This isn't Berlin or even Tripoli. It's the Sahara, the rear of the front lines. Why don't you just wear a sign that reads 'shoot me'? Because I assure you, they will, without thought, reason, and certainly without conscience or regret. No one appreciates, respects, or even *likes* the SS. They hate us. Hate us," he nodded, "fear, loathe, and despise us, albeit rightfully so. But then we're not really the elite are we, no. We're thugs. If you really want to get through this—out of it, *alive* no less, take a page from my book and lose the three-piece tattoo. The Wehrmacht rules North Afrika, trust me, it rules. *Rommel* wouldn't have it any other way."

"Are you sure ..." Faust accused.

"That I'm SS?" Eric laughed. "Oh, yes, even though you're not despite my arrogance and threats. It's less my attitude than ... well, my attitude," he dismissed. "My jokes and friendly nature, my soft, friendly hand. I believe you'll find they not only work, gentlemen, they're irresistible even at times. Like a bee to honey, a fly," he promised, "to my spider web. But then really, which of us do you really think these ... *pirates* will feel more comfortable with sharing their hopes, dreams, secrets, and schemes, even better, their *contacts* and connections? I'll give you a hint. It's definitely not *Himmler* or *Heydrich,* or either of you. I'm sorry, gentlemen, but I am here to market what you are here to destroy, and I'm afraid I win. You can have Alfred, but only after I'm done with him. In the meantime ..." he picked up the notebook and set it back down in Weiheber's lap, "you may keep *Charles* as your consolation prize. If there is a Charles, I expect to hear, see, and know nothing of him. Take care of it. Put him out of business and do it quick. That's the *deal* I am willing to make. The beginning, middle, and end of it. I suggest you take it."

"What is this?" Weiheber frowned at the binder.

"A novel," Eric assured. "Not exactly *Tolstoy,* but close enough. And now that that's settled," he settled back to light a cigarette and find his bottle of courage under the seat. "What's all this about some Hauptmann Reineke? What does he have to do with any of this, other than what he's told to do?"

Chapter Twenty-Three

Cairo
March 9

Even if he tried, Justin had no particular image of Joanna in his mind. No snapshot recollection of his stepsister, tender or otherwise. What he had was a responsibility he took seriously, one he felt deeply, and an old man given a second chance to right his wrongs and prove himself worthy before he died with his head held high. "Care to try that again, Mike?" Justin said as he sat there.

"No!" Michael assured. It was hard enough the first time. "Red's missing, Chuck, bottom line. They got her, they ain't got her, who definitely doesn't have her is you or I."

"That's ridiculous, Mike," Justin said. "Joanna is with Evelyn."

"London," Michael said and Justin's eyes brightened. "Supposed to be in London, supposed to be. Gramps thinks she's in New York with me, and therein lies the problem, because she ain't neither."

"Isn't, Mike," Justin corrected, tightly. "And why isn't she? I'm waiting, Michael!" he didn't wait long, but jumped up to loom over his desk, the stem of his pipe pointed in accusation.

"Hey!" Michael could jump, too, straight up to meet Justin head-on without flinching. "Try throwing your weight around this! She's not, OK? She's just not. She's in the ATS, all right? She's a driver in the ATS. You want a confession? Fine! I confess. You got me. I surrender!"

"Damn you!" Justin exploded, and his fist almost went through the table. Downstairs, covering the radio after Joe took off to help, Bobby heard bone or wood crack. It was probably both, and Bobby wasn't concerned either way. Wouldn't be the first time, probably not the last. Justin had a mean temper when aroused. A killer's instinct, and a killer's heart, and that was all right, too. Should have killed the Doc a long time ago and be done with it the first time he showed his spots like the Old Man had dropped Teddy Drake when he started carrying on. Just dropped him in his tracks and walked away without a thought to it despite their life-long friendship. Bobby shut the radio off, smoothed the report out neat for Justin when he came for it, which he would, and waddled over to check the Telex. There wasn't anything, not yet. When it came there still wasn't much, but there would be if Justin had to turn the planet upside down and shake it out, that Bobby also knew.

"Me?" Michael said as Justin whirled away from him to try and find the paper trail in among forty million others he had laying around. "Fuck you. This is all your fault, not mine."

"Is it now?" Justin said, and the words dripping acid.

"Yeah!" Michael assured. "Look, I didn't have to fucking come here. I could have just left you sitting with your head stuck up your ass—"

"Yes, well," Justin nodded, "you certainly took your precious time—"

"Ay!" Michael said. "I took all the fucking time I needed, OK? Who kept who sitting on their frigging thumbs for nine hours—"

"I don't care, Michael!" Justin turned on him.

Yeah, well, neither did Michael. "Look, screw the fucking paperwork," he tore a week's worth out of Justin's hand. "It's not going to change anything. She's gone, all right? That's what I'm telling you, she's gone, there's nothing you can do about it, not now, not ever, and it's all your fucking fault!" he screamed again. "I mean, for Christ's sake, Justin," he whined, "you've kept her locked up for years. First with Gramps, and then with Joe, and when Joe died, where did you put her? Back it jail! She doesn't belong in jail. She belongs out doing things. Seeing things!"

"And do you think she likes what she's seeing now, Mike?" Justin wanted to know. "What she might be doing now?"

"No! And that's definitely your fault," Michael insisted. "They took her because of you, they didn't need me. They could have taken her from England, Scotland—the frigging States, if I brought her home with me. They didn't need fucking North Africa! They didn't have to wait for her to come to them. You signed that warrant long ago, buster. You and that three ring circus of yours out there. Is you, ain't you? Will you, won't you fuck with me? Yeah, well, they fucked with you, didn't they? Don't look now, but they fucked with you but good!"

And Jesus Christ, Justin must have left him standing there for another frigging hour.

"Fuck!" Michael grabbed the Scotch winging it across the room.

"I got it!" Joe slid into home plate to take over for Laura confused and up on her feet, the dead receiver of her telephone in her hand as she tried to, Joe didn't know, call the fire department or something to come and turn their hoses on the Maj and the Doc going at it pretty good behind the closed door. The two of them, loud enough to be overheard, and angry enough to be frightening, he supposed.

"I'm serious," Joe flashed his very best grin, dropping Scarecrow in front of her for her consideration and gently removing the receiver from her hand. "I've got it covered."

"Yes, of course," Laura agreed, because really what else could she say? What was she supposed to say? Squadron Leader Charles emerged from his office at that point to head off at rocket speed the direction Joe had just run.

"Excuse me." Joe whipped a ring of keys off his waistband that Laura could quite honestly say she had never noticed him carrying before, to quickly lock the office door and hence the Doc inside. A loud "Fuck!" followed by the sound of breaking glass suggested Michael may have decided to go out the window, but Joe would check that out in a moment if only because if the Doc had sprung for a dive he wouldn't be going anywhere except maybe to the infirmary. "You hungry?" he turned his grin back on Laura.

"I beg your pardon?" she said.

"Hungry," Joe shrugged, trying to nonchalantly *move, move, move* her along without actually pushing her. "Got to be lunch time or something, right?"

"Lunch time ..." Laura glanced at the wall behind him and the clock that said not quite twenty past nine.

"What I mean is ..." Joe said, but changed his mind and cut the bull crap laying it out as polite and sweet as possible. "Look, don't take this personally but I need you out of here now. Try to stall me, and I swear to Christ I'll carry you."

"Quite all right," Laura stopped him there, collected her shoulder bag and left, leaving him to blow a low appreciative whistle after her with a shake of his head.

"Out of this world," Joe said. "Definitely out of this world—yo!" his hand connected with Scarecrow paused to take in the sights. "Escort her, man, escort her. We're talking out of the building and gone. On a boat back to England. Wherever." Scarecrow left and Joe sat down to hook the phone back up and get ahold of Bobby and forewarn him the Maj was on his way. He was already there.

"Yeah, OK," Joe took a breath. "Just give him whatever he wants," he said like he had a say in the matter. "I'm here, Laur's gone, everything's covered ... yeah, him, too," he turned around to look over the door in answer to Bobby's inquiry about the Doc. "He's in there, trashing the place and talking to himself. Thought he might have tried to make a break for it, but, I can hear him—what? You telling me you can't?" his temper flashed suddenly, not at Bobby but at the idea of someone messing with his equipment. "Oh, you turned him off," he nodded. "Yeah, OK, got it, guess so. I mean, who the fuck's he gonna call? I don't think so.

"I mean," Joe sat down with a wipe of his sweating neck, "what's the deal here anyway? What's this crap about the Maj's sister? Where's that coming from? Yeah, I got it," he nodded. "I'm fine. Count on me. I'm just saying this is crazy. It's nuts."

Crazy or nuts could describe her assignment, Laura supposed, as she propped herself at a local pub for a light early brunch, a healthy splash of rye whiskey in her juice cup, Colonel James Peterson at her side, flashy and dignified in his polished brass and grey temples. Condescending, certainly, for all his sympathy and attention, as they all were when they weren't trying to out-shout each other in their profanities and general rudeness.

"Really, what a vulgar world it has become," Laura remarked as she sat there.

"Vulgar?" Jim's brow arched. A kind brow it was, older, like an uncle's or a priest's. She really was being unfair to him and she softened. "Charles?" he said.

Her softness did not last long, Laura felt herself immediately bristle at even the name. "The world," she repeated. "For that matter, the war." She looked around the public house, crowded for this hour of morning, extremely crowded, from the looks of some of them, more than a few of them had been there, or elsewhere, all night.

"It's war," Jim chuckled.

"So it is," Laura acknowledged primly with a sip of her drink. "War." A vastly different war than the one she had left behind at home. The land perhaps decimated, in some ways desecrated, but not its people, their spirit or their morals. Here it was almost primal. "Why did you say Charles?" she asked.

"No reason," he shrugged. "Don't like him much myself, but he's not the vulgar sort, wouldn't think."

No, of course he did not. But then vulgar to a man meant something sexual. To where vulgar to a woman meant vulgar. "Fine," Laura said, "we'll compromise. He's a nutter."

Jim chuckled harder. "That's on point. Makes a fine living at it, too."

"Really," Laura said. "And what sort of fine living is that?"

Jim shut up like the proverbial clam. Really, it couldn't be more obvious, and really, that was the point, wasn't it? Yes, it was. "That's the point," Laura nodded firmly.

"No, it isn't," Jim tried to claim.

"Yes, it is," Laura insisted. "It's an assignment, not a game. Of course, I've no idea what my assignment even is, other than to sit there and be made a fool of on a regular basis."

"Look, luv," he patted her hand.

"Don't call me luv," Laura requested, "and for God's sake please stop patting my hand. I'm an officer in your bloody air force and it's high time the lot of you learned not only to accept, but to respect that. I'm not a secretary—for that matter, I'm not only a pilot," she reminded him, her Irish rising. "I'm a trained and experienced cryptographer. I didn't spend six months in Buckinghamshire warming the benches."

"Yes, all right ..." Jim nodded.

It was hardly all right. "And," Laura said, "I do seem to recall your saying not only what an ideal position this was for a woman of my skills, but what an ideal candidate I was, better than any other."

"Well, you are," he assured, "you are. Just takes a little time."

"Of course," Laura ignored him, "you did say woman, not officer, so I should have known right then and there, shouldn't I? Of course I should—except," she set her glass down sharply with a crisp nod of approval at the offer of a refill, "I can't even sit there and look pretty for your parade of brass flashing through, any more than I can do anything else, I'm not allowed."

"What do you want, luv?" Jim asked. "If I can do it for you, I will."

What did she want? Laura straightened up. What did he think she wanted? A transfer since an apology was certainly not in the offing. "What did you mean when you said it takes a little time?"

"He's one of those man-fellows," Jim downed his bourbon with a shrug. "You know how they are."

A man-fellow? Laura wasn't sure she knew what a man-fellow was, least of all how they were. "Oh," she sat up a little straighter as a thought crossed her mind. "Yes, well," she said briskly with a somewhat heartier drink of her tea, "daresay for all you don't know about Squadron Leader Charles, that's certainly one thing I did not know. Definitely," she shuddered. "What?" she said, but only because Jim was looking at her oddly. "Your words, not mine. I merely said he was vulgar. Who knew how so? Quite," she downed her tea, requesting another post haste.

"Oh, no, luv ..." Jim started to laugh once he figured out what she was saying.

"Please don't," Laura stopped him from elaborating. "Really, it's not anything I need to know."

And not anything he was going to tell her, other than she had it wrong. "All I'm saying is he's one of those opposed to women in the services—a queen? Charles?" he couldn't laugh any harder, though he certainly did try. "He's a bit queer, all right, but not in the way you're thinking. Likes them savage, naked, and wild, if you know what I'm saying."

"To the contrary, I'm quite sure I do not know," Laura assured.

"Yes, you do," Jim patted her hand.

"Fine," Laura said. "I know what you mean. I'm twenty-six, not thirteen. Old enough," she assured the barkeep apparently puzzled about her request for a fresh cup of tea, "to know precisely what you mean. Tea, please, yes, tea. Contrary to popular belief, we're not all alcoholics ..." she scowled at Peterson, fairly gasping.

"Charles?" Jim said for what had to be the fourth time with a shake of his head, marveling at the notion. "Talking out of your hat with that one, luv. It's rich though. That's pretty rich. Might be tempted to spread it around myself, if I thought it'd catch on. Be the end of him it would."

Laura was not talking out of her *hat* or any other object, inanimate, or otherwise. "Yes, well, that would explain the blonde then, wouldn't it?" she pursued the wild part of things. "Rather nicely."

"Blonde?" Jim frowned.

"Or perhaps not," Laura nodded firmly with an even firmer sip from her cup. "After all, such a man's man, one can't imagine why he would want her around."

"You talking about Julia?" Jim frowned, hard put otherwise.

"Yes, well," Laura dared say she wouldn't know, and didn't know if she was talking about *Julia,* or whomever, not having been introduced.

"Didn't realize you knew her," Jim reflected curiously on that with a wrinkling of his chin. "That's a bit odd, now that is a bit odd."

"Yes, well," Laura never claimed to know her. Seen her, yes, she had seen her. Once. Only once, and rather briefly, but still long enough to know once was enough.

"Right. Well, don't be too hard on her," Jim patted her hand. "There's more to her than meets the eye."

Yes, well, there couldn't be much more to her from what Laura had seen, however briefly, rather all of her right there to be seen.

"Fairly highly skilled lass herself," Jim assured.

"Obviously," Laura concurred. "Simply a matter of what sort of skills one is talking about."

"A pilot," Jim assured. "She's a pilot, luv. So see? Just need to bide your time, you'll get your chance."

A pilot? Laura almost choked on her tea. "A pilot?" she slammed the cup down before she did choke for that matter, pour the damn tea over Jim's head.

"Luv ..." Jim groaned.

"Oh, this is too much," Laura couldn't get her purse out fast enough, the change down on the bar fast enough, or herself out the door. "This is really too much."

"Laura!" Jim caught up with her, caught her by the arm, a step or two outside. "Laura, what in bleeding hell ..."

"A pilot?" Laura turned on him so angry she could barely get the words out. "That woman is a pilot?"

"Yes," Jim said. "Fairly decent one—Laura!" he protested, but only because she walked off on him again.

"How dare you," Laura sputtered as he trotted along besides her walking as fast as she possibly could in her tight skirt and stacked high heels. "Really, how dare you, all of you." She stopped, eyeing her father's oldest and dearest friend, God rest his wretched soul.

"What do you want me to do?" Jim asked again in all seriousness and understanding. "I will, if I can. Anything."

"What in bleeding hell do you think I want?" Laura snapped. "A transfer, of course. I'm sick to death of your 'Charles' and I scarcely even know the man."

"Right. Well, that I can't do ..." Jim scratched behind his ear.

"Oh?" Laura said coldly. "Why not?"

"It's not that simple," Jim said simply. "You know that. This is Charles's problem. Thinks because he says it is, it is, and it's not."

"What's that to do with me?" Laura asked.

"It doesn't," Jim said. "You're the right one for the post. So to hell with him. Besides," he smiled, "you're rather a brick. Wouldn't have put you there if I didn't think you couldn't be a match for him. I'm right, aren't I? Of course I am. Might even come around. Stranger things have happened."

"Come around," Laura said. "Dare I ask to what?"

"Just that," Jim shrugged. "Never had a secretary before, can't see why he has to have one now. It's rot. You know it's rot, and I know it. He's an arrogant bastard. Needs to be knocked down a peg or two."

“Well, if else fails, there’s always the Jerries,” Laura considered only half-joking.

“Exactly,” Jim chuckled. “It’s nothing personal, luv. Really, you’re taking this far too personally.”

“I beg to differ, but it is personal,” Laura corrected. “I shouldn’t have to defend wanting to contribute to your bloody war effort. At least be allowed to feel I’m doing something worthwhile to the best of my limits and abilities. But instead, I’m an object of ridicule, by, of all things, and if you’re telling the truth, a man who would prefer not to have a secretary. How absurd. How perfectly and utterly absurd. Quite frankly, if that’s all it is, your *bizarre* Mr. Charles is the one who is taking things far too personally, with the simple answer for you to do us both a favor and let him have his way.”

“Can’t,” Jim shook his head.

“Why not?” Laura insisted. “Surely you’re not suggesting he really does have the final say in whatever game the two of you are playing.”

“Clearly he doesn’t,” Jim smiled. “You’re still there.”

“Then why not?” Laura insisted. “And don’t give me your rot it’s not that simple.”

He shut up like a clam again, and so the point remained the point. Laura stared off down the street.

“Luv ...” Jim tried. “Now, don’t start crying on me, it’s really not worth it, it’s not. So he’s a prick. All right, he’s a prick. Just do your duty and leave the rest be.”

“Crying on you,” Laura said. Yes, well, crying, Laura could assure him was the last thing on her mind. “To the devil with you,” she said. “The lot of you. If you’re thinking I’ll likewise come around—”

“You will,” Jim nodded. “You will.”

“Like some second class citizen to you ruddy beggars?” Laura looked him dead in the eyes. “The devil I will. If you know anything, James Fillmore Peterson, you know that.”

Chapter Twenty-Four

"So!" Michael said when Justin finally decided to show back up to hunt up a pair of dusty knapsacks and some old rifle that hadn't seen action since the Crimean war.

"So what, Michael?" Justin emptied his desk into the knapsacks, checking the sight of his rifle on Michael's lapel.

"Put the gun down, Chuck," Michael nodded. "In the first place you never could hit the broad side of a barn."

"Yes, well, in the first place it's not a barn I'm looking at, now is it?" Justin countered.

"And in the second?" Michael thought he'd ask.

"Yes, well," in the second, it would be too easy, too damn easy. Justin set the rifle aside. "When I pull the trigger, is when you really have something to complain about."

"Ditto," Michael breathed, "save I'm the one with the balls to do it."

"Debatable," Justin said. "But that's all right, you'll do."

"Me?" Michael's head jerked up to stare at him. "You're kidding, right?"

"Do I look like I'm kidding?"

"No!" Michael snapped. "So let's can the witty repartee and get down to brass tacks. I'm here because I want to be here."

"Yes, well, you're here, Mike," Justin said, "because you have no choice and until I say otherwise. I don't give a damn what you or Roosevelt might have to say about it. That's something you should have thought about before you hired Joanna out to drive someone's car."

"I didn't hire her out, and not on your frigging career, Chuck. You can't touch me, you can't do shit."

Yes, well, the hell with his career obviously, so Justin didn't even bother mentioning it. "No, you did a favor for a friend," Justin had it down pat. "Mahlon McDowell, Colonel, USA, and his aide, Corporal Paul Reid. Of course, Reid was apparently SIS, and who knows who McDowell really was. Don't know yet, but I will."

"He's not a friend," Michael assured. "And fuck him along with everyone else. I've got one concern and that's Red."

"Yes, well, as I said, it's a little late for that." Justin laid it out for him in gory red, white, and black. "They brought part of agent Reid in, Mike, what was left of him. Whatever the beetles ate or didn't, they cut off his hands and hanged his head from the antenna wire."

"All right!" Michael shut him up. "Bottom line, what are we going to do? Got that? Do. What is the plan? If you want to drive something around the block, try a few hard and fast ideas."

Yes, well, the 'plan' Justin already knew, rather surprised Mike didn't. "I'm going to find the bastards and kill them, Mike, simple as that. Not quite sure what else anyone would expect me to do. You, Mike, are the bait to do just that. Better get packing."

And Christ if Chuck didn't leave him waiting there another frigging hour.

"Bait?" Michael said when Justin returned that time with a couple of sheets of paper in his hand to read while he lit his pipe and sat on his ass in his armchair.

"Looks like your McDowell friend ran with the Tobruk crowd," Justin pursued his own interest. "Tough lot, but that's all right. Aside from you, I've Joe and Bobby to spare. You haven't met Joe yet, but you will. He'll be along shortly."

"Lucky me," Michael agreed for some stupid reason. "Back to the fishing business. How am I bait? Apart from the obvious," he waved. "And don't even bother with that. You're not going to sell me out, Chuck. You and I both know that."

"And you know that for a fact, right, Mike?" Justin didn't look up from sucking up the words off the papers.

"Yeah!" Michael insisted. "So, talk to me. I'm trying to talk to you!"

"Yes, well, you'll probably like Joe," Justin suspected. "Same as he'll probably like you."

Either way it was another two hours before Michael met him, not that he was in a particular hurry to meet any more of Justin's friends. It was just an uncomfortable one hundred and thirty-five minutes of silence.

"I mean!" Michael said, "under the circumstances."

"Yes," Justin thought so, too.

"Right." Michael concentrated on polishing his shoes for a while. "Let's get back to fucking," he offered presently. "And speaking of fucking," he said, not that anyone was, "Ever fuck her?" he wondered with a flick of his head toward the silken legs he knew sat just outside the door.

"Who?" Justin said.

"The dame," Michael huffed. "The frigging dame who sits outside."

"Oh," Justin said. "No."

"That figures," Michael said. "Mind if I do?"

"I don't care what you do, Michael," Justin assured, and Michael shut up.

"Why not?" he opened up again seconds short of Joe.

"Why not what?" Justin said.

"Why haven't you fucked her?" Michael sputtered, not really understanding why he was bothering to talk at all.

"I don't know," Justin said. "Never thought of it, I suppose."

"That figures," Michael snorted. "You always were a queer bastard. Ever fuck Joe?"

"I don't know, Michael," Justin said, "why don't you ask him?"

Easy enough to do, considering Joe just walked in the door, however it was not the sort of question Michael wanted to ask Joe. Joe appeared to be a pleasant enough chap with a flashing, friendly smile and extended hand, and Michael could see no good reason to ruffle Joe's good nature with a question in such obvious poor taste. Besides, a darkly handsome kid of about six feet even, Joe had a waist as tight as Michael's should have been, a chest as broad as Michael's could have been, and arms bigger around than Michael's head.

"Joe," Justin introduced them, "Mike."

"Yeah, hey," Joe gave Michael's hand a hearty pump, and Michael was surprised to be listening to a voice as familiar as home.

"Jersey?" Michael frowned.

"Flatbush," Joe grinned. "You know, Brooklyn. New York."

"No kidding," Michael whistled. "Hey, I was born in Brooklyn."

"Yeah, I know," Joe's grin stayed. "The Heights. I knew your old man."

"My old man?" Michael repeated with a glance over the tattoos, but only because they were there. As in obvious. As in, the kid was half-naked. Not because he expected to see *Dad* carved next to *Mom* in a heart. "You knew my old man."

"Well, not *knew*, knew him," Joe admitted, "seen him around. It was a while ago. Couple, few years. '37, '38, something like that, before they took him out. Harlem, right? Up in Harlem?"

"Never fucking heard of you," Michael said, and that was the end of their conversation for a while.

Joe turned his attention to the crumpled typing paper he had in his hand and Justin. "This is yours, because, well, I kind of figured," he shrugged, "I might as well do something while I was sitting out there. Not exactly hard work, a monkey could do it."

"Thank you," Justin stuffed the report in his knapsack with all the others.

"Not that I mean the lady's a monkey," Joe hastened to clarify for whatever reason. "Definitely, she's not a monkey. She's ..."

"Temporary," Justin finished for him.

"Yeah, huh?" Joe laughed. "Aren't they all? That's the way it should be. Definitely the way it should be."

"Yes," Justin swung his knapsack over his shoulder. "Is that it?"

"Oh, yeah," Joe waved. "Everything's fine. Not to worry. Just saying I got rid of her. She's gone, history—not rid, rid, of her," he said, quick to clarify because Justin did sort of pause. "I mean, it's not like I killed her and buried her out in the yard. Christ, give me a break. I set it up for her to be transferred ... why?" his grin slipped in. "Having second thoughts? Thinking ... I don't know, you'll miss her?"

"No," Justin said, "but you might."

"Yeah, I might," Joe nodded. "Definitely. Too much though and I'll just go looking, know what I mean?"

"Yes, well, speaking of looking ... " Justin suggested as the phone rang.

"Bobby," Joe reached to answer it, apparently taking his secretarial duties as seriously as he took everything else. "It's OK, I got it. Pain in the ass, anyway. Reams me out for pestering him and now look who's suddenly in a hurry—what?" he said into the phone. "Turn the frigging thing back on and you won't have to ask if we're coming. Yeah, we're coming, on our way ... He's out in the yard," he explained to Justin. "That's why he's calling. Wanna talk to him?"

"Yes, actually," Justin agreed.

"Yeah, well, you're out of luck because he doesn't want to talk to you." Joe hung up the phone with a laugh, a snap of his fingers, and a point at Michael. "Yo. You're with me, let's go."

"Yes, well," Justin cleared his throat, not about to let that little business with the telephone just slide, "that'll cost you a few laps."

"I can handle it." Joe headed out, leaving Michael to look at Justin and Justin to look back at him.

"What?" Justin said.

"Nothing," Michael picked up his duffel. "Let's get on with it."

Siwa Oasis, Egypt
March 10

They got there at first light. The sun rising over the baked plains, scarred with reminders of last season's heavy fighting, life a few thousand feet away in the distance, churning away as it had for centuries. Justin stood solemn in the isolation, taking it all in. Behind him, Bobby waited, arms folded, propped against their jeep, Joe perched comfortably on the hood of his, Michael uncomfortably sharing his space with Joe's large pack radio *Christine*, his white suit, shoes, and Panama hat, dusty and dirty, his bladder on overload. "Siwa, huh?" Michael hammered his spine straight, prying himself out of the jeep to take a leak, looking out over the expanse of nothing stretched before him. Behind him a city waited, half stuck in the Stone Age, half not. Made sense to him, he supposed. Could be someone around who knew something, what's more, willing to talk, yeah, right. "Think I've seen this movie. What are we, a mile out of town? Is there some particularly special reason we just don't bite the bullet and go the whole hog instead of waiting for the guys in the shuttered car to come to us?"

"Yeah, well," Joe said, reminding Michael of a rule he probably never even heard of, "you know sometimes, Doc, a forward approach isn't necessarily the best."

"Uh, huh," Michael could have fun with that but he passed. "You mean because we're on the corner of first and the front lines? I don't know why that should concern anyone. There's four of us."

"Actually, Doc," Joe looked around, "out here the front kinda depends on what day of the week it is. Know what I mean? Not that the place hasn't seen its share of action like the rest of the world."

"Uh, huh," Michael looked up with the whine of a toy airplane overhead. On cue, another jeep appeared from nowhere, cutting across the sand on high as Lucky Lindy and his crop duster swooped into view, circling to land, and taxi maybe thirty yards before he got serious with the brakes. Justin lit his pipe, meandering to meet them.

"About time," Joe slipped off his perch with a grin for Bobby.

"Right about that," Bobby nodded tersely. "Now is not the time to try the lad's patience."

"No, it's not," Joe agreed, his knuckles cracking Michael's arm. "Yo. Put the package away. Let's go."

"Suck spaghetti," Michael said. "The crowd's forming as we speak. Think it's a little late now to be discreet, for that matter, in a hurry. It's ten-of fucking Tuesday. What happened to we'll know everything there is to know within an hour?"

"We do know," Joe assured. "Just tying up with a couple of the guys so we can do something about it."

"Guys, huh?" Michael adjusted his sunshades to ogle the jeep rolling in, Marlene Dietrich, shapely in her sweaty undershirt, sun-bleached hair, and copper tan, riding shotgun.

"Yeah, that's Jewels, Doc," Joe identified the mirage. "Julia. But, um ..." he cautioned. "Don't get any ideas. She's a lion poacher from Kenya. Takes her job seriously, in other words; know what I mean? She'll hang your hide right next to the rest of them."

"Sounds like fun to me," Michael headed for trouble.

"Yeah, right, in your dreams," Joe hitched up his pants and beat him to the draw.

"Hey, Joe, what do you know?" Julia slithered down to snake her way over and make his gun sweat a few bullets, her eyes green, voice husky, and chest breathing deeply.

"Aw, that's old, Jewels, old," Joe chuckled and probably would have squirmed a little in his shirt collar if he was wearing one. He wasn't as usual, settling instead for a disconcerted sweep of his lashes over the one semi-normal looking one of the group, if you didn't consider his oversized head. Another grizzly buzzard swung down out of the cockpit of the plane to join Chuck busy talking with some walleyed freak with a gold tooth in his mouth.

"Does it still work?" Jewels could be cold when she wanted to be, but then again, she could be real hot.

"Yeah, of course it still works," Joe's chuckle deepened, clearing his throat with a wave at the head. "Hey, Fred, how's it going?"

"It's going, lad," Fred nodded, looking rather like the cat who swallowed the canary to Joe, and so Fred had. Husband Number Two and counting for the bad lass with the good heart and generous spirit until she tired of the singularity clause of her commitment, which she would, but it still placed Fred a cut above the others, and he'd settled for that. "It's going."

"Yeah," so Joe had heard. "So, why you trying to give the guy heartburn?" he scolded Julia.

"Don't know what you mean," she was on a roll, "just because I love him, doesn't mean I can't love you ...

"Or you," she looked Michael up and down before sauntering on to see what she could do about lighting Chuck's pipe for him.

"Hey! Did you hear me say no?" Michael called after her, not too proud or shy.

"Yo!" Joe's hand cracked him in the back of the head. "Show some class. She's kidding."

"Now I know you're stupid," Michael assured. "I know a piece of fish when I see one and that is Moby fucking Dick."

"Um ..." Joe tried to hide his smile, but failed. "Blah, blah, blah. This is Fred, her old man. You know, husband?"

"And?" Michael waited for the punch line.

"And so I'm serious," Joe nodded. "Dead serious. Don't make me have to hurt you. Show some respect."

"Now you sound like my fucking wife," Michael moved on to see what he could do about helping Chuck figure out which one was the girl.

"It's water, mate," Pete hopped from the rolling jeep with his traditional offering of a bottle for Justin, this one labeled Scotch. "No cause for alarm for the safety of your gun or the mink collar draped over it."

"Yes, well, that's one way of putting it," Justin accepted the Scotch.

"Oh, what's another?" Pete unscrewed the cap of his canteen to take a drink with a laugh and a nod for the bottle. "I mean, it's water, just like this is. Bottled it personally myself not an hour ago."

"Yes, well," that much Justin had figured out before he took a swallow. "Kiss ass is another way of putting it. Quite all right, up to it or not, you're it. Nel's otherwise occupied trying to win a war."

"Oh, well, now, if I'm going to kiss an arse, I wouldn't look for it to be yours," Pete assured with a smile for Julia cozying her way into the conversation. "Am I right, or am I wrong?"

"Sounds good to me," she wrapped her lips around his canteen with reassurance for Justin. "It's water." And just to prove it she splashed a little on her throat and a few other overheated parts.

"Right," Pete took the canteen away from her. "Just been through that, luv. Let's not have the man repeating on himself."

"Been through that," Julia nodded at Justin. "Who's the porter?"

That was also one way of putting it, Justin supposed. "You mean Mike."

"If the suit fits," she shrugged, which from the looks of him it did.

"Yes, well, we'll get to that," Justin promised, more interested right now in his airplane, old, though it might be, old and painted to look like something it wasn't, which was German to the nearsighted and ill informed. "What happened?"

"Nothing," Julia said. "Hank said it sounded a little rough as I passed, I said it was just running a little hot. He took it up to see if it was him or me."

"And the verdict?" Justin asked.

"Needs oil," Hank tossed Julia the can.

"Who doesn't?" she caught it with a sharp whistle for the "boys" to give her a hand as she sashayed away.

"Right," Pete gave a whistle watching it walk away. "That's some wedding present, lads, I'm telling you. Make the Holy Lord rethink his bachelor ways." He eyed Michael muscling up, an angry look on his face. Pete wasn't too sure about him, right off. He looked like money and even more like trouble under his curls and tan. A small man in a sea of giants, even though he wasn't that small, but on the short side of average with a muscular build. Still he was apparently a little too small for his own liking from the way he moved in. The glasses lending a sense of respectability to his pretty face, the early crow's feet and tightness of the skin spelled dehydration or drink. It remained to be seen which, the same as it remained to be seen just how much and the reason. Want or need, the latter a definite problem, the former could be as well, depending again on how much. Justin was heavy with the Scotch. Pete, heavier and less fussy, satisfied with whatever tasted good, and most did. Neither of them drank when there was work to be done however, and neither of them watched the sun rise through the bottom of a glass when the work was over. Those who did were a problem.

Pete eyed Michael who looked as Italian as his name despite the blue eyes and blond hair. His skin near high-yellow like he might be mixed, it had to be the blond hair in contrast to the olive tanned damn near gold as oil since Pete doubted if Justin's family tree included some mulatto regardless of how smart this one was reputed to be.

"Is this him?" he asked Justin. "What's got your entrails in a knot? Could be somebody, I suppose, but most wouldn't think physicist, is my guess."

"Physicist?" Hank came up unexpectedly from behind, startled what with being regular army like Fred, if one considered the Black Watch and Long Range Desert Troops regular army, which they weren't. They were the ones who did the job after Justin analyzed the intelligence collected by his squad. Still, a physicist was up there all right, versus just keeping some ordinary pain in the ass on ice.

"Hey," Michael said, "it's a job. Somebody's got to do it."

Pete laughed. "Now that's a frightening thought. A real

frightening thought—what?" he said to Michael looking at him like he wanted to take somebody's head off, which Pete wouldn't suggest he try. "Got something you want to say there, or just a little indigestion?"

"Yeah," Michael said, "screw. That means scram where I'm from. Take a hike."

"Right," Pete nodded. "And I'll bet you've heard it often, too."

"Whatever," Michael turned to Justin. "Got a minute?"

"In a minute, maybe," Justin relit his pipe.

"It's all right," Pete retreated to say hello to Bobby and exchange photographs of some Yank named McDowell for those of a lass who could very well be their very own secretary Cain, some ten or so years ago.

"This him?" Pete looked over the picture of the Army Corp Engineer in his dignified getup and fun-loving expression. Getting on a little in years to change his mind and hence sides after a twenty-year career, in Pete's opinion. "Looks like an ordinary enough fellow. But then that's the whole point with these lads, isn't it? To blend in?"

"It's how they work it." Bobby was lost in his study of the worn photograph of the young lass. No doubt who she was, still stood the same way, held her head the same way, a serious look in her eyes, still had that as well.

"Sounds like the life of a coward," Pete handed him back McDowell's photograph for his scrapbook. Didn't need it, after all, what with the fellow likely dead for all his big ideas good or bad. "Right or wrong?"

"About which?" Bobby kept the picture of Laura, tucking it safe and warm, down in the pocket of his wet shirt. Pete eyed him. Soaked, Bobby was. Soaked and breathing shallow. He didn't belong out here, old and fat as he was. Seemed almost cruel of Justin to take him away from his overhead fans, and make him come, if he didn't want to. Give in to his whining, if he did want to, which Bobby probably did. Pete smiled. Knew few men who inspired that sort of loyalty. Few who'd kill themselves for you, in your stead, or just stop you from going off half-cocked doing something unlike yourself. It was one or the other, Pete knew that much as well, probably some combination of the two.

"It looks like her," Bobby was saying, "if that's what you're wondering. Could be, and probably is."

"Oh, now, I'm not wondering anything," Pete assured with a smile. "No more than I'm accusing, simply stating a fact—one I'd want to know," he pointed out. "So you either tell our boy Justin, or I will. Got enough personal problems the way I hear it, doesn't need any new ones, which that lass either is, or she isn't. Personally, I say she's not. But then I'm not so jaded as you might think. What I am is been around a while, longer even than you."

"Doubt it," Bobby disputed but only because he had close to twenty years on Pete.

"The hell I haven't," Pete assured. "Wore your damn flag for my nappy, and don't think I won't piss on it again as soon as this war business is over. Regardless, like you, I know all the devils, all the angels, and all the ones who don't give a damn about any of our crap. That would be that one," he pointed at Laura's picture, hidden away in Bobby's shirt and he could hide all he wanted to because Pete was serious; he would tell Justin if Bobby didn't. "Can't stake my life, and sure as hell won't ever stake my reputation, but what I do have on my side is my longevity, and I would have known, lad. Peter would have known if McShane's baby sister ever worked my side of the street. On that, you can stake whatever the hell you feel like."

"I'll tell him," Bobby said, and would, not because he felt pressured into doing it, but because he worried for Justin like some surrogate father. Pete could hear it in Bobby's voice when they talked over Joseph's radio. Bobby calling to tell him to make sure and bring the eye-opening photograph along with him, to where Bobby hadn't even wanted to hear about it for the last three months.

"Now, see?" Pete gave Bobby a friendly whap in the chest. "I knew you were an upright and outstanding fellow, same as me. Not at all like that Benedict McDowell. Brings shame to all his relatives his daddy left back in County Cork for the land of milk and plenty, sidling up to these Nazis the way he did, I assure you he do."

"Is that so?" Bobby said, not that he doubted Pete, or even particularly mistrusted him. He just knew him like he knew the rest of his clan, and appreciation or respect for Justin Charles, who he was, what he stood for, was unlikely. Bobby didn't give a damn about all the possible psychological reasons for Pete's exception for Justin, he just didn't believe it.

"Aye, it is so," Pete agreed, including how he and Justin together were a most unlikely cocktail. "But don't let my transgression go to your head. Liking one is not liking all of you. Peter just likes passion, that's all. Understands and appreciates it. Anytime you want to debate that, give me a call. Just make it, like I said, after the war."

Hank was thinking along similar lines, about the Yank engineer McDowell having more of a role to play in the drama other than an innocent bystander. "Anyone figure out yet what he was doing out here?" he recovered from his surprise in learning the race for the Atom bomb included the best and least likely of men.

"You tell me," Justin puffed on his pipe.

Hank scoffed. "Right. Could have saved himself a lot of time and trouble and just landed in Tobruk, if that really were his only idea. Didn't have to come all the way to Cairo and drive. But then that would have made for a different ending, now wouldn't it?" he nodded.

"That's the thinking," Justin agreed.

"Hey, whoa, wait a minute," Michael jumped in. "What are you saying? Mahlon sold Red? The fuck he did!"

Justin ignored him, walking with Hank to his jeep with a nod for Pete to quit antagonizing Bobby and put his muscle to work helping Joe and Fred with Julia's refueling. "How's the weather?"

"Little low coming in over the mountains," Hank unfolded the latest report. "She'll be fine though, unless you'd rather I took care of it."

"No, she'll be fine," Justin eyed Julia preparing to take the plane back up and once around for a test run. "Will need you and Fred to lend Pete a hand. You can head out as soon as we get these jeeps in. Have another fellow Nel out there. He's doing some reconnaissance, and after that should be heading to Jean Paul's place in about a week. That's an approximate. Nel has a new fellow with him, Jeff. A translator. He's bit inexperienced, but that's why he's with Nel. Shouldn't need your assistance with the language, but you never know. Either way, Pete will let you know." He lit his pipe.

"Whatever you need," Hank nodded. "Not thinking Jean Paul's somehow mixed up in any of this, are you?"

"Yes, well, no," Justin said. "Don't have much yet, but I doubt if it's anything to do with Jean Paul. Not that Mike's not pretty hot property, because he is."

"Aye, quite," Hank said. "That much I've got. A bloody physicist, no less."

"Yes," Justin said. "Shouldn't have overheard that, but you did, and it's not to be spread around. That includes Julia and Fred."

"Understood."

"Good. Unfortunately, for all Michael is, there's a lot more he is not. Took off for the States for a reason, and then took off from there, supposedly because of this. Might be true, might not. Something's in the works though clearly, as clearly wherever it started out, it ended up here. Need to know who, and need them all, fast as possible, and Mike can't be anywhere around, certainly not here."

"Right." Hank's eyes flitted for Joe's jeep. He was not against taking it in now and getting on with the job, not that a few minutes or even an hour would matter.

"But it's not a bad idea," Justin said. "Making use of Jean Paul," he clarified as Hank looked at him. "Since we also don't know what the problem is with Jean Paul, can't chance accidental involvement in any this, if only out of simple curiosity. Right now, Michael's a lot safer in Algeria than he is in Cairo, and I'd like to keep it that way until I know better what's going on here, damn Algeria. For the official record, Mike's a war correspondent, just moving him out for safe transport back to Gibraltar following a little trouble with his attaché. That's the story and we'll stick to it regardless of who asks. You can send a wire with reassurance to Jean Paul along with the sad news from home. Death in the family," Justin lit his pipe. "You can tell him it's my sister, just in case there's anyone out there tuning in."

"Be news if they weren't," Hank agreed.

"So it would," Justin said. "We'll see what comes of it. In the meantime, make sure Jean Paul gets the point I'm not in any mood to listen to any lip about Nel, any more than I am in a mood to entertain. I don't want or need the press underfoot, and so the correspondent is out. No action necessary. Just need a little time to make the arrangements, until then, it's hands off. If I need his help, I'll ask. Any complaints, he can send them to de Gaulle."

"Will do," Hank promised.

"Good. You can take care of that now if you will with Pete before he leaves. He'll get you the OK to send it out from Cairo. Once out there, Frank will handle general surveillance, as usual. Need anything, radio him. Pete's boss, but you're his second." Justin ogled Michael currently being held at bay by Bobby, which wasn't going to last long. Bobby didn't have the patience, and Michael, whether he believed it or not, was apt to end up shot.

"What?" Justin wandered back Michael's way, but only because Mike was definitely worthless dead.

"You about done?" Michael nodded.

"No," Justin assured. Not with throwing his weight around, telling people what to do, or with putting the blame where the blame belonged, and it was in Michael's lap. "There's no link between Joanna and I, certainly not in North Africa, unless you gave it up to your pal McDowell. The only possible link is in England, and even there he'd have to have more than just some key to an executive's toilet. You're in this, Mike, up to your neck, and I wouldn't look for Evelyn to cover your arse for you, not this time around."

"Guess again," Michael said. "Mahlon didn't do this. You're looking for a scapegoat to cover your own stinking smell, and he ain't it."

"Then it's you," Justin turned his back, climbed into the jeep, and sped away to cut Julia off at liftoff, catching her attention by crossing her flight path, the plane banging back down without damage or injury to either of them.

"That wasn't too bright, guv," Julia cut the engine and leaned out over her door to say. "Lose more than a tire that way."

"And you're going to have to do better than that," Justin countered. "Cloud cover's heavy and low over the mountains. No indication it's going to get any better by the time you're there.""

She shrugged. "Still nothing you couldn't have said with a kiss."

"Yes, well," Justin said, "afraid you're a bit out of my league."

“Oh, right,” she laughed. “Meaning, you’re a bit out of mine, and it’s a lie either way, but that’s all right, I won’t tell.”

“Yes, well,” Justin said, getting to back to why he was out there.

“Now we both know why you’re out here,” Julia purred. “You’re a camel, not a monk. Something else I know.”

“But won’t tell,” Justin suspected.

“Cross my heart,” she crossed and swore.

“Yes, well,” Justin said, getting back to the second reason why he was out there, his airplane. “You’re a little crowded with four, but weight’s fine. You’ll make Malta with no problem. Put her down though, should you have to, wherever you have to. Might not look it, but Mike’s a valuable piece of cargo.”

“Oh?” Julia glanced toward home field. “Who says?”

“I do,” Justin assured.

She smiled. “Well, in that case ... yes, sir.”

“Much better,” Justin approved. “You’re waiting to link up with Nel, should anyone ask. Hank and Fred will be along in a day or two to bolster your crew.”

“Curious more who might ask,” Julia admitted. “Heard from Pete a pack of lions couldn’t have done better job on the lad who was brought in from that lost convoy. No lions around here that I’m aware of so it must be the two-legged kind. Arabs or Jerry, you’re thinking? Or both? Jerry would have just left him, wouldn’t they? No reason to go through all of that.”

“Yes, well, it’s not a suicide mission, if that’s what you’re wondering,” Justin said.

She laughed. “No, luv, just curious, like I said. Sure you’ve got better plans for me.”

He did. “Algeria,” Justin nodded. “That’s where you’re headed.”

“Explains the mountains,” Julia resumed eying home plate. “Your Michael must be hot then, too hot for Cairo. Anything else I need to know?”

“He volunteered?” Justin said.

“Oh, right,” she scoffed. “Like the rest of us. But that’s also all right,” she teased him with her smile again. “Give that secretary of yours her cards and I’ll show you how well I can type.”

“Yes, well, haven’t the faintest ...” Justin had to say.

"And no reason why you should," she purred. "Ugly as sin under all that paint and padding; take my word for it."

He would. "Back to Mike. He's a war correspondent. Don't worry about the details, Pete and Hank will take care of that, and Mike's got his own rather healthy repertoire should anything unexpected come up. Rather the same as he likes to think he can take care of himself. He probably can, but let's save finding out. He is hot, and too expensive to lose, so, yes, Algeria's a better choice right now than keeping him here until we know exactly what's going on. Nel will take care of anything to do with Jean Paul, and Pete will take the reins if it turns out to have anything to do with you. Nel has a fellow with him named Jeff. Bit new, and so depending on what Nel does come up with, I might pull Jeff and put him with you. Pete doesn't like him, but Pete will make do, trust you can take care of that."

"Trust Pete more than I trust you," Julia suggested, though not to rub it in. "Said something about a lady friend of yours being in that Yank's car. Can't say I'm sorry to hear the worst."

"Sounds like Pete's had a lot to say," Justin agreed. "The car was a jeep, and, yes, my sister was with them. She's dead."

"Oh," Julia flushed. "Sorry. Didn't mean to be rude, no more than Pete did, I'm sure. Just talking, you know."

"Yes," Justin said. "That's about it then, other than I'll need Fred to take your jeep in. Mind? Pete also said something about a wedding."

She laughed. "Why? Would it matter if I did?"

"Yes, well, no. On the odd chance you do though—"

"What?" Julia leaned a little further out the window of the plane.

"Yes, well," Justin kept a respectable distance and firm grip on his reserve. "Bit of a drastic measure, isn't it? This wedding of yours? After all, there's no saying I wouldn't have come around."

"There's no saying you can't now," she assured.

"True," Justin said, and left before he made good on his threat, Michael throwing his weight in front of the jeep as he rolled up.

"Let's start over," Michael suggested. "Mahlon was an engineer. You know how many frigging engineers they have out here?"

"Yes, well, the only thing you're right about, Mike, is they used

Joanna to get to me whether they intended to or not."

"I never said that," Michael's hand sliced through the air. "I said it was your fault that's what I said, which it is."

"What's the difference?" Justin asked.

"All the world!" Michael insisted. "Mahlon wasn't big enough to be given the time of day!"

"Which I am," Justin nodded. "Be careful out there, Mike, because so are you." He drove off to collect Bobby.

"Careful out fucking where?" Michael barked after him. "Chuck!"

"Ready when you are—Doc, is it?" Pete interjected jovially from behind.

"Funny, you don't look like Chuck to me." Michael turned around to find Joe standing with the grinning walleyed freak, a mission on their faces. "What the fuck is this?"

"You mean the plane?" Pete glanced fondly back at Julia waiting patiently in her cockpit, motor running. "Well, now, that, Doc, is an *Applecore* what you call an *Albacore*. Don't let her swastikas fool you, she's born and made in the UK. That paint's only to help get us to where we're going without the problems we might have otherwise."

"We'll carry you if we have to, Doc," Joe added. "Swear to Christ."

"Huh?" Michael said.

"Just get in the plane," Pete translated for him. "Make it easy on yourself."

"I'll make it a lot easier," Michael assured. "I ain't fucking going anywhere."

"Have it your way," Pete sighed, and Michael woke up three miles high.

Chapter Twenty-Five

Justin was pensive, his face deadpan when he returned to Bobby and the jeep. That was all right from Bobby's perspective, the same as it was routine, including what Justin was thinking about, less the details that would be the business at hand. The personal angle, well, that was over and done. Gone with the Doc on his airplane. Bobby believed Justin got rid of the Doc for no other reason than to keep what was personal at arm's length, far as he could keep it. Couple of thousand miles away seemed just about right. The point Justin risked his career, quite possibly his life, should anyone find out he'd done all of that being who the Doc was, apparently made no never mind to him, much as it might to someone else, Bobby among them. Bobby was mad as hell with the Doc, and even angrier with Justin for risking his neck to save Michael's. Wasn't a fair exchange, in Bobby's opinion, the hell with the damn Doc.

"Where to now?" Bobby asked with an edge to his tone Justin noticed as he lit his pipe. But then Bobby wasn't Pete who took such things as anarchism in stride, or Hank who preferred not to know. Bobby was Bobby and Justin was probably guilty of anarchy or something similar for taking it upon himself to assist Michael with his disappearing act.

Justin was probably guilty of a lot of things. In contempt of every rule and regulation in the book, including the ones no one had thought of yet, when they threw the book at him when and if Justin should be found out. It did not change anything, would not change anything. Justin was Justin, the same as Michael was Mike and so forth.

So forth and so on. Justin thought of Evelyn, how to tell him about Joanna, what to say. He could not keep that confrontation at arm's length for too long regardless of how many miles away. It did not make Justin sad to think of Evelyn. It made him what he was, and that was angry. In an odd way angrier about Michael than he was about the disappearing Jerry depots and that probably made him angriest of all. Damn, Mike. Damn him over and over again. One of those things that also never changed. Justin did not like Michael regardless of what Evelyn might like to believe about the boyhood trio who grew up to be men. They were not Evelyn, Teddy, and Scotty. They were Justin, Joseph, and Mike, and Justin could not resist thinking how it might be easier on Evelyn if Mike and Joanna went down together. Would be sad, tragic, but also poetic. Evelyn liked poetry, the sight, and smell of flowers in the spring. Justin put and kept Michael at arm's length so he wouldn't kill him. Nothing poetic about that, just plain fact.

"Want to check the town yourself or leave if for the fellows?" Bobby was asking. "Either's fine with me."

Bobby was a damn poor liar. Nothing was fine by him the same as none of this was 'fine' with Justin. Bobby had as much on his mind as Justin had on his. The fact that Bobby was fidgety clinched that. Probably thinking about Pete, whatever the business was with Pete Justin hadn't failed to notice. As far as Siwa, yes, well, there wasn't anything in the town Justin personally needed to see. He had seen it all here, from here. He considered briefly how it was no one in or from the town apparently noticed a group, large or small, of Jerries being around, but then decided the answer was rather obvious. They weren't Jerries, at least not dressed like them if they were, and even if they were the town apparently preferred not to become involved. So, no, there wasn't anything the town could tell Justin he didn't already know, which was nothing.

"Yes, well," Justin supposed he could order some arbitrary group of residents lined up and shot for complacency or conspiracy, but that would mean Bobby had to stay out in the heat that much longer instead being on his way home to his fans. "Home," he answered from the looks of Bobby with his sweat dried to wrinkles on his shirt and drying as it dripped out from under his hat. "You all right?"

"Aye." Bobby borrowed Pete's gift of water to rinse his mouth and spit. "This little bit of sweat will do me good. Maybe even drop a stone or two."

"Yes, well, as long as that's all you drop."

"Same goes for you, lad," Bobby assured. "My arse and your neck go together, last I heard."

"So they do." Justin ogled Joe taking charge of packing Christine in the plane like she was made out of china.

"Then get going," Bobby suggested, "before you find my foot up yours. Worried about the heat, a little breeze would help."

"Yes, well, I wouldn't suggest it," Justin got down to business, climbed in the jeep, hit the pedal and took off like he was flying one of his airplanes, storming the dunes like you might a beach or a barn. Difference of course being they weren't in the air, but on the ground, sand, more specifically, and so it was a bit bumpy to say the least, the sheer weight of Bobby probably all that kept him from being thrown clear. "You're in enough trouble already for that telephone business earlier. Joe's up for a few laps and you can always join him."

"Well, now, I already knew what you were going to say, now, didn't I? So why waste more time, especially since I wasn't about to listen anyway? As far as Joseph, right," Bobby scoffed. "Lad could do fifty laps before he cracked a sweat."

"The devil he can," Justin said. "Five bob says he's down and gasping at twenty-five."

"Aye, and another five for every damn lap he makes after that," Bobby nodded.

"Deal," Justin said. "Now all we have to do is figure out what to get him for his wedding."

"You mean Christine?" Bobby chuckled. "Oh, well, now, that radio's all Joseph's got now that you gave his lady love her cards."

Had he? "Might have to try that again," Justin suggested. "I've no more fired Julia than I'm sure she's fired Pete despite Joe being in the picture and that bloke she decided to marry."

"Fred," Bobby nodded. "Aye, Fred. Not going to last any more than the first one so just leave it run its course."

"Yes, well, I didn't fire her," Justin assured. "Just a reminder who the boss is and that Hank isn't going to be aboard to bail her out. Need to be able to rely on her, and her judgment."

"She's fine," Bobby nodded. "Wasn't talking about her, anyway. Was talking about your secretary. She's Joe's love, or was."

"Oh," Justin said. "Right. Sorry. Forgot about her. And, quite. I gave her, her cards. Though I wouldn't be too concerned there either, they're pretty well stocked. Bigger and better each time."

"Beg your pardon?" Bobby swallowed the water he had been prepared to spit out again.

"Quite well stocked," Justin assured.

"Right, well," Bobby shifted uncomfortably in his seat, "looks good on her, just the same."

"Yes, well," Justin said, "believe it's she looks good on him, isn't it?"

"What?" Bobby said.

"Or maybe it isn't," Justin shrugged. "What do I know?"

"That's my question," Bobby insisted. "What the devil are you talking about?"

"Believe I was talking about Joe," Justin said. "Why? What am I talking about?"

"Nothing," Bobby assured. "Not your damn business, nor mine that damn brassiere of hers. I don't give a damn if it's bigger and better each damn morning she comes in. Which it is," he admitted. "Aye, it is. Noticed that myself."

"Right," Justin said after a moment. "Yes, well, no, I wasn't talking about that. For that matter," he assured, "believe I said stocked, not stacked. Pretty damn well stocked with them," he nodded, which they were, appeared to be. "No ruddy end in sight to them, apparently. Though I can't say I'm not surprised Joe even noticed a difference between them—the ruddy girls," he clarified. "Not the damn size of the last one's bristols."

"I understand," Bobby waved.

"Well, good," Justin said.

"Though I can't say I know what the devil you're talking about now either."

"Yes, well, that makes two of us," Justin assured. "Ruddy brassiere? The devil with Joe, can't say I'm not a bit surprised at you."

"Oh?" Bobby said. "Why? No one's that damn blind, lad, not even you."

"Yes, well, it's not a point of being blind," Justin said.

"Oh?" Bobby said. "What's it a point of being?"

"How the devil do I know?" Justin said, that time impatiently. "It's a point that's all. Think you'd have more damn important things to pay attention to, that's the bloody point."

"I'm old, not dead," Bobby shrugged.

"Apparently," Justin agreed. "Still, think we can save the damn subject for another day don't you?"

"No more dead than you, lad," Bobby suggested cleverly.

"Yes, well, if you mean the secretary ..." Justin assured.

"I don't mean the secretary," Bobby shook his head. "Mean Julia."

"Oh," Justin said. "Yes, well, then you're right. I'm not dead."

Bobby nodded. "So what's your point about no end in sight to them? The secretaries," he clarified as Justin frowned. "Not Julia."

"Just that," Justin said. "There's no ruddy end of them in sight."

"Except I don't know what you mean," Bobby said. "That lass is the only secretary you've ever had."

"In what way?" Justin requested.

"What do you mean in what way?" Bobby said. "In all ways. Every way. Three months, lad, almost," he nodded. "In and out, you're right, like a damn revolving door. But I don't know what you mean about 'secretaries' is what I'm saying. There's only been one."

"No," Justin said.

"Yes," Bobby assured. "Same one, lad. Same one."

"No," Justin said.

"It's the same damn woman!" Bobby insisted. "There a day, gone the next, and back again the day after that, you're right about that. For what it's worth," he scoffed, talking largely to himself, which was fine with Justin. "Can't even tell she's ever been here at all from the state of your office. In the same damn mess since we came here."

And it would stay that way. "Now, during, and after the next one," Justin assured.

"Same one, lad," Bobby shook his head. "I'm telling you, she's the same one."

"And I'm telling you she's not," Justin assured, and he had five more bob that said one of them was right. "Check the damn personnel files, and while you're at, check your damn blood pressure and heart, because one or the other's a bit off."

"Deal," Bobby accepted.

"Deal," Justin agreed. "Now, if your preoccupation with my secretaries is satisfied, think you're ready to tell me what the business was with Pete?"

"Preoccupation?" Bobby said, and Justin looked at him.

"Aye," Bobby sighed. "And, well, I wouldn't call it preoccupation exactly."

"Oh? What would you call it, exactly? Even Julia mentioned something about them for some damn reason or another. Joe, probably. Quite," Justin decided. "And the ever increasing size of their brassieres, no doubt."

"You're talking nonsense now, lad," Bobby assured. "Same as any 'business you're referring to with Pete."

"Meaning?" Justin said.

"Now, I don't know what meaning," Bobby shifted again in his seat. "Meaning just that. Nonsense. Want to talk about something that might not be, is this business with that Doc of yours. You sure you won't find it's you they're gunning for?"

"Yes, well, it's your job to make me sure, isn't it? Fair to say at the moment I'm not sure of anything, except that Joanna is not coincidence, and that it's not over."

"Whatever *it* is," Bobby agreed. "Other than the war."

"Quite," Justin said, "other than the war. I believe it's Mike, because it has to be Mike. Do more with him than they ever could with me. Only thing they'd want to do with me is put me out of business. Don't need Joanna to try that. It's all right, though. They want Mike and I want them. So, yes, I guess Mike is right, whoever they came gunning for, who they got is me." He turned the wheel of the jeep sharply as they banged their way up onto the road where he could finally pick up speed.

"Aye," Bobby stared straight ahead. "Well, we could always beat it out of him, lad, if you think he might know something more."

"Mike? That we could," Justin agreed. "But I doubt if he does. I don't think Mike hightailed it out of England because someone was after him, save for possibly Uncle Sam. I think Washington made him an offer he couldn't refuse and he went quietly and took off the moment their backs were turned."

"You mean he's telling the truth," Bobby said.

"I mean he's telling the truth," Justin agreed. "I think Mike was on the run, cooling his heels until the heat died down, next stop Peru. Something happened though he didn't anticipate. Obviously that was Joanna. It's the North Africa part I can't quite figure. If Mike left orders, Joanna should be in one of two places, home with Evelyn or on her way to Manhattan and him. He said as much," Justin frowned. "Mike said as much."

"What?" Bobby asked.

"Actually, if someone were after Mike," Justin thought, "the last place Joanna would be is home with Evelyn or on her way to Mike, least not straight away. Too risky. Whoever McDowell turns out to be, Reid definitely appears to have been SIS."

"Aye," Bobby nodded. "Thinking they brought her here?"

"To me, you mean?" Justin said. "It's possible—Son of a bitch," he stopped the jeep.

"What?" Bobby asked.

"Too many possibilities," Justin nodded coldly, "need more facts. McDowell isn't the only one who could have been in this up to his ruddy neck. There's Reid, too. SIS he'd have access McDowell wouldn't have. Still, damn Reid's access, there's no damn link between Joanna and I. There isn't."

"Aye, there is," Bobby disagreed, "she's your sister."

"My sister is dead," Justin reminded. "Been dead ten years. No, there's one link only and it's between Joanna and Mike."

"Well, it's no coincidence, lad," Bobby said. "No one brought the lass here save to get to you. That much I believe."

"Because she talked," Justin said.

"What?" Bobby said.

"Joanna," Justin assured. "She talked to Mike's ruddy friends."

"Willingly you mean?" Bobby said.

"Or otherwise," Justin agreed tightly. "Sure at some point it wasn't exactly over tea. In the meantime, McDowell either tried to get her the hell out of there, as Mike claims ..."

"To you, you mean?"

"I mean," Justin said, "it's possible they didn't know where the hell Mike was. On the up-and-up, they had to get Joanna out of there.

On the flip side, taking Joanna would definitely work to coax Mike out of where he was."

"And that means they were privy to a lot more than you think, lad," Bobby said, "because where they brought her is here. Good reason or bad, no reason save you."

"The States," Justin shook his head. "Safe passage to the States. Into Africa and out via Gibraltar."

"Aye, well, if she were on the continent maybe," Bobby concurred. "But she weren't, according to him. Should have just taken her to Greenland."

"Except that would have been—"

"Anticipated," Bobby said it for him. "Got it. All right. So McDowell tried to throw off whoever was after them by coming here."

"Possibly," Justin said.

"And definitely failed," Bobby nodded, "what matters most."

"Or succeeded," Justin lit his pipe and shifted the jeep back into gear, taking off.

"Aye, depends on whose side he was on, you're right," Bobby concurred. "It's all right, we'll find out. Good news is, you might not be in this at all, lad, other than by way of coincidence."

Oh, Justin was definitely in it. Maybe not at the start, but definitely now. "Why Cairo?"

"Instead of Morocco?" Bobby understood. "Bit odd, but could just be more of that 'anticipated' idea. If the Jerries were waiting for them here, which apparently they were, they sure the devil had a group of them waiting in Morocco."

"Why Tobruk?" Justin asked.

"Driving? Well, that doesn't make any damn sense," Bobby agreed. "Stupid and dangerous, to say the least. That McDowell couldn't seriously have thought he was going to get the lass clear across Africa without running into a problem or two."

"He was on the run," Justin said. "No plan, he was on the damn run and making it up as he went along. You're right. That lets me out of it, since I'm here."

"And on the run he should have stayed put. Here," Bobby assured. "There's enough of us here, that's for sure. Someone would have helped him out. Should have waltzed her into the nearest brass and hollered for help. No, he was on the wrong side, lad," Bobby promised. "Of that I am convinced. He might have worked to make it look good to those who were concerned on the London side, but once here, *bam!* Just took her. No one here to stop him. Not that he was aware, which he wouldn't be if you're right there's no damn link between you and her. It's the only way it plays out, lad. It's the only way it makes even the slightest bit of sense."

"Either that or the damn family's just cursed," Justin grunted.

"Well, I wouldn't say that." Bobby shifted a little in his seat Justin noticed.

"Still not quite right," Justin said. "Don't have it quite right yet."

"Well, no," Bobby said. "Of course we don't. But that's all right. You keep thinking it through like you are and I'll do what I need to do, and we'll get it done, lad, like we always do."

"So what was all that with Pete?" Justin changed the subject since this one was about worn out.

"Nothing," Bobby said. "You do have one problem with what you are thinking, lad, you know."

"Mike," Justin agreed. "Yes, I know. Damn pinching Joanna in hopes of having Mike show up. Mike did show up, in Cairo no less, where they should have been to snatch him as he stepped off his plane."

"What do you think that means?"

"Yes, well, I'm gambling," Justin said, "it means they actually have no idea who Mike is, not only not know where he was. The closest they got was Joanna, and, quite, they needed her to move onto Mike."

"Sounds reasonable."

"Yes, well, it sounds reasonable," Justin assured, "because it's the only way it makes any damn sense, if any of this makes any sense."

"It will," Bobby nodded confidently. "It will."

So it would. "Start with the patrol who found the jeep and Reid. One of ours, wasn't it? Wasn't the Yanks."

"No, it was ours," Bobby agreed. "Second wave of them coming in from Tobruk. Jeff was with the first one, just came in a day or so before."

"Jeff?" Justin looked at him.

"I'm checking into it," Bobby assured. "I'm checking into it. Confirming everything, from the damn report to Jeff's checking in."

"Let's start with Cairo," Justin agreed.

"Aye, and it's a lot of territory," Bobby reminded, "is all I'm saying. Going to have to be a little patient. Every damn job and agenda under the sun. But we'll find the one we want, lad, we'll find it. It's how it works. Someone knows, and someone will talk. They always do."

"Yes," Justin said facetiously, "and plenty of time to sort through it all to find it. You up to it?"

"Course." Few things Bobby wasn't up to. He took the picture out of his pocket.

"What's this?" Justin asked as Bobby handed him a photograph of some Catholic girl outside her school some years back. Quite a few years back from the style of the clothes and the general quality of the print, both somewhat worse for wear.

"That business you were asking about with Pete," Bobby nodded. "And before you say anything else, coincidence, lad, remember that. Said as much yourself, such a thing does exist."

"Yes, well, what else would I say?" Justin asked.

"I don't know," Bobby shrugged. "Recognize her? Could start with that."

Recognize her. The devil with her. Recognized the fellow standing next to her like a proud father or mate. Ian McShane. That was a name out of the past, an icy road, car accident, and occupants burned alive. Evelyn swore it was the Fascists, afraid of exposure by the honorable Charles, regardless of who they got to do the job. Justin swore it was McShane regardless of who wanted the job done. "What's the point?" Justin asked.

"You being facetious for a reason?" Bobby asked.

"Could ask the same of you," Justin assured. Of course he recognized her despite ten years and her curls dyed three shades lighter and stretched into an unnatural state until they looked more like cotton batting than hair "Who is she? Daughter would be pushing it. McShane's not Pete's age, and she's got to be close to thirty. Picture's not that old."

"She's twenty-six, lad," Bobby agreed. "Sixteen in her picture."

"I asked you who she is," Justin stopped the jeep hard. "Cain was the father's name."

"His sister," Bobby sighed. "Aye, she's McShane's sister. Fifth one or so in line between that string of fellows the old man sired. Six or seven all total, wasn't it, by the time he was done?"

"Eight," Justin said, before the cow laid down and died, the widower Johnnie not far behind. Stepped in front of a streetcar, some say deliberately. Others say he was drunk on whiskey and grief, and either way it left Ian in charge at seventeen or so years of age before the authorities stepped in to break the happy brood apart. Never got them all, some retreating to their lair to regroup after a few years, others shuttled appropriately off to the children's home, a flip of the coin which lot ended up the worse for it. Still, Justin didn't seem to recall stumbling upon some teary-eyed story of some bleeding heart taking pity on one or any of them. Raising them as one of their own while the rest of her clan eked out a living as best they could. Crime, largely, two of them dead before Justin ever heard the name.

"Where's Pete fit in?" Justin handed him back the photograph and lit his pipe.

"Messenger," Bobby shrugged. "Said she was her, I said she wasn't. Said he could prove it, and I said go ahead and try."

Looked like Pete won. "And Peterson?" Justin asked.

"Now that's interesting," Bobby agreed as if the rest of it wasn't. "Went through the first war together, it seems, Jim Peterson and her old man."

"McShane's old man," Justin corrected, finding that tidbit of information somewhat interesting, Bobby was right.

"Nothing more romantic than that," Bobby nodded. "Peterson went on to make a career out of it, Cain just went home. Happens all the time."

"Deliberate, in other words," Justin said.

"Peterson putting her with you?" Bobby said. "Aye, well, obviously it's deliberate, lad. Went through the war with her old man like I just said. Doesn't mean it has anything to do with her."

"Never heard of him," Justin said, meaning James Peterson and not until three months ago.

"Right. Well, he's obviously heard of you," Bobby said.

"Quite," Justin said, "and he should have listened to what he heard. So much for him keeping that career he's worked so hard to make. You tell him that?"

"I haven't told him anything. Thought I'd leave that to you."

"Thank you," Justin said. "I'll tell him."

"Right," Bobby said. "Before you do though, just remember it's a different world. This war, aye, it's making it different, but it was different already. Different for you than it was for your father. Different for him than it was for Lee and so forth, all the way back. Not taking anything away from you. You are who you are, and you've got a lot of leverage, lad, that you do. Just saying it's different, that's all. Lots of fellows out there who don't have your lineage, but have the same leverage and then some regardless."

"Rubbish," Justin said.

"That's what I thought you'd say," Bobby sighed. "Aye, and, it's all right. Do what you want to do, since you're going to do it anyway."

So he would. "That it?"

"Well," Bobby said, "from what I've been able to gather, it's her who sought Peterson out about five or so years ago, not the other way around." He smiled suddenly, chortled, for whatever damn reason that escaped Justin. "Fancies herself the next Amelia Earhart since the first one went and disappeared. Not just Peterson you've never heard of, apparently not heard of her either; the lass I mean."

"Yes, well," there was no reason why Justin would have heard of her. He was interested in who killed his father. Ian McShane was a man, forty years old himself by this point, thirty back then. Not some tot with his thumb stuck in his mouth.

"Well, she's no tot, lad," Bobby said. "Not then and not now. She got her A-levels. Graduated a year or two behind her classmates, I'll grant you, but still she did it."

"Despite her early upbringing and a couple years off for good behavior," Justin said. "Rot."

"Now, be civil, lad," Bobby suggested, "if you can't be anything else. I happen to like her. Not too proud or ashamed to say. I've kept my eye on her, that's true. But I happen to like her, no offense to you."

"Rot," Justin just said again.

"She's RAF," Bobby reminded, clarifying the earlier reference to Earhart. "And nothing to suggest she's any idea who you are other than her assignment."

"Coincidence," Justin said.

"Innocent," Bobby assured. "On her part, I believe she is. Unless you've a mind to think it's the Blueshirts what followed you to Africa, killed your sister to finish the job they didn't quite finish ten years ago. And if you've a mind to think that," he said, "I've a mind to tell you what I think about that."

"No," Justin did not think that. He thought what he said. Jim Peterson obviously had as little respect for his own career as he did for Justin's lineage and personal feelings, and Justin would take care of that despite the damn new world on the horizon. As far as McShane's sister, it was difficult not to think she enjoyed the joke at his expense as much as her pal Peterson. If he was wrong, he did not care. Beyond that, he didn't think much, somewhat preoccupied by a hollow feeling in his stomach he was unaccustomed to and did not like. "So what is Pete's point again in bringing her to light?"

"I don't know," Bobby shrugged. "Hates the Blueshirts, he says, you know that. Point of fact, that's all. Thinking more about my reasons for not wanting him to. She's a smart one, lad," he said. "Something you might want to know before you hang her. Never graduated college, but that's also more to her credit than against. Knew she didn't have a chance of getting some diploma despite all the protests about equality and I don't know what all going on at the time. But she has her commission, and where she did graduate from is Buckinghamshire, just finished a six-month assignment as a lead cryptographer."

"So she's a smart one," Justin agreed.

"Right," Bobby smiled, "before you hang her. Now you're starting to talk sense."

Not really. Now, as well as back when, Justin didn't care much for sense, only the common sort that held McShane responsible and guilty regardless. "McShane's sister," he said.

"Innocent until proven guilty," Bobby nodded. "Which, just for the record, Pete made a point of pointing out, wanted that clear."

“Well, it’s clear,” Justin assured, “and contradictory, considering Pete hates McShane.”

“Whatever, lad,” Bobby dismissed. “Leave trying to figure out the IRA. Asking me why Pete brought her to light and per Pete his information is for your information only. It’s no form of accusation, but rather believes she’s as innocent as I do.”

“Pete would know,” Justin agreed.

“Would,” Bobby assured, “that he would.”

“Doesn’t stop me from hanging her,” Justin said. “No more than Katy, Martha, and Liz being in that car stopped McShane.”

“Can’t do that,” Bobby shook his head. “That would be murder, lad, for all the wrong reasons.”

“The devil I can’t,” Justin said and drove, just drove, along the heated road for Cairo, Hank close behind in Joe’s jeep, Fred beside him in Pete’s.

Partisans, Rogues, and Thieves

Chapter Twenty-Six

Great Atlas Mountains, Algeria
March 10

By 1100 hours, Tuesday, Jean Paul Dumont received a transcript of a broadcast message they had intercepted, and was reported to have been issued by Justin in Cairo. It was Jean Paul's second urgent message of the day. Anna Haas, the Jewess he called Cassie, there since early morning to abuse him. As fast as her eldest son Abraham could fly her to Jean Paul's lair to scream about the weaknesses in Jean Paul's security network.

She wasn't the only one. The tone of Justin's message was threatening in that Justin apparently had men en route, and unclear in its references to some foreign correspondent and Justin losing his sister. The "men" had to be Reynolds for the same reason Cassie was already there: The depots. Jean Paul's delicate black face pinched with worries and concerns he should never have at his young age, but did. Had them since birth. Different ones, but trials just the same. His mother a Nigerian prostitute and slave, his father the crippled Algerian monk Pierre who bought her freedom for sixty pounds of salt. His father escaped. His mother died in Mussolini's camps during the Italian-Libyan War, where Jean Paul survived to grow up and fight for France, and watch them lose their war. He was not losing this one. Not to Hitler, or for Anna Haas. He didn't care what his father said. His father was in over his head.

"That's it?" Jean Paul demanded of his radio operator.

"Oui, mon caporal," she assured. "The signal wasn't very good."

No, and the subsequent translation into French made things worse. That much Jean Paul had figured out for himself. "Well, Justin isn't wasting his men entertaining some correspondent, and he didn't lose his sister here," he tossed the message to her, changed his mind and took it back. "Find out what this is actually about."

"The depots," she believed as Jean Paul believed. Reynolds was returning for one reason and it had nothing to do with some sister.

Jean Paul frowned at the message. He wasn't sure if Justin even had a sister. He tried to think of what else the reference could mean but couldn't think of anything. The foreign correspondent had to be Reynolds. He didn't need Anna Haas to tell him that.

"Find out," he said. "Confirm this is even from Justin. Ask them to repeat—radio Justin if you have to and tell him we've intercepted a message that has us confused—just find out. I can't argue if I don't know what I am talking about."

"Perhaps dead, mon caporal," she nodded.

"What?" Jean Paul said.

"Perhaps it is not lost, but dead," she closed her code book satisfied.

"It doesn't matter!" Jean Paul snatched the code book out of her hand, slamming it down and waving the message. "This matters. The depots are why Cassie is here. If this is Reynolds returning, do we know when? Do we know where? Do we even," he insisted, "really know why, and don't you think we should find out?"

"The depots, mon caporal," she smiled. "But it's all right. We will find out where, and we will find out when regardless of the silly English code."

"It's not so silly if we can't translate it," Jean Paul assured and left to see what he could do about winning the argument that mattered most. Anna. Anna, who wanted the depots safe and protected that Justin wanted located and destroyed. But then they were her depots, not German, mobile, temporary transfer stations, shipping supplies in, shipping them out. They only looked German for the same reasons she relied upon Jean Paul. Protection. Protection for her people traveling under Rommel's North African flag and the shroud of her beneficent le Metapel, safe passage south from the coast down into the interior and Eden. Non-interference guaranteed by Jean Paul's troops.

She was crazy. Jean Paul knew that regardless of what Justin might have figured out or guessed—which Justin apparently was onto something. Believed he was onto something worth his attention, and unfortunately, it was very much worthy of Justin's attention. Jean Paul wanted out of his arrangement with Anna for more reasons than his allegiance with Justin. What he had agreed to once had now happened ten times. If only Justin knew. There weren't two depots. There were ten, twenty, thirty, who knew how many. Jean Paul could not guess how many might actually be out there. He knew he couldn't close his eyes because when he tried all he could see was a line of German defenses, temporary or otherwise he had unwittingly helped to build and supply. Anna was like his father, believing what she wanted to believe not what was true. Eden was not Eden, and it was not innocent. It was German and out there somewhere. But taking Justin into his confidence was not the answer. If it ever had been, Jean Paul was three months too late.

Jean Paul crumbled Justin's message into a ball. He could never take Justin into his confidence, not then, not now. The people's fear, mistrust, and even hatred of the English was too great. They tolerated Jean Paul's commitment to assisting the English in their fight because they would not tolerate the rape and occupation of France and her Colonies by Hitler's Nazi. Betray their faith and trust in him as the son of some iconic monk they revered, and Jean Paul could forget it. Anna's threats of annihilation would come true. He would be ripped apart. His head sent to the English on a tray.

Jean Paul was no martyr or hero. He was a societal outcast, African, with handsome ebony skin, fine French features and bold white teeth. Apart from his name and accent, which were distinctly French, it was questionable how much of their blood he had in his veins. The closest Bobby Roberts could come to deciphering Jean Paul's background was that he was French Berber, whose pre-war history had him in bed with the Algerian Nationalists, a radical anti-French movement, increasingly popular among the disenfranchised Arab.

Cairo
January 1942
"So you're Dumont," Justin grunted, recovering from his surprise at finding some twelve year old sitting across from him.

"Yes," Jean Paul concurred without apology or embarrassment, and he was not twelve. He was twenty-one, and it was not his problem if Justin expected someone taller, older, for that matter whiter than Jean Paul was, which Jean Paul was none of those things. "And you're Charles. It's nice to put a face to the name."

"It can be," Justin sat back in his chair and lit his pipe. The face of this Resistance leader he cared about was the fact that it was radical, not the point that it was black. One who, in his present incarnation as folk hero, or whatever the devil Corporal Jean Paul Dumont was to his clan, with the invasion and fall of France had apparently decided he hated the Germans and Italians more than he hated his French half-brothers. In fact, three of Jean Paul's small round table of advisors who had made the trip with Jean Paul to Cairo, were French not just bone-white. Like their leader Dumont, deposed French army. That would be the society twins Pierre and Louis Forget, one of them an imbicile, Louis, from a war injury, both of them lieutenants, still in uniform, and almost as small and young as Dumont. Then there was a career sergeant Claude L'Heureaux whom Bobby dated to the Foreign Legion, and trenches of the First World War. L'Heureaux was dressed like Jean Paul in civilian clothes, rural, not urban. A big fellow by comparison, around the size of Pete, Justin pegged L'Heureaux as a bodyguard, and Justin would be right.

"So who was Dumont?" Justin asked.

"Come again?" Jean Paul's head tipped slightly to the side. Justin didn't say anything, but made a note the fellow not only spoke English surprisingly well despite the pronounced accent, but his choice of words indicated he had seen an American film or two, and so Jean Paul had. He had seen a few. With or without them he got what Justin was asking, what he meant. The English Charles trying to figure out just who was this Dumont that had the white boys answering to him instead of it being the other way around.

"My mother's pimp," Jean Paul smiled. He probably shouldn't have. The English did not like to think they were being ridiculed.

"She did not have a name," he offered, "not Anglicized, and so she gave me his."

"Touching," Justin sat forward in his chair, flipping through his manila folder not too obviously. A fourth member of Jean Paul's allied Algerian council who hadn't made the trip to Cairo was another Nationalist. An Egyptian woman, Moslem, Cassandra *X* as in no last name, or no known last name, or Cassie *X* as she appeared in print most often, who oversaw John Paul's extensive network of prostitutes. A fifth associate of Jean Paul's however, also a woman called Cassie for confusion's sake was where Jean's group really took a sharp left turn into the little known and under-appreciated world of Jewish Resistance. "What's this Cassie to you?"

"She prefers Cassandra, and I'm sure you know," Jean Paul assured with a gesture at the file. "You'll find her useful."

More like a pain in the arse. "Meant Haas," Justin said.

"Oh," Jean Paul said. He smiled. "Well, we don't talk about her."

For such obvious and good reasons as the hefty price on her head for consorting with and supporting known terrorists fighting their wrong and private war against the British who closed the gates of Palestine. "Make an exception," Justin closed the file.

"I can't," Jean Paul shook his head. "If you know about her, and apparently you do, you understand I can't."

Justin did more than know about her, he knew her personally. Anna Kassim "Cassie" Haas was one of Evelyn's old cronies he had met during one of his world tours some forty years ago. Entwined with Evelyn, Robert, and even Justin's father Henry with his India affairs, she was also one of Michael's pals following some stint as a visiting professor at one of his alma maters. Anna Haas was a piece of work, a fierce diva who managed in between her marriages and pregnancies to achieve renowned stature as a pioneer in modern cancer therapy. Currently she was nobody save for a nuisance, self-exiled from her native Berlin due to her misfortune of being a Jew. It was Justin's misfortune she decided to park her arse in Africa while waiting for the gates of Palestine to open for her boat people.

"We live in different worlds," Jean Paul offered.

"Yes, well," all that meant was Jean Paul lived on earth. Justin had yet to figure out what cloud Haas called home. Unable to see the world beyond her own nose, Haas's views were single-minded, unwavering and committed solely to her biblical chosen, the rest be dammed.

"It won't be a problem," Jean Paul assured.

No, it wouldn't be, not for Justin. He wasn't so sure about Haas who hated him and England almost as much as both hated her, but that was her problem. "Yes, well, it's not a problem," Justin assured, "as long as she stays out of this." Meaning his and Jean Paul's arrangement. "Get a whiff she's not, and all bets are off. She's a wanted criminal."

"So am I," Jean Paul agreed. "By the Germans," he clarified.

"Yes, well, who isn't?" Justin grunted. Still, he never thought of Anna Haas, not even in passing when Mike showed up, and Joanna turned up dead in North Africa, of all places. He probably should have, though not in any manner to imply Haas might somehow be mixed up in any of this, because she wouldn't be, definitely not anything to do with selling Mike out, whom she adored as she adored Evelyn, and therefore certainly not with murdering Evelyn's beloved granddaughter Joanna. All of that, and the fact Haas was a Jew precluded her from consideration. Had Justin thought of her it would only have been how there was a link to all of them in North Africa and it was Anna Haas. However being that it never crossed Justin's mind, at least not yet, the point was moot.

March 10

Justin should have thought of her, very true, if only in passing. Anna did hate his and his England's guts for the Palestine situation, almost as much as she hated Hitler and Germany. To where England refused, Justin could have helped them, but refused as well, and he should be the last one to denounce the concept of 'chosen', in her opinion, wearing the imperial power and attitude of his English Crown as his own. He did not like her because she refused to accept her role as second class to his first class citizen, which she would never do, unlike so many others who bowed and scraped—like O'Brannigan. Yes, Anna knew Peter O'Brannigan, too. She knew them all. Evelyn, Teddy, Henry, Robert, Martha, Katy, Liz, all of them. She danced at Henry's wedding, cried at his grave. Not so with Justin. No, to the contrary, if the young King Charles ever did topple from his throne, Anna would be right there, not to pick Justin up, but to laugh. Harder than the butchers who entombed her daughter in Poland, Hannah not her mother Anna when it came to her men.

Choosing to die by her husband's side rather than spit in his eye and leave him behind as Anna did with her latest fling, taking her grandchildren with her on her exodus, she thought to Palestine.

They did not make it, obviously, and who Justin did not know anything about being around were the boys, presuming they had more brains than their mother. They didn't, not his kind of brains. They were not only sons, they were brothers. To each other and to Hannah, the middle and only girl between Anna's four towering pillars of testosterone, intelligence, and strength with their Manhattan suites and Park Avenue addresses. Admittedly a life rather hard to abandon for the dunes of Hell, but you do what you have to do in this world, and Anna and her sons did it without guilt, apology, or looking back, just straight ahead to Israel. "Time to go home," Anna told her children like Moses told his. It was what they called her, *Moses,* not *Cassie* like Jean Paul and his French did, until more recently when they started calling her *Diana* after the Roman goddess whose Saharan temple she inhabited and controlled. Yes, Justin should have thought of her, if only in passing. She certainly thought of him and none too pleasantly.

Chapter Twenty-Seven

Great Atlas Mountains
March 10

"We are having some problems confirming the details of the transmission we intercepted," Jean Paul explained when he returned to his round table of lieutenants and Anna. "I need more time to find out what it is about."

"Oh, really?" Anna lifted a harsh brow, hardened and grey, and of little resemblance to the woman she was even five years ago, except that she was still ugly. Uglier at sixty-seven than she had been at sixty-five, or two, her iron-colored hair chopped like a man's, cooler under the wigs of the many characters she employed, her weight still heavy and large breasts staining her shirt with their sweat. "What sort of problems is this?"

"See for yourself," he handed her the message. She read it, throwing it back at him in disgust. "He is an imbecile to think you will fall for this trick. I know Justin, and I know his sister. She is home in England, diapering her dolls, not in North Africa. Isn't that right?" she challenged her son Abraham, tall and dashing in his cloak of Ishmael at forty-one. The hair black and skin browned, his medical degree home safe in his Manhattan suite, his face and flesh tattooed with the art of Arab pagans. She hated the tattoos, hated them, his life over, his career, condemned to the African wilderness and unhallowed grave. He spoke to her in her native German as much to soothe her as to annoy Jean Paul. Telling her to relax, keep still, not to tip her hand. She did not listen very well, furious over the complications of the SS, and now Justin, threatening everything she wished was only her depots. There was no separating Justin's sister Joanna from Michael, and no separating Michael from what he was.

A physicist. She had the sister Joanna brought by the SS. Michael had to be out there somewhere, alive or dead, and Justin would blanket the planet to find him to make sure one way or the other.

She returned to Jean Paul who looked surprised. "What? What's the matter with you? Did I say something you didn't expect?"

"Well, no," Jean Paul said, "perhaps a little surprised you questioned the reference to some sister rather than the foreign correspondent, which, yes, I agree with you. It is concerning, possibly an indication Reynolds is en route as you suspect." He frowned at the message. "Then Justin does have a sister."

"So?" Anna said as her son Abraham resisted the temptation to hit her over the head for opening her mouth so wide. "So I know his sister? So what?"

"Nothing," Jean Paul shook his head and sat down. "I guess you could be sympathetic?"

"Why?" she asked.

"I don't know," Jean Paul waved impatiently. "Because you could? It doesn't matter. It has nothing to do with us."

"I just said that," she agreed, "didn't I?"

Yes. So did he. He felt sorry though now that he knew it was a line in a message, not some code. He liked Justin when he met him. He liked him still. Anna, he felt sorry for, until he met her. She was not a woman who inspired pity, but was quite capable of taking care of herself. It escaped him why she remained in Africa, bent on protecting and assisting those who had escaped the Nazi, instead of returning to Europe to help those who had not.

That was a lie, actually. Jean Paul knew why Anna stayed. She stayed because she was not stupid, survived, and lived out of spite. Her power was limited to herself and her wits, her sons, and their wits. She did not believe in martyrs, fighting battles she could not win, but instead in winning those she could. She did not have a chance in Europe, here she did.

"If you want sympathy," Anna's hand flitted at Abraham, "talk to the psychiatrist. He'll give you all you want. Me, I could give two-shits."

Yes, Jean Paul got the message. "Why did you say trick?" he asked curiously.

She shrugged again. "Trap then."

"Trap," Jean Paul savored. It had to be her. French was his language. "Meaning?" he asked.

"Meaning just that," she snapped. "I know."

Jean Paul eyed her with a glance at the twins Louis and Pierre Forget and the long, thin frame of his whore Cassandra with a hook for a nose behind him. Cassandra was tense, Louis, his usual nervous, Pierre his usual deadpan. It was Cassandra who straightened up to dangle her jewelry over the wooden door they used for a table, her Egyptian breath in Anna's face. "How do you *know* anything?"

"Meaning?" Anna countered.

"Meaning this," Cassandra's fingers took the message out of Jean Paul's hand to wave it at her. "You know so much, you should be telling us instead of asking us to tell you."

Anna sneered. "You mean care, and I don't."

"She's lying," Cassandra said confidently to Jean Paul, and not so evenly to Anna. "You're lying, Jew. What do you know about this? What did you do this time for Israel?"

Jean Paul silenced Cassandra, waving her back to her post. Lying was a strong accusation, suggesting Anna might have something to do with the death of some girl was simply ludicrous regardless of how angry she was over Reynolds. "Let's not read into things," Jean Paul suggested. "Lose sight of what is important. Reynolds."

"Me?" Anna said. "Me lose sight?"

"Any of us," Jean Paul assured. "I'm sorry," he apologized, "it was confusing that you would say 'trick' or 'trap'. Let's talk—" he started to say again.

"Trick or trap," Anna interrupted him, "is what Justin does. Nothing is ever innocent, not some *sister,*" she waved, "or some *war correspondent,*" she waved again. "Trick, or trap, that is his forte. *Coup d'état.* You know what that is? Of course you do. You say you are allies. I say you wouldn't interest Justin unless there was something about you he did not like. His job is to infiltrate and destroy at any cost, you'll see. You are his means, not his partner. He wants the people kept in line, not inspired. If he tames you, he will tame them, because you will do it for him. I know," she smiled, "you're right. I do it every day, all the time."

And said it all the time, Jean Paul looked away from her again, over his small arrangement of advisors, the twins, very pro-British, like him, not partisans of Vichy control. His companion Cassandra? Loyal to no one except him. "There is no one here to divide ..." Jean Paul said carefully, turning back to Anna. "We are all on the same side."

"Oh, good," she said. "Because you forget it is you who guarantees me, not the other way around. And now because Justin speaks ..." she snatched the wire off the table to wave it like a flag. "You are suddenly frightened? Really, Jean Paul, if it is time for you to have a conscience, kill your own, not mine."

"That is enough!" Jean Paul snatched the wire away from her in frustration. "I am killing no one. If I ask questions, it is simply because I am asking you to verify information I have received—"

"About Justin," she nodded.

"About the depots!" he snapped. "And perhaps we can figure out what to do about Reynolds together. But I have to know, Cassie, what I am involved in. I have to know for a fact before this goes any further."

"Which you are asking me to explain, not verify!" she assured. "Me. Who is insane? I am a Jew. My daughter lies dead in their camps. Would I walk with the creatures killing my own? Help them? Hide them?"

"No, of course you wouldn't," Jean Paul waved. "No one is saying you are. But I have men, Cassie," he stressed, "talking about munitions depots, not supply compounds. Why are they saying this? Can you explain that to me, yes?"

"I do not have to," she refused.

"Excuse me?" Jean Paul said while Cassandra smiled satisfied behind him.

"You have an idiot by the name of Reynolds breathing down your neck," she assured. "Kill it."

"Kill it," Jean Paul repeated.

"Yes," Anna said. "Kill it, him, get rid of it."

"Actually, 'men' and 'war correspondent' are separated in the message," Abraham advised his mother who glared at him for talking out of turn. "That implies more than Reynolds are coming."

"Will you talk to her?" Jean Paul agreed with Abraham excitedly in French. "I can't kill Justin's men!"

"No?" Anna said. "Not even when they are plotting against you?"

"How?" Jean Paul insisted. "How are they plotting against me? Where is your proof for any of these accusations? Even if I agree with you Justin is not satisfied with the reports of the depots and this proves Reynolds is returning!" he waved the message which said no such thing. "We will take care of it. We will work together to take care of it. That has nothing to do with killing anyone."

She snatched the wire back to read it. Dissect it. Decipher.

"What?" Jean Paul insisted. "What is it you see in there that I cannot?"

"That's a good question. What is this?" Anna thrust the notice impatiently at Abraham. "You know Justin better than I do, you tell me. What is the meaning of his silly post script about his sister if it's not to include this one in his fishing expedition? Some sad note to a friend? I don't think so. That girl didn't come here alone. You know who she had to be with, and Justin will go where he needs to go to find him dead or alive, as would I. He will not stop at the border of Egypt. And if he comes here and finds those depots where do you think they lead? To us with his sister laying right there as well. So who is crazy to be concerned? Not me. You want to wait until Justin shows up on the doorstep? I don't. I want those depots safe."

"Yes," Abraham agreed in part. "But there are two separate issues here—"

"Oh, really?" Anna sneered. "I'm sorry, is there no girl at my compound?"

Dieter's compound, and, yes, obviously there was. "There are two issues here," Abraham said again. "The girl and the depots. Justin did not send the message to this one. They intercepted it as we did."

"And that's not intentional?" Anna said. "Justin just happened to broadcast instead of wiring this one directly?"

"Of course it's intentional," Abraham said. "Justin has dropped a fishing line to see who bites. The bait about the girl isn't meant for this one or anyone. He's stirring the pot to see what boils to the top."

"And that's not Reynolds Justin is talking about?" his mother's finger pounded down on the transcript.

Yes, Abraham believed it was, and he did not like the message at all. It was well crafted, deliberately vague on the surface, allowing the audience to read into it what they wanted to. Abraham read a lot. Justin was on the warpath. Disclosing the dead girl as his sister when for ten years, on paper for public knowledge, he had no sister, was bold. That bold, meant that angry. Men on route had to be Reynolds and his boys, the 'war', or 'foreign' correspondent Justin separated from the pack had to be whom? Possibly Mike? Abraham did not think so. Instead, who came to mind was O'Brannigan. Out loud, he said calmly to his mother, "We've been over that. Yes, it has to mean Reynolds is returning. Yes, Justin involved this one to throw a scare into him—about the depots, not the girl. In the meantime, Justin thinks the girl is dead. That's why the broadcast. Notice to whomever else intercepts. Not us. Let's leave it that way. Stick to talking about Reynolds and the depots. Do not talk about the girl."

"I want them safe!" Anna insisted. "We are between Vichy and Cairo, and Justin is out there. If they come here, kill them! Reynolds, O'Brannigan, whoever. All of them. Or I will let David off his leash and it will be over!"

It would be over all right. David was Dieter, who Jean Paul and his gang only knew as le Metapel, Anna's mysterious benefactor. She called him *David* not to say his name. There was another name she avoided saying and it was Mike. Justin wasn't the only one out there somewhere, so was Mike. Like his kid, Red, dead or alive, and yes, Justin would scour the planet to find out which, find out who, and certainly find out where. He was setting himself up as bait, taunting them, daring them. That was the message Abraham read in Justin's note. The fact Justin made sure his broadcast reached as far as Algeria confirmed Justin considered the French suspect, and that had to be the depots, not the girl or Mike. An assurance from Justin he knew things others did not think he knew, whether he actually knew them or not. Justin knew something or he would not be sending his men back.

That was how Abraham read it anyway, and he was confident he was right. The problem was his mother's point that there were depots. And this one, Jean Paul, apparently knew a lot less than he should about Justin's movements and motivation.

Abraham studied Jean Paul. Nellie Reynolds was Justin's blood hound, his Ace of Aces, but not his Ace of Spades. That was O'Brannigan, the head of Justin's death squad. Peter O'Brannigan wasn't en route because of some depot. He was en route to kill. Who? This one, Jean Paul? Justin wouldn't waste O'Brannigan on Jean Paul unless Justin knew a lot, if not everything about the depots, and if Justin did, he wouldn't need Reynolds, and even then it would be more of a revenge killing.

Maybe it was Mike, Abraham considered, and maybe it wasn't here at all, at least not Jean Paul specifically. But Algeria in general included in Justin's manhunt. Reynolds to find Mike? O'Brannigan to kill Mike if they couldn't get Mike out, or wasn't dead already? If the girl wasn't at Dieter's compound, while not completely out of the question, Abraham would say Vichy Algeria would be stretching it. It wasn't, and the facts supported one scenario. A plane en route that failed to show. Cairo to Gibraltar the route? Mike aboard, it probably had escorts across Libya, dropping off as they reached Algeria, and that was when they lost contact with the plane, forced down, shot down, or crashed.

"Jesus Christ," Abraham muttered, the odds good the story went something like that. Bottom line, Justin was out there, and that was not good. Anna had one thing on her mind, her depots, from there, Eden and Dieter. This idiot Jean Paul, had to know something more, and if he didn't, he should. Abraham turned uncharacteristically hostile and impatient on Jean Paul. "Reynolds is Justin's scout, but O'Brannigan is Justin's assassin. If it's not your neck he wants whose is it? *Le Metapel?* That's her concern. Something has to be out there, someone has to know something. She is right. You're not out here alone. Justin is too close for comfort whether it's Reynolds, or O'Brannigan, or whoever it is. Justin did not ensure the message reached Algeria for no reason. So, what happened? What caused Justin to send Reynolds back? Whatever line you are trying to sell Justin about the depots he clearly isn't buying it."

Jean Paul couldn't have played it any more convincingly in Abraham's opinion. He didn't know anything, less even than they did. Abraham sighed. It was a little late to try and pretend they didn't need Jean Paul regardless.

"We intercepted the same transmission," Abraham offered as Jean Paul stared at the wire. "That appears to be the extent of it. Justin sending Reynolds out is one thing, but O'Brannigan is another. O'Brannigan is here to kill. The question is who? Why? We assumed the death of this girl happened at home, but perhaps it didn't. Perhaps it was here, Cairo. What is the chatter over the last few weeks? Is this the first time you've heard any mention of this?"

"I don't know," Jean Paul said. "Cairo ..."

"Three-thousand kilometers," Anna shrieked in support. "Justin is not sending men three-thousand kilometers for no reason!"

"I got that!" Jean Paul assured. "And I don't know. We presumed this had to be about the depots. We were puzzled about the reference to some sister, but I don't think any of us considered ..." he surveyed the twins, but they were shaking their heads, confused as he was. "You know as much as we do. This is it, yes. The quality of the transmission was very poor—the Telex? Forget it. They're still trying to re-contact them and confirm, but so far that's it."

"The mountains," Abraham nodded. "We have the same problem."

"Yes, of course, who doesn't?" Jean Paul dismissed. "I am confused. What are you saying? Justin is investigating us for his sister's death? How? Why? What does that have to do with the depots?"

"It doesn't," Abraham assured. "It can't. It is the choice of men that is concerning—obviously concerning," his impatience returned, "especially if one of them is O'Brannigan."

"Yes," Jean Paul agreed, "that is a good question, isn't it? Especially since, I agree with your mother. Justin isn't sending men three-thousand kilometers to kill French or Jews in revenge for his sister's death—in Cairo!" he turned viciously on Anna. "What the hell is actually going on here? Palestine? What did you do?"

"Stick to Reynolds!" Abraham barked at her in reminder.

She ignored him, vehement as the Gorgon Medusa, her tongue whipping Jean Paul in counter attack. "What do you think? I am not waiting until Justin is banging on the door! I do not care about your British, or your Free French, I care about mine. Justin and his idiots are a threat to mine. Get rid of them!"

"Cassie ..." Jean Paul said.

"No!" she refused. "No, if you had done your job correctly no one would be confusing depots and supply stations—and I would not have the SS at my door!" she hissed. "Now, what do you think I should do?"

"SS?" Jean Paul stared at Abraham.

"Yes," Abraham sighed. "Yes. Somehow, the SS is also mixed into this. It's a mess, and this doesn't help," he threw the message back on the table. "Justin's fishing, maybe, maybe not. But he must think you can tell him something he wants to know otherwise this message would have never reached here. Reynolds at least has to be coming here."

"He's right," Cassandra said in Jean Paul's ear. "Why would the English be coming here except for you? They're right. The Jew is right. Kill them now, all of them, her, too. Do it!"

Jean Paul ignored her. "We'll find out," he promised Anna. "Talk to me. Calm down—both of us, yes," he agreed, "and talk so we can figure this out. Together," he stressed. "Together."

"Twice now you have told me," she fumed, "how Reynolds has been where he does not belong—"

"Yes, and we took care of it. The supply transfer is safe, the camps are both gone. I will put a stop to Reynolds, I promise you. Without killing him, I will stop him. A guarantee."

Her brow arched. "You mean my camps. You want blood, Jean Paul, le Metapel will give it to you, and it will not be mine."

Jean Paul straightened up. "I do not want blood. Is that a threat to me? Because I will tell you something, Cassie—"

No, she was telling him. "I will strike a bargain with you, Jean Paul. When I am confident, mine are safe, perhaps Justin will find he has his sister back. In one step, the SS have gone from Egypt to Eden. You are a smart man. Someone has to be supplying them with this information, the same as they are supplying Justin. Is it you?"

"No!" Jean Paul turned on Abraham. "What the hell is she saying? You have Justin's sister? Are you complete idiots?"

"Do we look like idiots to you?" Abraham said.

"Don't lie to me!" Jean Paul's fist hit the table. "I'm sick of it. No, you don't look like idiots, but apparently, you think I am some kind of fool, and I am not! You can tell me what is going on, or you can tell Justin, that is the only bargain I am willing to strike with you."

"Except they are supply stations," Anna jeered. "So what could be going on? Bullets for Rommel, or pillows for my children's heads?"

"Cassie, they are hardly pillows," Jean Paul ran his fingers through his hair. "I am asking you now about Justin's sister, I want to know what you did."

"No, they are munitions," she persisted instead. "Mine! To blow open the gates of Palestine Justin has closed."

Palestine. He knew it. "Justin did not close the gates!"

"His army did! And England is never wrong, never. Ask him!"

"Fine!" Jean Paul said. "His army closed the gates, and his army is the only one who can open them—not Justin! You kidnapped his sister?" he gaped at her. "Holding her hostage? I cannot believe this. And then you come complaining to me, asking me why he is coming here? Why the hell do you think he is coming, eh?"

"Take care of it!" she barked. "A good idea, if only to stop the French from hanging the great Jean Paul Dumont first!" She stalked out the door leaving him to stare helplessly at Abraham.

"She likes him," Abraham shrugged, sometimes wondering if his mother carried on the way she did, simply because she liked him. He lit a cigarette and sat down to think. "Le Metapel," he clarified as if he had to.

"Yes," Jean Paul agreed hollowly. "I got it." She was not alone. Just ask his father who revered and idolized him. Upheld and promoted him until he was more than just a sympathetic ear, but a legend, a god no one would dare deny, betray, or offend.

"Who else?" Abraham nodded. "The sword she can see in his hand, ready to strike, defend, whatever he needs to do. A true King. Not simply an aristocrat with a guilty conscious and Superman complex, which he is," he smiled. "Make no mistake. Superman. Immortal and invincible, just ask him."

Jean Paul looked at him tiredly, and Abraham felt almost as sorry for him as he did for Dieter. "A bad joke," Abraham apologized.

That wasn't it. "I'd rather not know," Jean Paul said. "We," he waved, meaning Cassandra, the twins, "would rather not know anything about le Metapel."

"Suit yourself," Abraham said, amiable to the blind leading the blind. It worked out better that way. "It doesn't change anything."

Of course it did. It changed everything. Confusing the lines between enemy and friend, creating a war no one could win. "Why?" Jean Paul insisted. "Why was it necessary to kill Justin's sister if this is all as innocent as you claim? Revenge for Palestine? Give me a break. Justin is not responsible for Palestine!"

"We didn't kill her," Abraham assured.

"No, of course not," Jean Paul nodded. "Your mother is just talking. She's upset and couldn't think of anything else to say. Abraham," he advised, "I really am not an idiot, and neither are you. Your mother is so concerned about being sacrificed she is willing to sacrifice anyone."

"Probably. But then it is only a supply station," Abraham supported the claim of innocence beneath the flag of the Afrika Korps. "We need it and le Metapel right now. When we don't, you'll be the first to know—or the second," he shrugged, since Dieter would be the first when his kingdom went up in smoke, the poor fool.

"A supply station with the SS at its door," Jean Paul said.

"More like the Gestapo," Abraham stood up. "Makes sense to me why she wants to end it here, now."

"And how does this end it?" Jean Paul insisted. "How does killing Justin's sister, his men, end anything? Punish, is what she wants to do. She wants to punish who she thinks is responsible."

"Which someone is," Abraham assured. "Make it Reynolds. Satisfy her. What can it hurt?"

"Us," Jean Paul said. "It can hurt us!"

"Not as much as it will hurt if Justin finds those depots," Abraham promised, "and definitely not as much if the SS finds any of us. Look," he said, "the kid's no one. She's a blind. Don't bite the hook Justin's dangling. She has nothing to do with you."

"You mean like you didn't bite it?" Jean Paul said.

"Oh, no, we bit," Abraham assured. "Hard, fast, and furious, and not about to let go."

"But why," Jean Paul insisted, "if your hands are clean."

"Ma wants to know what's going on," Abraham said simply. "No guess work. Justin is on to something. He thinks he is, anyway, and regardless of his reasons or plan, there is a link here linking all of us. You, le Metapel, the SS, AND me. The depots. So you take care of Justin's men, and we'll take care of the SS, because, well, let's face it. Regardless of anything else, nothing about the SS is coincidence. You know that. I know that. And, yes," he said, "le Metapel knows that. Their tentacles are everywhere. Even more than Justin's."

"I don't even know Reynolds or Peter O'Brannigan," Jean Paul stared dully into space.

"Lay it to Vichy," Abraham said. "In war men die, kid sisters as well. Either you do it, or we'll do it—"

"Or le Metapel," Jean Paul said sourly.

"Definitely," Abraham assured. "Without losing sleep. That altruistic nature of his extends only so far. I wouldn't look for it to include the ranks of England's 8th Army. He is still German, after all. But then, so are we," he shrugged and exited, leaving Jean Paul to stare at his trio of advisors.

"We cannot betray le Metapel for the English ..." Louis began carefully, positive Jean Paul could not seriously be thinking of taking such a risk with the loyalty of the people without which he could not survive.

"Shut up you fool!" Cassandra snapped. "We can betray whoever betrays us. It is all right," she reassured Jean Paul. "We will think of something."

"We have a day," he said. "A day. Two, if we are lucky. A week if we kill Reynolds. Another if we kill O'Brannigan. I have a headache," he sat down with a thud.

Chapter Twenty-Eight

The Fezzan
March 10

Joanna Lee was no longer sleeping. Her eyes were closed and she was lying very still, her chest rising and falling at regular intervals. Michael, you see, had taught her that. If you're going to pretend to be asleep, you have to do it right. People when they sleep breathe evenly, slowly, occasionally making strange sounds. The man, whoever he was, was in the room. Joanna knew it was a man because she seemed to remember a man, though not quite sure why. That was peculiar. Why didn't she remember? She did not know. The same if someone should ask her what she remembered about yesterday, for example, or the day before, did she remember enough to even know if she had forgotten anything? Days, weeks, people, places, things, it all seemed rather like a blackboard that had been wiped clean. Any trace of what had been written—was there any trace left? Heat. She remembered being hot for some reason, feeling hot. A stifling dry hot like one felt when they bent over an opened oven door, or the dusty plains of Queensland where she had been born.

She remembered thinking about Australia and home, about a day in the future, any day, Tuesday, why not? That if she thought about Tuesday, imagined herself there, this day would be over and she would be safe a week in the future where whatever one felt now they didn't feel anymore because it was over, finished, gone.

Not that it was, or had been a bad day. Had it? What was she thinking to even think that? Joanna did not know. Not what she was thinking, or what she was not. She felt odd, groggy, only half awake, and so not really, completely, pretending to be asleep. Just as everyone did the first thing in the morning before waking up to think anything. Before the world came into focus and dreams became dreams much to your disappointment and occasionally to your relief. She could tell she was on a bed of some sort, the mattress soft and thickly cushioned like a pillow, the sheets smooth. She could feel a hot breeze close by and an odd smell threatening to make her sneeze. That would be inconvenient, since surely the man would hear her unless he was deaf. Could he be deaf? Was it odd or just wishful thinking to wonder if he might be deaf? There was no rule saying he couldn't be deaf, if he was even really there at all.

He isn't really there, Joanna decided, shifting slightly to a position more comfortable for her back. He was a mouse, or perhaps a ghost. She had never seen a ghost, and while she might be nineteen, she still thought occasionally about them. He had to be one or the other, and she tried to listen closely to figure out which he might be, knowing she could always ask if she really had to. Muster her courage and call out, *"Who's there?"* Cry or scream if she did not like the answer. Fight, or die or just fall back to sleep. *God!* Joanna wished she was on her stomach. It would be so much simpler to pretend to be sleeping if she was on her stomach. She wouldn't have to worry if anyone was staring at her face. What if the man was staring at her face?

Let him stare, she decided. She hurt too much right now to even want to move and that was also very confusing. Why did she hurt? She had so much pain in the parts of her she could feel she could not help but realize there seemed to be parts of her she couldn't feel. Her legs for example, she could barely even find her legs, figure out where they were ... what *was* that smell? It really was awful. A harsh antiseptic filling her nose and tickling her tongue. She wouldn't be surprised to wake up and find she was in some hospital corridor—she was in hospital? That thought startled her even more than the idea of some man haunting her room. What on earth would she be doing in hospital? She didn't hurt that much, only bad enough to want to lie flat like the time when she was ten and fell out of the tree, the wind knocked out of her. Joanna tried not to open her eyes and check things out for herself. It wasn't easy being she was, by nature, a curious person. A kind of curiosity that occasionally got her into trouble ... *like the tree ...*

Joanna fell back to sleep, or she thought she might have because when she woke up it almost seemed as if she was pointing a different direction. But, no, she wasn't. She was still on her back, still inside the hot smelly fog. That fog would be there for days. She did not know that now, but it would. Sometimes less thick than others, and sometimes so thick she couldn't remember what she remembered one minute and did not another. Like the furniture. She always seemed to have trouble remembering furniture, where it was or that it was even there at all. That's what Claudia said. *"That child never pays attention. I don't know what it is."* She was better by now, of course, much better, far less rambunctious, much more mature, her nails less frequently dirty and broken, a solid steel barrette taming her wiry red hair ...

England before the War

"What if I cut it?" Joanna sighed as she flipped through the magazine of the very latest in glamour and glamorous dress, so tired of being thoroughly unglamorous and short. Horribly and thoroughly unnaturally short. It was so depressing. It wasn't like everyone around was so extraordinarily tall because they weren't. Michael certainly wasn't. But even next to Michael she seemed to disappear. Everyone having to look down to notice she was there. It really was time for a change. A desperately needed change and today was the day. It most definitely was. Why just today, this afternoon, Andrea, Michael's daughter and her best and only friend even though they were a solid four years apart, looked so pretty in her afternoon dress, long, and golden, like summer itself. It absolutely was time for a change.

"I need a change, Michael," she assured, "and I need it today." Tomorrow, of course, they would find her up on the roof where she belonged, lookout for Michael hiding out next to her, Andrea and her sisters Millicent and Heather down on the lawn taking pictures with their mother Claudia. "Michael," she insisted, "Michael, are you listening to me? I want to cut my hair, and I want to cut it today."

"Over my dead body," Michael took the magazine away.

"But it's 1937," Joanna stared in the mirror. "I'm fifteen."

"So?" Michael said.

Well, it was Claudia's point, actually, how she still looked so much like a savage. "Perhaps you're right," Joanna agreed as she turned this way and that way in the mirror. "I rather like it, actually. It's rather exciting to think of myself as—*savage,"* she shook her head just to be sure it was savage enough.

"Keep it up and we'll shave it," Michael picked up his razor to clean it, salvage what was left of it and her knees, which wasn't much, nope.

"You wouldn't," Joanna gasped.

"Oh, wouldn't I?" he countered. "You're two years into my first heart attack as it is. Christ," he shook his head at her bloody knee. "That's a hell of a hack job. I knew something was up when the buzzards started swirling overhead."

"I don't know about that," Joanna surveyed her handiwork. "I didn't do that bad."

"You did worse," he assured. "It's OK, it'll grow back."

"Grow back?" Joanna said. "But, I don't want it to grow back, Michael. That's rather the idea, isn't it?"

"The skin," Michael patted the sink. "Leg up, hold still, and pay attention because I'm only going to do this once. Hold still," he insisted. "Christ, which one of us is drunk?"

Well, she wasn't, of course, it was just the idea of holding still. Joanna wasn't very good at holding still, even worse when someone asked her to. The more they asked, the more she seemed incapable. Even by nineteen when she ought to be *years* into being mistress of Grandfather's house that had no mistress, Joanna still wasn't very good at anything she ought to be good at. She left such responsibility to Claudia who was really very good at everything from directing the cook to managing the horde of cleaning personnel ... That's what her mother had called them. "*Why, for goodness sake, Henry ...*" Joanna could hear her mother's clear, soft voice, unaffected and genuine. "*Who are all these cleaning ... personnel*?" Her ladyship Elizabeth Edwards not quite sure what else to call the overwhelming number of house staff with their military stiff backs. Henry laughed, chuckled as he always did, citing it to be as good a description as any, but then he always agreed with her mother, no matter what she said, why wouldn't he? Her mother was a beautiful woman in mind, body, and soul, slender and tall in her comfortable heels, elegant and respectable in her fine fitting suits and some saucy little hat she always wore perched to the side of her head.

Joanna remembered her mother quite vividly, the smell of her lip rouge, the touch of her hand. She remembered her father also, the first one, John, her mother saying *"John"* exactly the same way she said *"Henry"*. Kind and affectionate to them as they were to her, rarely with any sort of reproach. John was the broader of the two men, muscular, the younger of the two. Henry, a tall, dignified stick, his hair grey, and face defined with lines. A city man, to where John was an enthusiast of Nature, a fanatic for the wilds of the outback beyond their Australian ranch.

Joanna remembered the ranch, the lone tree past the fence of the corral where her father released the horses to run on the first day of spring. It was so exciting to watch, their eyes rolling and faces mad as they reared and pranced on hind legs. Too exciting, her mother would scold, for a young lady. But then her mother would be the one who decided they needed to have a fine picnic out by the tree with the ants and the birds and the leaves.

Her mother would be the one to support her daughter's claim it was a croc what got her father. He hadn't really drowned at all. Joanna stood up on the seat of her chair to reach the round wonderful looking buns in the bowl on the dining table.

"*Yes, that's quite true, isn't it?*" Liz thanked her daughter for the delicious roll and butter she passed forward. "*A crocodile did get John. Just in the way he would want to be gotten,*" she smiled at Henry seated across the table from her. A man she did not know well before her husband's death, but only vaguely. A look in her eyes telling him she also knew what she should not know, and it was the truth behind the life and death of Sir John Edwards. A fallen soldier in the savagery and shadows of the Outback and their ranch where he ran horses, cattle, and sheep, as opposed to Sir Henry who "*owned things*", Liz believed was what Henry had said when she inquired into the nature of his livelihood apart from Parliament's Back Benches.

"*Well, that's all right, I suppose,*" Liz agreed, "*if one can afford it,*" which she could. Her money, body, and soul, married to Sir John's for ten years, some old family money and John's astute mind for business leaving her financially quite well off. But that wasn't the point. The point was she had a daughter and she was naturally curious as to what made Henry Charles think he was not only qualified, but wanting the responsibility of rearing and providing for a daughter in the midst of a financial depression. A global situation so great and dire it affected Australia and England the same as it affected the very foundations of everywhere else. The world was on its knees, ripe for an assortment of sordid troubles. Henry snorted at the idea, comfortable in the simple knowledge the world and civilization would survive as it had survived all its catastrophes before, from the wars to depressions to the famines, uprisings, rebellions, and even plagues.

"*Yes,*" Liz recalled something about a Black Death, some four centuries past. "*Before my time, I'm afraid,*" she smiled. A subtle way of bringing to the table the fact that Henry Charles was older than she was. Quite old enough to be her father never mind her daughter's. A fact that had Henry stopping what he was saying about man, mankind, and Briton, to ask, "*See here, are you going to marry me or not*?" A proposal Liz naturally answered, "*Yes,*" though she cleared her hasty decision with Joanna while she helped her daughter straighten her bonnet and clean her dusty knees as best they could.

"*After all,*" Liz smiled at Joanna who looked so much like her father that any less strong woman would surely break down and cry, "*we can't have Henry knowing what grubby little beggars we really are just yet.*" Something which, yes, by some misguided social standards they actually were, what with preferring picnics out in the horses' corral to sipping tea any day. Still, it was something Liz rather suspected Henry wouldn't mind at all, such picnics. "*We'll save that for next week Tuesday when we sail to visit the ranch.*" she nodded in appreciation to Joanna climbing up on the chair to pin her mother's hat. "*What do you think about Henry*?" she asked Joanna just about then. "*You haven't said much.*"

He was nice, Joanna supposed, being only eight, and not really having thought about it. She crawled out from under the bed, still looking for her other shoe with little hope of finding it.

"*Yes, he is nice, isn't he*?" her mother smiled. "*Quite nice. I rather think we're going to have fun. Where's your shoe*?"

Joanna shrugged. *"I'll hop."*

"That will work," her mother agreed, *"but not on the stairs. Slide down the banister instead. After all,"* she smiled at Henry as Joanna whizzed past her, down the banister to land at his feet in the front hall, *"we can't risk breaking a leg. That wouldn't be much fun."*

"Nice hat," Henry complimented.

"Thank you," Liz accepted, and they went on to purchase Joanna's third new pair of shoes that week so they would look reasonably presentable for the Vicar who commented politely on how much Joanna looked like her mother, which was charming, but not true. Joanna did not look much like her mother at all, except for possibly in the eyes. Her eyes were like her mother's, a warm, soft, ordinary brown. Liz's flecked with intelligence and vigor. Joanna's? Liz smiled at her daughter with her restless independence exactly like her mother in that regard for all she favored her father John.

"Odd, but neither of you look like a rogue," Henry brought up the subject of Joanna's rather carefree nature later, after tea.

"Neither do you," Liz agreed. *"So that and a nickel will get you ... what is it?"* she verified.

"A cup of coffee," he smiled. *"See if any of us has made an impression on you, it's Mike."*

"Yes, well, I rather suspect Mike ..." Liz thought about the American doctor who was handsome, she supposed, she'd give him that, *"makes an impression on most people."*

"Good or bad?" Henry wondered solely out of curiosity.

"Well, both, I would think," Liz said. *"Whatever impression he's inclined to make at the time. Is he really an American gangster? I honestly couldn't decide if I was supposed to believe him or not."*

"Oh, no," Henry chuckled. *"No, Mike's a sort of chemist. Quite respectable underneath it all. Just his odd sense of humor. Don't let him trouble you."*

"Yes," Liz said. An odd sense of humor bristling with cynicism and, she would almost have to say, fierce hostility. He certainly did not seem to like his wife very much. A woman, Liz understood he had been estranged from for some time before reemerging quite out of the blue. He was a rogue, without a doubt. Not the sort of man one would think a woman of sense would be attracted to, though she was

apparently wrong since for all he did not seem to like his wife, his wife certainly appeared to like him, almost desperately. "*Trouble me how*?" she asked.

"*In any way,*" Henry assured, leaving Michael there and inquiring naturally on his own child, since they were on the subject of children. "*What about Justin*?"

"*Yes, of course,*" Liz smiled, thinking of the towering barnacle Henry had for a son, a young man who seemed so completely out of place around this Cambridge highbrow lot as his questionable friend Michael. No less of an adventurer than his friend Michael, she suspected, few responsibilities to tie him down, and strongly averse to acquiring any. "*Well, Justin I would rather suspect is you, isn't he*?" she said. "*Perhaps when you were somewhat younger, but definitely you.*"

"*No flies on you I see,*" Henry laughed. "*Quite all right. Might not look it just now, but he'll come around, the same as I did.*"

"*Come around to what*?" Liz wondered. "*Seems perfectly content to me.*"

"*Civilization,*" Henry patted her hand reassuringly. "*Nothing more drastic than that.*"

"*Oh, yes, of course,*" Liz said. "*Civilization. Evening suits and evening tea rather than tweed and a beaker of Scotch. He seemed perfectly well mannered and acceptable to me.*"

"*You like him,*" Henry said.

"*I do, actually,*" Liz agreed. "*Why? Don't you?*"

"*Very much,*" Henry assured. "*He's a good lad. No complaints.*"

"*As I rather suspect he knows how to wear an evening suit,*" she said. "*He simply prefers not to.*"

"*Right again,*" Henry said. "*So what about you? Who are you?*"

She laughed. "*Joanna. Yes, all right, you've caught us. I'm quite like Joanna or rather she's quite like me. Rogues, ourselves, if you care to be unkind, mavericks, daughters of the Suffrage, therefore, barbarians. I'm quite sure someone along the way has said so, or they will,*" she fairly promised teasingly. "*John, for all his adventure, was really the respectable one of the group. So if you've a mind to reconsider our engagement, perhaps you should do that now, before we're announced.*"

"Wouldn't dream of it," he assured, and six months later considering the grim end they came to, he rather wished he had. Bob and Martha mercifully killed on impact as the car went over the edge and the earthly world came to an end for the rest of them. Henry would have shot Liz, had he thought of it, the compartment already erupted in flames as he fought desperately in the few seconds they had to shove both Liz and Katy free. By the time, he did think of his gun, it was too late. He had already lost Liz through the opened door, the bullet jamming in the chamber, the gun dropping from his charred hand. Still who he felt sorry for most of all as peace came was that tot of hers Liz left behind to fend for herself, alone in her adventure her mother had quite innocently promised her would be fun.

"She'll be fine," Liz reassured Henry when they met along the High Road, Bob and Martha patiently waiting for Katy and them to catch up.

"How do you know that?" Henry asked, a cynic apparently even in the afterlife.

"Because I do," Liz said. *"She's my daughter, and we're rogues,"* she reminded him. *"You'll see. Joanna's quite clever, actually, quite self-reliant, she'll survive, succeed, I dare even say,"* she laughed quite proudly, *"where others less daunting would certainly fail. Largely, I suspect, because she doesn't realize she's not supposed to succeed. Never has, and hopefully never will."*

"To where apparently we're members of that less daunting group of yours," Henry grumbled, rather never dreaming he'd fail himself, and if he failed, never dreaming it would be this way; to this extent.

"Well, that's all right, too," Liz tucked her arm through his with a pat. *"After all, would you rather it be Justin?"*

"Myself, of course, naturally," Henry assured. *"Talking about you, Katy, Martha, even Bob. Not saying Evelyn, for that matter, Justin won't fare all right for himself, because of course both will."*

"Even come around," she agreed.

"What's that?" Henry said.

"Even come around," Liz smiled. *"Must have something to do with being a rogue themselves, can't ask for anything more than that."*

"The devil I can't," he corrected. *"What happened to happily ever after?"*

"We did live happily ever after," Liz nodded.

"Yes, well, wanted it to be longer then," Henry said. *"Six months? Barely got our feet wet."*

"Well, who doesn't want it to be longer?" Liz shrugged. *"Rather suspect most do, and some will."* She smiled down on the angel hovering over her daughter. An unlikely looking one, she had to admit. Though angels were apparently like that, coming in all shapes and sizes, and occasionally speaking French. *"Atta girl, Red,"* she encouraged Joanna, Michael quick to join in and drown her out with his cheer. *"Atta girl. Show them your stuff. Show them what you're made of. Fuck 'em, if they don't like it. Atta girl, atta girl, atta girl ..."*

The Fezzan
March 10

"Is Mademoiselle ready to wake up?" the man interrupted Joanna's oddly pleasant dream, his voice just above her head, and her entire body stiffened, turned into a board.

"It is after five o'clock." Joanna heard him say, the words in French and words she understood, but she kept her eyes tightly closed even when he told her his name. *Pierre.* That was right, too. *I remember you, Pierre,* she agreed, though not out loud. The only thing she said aloud was something Michael had taught her to say when she was only nine and so frightened in a sea of strangers without her mother to comfort her. Joanna Lee made her choice to cry or fight in the middle of Pierre's speech. She said, *"Fuck you."* Or roughly translated, told him to kiss her ass, go to hell.

Chapter Twenty-Nine

All of its translations were an interesting choice for the little mademoiselle who looked more to Pierre like someone's lost child than what instead? A sailor? Some prostitute in British school girl dress? Or perhaps it was simply she did not understand French and was so very much afraid?

Of course she was afraid, naturally terrified. Pierre nodded wisely. Her vulgar slang, while an odd choice, was significant in that she spoke it in English, helping him to assist in identifying her, which he wanted very much to do. He had noticed more than her fists yesterday. Her reactions to him, his voice, the awkward way in which she twisted her head, he was convinced she could understand him. To understand French suggested education, breeding. Important because he did not believe she lived here in European North Africa. Her skin under her sunburn was fair and tender, not harsh and heat browned. She was a young woman who traveled perhaps? With her husband, her family, or with her English troops? Pierre eyed her. Her fragile size and her youth were also extremely important, quite possibly the difference between her life and death. Small, she was not a child. What Pierre first suspected, he now knew from her body under its swollen black bruises. She was young, yes, but a young woman. Eighteen, nineteen years old or so he guessed, not fourteen as Reineke surmised and Pierre perhaps had been too quick to correct. The younger, the better if he hoped to convince Reineke to remand her to the children's camp where she would be safe from the soldiers until Pierre could figure out what to do. Anne, Reineke's little Anne, was eleven and no threat to him though the gun Anne carried was bigger than this English woman lying on the bed.

Pierre forgot about Reineke to concentrate on the woman, the voice he could barely hear and she could barely raise loud enough to talk. Whose English? British, Irish, Scot? He suspected Irish for the same reason Reineke considered Polish or Scandinavian. The light skin and red hair. Reineke was lying, a desperate attempt to delay the truth by pretending he had not decided what she was. Pierre was not lying. She was Allied, they both knew that, simply not whose or why. It was time to find out.

"So," Pierre teased, while Joanna stayed where she was, bravely on her back, her eyes tightly closed. "So," he primly approved, choosing the more formal Italian translation of her curse, "vai a fare nel culo? Mademoiselle proves she is not a child, but the adult. This is good. So, now, she will have no difficulty, but understand and listen when I say to her, it is time for her to get up, I have drawn for her a bath."

Joanna almost opened her eyes and Pierre knew it. She spoke French. That she could not hide and it was good. She spoke French, and he was French, and so they would get along fine. "I am sorry but we will have to speak in French, Mademoiselle," he offered apologetically. "Though I am French and can speak many languages, unfortunately, except for a few words, I do not speak English, but until recently there has been no need. Still," he said, when she continued not to respond, "for all I am sorry for, I am sorry most if Mademoiselle thinks she should perhaps sleep longer. Mademoiselle has slept long enough. It is dinner time, and she will have to eat, yes, but first, she needs to again bathe."

What he meant by her bathing again Joanna had no idea, but he obviously thought he meant something because he not only repeated it, he said it at least four more times. That was his problem. Hers was trying to find a pillow large enough to wrap around her head, covering her ears. Her hand reached out, bravely and boldly fumbling until she found one.

The sight was amusing to Pierre, offering her little protection, and proving only that she had courage enough to fight fights she did not need to win. Pierre thought again about the punches and kicks she threw yesterday. She was strong under her compact petite frame, athletically inclined, her spirit, brave and foolish at the same time. He did not have to be French any more than the men who beat and raped her were French. It was her good fortune he was.

"There is no reason for Mademoiselle to hide," he said softly. "You are quite safe. Any scars you have are only in the mind. How deep they go is up to you."

He touched her with something, it felt like a stick, and that was the trick to get her up fast. The pillow came off her head, her eyes open as she struggled to sit up, lash out at him with her fists and hoarse, harsh words she couldn't quite get out.

That was the plan, anyway. It changed the moment Joanna saw him. He was hideous. Not some disconcerting shadow she seemed to remember, a distorted figure she couldn't quite make out, but a twisted and misshapen man, hideously and horribly so like a gnome.

Why, exactly like a gnome! Joanna stared at him. Some horribly discolored gnome. Dark like a Negro, shrunken and old, and fat—round like a very fat round barrel, with a very large round brown face and two beady little black eyes peering out at her from inside some sort of hood. A brown hood. Brown as his skin and the odd looking brown sack covering him from his neck to his toes.

"Why ..." Joanna managed as she stared at him. "Why ..." she succeeded in choking out.

He smiled, leered at her in a disgustingly familiar way, his teeth old and discolored in his gums also tinged brown. "I am Père Pierre, Mademoiselle," he said. "A priest, oui, a bishop. And, oui," he granted, "to some I am a cripple, too. Washed before my seventh birthday, I was too young to endure the evil eye. Infantile paralysis," he winked, or at least Joanna thought he did. Perhaps it was her. Winking and blinking and trying to keep him in focus. "The community I was released to was the hospitality of the monks at La Trappe de Staouelli who gave me my name *Beausoleil.* Beautiful sun."

Cripple? Joanna frowned. He looked more like a midget. A fine one to talk herself, she knew that, but he looked more like a midget to her and a hundred years old at least.

Sixty-seven, perhaps. Pierre read her face, not her mind. Her height, and sixty-seven years old. Not a hundred as he might appear or the thousand Reineke feared he might actually be. A monk. Not some wizard, or a gnome, and not a Negro, simply an old, crippled French monk with a large French face darkened by age and the sun. Mademoiselle, on the other hand, was of the English upper classes despite her silent, tactless scrutiny—or should Pierre say because of it he knew this? She lived a life of privilege, wealth, and snobbery, all very clear. As clear as those bruised and loosened teeth of hers with their chipped enamel that had been cosmetically straightened, forced into place with steel and wire like his legs. "You have never heard of the monastery at La Trappe?" he smiled. "Where are you from, Mademoiselle? If it is not here, where?"

Where was a very good question. Joanna had no idea. Not where here was, or even what here was with her surroundings looming in the background of the man as unfamiliar as he was. She eyed him because he seemed closer than the room for some reason. Close enough to see him. If he was French, some kind of priest or bishop as he claimed she had no idea. She studied the massive crucifix dangling from the Rosary tucked in what looked like a black sash around his waist. She knew what a Rosary was because of Michael who had assured her they and a nickel for the streetcar would get him into Heaven, but she had never seen one so large. The long rope of dark brown beads almost touching the floor ...

The chocolate brown floor. It must be the room that made the brown so brown, almost black because everything else in the room was white. Huge white-on-white marble columns and high stone walls glistened crystal white in the sun streaming through a long row of paned glass widows with their airy white draperies dancing slowly in a warm, bright breeze.

Oh, but where was she was right. "I!" Joanna agreed in a whisper, uncertain if she was awake or still asleep after all. It was all so large, seemed all so grand. Even the furniture was white, gilded in platinum and gold. Not like home, at all. Certainly not Grandfather's with its mighty oak and mahogany halls. Or even Michael and Claudia's house built of that manufactured brick Grandfather loathed, proud, and high on its pastured hills outside Yorkshire.

But still, as fancy as Michael's house was, in some ways fantastic with its palatial baroque decor, it was far less fantastic than this. Joanna stared down on the soft, white bed, nearly as massive as the room, and swimming, simply swimming in white silk pillows. So many of them one could barely find the bed, her, or even notice the dressing table next to it ...

Joanna's head cocked, staring at the nightstand that was white like the rest of the furniture in the room. An odd green figure of a cat sat on top next to a large brass pitcher and bowl and a row of fluffy white ... pillows? She couldn't quite make out what they were.

"That is not important," the fat brown barrel informed her, and she looked up at him.

"What?" she tried to say, but he picked something up, his nasty, twisted hand coming toward her, and maybe to him it wasn't important, but to her it certainly was. How awful. Really, she couldn't think of anything more awful. So much worse than realizing wherever she was, she was hardly at home, but far, far away from Michael, Grandfather, and even Claudia. That hand coming toward her held a sheet. Some kind of sheet, silk white, or just soft cotton, and when Joanna looked down to see what he was going to do with it she realized she was naked, mother naked. Not a stitch of decency or clothes.

Joanna shrieked with her hoarse, sore throat and grabbed the sheet, tucking it around herself up to her chin until she looked like one of those mummies everyone went on about, and she had yet to see.

"I am a priest, not a man, Mademoiselle," the contemptuous bastard leered at her again, exactly like that hunchback in Michael's favorite film. She swung at him and missed but he retreated, disappearing behind one of the columns, his voice still close. "Mademoiselle does not have clothes. She does not need them, she needs a bath."

Well, she certainly had them when she came in there. Joanna kicked and pushed at the suffocating mound of pillows desperate to find them before he came back. He was back, quickly reappearing and waving something that was neither brown or white, and certainly threatening. She gasped and screamed again, waving at him to stay back. He would not stay back, but advanced, sweeping unconcerned through the pillows and bedding littering the floor like landmines. "What Mademoiselle wants is not important. Today, we are going to do what Pierre wants."

Fat chance of that. Joanna tried to grab whatever it was he had in his hand, and fling it away, as far as she could. He peered at her, his beady black eyes squinting like he needed glasses. "Mademoiselle, this is a blouse, not a weapon. I am not going to strike you with it. You are going to wear it."

That's what he thought. Joanna promptly kicked whatever it was off the bed as soon as he set it down.

"Mademoiselle," he sighed. "Mademoiselle, I am sorry, but your dress has been destroyed. Though, I think, oui," he said, "even if it were not, she would not want it, no. I think, oui, I am positive, Mademoiselle has seen enough for one so young."

Seen what? Whatever could he mean? She hadn't seen anything. For that matter, could barely see anything. Joanna realized that as she peered back at him. She could see in front of her, not very well, but she could still see. But when she tried to turn her head, even just tried to look to the side, the room turned dark, her sight fading, and she swooned.

"Oui, Mademoiselle," he said for some reason as if he were agreeing with her about something, "but it will pass."

When Joanna woke up the next time, it was dark and she was clothed, wearing something that felt like a cloth dress.

"It is all right, Mademoiselle," his voice assured and she jumped. "She will wear the sahariana and not worry about her modesty, for on one so small, it will be a dress." He struck a match for the lamp. Joanna could see the dancing flame of the lantern, watching it as it came closer.

"Oui," Pierre agreed, setting the lamp down on the nightstand, the light from the flame dancing on his face. "You want me to stay back, you want your dress. But no, it has been burned."

Burned? Joanna touched the dress she was wearing. It had buttons and seemed large, but was short, like a nightshirt. A man's nightshirt.

"Oui, burned," he nodded, "in the fire."

Fire? Joanna did not remember any fire. Odd though, because she did seem to remember smoke, a thin column of smoke.

"What do you remember?" Pierre smiled at her concentration.

What did she remember? What a rude and uncomfortable question, particularly since Joanna did not know the answer.

"It is all right, Mademoiselle," he reminded as she glared at him. I am a priest, not a man. Still, you will be more comfortable like this."

Comfortable? In what way? Joanna studied the dancing light on his face. It made her stomach sick and she vomited a spicy, acidic mixture of mucus and undigested blood.

"The ether," he said. "It will pass. I am not here to frighten you, but to help. But Mademoiselle must also help. She must listen to Pierre and do exactly as he says. She has been molested, oui, molested," he nodded as she looked up at him. "Sex with a man she does not like. Your life has not been ruined by your assault, but your body has been injured. This land is a desert, wounds do not heal here, they rot. The bath is to soothe this. It is la douche. Does Mademoiselle know what that is?"

Not even what he was talking about.

"I did not think so," he nodded satisfied. "Mademoiselle is English, not French. It is all right, we will help you." Someone touched her, it wasn't him, but a nun dressed in black habit and veil.

"Come, Mademoiselle," Pierre encouraged as Joanna stared at the sister. "Embarrassment is not worth your life. Sometimes a man carries with him things that have nothing to do with the desert or an unwanted baby, but disease, infection. Une douche is no different than any other medicine to protect you from this unnecessary fate."

She was standing up. At least Joanna thought she was. Her head felt lopsided and heavy, her stomach turning with dizzying nauseating pain. She swayed like she was drunk, veering toward the columns briefly bright white in the lantern flame before returning to the shadows. They were cold when she touched them and she shivered, clutching at the stupid shirt she wore.

"Let us help you, Mademoiselle," he encouraged, "be careful, there are steps."

She could see them, but that was a lie. All she could see was she was in a loo, some sort of loo, nearly as large as the room, and rapidly shrinking in size. She sank down to the floor, next to what looked like a flat commode, resting her head on the cool marble that felt good, peaceful. From there she found herself back in bed, vomiting at least twice more as the room turned bright and hot and then back to dark and cold. The sister in black was gone and did not return, and the strange ugly man did not speak to her again except to tell her she must rest and could not eat where he had practically insisted she eat before. She wanted to complain but was just so tired. When she tried to complain he ignored her and gave her a wet cloth to suck on. At some point she decided he was a priest, French, and this was all a dream. A very bad dream, very long. Eventually, she remembered another man. Some man with a hat leaning over her. It wasn't the fat priest, and he wasn't French, and she screamed, falling back to sleep as instructed when the priest answered her call.

Chapter Thirty

The Fezzan
March 12

Joanna lay in bed wide awake and alert. A quick survey of her surroundings when she woke up confirmed the strange fat priest was not there in the room that remained unfamiliar and unchanged from its cold stone and abundance of white except for what looked like a bundle of laundry folded neatly on a chair over by the linen draped windows. How tempting the windows were, how bright the world looked beyond them, even brighter than the room. Before she could make up her mind however if she dared to have the courage to get up and look out the windows, the priest appeared through the pillars and she was down under the covers if only in an effort to escape his annoying enthusiasm.

He was undeterred by her disappearing act. "Good morning, Mademoiselle," he greeted her like some upstairs maid carrying tea. Joanna had often wondered what it would be like to have an upstairs maid bring her tea. Tea in the morning and again at night, even at noon if she wanted it. Grandfather wasn't a supporter of such nonsense, as he called it. There was no flurry of personnel to greet Joanna when she arrived to live with Grandfather, as there had been to greet her and her mother when they moved from Australia to live with Henry. There was Maria the cook, and John, Grandfather's batman, and Joe who was her tutor, as well as Grandfather's personal secretary when he needed one.

"It is good to see you are awake," the priest continued babbling. "Today we have much to do. But first ..." his voice seemed to soften, fade away but then came back, loud as before. "Mademoiselle's clothes that have been so graciously provided for her."

Joanna had absolutely no idea what he was talking about. Her clothes? The blankets came off her head and she sat up, a bit too quickly for the liking of her stomach, but that was all right. Or it should have been. She stared at the folded laundry on the bed, from it to the windows and the chair whose large cushioned seat was now empty. The clothes on the bed were not hers. Hers were green. A putrid, ugly green, awkward and unflattering, but that was beside the point. These were ... well, like something Michael might wear on one of his big game safaris.

"Dress, Mademoiselle," the priest patted the laundry with that claw of his that Joanna swore an oath to bite off the first time it came close enough, "and Pierre will be right back with her breakfast. Oui, breakfast," he promised happily, "today Mademoiselle is to eat."

He was gone, exiting out of her sight to the right. Joanna heard what sounded like the latch of a door and turned quickly, far too quickly for her head. It was a door, there on her right. It was also not white, but brown like the floor, and quite tall. Very tall. Large and heavy with a high, brass latch that looked almost too high for her to reach. Joanna wished she had turned her head sooner than she did so that she might have caught a glimpse of what was on the other side. It was unnerving not to know. But at least he was gone, not simply hiding behind the tall white columns waiting to spring. If only there was a way to lock him out, make sure he couldn't come back in. If only there was a way ...

Joanna stared at the clothing on the bed, from the clothes to the row of paned-windows and the bright world outside wondering if she dared have the courage. She did. "Trousers?" she whispered as she reached cautiously for the bundle and found a pair of trousers under the neatly folded shirt. Trousers were certainly far more comfortable than that stupid skirt she had been forced to wear with stockings that did nothing except twist and tear. Though that was not to say had she been given a fresh skirt and stockings it would have stopped her from shimmying down the sheets, rope, pole, or nearest tree to make her escape, the farthest from it. She was up, and she was out of there—planning it, anyway.

"Atta girl ... atta girl ..." Joanna invoked Michael's cheer as she got up, discovering her ankles, knees, and even her wrist up to her elbow on her right arm, were wrapped in plasters and white gauze. She *had* been in hospital, as she seemed to remember. Injured in some way. The funny priest had said something about a fire. She did not remember anything about a fire, and certainly could not take the time to worry about remembering it now. She pushed the clean shirt aside. She was already wearing some kind of shirt and could feel more plaster and bandages wound around her back and right shoulder that hurt considerably.

"Amputation, kid," Michael cracked in agreement the day she fell out of the tree, *"it's the only answer."*

"I don't need an amputation, Michael," she assured him.

"*Oh, yeah*?" he said. "*Sez who*?"

"Says me," Joanna picked up the trousers. They were long and loose and threatening to fall down even though she rolled the waistband as tight as she could, and *damn!* Joanna could feel the dizziness start to swim over her. She hung on to the nightstand trying to clear her head. The floor rolling in waves under her feet as she clutched the trousers, trying to find her way to the windows, her hand stumbling along the nightstand, along the edge of the bed, and finally along the smooth slick surface of the bureau top where she came face to face with—

"My face!" Joanna gasped in the mirror. Half her face was gone, just gone, and in its place was some huge fat bandage wound around and around her head like a queer fat hat. "Michael!" she screamed, "my face!"

Joanna was in the loo so fast she could not remember how she got there. There were mirrors in the loo, she remembered them from yesterday, she must have seen herself yesterday—there were more mirrors than walls in the loo. Joanna grabbed the edge of what had to be the sink, staring at her horribly misshapen head and face. No wonder she couldn't see, the bandage did not only cover her head, it covered one of her eyes, her nose and mouth swollen under a hideous blackened purple bruise practically covering her face, neck, the whole of her body she knew if she dared to look.

"Mademoiselle should have waited for Pierre," the priest said quietly behind her.

"My face!" Joanna heard herself whine.

"Oui, I know," he sympathized. "But it will go away. It will pass. Come," he held out his hand.

Go away? Joanna's head tipped in the mirror. It was already gone.

"Come, Mademoiselle," he encouraged. "Your breakfast is here."

Joanna went with him. Why? To get away from the mirrors.

Breakfast was waiting on a silver tray with a porcelain bowl of mealy black puree and a round flat pancake of bread.

"Fool," the priest nodded as Joanna blinked.

The fool was he if he thought she was going to eat that. Joanna looked at him.

"*Fool* ..." Pierre emphasized with a smile. "A type of pudding. You use the bread. See?" he dipped the bread in demonstration. "Very good, no?"

Hardly. Joanna crawled back into bed. "I'm hungry," she said. "Hungry," she repeated as he spread his hands and she sighed. "Fine. *Affamé.*"

"Very good," Pierre picked up the tray, setting it firmly on her lap.

"No," Joanna pushed it away. "Food. Not that. I can't possibly eat that. For heaven's sake," she peered at it, "it looks like someone already ate it and gave it back."

"No," he said, and Joanna's stomach turned, "No, I do not think so. This has been prepared especially for you by me."

That was his problem. "Food," Joanna insisted. "I haven't eaten and I am very hungry."

"You have a concussion, Mademoiselle," he explained. "It was decided it was best not to feed you for another day until you were awake."

"I'm fine," Joanna assured.

"I know," Pierre agreed. "Even your throat. Very improved. You are talking."

Her throat hurt almost as much as the rest of her. "Food," Joanna insisted, and to make sure he understood she shoved the tray off the bed, the heavy silver clanging like a bell when it hit the floor, the bowl rattling before it broke, and bread unscathed.

Pierre sighed. “Mademoiselle must eat.”

“Food,” Joanna assured.

“Oui,” he nodded.

“And some water,” Joanna pointed before he left. “I’m quite thirsty.”

“Juice,” he nodded, “sugar for your strength, and perhaps later some tea with lemon and a little honey. It is better for your stomach.”

“Water,” Joanna said.

“Oui,” Pierre said and left.

While he was gone, Joanna debated about trying for the windows again but decided against it until she had some food in her, especially since only Heaven knew when she might be able to eat again. For a hospital, it was not only strange looking but distinctly inhospitable what with starving her to death for more than a day. She decided she wasn’t sure if she was in hospital after all and decided to ask him when he returned. Until he returned, she busied herself picking at her plasters to see what this business with burns was all about. She did not feel burned and did not remember anything about being burned. However since she had never been burned except for possibly touching the stove or clothes iron when she shouldn’t have, she wasn’t entirely sure what being burned would feel like. Her wrists were the easiest bandages to loosen and the wounds underneath the first one were certainly ghastly looking enough to have her quickly patting the plaster back in place, not wanting to know anything more. The priest was back with another, much larger tray, one he had to push in on a wheeled cart.

“What’s that?” Joanna blinked.

“Fool,” Pierre set a tray down on her lap identical to the one he had set there before. “When you throw this one, Mademoiselle, we have that one,” he pointed to the second shelf, “and that one,” he pointed to the third and final shelf of his cart, “and many others. I think however Mademoiselle will be too tired to throw too many after a while and will eat her breakfast as she should now.

“We also have,” he returned to his cart while she studied the tray on her lap, “some very nice juice. Kamar-eldin. Very good and very popular.”

“Kal ... kalmar ...” Joanna stumbled over it.

"*Kamar-eldin,*" Pierre smiled. "Apricot. And then we have some tea," he nodded. "A nice mint with lemon, or perhaps another. Mon capitaine prefers tea to the kamar-eldin which he finds too sweet, and so we have many teas here, from many places. The choice is yours. India. Russia. Even your England. Would Mademoiselle like a nice hot cup of English tea?"

"Well ..." Joanna considered, since anything might be helpful with a bowl of what, she insisted, looked like smashed black beans.

"Perhaps even a sip of coffee," Pierre nodded. "Oui," he decided for her. "A very small sip of coffee with sweet cream would be nicest yet. Mon capitaine loves coffee even more than tea, and so we have many coffees here, from all over the world. Spain. France. Italy. Africa!" he laughed at some joke Joanna would not have found funny even if she knew what it was.

"You are not eating, Mademoiselle," he noticed, "and you really must."

"All right, fine!" Joanna grabbed the bowl stuffing half a spoonful of the beans in her mouth that she promptly gagged right back out they were just so awful.

"Eat, Mademoiselle," he nodded as she sent the bowl flying. "Try some bread and a little juice."

The bread was flat and practically tasteless, the juice very sweet as forewarned. "I would really like some water," she reminded.

"Perhaps tomorrow," he nodded. "Water is very harsh."

"But I can have tea," Joanna said.

"Oui," he smiled.

"Good," she said. "May I have a glass of tea with lemon and a little honey but none of those nasty tea leaves?"

He thought about that. "Mademoiselle ..." he said.

"Please just bring me a glass of water!" Joanna snapped.

"Oui, Mademoiselle," he said.

"Thank you!"

Joanna sipped her water slowly from a glass that was a heavy crystal goblet and quite beautiful if she paid any more attention to it than she had to the spoon, the tray, or the bowl. She did not. Why would she? All of Grandfather's china was china, and certainly all of

Claudia's. All their silver, silver, and all of their crystal heavy, exactly like this one.

"So you see, Mademoiselle," Pierre was busily explaining something else she hardly cared about, "it would be much better to have the water fresh from the well. This water is kept in bags, and it is warm, the taste strong. It is not so strong from the well when it is cold."

"It's perfectly fine," Joanna assured, and it was. It was wet.

Pierre shrugged. "If Mademoiselle says so."

Joanna did, and that was all she was going to say, at least about that. "Where am I?" she asked.

Pierre laughed. "A very good question, Mademoiselle. Oui, a very natural one."

"Well?" Joanna said. "Am I at that place you talked about?"

Pierre frowned. "Place, Mademoiselle?"

"You mentioned a place," Joanna assured. "I can't remember what you called it."

"Nor I," Pierre shook his head in apology. "I am sorry, but I do not recall mentioning some place."

Well if he didn't remember, she certainly couldn't. "Well?" Joanna said. "Where am I?"

"Of course," he seemed to hesitate, but then sat down in the chair by the bed.

"Well, yes, I suppose that's all right," Joanna agreed, though it was a little close. "You can clean later. I want to know where I am."

"I, Mademoiselle?" Pierre chuckled. "No, the servants will clean, Mademoiselle. That is their job. Pierre's job is to take care of you."

"Servants?" Joanna said.

"Oui," Pierre nodded. "Servants of the house."

"Oh," Joanna said. "Oh, well," she tossed off, "I knew I wasn't in hospital."

"Hospital?" Pierre said. "No, you are not in hospital. You are in a house, oui, a building. A very big, very beautiful building. Pierre's ... and, oui, mon capitaine's home," he agreed.

"It's all right," Joanna supposed. Certainly, Michael's home was far more beautiful than this. "When can I leave?"

"Leave?" Pierre chuckled. "I think Mademoiselle should think about getting stronger and well before she thinks about leaving."

"I want to leave," Joanna assured.

"Soon," he nodded. "Very soon, Mademoiselle. You have Pierre's word. It is a promise. Now," he smiled again, folding his hands exactly as a priest might Joanna noticed. "I think we should talk. God's gift of language is a wonderful gift, and since you speak French so well, there is much we will be able to talk about."

"When?" Joanna interrupted. "When can I leave?"

"Soon," he nodded, again. "Very soon. When the time comes—you will be surprised how quickly the time has come when it is here, Mademoiselle ... Lee, is it?" he winked. "Oui, it is Lee," he agreed positively before she could speak. "Joanna Lee. So young and yet a nurse?

"No, you are not a nurse," he shook his head as positively. "It is not your age or your face that tells Pierre this, it is your actions. Your curiosity with the bandages, the way you sniff with your nose. That malodor you smell, is not bowel, Mademoiselle, it is sulphur. A salve under your dressings to help you heal—"

"I haven't the faintest idea what you are talking about," Joanna interrupted again.

"No, of course you do not," Pierre understood. "You have a concussion, Mademoiselle, as I have attempted to explain to you. You have struck your head, and you must give your head time to heal."

"The car door," Joanna nodded.

"Pardon?" Pierre paused.

"The car door," Joanna assured. "I struck my head on the car door."

"Really," Pierre pondered that thoughtfully. "You remember this, Mademoiselle? That is very unusual."

Was it?

"Oh, yes, Mademoiselle," he assured. "Extremely. Do you remember anything else?"

He'd like to know that, wouldn't he? Joanna could tell by his face he would. "Everything," she promised. "I remember everything."

"Most unusual," Pierre nodded. "Most unusual."

Maybe for him. For her ... well, for her it was a lie. Joanna did not remember anything, not even why she seemed to remember a car, but she did.

"Are you English, Mademoiselle?" he was asking. "Or possibly of English descent? That is still unclear to Pierre as it is unclear exactly who you are. Do you have an uncle, or brother, or father in the army, perhaps? If not, then who could Mademoiselle Lee be other than in the army herself perhaps as her title and clothes suggest—"

"Could you bring me some more water?" The crystal goblet bounced on the floor at his feet, rolling to a stop, quite unharmed.

"Four centuries," Pierre shook his head. "Mademoiselle, you have thrown four centuries onto the floor. Are you aware of this? Do you care?"

"No!" Joanna assured.

"You are not only bold and brave, Mademoiselle, you are very reckless and spoiled," he bent over slowly to retrieve the goblet with a laugh. "A dangerous combination. It is all right though, because so is Pierre, and neither would Pierre care. A secret, Mademoiselle, between you and I," he winked. "It is possible Pierre cares even less than you."

Joanna highly doubted it. "Is it too much to ask for you to give me some water and leave me alone?"

"Alone?" he said. "To do what, Mademoiselle?"

Wouldn't he like to know. Joanna slid down under the covers, pulling them up over her shoulders as if she was cold even though she wasn't, but fairly warm as the room.

"Escape," Pierre nodded. "Yes, of course. A soldier's duty."

Joanna wouldn't know. Only that escaping was something she was going to do.

Pierre smiled. "And escape from where, Mademoiselle? Here? Why? Pierre believes you are too young to be in an army, so it isn't duty, but simply a desire to leave us. How old are you, Mademoiselle? I am merely curious. If you tell Pierre how old you are, I will tell you how old I am. Sixty-seven," he nodded, not waiting for her. "Oui, Pierre is sixty-seven years old. So, how could Mademoiselle be angry, or frightened of such a frail old man? How could Mademoiselle be angry, frightened, or refuse to talk with a priest? Do they have priests in your village where you live, Mademoiselle? Are you Catholic? Have you ever heard of the Jesuit? That is what Pierre is," he nodded. "Oui, a Jesuit missionary. I have been one for many years, and I will be one for many more ... la Trappe," he remembered. "Oui, of course. Pierre remembers now," he laughed with a shake of his head. "He told Mademoiselle about the Monastery at la Trappe. Is this the place Mademoiselle was asking about? No, you are not at the monastery, Mademoiselle, but you are some place just as nice."

"I don't care. I want to leave," Joanna nodded. "I don't ..." Well, quite honestly there was something about the place she did not like. Something about it that frightened her even if she did not know why.

"Oh, but you do care, Mademoiselle," he corrected. "You care very much as you should. I want you to listen very carefully to me. It is very important you listen to me. In a few minutes, oui, a very few minutes, you are going to have an audience with mon capitaine. I have convinced him this is very important, and I am now explaining this to you. When you meet mon capitaine you must remember not to be frightened because there is no reason for you to be frightened. Of all the things you may or may not remember," he said kindly, "if Pierre could change one thing it would be who mon capitaine is, but he cannot. You are with the Germans, Mademoiselle, I cannot lie to you. You will see how true this is for yourself when you meet mon capitaine.

"I can swear to you, Mademoiselle," he swore as Joanna stared at him, "you are safe, because you are safe. Do you know what day this is, Mademoiselle? What day it is?" he repeated when she did not answer him. "It is Thursday, the 12th of March. You have been with Pierre and mon capitaine five days, and no one has hurt you, and they will not hurt you. You have Pierre's, and oui, mon capitaine's word."

She was in a room of books, just outside her door. From the floor to the ceiling, nothing but books tucked in massive white stone and dark brown wooden cupboards lining wall after wall ...

Our father, who art in Heaven ... Joanna prayed, even though she wasn't Catholic, or particularly religious as she walked out of the darkness of the books and into the sunlight with Pierre directing her around something she knew dimly to be a scaffold.

Hallowed be thy name. Thy Kingdom come. Thy will—

"Oh, my!" Joanna stopped suddenly when the brilliant sunlight streaming in through the windows blinding her, turned around to face her, turning into a man.

"Mademoiselle?" Pierre reached for her.

"I'm fine," Joanna pushed his hand away. "I'm perfectly fine." And she was. She was startled that was all. She couldn't half see and she just did not see him at first, though now that she did?

"Oh, my," Joanna blinked, her eye opening and closing like a camera lens. "Oh, my." Why he looked exactly like Michael. He was as tall as Justin and looked exactly like Michael, how perfectly ridiculous. He could not possibly look anything like Michael, and he did not. To the contrary ...

"*Sit down, Fraulein*!" the man who looked absolutely nothing like Michael while absolutely being the extreme height of Justin loomed toward her, his English awful, fairly incomprehensible, biting and clipped with a distinct and unfriendly foreign hiss.

"Over here, Mademoiselle," Pierre whispered in her ear, and Joanna found herself sitting in a chair next to Pierre, the two of them in front of a desk.

"Oh, my," Joanna stared at the overweight piece of furniture heavy on its stout short legs with savage talons gripping glassy white balls. More relics from a medieval manor, the furniture in this bright, white room was nearly all brown. Huge. Strikingly ornate with leather cushions instead of brocade satin, adorning high back chairs—

"Mademoiselle, relax," Pierre whispered in her ear.

Oh, but, Joanna couldn't. Not with some man looming over her, bearing down on her, insisting she talk while he talked at her with that harsh, nasty sounding tongue.

"I!" Joanna said.

"I am Hauptmann Reineke," he interrupted her coldly, though perhaps not quite as coldly as Joanna heard, or as abusive as his pronounced accent might suggest, and he was standing in front of what must be his side of the massive, frightening desk.

But that was not possible. Only a moment ago he was watching her from in front of the windows—

More windows. Joanna stared at the French windows that were exactly like those in the room she occupied, only these were much larger, many more of them, opened wide onto a balcony, the sun streaming in through the fine sheer draperies—

"Mademoiselle," Pierre said with a light squeeze of her hand.

Stop telling her to relax! Joanna could not possibly relax. "I!" she stammered hoarsely at the man who appeared to be waiting for her to say something, though God only knew what. "I!"

"*You*, Fräulein," she was violently advised, "are a guest." *Fine.* Joanna agreed silently. *Anything. Just sit down.*

He did not sit down.

Oh, please sit down. Joanna prayed. *Dear God, sit down.*

But he did not.

Perhaps he was incapable. Joanna stared at the straight stiff legs and high arched back with the cap on his head. She had seen that hat before. "I!" she said.

"*You*, Fräulein," She was again silenced, "are well."

The picture of health, feeling swell.

"And since you are," he advised her. And since she was currently occupying a space known as—"*There*!" his finger shot out and Joanna stared back at her room, a hundred miles away. There were a few strict and stringent rules for her to abide by, listen to, heed, honor, and obey.

"*None*," she was assured, too difficult, or strenuous as long as she did not mind the pain. She was ill—which did not make *any* sense since he just told her how well she was. And though ill, he expected her to do precisely what she was told—

"Sit back in your chair, Fräulein," Reineke ordered, "you have not been dismissed."

Except Joanna did not know she was out of her chair. All she knew was he grew taller with every word, his head higher in the air.

"The Holy Man has been given to you for guidance," Reineke continued in his notice to this appalling example of Allied frailty and German strength. "Do you understand?"

No, Joanna did not. Not one bloody word.

"I have asked you a question, Fräulein," Reineke impatiently repeated. "Do you understand me, or do you not?"

"Yes," Joanna croaked, and his head came down from the ceiling to glower at her.

"Indeed," Reineke cocked a brow. One word was not sufficient to determine either her racial background or enemy affiliation. "Beginning today," he said, carefully, watching her, "you are to be exercised." He raised his hand; Joanna had no idea why. "Your energy is returning," was his observation in contrast to the Holy Man's who maintained she was too weak to do much more than scream and cry. "I expect it to be put to a more useful purpose than the disruption of my staff. Do you understand?"

"Yes," Joanna croaked, though hardly understanding at all.

"Indeed." Again, one word was not sufficient. Reineke wanted to hear her voice, suspecting the Holy Man was in error with his presumption she was English. The voice Reineke had not heard, nor listened to had not sounded particularly English to him. The only thing it sounded was hoarse. That was understandable, considering her condition, and due to her condition, he could extend her a degree of compassion and pity. The girl was indeed small. Not much above the height of his knee. A true elf.

Another elf.

He was tired of elves.

Indeed.

"Do you have any questions, Fräulein?" Reineke asked before he sent her on her way, his voice bored and tired.

There was no answer from the elf.

"Indeed, do you have any questions, Fräulein?" he snapped, and Joanna sat up straight in her chair.

You bastard. She glared back at him. *You bloody bastard.* She watched that head of his go up in the air, and he could stick it up ...? Somewhere unpleasant, as Michael would say.

"That I have," Joanna assured, and was on her feet, seizing the edge of his desk in her savage broken claws, "where the devil am I?"

She was going to hit him. Reineke's eyes flew open. The little elf was going to attack him, leap to the top of his desk and spring.

"I asked you a question," Joanna nodded. "And don't you tell me you don't know!"

Definitely British. Of the lowest social rung. Reineke glared at

Pierre busy admiring the arm of his chair. The girl was a servant, no mystery in that. Not a nurse or some secretary, but a scullery maid, sold into servitude to the American who brought her along to scrape his boots and please his lap.

"Oh, hello in there, Captain," the girl continued her jeer, "Anybody home in there, Captain? Cat got your tongue?"

It most certainly did not. "Sit down, Fräulein," Reineke ordered with an insistent point at her chair.

"It's Frau, Captain," she taunted him. "I'll thank you to remember that."

"You will indeed thank me, Fräulein," he assured. "And you will indeed sit down—*NOW!*" he barked, and Joanna sat down quickly.

Elves! Reineke glared at Pierre. Elves, indeed. As if he needed any more elves. "Fräulein," he said.

"It's Frau, Captain," she assured, bold and brazen.

"Fräulein," he ignored her, elves notorious liars, "you are in North Afrika of the continent of Afrika under the jurisdiction of the Third Reich. Your interests, preferences and indeed, politics, are irrelevant to where mine rule. Continue to conduct yourself as your mother, and you will be treated the same. Conduct yourself as your master, and you will be treated with a similar regard. I trust that answers any question you may have."

She did not answer him.

He did not think she would.

"If there is nothing else," Reineke concluded sharply, "you may consider this interview over, you are dismissed."

"Mademoiselle," Pierre was at her side.

Over? Joanna stared at him. But that was ridiculous. He hadn't said anything, nothing at all, just something about her mother, and whatever could her mother possibly have to do with any of this?

"Mademoiselle," Pierre coaxed, but Joanna pushed his hand away.

"I remember you, Captain," she stood up, and his eyes narrowed, she watched them narrow until they were little more than slits in his glowing yellow face. "Don't think I don't. Cat got your face, Captain? Cat scratch your chin?"

"There are steps, Mademoiselle," Pierre cautioned.

"I see them!" Joanna assured, and she did. She did not remember them, but that they were there now did not surprise her.

"Fräulein."

The Captain was in front of her, holding something out to her, her silver tags. Tears welled in Joanna's eyes.

"I understand these are yours, Fräulein," he said.

That they were. Michael had given them to her for Christmas as a joke, a stupid, little joke.

"You may have them, Fräulein," his head tipped.

Joanna's chin came up. "You may have them, Captain," she corrected, "as a souvenir."

"Indeed," he said, and put them in his pocket, motioning for Pierre to take her out of there.

Joanna burst into tears on the other side of the door, choking and gasping and vomiting up what little breakfast she had eaten. When it was over, she laid there exhausted and defeated, obediently agreeing to the priest bringing her food.

"No horses," she requested as Pierre's hand touched the latch.

"Pardon?" Pierre said.

"No horses," Joanna said. "Michael's told me how they eat horses, horrid fiends they are. I don't eat horses. I can't."

"No," Pierre smiled. "No horses. A little lamb, perhaps? Does that sound nice? Even if you vomit it has more nutrients and fat that you need."

Lamb? Why, yes, sounded wonderful actually. She loved lamb. "Yes, that's fine," Joanna said. "Quite fine. I'll have the lamb."

"Very good," Pierre inclined his head and left for her lunch that would be goat, not lamb, as it had been black beans for breakfast.

Chapter Thirty-One

"Horses, indeed," Reineke was annoyed.

Pierre kept diddling around the kitchen.

"Eating horses," Reineke sputtered.

Pierre laughed. "Mon capitaine, many people eat horses. It is not only the German. It was not the German who thought of eating horses first."

Germans did not eat horses. A thousand years ago perhaps, but not today that was Allied propaganda. It served the woman right to be eating goat. He hoped it made her sick, violently ill. "Horses, indeed," Reineke spit.

"Mon capitaine was listening again," Pierre clucked.

Le capitaine was not listening. Le capitaine could not help hearing. The woman's voice boomed with the power of a baritone, pounding in his brain. People not listening in Tunis could probably hear her. The daughter of someone, the wife of no one, and both of them probably gave her to the beastly Germans. "Horses, indeed," Reineke snapped. "The walls are not made of stone."

"Oui, they are," Pierre nodded. "But even at their thickest, they can be made thin when the ear is pressed against them."

Indeed. Reineke hoped Pierre ate goat and got sick. "Escape?" he demanded. "The woman plans to escape to where?"

"Who knows, mon capitaine," Pierre slapped Reineke's hand reaching for the plate Pierre was preparing for the woman. "From here for somewhere, yes, oui, obviously, perhaps even anywhere."

"Indeed," Reineke said his sharp tone for the slap. "The Kufra is less than a three-day ride."

"Ambitious, but perhaps possible," Pierre agreed. "Depending on how you ride, it could be one day or two weeks. Mademoiselle has been with us for five days. Have you had any reports of the Allied or the French in the area? No. And neither will you because it is not the Cufra."

"Indeed," Reineke said. "*Cairo* could be two weeks or one day, depending on how you ride."

"True," Pierre smiled. "But what does it matter, eh? Mon capitaine, like Mademoiselle, does not care, and when one does not care? One does not care," he shrugged. "Unless ..." he came at Reineke with a peer. "Mon capitaine has decided to care and give himself more problems?"

Le capitaine had no problems, and he did NOT care. It was simply an interesting point. One he felt he should point out. "Indeed," Reineke said. The Holy Man should be pleased. It meant he was considering believing him when he said the woman had not come from the Kufra. The Kufra, Reineke felt to be part of his backyard, regardless of how long it took, or did not take to get there, and he would not appreciate Allied beasts roaming around not eating horses.

"When did she become a woman, mon capitaine?" Pierre asked. "Rather than a girl? I am simply curious. You cannot exchange what has happened to her simply by changing her age. Rape is still not sex."

"I have no idea what you are talking about."

"Perhaps," Pierre shrugged. "But I saw your face, mon capitaine when Mademoiselle mentioned the scratches, but I would not be alarmed. I also saw Mademoiselle's face. She does not remember you. She knows she does not remember you because she knows she would. Who she is frightened of is not you, it is the uniform."

"Germans," Reineke inclined forward, "do not eat horses."

Pierre sighed. "Mon capitaine, Germans do eat horses. On the outside, many people eat horses, the same as they eat lion, elephant, monkey, or rat, and of these people are Germans.

"On the outside, mon capitaine," he said, "Germans do not live in gardens or have rendezvous to go swimming with children.

"On the outside, mon capitaine," he claimed, "the German is not mon capitaine's German. But how can Mademoiselle know this? How can anyone? How can they care? In one-hundred years perhaps, yes," he agreed. "In one-hundred years when it is over, someone might say,

'Oh. There once was a German who lived in a garden and went swimming with children'. But that is not today, mon capitaine. Today they do not know, and cannot care. And why should they? Ehiwaz, you claim for your coat-of-arms? No. Ehiwaz is an honorable and ancient symbol of defense. Your coat is not Ehiwaz; it is a swastika, a symbol of domination."

Indeed. The Holy Man probably ate horses.

"But!" Pierre could be generous too, "To help with mon capitaine's wounded pride, I think mon capitaine should know, I believe Mademoiselle has noticed how pretty he is?"

The woman had done what? "Indeed," Reineke left the goat where he had dropped it on floor.

"Oui," Pierre slapped Reineke's wrist in punishment a second time. "I saw her face when she saw you. She did not expect you, and she was very surprised. Very, very surprised," he laughed. "But that is not so strange, mon capitaine, it is simply a matter of fact. Mademoiselle does not remember mon capitaine, and mon capitaine is pretty. He is extremely pretty—

"Especially, eh?" he gave Reineke a knowing crack in the ribs with his fist. "When he is standing in the window with the sun, and he is already the color of the sun, and he makes sure you notice this because he stays in the window, he does not sit down? Glorious, mon capitaine, oh, so, glorious, oui, very, very clever. A man so glorious, how could he be evil? I noticed you did this. I did notice. But, so what, eh?" he shrugged. "Who cares? All Mademoiselle would notice is a pretty man. A horrible, oui, very pretty fiend."

Indeed. The woman noticing he was pretty was of little importance to him. Pierre saying she noticed he was pretty was probably a lie. Pierre was an elf, and this elf Reineke knew well. He was also carrying his elfin tactics over to the woman, and Reineke could sympathize with her in wanting the Holy Man to leave her alone. He was obnoxious. Deliberately sweet and coyly misleading the woman into believing there would soon be some miraculous change in her situation.

"But of course," Pierre defended himself and his tactics. "She is drawn to Pierre despite her convictions to the contrary. I am the only one there, mon capitaine. I am available to scream at or to cry with, and I must encourage her to do both for the sake of her mental health, not only her physical. I have told Mademoiselle she is safe, but she must believe she is safe. You?" he sniffed. "Who cares about you? She does not like you. You will see. By tomorrow, she will be plotting your death with I as her assistant. It will be a tempting offer, I must admit."

"Indeed," Reineke said. Pointing out the Holy Man's conniving and devious scheme was *his* point, including how it had not gone unnoticed by him. Reineke was positive, the Holy Man in his plots to glean acceptance, would get what the English called comeuppance. "You are manipulating her."

"No more than I am manipulating you," Pierre assured. "You believe she is a threat, I tell you she is not a threat, and you will see this for yourself."

"Indeed," Reineke said.

"You are jealous, mon capitaine," Pierre laughed with a waggle of his finger. "I have told you this many, many times before. You are a very jealous man. You strut your pretty face because you want Mademoiselle's acceptance and appreciation for yourself and I am taking it from you. Too bad! Learn the facts of the life you embrace. 'Beauty is in the eye of the beholder'. In the eyes of all, I am who is beautiful, not you. With you, it is just a face."

Hardly. Reineke's desire to be accepted and appreciated was not jealousy. It was nothing less than deserved, right, and fair. One hundred years from now was not sufficient for people to know there once was a German et cetera. Yesterday was not sufficient. Not all Germans ate horses. He had never eaten horses. He had lived among gardens all of his life and the mere onset of global war was, in his opinion, little cause to change. If the woman thought until her death he was a fiend then this was upon the head of the woman and her ignorance was of no importance to him. Her thinking on the whole was not important to him.

Though this would be the second time the Holy Man had alluded to how his physical appearance might be useful in persuading the woman ... from what? Attempting suicide?

Interesting. Reineke puzzled about it for a moment, but only for a moment. In fact, even thinking about it brought immediate guilt.

He could do precious little about his being pretty. It was obvious though the woman was not pretty under her bruised and swollen face. But was plain, even unattractive and therefore spared the full horror of her disfigurement. One cannot disfigure what is already ugly. It was not catastrophic what had happened to her, it was unfortunate.

And that itself was unfortunate. It would take more than a simple effort on his part to change his disinterest in women who were not pretty. His recently acquired compassion for mankind was just that, recently acquired. Only with age came wisdom, and he was not yet old. In his still youthful state, he found great difficulty extending to women the right not to be as pretty as he was even though historically speaking with the coming of age he was finding few women were as pretty as he. Even as compassionate and understanding as he knew himself to be, his ability to consider extending such a compromise to the enemy would be a true test indeed. One hundred years? They could take two. This was his garden, his swimming hole, and his children. That was his Holy Man, his apartment, and now his guest. It was not his vanity that wanted the woman to know the kindness and help extended to her came from him, not simply the Holy Man. It was his ardent respect and appreciation for the truth.

"Indeed, I am a truthful person!" Reineke snarled at Pierre. It was he who called the Holy Man. He who routed the SS. He who supplied the sutures and bandages for her head. She was sleeping in his bed, drinking his water, and eating his goat. It was not strange or bizarre for him to want her to know the bounty she stumbled upon had come from him! They could take three-hundred years! The woman probably ate horses. Anyone as vulgar as she was, probably ate horses for breakfast. He could understand any desire the Holy Man might have to punish her for her violent and abusive behavior. SHE was obnoxious. "Horses, indeed," Reineke snapped. He just might feed her horses and laugh while she—what had the Holy Man said? Something about the woman's mental state? Indeed. If she found herself in some state of nervous collapse due to him, what sort of condition would she have found herself in had he left her in the cellar, ropes around her, with not even horses to eat? Mental state.

Her mental state had nothing to do with him, but rather with her Allied associates failing to supervise some *girl* who obviously couldn't take care of herself. He maintained she was a *girl* despite her claim of marriage, something that only proved she was sexually mature, hardly chronologically.

"Michael," Reineke snarled at Pierre. "Michael, indeed." The woman had called him *Michael* in her confused and unconscious state, and he had not understood. However, he understood now, and it was an insult. This *Michael* was obviously a heathen. Enjoying the company of other heathens too busy devouring horses to even notice one of them was lost to the desert. "Who is *Michael?"* he demanded of Pierre.

"I do not know, mon capitaine," Pierre assured. "It is the first time she has mentioned the name, any name. Perhaps it is the dead American? She has not asked about him, or anyone. And so perhaps she knows, whether she remembers or not, her people are dead."

"Yes," Reineke scowled. "Obviously, yes" It was the dead American with the bones sticking out of his head. "The woman's hair is to be washed."

"Pardon?" Pierre blinked.

"The condition of the woman's hair," Reineke assured, "is disgusting. It is filthy. It is to be washed before any exercise."

"Oh," Pierre said. "Well, I do not believe she will not allow it, mon capitaine. She is very protective of her head."

"Do it!" Reineke barked.

"Oui, of course, whatever you say," Pierre shrugged.

He was staring at him again. The Holy Man was staring at him. Why NOW was he staring at him? Every time he opened his mouth, the little man did nothing except stare at him. The goat was off the floor—from where he had flung it. Its little round circle of grease was off the floor—from where he had wiped it clean. Her goat ... Her goat on the tray was cold, its fat congealed, hardly appetizing and bound to make anyone sick. You do not serve cold, congealed goat to someone who has been ill and expect it to do anything except come back at you. "That is cold," Reineke pointed in accusation.

"Oui, mon capitaine," Pierre agreed, "but it does not matter, for Mademoiselle will not eat it."

Not eat it? Then why was he giving it to her? "Why?" Reineke insisted.

"Pierre has been gone so long," Pierre shrugged, "she will be sleeping—or she will be awake," he smiled, "and will know Pierre has done other things except to find her something to eat, and she will hit him with the tray."

That woman was one of the most uncivilized persons Reineke had ever met. Offending every decent and respectable quality he had—and he had thousands—causing his perfect and glorious skin to crawl.

"One-hundred years from now," the Holy Man was saying, except Reineke had decided to leave the kitchen regardless of what he was saying, "the people who believe in the German and his gardens, will never believe in mon capitaine, never."

"Indeed!" Reineke kicked open the door of his villa to stand on her grand stairs before her magnificent courtyard and scream at the sand if he thought it would listen, except he knew it would not. He had things to do, things he should do, and did not want to do a thing about them, which was why he had called for the Holy Man, earlier, to tell him just that. He was not doing anything after lunch. He was going swimming with the children, leaving the woman the freedom to roam the upstairs halls for her exercise, unencumbered by intimidating armed personnel. However, the Holy Man who hated the war was always the first to point out there was a war, and in war, men did not find the time to do the things they liked to do. The Holy Man was wrong. There was no war, not here. Here, they were simply piling things up for when the war would start again. Let it start again. If they needed him, they would find him, swimming with the children. Ha! All his boxes and barrels of munitions were ready and stacked, his waterholes counted and still full. He remained committed to killing the soldiers who had jeopardized his compound, and he had run out of things to make rules about.

The French windows in his office and the ceiling were both under repair. An *enormous* scaffold filled the room, and did you notice? Reineke sneered at the desert. That idiot woman almost walked into it? Was she blind as well as ugly? She had the grace of one of the Holy Man's goats. Did she think he failed to notice she had little idea how to walk? Had no one ever taught this woman how to pick her feet up? She was undoubtedly a trick of the Gestapo, hardly some Allied spy or anything. He could see the Major planning his plan. Make sure all the boxes and barrels are present and accounted for.

Make sure all of the watering holes are bubbling and full. You already know he will kill the soldiers, and what could there be LEFT to make a rule about? So give him a corn for his toe, and call it a woman. No one can ignore a corn. Ha! But did they know what giving him such a corn would cause him to do? Could they have known it would cause him to blow up his ceiling, decorate his French windows with Thiele, and give the corn to his dwarf of a French priest? He doubted it. With everything done, he could stop any new things to do by placing them all on radio silence where they remained, giving him more than sufficient time to go swimming. *Ha!* On radio silence should the war begin again, no one could tell him, he could not hear them, and he would not hear them until he wanted to hear them, which he did not want to do, he wanted to go swimming!

But.

There was one thing still that should be done.

"THIELE!" Reineke shouted, surprised the man's wife sitting at home in Stuttgart did not look up from eating her solitary lunch.

Thiele listened patiently. He examined obligingly the silver dog tags thrust into his hands, agreeing they were not of a style common to Allied necklaces.

"They are ridiculous," Reineke assured. A passion for trinkets did not excuse turning precious metals into garbage.

So was Reineke's request ridiculous in Thiele's opinion. He had a thousand things he needed to do other than waste time with some ugly and offensive piece of jewelry.

"Give them to someone else," Reineke ordered. Thiele was off to the Kufra with a patrol where he would turn over every stone, sift every grain of sand until he had proof there was or was not a band of roving saboteurs, French, British, or Chinese, Reineke really did not care. The Kufra was minimally, a three-day ride going, and a three-day ride back, therefore Reineke had better not see Thiele for a week.

"A week?" Thiele gasped, he had a thousand things to do!

No, he did not. The only thing Thiele had to do was what Reineke told him to do.

But Reineke had a thousand things to do! Thiele insisted. They were conducting their first shipment of munitions to the farthest camp.

"Indeed." Reineke told Thiele five days ago they were not shipping any munitions, at least not now, not until Reineke was ready.

"Ready?" Thiele sputtered. "The war is coming!"

"It is not here yet!" Reineke snapped. He knew precisely when the war would be there, which Thiele did not, and since Thiele did not, Thiele would do what Reineke told him to do, not what he thought he should do. Come May, Thiele was scheduled for a short, personal leave. Reineke knew, come June, and for months to follow, he, personally, would have no such luxury. And since he would not have one then, he would take one now.

He needed one now.

He wanted one now.

And he would have one now!

But, he was playing into their hands! Thiele moaned.

"Indeed," Reineke raised a haughty brow. Whose hands? With what? He had nothing to play into their hands with. He played with no one's hands except his own. And his own were going to be playing with the children in the game known as swimming.

Only this, he did not tell Thiele, though he was tempted. Thiele's ideas on war were even stricter than the Holy Man's. Little did either of them know however, how many blazing battles Reineke had actually been involved in, and how, in the heat of those battles, should he, Baron Dieter Reineke, decide to put down his gun, stretch out his legs and have a cigarette, he would do precisely that, and dare the bullets whistling by to strike him.

And not one would.

Not one ever had! That was proof of something. Even inanimate objects, deadly, little lead and copper pellets were frightened of him and did not dare stop him from doing precisely what he wanted to do, when he wanted to do it.

But this again he did not tell Thiele. The only thing Thiele might have found it to be proof of was that Reineke had eaten rancid goat, and had precious little time left to decide who did what when before he died of the Holy Man's poison.

But, goat, away! Thiele away! Reineke was off, retreating inside his villa, with only one thing left to be said.

"Anyone," he vehemently informed, finding half-eaten horses was to leave them precisely where they found them.

ANYONE caught eating horses would be shot. No questions asked, reasons, or excuses accepted, end of discussion.

End of something, Thiele was sure. Upon storming away, in his heart, Thiele was convinced taking a patrol and departing just might be the best thing to happen to him. They just might find Allies swarming all over the Kufra and he might never return, never mind in a week. Thiele was not immune to puncture by deadly little pellets. Bullets did not heed him.

Chapter Thirty-Two

March 12
The Tell Atlas, East Algeria

Less the necessary stops to refuel and cool its engine, Justin's reliable Applecore made it across Libya into Algeria in just under thirty-six hours to sit there and wait, landing along the northern folds of the Atlas, Algeria's brooding mountain range. It was still winter but not cold, the air fragrant with cedar and pine under the cool shadows of dwarf palms like a line of fat-bottomed women standing there. Three and a half days, eighty-four hours—count them—since he came into Cairo, sitting around doing nothing, Michael was in a sour mood. Chuck's buddies for all their cartoon qualities were a tame lot. Ate, slept, took turns at watch and occasionally kicked a ball around, dull as housewives. Michael was angry and anxious, edgy like a kid stuck inside on a rainy day.

"Nice night, huh?" Michael solicited one particularly voluptuous tree, but she kept her opinion to herself. "Mind if I join you?" he invited himself, anyway, and Pete glanced over from where he lounged on his blanket.

"Mate ..." Pete turned from Michael to Hank who had seen to rejoining them about an hour ago by way of the Applecore's elder sister, a Swordfish, or Stringbag as they were affectionately called by Hank's lot. Hank did not fly that relic into Malta from Tobruk, though. It did not have the range, the devil with the ruddy Applecore cutting it close, or the range from Malta to there. So, Hank and Fred had to come in from Frank's place out on the Saharan Atlas, picked his Stringbag up there after catching one of the long range flyers out of Cairo to get them in quick as possible. Pete smiled. Justin was moving Hank and Fred into the ranks of his irregulars fast. He wondered how Bobby felt about that since Bobby did not like sharing with outsiders, especially the regular kind, which Hank and Fred most definitely were.

"Tree, mate," Pete spelled out in sign language for Hank when Hank looked up from playing solitaire in reply to the piece of rock Pete tossed killing Hank's Queen of Hearts dead between her eyes. "Tree. He's talking to the damn tree."

Hank looked over in time to see Joe followed by Julia emerging from walking the perimeter.

"Never mind," Pete rolled over on his blanket as Fred got up with a stretch to take his turn patrolling after giving Joe a wave, and his wife a kiss hello, and Hank returned to his solitaire as disinterested as when he first looked up.

"Ay!" Shortly thereafter, the Doc apparently decided he was bored with life and living, his swift kick catching Pete in the bony seat of his pants but only because Hank was sitting on his duff and Pete's was pointing Michael's way.

"What the hell are you looking at?" Michael sneered as Pete rolled over to prop himself up on his elbow and look the Doc over before he killed him. "I'm the one who almost broke my toe."

"Break more than that," Pete promised, "if you ever do that again."

"Save it for my mother," Michael squatted down, willing to bet like everyone else Pete had his price, and Michael was willing to meet the asking price and buy his way out of there for wherever. "Think it's time for a change—"

"Well, now, give it a minute, Doc," Pete nodded, "and it'll be as different as night and day. Algeria's one of those country's with a climate that changes as you change. What you think is snow on those branches over there, walk a few miles and it'll be flowers of peaches, apples, cherry, and pear," he smiled. "Or weren't it the weather you were wondering about?"

"Let's start over," the Doc sucked at the inside of his mouth like he was sucking on tobacco when he could probably stand a taste of something a lot stronger. This boy had a thirst on him. Pete had noticed that immediately. The Doc hadn't drunk much, and maybe he should to keep him from being so mean, the burnished apples of his cheeks tight and inflamed as his temper. Come to think of it, Pete had yet to see the Doc in anything but a bad mood, not so much as even try to smile in the face of adversity like they say one should. He had a sense of humor, or at least thought himself funny with things like the kick he gave Pete in the seat of his pants and clever double-talk, but he wasn't funny. He knew it, Pete knew it, Joe and Julia meandering their way over knew it. A flicker of apprehension in Joseph's eyes, clear annoyance in Jewel's for the Doc trying to show off. Even Hank was inspired to forego cheating himself at solitaire and get up, wandering Pete's way, nonchalantly shuffling the deck, his weight and reason shifting to Pete's side.

"Look," Michael said, "I think we both know Red being shanghaied has got about as much to do with Vichy as I do, which is nothing. So the way I see it—"

"Oh, well, now, that depends," Pete agreed easily, "on how you want to look at it—"

"Dead on!" Michael snapped. "You think I don't fucking know who I am regardless of who else does or doesn't? You think I don't know I'm out here for my health and not much else?"

"You don't look that healthy to me, Doc," Pete advised. "I've seen worse, admit I have, but I've also seen a lot better."

"And I get worse," Michael assured, "before I get better. So let's cut the crap. I want out, and I've got two big ones that say I'm up, I'm out of here. That's five-hundred each for those who are listening."

Four-hundred each if they were feeling generous and included the quiet one with the over-sized head who also showed up when Hank showed up and was around somewhere, on watch, patrolling the perimeter while his wife played house with Joe. Even Michael had to shake his head at that one, yeah, he did, but only in fond memory. "So, any takers?" Michael looked around, 'cause like he said, everyone had their price, this group hardly the exception. "Going once, going twice ..."

"For where, Doc?" Hank asked, though not to suggest he was seriously considering it, which he might be. The same as the rest of them were in the back of their minds. This fellow was a pain in the ass if he were nothing else. Trouble, not just stupid with trying to be funny.

"What do you care?" Michael countered. "I mean personally? Just out, OK? Back, how's that? Take me back to Cairo and I'll take it from there.

"I mean," Michael pled his case, and to an extent even sounded legitimate. "I've got a kid out there somewhere that until someone proves to me otherwise I say is alive. Because I'd feel it, you know?" he said, hell, what anyone in his position would say, did say. "I'd know," he assured, "whether she was or she wasn't. That's all I care about, *all* I care about. I don't care how long it takes, a month, six. Fuck, it took Noah forty fucking years to get where he was going and he had divine direction, so, screw Chuck."

"Moses, Doc," Joe chuckled, glad Pete also felt inclined to laugh even if Julia and Hank did not. "Think you mean Moses. Noah was the guy with the ark."

"Ark, huh?" Michael eyed Pete. "Little wonder it took him forty fucking years."

"Whichever," Joe's hand clapped down on Michael's shoulder in a friendly though firm gesture even though he knew the Doc didn't mean any harm with that kick in Pete's behind nah, he didn't. Joe was confident about that. The Doc was just angry, mouthing off because he was angry, probably feeling helpless, yeah, that was it. Helpless, sad, and grieving, and this just hanging around waiting would kill anyone, get under anyone's skin especially when no one was even really sure exactly what it was they were waiting for, certainly not for some kid to show up, blow in like Dorothy from Kansas. She was dead. The Doc was just having to come to terms with that, on the verge of coming to terms with it, and it wasn't easy, no, it was not. "We understand, Doc," Joe assured in his friendly way. "We do. Talk, if you want to talk—"

"Think fuck off will work?" Michael lunged for Pete and ended up with what turned out to be a load of Joe. But only because Pete was fast, Hank even faster, in a better position to put himself between the Doc and Pete since he was standing and Pete was sitting down. Joe perhaps the fastest of them all, much to his chagrin, because it was his chest hair that wound up snarled in the Doc's fist instead of the Doc's neck twisted in Pete's because there was no way in hell the Doc stood a chance to get his hands on Pete first.

"Joe!" Julia yelled, which had Pete and Hank forgetting about challenging Michael and reaching for her before she made matters worse by shooting the Doc, Joe gasping, "Whoa, Doc!" with a grab for Michael's wrist before Michael tore a few tattoos out by the roots, the pain instant, stinging and burning hot.

"Serious, Doc, let go of the hair—do it you dick-ass motherfucker!" Joe grabbed Michael by the hair on his head, "before I fucking kill you!"

"Fine!" Michael gave him back his wool. "Now fuck off before I get nasty."

"You, too, lad!" Hank advised Joe to give up the ghost before everyone ended back up in the tussle they had all just worked so hard to stop.

"Fair enough," Joe released Michael to surrender to Julia's worries that he wasn't, he didn't know, the man he was when he started out or something. "I'm fine. Serious, I'm good. Just ... wow, yeah," he noticed what she was in a sweat about and it was his blood, couple of little bright dots from where the Doc won and the hair lost, "get me some alcohol."

"For the Doc, too," Hank suggested as she headed for the medic-pack, only he meant the drinking kind.

"Aye, some of Peter's rum," Pete seconded with a smile and a wink at Michael. "Demon rum, Doc. Call it that, because that's what it is. Potent, just the way Peter likes it."

"Yeah, well, don't get your hopes up," Michael ran a hand through his mop of oily curls to make sure they were still there, which they were, like Joe's chest, missing only a few.

"What hopes are those?" Pete asked. "That it gets worse long before it gets better, because you know damn well how it does, don't you?"

"You know," Michael said but only because he felt he had to say something, wouldn't be in character if he didn't, "there's something about you I don't like."

"Oh, well, now, that's all right," Pete sat back down comfortably on his blanket, inviting the Doc to join him for that nightcap, "because there's everything about you I don't like. Not one thing," he assured Michael. "You're stupid, for one. If you weren't you'd know no one ever gets the upper hand on Peter, death wish even to try. I mean, look at me, Doc, have a good look," he smiled while he checked on the order for spirits he had placed. "How's it coming there, luv? Give Jewels a hand, won't you?" he petitioned Hank uncertain about leaving Pete and the Doc alone even for the minute it would take. "Can't have the Doc coming down with the shakes when there's no reason, none at all, Joseph will keep, he'll keep. Live even."

"Not him I'm worried about," Hank countered pointedly.

"Oh, well, I don't know why," Pete smiled at Michael sitting down, right there on the blanket across from Pete. The Doc had balls on him if he had nothing else, aye, he did. "Nothing wrong with the Doc, just like Joseph was saying, that wouldn't be wrong with any of us. Why, I remember when my old lady died ..."

"You talking about your mother?" Hank said, not to be wise, just curious since the Pete he had come to know had lots of old ladies, most he didn't even know their names.

"No, I mean yours," Pete cooed, "and a pitiful sight it was, too."

"Aye, and worth it to get away from you," Hank assured as he retreated as asked, figuring Pete had enough brains to behave even if the Doc didn't.

"No doubt about it," Pete continued to smile at Michael. "No doubt about that at all. Where was I? Oh, that's right. Look at me, Doc. I mean take a real good look," he nodded. Past Pete's bristle of whiskers starting to sprout, the same as the Doc had a few of his own, thicker and darker than Pete's reddish-blond two-day growth on his upper lip and cleft-chin adding a devilish look to his devil-may-care.

Beyond the well-worn cotton shirt no dirtier than the Doc's Italian silk, the semi-automatic strapped to his thigh ...

Jesus frigging Christ, Michael got the point. The guy had a brand burnt into his left tit never mind some pec-load of tattoos, the scarred circles of flesh visible as he bent over to borrow Michael's cigarettes and strike a match. "Yeah, what about it?" Michael said. "Think because I'm not a fan of self-mutilation I'm not as tough as you?"

"Self-mutilation?" Pete glanced down to his breast. "Why, that isn't any self-mutilation, Doc. That's a birthday present from my old man. Poor as we were at the time it was all he could afford. Had a farm, we did, long before I was born," he assured lest Michael confuse him with some country gent instead of the city born and bred fellow he was. "I never saw it, that's for sure. But we had a farm, and all my father could hope to do was burn her into my soul. You following me?" he asked, just like the Doc had asked them to follow him. "Right there should I ever chance to forget, need do nothing except look down."

"You going somewhere particular with this?" Michael checked.

"No, but you are," Pete promised, "if you ever pull a cockamamie stunt like you pulled on Joseph again, try it and see. Try it on me. Go on, grab a handful and see what happens. I don't give the King's ass who you are, save stupid like I said. Should have just stopped with asking me to get you out of here. I'd have taken you anywhere you want to go for less than half your two-thousand and take my chances on finding myself on the wrong side of Justin. It wouldn't be the first time, he'd tell you that himself, and sure as hell wouldn't be last, he'd tell you that as well."

"Let's leave Chuck and back it up to my ticket out of here," Michael suggested, "if you're serious."

"Oh, now, I was serious, Doc," Pete swore. "Take convincing to be serious again. But don't let that stop you, go on, give it your best. Convince me. The only problem I can see facing either of us is that airplane reliable as she is, isn't any help."

"Oh, yeah?" Michael said like he had wings on his back to go along with his name. "How so?"

"Oh, well, how so is that she's an airplane," Pete reminded, "not a jeep. No one's ever going to corrupt Hank. He's not us, he's RA. Black Watch. Got Justin's morals and commitment. Even Jewels isn't going to be quick to comply. Before this job she was looking at ten years—"

"I can handle it," Michael assured.

"Think so I'm sure, but she's not as easy going as she looks."

The hell she wasn't, but that was beside the point. "The plane," Michael said. "I can handle the plane."

"Really?" Pete smiled. "Is that so? You mean to say you're a pilot, Doc, on top of everything else?"

"I'm a lot of things," Michael assured.

"Are you now, Doc?" Pete smiled in the direction of Joe heading back to them on a fast trot, the Doc's nightcap in his hand. "Are you, now?"

"He serious?" Julia snatched up Pete's concoction, sloshing it into the tin beaker Hank held out.

"Pete?" Hank said. "About what? Some fellow seeing pink elephants if he doesn't have enough to drink? I don't know. Know the fellow's an arsehole, that's what I know, whether he does or doesn't need the stuff."

"No, you're right, Pete can't be serious," Julia decided. "I mean, the guv would know, wouldn't he?" she frowned at Joe. "Say something about it you would think."

"What?" Joe finished wiping his chest down with iodine. "The Doc? Nah, he's fine. Just him, you know, just him."

"All right, just him," Hank accepted. "Only problem is Pete's just Pete. Start bragging about how tough you are Pete's apt to show you how tough he is. He's not good at sitting in a foxhole. I don't care who else is or isn't. Pete's no good at it, you can see that."

"Huh?" Joe said.

"Sitting in a foxhole, lad," Hank assured. "Just sitting there waiting, pressure mounting, turns minutes into hours, after a while it even gets to the best. Pete's hardly the best. He's pressurized long before some fellow starts bandying about the size of his bollocks."

"Yatata, yatata," Joe took the bottle of Pete's rum, heading back to the Doc and Pete. "It ain't the booze, it's the Doc. That's the way he is ..."

"I'll second that," Hank snorted, offering Julia a turn at the beaker Joe left behind. "Think that lad is going to have to do better than that if he ever wants to run for President."

"Ta," Julia shook her head. "I'm fine."

"You sure?" Hank chuckled. "It'll put hair on your chest."

"Oh?" Julia laughed. "Think you're the one who's going to have to do better."

"Aye, well, I'm not good at politicking," Hank assured. "Don't even pretend to be."

"No more than Pete is at foxholes." Julia wrapped her arms around herself to calm the shivers that weren't because she was cold, but worried and wondering and not liking the feeling. "Is rather like sitting in a foxhole, isn't it? Don't suppose this waiting would go any faster if any of us knew what we were actually waiting for," she looked Hank over. "Know what I mean?"

"I do, and I can't answer you even if I could, and I can't," Hank said.

"Why?" Julia asked. "This Doc's too hot for Cairo, there's got to be a reason why he's too hot. Figure out who he is, probably figure that out as well ... only problem is I can't figure who he could be, other than a damn pain in the arse," she took the beaker from Hank, a smile on her face as it passed through her lips. "Warm the cockles, Pete's right about that. With a little luck, it will knock the Doc flat over on his. In as bad shape as Pete seems to think he is, it can't help but knock him flat."

"Think that's more it," Hank took the beaker back.

"What is?" Julia said. "Babysitting some drunk? Pete will put a bullet through his own head, never mind anyone else's."

"Or at least a pain in the arse," Hank nodded. "Think he's less hot than a pain in the arse the Major doesn't want around. I mean," he scoffed, "he seem like the sort of fellow to you, you would put your career on the line for? He doesn't to me, and I wouldn't."

"Put his career on the line?" Julia said, concerned. "The guv?"

"He's fine," Hank assured. "Think he's trying to teach that Doc a lesson that's all. Sit him out here and see how he likes it. Looking over your shoulder every five minutes, wondering who's out there, *if* anyone's out there. Which direction the damn bullet's going to come from, if it's going to come, which you know damn well it is, and if it's not, what is? Hell, if the Doc weren't a drunk when he started out, he'll be one by the time he goes home, especially if he spends much time drinking this stuff."

"Quite," Julia said. Pete's rum was as potent as he claimed, and Hank's lips, if they weren't numb they were getting a little loose. Julia watched him closely.

Hank knew she was. He smiled. "Tell you this much, luv, so you don't ruin your looks wondering, it's him who got the governor's sister mixed up in the mess she found herself in. Him who got her killed, that Doc sitting right over there. So, quite. The boss doesn't want him around, no more than I would, for the single reason he's apt to kill him never mind anyone else."

"You're lying through your damn teeth," Julia accused after watching him a little longer.

Hank laughed. "No, I'm not. Anyone come by to trouble you about him, you just send them on to Pete or me. Just tell them you don't know, but we do. Point them in our direction, and we'll take it from there. That Doc, I can promise you won't live long enough to ruin anyone's career, including his own. No one's going to have to worry about that."

"Babysitting," Julia nodded, "babysitting. Isn't that rich. I owe Justin one, I do."

"Oh, right," Hank laughed again, handing her the beaker, "Remember that and you might not be back with us so quick the next time."

"Here you go, Doc," Pete took the duty from Joe handing Michael a cup, and pouring himself a little of his dynamite. "Good as new in less than a minute, you'll see."

"Uh, huh," Michael said, "think we covered that part and had moved on."

"So we have," Pete agreed. "Doc was complaining again how he would prefer to get cracking and take care of these Jerry fellows ourselves," he explained tentatively to Joe carefully watching Michael's reaction. "Thinks he can get you interested in listening to him the same as he has me."

"Oh, yeah?" Joe grinned at Michael. "Why? 'Cause you think I'm stupid or something?"

"Yeah," Michael said, "actually. I mean, I don't suppose it's occurred to either of you zeroes that whatever scent Chuck thinks he's on is the one to get him off the track, rather than on it?"

"Oh, well, now, that would be a little strange, wouldn't it?" Pete considered the notion of being taken for a ride. "For Jerry to try and throw somebody off a track he just did his damn best to get them on?"

"Not so strange," Michael hinted, "if all they wanted to do was bust Chuck's balls. Maybe all they ever wanted was to pinch Red, slit her throat, to show Chuck he ain't the king of the mountain. Not this one."

"Now that would be a really stupid thing to do," Pete nodded at Joe nodding back.

"Too late, even," Joe agreed.

"Aye, a lot too late," Pete poured himself a little more rum with a laugh. "It's Charlie's attention they got whether it's Charlie's attention they wanted or not—not to say you don't have a point, Doc," he poured Michael a second dose, dry as the Doc's cup had been now for a while. "Doc's got a point, Joseph, he does. All this time wasted wondering if Jerry's up to finishing what he started, or what he's up to when we could just go out there and find out for ourselves."

"Yeah, you've got a point, Doc," Joe agreed, "on top of your head, and whatever scheme you're rattling around in there, just don't, OK? Don't. If we sit here two days, we sit here two days. If we sit here for ten, we sit for ten. You don't like it, I don't like it, nobody likes it, but that's the way it is. OK?"

"No!" Michael assured. "But, then, hey, unlike you, I would notice if someone puts a bullet through my brain."

"Nah, I'd notice, Doc," Joe helped himself to Michael's cigarettes, tossing Pete one as well. "Pretty sure I would—Pete might not, but I would."

"No, I'd notice, lad," Pete assured, accepting a light. "Maybe not if it were your brain, but definitely if it were mine."

"Whatever," Joe dug in his pocket for the deck of cards he happened to have. "We stay until the Maj says go, and then we go, not before."

"Maj," Pete scoffed. "Come off that Major business once and for all, can't you? He's a damn governor like Jewels says. You even know what a damn governor is, boy? Prison warden. What Justin is, and where we are, prison."

"Yeah, I know what a governor is," Joe assured. "You know what happened to the last fucking asshole who called me boy?"

"Nothing," Pete assured, "just like what's going to happen to me.

Where were we?" he helped himself to another of Michael's cigarettes to save for later. "Talking about Charlie, weren't we? And you should know, Doc how *Charlie* do mean *fool*. You know that, right? Sure you do. But if you think Justin's the fool, what do you think they are who started this?" he wondered.

"Sick bastards," Michael assured, not surprised to find it was contagious.

Pete laughed. "You do have a knack for stating the obvious, Doc that you do."

"Yeah, well, there's obvious, and then there's obvious," Michael suggested. "Know what I mean?"

"No," Peter shook his head, "can't say I do."

"Think about it," Michael stretched out, tucking his hands behind his head. "Let me know."

Pete eyed him. "Lying through your damn teeth about being able to pilot that plane, aren't you, Doc? Trying to make a fool out of Peter?"

"You tell me," Michael's perusal of the stars ended at Julia having a chit-chat with Hank, probably not about rules of some card game. He sneered. "What's she doing, taking a break?"

Pete looked over. "Jewels? Well, now, I can't say I know what you mean by that either, Doc," he advised.

"Now I know you're stupid," Michael assured. He nodded at Joe. "That goes double for you. Yeah, I can pilot a frigging plane, so do you want in, or don't you? That's what we're talking about. Me out of here, into the wide blue yonder."

"Um ..." Joe said. "No, I'm not stupid, Doc. And, yeah," he said, "you're right. Jewels is taking a break. From me."

"You mean kind of like dress rehearsal for when her old man comes back in?" Michael aimed to hit below the belt.

"Um ..." Joe said with a glance at Pete shaking his head.

"Don't do it, lad," Pete advised. "Do not. Justin will ask how the Doc got his neck broken and Peter will have to tell him, he will. But then while Peter will do most anything for you, die, even, if he's asked to, what Peter will not do is find himself back in jail for you."

"Fair enough," Joe accepted. "Yeah, Doc," he told Michael. "Yeah, actually, until Fred comes back in. You're right about that, too. Next question?"

"That's probably it," Michael said. "Just checking. After all, I wouldn't want to accidentally ruin anyone's fun by talking out of turn."

"No chance of that," Pete shook his head. "None. You've got it all wrong, anyway."

"I do, huh?"

"Aye," Pete said. "Joseph's a lifer, Doc, like I am. Who's not is Jewels. Who's certainly not is Fred. He's regular Army. And apart from Fred's the one who asked Jewels to marry him, what would you like Joseph to do? Tell the lady she can't have a life after she's paid her society dues and is out of here?"

"Is that the way it reads?" Michael verified with Joe.

"Yeah," Joe said. "That's about the size of it."

"Well," Michael said, "I've heard better, and I've heard worse."

"Knew you'd understand, Doc," Pete nodded. "Same as I'm sure you understand any momentary urge on Joseph's part to kill you. He tells me, like he says about you, it's just got something to do with him being Italian ... now is that true, Doc?" Pete just thought he'd ask since they were on the subject. "I've often wondered about that. Are you inclined to kill and not ask first just because you're Italian? Or is that just a load of what you Yanks call bullshit?"

"It's true," Michael said.

"Right," Pete smiled. "Sounds like a small man's disease to me." He stood up to hitch his pants and stretch his lanky limbs, tall enough at six-one in his boots. "About time to police that perimeter again, isn't it, Joseph?" he reminded with a tap of his watch. "Tea time's, over."

"Yeah, we're on it," Joe put away the cards. *We*, of course, meaning him and Julia, leaving Michael to hope the *perimeter* could take care of policing itself.

"What about you, Doc?" Pete asked.

"Huh?" Michael looked up.

"Want any more of this?" Pete dangled the rum before he put it away for the night. "Sure you do," he said, "same as Peter does. And then we'll take our guns out and see which one of us can hit that notch on your tree with our eyes half closed. Those the kind of games you like to play, Doc? Like they do in films? Is that what you think this is? Make-believe? Is that who you think you are with your prissy white collar and high-buttoned shoes, mouthing off about wanting to do this and going to do that? One of those gangster fellows? Like Bogart?" he poured some rum. "Or that Mick, what's his name? Cagney," he nodded. "Right, that's it. That's who Bobby says you think you are. James Cagney. How the hell old are you anyway, Doc? Forty? Shit, I'm forty-five. Been in jail half my life and still I look better than you. About time you grew up, isn't it? You'll never be a tall man, I don't care how much you pay for your shoes, but it's never too late to change, especially for something as big as this."

"Better question," Michael said, "you believe that schlock you spieled off?"

"Which schlock's that?" Pete asked, like he didn't know. "The one about Joseph and my girl Jewels? Well, now, it doesn't matter what Peter believes, now does it? Understand me, don't get me wrong. I like Fred, I do. I like Joseph. I even," he handed Michael one for the road, "could consider not hating you. But who I like most of all is Jewels.

"Aye," he shook his head, cuddling his bottle as he stood there, thinking about more than constellations. "I like Jewels. Fine lass. Mighty fine lass. Good, too, she is," he assured. "Talking about more than the services she provides. She's a bushranger—that's a bandit, Doc," he clarified. "Here in Africa that usually means poacher. Her father taught her everything she knows about her airplanes. Just playing firefighter out in the wilds of Kenya wasn't her interest, that's all," he shrugged, "can't fault her there.

"No, cannot," he shook his head. "No reason in the world to want to hurt or upset her, but then," he smiled, "she isn't doing anything a man doesn't do, and she's living in a man's world, so why not?

"Aye, why not?" he went back to hugging his bottle briefly in the moonlight thinking about things before he thought of something else. "Joseph?" he picked up his two-way.

"*Yeah*?" Joe answered on his end, sounding normal, too, except for his groan. "*What*? *I passed your final exam, too, didn't I*? *Yeah, I did. Not going to have to worry about mutiny or whatever the hell it is you're concerned the Doc might be able to talk me into.*"

"Aye, you passed," Pete assured with a wink at Michael ogling him with that mean look of his. "Remind me to talk to you about a fellow later," he said, Hank rejoining them with a frown. "Fellow by the name of Cain. Ian McShane Cain."

"*Oh, yeah*?" Joe said. "*Why*? *Something important*?"

"No," Pete said, "just remind me."

"Now, why do I know that name?" Michael asked as Pete lit a cigarette and Hank sat down to play his cards.

"Well, I don't know the answer to that, Doc," Pete assured, "haven't the faintest. McShane's IRA born and bred same as I. Neither of us has ever been to Brooklyn that I'm aware of."

"That's why I know that name," Michael said. "Go on, tell me. Tell me Chuck's plucked him out of some steel cage, and I am definitely thumbing my way out of here to have a chit-chat."

"Oh, well, now," Pete smiled. "Fellow's first got to be in a cage, doesn't he? And as allergic Pete is to steel bars, I've heard McShane's highly allergic."

"He's allergic to more than jail," Michael assured.

"Is he?" Pete said. "Well, I guess he is," he shrugged, "if you're talking about working off a sentence or two by doing a little work for the Crown. No, that's not McShane's game. But then he's not seen the light Peter has, doubt if he ever will."

"Oh, yeah?" Michael said. "And what light is this? The one where they flip the switch, or the one at the end of the rope?"

"No," Pete said, "It's the same one as I told Justin, if I don't like the idea of handing my Emerald girl over to some Brit, I sure ain't going to hand her to no German, now, am I? Fallacy, Doc, the idea of neutrals, is. Ain't no one neutral—except for maybe the Swiss," he shrugged. "But considering it takes twenty minutes to open one of those damn knives of theirs, that about explains why. But as far as anyone else? It's a fool's notion, because if you think Hitler's going to stop at that border of Erin and Blighty and not want to step over it, I've got a bridge I want to sell you."

"And after it's over?"

"Now, that is a different arrangement," Pete nodded. "Yes, it is. Justin and I are going to have to take a look at our contract should the two of us come out of this alive, that we are, and that we might. We just might." He thought about that, returning to the present with a smile for Michael, and a spray of smoke from between his teeth. "You know war is a game of poker, Doc," he said. "Took my innocence, Justin did, when he told me that, but he's right. Something less than a fool's ass thinks war's chess. To the contrary, it's all in the luck of the draw. After which," he downed the rum, "the only strategy you have is how good you gamble, how willing you are to bet your shirt if need be, and how well you bluff."

"Justin," Michael said.

"Justin," Pete assured. "Man's an addict, a veritable addict—talking about gambling, Doc, not drink or drugs like you and me," he clarified. "He's a gambler, sinister one, at that. Sure you must know that what with being such good friends and all. Bet the lot of us fifty quid apiece none of us make it out of here alive himself included, and personally, I'm on a mission to prove him wrong, same as he's on one to prove it's possible. Not saying we don't like each other," he shrugged. "Not saying we do. Got nothing to do with it, either way. Honor among thieves, that's all, honor among thieves. You've heard of that, right, Doc?" he asked. "Or did you really think one of us would sell another of us out just to give you some damn ride home?"

"Oh, yeah," Michael said, "goes something like, *'once upon a time'*. He fried his father, for Christ's sake. Chuck's! Give me a fucking break 'honor among thieves'. You're a fucking coward, that's what you are, you're yellow!"

"Who did?" Pete smiled easily. "McShane? Well, I guess you read the papers, Doc, and congratulations to you, too, considering half the world's population can't even read at all, our man Nellie among them. True," he nodded, "it's true. Though even still, even Nellie, I believe will tell you, honest fellow that he is, and being able to read it for himself or not, don't think the papers said anything about McShane being convicted of killing Justin's daddy, though I understand he was accused."

"Accused?" Michael said. "*Accused*?"

"On the other hand," Pete nodded, "I guess whether McShane did the duty himself or not, or just stood accused, who he couldn't have killed was that little baby sister of Justin's since we're running around, chasing after the ones who have killed her now ...

"Or we will be, Doc," he promised, "we will be. You might get that wish of yours after all, ever think of that? Might get that wish of yours of 'doing something about this' without having to lift your little finger to go find it, as it's apt to come to you all on its own. And then we'll see, won't we? Just which one of us is yellow like you say."

"If you're talking about Jean Paul," Hank put in, "be interesting to see if that prediction of someone coming turns out to be right. Charlie's got a stick up his arse about Jean Paul for some reason or another, and he won't be satisfied until he pulls it out. Hang Jean Paul for this, hang him for that, we wouldn't be out here unless Charlie thought there might be a reason to hang him, you're right about that."

"Now, see, Doc," Pete pointed. "There you go. Jean Paul Dumont as far as anybody knows, is Justin's right hand man, and so it's what I've been saying. My boy Justin's a sinister bastard. Could be why I like him, could be at that, could be why he likes me. Not saying either of us do, not saying either of us don't. It's up to those who believe, and those who don't."

"You do," Hank assured.

Pete laughed. "That's something else war does, Doc," he advised, "makes for strange bedfellows. Though you know that already as well, don't you? Sure you do. What with the two of you being such good friends and all, because there is nothing stranger than the two of you being friends—damn. You and Justin? Lord." Pete sat down to lie down on his blanket and close his eyes.

"Does this mean I don't get ride home?" Michael confirmed.

"It means you get to live, Doc," Pete assured, "to where an hour ago Peter was going to kill you but settled for his rum instead so he'd be sure not to care if you lived or died. No, you don't get your goddamn airplane ride. Stupider than I think you are to believe that bullshit. But thanks for the information, and thanks for reminding me. Hank," he said, "Doc here's apparently a pilot. Thinks he can fly one of those airplanes out of here himself. How long it take you to put the distributor caps back on, should you have to take them off?"

"Twenty minutes?" Hank shrugged. "Give or take."

"That's too long," Pete said. "It doesn't take but a second or two to unlock a pair of cuffs, so be a good fellow, won't you, and chain the Doc up to his favorite tree over there for Peter so the rest of us can get some sleep—that all right with you, Doc?" he asked. "Wouldn't want to upset that killer Italian temper of yours while I lie here unsuspecting with my eyes closed only to have my head bashed in by some rock you got sitting close enough to you to grab—go ahead and try it, Doc. Do it. And then take off in one of those airplanes. Shit. You really are an arsehole, aren't you? Stupid, and a loud mouth coward to boot. Shit," he said again. "Jean Paul answer that broadcast of Justin's?" he asked Hank before he fell asleep. "Is that it?"

"Before we even got into Cairo with the jeeps," Hank said. "Waiting for us when we got in."

"That's too bad," Pete said. "I kinda liked him, I did. Aye, well, we'll see what Nel turns over and take it from there. The Doc might be heading back to Cairo faster than he thinks so we can get on with things here. That he might be."

Chapter Thirty-Three

The Fezzan
March 13

"Oh, my!" Joanna gasped as she stood on the long, narrow balcony outside her room overlooking the vast marble world sprinkled with twisted trees and chips of white sand glittering like ice in the sun.

"It is pretty, isn't it?" Pierre agreed proudly.

Pretty? Joanna touched the balcony rail warm with captured heat. "Well, I don't know," she said. "I ... don't know ..."

"Miraculous, oui," Pierre nodded. "Glorious. Though the hillside is not marble, this structure is, yes."

Hillside. Joanna stared out at the jagged white mountain so close and tall she could not see the top of it as it disappeared into the sunlight.

"A composition principally of limestone," the funny little priest was busy explaining, "not uncommon in the desert—"

"What's not uncommon?" Joanna asked, absently.

"The wall, Mademoiselle," he said.

Wall? Joanna looked at him. "Wall? What wall?"

"That one," he pointed to the mountain. "Her trees are olive, some of them a thousand years old. Cyprus, naturally. Date, fig—"

"I don't understand," Joanna interrupted. "Are we in a valley, some sort of valley?"

"Valley?" Pierre smiled. "What valley is this?"

Well, Joanna hardly knew what valley. How could she? She looked around at what wasn't at all familiar, but seemed as if it should be, and in an odd way, it almost was.

"I ..." she said.

"Do you mean like Egypt, Mademoiselle?" Pierre asked. "Egypt and her Valley of Kings? Have you been to Egypt, Mademoiselle?"

Yes, Joanna had been to Egypt. She was in Egypt ... wasn't she? She frowned because where she had been in Egypt it certainly did not look anything like this.

"Perhaps you are thinking about Rome?" Pierre pursued. "Has Mademoiselle never been to Rome to see her coliseum? Or Greece, her amphitheater?"

"Rome?" Joanna stared out over the balcony, uncomfortable with the mountain so close particularly now that the priest had mentioned it was a wall, and what an unpleasant thought that was. Surely, it couldn't really be a wall, could it? Any more than she could be in Rome, could she? Surely, he wasn't trying to tell her she had been spirited away from Egypt all the way to Rome, was he? "I'm in Rome?" she gaped at him.

"No, Mademoiselle," Pierre chuckled. "A comparison only, an example. This is a valley of the gods, oui. Jupiter. Venus, Apollo, and, of course," he smiled, "Diana. Goddess of the moon, the hunt, children," he nodded. "The Egyptian artifacts are restricted to the house, and are decorations only like mon capitaine and his Germans."

That all sounded too terribly involved to Joanna. "Why are you calling it a wall?" she asked.

"The hill?" Pierre said. "Because that is what it is? That is what it is like?" he shrugged. "All around us like a wall."

"All around ..." Joanna repeated. She leaned over as far as she could to see to the side but she couldn't see much that looked any different to her.

"Oui," Pierre continued talking. "Protecting her magnificent display of Roman splendor and opulence." He laughed. "That is what this is, Mademoiselle, yes," he assured, his hand sweeping out. "A gateway, a temple, a meeting house, a city. Mon capitaine is unsure, but then he is an architect, not an archeologist. And really what does it matter anyway, eh? It does not. Come ..." he drew her away from the balcony rail back into the cooler sunshine of her room. "Come explore Pierre's castle. Come see where you are inside, and perhaps tomorrow we will look outside. The Roman and his ruins are scattered from one end of this desert to the other. But this house is still unique, and it is the house I want you to see. It was resurrected by the Moors, renovated by a man from Istanbul ..."

"What?" Joanna said.

"Istanbul," Pierre smiled. "Constantinople to the Eastern Roman Kings. A seaport in Turkey. Rome was an Empire, Mademoiselle, not merely a city. You must know this. A very famous and wealthy shipping owner restored this home for his thousand wives. I do not know his name. If I did, I have forgotten it. It was so long ago, four-hundred years at least. So many guests Pierre had before then, so many guests since. He cannot remember all of them ..."

Joanna snatched her hand away and he laughed again, teasing her with that ugly little wink of his. "Mon capitaine does the same thing. That is interesting to me, curious for a race of man who believe in God to believe also in the supernatural. Tell me, what is frightening to you? That Pierre has been here forever, since the time of the Roman Kings. That he is telling the truth? Or that he is telling a lie?"

Joanna hardly cared either way. "You said I could see the house. I want to see the house. I don't care who built it."

"The Romans, oui," Pierre nodded, "and the Moors. A Moor is of a race similar to the Arab, Mademoiselle, if you do not know this. A pagan, if he has not found God, a Muslim, if he has. An ancient people. Descendants of the Arab and mysterious Berber who populated the whole of the coast of Afrika across the Straits of Gibraltar to Spain."

"The house," Joanna said firmly. "Show me the house."

"Of course," Pierre smiled.

They went out into the library where Joanna had met the Captain the day before, and thank heavens he was not there now, as Pierre had promised her he would not be. Pierre discouraged Joanna from exploring the library however, and that was fine with her. She was not interested in exploring anything, just wanting to see where she was. The library was huge, even larger than Joanna remembered. Overwhelming and intimidating in its size it looked like a church. The only thing she could think of as she stared up at the domed ceiling high above her head. Her room a box by comparison to this one, her ceiling was rather flat except in the chamber off the loo where the priest slept. Until he told her that and showed her his sleeping room, Joanna hadn't even thought of where he lived or slept. Why would she? She should have been upset to learn he was living so close to her, just around the corner in her room, but she wasn't, and like everything else she was feeling she wasn't quite sure why.

There was another room off the library, adjacent to hers. Half the size of the library and four times the size of hers, it, too, had a high domed ceiling, and those same French windows lining two walls, not only one wall as they did in her room. It was practically empty except for a large bureau, and equally large bed, a crucifix of wood and gold lying on top of a small night table.

"Oh," Joanna stopped short at the sight of the crucifix. "Is this your room?"

"Pierre's?" Pierre smiled. "No, as I explained to Mademoiselle, I am sleeping in the small room until Mademoiselle is completely well."

Joanna meant did he sleep there otherwise. Honestly, one of these days people were going to stop speaking to her as if she was stupid. She was not stupid. "Never mind," Joanna said. She picked up the crucifix that was very pretty and quite heavy, and unfortunately, not really the sort of thing she should consider using to bash in someone's head. She sighed.

"A reasonable question though to ask," Pierre agreed. "It is very simple like one could expect for a priest."

Yes. "It's big," Joanna said aloud.

"Yes," Pierre said. "Space is deceiving when it is empty, and mon capitaine likes space. He removed most of the furnishings from this room, as he did from the library. Antiques are ghosts of the past he claims. They haunt him, he cannot think."

Joanna was not listening. Bigger and brighter than her room, it was cooler with the cross breeze. She hesitated in approaching the windows though where she could see the balcony through them, but also the mountain wall that did appear to be surrounding them, at least on two sides. "May I go outside?"

"On the balcony? Do you want to?" Pierre asked.

Joanna was considering it. "Can we change rooms?"

"Pardon?" Pierre said.

"Can we change rooms?" Joanna asked. "You can have mine, and I'll take this one—you'll still be close," she assured when he did not answer her. "For God's sake, they're not that far apart. It's just ... well, it's more respectable," she said if he wanted to know the truth. She wasn't entirely comfortable with knowing he slept around the corner in the small room he called an alcove or something like that, even if she wasn't upset about it.

"Yes," Joanna decided. "Yes, I think I would like to have this room and you can have mine. We'll exchange."

Pierre smiled. "This room? No, you cannot have this room, Mademoiselle. It is mon capitaine's room, and he not only likes his space, he likes his privacy. The crucifix, oui," he indicated the cross she clutched in her hand, "that is Pierre's. I gave it to mon capitaine for the simple reason le Christ is a ghost of the past who should haunt him."

He was an absolute beast. "Beast!" Joanna threw the crucifix on the floor.

Pierre chuckled, evil in his laugh and twinkling eyes. "You said you wanted to see the house, Mademoiselle. This room is part of it ... and, yes, it was Pierre's room," he agreed. "It is simply on loan to mon capitaine, as yours is on loan to you—"

"I don't care!" Joanna hissed. "I hardly meant ... well, I certainly hardly meant ..." she took two wild, faltering steps forward, two wilder, faltering steps backwards, as she tried to collect her bearings and simply get out of there.

"I mean, I hardly knew!" Joanna crashed into what turn out to be a wardrobe trying to get through it, fight and find her way out, a row of Captains standing at attention, meeting her, greeting her, dressed in white, beige, green, black, and blue—"Pink?!" Joanna stared at the gaudy pink strip running down the leg of the dark green trousers. "Pink?!" she clutched them.

"Oui, pink, Mademoiselle," Pierre agreed. "Is there something about the color pink you do not like?"

What is he? An organ grinder? Joanna heard Michael crack in her head. She stared at Pierre.

"Pink is for Panzer, Mademoiselle," Pierre explained. "The color of the Panzer. Mon capitaine is a Panzer Commander—or he was," he snickered. "Mon capitaine is too much like Pierre to be anything but what he is. He does not listen any better than Pierre, and neither does he care to learn."

"I want to go," Joanna whispered.

"Oui, of course," Pierre gestured, "come. Leave that. Pierre will take care of it ..." he pushed the clothes back inside, straightening them neatly. "Panzer is armor, Mademoiselle, tank. This black one?" he pointed at something, Joanna had no idea what. "That is Panzer. No buttons to hinder the man or his operation. Very practical, very attractive, and very ..." he winked, "a very nice target to shoot at here in the desert, and therefore very stupid like all Germans are ... as they are morbid, oui. That is the word. Morbid. A man whose favorite color is black is morbid. He is not flamboyant as mon capitaine thinks he is. He is not exotic, or dramatic ... he is morbid."

"I want ..." Joanna closed her eyes.

"Oui, you want to go," Pierre nodded. "We are going ... you see? The door is right here ..."

They were out of the room and back into the library. "Where do those lead?" Joanna stopped.

"Pardon?"

"Those!" Joanna stumbled forward, stumbling down the stairs.

"Mademoiselle!" Pierre caught her. "Be careful, you must! Remember, there are steps—"

"I'm fine!" Joanna slapped his fluttering and flapping hands away. "I want to know where those doors go ... where they lead ..."

She reached them, grasping their twin latches in her hands, and the latches were huge. Joanna stared up at the doors that had to be exactly the same massive height of those found in a church. She turned sarcastically on Pierre. "Where do they go? To his toilet?"

"Pardon?" Pierre said. "No, Mademoiselle, mon capitaine's toilet is in his chambers, as is yours ... would you like to go to the toilet, Mademoiselle?" he asked solicitously.

No. Any water Joanna might have had in her was sucked right out of her the moment she realized she was in the Captain's room barely spitting distance from hers. Just sucked right out of her, leaving her bone dry and breathing harshly. "Where do they go?" Joanna rattled the latches. "Where?"

"The hall, Mademoiselle," Pierre said. "Oui, the corridor. Would you like to go out into the corridor?"

"They're locked!" Joanna said.

"Oui, but a simple solution."

Pierre produced a key, and the mezzanine Joanna stepped out onto was so much more enormous than the rooms, looking up, around, and even more so looking down.

"I! Oh, my ..." Joanna said as she stared at the towering columns, brilliant pink and fat, trimmed in green and gold.

"Oui, pink, Mademoiselle," Pierre nodded as Joanna dared to touch the polished stone. "I hope you do not mind. The Moors, too, they like pink, what can Pierre say?"

"Oh, my ..." Joanna said, breathed, as she dared to step and look over the rail, down onto the highly polished floor of pink glass ... too far to jump. *Fifty?* she tried to calculate. *Maybe fifty?*

"Oui, many meters, Mademoiselle," Pierre read her face and took her by the arm. "As from your balcony, you could not entertain any idea of jumping, only to your death."

Joanna could entertain any idea she liked. "It's sand," she assured, absorbed in the flamboyancy of the hall.

"Pardon? Sand, Mademoiselle?" Pierre said. "No, it is marble."

"Outside," Joanna assured.

"No, it is marble, Mademoiselle," Pierre nodded. "The sand is simply a dusting, a little here, a little there. But the grounds are marble, Mademoiselle," he promised. "Crushed marble, a deep bed of marble, trees, and, yes, limestone to support the villa. A structure such as this could never be built on sand."

"Oh," Joanna said and frowned, thinking about that.

"But it is all right," Pierre patted her hand. "We will think of another way."

Quite. Joanna eyed the twin staircases around the mezzanine on the other side, trying to count the number of steps and coming up with thirty-five before they reached a large landing where they merged into one about half-way down.

"This is the Roman atrium," Pierre was saying, his arm up and sweeping around again, "the entrance way to his temple or palace. This floor is the mezzanine with mademoiselle's chambers, mon capitaine's, and his library, and oui, several smaller vaults—you see all the little windows, Mademoiselle?" he called Joanna's attention to the row of tiny keyhole shaped windows lining the walls below the ceiling directly above her. "From the time of the Moor until this last century the atrium, the vaults, this entire section of the villa was never open as the Roman intended, instead a secure, private box.

"Oui, like a box, Mademoiselle," he nodded. "A giant box protruding on the outside ... you will see. Inside, the same. Walls, not pillars, all around you. Can you imagine? Only those tiny windows for light?"

"Well, no, actually," Joanna said honestly, "I can't."

"Neither can Pierre," Pierre assured. "I would think ugly, not beautiful like this."

"Where do those steps go?" Joanna pointed ... well, really in both directions. One set on the left and another on the right curve of the mezzanine there were narrow staircases leading up somewhere.

"Those?" Pierre said. "To the towers," he shrugged. "A series of smaller rooms used for storage that is all. Similar to any other house."

"Oh," Joanna said. "Well, can we go down?"

"Down?" Pierre smiled. "To the outside? Yes, we can do this. Perhaps tomorrow. Down to the outside ... or even better," he waggled his finger in delight, "instead of the front, down through the gardens so much prettier."

"Gardens?" Joanna said.

"Oui, gardens, Mademoiselle," he assured. "Fifteen different gardens and a magnificent arboretum. Not too many interesting plants or trees, but magnificent colors of stones and interesting places to sit ... Come, I will show you ..."

He led her away from the sweeping staircases where she wanted to go, along the mezzanine, passed the flight of steps leading up, through one of the high arched doorways. Joanna found herself on another balcony facing the hillside, overlooking a series of broken low walls that went on and on in through trees, and, yes, what did appear to Joanna to be more stone than sand. It was interesting she supposed, certainly bright and sparkling as everything else in the sunlight. She thought of something, realized, actually. She looked at Pierre. "What did you mean we'll have to think of something else?"

He smiled. "I do not know, Mademoiselle, could you explain?"

"When you were telling me how I couldn't jump down."

"Oh," Pierre said. "Well, yes, Mademoiselle, we can walk—you do not have to jump."

"Oh," Joanna said. "Oh, of course ... well," she said. "Can we go down? Why can't we go downstairs now?"

"Did Mademoiselle notice the lights?" he ignored her, guiding her back through the arched doorway to where they had started so she could see the lights. They were boring. Ugly. Half expecting crystal chandeliers from the tone of his voice, the lights were simply large and metal woven with fat short unlit candles, suspended from thick ropes tied in the walls and hanging like nets over the center of the hall.

"I really want to go downstairs," Joanna repeated.

Pierre sighed. "No, Mademoiselle, I do not think this is wise, not today."

"I know the stairs are large," Joanna assured, only half blind.

"They are larger than large," Pierre agreed, as everything in the place was bigger than big except for perhaps her and him. "And you are not blind under your bandage, Mademoiselle," he promised her. "I swear to you, a cut above your eye, not through it. But, today is the first day you have walked any distance at all ... and, oui," he approved, very pleased, "you have walked very well, a very good exercise. But now I think it is perhaps time to take a rest. The steps are not only very large, they are marble, and they are slippery as if wet, as if ice, as if glass."

"Well, I'm going down," Joanna took a step to prove she did intend to do it.

"Mademoiselle!" Pierre implored, but then stopped. "Oui, Mademoiselle," he agreed, rather than attempt to wrestle her to the floor, "if you insist."

"Thank you," Joanna said, because she did insist even though the funny thing about steps is if you haven't walked them in a while, they seem to grow as you step.

"But carefully, Mademoiselle," Pierre reminded. "Walk carefully. Remember they are large, flat, oui, but marble, smooth like glass. Take two steps if you have to before you step down."

Two steps before stepping down were too many, and one step not enough. Joanna was already tired in spite of her insistence before she started down the stairs. Dizzy when she looked down to watch where she was going when she hadn't been dizzy at all when simply looking straight ahead. The palms of her hands sweating and damp as the soles of her bare feet before she took her first knee-rattling step, she was determined though. She grasped the smooth banister she dimly noticed was wooden not stone, but smooth and polished just the same. Longer than long, she managed what seemed like a hundred steps before she paused to take a breath less than halfway to the landing less than halfway down the stairs.

"Mademoiselle?" Pierre clung to her arm on her blind side, worrying and nagging every step.

"I'm fine," Joanna breathed, "quite fine." And she was. Exhausted, but quite fine, and certainly not hard of hearing. "What was that?" her head snapped up as a distinctly loud *crash!* rattled the air.

"Pardon?" Pierre said.

"That noise," Joanna insisted. "That ... well, *bang* actually." It was definitely some sort of bang, something banging into something else, and therefore definitely not something she had done unless she had quite unknowingly fallen down. "Well?" she demanded, after quickly checking to ensure she hadn't fallen but was standing quite firmly in place.

"The front door," Pierre shrugged, too old and small himself to pick her up and carry her away.

"The front door?" Joanna repeated. "You mean the wind?" she clutched him.

"No, I mean the front door," Pierre shrugged, as was the sound Joanna heard now that of a booted foot hitting the first of the stone steps.

Reineke did perhaps shut the front door loudly causing it to *bang* rather than *click* in place. He was not paying attention to the door.

He was thinking, obviously thinking of other far more important things because his hat was in his hand, not on his head, and he loved wearing his hat on his head, if only because he loved taking it off.

His attack on the stairs was not unusual. If he had been meant to walk in mincing little steps, he would never have been given legs so long, the same as if his head was meant to watch his feet, he never would have been given a neck to hold it up and erect. And hold his head erect he did, quickly, snapping to attention when he realized the stairs were covered with elves watching him.

To have moved the wet strands of hair hanging in front of his eyes would have been to admit they were there, and so instead up in the air went his head, behind his back went his hands, and he walked up two more steps, slowly, to the landing, watching the elves watching him. It was a ridiculous little climax in the navel of the stairs. A bruised woman choking the banister, the Holy Man contorted in a grin beside her, too ridiculous for words, except for perhaps one.

"Fräulein," Reineke acknowledged Joanna unpleasantly, the one word a dare, daring her to strangle the banister, release it, go back up, or continue down. It dared her to do anything, perhaps even breathe.

Joanna Lee enjoyed breathing. In remembering that, she, too, remembered how she had a neck. Perhaps one not as long as his, perhaps not quite as sturdy, but certainly capable of holding her head up, which she did, promptly. She stepped to walk, not run, down the stairs, since running would have been far too chancy. She was confident however that with his hair hanging in his eyes blinding him, he would be unable to tell if she hobbled, skipped, or strolled.

"Captain," Joanna croaked in reply, sounding more like a frog than a queen but that was all right. He was the one who had told her she had been ill and so perhaps he would think she had a cold. She paused one more time, to hug the newel post as the first staircase ended to merge with its twin at the landing in the middle of the stairs. But it was the Captain, though, not her, who stepped aside to allow her room to stretch for the rail. She reached it without tumbling over on her face, and she mastered the rest of the stairs, all the way down to the floor. Using a banister did not make her sissy.

Anyone with half a brain used a banister. If they weren't necessary, there would be no such thing.

A soldier approached her through a fog, opening a door and she and Pierre were outside.

"Indeed," Reineke's gaze followed them until the door shut behind them. Turning back, he looked up to where Thiele would have stood annoyed, but the mezzanine was empty. Thiele was en route to the Kufra. Reineke ascended the stairs, disappearing down the mezzanine and into his office.

"So, you see, Mademoiselle," Pierre announced happily as they stood outside in the hot, stifling air, "if the winds should come to annoy us, it would be but a breeze with such a mountain to protect us."

She was in a prison. Sun did not shine on the porch of the mansion. Only weak streams of light tried desperately to sneak their way between the tight columns encircling the porch and stone steps like bars. Cold and ancient, the marble was lifeless without the sun to illuminate it, scarred with embedded ugly black lines. The little man had lied. It wasn't beautiful, but frightening in its desolate silence and overwhelming size. The huge white wall and mountain loomed all around them, high in the blazing cloudless sky.

"I want to go back," Joanna said.

"Back?" Pierre smiled. "Oui, in a little while. Come and sit, rest for a moment ..." he took her hand. "This is the mezzanine above us. The vault that is the library, mon capitaine's and Mademoiselle's quarters. These columns the legs that support it ..."

"I don't care," Joanna snatched her hand away. "I want to go back. There's nothing to see."

"Oui, of course," Pierre bowed his head.

She would not remember the stairs.

"By tomorrow the woman's hair is to be washed," Reineke stalked back and forth. "By tomorrow the woman is to have shoes. She had difficulty walking. I saw her. Fix her!"

"She will not allow it," Pierre explained. "Two days I have argued to change the bandage on her head."

"Do it!" Reineke insisted.

"Oui, do it," Pierre shrugged. "As far as the shoes ... perhaps Anne can find a pair for her to wear ..."

"Indeed ... and as far as this!" Reineke snatched up the heavy crucifix he found on the floor of his chambers. A crucifix that had never been there before, that he had never seen before in his life, but did not have to look far to know how it happened to be there now.

"You said I could show her the mezzanine, mon capitaine," Pierre reminded. "This is the mezzanine, part of it."

"Not my quarters!" Reineke assured. "Are you out of your mind?"

"No, I am not out of my mind," Pierre shook his head.

No! He was playing games—some stupid, idiotic game!

"It is not a game, mon capitaine. Mademoiselle is frightened ... She is extremely frightened," Pierre assured. "I am very concerned about this. I have been trying to explain to her, but she is not listening, and I thought if I could demonstrate for her that though I am there with her, and you are here, she is safe. No one is hurting her—"

"Get out!" Reineke ordered.

"Mon capitaine, if you think, you will understand what I am saying—" Pierre insisted.

"And take le Christ with you!" Reineke fired the crucifix through the French windows of his quarters, over the balcony and out into the desert night, daring the wrath of the heavens and hells to strike him dead for the blasphemous act, which, they would not do.

"So now you have two panes to fix," Pierre clucked with a shake of his head. "I swear to le Christ, mon capitaine, between the two of you, you and Mademoiselle have inflicted more damage than four centuries has managed to destroy."

"Get out!" Reineke pointed.

"I am going," Pierre assured.

"Good!"

Chapter Thirty-Four

March 14–15

Joanna sat on one of the low stone walls in one of the villa's large courtyard of gardens. What particular type of stone the walls were Pierre apparently did not know or he would have told her. He knew about the gardens though, and he was right when he said she would not see roses or lilacs or grass. Instead, desert flowers were of their own variety. All fairly awkward and dull as they struggled to survive entwined around the roots of olive trees embedded in their beds of stone sand absent of color except for the incessant milky pink and yellowish white marble brightening with the sun and fading with the shadows. Pierre disagreed, telling her desert flowers were not only beautiful, but could fly.

"Did you know flowers fly in the desert, Mademoiselle?" he tempted her. "Spread their wings and take flight?"

No, Joanna did not know and was not interested. The murky fog of confusion returned to surround her in the hot bright sun hurting her eye. Pierre held a funny umbrella over their heads, but it did not help much. She felt awkward sitting with him as if she was doing something wrong.

"They do," Pierre assured her how desert flowers fly. Beautiful colorful petals people call butterflies migrate in the desert, thousands of them, along with birds and eagles, hawks and hens.

"Would Mademoiselle like to see some of these?" Pierre invited with his smile, not that Joanna's answer was important. Pierre decided that tomorrow she would see his funny hens.

"Oui," Pierre decided that tomorrow they could go for a short walk in the gardens farther away than the ones they were sitting in today.

"More gardens?" Joanna yawned, much too sleepy to try to escape this morning as she had promised herself she would do as soon as she was outside. Tomorrow however would be perfect.

"Oui, more gardens, Mademoiselle," he promised. "Prettier than these."

"In what way?" Joanna looked around, thinking of Grandfather's gardens where, when she was young, it would take John, Grandfather's man, and Maria, the cook, hours to find her hiding among the hedges. There weren't any hedges here only the gnarled trees that would work well as a cover if there were more of them. "Do they have trees, like the trees over there?"

"There are thousands of trees here, Mademoiselle," he assured. "Palm, olive, fig."

On the wall, yes, Joanna could plainly see. A fat forest of thick green leaves. But the wall that had seemed so close from the balcony of her room was really a mountain and rather far away. The grounds around the house were flat and open. She needed the trees to get to the mountain with its palm trees where they would never find her.

"And very beautiful," he maintained. "This is an oasis, Mademoiselle. An island of land in a sea of sand. You are in North Africa, as has been explained. There is a lot of sand in North Africa. Not too many trees except in very special places like this;" he beamed. Very proud of his stone world regardless of how boring she considered it.

"An oasis," Joanne repeated, having heard of an oasis, even before she came to Egypt, and actually finding them much larger than she thought they would be for some reason. She shrugged and absently ate one of the olives Pierre brought along as a treat. It was tart with a large pit. She gnawed on the meat, working the pit into the side of her cheek and sucking on it like a lozenge. "How long have we been out?"

"Oh, twenty minutes?" Pierre guessed. "Perhaps a little less."

"I want to go in," Joanna said. "It's too hot out here." Which it was and she wanted to think. She could not think out there in the heat.

"Oui, of course," Pierre agreed without an argument. "We will come outside again later today when it is cooler, and perhaps earlier tomorrow morning when it also cooler, so you can spend more time outside in the fresh air."

Joanna made it to thirty minutes when they came out after dinner before it was dark. Almost an hour the next morning, when they came out much earlier, and it was not so baking hot, though not as cool as early evening the night before. Joanna decided early evening would be the best time to escape, under the cover of the trees while it was still light enough to see and find them, and under the cover of darkness from there when it fell. In the meantime, it was morning, and she got to see the hens, which were cute for hens, brown and fat like the priest and almost as talkative as he was, scolding, clucking, and pecking at her in their funny way.

"How big is the island?" Joanna popped another olive in her mouth as they sat on the low stone walls of the garden where the hens lived, walking in and out of their homes situated inside the little odd cut-outs lining the base of the walls. "I see trees over there, is that where the other gardens are?"

"Oasis," Pierre smiled. "Like an island, oui, yes, as I explained. But the sea surrounding us is sand, not water."

Joanna tried to imagine that, but couldn't. She did not remember Siwa, not its name or that she had been there at all. If she had, she would know the Siwa Oasis was very large, occupied by a town and an entire community. Cairo she remembered, but it was a city with city buildings, exotic and congested with traffic and people. "Well?" she said. "How big is it?"

"Oh, very big," Pierre said, "with many more gardens and trees, this is correct. If you could travel to the other side you would see how large."

"The other side?" Joanna picked up on that. "The other side of what? The wall?"

"Oasis," Pierre smiled. "The other side of the oasis where mon capitaine believes an entire city once stood."

"A city ..." That changed things. Presented possibilities Joanna had not considered—at least not here. She had certainly considered them once she got out of there to where there were people and things one would find in a city, yes, such as a telephone. "Can we go there?"

"To the gardens where there are more trees?" Pierre smiled. "Oui, yes, perhaps even tomorrow. You see how much stronger you are today? Every day much stronger than you were the day before."

"To the city," Joanna said. "To see the city?"

"Pardon?" Pierre said.

"The city," Joanna swallowed the olive pit she had in her mouth.

"Oh, Mademoiselle," Pierre protested.

"What?" Joanna said. "You said there was a city. I want to see it."

"The pit, Mademoiselle," Pierre insisted, annoyed and, of all things, helped himself. Started snatching up the fresh olives he had collected, and the ones from the house he had given her and she had piled up on her lap. "You know you are not supposed to eat the olive pit. Really, Mademoiselle," he shook his head, "I do not understand this. I do not understand you ..."

Oh, well, excuse her. The next time Joanna would be sure to spit the pit out on the ground. For that matter as of right now throw all of the olives on the ground since he was so clearly effected by them he was snatching and grabbing at her with those hands of his that he should really learn to keep to himself.

"We were talking about the city!" Joanna slapped his hands away proceeding, yes, to clear her lap of the whole lot of olives, sweeping them off and onto the ground.

"What city?" Pierre scoffed as he gathered the extent of the olive collection he had managed to save into the little cloth napkin he wore over his lap, pulling it closed and tying it up in a protective knot. "There is no city."

"Oh, really," Joanna said. "Well, you said there was. So what happened to it? Where did it go?" she insisted. "In the last five minutes, where did it go?"

"Nowhere," Pierre assured. "That is not what Pierre said—"

"Yes it is!"

"No, it is not!" Pierre snapped, slapping the little bundle of olives back down on his lap with his frustration. "That is what Mademoiselle heard, that is what she thinks. It is not what Pierre said. Pierre said there once was a city—*once,* Mademoiselle. Possibly once, yes, and possibly once, no—and Pierre does not want to talk about it either way," he assured as Joanna stared at him. "No, Pierre wants to talk about this, Mademoiselle," he waved the olives threateningly, "this!"

"Excuse me?" Joanna said.

"There is no excuse," Pierre corrected, "No there is not. What do you want to go to the city for, eh, Mademoiselle? So you can spit olives, swallow them or throw them on the ground?" he waved the little sack.

"Please stop doing that," Joanna requested.

"Is that what little girls do when they go to the city, eh?" Pierre insisted. "No, that is why little girls do not go to the city until they know how to behave!"

"I said, please stop doing that!" Joanna snatched the waving sack out of his hand and threw it on the ground, and the two of them sat there, her looking off in one direction, having no idea where he was looking or what he was looking at if anything. Tears clouded Joanna's eyes, both of them, the one under the bandage, and the one that wasn't.

"Mademoiselle ..." Pierre said gently when Joanna looked down on her lap, picking at her hands, the cuticles still very dry and split.

"I want to go back to the house," Joanna replied.

"Oui, this is fine," Pierre nodded, "but I think it is time you and Pierre had a talk."

"I said, I want to go back to the house," Joanna repeated. "If you don't take me I'll go there myself. I remember the way—it's right over there," she pointed only half blind. "I can see it."

"Oui," Pierre agreed.

"Well, then?" Joanna said.

"Of course." Pierre rose and smiled however forced the air might be between them as they walked. "We will come out again in the evening after dinner, before dark, as we did last evening."

"Perhaps," Joanna said.

"No perhaps," Pierre said. "Definitely, Mademoiselle. This is the exercise regimen, at least for the next few days. After that—"

"Or what?" Joanna stopped. "You'll start throwing olives again?"

"It is not Pierre who threw the olives," Pierre shook his head.

That was beside the point. "I think you're right," Joanna agreed. "I think it is time we had a talk."

"About the city?" Pierre smiled. "Or that there is no city? Which there is not."

"Fine," Joanna said. "So there is no city." She did not want to see his stupid city, anyway. It was just an idea, and since it was a bad one, she would think of another one, confident it would be much better.

"Of course it is not fine," Pierre understood more than she might think he did. "But we will talk about that too, when we talk."

"I think you're the one who's not listening now," Joanna said. "I'm the one who wants to talk to you."

Yes, Pierre knew that and he suspected it would be something about her right to do what she wanted to do, her right to decide what she wanted to do as she got stronger every day. Mentally and emotionally though her strength festered in stubbornness frustrated and stagnated by fear.

It did not matter. In another moment, none of that would matter, as they were not the only two people who cared about what they wanted, regardless of what others may want.

"Mon capitaine!" Pierre suddenly gasped and before Joanna could even finish turning around to see why he was gasping, she was drenched in water pouring down over her head drowning any sound she might make. Pierre jumped as she jumped, he almost as wet as she by the splashing water.

"God!" Joanna gasped, water streaming down her face, in her eyes, her nose, mouth, gagging her. She was soaked. Her shirt, pants, an entire bucket of cold water dumped over her head, saturating her, Pierre, and the ground around them.

"Fräulein." The Captain was in front of her, holding the emptied bucket. An Arab standing next to him took it away to hand him something in exchange. He took it and grasped her wrist, forcing her hand open, slapping the object down. It was a bar of soap.

"So far my men, Fräulein," he said, cold as the water, "have been fortunate to escape the plague lice. I suggest you do the same."

And he was gone.

"Bastard!" Joanna screamed after him. "You rotten bastard!"

Back in her room, Joanna would never stop crying, destroying everything in sight until she made herself sick enough to vomit, and when she finished choking with dry heaves she washed her hair, and it felt good, marvelous.

"Is there anything else Mademoiselle would like to do?" Pierre asked as Joanna sulked at the French windows, waiting for her hair to dry in the sun.

She did not answer him. He toddled around for a while longer, rearranging things before he sat back down asking again and that time, yes, she answered.

"What do I look like?" Joanna asked.

"Hm ..." Pierre surveyed her. "Pretty bad. But it will get better. Pierre is not concerned. Do you want to see?"

Hardly. What she looked like with bandages on was bad enough. Joanna wasn't ready to see what she looked like underneath them.

"Well, this is all right, too," Pierre agreed. "You do not have to see now. You can see at any time. Tomorrow, the day after. Each time, like you it will be better ... In the meantime, I have a new hat for you," he held up her new plaster bonnet since the other one had been ruined by the water.

"It looks different," Joanna said.

"It is different. Not quite so big. It is this week's fashion." Pierre smiled. "Each week a new fashion, how is that?"

Well, it wasn't funny. "That's not funny," Joanna said.

"No, it is not funny," Pierre agreed. "But it is true. I think we can even make a little less bandages around the eye and the chin. How is your sight? Can you see?"

"It hurts," Joanna assured.

"Because you are in the sun," Pierre said. "Trying to see in the sun with an eye that has not seen anything in a week. Come out of the sun so it will not hurt ... and so," he cautioned, "you do not hurt it."

"I'm drying my hair."

"It will dry over here, out of the direct light," Pierre assured. "There is sun over here as there is sun everywhere."

There was more sun at the windows. "No," Joanna said.

"Yes," Pierre said. "Come away now and sit over here and in one hour, less, your hair will be dry. When it is, we will put your new hat on and see how many bandages we have to add to protect your eye—and to keep your hat on," he winked. "We cannot have it falling off, not even in the bed. You need it to protect your head."

Joanna had stopped listening at the hour it would take her hair to dry. Her hair took four hours to dry. Sun, rain, snow, it took four hours.

"Mademoiselle ..." Pierre said.

"Fine," Joanna got up and went over to sit in the chair by the bed. "My hair takes four hours to dry. The only reason it will take an hour is because you cut it off."

"Less than an hour, Mademoiselle," Pierre assured. "Nothing takes four hours to dry in this desert, not even a lake if we had one; which we do not," he winked. "It left with the city."

That was also not funny. "I don't care about your stupid city," Joanna reminded.

"No," Pierre agreed. "And Pierre did not cut off Mademoiselle's hair, only what he needed."

Well, he needed a lot of it. Joanna could not believe how much of her hair was missing when she washed it. Almost the entire right side of her head was shaved bald, down to these bristly nubs like Michael's beard in the morning.

"Is that what you wanted to talk to Pierre about?" Pierre asked.

Hardly. "Save it for Michael," Joanna assured, because believe her, Michael was going to ask.

"Michael ..." Pierre said. "Yes ... Mademoiselle said something about a Michael, I believe, once before."

Joanna scoffed. "Try a hundred times."

"A hundred times," Pierre said. "Really. Well, perhaps then it is true Pierre has not been listening because I remember Mademoiselle saying something about a Michael only once."

Joanna tossed her drying hair. "That's not the point."

Pierre smiled. "No. No, of course it is not. But it is perhaps Michael Mademoiselle wishes to speak to Pierre about? Do I have this right?"

And how. Joanna turned around and sat up straight in her chair to face him squarely. "You think I want to escape. You think I want to go to your city because I'm planning to escape."

"Oui," Pierre agreed. "We have talked about this," he chuckled. "That is something Mademoiselle has said to Pierre a hundred times even if she has not said it out loud each time. It is always on your face," he nodded, "in your eye. I can see it very clearly."

"Well, you see," Joanna said, "that's where you're wrong. I only told you that ... well, to throw you off the track," she claimed.

"Really," Pierre said. "That is interesting because Mademoiselle had Pierre completely convinced. That is very true."

"Well, that's more to the point," Joanna said, "because I don't have to escape. Michael will be coming here."

"Really ..." Pierre said.

"Yes," Joanna stopped short of saying to rescue her because she did not like to think she might have to be rescued, that was too frightening to think about. But for Michael to come there and take her home, yes. That was quite comforting to think. Even if he had to come and take her out of the sand when she climbed over the mountain since apparently there was no city for him to come to, it was still a very comforting thought. "So you can stop saying 'really' because it's true."

Pierre nodded, leaving it up to Joanna to speak again if she wanted to speak. She did.

"What did you want to talk to me about? The olives?" she sneered, finding it silly.

"Oui, Mademoiselle," Pierre said.

That figured. "You know the only reason I threw the olives away is because you ... you were winging them around," she waved in demonstration. "I asked you to stop and you didn't and so I threw them away."

"Pierre was excited," Pierre explained.

"Well, what's that to do with me?" Joanna said.

"Everything, Mademoiselle," he assured. "Everything." He got up and waddled over to sit down on the bed. Joanna flinched when he got up and wasn't exactly comfortable when he sat down on the bed to study her. "Mademoiselle ... " he said.

"I really do not think you should be sitting on the bed," Joanna interrupted. "I'm not sure it's proper. I mean, I realize you're old, and a priest, but I still do not think it's proper."

He ignored her. "Mademoiselle," he said, "I would like you to focus on something for me, if you can. I would like you to forget about me, this room, this space, everything. Clear your mind, and think about you, only you. While you are thinking, I want you to remember how you are a young woman, not a little girl, and to leave the frightened little girl behind you regardless of what has happened to her, what may have happened to her, and what she is so afraid will happen to her—it does not matter. I want you to think about you, only about you--just for today," he smiled. "This afternoon, a few hours. Would you like to try that? We can talk about it afterwards, if you like. What you did not like and what you did like about our little experiment. Does this sound interesting to you? A challenge you might like? One that you create, meet, and win? What do you think about what Pierre is asking you?"

What did she think?

"Mademoiselle?" Pierre encouraged. "It is really not difficult for you to answer that simple question, is it?"

That was her business. "Michael will be coming here," Joanna repeated. "That is true."

Pierre nodded. "And this Michael—" he said.

"He's not *this* Michael," Joanna interrupted. "He's Michael. Just Michael."

Pierre nodded again. "Is your friend Michael in the army?" he asked.

Oh, well, now, Joanna might be stupid in a lot of ways as she understood she was, but she wasn't quite as stupid as all of that. Her chin jutted forward, unintentionally, unknowingly, but it jutted forward and was noticeable to Pierre when it did. "You'd like to know that wouldn't you?" she said.

"Oui," Pierre agreed. "I would. Mademoiselle has mentioned Michael, as she said, and Pierre is curious, yes naturally if your friend Michael is in the army ..." he hesitated, but only briefly and not so Joanna noticed at all. "An American, Pierre understands—if Pierre understood Mademoiselle correctly."

"You certainly did," Joanna assured.

Pierre nodded but refrained from saying anything, wondering only if she knew her friend Michael was dead, killed in the courtyard.

If she had perhaps witnessed the brutality of his death, or if she knew nothing about it at all ... other than he was with her. Pierre studied her, curious because if she did not know or remember his death, she should be asking where he was.

She would be asking where he was, but she wasn't. This Michael was not the man who died in the courtyard, his body burned and ashes scattered, that was someone else. So who was Michael? The other blood? The third person? The same rule would apply. She should be asking where he was and she wasn't. She was telling how he would be there.

"As far as in the army," Joanna tossed her drying head, "That's for me to know and for you to find out."

"A reasonable response, Mademoiselle," Pierre smiled, "though most would probably not speak it aloud. It's all right though," he assured, "it is however fair for Pierre to presume Michael will not like Pierre when he comes?"

"He will positively loathe you," Joanna promised.

"I am sorry to hear that," Pierre said. "I would have hoped that when your friend came and Pierre explained why he cut your hair, he would understand."

"I don't think so," Joanna said.

"And I would have hoped," Pierre said, "when your friend saw how you have been cared for and not hurt, he would say thank you and understand how Pierre was not your enemy."

"I do not think so," Joanna said a little stronger that time.

Pierre smiled. "No, of course not," he agreed. "Pierre is a collaborator. That is not too difficult to see ... do you know what a collaborator is, Mademoiselle?" he asked when her resolve faded away to her blank uncertain expression.

"Well, yes," Joanna said, "sort of—I know it's not very nice," she assured. "It's not a good thing to be."

"And most would agree with that, Mademoiselle," Pierre agreed, "regardless of the nature of the collaboration. But, you see," he said, "Pierre disagrees with them. Pierre says the purpose of the collaboration is not irrelevant, it is everything. The reason, the goal—everything. I am a survivor, Mademoiselle. Oui," he assured, "I am a survivor exactly like you, and it is exactly what you are going to be.

"Now," he said, "you will listen to me, and you will be the young woman you are when your friend Michael comes to take you home, or if it is you who goes to him. You will be the young woman you are, not the frightened little girl who swallows olive pits and throws dishes because she is too afraid to do anything else."

"I really do not like you," Joanna said.

He smiled. "Oui, I know. But you will," he promised, and *whisk*! he was gone, just like that. Up, off the bed, and gone, leaving her there without a word.

Chapter Thirty-Five

Reineke laughed. He walked away from the woman into his villa and laughed a deep, honest laugh. The sight of her confused and outraged, soaked like some drenched cat, was sufficient to do away with all the nerves she had caused him these past days. Gone was the thorn in his side, the corn on his toe. He had no more reason to be frightened of her, than he was frightened of Diana ...

And he was frightened of Diana. "Indeed." Reineke stopped laughing. The woman was death disguised as a child, hanging there, waiting for him to surrender to her Allies out there somewhere. The only way he could hope to emerge from this was to send her away, except she was not his to send, and send her where? Heeding the cry of the Holy Man for leniency would be a gamble with his life. He knew what this woman was, and she was not just some Allied prisoner brought to his complex for reasons and purpose unknown. She was someone, some plan. There would be nothing at the Kufra except sand, plenty of sand. Le capitaine Reineke's holiday was over. He had only three days.

"Indeed," Reineke picked up his Colonel's terse reply to the notice Reineke had decided to delay the scheduled shipment between camps. It asked pointedly how long Reineke planned to remain on radio silence.

It suggested Reineke rethink his decision to delay all of the shipments. It informed him there would soon be a tête-à-tête that regardless of how informal would require his attendance nevertheless. A certain SS Major was understandably ruffled over his mistreatment during his visit to Reineke's compound. Herr Oberst Alfred Schönfeld, Reineke's Commanding Officer, wasn't necessarily interested in SS Major Hanse Weiheber, his complaints or his demand for Reineke's arrest. Their tête-à-tête already concluded had left Weiheber additionally ruffled. But then Hauptmann Reineke's characteristics of a proud, independent peacock were not characteristics belonging to him alone. Oberst Schönfeld did not care about Reineke shooting out ceilings above the heads of SS officers. He did not care about the SS at all. He did care very much, however as to the reasons why Reineke, an intelligent, and talented officer, found it a continuing need to indulge himself in such antics. Oberst Schönfeld did not reprimand, this project had no such clause, and Reineke was not the proudest, most independent, or even the most original officer with orders for men to be shot who failed to live up to expectations, he was simply the most unruly.

Fortunately, however, Oberst Schönfeld liked Hauptmann Reineke, which was why he was urging Reineke they meet at the very same desert village recently visited by SS Major Weiheber, and Reineke had three days to comply with the request.

"Request!" Reineke dropped the communiqué on his desk. He had three days to think of an alibi, compose a defense. A point sure to be discussed was Reineke's intentions with the SS prisoner, though that would only be a formality. Schönfeld, familiar as he was with his handpicked squad, was capable of understanding, if not predicting Reineke's reaction to the SS bringing some Allied prisoners to his highly sensitive compound. Reineke taking the surviving prisoner away from the SS was undoubtedly in spite, a form of punishment for the SS indiscretion. Taking the knife away from the SS that they hoped to plunge into the project by appropriating his complex, and plunging it instead into them, leaving them to explain the loss of the prisoners to their superiors regardless of what Reineke might have to explain to his.

Reineke eyed the message. If Weiheber had attempted to fuel concerns over Reineke's stability, or worse, his loyalty, with stories of the Holy Man and his children, he would have come away severely disappointed. Schönfeld already knew of them. Earlier inquiries into the issue had been quelled with a stare and short, clipped, reminder it was Schönfeld's idea to avoid notoriety for as long as possible, and what better way to ensure this than to keep oneself disguised as a native watering hole?

"Indeed," Reineke might decide to employ that excuse again.

Incorporate this new situation into his already existing rationale, reminding Schönfeld it was the SS who insisted there was an Allied troop somewhere in the immediate area.

"You hang yourself, Herr Major," Reineke suggested. "Not I." Schönfeld was not about to question one of his top officer's decision to tread slowly under the circumstances Weiheber presented.

In the event Weiheber decided to retract his claim of Allied presence? "Indeed," Reineke moved around his library, pensive. Perhaps he would simply remind Schönfeld of his passion for security regardless. Schönfeld would probably not care if Reineke decided elephants would prove useful as a façade, as long as the munitions were where they were supposed to be. They would be. Any way possible Reineke would ensure the hijacking of the munitions from the Italians remained on schedule, whether or not delivery was delayed by a few days if he had to shoot them all.

And he just might shoot them all, beginning with the woman screaming on about her wet head. "Indeed!" Reineke abandoned the library, escaping to his quarters, but stretching out on his bed and massaging his temples made no difference.

Another door between them made no difference. He sat up. He should just get up, go back through the library, into the apartment, and shoot her. He could explain her death to the children that she had died of her illness. Diana would probably not care if she died since she already wanted her and anyone else dead even remotely linked to rousing the SS. Who would care was the Holy Man, and in retaliation, Pierre just might shoot him.

But not if Reineke shot Pierre first.

Yet, if he shot Pierre, Diana would shoot him.

And if Reineke shot Diana, Anne would definitely shoot him—or shoot at him, which, if she did, Thiele would shoot Anne, and then Reineke would have to shoot Thiele.

"Indeed!" Reineke jumped off his bed. It would be distinctly risky trying to get away with killing *two* First Officers so close together. He barely got away with the first.

"Indeed," Reineke smiled in the mirror. "'Watch my Hauptmann Reineke, for he is all that he appears to be and more.'" And so they did watch. Only Pierre liked what he saw.

Diana watched, only she liked what she saw.

Thiele, the same, and so Schönfeld lost whatever control he hoped to gain by assigning his personal aide Heinrich Thiele as Reineke's new First Officer because even if Thiele knew it all, which he did not, he would not believe it.

"Indeed," Reineke smiled in the mirror. "You cannot trust your Hauptmann Reineke, you should not. He can change, if he has to."

He could change into whatever he had to, if he had to.

"Indeed," Reineke stared through the walls of his chambers out to the message lying on his desk. Odd thing was Schönfeld knew Reineke shot and killed his First Officer and why. Odd thing was Reineke knew Schönfeld knew.

Odder yet, Reineke knew when he met them, Schönfeld, Thiele, Pierre, Diana, or Anne, like each other or not, one or the other, would someday have to shoot the other. Odd thing was Reineke knew which of them it would be who shot first.

"*Return the woman*!" Diana bore down on him from her Temple, harsh and uncompassionate as her cold, marble stone. "*Return the woman, Dieter, to the SS and let it go, do not be a fool. I will take care of the SS, not you. The Holy Man will find you dead at the foot of my statue if you defy me, a bullet through your skull. The children are dying by the thousands. You cannot exchange one life for the seventy-five under your care. Return the SS prisoner, or I will kill you. Your complex, little more than a memory buried in the sand.*"

"Indeed," Reineke picked up the message from his desk. He had only three days and not an idea in his head, or so he thought.

No, Joanna wasn't angry with the little priest for leaving her without a word to go off like that and then as suddenly show back up. She was frightened. What did he mean by a ride? A ride where? Joanna did not want to take a ride. Could see no good reason why she should agree to take a ride anywhere, especially when it was a soldier playing driver and the car was a wagen.

But Pierre was emphatic, the young soldier nodding, "*Ja*! *Ja*!" to Pierre carrying on in some queer, foreign speech.

"Get in, Mademoiselle," Pierre instructed her, the soldier nodding, "*Ja*! *Ja*!" as Joanna obeyed.

Reineke left his quarters paying no particular attention where his walk brought him. He was back again in his chambers around three o'clock, still thinking. What else was there for him to do? His most recent thoughts suggested he should interrogate the woman more fully. Demand to know everything there was to know about her so he could orchestrate an appropriate response instead of attempting to guess what significance she was to the SS who involved and endangered him with their invasion of his compound. The Holy Man would be upset, but the Holy Man was a fool if he thought le capitaine did not want to know everything, because he did.

"Indeed," Reineke rapped swiftly on the apartment door.

No one answered, so he knocked again, and no one answered.

Catch them outside? With luck in the gardens? Far away from the ears and eyes of his staff? It was better still. He could put the woman up against the wall, his hand fastened around her throat, demanding to know why he had been chosen for sacrifice.

No one moved in the gardens nearest the mansion. Reineke walked quickly to cover another garden, but it was taking too long and thoughts were beginning to grow ...

"Where is the Holy Man?" he demanded, the soldier he attacked getting as far as, "The children!" and Reineke started to run.

"Dieter!" Anne was sitting in her favorite spot on the edge of one of the wells.

"Dieter!" she jumped up, dashing to meet him as she usually did, her long black hair flying behind her.

"Where is he?" Reineke insisted, Anne's flushed face paling to confusion, her arm he twisted, hurting her.

"Dieter!" she said. "Dieter, you're hurting me!"

"Where is he?" Reineke hissed. "Where are the Holy Man and the woman?"

"At the house!" Anne's snapped, meaning the Holy Man's hut, her black eyes narrowed and voice angry and emphatic. "Dieter, let go of my arm or it's not that woman Thiele will find dead!"

"Go and get him," Reineke released her. "Do it! Go and get him—MOVE!" he barked when she stood there. "Idiot!" Was Anne turning idiot on him, also?

Apparently, for she was taking far too long, and Reineke was running again, chubby legs, all different sizes, and ages believing it a game, following along, imitating the wild stride of his boots.

He was almost to the Holy Man's house, near another well. The trees parted, he could see more children gathered in a group outside—

The sun's reflection caught the armor of the idle wagen and the soldier playing with Aliza, the two year old, seated on the ground, helmet on her head.

"Hauptmann!" the soldier jumped to attention, failing in his attempt to snatch his helmet from the child before he could be found out.

"Indeed. Where is the woman?" Reineke replied.

Not more than twenty meters away. Reineke took the helmet from Aliza for protection, but the woman was too busy braiding the hair of one of the girls to notice him. A select army of the Holy Man's elves crowding around her, listening to her highly animated and inaccurate recital of some fairy tale.

A very select army of elves. The Holy Man was not a fool. Not one child spoke, or understood the prisoner's English.

"Mon capitaine!" Pierre greeted him happily, poised to present some elaborate lie, but it was unnecessary. Somewhere in the twisted story the woman was telling, Reineke stopped thinking of interrogation and returned to not caring why the SS had brought her there. She was hardly death, hardly dangerous, to him, or anyone else. She was simply a very small, very young woman, with a big, bright white bandage wrapped tightly around her damaged head.

"Mon capitaine?" Pierre frowned.

"Diana," was all Reineke said, and walked away.

One hundred times of reassuring Joanna of her safety and his as he rushed her back to the wagen, was not enough, but Pierre gave up, abandoning Joanna to her fear.

One hundred times of reassuring himself all would be well as he hiked to meet Reineke was also possibly not enough.

Reineke confessed to Diana in her Temple how he had lost his mind.

He avoided Pierre until long past dark, hoping the little man would give up and go away. But if the Holy Man had nothing he had patience, and a temper.

Chapter Thirty-Six

"So!" Pierre exploded. "It is a trick! I should have known mon capitaine keeps Pierre waiting for such a long time for no reason except to punish him for taking Mademoiselle to the children. You think Pierre is stupid? He is not! It is mon capitaine who is stupid."

"I do not think you are stupid," Reineke dodged the rock Pierre threw. "Put those down!"

Pierre would not put anything down. "You say, Diana. Oui, come to Diana, and so Pierre comes, and where is mon capitaine, eh? Nowhere. And you say it is not a trick? Ha! It is."

"I have not had the chance to say anything," Reineke managed to get ahold of Pierre's wrist. "If you stop fighting perhaps I will have a chance. Put those down!"

"So," Pierre raised a poisoned brow at the fingers clamped around his withered bones, "Mon capitaine has changed his ways. He beats now on children and old men. Anne will have a mark by morning."

He had not meant to hurt Anne. "For which, she can blame you," Reineke gave Pierre back his arm with a huff. "I did not mean to hurt Anne." He lit a cigarette, turning the collar of his jacket up against the cool air that felt good, but cold. He should have worn his greatcoat. "What?" he said to Pierre. "I did not mean to hurt Anne!"

"No excuse," Pierre waggled his finger. "It matters not what mon capitaine meant to do, it matters what he did."

"Indeed. I have not *done* anything," Reineke assured. "I have been thinking that is all, thinking. Yes."

And he was still thinking, everything from the smallest detail to the grand plan rattling around in his head, all of it needing the Holy Man.

"Ach, thinking," Pierre was already bored. "Mon capitaine is always thinking. So much so one of these days his head is going to explode."

"Indeed," Reineke said. "A week ago you told me I never think at all."

"Oui," Pierre agreed, "and you have not stopped thinking since then."

True. A week. One week. Perhaps he was thinking too much. He never took a week to decide anything. "I am here to talk now."

The Holy Man was never satisfied, complaining regardless. "Ach, talk. What do you want to talk about, eh?" Pierre sneered. "What is it the detective who does not want to know anything, want to know now? I took Mademoiselle to the children, you know this, you caught me.

"Oui, you caught Pierre," Pierre agreed. "And big deal for you. I am taking her again. You know this now because I am telling you this now and there is nothing you can do about it."

There was, of course, something Reineke could do about it, but that was not what he was there to talk about. "Your friends," Reineke nodded. "I want to talk to you about your friends."

Pierre frowned. "Pardon? My friends? What friends? I have no friends. What are you talking about?"

"Your friends," Reineke insisted. "I am talking about your friends in the west. You have friends in the west who come this way."

"I have no such friends," Pierre waved such nonsense away. "Mon capitaine is crazy, intoxicated or something. Deranged. I do not know what he is talking about."

"I am talking about the west!" Reineke barked.

"What west?" Pierre barked back.

"Algeria!" Reineke threw his hands in the air begging Diana for her assistance but she could do nothing. She was, after all, only stone, silent on her pedestal, guardian over the rubble and ruin of her temple around them. He stared up at her.

"So now mon capitaine is a maniac, screaming in the wind," Pierre shrugged in agreement. "It will do him as much good as the punishment he hoped to inflict by keeping an old man waiting out in the cold."

The man was impossible. "Holy Man," Reineke warned, "I am not a man of your patience, or convictions."

"So now it is Holy Man," Pierre nodded to Diana. "Always when mon capitaine wants something he invokes 'Holy Man'."

"And always," Reineke countered, "when the Holy Man is interested, he pretends he is not."

"What interested?" Pierre scoffed. "Interested in what? What is there for Pierre to be interested in? Some friends he does not have? In some country to the west?"

"Algeria," Reineke assured. "Algeria. Algeria. *AL-GER-I-A*!" he screamed, and Pierre winced.

"Oui, thank you, mon capitaine," he nodded, "but the ears, please. Pierre is old, he is forgetful, but he is not deaf. Talk. Do not scream." He sat down, perched on the base of the pedestal's steps, inviting Reineke to join him.

"Thank you," Reineke said.

"But!" Pierre reminded, that deadly finger extended with its claw, "I tell you this, I tell you now, if it is a trick, I will shoot you dead."

"Indeed," Reineke blinked. "Earlier today I thought of shooting you."

"Oh, please," Pierre had no patience for this nonsense of his. "Mon capitaine will never shoot Pierre, he likes Pierre. Two months ago I tell you myself to shoot Pierre. It is better if you shoot Pierre. But you say 'no. I cannot do this. Pierre is good. A man of God ... '"

He was the witch Merlin simply French and brown. "Algeria," Reineke said, a far safer subject.

"Algeria," Pierre surveyed him. "What about it? I know nothing about Algeria, and why should I, eh? What is Algeria to me? A country, that is all."

"It is your country," Reineke nodded.

"My country?" Pierre said. "No, Algeria is not my country. Here is my country. Only here."

"And in Algeria," Reineke nodded, "are friends of yours."

"These friends again," Pierre's eyes rolled "What is it to Pierre if mon capitaine thinks I have friends? It is nothing. One friend, two friends, probably no friends," he assured, "since you are here, and so what? Pierre has too few friends living in Algeria to matter to anyone, least of all you."

"And when is the last time," Reineke suggested cleverly, "you saw them, eh, Holy Man? Your too few friends living in Algeria?"

"The last time?" Pierre considered. "A long time, oui. This morning, at least."

What? Reineke stared at him.

"That is a long time, mon capitaine. Oui, many hours ago already."

"Hours?" Reineke repeated wearily.

"Oui," Pierre assured. "So close your mouth, all right? You look too stupid with the mouth hanging open like that. What is that, eh? What kind of soldier is that? Not a very good one."

That was Pierre's opinion. "This morning," Reineke said. "You saw your friends this morning."

"I said I did, yes," Pierre said. "Why? Is this some surprise to you?"

"Should it be?" Reineke closed his eyes.

"No!" Pierre laughed. "But then mon capitaine knows Pierre, he does. And Pierre has friends, he does—friends who come as friends this time, mon capitaine," he pointed out. "Concerned naturally for the safety of Pierre and his children since mon capitaine's police have been here. I tell them for now how it is nothing. How Mademoiselle is nothing, only one of mon capitaine's whores. What I tell them later we shall have to see."

"What?" Reineke felt his brain reel. "What?" he said.

"Mon capitaine doesn't have whores?" Pierre said.

Of course he had whores. "Are you insane?" Reineke sputtered. "That child one of my whores?"

Pierre shrugged. "Oh, well, what would mon capitaine have preferred for Pierre to have said to them? That the SS brought her? Beat and raped her? A young woman? A neutral? Mon capitaine would have nothing to worry about if Pierre says this to his friends because there would be no more mon capitaine."

"Neutral?" Reineke frowned. "Are they talking of the Swiss? The Red Crescent Society? Are they sure? What would she be doing here?"

"Comme ci, comme ça," Pierre waved. "They are sure enough—as is Pierre," he assured. "She is too much Mademoiselle to be anyone of any importance to anybody. You know this. You must have realized this—and, it is why!" he clouted Reineke, "Pierre takes Mademoiselle to the children in hopes they can reach her, which Pierre cannot do no matter how hard he tries. She is too frightened, trapped in her fear, like a child in a temper tantrum who does not know what to do, which she does not."

Except continue to scream days, evening, and nights rattling Reineke's teeth and his nerves. "Talk to me about Algeria," Reineke requested. "We were talking about Algeria."

"Oui, we were," Pierre agreed, "and mon capitaine is right. Algeria is a country, and it is to the west of here."

"And in it," Reineke said, "are friends of yours."

"Oui. Not as many friends as here, but yes, I have friends, this is true. I have lived in this desert all my life, sixty-seven years."

At last. "And those friends," Reineke treaded carefully, "how far to the east would they, could they go?"

"Why?" Pierre said.

"Why?" Reineke jumped up. "Because I want to send the woman away! Is that reason enough?"

"I don't know," Pierre said. "What do my friends have to do with Mademoiselle? Nothing."

"Everything," Reineke assured. "I want her gone. I want her out of here."

"So?" Pierre said. "Send her out of here. Call your trucks to come back and take her away."

"Not to the camps," Reineke waved impatiently. "Home! Except I do not even know where her home is, I need you to tell me."

"I?" Pierre said. "And I could do this how, eh? Pierre is what? A seer? A prophet? No, he is not."

"But you could find out," Reineke insisted. "Your friends could find out."

"So, if they could," Pierre agreed. "So what."

"So if they can," Reineke snapped, "they could take her there! Home. I am talking about you, your friends taking the woman home!"

"Ah, ha!" Pierre declared. "So it is a trick. A bullet through the heads of Pierre and his friends who are so stupid they will walk right into your stupid trap. I do not think so."

"It is not a trick," Reineke groaned. "Will you stop saying it is a trick? I do not care who they are, where they come from, or where they go. I simply want the woman out of here. You have to do this for me, you must!" he insisted. "I want to send the woman home!"

"Oh," Pierre said. "Well, in that case—all right," he agreed.

"What?" Reineke blinked. "All right?"

"Oui," Pierre smiled. "All right. I will do it. Yes, naturally. To defy Diana will not be easy, but it is possible. Perhaps a good friend who does not care too much about his life could find out some information for mon capitaine."

"The east!" Reineke anxiously supplied.

"East?" Pierre said. "Why not the west, eh?"

"Because it cannot be the west," Reineke sputtered. "Do not be absurd. The woman is British. They are in the east, the French are in the west—Holy Man," he warned, "this is something you already know."

"I do?" Pierre said. "I know there are many, many English in the west that is what I know. Husbands. Wives. Children. Families—"

"Not in uniform," Reineke snapped. "That woman was in uniform. Thiele is right. She is a soldier regardless of what kind. Your friends are lying—as are you. She is no neutral."

"Ha!" Pierre said. "Thiele is not right. Mademoiselle is not a soldier *AND!"* he said. "Mon capitaine is an idiot if he thinks there are no soldiers in the west other than his, because there are. British, oui. Arab, yes. And, of course, naturally, French. Because they do not wear a uniform, mon capitaine thinks they cannot? HA! Well, I tell you this, they did wear a uniform, and they will wear one again—the uniform of France!"

They could put them on tomorrow for all Reineke cared. "I want the woman returned to where she belongs," he said. "It is not here."

"That is true," Pierre agreed. "And mon capitaine is probably right. It is probably the east."

"Thank you!"

"Though it could be more north," Pierre considered. "Oui, it could be Tobruk—Your uniformed army still does not have that one," he pointed out. "Are you sure this is the same General Rommel who took France? Because he is not doing so good here. No, he is not."

"Indeed," Reineke said.

"But you are right," Pierre nodded, "it does not matter. What matters is we cannot send Mademoiselle to Tobruk. There is fighting there, and she is a woman, and so we will send her to Egypt. Oui, to Cairo. This is what we will do."

"Cairo?" Reineke weighed that. "I had not thought of Cairo."

"No?" Pierre said. "Really? There is another country to the east of here that Pierre is not aware of?"

"Do not be coy," Reineke suggested. "Of course, there is no other country. I simply had not considered Cairo." He was not sure what he had considered other than simply sending the woman away, just away.

"No," Pierre agreed. "There is only Egypt, and in Egypt there is only Cairo. So how is mon capitaine to do this once I have his information for him? Have you thought of this?"

Him? "I?" Reineke gasped. "Not I, you! You are to take the woman."

"Oh?" Pierre said. "Oh, no, no, no, mon capitaine, wait a minute. Find out for you where the Allies are so you can avoid them? Yes, Pierre can do this. If they are out there, you will know where. If they are not, you will also know that. But to take the woman for you? No. No, Pierre has no friends who have the ability to do this."

"But you have to," Reineke insisted. "I certainly cannot take the woman to Cairo. Are you mad? It has to be you!"

"Oh?" Pierre said. "How? Pierre is not only a magician, he is also invisible?"

"Far less visible than I," Reineke assured.

"Well, yes, that is true," Pierre agreed. He frowned, thinking and deciding with a clap of his hands. "All right!" he accepted, sealing the agreement. "I will do it. I will find a friend who can assist and I will take Mademoiselle to Cairo. Now all we have to do is figure out how mon capitaine is going to explain to his army what has happened to Mademoiselle. You have thought of this, right? Where has she gone?

Where has she disappeared to? She is under your authority, mon capitaine, not mine. She is a prisoner of the SS. What are you going to tell them has happened to her? I presume they will question you on this?"

Reineke hesitated.

"And?" Pierre said. "What is your plan? Claim she has died?"

And Reineke stared down at his feet.

"No ..." Pierre said softly. "No, that is not your plan. There is something else mon capitaine is not telling Pierre."

Reineke groaned again. "It is not a trick. Before you start with saying how it is a trick, it is not a trick. The woman cannot simply disappear."

"But that is what she would do with me, no, mon capitaine?" Pierre said. "No," he nodded when Reineke did not answer him. "That is not what she would do. All right, what is it actually that mon capitaine wants to do?"

"Holy Man?" Reineke said anxiously, afraid the priest had already changed his mind.

"No, it is all right, mon capitaine," Pierre nodded. "Just tell Pierre what it is you want to do."

"My supplies," Reineke explained, started to. "No, wait!" he stayed Pierre's immediate irritation. "Allow me, please? I was scheduled to transfer the supplies that arrived Thursday. I did not do this naturally."

"Naturally," Pierre agreed. "Either because Mademoiselle was not ready to leave with the trucks or because Rommel is not yet ready to receive them. Which do you think is the reason why?"

Reineke looked at him and Pierre smiled. "Continue, mon capitaine."

"But the next shipment I have to deliver," Reineke assured. "And I was thinking ..." he hesitated again. "I was thinking how the two could possibly go together?"

"Together?" Pierre frowned. "Mademoiselle and the trucks? I do not understand. This is what mon capitaine originally planned, to send Mademoiselle by his trucks to the camps."

"Not exactly," Reineke silenced him. "My superiors are asking me about my delay. I can say I was concerned about the threat of

Allies—I *am* concerned," he assured, "about the threat of Allies. But I can fault the SS for bringing the prisoners here. They insist they are Allied spies. I can say I believed the SS claim of captured spies. I have already sent Thiele to investigate the Kufra. This can only work to our advantage."

"As an example of your fear," Pierre nodded.

"Concern," Reineke corrected, "And, yes, it is. This is a prime oasis, not yet charted? Twelve hundred kilometers from the Kufra? Almost as large an area? Fear of my compound's discovery by the Allied or French would be and is natural."

"I understand that, mon capitaine. As I understand, we are now talking about things Pierre is not interested in knowing. He has nothing to do with what mon capitaine does or does not do with Thiele, or his supplies—"

"You have everything to do with it, and you know it!" Reineke jumped to his feet. "We have been in Libya for over a year and I am the first to find this paradise?"

"Oui," Pierre chuckled. "Mon capitaine is the *first* except for the Egyptian, Roman, Moor, and Turk."

"Indeed," Reineke said coldly. "The *first* except for the Arab and the French."

"And the Jew," Pierre smiled, and Reineke paused. "Yes," Pierre said. "But this is also all right, mon capitaine. As difficult as it is for you to say Jew, not Arab, it is for Pierre to say munitions, not supplies. Both are difficult as both are true, and so both tell lies."

"We are twelve hundred kilometers from the Kufra," Reineke replied, "where the French destroyed my airstrip—"

"My French, and Germany's airstrip," Pierre agreed.

"My airstrip," Reineke snapped. "Indeed, I am German. And that is neither an apology nor a lie. My point is, the French destroyed the airstrip and never bothered to look anywhere else for German installations?"

"Of course they did," Pierre shrugged. "What would it matter? Mon capitaine was not here then to be found."

"I am here now," Reineke assured. "And by some divine chance, your French continue to be content only watching the Kufra?"

Pierre laughed. "Oh, mon capitaine wishes that were only so."

"Indeed, I wish for our plan to work," Reineke said. "I wish for our lies to be believed. I do not think anyone is going to do that without some form of proof in support of our claim of danger."

"Mon capitaine's claim," Pierre corrected. "Mon capitaine's plan, mon capitaine's lies. You are the one in danger, not Pierre."

That was only too true. If it was not from the Allied or the French and now the SS, it was also from *der Jude*. Reineke lit another cigarette uncomfortably aware of the statue Diana looming above him, muscle and power etched in her stone flesh. "We are twelve hundred kilometers from the Kufra," he said again, "and the French who are everywhere leave you to be the only Frenchman to ever find and settle here."

"Pierre is so lucky," Pierre grinned.

"I wish to be lucky," Reineke assured. "Indeed, I wish to continue being *lucky*. Why else would I advocate such caution except to ensure your French continue not to look around?"

"They will never look here," Pierre promised. "Mon capitaine is safe forever from any Allied, British or French. Diana?" he considered her statue. "There, mon capitaine may have a few problems, oui. She is not as liberal as I or you, only when it suits her needs."

"And in the meantime who the SS will question is not Diana or you, but I," Reineke assured. "They will want to know why I am safe, not why you are safe twelve hundred kilometers from a French installation, in a world where the French are everywhere."

"True," Pierre said. "But it is Paris the city that fell, mon capitaine, not her spirit or her people."

"And the answer is," Reineke ignored him, "is because I have insisted upon protecting and preserving our anonymity with the utmost vigilance, which the SS, in turn, have threatened to destroy."

"This surprises you?" Pierre said, and Reineke just looked at him again with a tired expression.

"No," Reineke said controlled, "it is simply a matter of manipulating the obvious to suit our needs."

"Pierre is trying to protect his children, mon capitaine," Pierre assured. "I do not know about you."

"The same," Reineke said. "Along with my complex, and, yes, my men. The SS are a clear danger to us both."

"Oui, mon capitaine," Pierre agreed. "You are our cloak as you are for Diana."

"And you are mine," Reineke assured.

"So back to the beginning," Pierre requested. "What does any of this have to do with Mademoiselle?"

"Horses," Reineke said.

"Pardon?"

"Horses," Reineke nodded. "For a caravan of scouts, guards—listen to me!" he asked. "It will soon be summer. You have told me of the caravans that travel the roads, every year."

"Oui," Pierre said, "of course. In search of water."

"But what if they do not travel south to the Kufra or Ghat?" Reineke suggested. "But north, away from here?"

"Why would they do this?" Pierre frowned. "The Kufra or Ghat are much closer than the coast."

"Because I want them to," Reineke said simply.

"No," Pierre shook his head. "No, I am confused, mon capitaine. There are few caravans that come this way, ever, few camels, less horses. They cannot cross the sea without risk of death."

"There are hundreds," Reineke insisted. "And they can cross the sand sea the same way I can."

"Except they do not know these roads, mon capitaine," Pierre reminded. "These are your roads I have given to you, no one else. That is true, not a lie. Anyone on those roads except for you would be killed in an instant."

"Yes," Reineke said sourly, "anyone except for the SS."

"That was not Pierre's decision," Pierre waved, "clearly. I do not understand why Diana did not kill the SS any more than you understand, except to investigate their intentions and association with you. Not everyone apparently believes in mon capitaine despite what Pierre tries to do."

"And killed by whom?" Reineke interjected. "Eh? Killed by whom, Holy Man? Who would Diana use?"

"Arabs, yes, naturally," Pierre agreed, "less attention."

"On horseback," Reineke smiled. "A reasonable masquerade."

"Perhaps," Pierre shrugged. "Until mon capitaine's Germans decide to annihilate the Arab along with der Jude and the rest of the civilized world, and then, yes, mon capitaine will have to think of someone other than the Arab for his ranks to impersonate."

Reineke ignored the bait that time. "My Colonel will not order the compound dissolved because of some Arab population potentially troublesome, or not—which!" he pointed excitedly, warming to his scheme again, "he could do if he believed the danger was from your French. So disguise your friends as Arabs on horseback, traveling my roads, and there will be no difficulty."

"I already do," Pierre assured. "And you are right. It is very simple, without difficulty."

"Indeed," Reineke just sighed, exhausted. "I surrender. I am no match for you."

"And a few real Arabs, too," Pierre laughed.

"I will take either," Reineke nodded. "It does not matter. French or Arab, I will take both, whoever is willing, however you can arrange it. I will arrange a similar tactical diversion of scouts dressed as Arabs on horseback to escort my caravan, identical in the manner that they protect my complex here."

"Except a horse is not feasible," Pierre said. "He cannot cross the dunes."

"I want horses," Reineke insisted. "I do not have two months to wait for some camel to deliver the girl or my supplies."

"Well, what you want, and what you can have are two different things," Pierre said. "To begin with, I know of no such person who can provide you with so many horses—"

"Not many, a few," Reineke corrected. "I have trucks. *Trucks!*" he insisted. "The supplies will naturally be carried on the trucks. The horses are only a diversion."

"But I know of no such person," Pierre maintained.

"But you can find one," Reineke hissed. "If anyone could, you could. Who are your horse traders, then? The highest, you claim, of the desert Sheiks. You must know of such a person, you, who claim to know everyone."

"And if I did?" Pierre said. "Why should he help you? Who are you to him? Nothing!"

"You could explain it to him," Reineke said. "Tell him of my plan for the woman's return."

"Except!" Pierre pointed, "mon capitaine has yet to talk of Mademoiselle. He is ranting only about his supplies, transferring them from here to there to where, eh, mon capitaine? The front lines! This Pierre knows. Oui," he assured, "that is what is important to you. It is your plan. This has nothing to do with Mademoiselle, but everything to do with your supplies—which are munitions, mon capitaine," he assured. "Guns and bullets to kill the very children you claim to want to protect. Their mothers, their fathers, brothers—"

"A plan that includes the woman who will travel with them," Reineke grabbed the flailing hand. "To be returned to the SS. Only the caravan will be attacked, the woman kidnapped, and the SS killed, my supplies secured safely by my men."

"Pardon?" Pierre blinked.

"By your French dressed as Arabs," Reineke assured. "There is a distinct and very real potential for trouble with the scattered nomad tribes, a point my subsequent investigation into the attack will reveal. I will advise my Colonel how going forward, further precautions must be taken to ensure it does not happen again."

"Oh," Pierre said.

Yes. Reineke took a deep breath, his body hot and perspiring in the cool air. "Well?" he asked. "I presume they will take her?"

"The Arab?" Pierre said. "Yes, of course, for slavery."

"To freedom," Reineke corrected. "The Arabs are your French."

"I understand," Pierre nodded.

Did he? "I will insist the SS come—indeed, I will demand Herr Major return and collect her personally," Reineke assured. "So what is your answer, eh, Holy Man? Will I have my masquerade of horses? In exchange for granting the woman her life?"

"I do not know," Pierre shook his head.

"What?" Reineke sputtered. "What do you *not know*?"

"I do not know that is what I do not know!" Pierre insisted. "You are talking about using soldiers, and in talking of soldiers you are talking of death."

"The SS," Reineke swore. "No one will die except for the SS."

"A difficult promise to keep," Pierre said, "when you are talking about an attack upon your caravan by bandits you have employed, and who your soldiers know nothing about. And so what will your men do? Nothing? Stand there and allow the Arab attack? No, they will fight back. Kill, as will the Arab kill until how many are dead, apart from the SS? How many Germans? How many French? Possibly even Mademoiselle herself?

"No, mon capitaine," Pierre apologized. "I am sorry, but this is not a situation you can control to the extent you wish to control it. It will be a massacre, not a rescue, and I am a priest. I know you laugh and I laugh when we say I am a priest, but I am a priest, and a priest does not kill. He does not involve himself in war. You say Algeria is my country? I tell you a priest has no country. The world is his country. It was given to him by God to help, not destroy it.

"So, no, mon capitaine," he said, "I am sorry. I will try to think of a way to help you for it is good this thing you want to do to save Mademoiselle. It proves to Pierre again how you are the man I believe you are. But killing, mon capitaine? I am sorry, I cannot kill for you."

"Not even Germans?" Reineke said quietly.

"Pardon?" Pierre said.

"Not even Germans?" Reineke seized him by that sackcloth he wore covering his twisted bones. "German soldiers? Police? Not even a Major and his Leutnant and entourage of SS?"

"Mon capitaine ..." Pierre whispered.

"I am trying to save your life," Reineke pleaded. "Diana's. I am trying to save mine. I will change the plan, think of another way—indeed, return the woman myself to the SS, if I have to. Arrange for a rendezvous with them somewhere—but I want them dead! I want the SS dead. Can you do it? Will you do it? Attack and kill the SS and return the woman to where she belongs? Could you do it if only the SS were to die? Indeed," he said, "are you so certain you cannot kill even for your children, Holy Man? Could you kill them all if it guaranteed you the lives of your children?"

"For the children, mon capitaine," Pierre replied, and Reineke held his breath, "I could kill even you."

Reineke was certain he would. "Holy Man?" he said as Pierre moved away from him beyond the towering shadow of Diana, into the ring of trees surrounding them.

"I must go, mon capitaine," Pierre nodded, "it is very late. It is tomorrow. I am sure it is tomorrow already."

"We will talk?" Reineke anxiously verified.

"We will talk," Pierre agreed. "Once more before the sun rises, now I have to think."

"I will send my car for you," Reineke offered, afraid to let him go.

"That is not necessary," Pierre declined.

"But it's twelve kilometers," Reineke stared at those crippled legs.

"It is not necessary," Pierre repeated and vanished.

It was some time later when Pierre made himself comfortable in the library. It was Monday the 16th of March, 1942. They argued for hours until Pierre left to arrange for the horses, and Reineke was in the apartment, staring down on the woman sleeping.

"*Mon capitaine is a man who sits on a fence.*" Pierre's voice echoed in his head, but the accusation was unfair. He did the best he could. It was Pierre's misfortune to owe him, not the other way around.

"As will you," Reineke whispered at the woman. "So if I am so wrong, how can what I do be so right?" It could not be, and yet it was. If he counted them all, it would be nearly as many lives spared as the number of his men. And while it might eventually cost him his own, it would not be today, or even the next, and certainly not for her. He had much to do after her.

"Indeed," Reineke said. "Who are you? What are you doing here? Where are you from?" Out there in the sand, long before he arrived to find her here, he knew he would find disaster when he walked in.

"Are you France?" he wondered. Was Diana right when she claimed his compassion was guilt, his rage, battle fatigue?

"No," Reineke said. "No, you are not France." The horror of France inspired him to grant life. This woman inspired him to murder with such passion and desperation he could not explain if he thought on it for a hundred years.

One hundred years and no one will ever believe in the existence of the German Captain Reineke, for in fact he was a German, and ones like him did not exist.

"I exist," he told the woman, so strange to watch her sleeping with her mouth partially open.

"I exist," he assured, and decided to order her water heated for her bath before he woke her up to show her.

Chapter Thirty-Seven

The Fezzan
Territorio Militare, Libya
Monday, March 16, 1942

"It's Joanna!" Joanna corrected her name, the smile thickening on the face of the ugly old crone who said it wrong.

"He says it's Johanna," chimed the little witch standing next to her with the straggly black hair.

"It's Joanna," Joanna insisted. "I ought to know what my own name is, oughtn't I?"

She looked around the garden she had wanted to see, the one past the trees. Now however Joanna was quite positive she did not want to be there. "Where is Pierre?" she kept her backbone straight and chin in the air. "I want Pierre."

"We don't know any Pierre," the little witch informed with a sneer. "If you are speaking of the Holy Man, he has been sent away."

"Excuse me?" Joanna said. Nothing like letting someone know right off whose side you're on, Joanna supposed, mustn't waste time wondering. "Away?" she repeated, her heart pounding harder if that was possible. "Away? What do you mean away?"

That was a very good question. One the crone Anna Haas did not have the answer to yet, and had asked herself that morning. Perhaps not as desperately as this one standing in front of her, but definitely as interested in the whereabouts of the Holy Man Pierre. Anne, the little witch Joanna eyed with a mixture of hate and misgiving, also did not know the answer, though down at the Temple Diana early morning, to present Dieter's request for Mirabel to come to the house to play nursemaid to Evelyn's granddaughter, old enough to take care of herself.

Or she should be. Anna eyed the pint-sized package trembling in her bare feet. Justin's stepsister and Evelyn's pride and joy had to be twenty or so by this time, and so Anna's question to her granddaughter Anne for an explanation for Dieter's request for Mirabel, was at least reasonable.

"I asked you why?" Anna repeated her question to Anne playing messenger for Dieter and his order for a nanny. "Dieter has suffered Pierre for three months. He had to pick today to kill him?"

"Well, no, I don't think that's it," Anne laughed. "I guess Pierre's just not there."

"I got that," Anna said. "It's my guess he'll be back. Why does Dieter want Mirabel?" she asked a third time. "What are he and Pierre up to?"

"I don't know," Anne shrugged with a nervous tuck of her hair behind her ear as she stood there trying to convince her grandmother of her innocence. "He seemed nervous about something."

"Nervous," Anna digested. "Dieter, nervous. Well, at least that much is normal." She eyed her granddaughter. "Continue. How is Dieter nervous? In what way nervous? Nervous like you? Or a different kind of nervous?"

Anne flushed. "I'm not nervous."

No, she was eleven and in love and therefore protective, defensive of her crush, and very jealous over what she perceived as preferential treatment for the woman up at the house. "You remember Andrea, don't you?" Anna asked. "Michael's daughter Andrea? The one with the doll you threw in the water?"

"The one who screamed?" Anne frowned, remembering the story, not necessarily the event.

"Right," Anna nodded. The one who had screamed like her granddaughter had killed her first born. "It's all right," Anna shrugged in forgiveness. "She was only five."

"I was two," Anne glared, so like her grandmother in holding a grudge.

"Almost as old as Dieter," Anna agreed. She waved with a gesture toward the other side of the oasis and Dieter's villa. "The woman is the other one. The older one. The one with the red curls."

Who, yes, looked something like a doll herself, at least back then. "Henry and Liz's daughter."

Anne frowned. "The one the Irish killed?"

"Fascists," Anna assured.

"I thought it was the Irish."

"Fascists, Irish," Anna waved again. "We'll leave Justin and Evelyn to debate which. What did Uncle John say about Dieter's request for Mirabel? Did you go to John before coming to me? I don't care what Dieter told you. This is what John is for. This is his job. He is the manager, not me. I am the boss."

"I can't find him either," Anne admitted.

"Really ..." Anna said, now this was starting to get interesting. Dieter and Pierre, they could be up to anything. But John? Her relaxed and easygoing and levelheaded son John not quite himself since Michael's Red showed up half dead in camp. "Oh, Abraham!" she let out a bellow for her eldest with a point at Anne. "I told him, I told him to keep an eye on John—Abraham!" she screamed at the top of her lungs, his lawyer Martin heading toward her on the run to plead his brother's case.

"Go find your uncle Abraham," Anna directed Anne.

"Do you think the SS are organizing to return?" Anne wondered.

"We should be so lucky." Anna headed for home to find her wig because a nanny Dieter wanted, a nanny Dieter was going to get, only not Mirabel. "A ride," she ordered Martin to bring up the car. "Yes, a ride. What do you think Anne and I are going to do? Walk?"

"Where's the woman Sotma?" Anna rifled through her trunk. "Were you playing with her again?"

"Who?" Anne followed her up the stairs and inside.

"Who," Anna said. "That's not too obvious. The woman Sotma. My wig." The grey witch of Eden. Pistol-packing mama of the camel set. Bonnie to the Holy Man's Clyde. "I've been dreaming about Michael," she nodded to Anne. "Again last night." His energy contaminating hers since realizing his connection to their unwanted houseguest. "He would be right. This is a fucking mess. " She took off her bra, hoisting her skirt to find a more comfortable place to wear her gun than stuffed in her ample cleavage. "What?" she said to Anne watching her. "Too much? Too much is those stupid tattoos your uncle Abraham has carved in his face. He's never heard of *Rubenstein*?" she darkened the shadows under her eyes.

"Lucky if the SS returned?" Anne questioned.

"Everything is relative," Anna assured. "I thought I told you to find Abraham? I'll take care of Martin, torture him for practice."

"I'm looking for the woman Sotma."

"I'll take care of that, too—what?" she said when Anne hesitated. "Tell me you don't know where Abraham is either?"

"No," Anne shook her head, "I do. It's not that, it's Dieter. Do you think he knows?"

"About the Holy Man and Uncle John leaving us for greener pastures? What do you think?"

"Well, yes," Anne said, scoffing at her grandmother's ignorance, "of course Dieter knows the Holy Man isn't here. He wouldn't be asking for Mirabel if he didn't. I mean about the woman, does he know who she is."

"Joanna Edwards," Anna offered.

"Dieter said her name is Lee. Johanna Lee," Anne nodded, and so naturally that was who she was.

"Lee, Edwards," Anna dismissed. "That's just Justin trying to make what's simple complicated—no, Dieter does not know anything about Johanna Lee, and we are not going to tell him," she assured. "No more than we would ever tell Justin about Dieter, now would we?"

"No," Anne scoffed again.

"Stop that," Anna suggested. "Dieter might be your lover, but I am your grandmother."

"He's not my lover," Anne blushed and took off.

"Yet." Anna found her wig, fashioning it in place, exactly what she felt like doing at nine o'clock in the morning and 83 degrees in the shade.

"What?" Anna said when she walked down stairs to her middle one Martin with the Polish blond hair and German attitude plowing a trench in the sand as he paced back and forth like a jackal.

"My question," Martin assured.

"Oh," Anna said. "Well, it's a good one. There is a rumor going around Dieter and Pierre may be up to something. Is this a surprise to you? It's not to me ... John," she admitted, "is a surprise to me."

"John?" Martin said.

"Hold that thought," Anna requested. "What?" she asked Anne, back already and breathing fast.

"It's the SS," Martin insisted, his usual bundle of joy. "It has to be."

"No, it doesn't have to be," Anna disagreed. "I said what?" she repeated to Anne. "Don't listen to Martin, it's not the SS. Abe's probably with Mirabel, but you didn't hear that from me."

"I know that," Anne nodded.

"Of course you do," Anna said. "Then what? No one's mad at Dieter. It's not his fault Pierre is senile and your Uncle John decided to have his mid-life crisis now. It happens. To the best of us, it happens. You'll see."

"I almost forgot," Anne said. "Dieter said to tell you she speaks French."

"Who speaks French?" Anna said. "Red?" Not that she should be surprised. Lee had money, breeding. People with money and breeding spoke French.

"Johanna," Anne huffed. "It's Johanna. That's what Dieter calls her."

"My mistake," Anna apologized. "Anything else? Nothing else you or Dieter want or need? Should Martin go get a pen?"

"No," Anne laughed. "He's just nervous, like I told you."

"That's true you did," Anna said. "And I will undo whatever it is Pierre did to make Dieter nervous. Until then Dieter can manage—after you find Abraham," Anna caught her by the arm before she fled. "You go to Dieter only *after* you find Abraham. Him, you tell his mother says he smells like fish and for Mirabel to get down to the house before Dieter comes apart at the seams. I'll be there after I decide who to kill first."

"I will," Anne promised and took off again.

"Actually, you can tell Abe, yourself," Martin said with a flick of his head for his brothers Abraham and Jacob the youngest and medical school dropout as he had also rushed with his brothers to answer his mother's screams for assistance in Poland, not that you'd know that now. The two of them on a leisurely stroll through the backdrop of the Roman tenement block as if they didn't have a care in the world.

"I will," Anna assured. "Fish," she told Abraham. "From here, I can smell fish. The two of you."

"I'm here," Abraham calmly replied. "What's wrong?"

"Oh, I don't know. Let me see ..." Anna pulled out her cigarettes and her favorite telegraph, unfolding it carefully.

"Oh, Jesus Christ," Martin hung his head, "not again."

"Relax," Abraham advised him. "Ma," he said, "I think it's time to let it go, we've heard it enough."

Oh, that was impossible. If Anna read Justin's response to Jean Paul's request to repeat and clarify his broadcast fifteen more times than the times she had already read it, she still would not be tired of it, and she wasn't, so she read it again, as usual out loud.

"Flash. An American war correspondent is continuing with his assignment following an Arab attack on his convoy in the Western Desert. STOP. Details to follow. Don't bother me with any more stupid questions. I am in mourning. My sister is dead."

Anna folded her telegraph neatly putting it back in her pocket with a pat. "I added the postscript."

"Yes," Abraham knew that. "Jean Paul was foolish—"

"Foolish?" Anna challenged.

"Fine, naïve. Jean Paul should not have contacted Justin. It makes him appear anxious."

"Stupid!" Anna assured. "It makes him stupid!"

"All right," Abraham said. "I still say it doesn't mean it's Michael."

"Of course it's Michael!" Anna spit.

"And Justin's finally gone over the edge, like the rest of us," Abraham turned to Martin with his constipated expression. "What's really going on? Is it Reynolds? Has it been confirmed he's back?"

"More like the fucking asshole's gone MIA with John," Martin flicked his cigarette away, "if you believe the kid."

Abraham believed Anne without question. It was the first part that threw him. "Dieter?" he said, not sure if he had realized John and

Dieter knew each other beyond Dieter's uniform being a pretty good indication he was King of the castle regardless of who carried on like she was Queen of the world.

"Pierre," Martin assured.

"And John!" his mother kibitzed. "I told you to watch him. I told you. John is not like you or Martin. He's sensitive like me, Jacob—"

"All right!" Abraham said. "Ma, I'm trying to think."

"Oh, now you think," Anna said. "Yes, of course, now the psychiatrist thinks—that girl is Red! Michael's Red—"

"And that's enough!" Abraham insisted. "If John's with Pierre they can't be far."

"They're at the town," Martin assured. "It's the frigging SS. It has to be. En route or already here."

That of course was possible. But Abraham did not think John would just go without a word—"The damn plane!" he said and took off, his long black hair flying and billowing robes catching the wind like sails, Martin on his heels, his mother bellowing, "And that's another thing I could have told you, *Dr. Einstein*!" before turning her fury on Jacob.

"What?" Anna demanded. "Don't worry. You're next."

"Martin could be right," Jacob said.

"About the SS? He could be," Anna agreed. "But he's not. We would hear Dieter's guns from here."

"But maybe they're not here yet ..."

"I said Martin's wrong!" Anna snapped. "Anything else? I noticed you didn't go with the boys. What do you know that they don't?"

"Nothing," Jacob said. "Only that something is going on ... the girl is with the kids."

"Joanna?" Anna said. "With Pierre's children?"

"Yes," Jacob said. "It's why Anne's looking for Mirabel. She wants her out of there. She's mad."

"Oh, really ..."Anna said, her granddaughter Anne apparently like her in more ways than one. "Well, it looks like Martin could be right after all."

"The SS?" Jacob said.

"Close enough," Anna said. "Go get your brothers. Tell them the SS they're looking for is about that tall and eleven. I'll go rescue

Michael's Red—and then we'll have a meeting. A family meeting. Dieter and Pierre, too, and decide what to do about this once and for all!" she assured as Jacob took off, not quite in the image of his brother Abraham or nephew Hanuk with the flying black hair and colorful robes, but close enough. Jacob still had an innocence in his face his brothers had outgrown or lost and his nephew Hanuk never had. Anna took Hanuk with her to the Holy Man's village.

Abraham ran too fast and long and all for naught. Out of breath, with a sharp pain in his side he careened into the family garage. The kübelwagens was gone an empty can of petrol left on its side in an evaporating stain of fuel, and several more Jerry cans missing. John was en route to the plane.

"Shit," Abraham hung onto the fence post catching his breath.

He could say that again. Martin kicked the evidence halfway across the stall.

"All right," Abraham gasped out, "that doesn't help. Maybe John's just humoring him."

Martin sneered. "Oh, yeah, how?"

"How the hell do I know," Abraham snatched up a two-way radio to try and reach John before he took it too far. It was a long shot unless John was still in the immediate area, but it was worth a try. The stained sand suggested John was careless, had fueled the wagen in a hurry. The fact that the stain was still there suggested it wasn't that long ago. "Just pick that stuff up," he instructed as he tried to get John to answer.

"Good luck with that," Martin collected the can with a scowl at the wasted fuel, precious as water. "He's gone for that fucking son of his to put the pressure on. Trust me, Dieter doesn't have to kill him, because I will—anything?" he checked.

"No," Abraham shook his head, but tried one last time before he gave up. "He's out of range."

"Well, I could have told you that," Martin assured.

"Get in line!" Abraham took off for the short-wave that would reach John in Timbuktu, if he wanted to be reached.

"What's going on?" Jacob caught up with them.

"Armageddon!" Martin snapped.

"What?"

"Yale!" Martin assured. "Brothers of the ivy, brothers on the field—'*Bow! Wow! Wow!*'" he beat his chest to Porter's cheer.

"Knock it off!" Abraham blew a sharp whistle, trying to do something constructive in case neither of them noticed. He barked into the radio, demanding John respond. John didn't, and Abraham threw down the headset to sit there. "Mike's kid," he explained to Jacob. He lit a cigarette.

Jacob nodded. "She's with the kids."

"Joanna?" Abraham looked at Martin. "Dieter would never agree to that unless he knew Pierre wasn't going to be around."

"And Ma said to tell you ..." Jacob said, making sure he covered it all. "Anne's the SS you're looking for. Anne's the one who wants Mirabel, not Dieter. There's a family meeting as soon as she rescues the kid—Dieter and Pierre included—"

"Good luck with that one," Abraham agreed with Martin's scoff.

"And you smell like fish," Jacob laughed. "Fish."

"Grow up," Abraham flicked his cigarette at him.

"So where's John?" Jacob asked.

"Gone with Pierre for Jean Paul," Abraham got up.

"Why?" Jacob said.

"Hannah," Abraham assured. It wasn't Mike John lent a helping hand to, it was Hannah he worked to avenge, his twin, separated only by birth and now death. The Holy Man was good. He knew his audience he knew his mark, which of the brothers to go to for assistance, at least at first. Abraham shook his head. "I have a feeling there's something in the cards for the SS they don't quite expect."

"I'm in," Martin assured regardless, without hesitation.

"Me, too," Jacob swore.

"Now all we have to do is convince Ma," Abraham agreed.

"And Dieter," Jacob said.

"Dieter knows," Abraham promised. "Dieter knows."

Chapter Thirty-Eight

The small size of Evelyn's and Michael's bundle of joy was perhaps slightly unexpected. Anna would have thought the child Joanna had grown a bit more than she had grown in the ten years since Anna had seen her. The big white bandage, bare feet, and rolled-up pants legs several inches too long just added to the sad picture of a pathetic little waif. Anna felt a pang of conscience and that's when she knew it wasn't conscience, just the heat of the morning sun. She was too old, too jaded to have a conscience, develop one. John was the one wrestling with an ethical dilemma, not her. She was hung over from her unplanned trip north to Jean Paul and the unexpected delay when the plane developed trouble, turning a day into three, before she moved on from Jean Paul to her constituents to discuss the situation with them. Another seventy hours before she was home to find her sensitive John had traded in his dentist drill for the lion's shawl of Hercules, pulling Mike's kid back from the jaws of death since he couldn't pull his sister Hannah. Anna also knew it was Hannah pressuring John to respond to this one's plight, not Michael. She didn't need Abraham's couch to tell her that. She knew her sons, all of them, even the adopted one. That was no pathetic waif standing there. That was trouble. Dieter would never recover from everything that girl represented, he would never survive. She had to go.

"He calls her Red," Hanuk's voice penetrated her observation.

"Dieter?" Anna said in disbelief. That was grossly out of character regardless of the color of the girl's hair.

"No," Hanuk laughed. "John."

"Oh," Anna said. "Yes, of course; I know. Who hasn't? Who can't? That's Michael talking, Yale. John doesn't really know anything about Red, no more than the rest of us. I thought I told you to keep an eye on him—John," she assured Hanuk looking at her.

"No, you told Abe."

"Abraham was with me," she silenced his excuses with a wave. "How could Abraham keep an eye on John if he was with me?"

"Point," Hanuk conceded.

"Yes, and the next time pay attention. I don't care who I am talking to, I am always talking to you. John's taken the Holy Man somewhere. Probably to Jean Paul."

"You're kidding!" Hanuk said.

Yes, she was kidding. That's what Anna did. She kidded around. Made up stories, excuses ... lied to her grandmother. She eyed Anne racing breathless into the children's town to stop short and crawl the rest of the way when she spied her grandmother haunting the trees.

"Did you find Mirabel for Dieter?" Anna asked when Anne slunk her way through the undergrowth.

"No," Anne said. "She refused until she heard directly from you."

"She's right," Anne agreed. "Do you think that one over there might have something to do with why Dieter wants Mirabel?"

"The girl from the house?" Anne turned around to look.

"No, the man in the moon," Anna turned her back to face her. "What is she doing here?"

"That's exactly what I would like to know," Anne assured with a lot more spirit, more like her old self. Not some frightened little worm afraid of being caught in a lie.

"Well, why don't we go find out?" Anna took her by the shoulders aiming her that way, out of the trees.

"Hanuk, too?" Anne eyed her brother's sub-machine gun longingly.

"No, Hanuk can stay here," Anna said, "just in case she turns out to be as dangerous as she looks."

"Oh, she's not dangerous," Anne guaranteed, "she's a moron."

"A moron," Anna said. "That's different. She speaks French, though, remember? Dieter told you how she speaks French? Not too many morons speak English and French. Are you sure she's not confused or something like that ... she looks confused to me."

"She's not confused," Anne assured. "I've watched her. She screams and cries and staggers around. No one will go near her. They're afraid of her. She even chased the wagen until she fell down."

"Really ..." Anna said.

"She's definitely a moron," Anne promised. "You'll see."

"That's too bad," Anna said, "because I was thinking as long as she is here we might put her to work."

"Work?" Anne said.

"Work," Anna assured, spraying a little more camel urine in her hair. It was a wonderful deterrent, good for keeping people at arm's length if only temporarily while conducting or completing an observation. "And you still say she speaks French."

"She does."

"That's good," Anna said and Anne groaned, "you need the practice."

"I am the woman Sotma," the crone announced unpleasantly, Joanna sneezing at the foul stench surrounding her. "You are Johanna, as the Hauptmann explains."

"The devil with him," Joanna wiped her nose. "I want Pierre!"

But the creatures only looked between each other, turning on their heels and moving away, taking their horribly unpleasant smell with them.

"Hold it!" Joanna hollered after them, pausing to sneeze again and wipe her raw, runny nose already sore from hours of crying.

"I!" Joanna had said when rudely awakened from her uneasy sleep to find the Captain there saying something about giving her a bath to the cloaked figure standing next to him and who did not even look remotely like Pierre, but was large and dark with a bucket of boiling water in his hands.

"Oh, right!" Joanna was off her bed, in the loo and back out in a flash, six inches of straight-razor in her hand, quite prepared to slash the two of them to ribbons if they did not get out.

They did, though the Captain wasn't gone long. Two gulps and her breakfast was torn from her hands and she was ditched screaming first in, than out of a wagen in the middle of the broken down ghost town Pierre had brought her to yesterday. Stranded for hours on her own until these two showed up supporting the Captain's decree of the Fräulein spending her day with the children.

"In a pig's eye," Joanna boldly took up her trudge after the two circus freaks who scared the daylights out of her when they swooped down through the trees, accosting her. "I don't feel like playing! Where is Pierre?"

"You are not here to play," the crone informed with a sudden stop and lurch back in Joanna's direction, her long unkempt grey hair and great hooked nose stuffed in Joanna's face, her large pendulous breasts swinging freely under her thin shapeless tunic.

"I!" Joanna stammered, but only because the woman really was very ugly if not too tall and broad to really be a woman if it wasn't for those big fat bazooms as Michael called them.

"You are here to work!" seconded the little witch with a toss of her hair and hostile glint in her sunken black eyes, her bony finger jamming meaningfully into Joanna's shoulder.

"That's enough," Anna slapped her granddaughter's hand.

"Drop dead!" Joanna pushed her hair out of her eyes, ready to go a round if she had to. "For the last time, where's Pierre?"

But the creatures turned their backs on her again, vanishing back into the heavy forest of trees.

"Oh, my!" Two steps into the woods, Joanna was certain she would find herself lost forever, but two more steps and she was out of the forest and standing in a large open field of yellow sand in front of a long stone barn. "A carriage house," she breathed in amazement, tripping over a heavy root and stumbling to stand up straight. Grandfather had one of those.

The crone was there, outside, thundering in a mighty roar and sharp clap of her hands, the doors to the carriage house opening with the help of two young boys, roughly the same age and size as the wretched little girl.

She roared again, waving for the boys to come outside, a few other children appearing in answer to her call, and Joanna dared to take a step, several new unpleasant smells greeting her in a rush, permeating the hot, still air.

"Alcohol!" the little witch shoved something at her as Joanna sneezed several more times. "You have to sterilize your hands."

"I have to do what?" Joanna pushed her aside to stare into the barn that was one great big room, ten cots in two neat rows on either side lining the walls with long white sheets hanging down like curtains between them.

"But they're sick," Joanna gasped at what were children lying in the cots. "I don't understand. What is this?"

"None of them are sick," the witch snapped. "They are tired."

"Tired?" Joanna repeated. One of them certainly looked quite tired, lying on a cot set apart from the others, over in the corner, surrounded by what appeared to be a movie set straight out of Frankenstein with tubes and ... things. "Oh, my," Joanna whispered. "Oh, my, what is this?"

"No, that's all right, let her," Anna stopped Anne from leaping on Joanna's back and wrestling her to the ground as Justin's sister took off down the aisle to check things out for herself. "Let her see. Just stay with her. Stay with her."

"Oh, my," Joanna stared down on the little bronzed girl with black hair and round black eyes, all bundled up and hooked up to rubber bags and tubes. "Yes, hello," she swallowed as the girl smiled at her. "Hello. Are you all right? Is ... is everything all right?" she stared around at the equipment.

"She will not understand you," gloated the witch who had insisted upon following her. "I'm the only one she understands, except for Sotma."

She wasn't alone. The crone was on her second go-round of a speech several of the others didn't seem to be catching on to.

Joanna ignored them both, the witch and the crone. She smiled again at the little girl still smiling up at her. "I'm Joanna," she said. "Who are you? Can you tell me? Do you know where we are? Is this a hospital? It looks like a hospital to me."

"I told you!" the witch cracked Joanna sharply on the arm, "she doesn't understand you."

"I know what you told me!" Joanna shoved her roughly away and Anna decided it might be time to join them. "But she can certainly understand when someone's trying to be nice, can you?"

"Maybe," Anne shrugged, but if Anna read her granddaughter's expression correctly, that wasn't exactly on her mind. "She is Adva. She is six. I am eleven. I am Anne. If you don't do what I say, I will kill you."

"Give it your best shot," Joanna invited. "What is this place? A hospital?"

"Why don't you tell me?" Anne yanked the sheet off Adva and Joanna felt her breakfast come up in her throat.

"Oh, my God!" she stared at the missing leg, half of it just not there, and if she wasn't so shocked surely she would have fainted dead away.

"She fell," Anne explained callously as her grandmother snapped her fingers in a silent suggestion someone in the audience go get Hanuk.

"Fell?" Joanna stammered. "Fell?"

"They tried to let her keep it," Anne said. "But it didn't work so they had to take it off."

"What?" Joanna gasped, not that she couldn't see what the horrid child meant. "Off? What do you mean off? Who ..." she started to back away. "What are you talking about? What are you saying? Who took it off? Who said they had to take it off ..." Joanna backed right into the crone, turned around and stared at her and then fled, blindly running out of the barn.

Anne smiled up at her grandmother not exactly smiling down on her. "Actually, she's the one who threw Andrea's doll in the water. It wasn't me."

"So now you're even," Anna agreed. "Now go get her and apologize. Do it, even if you don't mean it."

"I won't mean it," Anne looked down at her feet.

"I can see that," Anna said. "Did you mean to tell me Dieter wanted Mirabel because the SS were coming to lunch?"

"I didn't say that," Anne looked up. "Uncle Martin said the SS were coming. I said Dieter wanted Mirabel."

"Does he?"

"No," Anne admitted. "He told me to get Mirabel when he brought the woman here."

"Why?"

"I don't know," Anne shrugged. "For the woman, I guess. I thought it would be a good idea if Mirabel took her back to the house."

"What else did Dieter say?"

"Nothing," Anne said. "Just something about the woman was to stay with us until the Holy Man came back because he didn't want to leave her alone at the house. I stopped listening when he said she was little like us and we had to be nice to her. She's not little like us. She's old."

"Older, perhaps, but not old," Anna looked over as Hanuk rushed in. "All right, go," she flicked her head at Anne.

"Fine," Anne sighed, "I'll bring her back."

"In one piece," Anna assured. She took the gun away from Hanuk gagging on his grandmother's smell and confused as to why he had been called when there was no blood or bodies. "Go with her," Anna instructed. "And mind the theatrics," she said, "a little goes a long way."

"Right!" Hanuk took off, not fast, but not slowly either.

"Yes, we'll, see, won't we?" Anna agreed with a glance down on one of her Captains of the Guard tugging at her skirt. "What?"

"John said to tell you he took the Holy Man to Algeria to see his son."

"Oh, he did, did he?" Anna thanked her informant who at least knew what was going on even if no one else did. "Is that why Dieter calls for Diana in such a panic?"

He wasn't too sure about the Dieter-in-a-panic part. "John said he would explain when he got back."

"I can't wait," Anna handed him Hanuk's sub-machine gun. "Take this to Abraham and tell him what you told me—can you carry it?"

"I think so ..." he slung it over his shoulder, half bent under the weight.

"Tell me if you can't."

"I can," he straightened up, confident.

"Good." Anna found her cigarettes, adjusted her heavy wig, and meandered out to ensure Mademoiselle Lee made it back to the hospital in no worse condition than when she left.

Joanna stumbled through the trees. Tripping and fighting until she was out of the woods, sprawled on the sandy ground of the town square, her brain screaming and chest heaving, wheezing and gasping for air, struggling to get to her feet, heaving herself forward, staggering over the dragging cuffs of the trousers. She hit the ground again, pushing herself up on her knees and then over, down, collapsing into a seated position, her back resting against something hard and wet. It was the well.

"It's a hospital, you idiot."

The dirty boots of the witch materialized in front of her. Joanna's heels dug into the sand, scrambling to climb to her feet with the assistance of the well. "Get away from me ..." she said.

Anne sneered. "It's only a hospital," she repeated, scornful and disgusted, her arms folded. "You have two very large cuts under your bandage. Another on your shoulder and another on your knee."

"I said, get away from me," Joanna insisted.

Anne ignored her, counting off on her fingers. "Berthe, Jean, Isabel, and Irma have dysentery—Have you ever had dysentery?" she stuck her pointed face in Joanna's, regarding her suspiciously.

"What?" Joanna stammered.

"It happens," Anne shrugged, though of course it had never happened to her. "Everyone here is tired from something and needs help—"

"Including you!" Joanna interrupted her viciously, "Get away from me before I ... I ..." she looked around wildly for something, anything to use in defense.

Anne smiled. "What about measles? I know you've had measles, as old as you are? Good. You can help with the measles cases—"

Joanna settled for her backbone since there was nothing else around. "I'm not helping with anything," she assured. "Now you get away from me you little witch before I ... before I dump you in the well!" she promised. "And we'll see who needs your stupid hospital!"

"You did," Anne said. "And now it's your turn to give back. My father says you're here to help."

"What?" Joanna said. "What?"

Anne shrugged. "He says you are nice. I can't see where you are so nice. I don't see where there's anything special about you at all—come on," she grabbed Joanna's wrist. "You have to wash first. You can't touch anything until you wash. You are to do what you are told, or I will slit your throat from ear to ear, Johanna Lee, and there's not too much you can do about it—ear to ear," she promised viciously, drawing a line across her throat with her finger, "while you sleep!"

"I don't think so!" Joanna hauled off and cracked the little monster across the face as hard as she could, and they were down in the sand wrestling to be the first to rip each other's head off.

"Hanuk," Anna gave her grandson a nudge as he laughed at the two little cats. "Don't stand there, Lee's no match for her."

She wasn't? Joanna had Anne by her hair, cramming a fist full of sand into her mouth.

"Or vice-versa," Anna shrugged calmly as Hanuk snapped to attention, terror on his face, diving to his sister's rescue, prying the two cats apart.

"I hate you! I hate you!" Anne screamed at Joanna, choking and gagging, and spitting sand as she fought to free herself from her brother's arms.

"No, it's all right, she's all right," Anna waved Hanuk to take Anne out of there while she took care of Justin's little she-devil falling over the trousers six inches too long, her face flushed as red as her hair.

"Who taught you how to fight like that?" Anna set Joanna upright, amused by the hellion panting and gasping in her unsteady stance but ready, oh, yes, very ready to fight the world. Anna was inclined to think of Michael rather than Justin as Joanna's trainer. "Anne should have been able to snap you in two," she assured.

Joanna stared at her, staggering back a few feet to eye the crone and the cigarette dangling from her broad flat hand.

"No, it's all right," the cigarette waved in reassurance, "don't worry about it. You hurt her pride, not her. She's angry," the crone shrugged, taking a deep draw on her fag. "She thinks you're here to hurt him, and she likes him. What can I say? Eleven's eleven. Or it used to be. Nowadays it's sixteen. Cigarette?" she offered Joanna, nodding in approval when Joanna did not answer. "Smart girl. I should stop myself," she took a second, deep draw, coughing half of it back out.

"You speak English," Joanna whispered. A week of self-conscious French, her own words sounded unfamiliar and awkward as the crone's with her halting, foreign monotone.

"So do you," Anna nodded.

"You're not French," Joanna said.

"No," Anna doubted if she had one sweet, pleading 'oui' in her. "Neither are you."

"You're a Moor," Joanna decided.

"Close enough," Anna ground her cigarette into the sand with a critical look over the bandaged head reeking of Pierre. "Let's go. I want to see what you look like under there."

"What?" Joanna gasped, her hands flying to protect her head.

"No, you don't need it," Anna plucked the skullcap off with one quick snatch tossing it to Joanna who aborted her shrill scream to stare at the bowl-shaped bandage in her hands.

"All right now?" Anna said. "Your head's there. You know that, right? Good," she approved when Joanna did not respond, but she also didn't scream. "Now, let's go. Come on. We're going back to the hospital."

"Oh, I ..." Joanna managed. "I can't."

"Oh?" Anna said. "Why not? What are you afraid of? Adva? There's no reason to be afraid of Adva. She's five years old—"

"Six," Joanna whispered.

"Is she?" Anna said. "How do you know this?"

"That ..." Joanna pointed in the direction some ... well, some native, she supposed, had carried off the little witch. "That horrible little girl told me."

"Anne," Anna agreed, looking in the direction herself.

"Yes, Anne," Joanna replied, studying the crone.

"What?" Anna said.

"I ..." Joanna said, really not certain herself. "I'm not sure."

"Of?" Anna said.

Of? "Well, I don't know," Joanna said. "I mean, I don't think I understand ... any of this," she whispered, more to herself.

"I see," Anna thought about that. "Well, what is it about this you do not understand? Dieter? That's not too hard. No one understands Dieter, not even Dieter. He spends his life trying to, and you would, too. Do you have a lifetime to spend trying to understand Dieter?"

"Well, no," Joanna said. "I mean, I'm not even sure I know what a Dieter is."

"Good girl," Anna approved with a guiding, encouraging pat on Joanna's shoulder. "Let's go. I am sure the Holy Man has explained to you all about the desert. I want to take a look at that eye and that head of yours and see if we can remove those sutures. If we can, we will. If you need a new bandage, we will give you a new bandage. A smaller one—"

"Why are you talking to me the way you are?" Joanna interrupted her.

"How should I be talking to you?" Anna asked. "Like you are a child or stupid? Are you stupid? A moron?"

"No, of course I'm not a moron," Joanna stared in the direction of the carriage house.

"I didn't think so," Anna said. "They don't think you're a moron either. They're not sure what you are. Neither am I ..." She studied Joanna with the influence of Justin written all over her not only Evelyn and Michael. Her name should be Edwards, not Lee. What went on in that house over the last ten years since her parents died? Or maybe it was just that the parents died, Evelyn, instead of Justin, adopting her either on paper or off.

"Other than your name, of course," Anna agreed. "I know your name. Johanna Lee—to a German it is *Johanna*," she silenced Joanna's protest. "He's not trying to be rude, just German. Like Fräulein and Mademoiselle. It's the same thing. Just one is German and the other French"

"Why did Pierre tell that girl I was here to help but he didn't tell me? I haven't even seen Pierre ... I can't find him," Joanna looked down, picking at her hands, "I haven't been able to find him since they took him away."

"Who took him away?" Anna asked carefully.

"The Captain," Joanna nodded. "I tried to tell him it was my fault. I'm the one who wanted to see the gardens. But he wouldn't listen, he was so angry ..." she burst into tears, sobbing until she stopped, her bruised and battered glare fixed on Anna. "Don't you care?"

"How long have you been out here?" Anna asked.

"What?" Joanna said.

"How long have you been out here?" Anna repeated.

"Well, hours," Joanna said, guessed, actually. "I don't know; hours."

"Hours," Anna said. "Out here," she indicated the square, broiled in the sun.

"Well, I was under the trees, for a while," Joanna agreed. "I fell asleep under the trees for a while—I'm not talking about me," she snapped. "I want Pierre! Even that ... that *witch*!" she assured, "called him her father, and she's right, he is her father—*their* father. It's not right the Captain took him away because of something I did!"

"The Holy Man is fine," Anna assured.

"No, he isn't," Joanna insisted. "The Captain took him."

"No, he did not," Anna said. "The Holy Man is fine. There is a sick child in one of the villages. He is at the village."

"Villages?" Joanna repeated.

"Yes, villages," Anna agreed. "There are villages, of course there are. Not too close," she said. "But there are always villages."

"But ..." Joanna said. "But I don't understand. I asked him about the city ... he said there was a city," she said, "but then he said there wasn't."

"City?" Anna said. "Oh. He probably thought you meant here. The children's camp," she agreed. "Yes, this ... well, as you can see," she said, "this probably once was a city, but it isn't anymore."

"Oh ..." Joanna looked at all the broken buildings crowded around. "Oh, yes, of course. How silly of me ..."

"So, come on," Anna encouraged, "One foot in front of the other, before you do end up with an infection and have to have all your hair shaved. I can't cut your head off, so we have to fix it where it is."

"Cut?" Joanna swayed. "Cut my head off?"

Anna frowned. "I said I can't. I didn't say I was going to. What's wrong with you? How long were you in the sun before you fell asleep under the trees?"

"I ... I don't know," Joanna said. "I don't ... I just ..." she stared off.

"Uh, huh," Anna followed the stare. "Adva fell on the rocks," she explained, surprising herself that she did. But there was something almost infectious about Justin's sister. Maybe it was Evelyn, or just Michael. She knew it wasn't Justin encouraging her to soften her stance on sacrificing Joanna for the sake of the masses. "Cut her foot, not very deeply. That was four months ago. Two months ago I had to amputate her leg."

"You amputated her leg?" Joanna blinked.

"Yes," Anna said. "Why? Did you think the Germans did that to her? They didn't. But, you're a smart girl. They do a lot worse than that. They're not very nice. Don't let anyone ever try to tell you they are.

"Oh, I know," Joanna said. "I know. They killed Joe."

"Joe," Anna repeated, thinking about Justin's message of an envoy and the gruesome details her agents had secured about some impaled head. Offhand, she did not remember the name that had been assigned to the dead officer, but it wasn't 'Joe'. "A friend of yours?"

"Oh, yes," Joanna nodded. "Yes. A very good friend. My ... my husband," she stared down at her feet again.

And so the adopted name *Lee* made sense after all with or without Justin's thumbprint. It was probably with it as Joseph Lee was homosexual. The girl was right though, telling the truth. Joseph Lee was dead. Anna remembered hearing about that in a wire from Michael he sent Otto, John's father ... last year? Close enough.

"Mine, too," she nodded.

"What?" Joanna said.

"But like Adva," Anna assured, "like me, you will live."

"Are you a prisoner, too?" Joanna asked finally brave enough to ask what she really wanted to ask the woman. "Are you some sort of prisoner?"

"There are different sorts?" Anna thought about that. "Interesting. I guess there are. No, I am not a prisoner."

"You're not?" Joanna blinked, hardly expecting that to be the answer.

"No," Anna assured. "And neither do I want to be one. So listen to me, Johanna Lee, very carefully. The Holy Man and I were here when the Germans came, and we will be here when they leave. Don't betray us or our children to anyone ever because we don't want them to be prisoners either."

"Betray?" Joanna repeated. "How could I—"

"Should you ever leave," Anna shrugged.

"Oh, I am leaving," Joanna assured. "I am definitely leaving."

"I believe you," Anna said. "Something tells me I might not have a choice. Regardless, don't betray us when you do leave. Don't ever tell anyone about us, and we won't ever tell anyone about you. The Nazis have long arms. They have very long arms ..." she guided Joanna back inside the carriage house, bandages, scissors, and tins of shining steel instruments all sparkling clean beside a row of basins.

The crone removed the sutures and gave Joanna a new bandage, much smaller than the helmet she had been wearing and an actual eye patch to protect her eye from the sun and sand. After Joanna rested and after lunch, she did come up with enough courage and interest to help with some very basic chores under close supervision of the witch who remained very unfriendly but had curbed her ghoulish wit. She stayed in the ancient city until the car came for her around six o'clock to return her to the house and her supper. There was still no sign of Pierre. Joanna ate her dinner listlessly, falling asleep early with a pounding headache and a sick stomach, still feeling very frightened, and very much alone despite the reassurances of the old crone and unexpected companionship of twenty-two small children, including the horrible little witch with the extremely handsome older brother, very close to her age.

Chapter Thirty-Nine

The Tamanrasset Region, Algeria
March 16

His father looked good for a crippled old man. Well-fed, and clear in his eyes, rested, despite the length and discomfort of his trip. For that reason alone, the hardship of the trip, Jean Paul agreed to meet his father ... was it halfway between their two worlds? Jean Paul did not know, and under different circumstances, would have killed to find out.

He went south, was all he knew, away from the cold Atlas Mountains, to the ancient dry river bed of the Tamanrasset where the madness of Nature transformed the desert into a grotesque alien world of bizarre rock formations and colors. John, Cassie's second son, a healthy, solid man of thirty-seven was with the Monseigneur Pierre. With brown hair pulled back in a short tight queue and his father's German-blue eyes, John looked less influenced by his ancient heritage than his mother or brothers Abraham and Jacob, and less Aryan than the Pole Martin. But desert soul or not John had closed his Manhattan dental suite, as Abraham had closed his medical practice, Martin, his law firm, Jacob cutting his junior year at medical school short, to help his brothers attempt the impossible and fail. His sister's refusal to leave Poland her death warrant, his mother's courage and nerve to leave her daughter Hannah behind to the fate she chose, and take her grandchildren, their guiding light to a new life regardless of the continuing struggle to get there.

Of Anna's four sons, Jean Paul probably respected Abraham the most, and liked the softer, clearer-thinking John the best. The fact it was John acting chauffeur for his father surprised Jean Paul, though who he would have expected instead, he did not know.

Jacob, perhaps, Jean Paul contemplated. Jacob, his mother's hopes versus Abraham her intelligence and skills, Martin, her calculating mind and cruelty, and John her sensibilities and common sense. What had happened to John? Jean Paul did not know this John Haas, the one who took chances like this one. Bold and foolishly confident, smiling behind the smoke of his cigarette when Jean Paul arrived.

"I am too young for this," Jean Paul said in greeting to his father.

Pierre did not rise up from the floor, but sat there like a monk, chuckling softly. "So then you have the advantage over me. When it is my trial no one will shake their head and understand how it is my youth that makes me innocent, for I am old, and must be wise."

"They will hang me anyway, Monseigneur," Jean Paul walked a few meters away to glance out the opened broken window of the outpost, over the makeshift airstrip that seemed almost crowded with their two planes.

Pierre observed him, and he looked well, his son, Pierre supposed. The boots he wore, new, his back straight and muscles tight in his slender arms. "Perhaps," Pierre agreed, choosing this time to stand. "Perhaps they will. Here."

But not in the eternal world, Jean Paul understood. No, they did not hang fools in his father's eternal world any more than they hanged heroes or slaves. "And why are you here?" Jean Paul turned around, asking almost impatiently though he had just spent twelve hours to get to him and it wasn't unreasonable to at least give him a few minutes to talk.

The saintly hands spread. "To visit. To see how you are? To tell you how I am? To ask," Pierre nodded, "a small favor."

It was Jean Paul's turn to smile. "Don't tell me our numbers have grown so much as to encroach on Eden?"

"Oh, no," Pierre shook his head. "No. Many, many miles away. Many, so many, I cannot count. It is why, yes, I have come to you. We must close the miles, the distance between the two of us."

Must they? Jean Paul ignored his father's gesturing head and hands to study John with his blank expression. "Why? In which direction?" Jean Paul asked.

"North," Pierre beamed. "I wish to go north."

Did he? Funny, but John did not look like a Judas who would sell his sister's soul for some pagan Aryan god, no more than his father did. "You think this is right?" Jean Paul challenged John in English with a flick of his head at Pierre. "Your mother using some old man to deliver her message? I know Reynolds has been confirmed. I also know our agreement was I would take care of it. Why are you unleashing le Metapel?"

Close, but no cigar, John almost said, but didn't. "I'll wait outside and let the two of you talk," he offered and exited.

"Screw you," Jean Paul muttered and eyed Pierre. "You are not here because of Reynolds?"

"What is *Reynolds*?" Pierre asked.

"Who," Jean Paul waved and sat down on the floor. "*Who* is Reynolds. Sit down old man, sit. Why then are you here?"

"To go north," Pierre sat.

"North," Jean Paul said. "Many times you go north. Why this time do you come to me?"

Pierre grinned. "Because I do. And it is nice, no?"

"No," Jean Paul assured. "You are too old for this."

"Ha! Ha!" Pierre winked. "So, then, I have the advantage over you. They will hang me sadly, saying how Pierre was a sick old man with an illness in his head."

So they would. "I will not open the north for you," Jean Paul refused. "You do not realize what you are asking."

"Oh, but, Jean Paul!" Pierre protested.

"No!" Jean Paul's temper flared though he had sworn to himself before he arrived he would keep it in check out of respect. But that was very difficult when his father did not respect him, or even himself. "You forget, Monseigneur, I fight the Germans, I do not protect them. Tell that to Cassie when you go back." He found a cigarette, lighting it.

"And who is Cassie?" Pierre asked curiously.

"Diana," Jean Paul exhaled with a nod.

"Oh," Pierre said, "that's interesting. Cassie—"

"No it isn't!" Jean Paul snapped. "It isn't interesting, and it isn't innocent. She is using you. You don't understand why you are here, but I do. The threat Reynolds is to be annihilated, the north opened for le Metapel to ensure it is done—Monseigneur," he said, "how could you not know the people you consort with other than you do not want to know?"

"I know you fight yourself," Pierre smiled, "as much as you fight me."

"I do not fight myself," Jean Paul assured. "And I did not come here to fight with you." He shook his head.

"Oh, but you do," Pierre said. "I am not here for Diana, I am here for God. The package I propose for you to carry north is not German. It is not of the Germans. It is young and it is innocent."

"What?" Jean Paul said.

"So much younger than you," Pierre assured. "And if you are young, what is she, eh? Oui, she! A woman, Jean Paul. 'La petite Mademoiselle'. So, stop this, eh?" he requested. "Do not roll your eyes disgusted and scold your father because Pierre is tired of this. No one listens to Pierre anymore. It is always a fight. A simple request for assistance, and a fight."

"A package?" Jean Paul stared at the doorway and John outside somewhere. "Monseigneur ..." he said carefully, "I do not understand. You have thousands of supporters, more than I will ever have. Why have you come to me—why do you persist in aggravating me?" he turned back on Pierre.

"Because I like you," Pierre grinned.

"Like me," Jean Paul ran his fingers through his oily black curls. He was a half-colored man born of a Nigerian whore to fat businessmen impregnated by their priest. If his father ever considered him at all, he doubted very much if he would have been born.

"Oui, of course," Pierre nodded. "Even though you fight me, which you do if you fight what le Metapel wants to do."

"Except I do not believe in your le Metapel," Jean Paul reminded. "His powers or his claims. He is Lucifer, the God, Herod, le Christ."

"Blasphemer!" Pierre jumped up, his hand cracking Jean Paul's face. "Jean Paul, I am bringing you a package, that is all, and it is final. I tell you explicitly how it is not of the Nazi, and it is not! You will help though you refuse, I will see to that! Your war is not a man. That which is not a man, you are making a man. You are taking the mark of the Nazi and placing it upon yourself! You are the worst of the devil's children who do this. You, who know the Nazi for what they are, embrace its plague of bigotry and prejudice for yourself. You have no excuse for your ignorance, and your prayers for victory will fall on deaf ears because He who is God knows the liar that you are. You think you are fighting evil, my son? You are fighting only yourself!" With fury, Pierre wrapped his robes around his trembling frame, returning to his spot on the floor.

"Are you finished?" Jean Paul asked quietly.

"I think so," Pierre nodded. "Oui," he looked at Jean Paul with a grin. "I practiced before I came. Rehearsed. What do you think?"

"Effective," Jean Paul agreed. "Very dramatic."

"A little, perhaps," Pierre shrugged. "But I am old. And I am French. So, come," he encouraged Jean Paul to sit close to him and not fight anymore. "Come and we will talk. I did not raise you to be so cold like this."

"You didn't raise me!" Jean Paul stared at him. "From a baby to a man, I never even met you until this war."

"Eh, so what?" Pierre dismissed that unimportant detail. "I will raise you now, how is that? Sit and talk with your father, this is very important to him."

"Fine," Jean Paul agreed, "Fine," and it was a mistake, though an unexpected one.

"Are you married yet?" Pierre peered at him.

"What?" Jean Paul felt his jaw actually drop.

"No, no, no!" Pierre stayed him from running away. "Let me explain to you why I ask this. I have a reason, oui. A legitimate reason—"

"Save it!" Jean Paul stopped him. "Save your breath. Yes, I am married," he lied. "I am married."

"To whom?" Pierre shut his eyes, not wanting to think about the ugly beanstalk outside twenty years older than his young son. "To that nose standing out there? I do not like her, no. Pierre does not. She is not the woman for you."

"Father," Jean Paul tapped him on the shoulder. "You do not even know her. And she is not a nose. Please do not call her that. She has a nose, yes, but she is not a nose. There is a difference."

"No, and I do not want to know her," Pierre said. "I have found another Mademoiselle for my son. And I want you to take this Mademoiselle, assist her, protect her, and bring her home. And, yes, oui, possibly," he shrugged, "with a little luck, a little help, a little guidance, you will both fall in love along the way and get married. What do you think?"

What did Jean Paul think? "A very bad American movie," he nodded.

"Pardon?" Pierre said. "What does that mean?"

"No," Jean Paul assured and stood up. "It means no, father. A big no—I have to go," he said. "I must. Find ... yes, find one of your other sons to take your package," he suggested, "because this one is not going to do it."

"I have no other sons," Pierre assured. "I have one. And you are saying no to your father?"

"I would probably say more if you weren't my father," Jean Paul admitted. "Yes."

"Oh," Pierre said. "Oh, well, it is not necessary," he assured, "because your father is not serious about marriage to Mademoiselle, no, of course he is not. It is a small joke, naturally, to lighten, how you say? The air."

"The air is fine," Jean Paul assured.

"No, it is not," Pierre shook his head. "And Pierre is not joking when he says you are to take Mademoiselle. He is not joking when he says you must stop fighting yourself and fight evil where you find it, regardless of its name—"

"Father," Jean Paul stopped him. "I am a soldier, not a priest. My enemies do have a name and I cannot afford to be concerned or even consider someone's soul. If I do, it will be I who ends up dead, not them. Is that what you want?"

"No, of course not," Pierre said. "Why would you even ask me such a ridiculous question?"

"Then understand, father," Jean Paul nodded, "that a war is a war, it is nothing else. *Le Metapel*? Non! He is a Nazi. Tell him to join the Resistance if he is as good as you claim ... Something," he assured, "you know he will never do, and you know why, the same as I do. He is using you, father, using you, and he is trying to have you use us."

"I know this is what you think," Pierre agreed.

"Good," Jean Paul cut him off. "I have to go."

"No, wait!" Pierre hoisted himself back to his feet quickly. "Jean Paul please wait, you did not come all this way just to leave!"

"No, I came all this way because I am an idiot," Jean Paul stopped in the doorway, "As much as I accuse you." He looked at Pierre. "I am an idiot, as much as you."

"No," Pierre smiled, "you came this long way because I am your father. It does not matter if I knew you as a baby or as a man. Flesh of my flesh, you are my son, Jean Paul. I know you are young, and it is difficult for the young to understand sometimes, but mon capitaine is not the Nazi, though he wears the uniform, as you are a soldier, though you do not—"

"Father ..." Jean Paul said.

"All right!" Pierre snapped. "So mon capitaine is trying to win his war! Eh, so what? That is what he wants to do in the morning, in the afternoon it is something else, and in the evening something else. The soldier is but a portion of the man. Mon capitaine is as righteous as you—more righteous than you are because though you are French he would never kill you, never, not I, Diana, or the children! What do you say to that? Join the Resistance? No, of course mon capitaine will never join the Resistance. He is German, and the light you want him to see would destroy him, a bullet through his own skull."

"Father, le Metapel is extremely clever," Jean Paul nodded. "I do not dispute that."

"Benefactor," Pierre corrected. "Oui, protector, provider. I refuse to argue with you anymore. You will do as you are told and take the package I give to you, or bring dishonor to your father if you refuse!"

"Of course I refuse!" Jean Paul snapped. "Father, you forget, I am allied with the English. I cannot use Justin's sister—Justin's own sister to trap him and kill his men, are you insane? Are you?" he insisted at Pierre stood there frowning at him as if he had two heads instead of the one stupid head he did have.

"Package, Monseigneur?" Jean Paul said. "Woman—sister!" he assured. "It is the sister, yes? Right? Mademoiselle ..." he could not think of the name. "Lee, is it?" it came to him. "Mademoiselle Lee? I know all about her," he nodded. "*All* about her."

"Well then you know why I am here," Pierre shrugged.

"Good God," Jean Paul hung his head. "Yes, good God, father, good God."

"My son, I know you allied with the English," Pierre assured him. "That is why I am here. Mon capitaine wants her to go back to the English. He wants to send her home—oui," Pierre smiled as Jean Paul turned his head to look at him. "Mon capitaine wants to save her—he did save her," he assured. "Rescued her from death and he is angry, very angry at what has happened. Such a young woman? An innocent woman, victim of soldiers and war, rescued by mon capitaine, my son. Le Metapel. Diana knows nothing of why I am here. I am here on behalf of mon capitaine, only. He wants you to take Mademoiselle home. So, what do you think, eh?" he grinned. "Now, what do you think?"

What did Jean Paul think? "Is any of that true?" he asked. "Any of it?"

"It is all true," Pierre said. "Ask John. He stole the plane to bring me here. I told him, mon capitaine wants to send Mademoiselle home. Go steal the airplane and bring me to Jean Paul—because how else was I going to get here, eh?" he peered at Jean Paul staring at him. "Your father is a priest, not an angel yet."

"That is not true." Jean Paul said. "It isn't."

"It is," Pierre assured. "So you see? If you refuse, you are not only defying your father you're denying this woman's—who did you say?"

"Brother," Jean Paul nodded.

"Pierre does not care," Pierre silenced him. "Not anything about this woman at all, and neither does mon capitaine. Ha! Ha!" he laughed. "What do you think of that? Mon capitaine could not be more disinterested even than Pierre in anything about this woman at all.

"Not to say Pierre isn't a little bit interested," Pierre peered at Jean Paul. "Brother? How do you know this? Who is giving you this information? Diana? Ach, poo! Diana!" he spit. "It has nothing to do with Diana. Mademoiselle was brought to mon capitaine. She is his to do with what he wants. Brother or no brother."

"Brother or no brother who is British Intelligence," Jean Paul assured. "Father, you have the sister of a British Intelligence officer!"

"I do not care about that." Pierre waved. "I have the prisoner of the SS Gestapo. What do you say to that?"

"Gestapo?" Jean Paul frowned. "That is also true?"

"Very much," Pierre assured. "The Gestapo brought Mademoiselle ten days ago to mon capitaine, who knows why—Except," he pointed, "if they find le Metapel, they find your father. You realize this, yes?"

"Oh, I realize that," Jean Paul nodded. "It is you who doesn't realize the danger you are in."

"The danger my children are in," Pierre corrected. "And mon capitaine is trying to protect them and your father. Mon capitaine is not a fool. He knows the Gestapo have come for a reason."

"Well, he knows more than I do, if he knows the reason," Jean Paul rubbed his face as he paced back and forth. "Father, something is wrong. Something is very wrong. They took this woman from the Siwa in Egypt. I want you to leave there now. Since you are here, John does not have to take you back."

"Leave?" Pierre echoed.

"Yes, leave!" Jean Paul insisted. "I want you to leave! We will take your children for you to a safer place."

"No, never," Pierre refused. "I am not leaving mon capitaine."

"What?" Jean Paul said. "Don't be ridiculous!"

"I said no," Pierre assured. "So there is trouble. Of course, there is trouble. You think you can have a war without trouble? I don't think so. Who is this brother, really? What of him? Perhaps he is the trouble. Is he looking for Mademoiselle?"

"Of course he is looking," Jean Paul groaned. "Not for her, but for her body, yes. Her bones. The men who killed her."

"She is not dead, no," Pierre shook his head. "Very much alive."

"I know that!" Jean Paul snapped. "Yes, thank you, but I think even I know you wouldn't be asking me to go through all of this for a corpse. I do think I know that."

"OK," Pierre shrugged.

"No, it isn't *OK*," Jean Paul insisted. "It is far from *OK*. Father, what is the matter with you? I just told you this man is British Intelligence. Of course he is looking!"

"And what will he find? Eh?" Pierre smirked.

"Find?" Jean Paul echoed. "Nothing! Obviously nothing if you have her. That is not the point!"

"It is the point, and it is good," Pierre assured.

"Good?" Jean Paul smacked himself in his forehead, his hand sliding down to hold his face as he shook his head. "No, it isn't good. Nothing is good. You are in danger!"

"Then take Mademoiselle as I ask and remove the danger. Mon capitaine plots to kill the SS, which he will do, oui. So, do not talk to me about who is Nazi, and who is not. Give mon capitaine one week, possibly two. Plenty enough time for my son to take care of the danger on his end so Pierre can bring Mademoiselle to him, and he can return her to wherever she comes from—Siwa, you said?"

"Siwa," Jean Paul agreed. "Yes, Siwa. And only you know how close that is to Eden or how far."

"Very far!" Pierre laughed. "Very, very far!"

"Well, that's hardly of any consolation," Jean Paul said, "possibly more suspect. Why would they bring the girl from the Siwa to wherever you are? There is more to this, father. There is much more to this than either you or I know ..." he stared out the door at John talking with Cassandra. It was little wonder Cassie was so upset, possibly knowing as much or as little as he knew and suspecting anything else, everything else.

"This brother ..." Pierre said. "Michael, is it, you said?"

"Justin," Jean Paul said, but then looked at Pierre suddenly. "I thought you did not want to know?"

"I don't," Pierre assured. "Mademoiselle has mentioned the name Michael, I thought perhaps it might be him."

"Oh," Jean Paul said. "No."

"Well," Pierre shrugged, "whatever his name, perhaps he is wrong. Perhaps Mademoiselle is not from the Siwa."

"No, she is from the Siwa. Or someone was. Father," Jean Paul said. "You have no idea what these men did. They brutalized them, cut the page who was with them to pieces. Dismembered and decapitated him, hanging his head from the radio antenna. Now tell me what I should think of the immortal souls of your precious Nazi?"

"I think," Pierre said quietly, "what I have said. It is terrible, horrible, and Mon capitaine has sworn to kill the SS who did this."

"We'll see," Jean Paul said.

"We will," Pierre agreed. "So what are you going to do? Are you going to listen to your father and take Mademoiselle?"

Do? Jean Paul had no idea what he was going to do. "I can tell you what I am not going to do," he said. "I am not killing the British Intelligence for you, some girl, or Diana! Off with his head, Jean Paul. Don't even think twice," he nodded. "But, that's all right, father, really. Don't you or Diana think twice either, it's only war."

"I am not," Pierre promised. "Do what you want. Just take Mademoiselle and give her back to her brother—he is in Egypt as well?" he verified. "He is not? Tell him to go back there. Mon capitaine wants Mademoiselle to go to Egypt, far, far away from him. She upsets him, interrupts him, he cannot think with her around. But then he is embarrassed. Oui, very embarrassed," he clucked in sympathy. "Ashamed. He wears the uniform of the men who attacked her, and when he looks at his uniform, he cannot look at her ... which," Pierre acknowledged, "is good because Mademoiselle is not fourteen as he thought, but nineteen, and mon capitaine is a whore. To tell mon capitaine to stay away from a woman is to tell a cat to stay away from cream."

"His evening decision?" Jean Paul proposed sarcastically. "As opposed to his morning decision of fighting a war, and the afternoon one of killing the SS?"

Pierre laughed. "Oui, yes, absolutely. In another time, another place, definitely—and, of course, with a different woman," he assured. "Not with Mademoiselle, of course, no, never. Do not concern yourself. She is injured in the first place, oui, very badly injured. Very nearly killed. But, she is fine now, do not worry, your father is just talking."

So Jean Paul noticed. "Probably from the accident."

"Pardon?"

"Accident," Jean Paul said. "The jeep was smashed. They could have smashed it afterwards, but why?"

"Really?" Pierre said. "You think Mademoiselle crashed in a jeep?"

"She was the driver," Jean Paul shrugged. "I don't know. It's all conjecture—forensic evidence, if you believe Justin's science. I don't know ... I don't care," he said. "Father, I am truthfully more interested in why Justin's sister isn't dead, as I know Justin will be."

"Coincidence perhaps," Pierre shrugged. "Perhaps not. She was almost dead. Does that satisfy you?"

"No," Jean Paul assured. "What would satisfy me is for you to leave. If your capitaine is as powerful and as strong as you claim, he can survive without you. Let him fight his own battles."

"No," Pierre said. "This battle mon capitaine is fighting is not his, it is Pierre's. He does not have to protect your father. He can as easily kill him. He does not have to return any woman. He can as easily kill her. And!" he assured, "If some brother comes, he can as easily kill him. Understand, my son, mon capitaine chooses not to kill—except, of course, naturally," he agreed, "the SS. But that is understandable."

"Oh, yes, yes," Jean Paul understood that completely.

"Good," Pierre said. "So take your father's package before her bruises disappear and mon capitaine realizes she is not fourteen, but a woman. His decision today is to be an Avenging Angel. That is what he has decided. That is who he is today. I cannot guarantee tomorrow."

"You should know," Jean Paul agreed.

"Oui," Pierre winked, "I should. So do it. Do as I ask. Will you?"

"Of course," Jean Paul sighed. "Yes, of course. What choice do I have?"

"Really?" Pierre beamed. "You are not joking with your father?"

"Yes," Jean Paul said, facetiously, "I am joking. I am going to leave Justin's sister with the Germans. What do you think?"

"I don't know," Pierre shrugged. "So much time complaining you'd think my son did not like his war. I don't know why. He has a woman standing out there waiting for him whom he thinks is beautiful, and his father knows is ugly. She holds a gun instead of a child, wanting to kill your father, but have you heard me mention any of this to you?"

"Cassandra," Jean Paul glanced at the door. "And, yes, she does want to kill you."

"Oui, of course," Pierre could understand that. "Naturally. A marriage made in Heaven. My son and his wife."

"Companion," Jean Paul corrected. "I am not married, and Cassandra is not twenty years older than I am."

"There is hope yet," Pierre grinned. "And, yes, she is, my son. But have you heard your father say any of these things to you?"

"Yes," Jean Paul assured. "But then I am not deaf. *Like* my war? You really think I *like* my war?"

"What about an opportunity to kill the SS?" Pierre asked. "You think you might like that? And not only the SS, but a few of his soldiers mon capitaine also wants dead because he does not like them either."

"He is killing his own soldiers," Jean Paul said.

"Oui," Pierre nodded, "he is. He would have killed them the day the SS came, but he had to think. Of course," he shrugged, "he takes too long to think and now he is frustrated. He wants it all over yesterday."

"He is out of his mind," Jean Paul said. "Father, the man is out of his mind."

"Mon capitaine?" Pierre said. "Oui, possibly. But no more so than you, no more than I. Do what he wants," he encouraged. "He will do it with or without you, whether or not you agree. Go to the people and tell them. *Le Metapel* needs your help. He has helped you, and now it is your turn to help him. See what happens."

"I already know what will happen," Jean Paul assured.

"Oui, of course you do," Pierre laughed. "So do I. They will help him absolutely, from the north to the south, the south to the north. From you I am going to Ben Akach to borrow his horses that he will give to me. A truly honest man Ben, he cares only for money, not you, not I. And his blessings are many because he does not lie. But come, my son, come," he rose stiffly from sitting so long. "We have no time to talk of Ben. I know that disappoints you ..."

"Actually it does," Jean Paul said, he rather liked Ben.

"Of course it does," Pierre smiled. "It is nice to know there is one of your father's friends you do not despise. Mon capitaine wants this rendezvous with Mademoiselle and the SS to be at a hospital."

"A hospital?" Jean Paul repeated.

"My son," Pierre huffed.

Jean Paul stopped him. "I was going to say that is not a bad idea."

"Oh," Pierre said. "Oh, oui, of course," he assured, "mon capitaine's ideas are always good. This hospital is to be in Gadames."

"Gadames?" Jean Paul startled.

"My son," Pierre reminded, "you just said it was a good idea."

"The hospital," Jean Paul agreed, "yes. But, father, I am a faction of the Free French, I am not Charles de Gaulle. I cannot issue an order, controlling the area of Gadames."

"You misunderstand," Pierre shook his head. "Mon capitaine does not want you to control it he wants you to attack it."

"Attack it," Jean Paul said.

"Oui, attack," Pierre nodded. "Attack the hospital and kill the SS. Have you been listening to anything I have said?"

"No!" Jean Paul assured. "And I am still trying not to. Father, I could produce a film showing Justin Arabs attacking the American consort, his sister traded to Germans. From Germans to an Italian field hospital waiting to be remanded to the SS and a squad of dead Germans after the attack and Justin will still never believe any of this. Any of it!"

"Justin?"

"Her brother," Jean Paul reminded. "Someone you really do not want to aggravate, trust me."

"Well, I am not going to aggravate him," Pierre assured. "I have no reason to aggravate him, unless, of course, he aggravates me. Who is this Michael Mademoiselle mentioned?"

"Michael?" Jean Paul frowned. "I have no idea. Why?"

"Not important perhaps," Pierre dismissed. "What is important is we must plan."

"It cannot be Gadames."

"No? Where can it be?"

"I don't know," Jean Paul said. "I have to think."

"You cannot trick mon capitaine," Pierre warned. "He will know if you attempt to."

"And I will know if he attempts to trick me," Jean Paul assured. "All right, maybe it can be Gadames. You are really going to encourage Justin's attention with all of this, but fine. Fine," he said, thinking beyond the moment to Reynolds and the issue of the depots. "It's really not a bad idea. Perhaps good for all of us. It's possible I can convince Justin the depot was a field hospital. German. Italian. I don't know!" he waved, disgusted. "International Red Cross! The man can't even read."

"Pardon?" Pierre said. "Mademoiselle's brother cannot read?"

"No," Jean Paul said. "Never mind, it is not important. I have to go, father; I do. I am two days late for my next argument. Good God," Jean Paul massaged his temples. "First it's Anna, and then it's sand in the oil pump, and then it's you."

"There's sand in the oil pump again," Pierre nodded. "John says we are here, but we cannot go back. We are what he calls *stuck*."

"No, you are not stuck," Jean Paul scowled. "I have a plane you can use. Have John bring your things. We'll take you to it."

"Things?" Pierre said. "I have no things. I am all I have brought with me."

"And it is enough," Jean Paul assured. "It is more than enough."

Chapter Forty

John limped the plane into the Tamanrasset where Jean Paul ended up being hours late and whether he eventually showed up or not, John wasn't ready to give up on the oil pump if it meant the difference between flying the five hundred miles home or waiting a day for Abe to come and bail them out. Likewise, Jean Paul or no Jean Paul, John wasn't ready to give up on getting Mike's kid out of the mess she was in by some method or means. Of course, clearing the oil filter couldn't guarantee the system wouldn't fail again on the way home, forcing John to have to put the plane down before reaching the oasis, no more than Dieter's ambitious scheme to slaughter the opposing team's offense would guarantee he'd win the game. It was all chance, a gamble, the ultimate outcome anybody's guess.

When it came to being stranded versus chancing it and crash landing when the pump failed, they got lucky. Jean Paul did show up and John's attention switched from working on the pump to coveting Jean Paul's plane. Unlikely Jean Paul happened to be carrying spare parts for a British Stringbag, or knew where they might be secretly buried in this place that came equipped with a packed sand landing strip and a solitary lean-to set to blend into the rocks, there was always Jean Paul's plane itself John could take. At the point of a gun if Jean Paul failed in considering his elderly father, offering the plane to the old man, and staying to call his buddies to come bail him out rather that it being the other way around. After all, regardless of whatever else Monseigneur Pierre Beausoleil was, he was Jean Paul's father. An old, crippled man, twisted in deformities and arthritis that had to have him in constant pain. But he toughed it out every day at the oasis, and throughout the torturous plane ride. It impressed John and it remained to be seen what impression Jean Paul had of his father.

In the three years John had known the two of them, he had never seen them together. When he did, it was interesting to notice how much Jean Paul looked like his father in his face, at least when together in the same room. Apart, no, John had not noticed a resemblance beyond they were both short dark men, and both tough, spirited, if John wanted to be literary. Side by side though, there was an obvious physical resemblance, even if one never reached the conclusion of father and son.

Good luck continued with it obvious within a few minutes of watching their interaction that Jean Paul would offer his plane to his old man. John smiled at Cassandra as he walked out of the shack to wander around outside smoking his cigarette waiting for Jean Paul to succumb to the pressures of Pierre, also inevitable.

She was an exotic looking woman, Jean Paul's Cassandra with her wrinkled black hair and footlocker of brass jewelry. But the fatigues and the sub-machine gun put a kibosh on any fantasy of her breaking into a belly dance, much to John's dismay. Still, she looked like she had been born to the place whether or not she had been born to the role. Sort of a vice-versa to his brother Abe who took to his life of Desert Sheik like a born natural, and perhaps he was. Distinguished and dignified with his maintained European manner despite a few years of the States and Manhattan under his belt, Abe had always qualified as the true alien of the brothers. His father a half-caste Anglo-Indo-Turk Anna married one summer abroad in India while working on a doctoral dissertation. Hannah's first husband and Jacob's father were also Oriental half-castes, two more Anglo-Indo-Turk plus Sudanese when it came to Hanuk and Anne. Jacob, a perpetual rookie to the streets of New York where he endeavored to blend in by adapting and imitating a Hollywood inspired interpretation of the real thing, in North Africa Jacob imitated Abraham's flamboyance, to where Hanuk, Hannah's son, as his Uncle Abe was simply a natural, and Anne, like her grandmother Anna, simply wild.

Twins John and Hannah were Anna's only two full-blooded Germans with Martin's father, as with Hannah's second husband, Polish. John and Martin transplanted in New York early the same as Jacob, it was the subways, the city lights, and nights John took to like a native. He roomed with Michael at Yale, a big college in the middle of a tiny city set out in staid Connecticut, and while John might prefer Justin's demeanor overall, back in the good old days, and provided Mike stayed away from the hard stuff and hence the attitude, Michael was a heck of a lot of fun. John hadn't seen Justin in years, Mike, not since John hung the "Be Back after the War" sign on his office door and headed for the homeland, with little or no interest in rekindling any lost or dormant friendship, especially with Justin aka Chuck. But then, for all the transgressions John could forgive Michael, there was a bigger one standing between him and Chuck. Palestine.

Not saying Justin could do anything personally about the situation, Justin could, in John's opinion, admit, or at least acknowledge, closing the gates wasn't the greatest idea, but in fact passive support of genocide. Justin never would though, either because he couldn't, or wouldn't. In public or private, a company man to the very end, the Crown never wrong.

"Oh, what the hell," John figured he may as well have a go at the oil pump again as it gave him something to do. Pierre was taking longer than expected to convince his son he was on the side of good not the side of the Jerries whether or not this one happened to be a Jerry. It might help if Pierre didn't insist on speaking in parables, except he wouldn't be Pierre if he didn't. John ditched the cigarette, and stuck his head back under the hood, Cassandra joining him with what she apparently considered encouragement.

"We are doomed."

John laughed, inheriting his mother's wry, somewhat dry sense of humor, not only her brains, and hoping the lady didn't take it the wrong way. "You read palms, too?"

She eyed him, the kind of eye that makes your skin crawl, not necessarily in a bad way. John could appreciate what Jean Paul saw in her. He saw it also, though doubted if he'd get it free.

"Long life," she disclosed after she grabbed his hand and spent several seconds massaging his destiny.

"That's an improvement," John approved.

"Or it could be," she warned, liking to torture her victims. "Three children," she nodded as if John should prefer fatherhood to throwing himself on a grenade, John would take the grenade.

"Two," John corrected and neither of them his. "Hannah had two children."

"I see three," she curled her fingers over his into a fist to show him the proof. Three wrinkles at the base of his little pinky.

Well, two children *plus* one visit from the SS ten days ago and one Jewish mother who apparently could not keep her mouth shut. John did not envy Abe that trip north. It must have been a doozy. This lady was keen to Red, and John was keen to being had by Madam Zelda who was definitely living in a third world if she thought she could put something over on him. "Well, if there's a blonde in there, you could be on to something," John settled back against the plane to enjoy the show, but then it was a heck of a lot better than fooling with the oil pump.

"You like blondes?" Cassandra asked.

Honey, I like anything I don't have to pay for, John did not say. "Like every other red-blooded American," he agreed.

"You're Jew," she said.

"German Jew," he clarified. "Full blood. Which, by the way, Cassandra was Greek, not Egyptian."

"Trojan," she gave him back his hand. "And they didn't believe her either."

Like John said, the kind of look that made your skin crawl. He went back to work on the pump. Pierre emerged from the hut eventually with Jean Paul, as predicted it inevitable Pierre would get his way. The old goat really a persuasive and powerful personality. That is, if his audience was up to being persuaded, a category Jean Paul fell into, though he didn't seem overly happy about it. The look on Jean Paul's face John personally knew well having seen it on his own, as he had seen the one on Pierre's face on his mother who personally took no chances with her audiences, but carried a gun.

Kind of like the way this Dieter guy operated apparently. If you couldn't sway them with words, you could always shoot them. That was fine with John since the fellows on the receiving end of Dieter's annoyance were not only Germans, but SS.

"Where to?" John straightened up with a grin, foregoing worrying about the future to concentrate on the present that in another thirty seconds included a jeep swollen with six of Jean Paul's finest, appearing seemingly from nowhere, and who John knew had to be out there. The spare plane, John clearly knew nothing about, but soon would, down along the avenue of rocks that looked like Alice's Wonderland, hanging a right at the upside down mushroom. In the meantime, Pierre hobbled for the emptying jeep with a wave. "Ben."

"Ben?" John repeated to Jean Paul. "Akach?" he stared at Cassandra. Maybe he should have paid closer attention to her prophecy of doom. All of them, Abe included, fair to say, small potatoes with their theatrics to where the 'real thing' Ben Akach, wasn't as much a sheik, as he was a bandit. Grown fat and old on his enemies scalps, hardly their souls.

"Something wrong?" Pierre said as John groaned.

"Meaning apart from collaborating with Germans *and* Arabs?" John said. "Yes. You don't have to live with her." He swung up into the jeep after giving a helpful boost to Pierre and a reassuring nod to Jean Paul. "I have him."

"Your mother?" Pierre said.

"My mother," John assured. "It's all right. There's always a chance I won't live long enough to regret it."

"Are you thinking of changing your mind?" Pierre asked.

No. So Pierre could save the psychology and his toothy grin. If John were up to changing his mind, he wouldn't be here in the first place. He'd have just told the old guy no when he came to find him (and *maybe* Martin) as John was the man for the job, not Abe.

True. Abe was not the man for the job. Abe would never have done this. Apart from definitely tattling to Ma, Abe would have tried to talk Pierre out of it, possibly talked Pierre into at least thinking about it, and thinking Pierre did not need to do. Pierre thought as he talked, constantly. All in parables. John had hours' worth of parables by the time they touched down to meet with Jean Paul. The old guy talking as much to John as John was convinced he was talking to himself, possibly to convince himself this was the way to go, the route to take, which it either was or wasn't. John would settle for it being the right one because he didn't have a better one and the one as described suited him just fine. It got a little screwy in that Dieter was apparently the orchestrator, not Pierre. But Dieter was already a little screwy. That much John knew even if he was the DDS, and Abe was the MD, PhD in psychiatry who knew Dieter, which John did not, and did not need to, not well or personally. John was doing this for John, not Dieter, or Pierre, *maybe* for Mike, and definitely for Hannah. John did not have to lie-down on Abe's couch to come to the realization of how powerless he had felt in being unable to do anything for Hannah, and the anger he still felt.

"Michael?" Thirty-seven year old John Edgar Haas lied deadpan to twenty-one year old Jean Paul Dumont when Jean Paul asked rather offhand if the name meant anything to him as they rode the yellow-brick road to Jean Paul's spare plane. "Can't think of anything. Possibly one of the guys? Who knows."

"But you know him," Jean Paul verified.

"Chuck?" John said. "Yes, ten years, or so ago. I was at the wedding, flower girl. Why? What's Ma's preference to letting the kid off the hook and putting the SS on one? I mean, since we're on the subject," he smiled at Jean Paul.

"To kill them."

"Chuck?" John laughed until he ran out of wind. "Yeah, OK, Ma's dreaming because that will never happen. We'll stick with Dieter's plan as the better of the two."

"It will never work," Jean Paul had possibly been playing house with Cassandra a little too long.

Well, *work*, in John's opinion was relative. If by *work* Jean Paul meant would Justin not believe there was as much of a reason for his sister showing up alive as the reason she had for turning up dead? Probably not. Would the SS give up and go away simply because Dieter took out a platoon? Definitely not. But John was a firm believer in that ol' Hollywood adage *"I'll think about that tomorrow"* and in the meantime the kid would be whisked back to Kansas where she belonged.

"We'll make it work," John boosted the old guy into the plane and after a quick lesson from Jean Paul, took off for Ben Akach.

"What wedding?" Pierre asked above the rumble of the plane.

John smiled. "Speaking of noses."

"What?" Pierre said.

"Noses," John carefully checked the lay of land around him with an eye out for a convenient place to set down before the night closed in and the oven-like atmosphere turned to ice. He estimated he had about an hour or so until that happened. "Look, I'm going to have to put her down in a little while. I'm instrument trained, but I'm also close to spent, so if you've got any favorite spots, now's the time to say so."

"No, this is fine," Pierre nodded. "It's fine. Anywhere."

"You're sure?" John said. "I don't want any surprises."

"I am sure," Pierre said.

"OK," John said. "I'll hold you to that, and we'll take her up again in a couple of hours just to be sure, unless you think you can talk your friends into coming to us, can you?"

"Who knows," Pierre shrugged. "They are around, yes, of course, if that is what you are asking. They are everywhere."

"Like horse shit." John found a reasonable place to land about a half an hour later. Banging her only a couple of times, not hard enough to injure anyone or anything, the sand was firm enough to be able to take off without difficulty unless the wind shifted direction and they found themselves buried up to their necks, not a pleasant prospect.

"Speaking of unpleasant thoughts," John tightened his cloak around him because when the temperature dropped, it dropped fast and low. "You know those names you've been asking about?"

"Chuck?" Pierre said, looking rather like a beaver when he said it.

"Justin and the other one. Michael," John assured. "And you didn't hear it from me. In fact, you didn't hear it at all, ever, so stop asking about them. Cease and desist. Don't ask, don't talk, don't tell. I don't care if Dieter promises you season tickets to the moon and the SS give you lead feet. It's a long walk home. A *long* walk home."

"So who's Chuck?" Pierre asked, and if he wasn't so cute, John might have to smack him.

"Justin," John said. "Mademoiselle's brother. Call him Justin."

"Why?" Pierre said. "How many brothers does she have?"

"Why?" John smiled. "You have something against big families?"

Pierre folded his arms, a sight almost as comical as his fight with the word *Chuck*. "You are as disrespectful of the Holy Man as his son. A simple question that is all. Pierre is confused. One man, so many different names."

"You're not confused. Calling Justin Chuck is no different than Dieter calling you the Holy Man. Same person, different name."

"Are you telling me the truth?"

"Well, I either am or I'm telling you what I want you to believe is the truth," John agreed. "Your turn to talk to me about bruises."

"Bruises?" Pierre wrinkled his nose.

"Fading ones," John nodded, and so maybe it wasn't a safer subject. "Fading ones, nineteen year old girls, and male whores." And, yes, possibly the gist of what he was saying got a little lost in the attempted translation from English to French. "I was eavesdropping," he explained. "You know, spying until Cassandra caught on and I had to move on to something else."

"All right so you were spying," Pierre said. "This is news?"

"No more than you are to me," John smiled.

"Wrong," Pierre corrected. "Pierre does not spy, he pays attention."

"And the difference is?" John wondered.

"The difference is," Pierre assured, "I am not going to tell mon capitaine anything about soldiers, though it is you who tells my son about these men. How is it you know anything about this? These brothers of Mademoiselle, *Chuck* and Michael?"

"Well ..." John said, thinking carefully, "not excluding Yale 1926, it's a long story. A small world, but a long story, and I'd really rather hear the one about our aspiring Lothario, because let me tell you something, *stupid*, would not be the word. *If* you follow me?" he looked meaningfully at Pierre from under his arched brow.

"Follow you?" Pierre said. "I am not following you anywhere. I can't even understand you. Speak French."

"I'm trying," John assured. "Learn English."

"No," Pierre said. "No, I do not want to learn English. It is an offensive language mon capitaine says, good for business only and vulgar otherwise."

"OK ... We'll leave that for now and return to the matter at hand. Fine," John nodded, "we'll consider Dieter an accomplished Lothario, not to suggest otherwise, and not to deny him his due. But I don't care how long it's been since it's been aired out, he's to keep it zipped, as in his pants, if he has to nail it down. The heck with Joanna being Chuck's sister, that's Mike's kid."

"Kid?" Pierre said.

"Child," John clarified. "Like yours are to you, and therefore, off limits, because while I might not kill him, I will definitely deck him, as in lay him out flat if I find out he's so much as flicks a lash in Red's direction. But then, like I said, *stupid,* would not be the word."

"Mon capitaine is not stupid," Pierre sniffed.

"I know," John assured. "It's not the word."

"No, the word is dégoûtant," Pierre agreed, "disgusting, which is what you are to even suggest such a thing. What would Diana say if she heard you, eh? Mon capitaine is a lover of women, not children."

"Short," John countered, "does not a child make. And you don't want to know what Diana would say."

"No," Pierre patted his arm. "And don't worry about it. Take mon capitaine to Tunis and Cäcilie and everything will be fine, you will see."

"I believe you mean Gadames," John reflected on the request. "And I don't even want to ask about some Cäcilie."

"And you think mon capitaine is going to get his money how?"

"The company payroll?" John joked. "I don't know. How much money are we talking about? For what? Cooperation from Akach? You ought to be able to fix that."

"Twenty thousand pounds," Pierre assured. "That's a lot of money."

"Yes, it is," John whistled. "Wow. Maybe I do want to ask. For twenty thousand, I'd probably take Dieter to Texas."

"Tunis will be fine," Pierre nodded. "I will keep in mind the price of your soul is so cheap."

"Twenty thousand is not cheap," John assured.

"For a band of Arabian horses?"

"It's still not cheap. He could probably import his own stable for that price tag."

"Oui, possibly," Pierre shrugged, "but this way he doesn't have to."

John laughed. "I noticed you didn't ask what stable?"

"No," Pierre said. "Now you tell me what that witch read in your hand other than death and destruction?"

"Long life, lots of happiness," John shrugged. "The usual spiel. Why?"

"These brothers, of course," Pierre waved. "You have me very worried about this. Are they going to come?"

"Never," John promised. "Nothing to worry about."

"Well, I hope that is true," Pierre said. "Mon capitaine needs someone to help him kill the SS he can trust. Abraham can't do it. Not with that stupid tattoo in the middle of his head. Too recognizable."

"Actually, Abe can't do it, because he won't, so you're stuck trusting me." John lit his cigarette, the wind starting to change and so they were going to have to get going sooner than he wanted. "As far as Abe's tattoo? Too recognizable for whom? Give me a break. Half your buddies out here look like Indians in a B-Western. Abe's just trying to blend in. He gave the war paint a chance, but two hours out on this beach, and he's got more than mascara running down his cheeks—actually," he leaned forward suddenly with a sly, teasing wink. "I think he's allergic, but he's too much of a *guy* to admit it.

"Still," he straightened up in all seriousness. "I think Abe's comfortable with being denied burial in hallowed ground in lieu of finding himself buried out here in the middle of a sand dune. Particularly since," he teased again, "apart from this hair-brained scheme, your Arab pals and us aren't exactly kissing cousins, now, are we? I am all for letting some Tuareg outlaw take the heat for me, or off me, whichever the case may be. No, you name the time and place and I'll be there."

"Thank you," Pierre said, about the only part of John's speech he understood.

"It's OK," John shrugged. "It's the least I can do for Hannah. Anything else?"

"No," Pierre said. "I was just thinking how my son and his wife make a lovely couple."

John snickered. "Yeah, actually, I was thinking that myself. She's got twenty years on him, if she's got a day. Freud would have a field day with the two of them, never mind mon capitaine Heart Throb turning out to be a wolf in sheep's clothing."

"No idea what you are talking about," Pierre shook his head. "None. Mon capitaine, yes, at least I can understand him."

"Well, that's only because somewhere along the line the two of you confused the North African Campaign with the Crusades when men did things like slay dragons and rescue maidens," John stretched, rising to scatter the campfire.

"You think it is acceptable what happened to Mademoiselle?"

"Oh, no," John said. "Definitely not. No more than I think it's acceptable what's probably happened to Hannah. Rape, and a knock on the head, hopefully the extent of it, though I highly doubt it. So, yes, definitely, I think the bastards responsible should be shot and a few other things. That's why I have a nagging concern about Mike and Chuck."

"Oh?" Pierre said.

"Something to do with brothers and sisters?" John hinted. "Never mind kind-hearted strangers?"

"Oh," Pierre frowned.

"You see?" John smiled. "You understand the other side more than you think you do. I mean, come on, if Dieter's seeing red, what do you think her brother's seeing?"

"But mon capitaine is innocent," Pierre protested. "It has nothing to do with him."

"Right," John sighed. "Well, unfortunately mon capitaine is wearing the wrong color uniform and apart from it clashes with his eyes, there aren't too many guys out there willing to check name tags. But, then," he winked again, "methinks that's why he's got you and I doing his dirty work for him. There's a few grey cells under that powder blond head of his firmly working and living in the real world whether he wants to be here or not."

"But you still say this Chuck will not come?"

"I am positive," John assured. "They don't know where this place is, if it even exists, and they will never know or find it. Other than that, Mike's got the bark and bite, yes, but he doesn't have the connections, and Chuck's got the same problem we have with avenging Hannah, bigger priorities. I don't think we'll pull the wool over anyone's eyes. That's a pipe dream. But knowing something's not kosher, and knowing what's not kosher is two different things. The key is not to rub Chuck's face in it. We keep that in mind and we, and le capitaine, might come away scot-free." He eyed the old guy. "I am concerned who might have to work a little harder than the rest of us to keep his head above water is Jean Paul. I don't know what his deal is with Justin, but I do know he's foolish to bank too much on having one. He needs to back away, slowly, but he needs to back away. If Ma hasn't told him that, I'm telling you now. Do not trust Chuck. He's a loner. There are no partners. Chuck is a loner, and he plays hard, mean, and for keeps."

"My son is young," Pierre nodded.

"Yes, he is," John agreed, refraining from saying maybe a little too young, definitely to butt heads with Justin. His mother however was nuts, flat out crazy to order a hit on Justin's men unless she was willing to go the whole nine yards and hit Justin himself. Abe was who surprised him though. Abe couldn't possibly have agreed it was the best idea whether or not he disagreed with this scheme when he found out about it. John was a little anxious himself to get back and find out what the deal was with Reynolds being confirmed, or if Jean Paul was just trying his hand at manipulating his old man instead of it always being the other way around. He smiled with a pat on Pierre's back. "In some ways, he's young. In others, he's the average age of every other Tom, Dick, and Jean Paul out here. Just keep nagging him. He'll be fine. Let's go."

"Is that why my son is sleeping with his mother?"

John laughed. "All men sleep with their mothers, and all women sleep with their fathers—yes, thank you Sigmund Freud," he saluted the master of psychological masturbation. "Obviously you never met my mother or you would have refined your hypothesis."

"No idea what you are saying," Pierre shook his head. "I have no idea."

Chapter Forty-One

Great Atlas Mountains
March 18–25

The door of the adobe hut creaked open on its hinges, the rapid procession of Justin's Field Marshal Jean Paul and his small staff of twin lieutenants descending to meet the giant Reynolds waiting in the barnyard. Jeff ignored the twins, his mouth twisting in a crooked sneer for the dapper Dumont. He had not expected Jean Paul to be African. A head of black curls mismatched with his thin lips and narrow Alpine nose. A different man and Nellie probably would have burst out laughing at the insolence of the three men he could snap in half as easily as he snapped his fingers. He wasn't a different man, he was Nellie, calm and coolly bemused as he was about everything.

"Sit down, sergent," was Jean Paul's only greeting. He said it in English, his accent thick, distinctly French but comprehensible, a fist full of papers in his hand, and sour expression on his face. It was interesting for Jeff to watch Nellie bend to Jean Paul's ego. The little

Algerian emphatic and underscoring how the agreement to meet was not an open forum or invitation to debate. This was Algeria, and in case Mulrooney or Reynolds did not know, Algeria had no obligation to extend itself to any of Justin's men, but instead it had a choice. Here in this particular underground cell, Jean Paul Dumont was the chosen, David to Reynolds's Goliath, and the ancient ones would watch their giant fall again if Reynolds took one more step into Jean Paul's territory unescorted.

Ten minutes of listening to what was largely rhetorical chatter about territory and lines, Jeff felt obligated to propose he had heard enough. He already wanted out of there and back to Cairo for his own reasons, and so if Jean Paul wanted them to leave that was fine with Jeff. A week ago, Jeff briefly thought he had a chance to get out from under the unexpected detour in his plans when ordered out into the field with Nellie. He was wrong. A day after they got into Algeria, a Captain "Frank" of the Black Watch showed up to pick them up and drop them down in the Great Atlas cold with snow two thousand feet up.

Four days on their own until they came upon the first troop of Resistance comprised largely of cereal farmers off the plains, it was doubtful to Jeff if they shared a brain among them the size of Nellie's. He would have turned his gun on them, but Nellie stopped him. A response Jeff would have thought was uncharacteristic, but Nellie seemed fine with their leisurely pace. Even when they finally navigated their way to Jean Paul's nest two days ahead of the original schedule, only to sit there and wait for Jean Paul to show up on time for an appointment he could not have known he was slated to have.

Jeff's head cocked, a tell he could not keep in check despite his resume of personalities and identities. Jean Paul Dumont black or white, Jeff was looking squarely in the face of Charles' vital Algerian connection. Where he hadn't before, Jeff now knew who Dumont was, what he looked like, where he was, and how to get there whether it was 'headquarters' or just some convenient corner. It was information Jeff could use, information he could sell, and unfortunately his contacts were in Cairo, not here.

"This is rubbish," Jeff interrupted Jean Paul's prattle, picked up his rucksack and marched like the prissy little prick he sounded for the door.

"Excuse me, Lieutenant," Jean Paul interrupted himself mid-sentence. "I haven't quite finished with the rubbish."

John Paul watched the lieutenant throw the rucksack down and turn to challenge Reynolds: "It isn't?"

What would Reynolds say? The lieutenant's arrogance and his dismissal of Jean Paul supported the accusation of Justin doing just that: dismissing the French and crossing a line. Jean Paul did not know Jeff Mulrooney. He had heard of him naturally, but only vaguely, the same as he heard of most of Justin's field specialists. This Mulrooney, who was reportedly new to Justin's outfit, was also a little different than the usual rough crowd that seemed to surround Justin. He looked like an officer, polished and inexperienced in the field, pale against the robust tans around him, his skin reddened by the Atlas wind. What was his point though, his purpose, role, particular skill? Justin was a man of precision. Discounting the basics of survival ability, a reasonable degree of strength and intelligence, Justin's men were distinctly singularly focused, possessing a clear and honed skill. There were no Jacks-of-all-Trades, but masters only. Two masters together were powerful, three formidable. One on his own, a mission. A specific mission.

There were two masters standing there. Reynolds and this new one Mulrooney, not O'Brannigan as Abraham had theorized. Who was Mulrooney? What was he, his contribution to Reynolds, Justin's blood hound? It wasn't diplomacy despite the lieutenant bars. The rude and arrogant Mulrooney could almost be said to be a message from Justin how he was not in a diplomatic mood. Still Mulrooney had to have an actual reason for being there, other than it was likely he could read, to where Reynolds reportedly could not.

Language. Jean Paul hit upon the answer, grabbed a pencil and scribbled it down, passing it to his Lieutenant Pierre Forget with a sharp silent nod issuing the order to spread the word. They had an interpreter in their midst. Justin's interest in the rumors of depots had become focused and he was determined to hunt them down. Reynolds there to track and intimidate, Mulrooney to listen and understand.

Reynolds did not answer Jeff and that had the lieutenant rolling his eyes and sitting down on his rucksack with a huff in a display of unschooled temper and frustration. Jean Paul smiled because if the spoiled officer was frustrated now, just wait.

"I would have to say, no," Jean Paul offered as answer for Reynolds's silence as Jeff glanced at the message Jean Paul handed off to one of the twin lieutenants who immediately left. "It would seem your sergent Reynolds is in agreement not only with me, but also with your commander Justin who likewise apparently does not believe any of this is rubbish ...

"It is all right, Lieutenant," he assured as Jeff opened his mouth, "regardless, I do agree the reports of transfer stations are dubious."

"Depots," Jeff snapped. And the reports were hardly dubious, they were fact. Jeff knew it for a fact. Two convoys had slipped in and out unnoticed through the tight lines of French control. Dumont was lying to cover his arse to his superior English constituents who were hardly superior to Jeff. He wanted to tell Dumont that, how much he knew, see his face when he told him. Jeff controlled himself however and didn't. The French bastard's market worth was higher in business connected to Charles, than out of business, the connection severed by Charles.

"They would have to be transfer stations, Lieutenant, or they would still be there now," Jean Paul replied.

"Call them what you want to," Jeff assured. "I believe you'll find Squadron Leader Charles is much more interested in where they came from and went. Sergent Reynolds and I were in the foothills for four days, and you're right, there isn't anything there—now," he stressed. "With little supporting evidence anything has been moved in or out of the area, which there would have to be, certainly for something as substantial as a convoy."

"And what does that tell you, Lieutenant?" Jean Paul asked.

"It tells me," Jeff stood up, "if the reports got the coordinates wrong, you are choosing to overlook the fact Sergent Reynolds was personally at the second site."

"And sergent Reynolds, as with all English, is infallible," Jean Paul waved. "I have that as well. So where's the argument?" he asked. "You have your stated position, I have mine. As far as authority to be here, you have no authority to be here. Until England invades Algeria and I am given orders by General de Gaulle to obey without question, you come to me and you ask—which you did," he granted diplomatically, "a little late if you were in the foothills for four days, but you are here now, and now we will work it out together."

"Mighty big desert out there," Nellie spoke up, apparently adding his support.

"Yes, sergent," Jean Paul nodded. "You're in the mountains, right now, but I understand what you mean. It is a very big territory. The coordinates could have easily been wrong."

Nellie frowned, his eyes shifting to Jeff. "Johnnie just put his words in Nellie's mouth?"

"Yes," Jeff assured.

"No," Jean Paul corrected, "I did not say you did not see what you saw, sergent. I said where you thought they were, is in question."

"Charlie wants to know where they went," Nellie said simply.

"Yes," Jean Paul said. "And determining where they were—or you were—is the best way to help with that—unless you were in the foothills for some other reason?" he confirmed with Jeff.

"No," Jeff said smartly in time with Nellie who assured, "Aye."

"I'm sorry, but which is it, sergent?" Jean Paul said as Jeff looked at Nellie and Nellie straightened up from leaning back against a goat cart, smiling with his half-ass easy smile.

"Mighty big desert out there," Nellie replied. "Charlie has the idea even you superior French rats could stand a hand or two in looking for a lost little lady."

The lure of reclaiming the invaluable link to the scientist was incapable of being overshadowed by anything, and was the principal reason Jeff wanted to be in Cairo, despite the unanticipated opportunity of meeting Dumont. To hear Nellie suddenly speak however of something Jeff had presumed to be lost in Charles's extensive archives for no less than a month, Jeff was thunderstruck. His Mulrooney mask ripped away, face redden, and dumbfounded if anyone happened to be looking at him. They weren't. Jean Paul Dumont and Sergent Reynolds were focused on each other, the remaining Lieutenant Louis Forget simply silent.

"Got the wire, didn't you, boy?" Nellie continued with his half-ass easy smile. "Asked about it even."

"Sergent ..." Jean Paul shook his head. "I think something has been confused ..."

"And Charlie's inclined to agree with you," Nellie assured. "A month out, could be anywhere."

"No little lady!" Jean Paul snapped, had wandered from Egypt willingly or otherwise onto this side of the line. And there was a line. Jean Paul clearly defined the line a few moments ago. Reynolds had a short memory.

No, Nellie did not. Ol' Nellie just had a hard time swallowing how two munitions depots and now a little lady were bound to be found anywhere other than the land of Monsieur Dumont.

"Boy?" Nellie smiled, waiting for an answer he wasn't going to get, not one he liked.

"Sergent, this is absurd ..." Jean Paul's waving hand much more emphatic the second time. "Absurd!" he insisted. It was also too bad if Reynolds doubted the power the petite Dumont wielded, because unless Nellie and this Lieutenant Jeff Mulrooney were prepared to go to war with a thousand Frenchmen strong, like it or not, they were going to have to forego their independent ways.

"That sound like a threat to you, boy?" Nellie looked over at Jeff eyeing Jean Paul as if Jeff was trying to decide that himself.

"Yes, it does, Nel," Jeff smiled. "Yes, it does."

"And it is!" Jean Paul clarified for the two of them. If Reynolds and Jeff were serious about wasting their time looking for Madame Lee, depots, or anything else, then they were going to have to click their heels and fall in step with Jean Paul's troop of sewer rats for however long it took the saga to end. Mighty immense was the sea called the Sahara, Reynolds was right about that.

"Madame Lee," Jean Paul said one too many times, but he did not realize it, "could be anywhere. Benghazi. Tripoli. Tobruk. Morocco, Casablanca, still in Egypt," he waved. "She is not on the continent, she is under it. She is dead." Though for Justin, Jean Paul would extend the few men he could afford to try and lay matters to rest.

"So, which is it?" the knuckles of Jean Paul's tiny black fists pressed down on the wood of the door he used for a desk. "Do you wish to ring Justin and tell him you are leaving? Or do you wish to ask his permission to stay? I would calculate your agenda is going to take you a lot longer than *four* days."

Neither of them answered, and Jean Paul checked his watch. It was one o'clock in the morning, Algerian time, March 18th.

"Fine," Jean Paul said. "Then you leave with the sun—five hours—to meet your chauffeur Frank and get out of here. You don't like it, too bad. Justin doesn't like it, tell him to come here and complain to me himself. The choice isn't his, or yours, it is mine." He stalked out with a bark for Louis to follow.

"You about ready there, boy?" Nellie hitched his pants again, checking with Jeff.

Jeff was silent, quiet for a moment, thinking, studying the space Jean Paul had occupied, running the scene back over in his head. Jean Paul was angry about the pursuit of the depots, wanting them out of there. He exploded when suddenly hit with the story of some girl, emphatic but as suddenly changing his tune, inviting them to stay. Jean Paul thought they were idiots. Charles arrogant, Nellie a dunderheaded arsehole. Nellie was right about the depots, so was Charles. Jean Paul knew it. Could he also possibly know something about the girl? Charles apparently believed or knew the girl had been brought west. Tunis or Tripoli, yes. But, Algeria?

"Oh, I'm ready, Nel," Jeff assured. "I am ready." He raised his foot, shoving the door off its stone foundation, an old soiled and stagnant well. The door fell over onto the dirt floor with the thud of a coffin lid.

Nellie chuckled. "What you do that for, Holly? Think someone was hiding under there?"

"Felt like it," Jeff shrugged, snatched up his rucksack and followed Nellie out. They did not go far.

An hour later Jeff was freezing, sitting in the jeep watching Nellie who found this a perfect opportunity to polish and clean his gun by the light of the stars as he sat there on the ground.

"Nel," he complained, "I don't think Jean Paul meant we had to wait out here for dawn."

"Cold are you?" Nellie chuckled. "Put one of those blankets on. What do you think they're there for?"

Jeff would put all of them on if they would help in his attempt to convince Nellie he was not the man for this and needed to return to Cairo. As it was, Jeff did wrap himself tighter in the blanket he was wearing. "It's not that, Nel," he assured. "Quite honestly, I'm not the sort to sit quiet for this. Bit surprised I have to say that you are."

"Not sure what you mean. Nellie thinks it was fine of Johnnie to come all the way from wherever he was to meet with us himself."

"Took his bloody time about it, didn't he?" Jeff accused.

"Did he?" Nellie finished his gun, putting it away, the wood of a matchstick dangling from his mouth as he looked around their surroundings that was nothing but pine trees. Big ones. Evergreens.

Proud and congested. "Never know this place was here at all," he nodded, "big as it is. Go right past it on the road not too far away and never know unless Nellie was looking."

"So?" Jeff said.

Nellie smiled, still smiled since he hadn't yet stopped smiling. "Well, now, I guess Johnnie coming when he did couldn't be helped. Busy, like he said, very busy. Got those whores of his and his men. The lot of them working like dogs."

"Right," Jeff said. "Which explains why two depots disappeared under their nose—and what about this other business, Nel?" he insisted. "What you were talking about, some girl. Quick to brush that off too, yes, he was quick."

"Noticed that, did you?" Nellie nodded.

"Hard not to," Jeff grumbled. "Acting like we were fools—spoke to you, Nel like you were a fool."

"Nellie's no fool," Nellie assured. "Johnnie's stomach went cold; Nellie could feel it. Wanted to run."

"Did he?" Jeff said.

"You didn't sense that?"

"How do I know," Jeff dismissed. "Not even sure what you were talking about, Nel, myself. Jean Paul might not have been sure himself. That could be what you sensed."

"No, he's sure," Nellie nodded. "He's sure."

"Of what?" Jeff asked. "I don't suppose you mind telling me what you and Jean Paul are so sure about. I mean, I'm only out here with you, Nel—freezing to death as it is," he complained again, wrapping himself tighter. "But why concern yourself with me."

"You'll be fine," Nellie promised.

"No, I won't. I'm not going to be able to do this, Nel, I'm telling you now. It'll be the death of me—damn near dead already—me," he assured. "Me. I'm damn near dead, not some damn girl, dead a year or so, or whatever the devil it was you were saying."

"Month, boy, month. Not a year, a month."

"Close enough," Jeff nodded. "Jean Paul thought we were idiots. I'm telling you that's what you sensed. Didn't have the faintest idea what you were talking about, no more than I do."

"Save he's lying, Were right there in the wire Hank sent."

"What was, Nel?" Jeff asked. "What was in the wire? For that matter, what wire? Hank sent a wire about some dead girl? Why?"

"Charlie," Nellie assured. "Charlie's sister."

She was who? "What?" Jeff said.

"And she's dead," Nellie said. "Charlie's looking for those who killed her. Never find them," he stretched. "But Nellie can't blame him for wanting to look—what?" he chuckled as Jeff threw his blanket off, sitting up straight. "Johnnie's lying, boy. Telling you now. His stomach went cold."

"What do you mean what?" Jeff said. "Nel, we've got to go back to Cairo. We've got to go back and help Charlie—are you sure that's Charlie's sister who's dead?"

"Nellie would think Charlie would be sure, boy, even if Nellie had no idea."

"No idea of what, Nel?" Jeff pressed. "No idea Charlie had a sister?"

"No," Nellie shook his head. "Had no idea."

Well, that was probably because Charles didn't have a sister. He was just trying to be clever. "Nel," Jeff said, "don't take this wrong, but some girl, any girl, even if she were Charlie's sister, what would that have to do with Jean Paul?"

"Don't know that one," Nellie agreed. "Frank said to mention it to Johnnie and see what he says—and he lied, boy, he lied."

"I know," Jeff said, "his stomach went cold."

"It did," Nellie assured.

No, it did not. Jean Paul had looked at Nel like he was crazy, and with that Jeff agreed. "Nel ..." he said.

"Where you want to go now, boy?" he chuckled. "Want to get moving about the depots, want to go back to Cairo—"

"I do, Nel," Jeff said. "I want to go back to Cairo. I'm not going to be able to help out here about the depots, but maybe there's something I can do in Cairo to help Charlie about his sister—did they find her, Nel?" he asked. "You're not saying they found her, are you?"

"Don't believe they have found her anywhere."

"Oh," Jeff said. He scoffed. "Well, you know what Jean Paul's going to do don't you? He's going to dig up some old cow bones and present them to you as Charlie's sister to satisfy you."

"Johnnie can do what he does but Nellie isn't leaving," Nellie assured.

"Lead you astray, Nel," Jeff promised, "that's what Jean's going to do. You know, Nel," he said, thinking about it. "This could be a ruse, Charlie putting his sister in Jean Paul's face. Get him all upset and wondering about something that doesn't mean anything to him. Get him running around making sure there's nothing out there that could possibly link his lot to Charlie's sister, forgetting all about covering himself where he might want and need to. The depots, Nel."

"It could be," Nellie agreed.

"But why would Charlie do that?" Jeff asked. "Get Jean Paul in a dither about something that can't have anything to do with him?"

Nellie frowned finding that a little complicated.

"Never mind," Jeff said. "Just thinking out loud. I mean, clearly Charlie thinks there's something wrong about Jean Paul's story with the depots or we wouldn't be out here, Nel."

"I saw the depot, boy," Nellie reminded.

Yes. Jean Paul was careless, letting them slip by, and so Jean Paul lied, was lying. Jeff went over that again in his mind. One depot, ten depots did not mean they had anything to do with Weiheber and his fixation on complexes. The girl however could have nothing to do with Jean Paul. Charles planted that seed deliberately to create a blind, turn attention away from Cairo. Jeff had to get back to Cairo.

"I remember the story, Nel," he settled uncomfortably in the backseat to get a few hours' sleep. "Now that you mention it. That happened when I came in. Some fellows found a convoy ... out on the Siwa, I believe it was. Been attacked by Arabs. Really cut them up, mutilated them like Arabs do. Thought they were Yanks, though, Nel," he said, "not us. Could have sworn they were Yanks like the one who came in the day we left. The one who hounded Bobby until Bobby locked him in a room? What was his name? Sullivan?"

"You mean the Doc?" Nellie frowned and Jeff almost had to stuff his fist in his mouth not to yell out.

"Doc?" he yawned. "That wasn't a doctor. You must be talking about someone else."

"Wouldn't know," Nellie said. "Only one fellow came for Charlie when Nellie was there. Aye," he chuckled, "remember Bobby locking him in a room. Wasn't anything special, you're right about that. Charlie didn't even want to see him, didn't even care. I remember though, Doc Michael, that's what he said. Like it should mean something to Nellie, which it did not."

"We should go back to Cairo, Nel," Jeff muttered dreamily before he fell asleep. "The depots are gone, if they were ever there at all, which I like you, believe they were. But they're gone, Nel, so what's the point of all of this? Should grab Jean Paul and haul his arse back with us to Cairo to tell Charlie exactly what he wants to know. Not going to get anything done playing Jean Paul's game that we are definitely not going to do."

"You're exactly right about that, boy," Nellie agreed, and with surprising grace and speed for such an enormous man he was up, had his gun, slipping behind the wheel and slamming the accelerator down.

"Nel!" Jeff flew off the backseat, hit the floor and righted himself screaming, "What the hell, you goddamn fool!"

"Put that rifle of yours to work, boy," Nellie answered, "and keep them back."

Chapter Forty-Two

"Well, at least we are not the only ones who make mistakes," Jean Paul sputtered as he stalked away, trepidation in the eyes and quick steps of Louis following him. "Abraham is wrong in his guessing games—does that look like O'Brannigan with Reynolds?" he turned on Louis.

"Oh, no, mon caporal!" Louis agreed, the child-like innocence in his voice bringing Jean Paul up short. Louis did not know Reynolds or O'Brannigan and he probably did not remember Abraham being there, if he remembered who Abraham was without prompting.

"Thank you," Jean Paul smiled and Louis beamed. "I knew I could rely on you. This is why I deal in facts. Only facts. Mulrooney is not death by a bullet. He is death by someone's loose mouth. Some idiot farmer or some child on the street—he is an interpreter," he clarified for Louis who had no idea what he was talking about and had not read the note passed from Jean Paul to Pierre Forget—who was now back, standing there waiting his turn, waiting to report. Jean Paul turned around. "Done?" he asked.

"Oui," Forget handed him the dispatch he had issued. "I sent out his name, his description, what else can we do?"

"We can keep them close, control them, and shut them down," Jean Paul assured. "But, yes, you're right, beyond that there is not too much we can do. We speak French, we speak Arabic, the people are not going to stop speaking, and when they do speak we can ask they think before they speak, and hope for the best." He nodded, making a few notes on the transmission. "They say they were in the foothills for four days—were you there for that? Hear them say that? I'm sorry, I don't remember. What do you think?"

"No, I had left," Forget said, but he thought about it now that he knew, calculating the time line from the point of Justin's broadcast.

If Charles waited a couple days before issuing the broadcast to give them a cushion of time … I don't know," he said. "The lieutenant would be more sunburned if he were out in the desert for any length of time, not only from the wind. He is very light. They flew them into the Atlas. The Black Watch as usual."

"Louis?" Jean Paul asked, handing Forget the dispatch with his notes.

"I agree," Louis nodded.

"So do I," Jean Paul assured. "And of course flying them in, they could have been in the foothills longer than four days." He thought about that.

"Longer than four days we definitely would have heard something," Forget offered to Jean Paul thinking.

"Two days and I would have hoped we heard something, which we did not," Jean Paul criticized. "But, no, that's not it. I just don't like him. The Lieutenant," he said. There was no reason for anyone to like Reynolds, and no one did. But there was also something about Mulrooney Jean Paul did not like. "I don't trust him. A guess? Yes, I know," he nodded at Louis. "I sound like Cassandra when we should only be dealing in facts."

"The girl is a fact," Louis hesitated.

"Girl?" Forget frowned.

"Yes. They mentioned Justin's broadcast," Jean Paul explained. "Very good, Louis. Madame Lee. Reynolds did—did you notice his face?" he asked Louis. "Mulrooney's? I don't think he knew what Reynolds was talking about."

"But that is serious," Forget said.

"No, it is a ruse," Jean Paul shook his head.

"All right …" Forget said uncertain, and unconvinced.

"I did not say the girl was a ruse," Jean Paul assured, "I know she is real. But this … connecting or somehow fitting her into here? Vichy? No. If I believe Cassie, and I do believe her, no. Whatever Justin is saying or doing, it is a ruse for some reason. I do not know why and I am concerned, like Cassie, it is the depots, yes. Justin using this girl as his excuse to be here."

"She is not here," Louis shook his head.

"No," Jean Paul agreed. "Louis, you are right about that."

The fact she would be there a week from now, two weeks? Knowing his father it could be tomorrow. But it was still a future fact not yet happened, and wouldn't Justin be in for a shock when it did happen. A comeuppance. So much for his being so clever. Touché.

Jean Paul stopped gloating to focus, yes, on facts. He had not yet told Forget of his meeting with his father, he probably would. Louis was a lot more questionable. Claude, he would definitely tell when he got the chance.

"Another thing," Jean Paul said, "I don't care what anyone says, or who says it. In case you people have not yet realized, it is not we who need Justin, it is Justin who needs us."

"Very true," Louis nodded.

"Yes, it is."

Jean Paul headed for his plane. Up ahead he could see Cassandra moving in from the shadows to join him, but not this time, he was going to have to tell her. Louis's smile faded to anxiety as Jean Paul turned away and Louis turned to his twin, seeking confirmation in Pierre's strength.

"Don't worry about it," Forget offered.

"No, don't," Jean Paul called back to them. "Let's go."

"Oui, mon caporal."

They fell in step behind him, Louis explaining, "I was thinking of the Jew."

"Cassie," Jean Paul corrected. "Now, you sound like Cassandra."

"Sorry," Louis apologized.

Forget wasn't sorry. "Are you sure about this, mon caporal?" he asked. "About the Jewess? It would explain the English attention very well."

"The girl Cassie's revenge for Palestine?" Jean Paul said. "Yes, it would be, but it did not happen. Cassie is not involved in this any more than we are except on the peripheral."

"You are sure," Forget reiterated.

"Yes," Jean Paul nodded, "Yes, I am sure, and I do not want to hear anything more about it. I realize Cassie knows these people—claims to know these people and perhaps she does. True or false including how well, I have no idea, and do not care. This is not our issue, it is Justin's issue."

"But they are here," Forget said. "Reynolds."

"He is here about the depots," Jean Paul maintained. "And we will shut him down—you understand that?" he confirmed. "Shut him down, not kill him. That is another thing I do not want to hear anything about for any reason—including le Metapel," he advised the two of them. "Not his worries, his glory, or his name, ever again. Once we are through with this, we are also through with him. Do you understand?"

"Oui, mon caporal." Louis nodded and Forget was silent because it was a ridiculous and impossible request. The people knew of le Metapel, thousands of them, in the huts, and in the desert, and even in the city. Jean Paul was probably exaggerating his father's abilities, though he doubted it.

"All right," Jean Paul said. "Louis, let's go."

"Me?" Louis said.

"Yes, you, Come along. We'll talk," Jean Paul promised Pierre.

"Oui," Forget agreed.

"No," Jean Paul turned to Cassandra last to deny her. "Not this time. You and Forget find the rest of them—including O'Brannigan. Unless Abraham is completely wrong, and I don't think he is, there are others out there, probably not far." He swung up into the plane with a sigh for Louis standing there like a lost little child. "Get aboard, Louis."

"Oui," Louis got aboard as requested. "Where to?" he asked curiously as Pierre turned the propeller with a wave everything felt fine, and the engine caught quickly, sounding good.

"Gadames," Jean Paul nodded.

"Gadames?" Louis repeated.

"Yes," Jean Paul said. "Gadames, Gadames, Gadames," he waved back to Forget who stepped out of the way. "I said once it is over, it is over. It is just not over."

"Oui," that to Louis made sense.

"Yet," Jean Paul twisted the radio on, not wanting to listen to anything except the static over the headset. "Claude?"

"Here, mon caporal," his sergent answered immediately.

"Cassandra and Forget will keep an eye on the English, you, too. I do not trust ..." He shook his head. "I do not trust that skinny one not only Reynolds. I do not like him. See what you can find out about him if you have to break his wrist to do it."

"*Oui, mon caporal,*" Claude promised. "*Vive la France.*"

"Yes, of course," Jean Paul muttered. "Vive la France, Claude," he agreed, and signed off, the plane puncturing the night sky.

His experience dating to the first war and the Foreign Legion Claude L'Heureaux stood taller than the average Frenchman, strong from his outdoor life like a fisherman or sailor, grey salting the black wave of his hair. "He is young," Claude smiled at the radio operator Janelle, a pretty girl with a round face, large breasts and good hips. "Don't worry."

"Oui," she said, not worried about anything.

"See if you can find their signal," Claude turned to climb down from the radio tower. "Since Reynolds is here perhaps they will be broadcasting and we will get lucky and be able to track them ..."

"Sergent!" she called to stop him.

"Yes?" Claude looked up.

"Perhaps since Reynolds is here we should broadcast to them, eh?" she smiled over the rail. "And track when they answer?"

"Good idea. Try both. One should work."

"But what should I say?" she asked. "I cannot tell them where he is. To tell on him, is to tell on us, yes?" she laughed.

"No," Claude agreed, "that we cannot do ... I know," he said. "Announce we are executing them at dawn—for extreme ugliness. This way the others out there will know it is true that we have them." He jumped the last few rungs to the ground and took off to meet Forget when he drove in, since Louis had apparently accompanied Jean Paul.

"Use your radio!" she shouted after him. "What do you think you have it for? To you, too," she returned his wave and went back inside to transcribe her message. "Very ugly," she wrote. "*Very* ugly," stabbing a period on the end, satisfied. Ten minutes into her dissertation on the ugly English, however she interrupted her sultry pillow talk for a special announcement of particular importance.

"Sacré!" she gasped, the sounds of a rifle firing an alarm preceded shouts as Yvette and her squad briefly appeared below before vanishing into the trees. Ten minutes after that Cassandra nearly scared her out of her life as she clamored up the ladder like a monkey.

"Nel!" Jeff shouted as Nellie took off. "Nel, what the hell!"

"Get on it quick, lad," Nellie advised, barreling through the evergreens to hit a dead end, swing the jeep around and head off, trying again.

"Nel!" Jeff bounced as the jeep bounced unable to maintain position.

"Said you wanted to leave, boy," Nellie said. "Pay attention in case someone tries to stop us."

"I know what I said!" Jeff swung the gun strap over his shoulder and under his arm to keep his rifle from flying out of his hands, bracing himself as best as he could, watching the back, sides, poised to drop whoever of Jean Paul's group showed up to stop them. "Gosh, though, Nel, when you decide, you decide."

"Aye, well, you were the one complaining about wasting time," Nellie reminded.

"True," Jeff shrugged, his eyes darting and alert as the jeep bounced and bumped violently over ruts and rocks, smashing its way through the brush, the windscreen long shattered in a spray of glass and leaves. "I think we took them by complete surprise. I don't see anyone."

"They're there," Nellie promised. "If only for show, they're out there."

"Show?" Jeff said a moment before the first bullet missed them, overshooting their heads by a mile.

"Show," Nellie assured, highly doubting even a French boy had aim as bad as that.

"My turn!" Jeff laughed and took aim, hitting the lead jeep dead center through the driver's windscreen, sending the jeep careening half way up a tree before it flipped.

"Whoops," Jeff bit his lip. "I hit the radiator, Nel, and he lost it."

"That's all right," Nellie was not disturbed, and certainly not about to slow down and turn around to look. "They'll either stop or keep coming."

"They stopped," Jeff nodded as the two remaining jeeps of the pack reigned up short to check for survivors, leaving them home free. "Guess they weren't really serious about stopping us, you're right."

"That's exactly right," Nellie assured. "Exactly." And in an hour, they were miles away, soon to be farther.

"Mon Lieutenant!" A panic-stricken Claude rushed to pull Forget from the wreckage.

"No, I'm fine! I'm fine!" Forget reassured, angrily dusting himself off with a useless check of his driver who was dead instantly as the bullet sliced through his throat, severing his spinal cord and taking his head almost off his shoulders as it exploded out the back of his neck. "Son of a bitch!" He spit after Nellie and Jeff and their long-gone jeep. "Go after them, go!" he ordered the others. "And give me that damn radio!" he snatched the walkie-talkie from Claude, shouting for Jacques to answer him, the heat of Cassandra's breath searing.

"It's all right!" Claude held her back. "We'll get them!"

No, she would get them, personally, already spinning her jeep around heading back to the radio tower.

"Go help her," Forget flicked his head at Claude. "I'll be right there." He wiped the sweat from his cheek with the sleeve of his jacket. It was blood. Either his or his dead driver's.

Cassandra pushed Janelle out of the way, her fist slamming down on the console. "Infidels!" she screamed over the radio. "Surrender or die!" She turned on Janelle, shoving the receiver toward her. "Find them!"

"Oui, Madame!" she nodded, Cassandra stalking back and forth behind her until she did.

Claude and Forget joined them shortly to smoke cigarettes and foul the air with their tension, and about two hours after that, "I have something!" Janelle announced.

Claude threw his cigarette away to listen intently at the faint though shrill almost whistle-like sound. "Homing device," he determined.

"Yes, I think so," Forget agreed.

"Like they use when they drop supplies," Claude explained to Cassandra.

She understood. "What is their range?"

"A couple of kilometers perhaps," Claude said. "Like a small radio. With a mast like ours though, seventy feet?" he looked up. "It's difficult to tell. They could be twenty kilometers from here. They operate on a battery however, so there isn't much time—Cassandra!" he barked as she jumped for the ladder.

"Find Reynolds," she ordered, "I'll find the others. And you," she included Forget in afterthought, "stay here."

"It isn't intentional," Claude mentioned when she left. She dismissed them all really, not only Pierre.

Pierre Forget did not care if it was. He was not his brother Louis. Louis had been firm, like Jean Paul, less impatient at times, stronger at others. Pierre was plodding, careful. In twenty years, the two of them would have been Claude, simply not as tall.

"Let her have her fun," Forget shrugged. "Find Reynolds, yes," he agreed. "And stay with him," he ordered, as Claude's smile touched his eyes. The big Irishman was stupid if he thought he had gotten away so easily for no reason. There was a reason. The same reason Claude had been kept in the background out of sight. "I'll let you know when, and I'll let you know where."

"Gadames," Janelle shrugged.

Forget rolled his eyes at her and the idea. "We'll see. *Le Metapel* has either been out of touch or is interested in losing more than one supporter."

He startled her. "Lost one?" she echoed. "Who? Us?"

"Yes," Forget stared at the radio, bitterly.

"No!" she howled. "What about Yvette?"

"Yvette is fine. Reach mon caporal," he instructed. "Tell him he has a reason to defy Justin now. Henri is dead, murdered by sergent Reynolds and that other one, the Lieutenant."

"I hate them!" she screamed. "I do. I do not like them!"

The British? Who did? But Forget was less interested in revenge than in corralling them before anyone else was hurt. "And keep monitoring for any signal. Reynolds has a radio. We did not take it. I do not want excuses, I want results."

"Kill them!" she supported Cassandra as he left, jumping, as they all did, the last few rungs to the ground. "If you don't, I will!"

No. Forget could not support that. They were killing no one. Though it was tempting, he had to admit. Very.

"What?" Jeff gaped at Nellie talking about Jeff taking the high road for Pete while Nel took the low in search of the depots.

"Now, boy," Nellie said, because who had the say was Nellie who could move faster without Jeff with his limited experience. "Said yourself, boy, how you're not able to do this, and you're right," he chuckled. "Don't know what Charlie was thinking about sending you. Too far into the interior, and you will die. Probably within days as that sun eats you alive.

"Faster to where, Nel?" Jeff insisted. "Faster to where?"

"The depots, boy," he assured.

"But they're gone!"

"They're not gone, boy," Nellie promised. "The first one might be, but the one Nellie saw wasn't gone until he went to see if it were gone, and from there where it went. So, gone, no, moved, aye. Moved and out there somewhere, boy, you're right about that," Nellie patted Jeff on the back, pressing one of Charlie's little trinkets into his hand.

"What the hell am I supposed to do with this?" Jeff stared at the homing device no bigger than a matchbox camera, his eye on the radio, practically salivating as he threw the toy away, which was foolish because now he was going to have to wander around looking for it. "I want that radio, Nel," he assured, so much so he even drew his knife. "Swear to God, Nel, I'll cut you if I have to, you can't leave me here like this."

"Boy," Nellie chuckled, "now you'll be fine, boy. Nellie needs his radio—"

"They'll kill me!" Jeff hissed.

"Frankie'll hear you and be sending out his own beacon for Pete long before that," Nellie promised. "Just stay where you are—"

"Where the hell would I be going?" Jeff snapped. "I'm serious, Nel, I'll kill you unless you take me with you. Blow your damn head off. They'll never know it was me, they'll think it was Jean Paul—I'll tell them, Nel," he swore, "it was Jean Paul."

Nellie chuckled. "Just find that device as Charlie calls it and stay right here as I told you. My girl might be good at finding things, but she ain't that good. Will need a little help.

"Girl?" Jeff said. "What *girl?* There's no place for Frankie to land here." He raised his rifle. "I'm getting in the jeep, Nel, or you're dying right here. Which is it?"

Nellie chuckled, one hand on the gearshift, and the other on the wheel, "Boy, you know you should have been an actor, Joey's right about that." He took off. And in one scenario Jeff killed him, killed Nel where he sat. In another, the rifle jammed as he pressed the trigger.

"What the?" Jeff stared at the rifle. "Nel!" he screamed, "Nel!" pressing and pressing, but Nellie was long gone. "Son of a bitch!" Jeff started to run after him but stopped, darting back to kick and dig through the underbrush looking for the homing device. He found it, tossed his rifle to side and snatched up the machine gun Nel had been kind enough to leave him, and sat there wondering what the hell to do now.

March 20, 1942

Two days after Nellie dropped Jeff off on the corner of the Sahara and the Tell, he joined up with a renegade group of French Resistance much more to his liking. There were a couple of interesting things happening in Algeria other than the usual. Last month some locals claimed a row of trucks got stuck, bogged down in the mud after a heavy rain, until they also disappeared for nowhere, much like the depots had. Nellie liked the report even though the details placed the convoy much farther west than the areas of the two lost depots.

Other than that item, Nellie's gathered general information including the occasional mention of Jean Paul's name. Charlie's Johnnie apparently got around a lot, reportedly seen in several different places over quite a stretch of land recently. Nellie couldn't help wondering if Jean Paul continued to check into the reported depots including where they went despite his formal rejection of the claims.

"Well, now," Nellie whistled. That was interesting. Jean Paul was definitely not keeping Charlie advised of his actions. The question was why? The only answer Nellie could see was that Jean Paul was covering up for the sloppiness of his troops. Most importantly there was the possibility Jean Paul was holding back actual information on the depots from Charlie, whether or not Jean Paul continued to investigate on his own.

That was not good. That was not how Charlie operated. Nellie was distracted from the issue of Jean Paul's actions however when the first of several rumors started coming around about a new installation.

March 25, 1942

A week to the day Nellie abandoned Jeff, Nellie and his group of French first heard of the British supply convoy managing to make port at Malta despite heavy Italian opposition. Nellie was less interested in the convoy story than the reported ripple effect through the resistance pocketing Vichy and Italian-German controlled western Libya and the upsurge in organized or disorganized attacks ranging from rock throwing to attempted sabotage on known or suspected enemy installations or sympathizers.

Pretty routine, a report of a suspected encampment on Libya's inland shore, seventy miles south of the coastline stood out. Deep, it was several hundred miles the wrong direction Nellie was planning on going, and several hundred miles back the way he had just been. Nellie waited a couple of days to see what else trickled in before he flipped a coin to decide if he should continue forward or start to backtrack. It came up heads and so he started back slowly at first to take another look over the whole area.

And then faster when rumors grew with the reported sighting identified as everything from a field hospital, set up by one of those international health organizations worried about protecting civilians in a world where no one gave a damn, to troop movement, to a new fixed installation to assist in stabilizing the area. Still ...

"Strange though, isn't it?" Nellie mentioned the idea of a field hospital being particularly interesting in an area that might be unstable but hadn't seen a real fight in a long time. He wondered aloud if perhaps it might be a third depot. The collection of rough riders Nellie rode agreed with him the reporting was interesting and possibly suspicious as he suggested, especially the one calling himself

Claude who was as mean as Nellie.

"One way to find out," Claude's French sneer matched Nellie's Irish one.

"Aye," Nellie smiled. "So there is." They headed north.

Chapter Forty-Three

The Tell
March 18

"Um ..." Joe scribbled out Frank's coded message banging in over the wireless about an hour before dawn.

"Um ..." Joe said, the part about Frankie dogging the Sarge's footsteps making sense, it was just the part about the Sarge going AWOL that did not. "Pete!" he gave a holler half-tempted to dial the Maj's hot line without waiting the two seconds it took for Pete to come on the run, clutching his gun, hanging onto his hat, and trying to button his trousers. He gave up on the hat.

"Wow, sorry about that," Joe apologized, not for the scare, but for the unfortunate head of hair Pete hid under his beret where the sun did not reach. The mop more grey than red or blond, Joe would have thought as old as Pete was, he'd at least have the decency to be bald.

"Oh, now, you better not be sorry, lad," Pete suggested, after seeing the place was not on fire, which you never would have known it wasn't, not by the sound of Joe's war whoop. "What anything better be is damn good. There's a few things Nature does not appreciate being interrupted—I've got it, I've got it," he took the lad's piece of paper before Joe crawled out of his skin, jiggling around like a nervous cat. "Better stop listening to that whore, lad, I'm telling you. She's doing things to you whether you want her to or not ..." he nodded as he read what did not surprise him whether it surprised anyone else or not.

"Nah, it's from Frank," Joe assured.

"Aye. I think I know that by the tenor," Pete suggested with a shout for Julia to put in an appearance.

"But, yeah, you're right," Joe said, "I mean about the whore, she's been on."

"Well, I'm sure she is on, lad," Pete agreed. "On something that would kill any ordinary man. I still ain't giving her my surrender for her fanny. Ain't no one's fanny worth that, I don't care if I can stick my whole head in it and half of yours, and I would suggest you decline as well. Lass!" he finished with a second call for Julia to get her sassy tail ready to take a ride and pick up Nellie's Holly before the French mistook him for breakfast. "Where the devil is that girl?"

"Um ..." Joe looked around before settling back on Pete.

"Pussy," Pete nodded. "Fanny is pussy where I come from. Don't get any funny ideas about Peter. Hank's the one on watch with Fred, not me."

"Yeah, I know," Joe said to both actually, "talking about Jewels. She's not with you?"

"Went for a slash, lad," Pete assured. "Like I said there's a few things Nature does not appreciate being interrupted, when you get to be my age that one's close to the top of the list."

"What's first?" Julia strolled up, still in her long-legged skivvies with her hair pulled back in a ponytail adding to her look of wanton innocence.

"Why, good morning Mary Sunshine," Pete passed her Frank's love letter. "It's not the Armistice."

"Stupid Mick," she agreed upon reading about Nellie's transgression, borrowing Pete's lighter and setting the note ablaze.

"Oh, well now, and that's coming from a lass who has her own mind," Pete smiled "And here I thought you of all people would understand."

"What? That Nel's as crazy as you are?" she tossed him his lighter. "Anyone call the guv? Tell him he's at war with Algeria?"

"Now, that's a little premature," Pete believed. "Sure Nel thinks he has his reasons." Not that he'd ever met a Mick who needed one of those she was right about that. "What about it, lad?" he petitioned Joe. "Think you can raise Cairo without setting your little Christine afire?"

"Um ..." Joe glanced over at his radio waiting patiently as always for him to warm her tubes. "Yeah, sure. Want a voice?"

"A voice?" Pete said, not that he didn't believe him. "Now, I'll take a voice, lad, you know that. Typing is not exactly my forte."

"Speak Swahili?" Joe grinned.

"Swahili?" Pete paused. "No, I don't speak any damn Swahili. What the devil do I look like to you?"

"Well, then, I guess you're just going to have to hunt and peck like the rest of us," Joe tossed Pete the code book he kept stuffed halfway down his pants, figuring if he was going be searched he might as well enjoy it, and meandered toward Christine.

"Samahani," Julia tapped on his shoulder.

"Um ..." Joe wet his kisser, with a quick check around of the peripherals and any sign of Fred. "Is that Swahili?"

"Um, hm," she nodded.

"Yeah, well ..." Joe cleared his throat, "I still think we better type it rather than try anything cute. The Maj's already going to be pissed over Nel, let's not put him through the roof."

"Right," Pete shooed her away. "Think of his heart, lass, and mine while you're at it, and go get that engine of yours ready to take Joseph out of here before Nellie's little Nancy has the French up his arse—or his battery runs down," he shrugged at Joe. "One or the other. I'm not fussy. How you doing?"

"Meaning?" Joe said.

"Meaning the damn radio. She feel like being compliant?"

"Just waiting for you," Joe nodded.

"All right," Pete thumbed through the pages, looking for this week's special. "Get out of here like I said. Ol' Nellie's right about one thing, not going to a win a war sitting on your damn bum, no, you aren't—yo, Joseph!" he let out a sudden whoop of his own.

"Yeah?" Joe turned around.

"You like that boy," Pete reminded. "You like that bitch of Nellie's as if he were your own best mate. And that goes double for you," he assured Jewels when she emerged dressed for work, and only because he knew her better. "I don't care if the two of you vomit, you don't vomit in front of him."

"Um ... OK, got it," Joe pulled the ponytail out of Julia's hair as he sauntered away, snapping the band playfully until she had enough and took it away from him.

"Aye, now all I got to do is figure out what to do with you should that proverbial shite hit the fan," Pete agreed as he stepped over Michael rather than on him. The Doc laying there in wait of news, bad or worse, sunbathing in his suit that was little more than a rag by this time with his hat over his face.

"I'll make it easy for you," Michael moved the hat, but that was all.

"And I think you better mean that," Pete nodded, pausing to call Hank and Fred in from the cold with the notice Nellie had decided to go it alone. "I really think you better or else find yourself in a world of trouble."

"That much I got," Michael sat up.

"Oh, you do, do you?" Pete said.

"Yeah," Michael said. "Can't figure though how you could be with Justin all this time and not speak Swahili."

Pete smiled. "Aye, well, I do speak it, Doc, actually. Or I did. I just can't spell it."

Michael nodded. "You're right, though. First time, but you are. He is a bitch, as in a fag."

"Aye, well, you're one up on me there, Doc," Pete admitted, "because I sure as hell have no idea what you are talking about, but that's all right. Give me ten minutes and we'll start over. I want to finish making Justin's day before someone decides to make mine," which Pete had a feeling was going to happen, as he had a feeling he knew what Justin was going to say, and damn if he wasn't right about both.

Cairo
March 18

"*Any particular idea about the Doc*?" Bobby added Pete's particular flavor back into the cryptic message, still longer than most, as he read it to Justin sitting at his desk.

"*Should I wait for theirs to come to me or should I send mine home to you*?" Bobby tried to speed it up and gave up. "He wants to know what to do, lad."

"Yes, well," Justin lit his pipe, rising for his maps. "Sure Nel's not lost his mind."

"Right," Bobby scoffed. "Sure of that myself including that's not the answer Pete wants."

"Yes, well," Justin said, "as far as Pete, for that matter Michael, Mike has a knack for stepping in shit, as he calls it," though usually somewhat more colorfully, "without help, and apart from how it sound's, it's supposed to be good luck."

"Right," Bobby abstained from expressing any opinion.

"Trusting Mike's instincts for survival will stop him even if his mouth can't ..." Justin eyed his maps, Frank's latest report put Nellie about two hours south of his last position where he had deposited Jeff. That was interesting. Suggesting either Nel had decided to go on a rampage, which Justin continued to believe he had not, or that Nel was onto something that took him away from chasing his depot—possibly taking him deep, or he never would have left Jeff. Justin flipped a coin and for some reason it came up tails. He thought about that.

"Aye, well, you know him better than I do," Bobby's voice penetrated, talking about Mike.

So Justin did. He knew them all, some longer than others, but all of them long enough. "It's a red herring," Justin decided, knowing he was right when he said it.

"Beg your pardon?" Bobby blinked. "Where'd you come up with that?"

"Nel," Justin assured. "Nel didn't get his information from nowhere. It had to be Jean Paul. They're trying to separate them. Nel from the others. Tell Frank to stay close, and Pete to surrender."

"Oh, well, now," Bobby said, "I don't have to tell you Pete's not going to think too highly of that."

"Yes, well, I don't care what Pete wants, now do I?" Justin replied. "He's to lay down with the rest of them, and I mean all of them," he pointed his pipe just in case Bobby had decided to go deaf on him. "Hank, Fred, Joe, and Julia." Michael, of course, went without saying.

"Julia?" Bobby didn't give two shits about Michael, said as much in the way he said it, not who or what he was, and what it could mean if they lost sight of him.

"She'll be fine," Justin sat down.

"Now, you don't know that," Bobby argued for argument's sake. "Either way you can't ask her to walk in there when you, yourself, have no idea what to expect especially since you just got through saying it's Jean Paul, trying to lead Nel astray."

"It's a whore house," Justin picked up a report he didn't have the slightest bit of interest in, only an interest in shutting Bobby out. "If they bring them into Jean Paul's place, that's what it is. A brothel.

"As far as Jean Paul," he said as Bobby snatched the report out of his hand, "I said I don't want them separated that's what I said. Whether or not Jean Paul's decided to sell his soul—"

"He's covering his damn arse, is what he's doing," Bobby snapped. "You know that as well as I do. He's no damn partisan any more than the heat's gotten to Nel."

"Quite," Justin said. "And since Jean Paul isn't a partisan, I rather doubt if he'll try anything as flagrant as *shooting them at dawn for being ugly.*" He quoted Frank's transmission of the French bulletin. "It's a wild goose chase. Jean Paul probably thinks Nel will tire, which he won't. But he'll also be out of Jean Paul's hair for a while so Jean Paul wins in the end, either way."

He took the report back from Bobby that he had, yes, at least a passing interest in as it mentioned not only Hitler's announcement of the planned annihilation of Russia, but also the convoy operation scheduled to supply Malta which it would be a minor miracle unto itself if it managed to make port. But that was someone else's headache not Justin's. His was not losing Michael to enemy or friendly fire. He tossed the report aside with the rest of them. "Now that that's settled ..."

"Ain't nothing settled, lad," Bobby assured.

With Jean Paul? No. But Justin would take care of that, or Nellie would. He'd give Nel a few days to see what he came up with, if he came up with anything, and take it from there. As far as anything else? "Yes, it is settled. If Pete says no, tell him I say yes, that ought to take care of that."

"Take care of nothing," Bobby turned on his fat, "if anything happens to my girl Jewels, you better make yourself scarce because he'll hunt you for the rest of your life, however short that might be."

"She's Fred's lass," Justin picked up his breakfast tea piss warm and probably poisoned if it came from where he suspected it came from, which it did. He drank it anyway, just to prove he had the nerve even if Cain didn't.

"Him, too," Bobby assured, "and me. We'll all hunt you down."

"Yes, well, if that's all," Justin nodded.

"No, it isn't all," Bobby slammed the door behind him. "All is telling you to go to hell and meaning it, which I do. I do," he assured Laura there early for some reason, begging her pardon for his language.

"Oh, no, that's quite all right," she promised, probably just glad to find someone who agreed with her.

"Aye, well, there's probably more than one who does," Bobby grumbled as he waddled away. "Pete undoubtedly among them."

The Tell
March 18
"Right," Pete crumbled Justin's order to surrender. "Now how did I guess that?"

"Makes sense," Hank shrugged, his RAF eagle getting in the way of his balls.

"Does it now?" Pete ogled Michael looking back at him, the Doc trying to look especially mean, and they'd see how long that would last, now, wouldn't they? That they would.

"What?" Pete's chin jutted forward. "Aye, you, I'm talking to you, Doc. And does that make sense to you? It doesn't to me. Makes more sense to kill you and then we wouldn't have to worry about anything, no, that we wouldn't," he assured and Fred laughed like he thought Pete was teasing.

"I wouldn't," Pete advised and Fred's expression changed from mirth to uncertainty. "No, that I wouldn't," Pete took off his beret, wiping his forehead. Getting hot as hell already and it wasn't but six in the morning, or maybe it was him.

"Right," Pete set his beret back in place. "Well, I guess someone better tell Joseph." He took the duty on himself, finding the frequency and blowing a sharp whistle into the microphone when Joe didn't answer the first time.

"Joe!" Pete insisted. "Joseph, don't make me stay on here any longer than I have to—is this damn thing even working?" he gave Christine a whack.

"It was ..." Hank offered his expertise, and that was neither the question nor the answer. Pete knew it *was* working. The issue was whether or not it was working now?

"No, I got it, I got it," he waved Hank's hands away, like they say too many cooks. "Can't be there yet—how long has it been?"

"An hour?" Fred shrugged at Hank. "About that."

Since Pete had first sent his signal out to Justin. And about an hour since Nel decided life wasn't complete without that Victoria Cross.

"That's two hours, lads," Pete nodded, "two. Not one, two. That damn homing device is rundown by now. They've lost Jeffrey. They're looking for him. Joseph!" he tried raising Joe one more time with exactly the same result.

"Right," Pete sighed, making the decision that had in actuality already been made. "All right, Joseph," his finger clicked the button, "if you can hear this, the word is surrender. Got that? Surrender. The man says lay down, put her down, whichever is more applicable to your current situation. Down, and on your belly. We'll see you when we get there, on our way soon ourselves." He signed off, staying there crouched for a moment before he yanked the cord out and sent the microphone flying, his foot through Christine's front-piece as he rose, hard enough to bust more than a couple of things and shove her back a few feet, and then he lit a cigarette, his hand stuffed under Hank's nose. "Give me those damn cards of yours," he requested. Hank did and Pete nodded again with a suggestion someone should see to Christine before Joe had a canary wondering what happened to her as he sat down to lay out the cards like they were the tarot, capable of divination.

"One question," Michael said.

"Right, I know," Pete assured, "you want to know when. Shouldn't be long. An hour, maybe. Couple or three. Your Justin's probably got a damn sign out there pointing which way to make sure Peter does what he is told. It's all right, though," he nodded, "yes, it is. Peter knows who the boss is, the same as the boss knows someone frying his daddy is the least of his concerns should things not go the way I think they should."

"He's worried about Jewels," Hank explained to Fred in, offside Pete's arse.

"I heard that," Pete assured, "and no I'm not. That's Fred's concern. My concern is you," he looked at Michael before he looked back at his deck. "And since we're waiting, while we are, I don't suppose any of those many talents of yours include French? Because mine sure do not. No, that's for you rich boys and otherwise intelligent folks."

"French," Michael said.

"French," Pete assured. "They're on their way. Sure you must have figured that much out, if not, you will."

And he heard the click of the gun in his ear before he felt the barrel touch his cheek, saw the boot come down in front of his face, its toe touching his spread of cards before he saw anything else. But that was because he did not look up with Hank's muttered alert, "Here they come," after what had to be at least two hours more spent waiting, probably closer to the four it seemed, and the forever it was either way.

"Aye," Pete said in answer to Hank, the Doc somewhat more demonstrative in his reaction to being descended upon by a rampaging group of vineyard workers and whores, up on his feet before anyone arrived to help him, barking, "What the fuck?" and yelling, "Watch the suit! OK? Watch the frigging suit!" to the assortment of arms groping him for weapons of which he had about six if you counted his mouth.

"Damn, Doc," Fred whistled as he was pulled away, his arms and rifle passively up over his head until someone took the rifle, his arms yanked rudely down, a club cut from a decent sized branch of wood slammed under them, across his back, and lashed up tight just like in the old days.

Hank was a little slower, though also up on his feet on his own, not even bothering with his gun just leaving it laying there. Pete continued not to look up, his eyes on the boot coming down in front of him, and then the bend of a knee, and then her face, which was ugly, yes, it was. Ugly as sin, as they say, like some old middle-aged witch with her sunken hollow face and snarl that didn't do anything to help her and probably wouldn't make much of a difference if she had washed before she came.

"That's right," Pete said, not in reply to her hiss and twisting neck spitting, *O'Brannigan*! "Get it out of mine, because if you think I won't smash something as ugly as that, you got another think coming—tell her," Pete petitioned Michael. "Tell her what Peter said."

Pete wrenched his arm away from the hand trying to pull him up. The Doc already having attempted something similar with the wild right cross he threw, and was currently in the process of being subdued. Pete's face briefly registered a consideration of respect for Michael who apparently wasn't all bark, but had a little bite in him.

"Fuck you!" Michael screamed, not at Pete, but in general, his too-tight shirt splitting and spitting its buttons under the force of his arms being pinned back, the pole rammed into place, exposing his muscles and muff of chest hair. Pete shrugged, having seen better chests and having seen worse as he was hauled to his feet whether or not he wished to be, the bitch following, rising as he rose, keeping him in her sights. "Then I'll tell her," he said, and did. Grabbed that snarling face of hers, clenching it in his hand, and she should consider herself damn lucky he didn't snap her neck as he sent her sailing backwards into the dirt and the arms of her constituents where she belonged.

"Now, get it out of mine!" Pete said as those who didn't jump for her, jumped for him, and they could kiss his arse along with her.

"Jesus Christ," Hank muttered with a bark, "Pete!"

"What?" Pete snapped. "I don't give a damn what she's got between her legs, damned if I do. Thing's rotten as she is. Tell her that for me, too," he nodded at Michael staring at him, which he should be the last one to talk about someone putting up a fight after being explicitly told to go quietly by the boss man. "Go on, tell her, can smell her damn stink from here."

Michael told her, in French, and it was time for a few others to stare at Pete. Which, they could also stare all they wanted to, the same as her.

"Thank you!" Pete said.

"Don't mention it," Michael assured.

"Aye, don't," Hank advised when Pete joined him on the back of a jeep, tossed there like the rest of them however mad that might make him, which it did. No angrier than he already was, which if he were any angrier he'd be foaming, having one of those flashbacks to some past unpleasant experience that had happened to him like Fred was trying to con himself into believing as an explanation for Pete's ungentlemanly behavior. "He told her you want to sleep with her."

"Did he now?" Pete said.

"Yeah!" Michael said. "And do something about it, you fucking fruitcake, I don't think so. Knock it the fuck off!"

"Piss on her, more like it," Pete assured. "But that's all right, yes, it is," he nodded around, "tell her that myself and then do what the hell I like—which is piss on you!" his boot hit the side of the jeep.

"Ay!" Michael said. "What'd I just say?"

"Don't give a damn what you said," Pete assured. "Ain't nobody here give a damn what you say. Go on, ask them. Ask them!" his boot hit the jeep again. "You know that is what is the matter with you Italians, yes, it is ..."

Pierre Forget had a headache by the time they got back to camp, and he already had a blistering one before he left.

Chapter Forty-Four

"*Joseph*!" Pete insisted over Julia's headset, but if he said anything else, it was drowned out by Joe screaming "Pull up! Pull up!" as Julia pulled off a hairpin turn through a narrow aisle of cypress and firs, the tip of the left wing nearly perpendicular to the ground, before she headed *up*! *Up*! the tires ripping through the top branches of an unforgiving wall of green, showering the forest floor in a burst of confetti and bending one of the struts.

"Damn!" Julia punched the dash. "You all right?"

"Fine," Joe nodded. "I'm fine." Maybe a little surprised to find he was still inside the plane, but other than that he was fine. "You?"

"Bent the damn wheels," she cursed. "Could have been worse, could have lost the tail—" she stiffened, clapping her hand to the side of her head, listening to the headset.

"What?" Joe said.

"It's Pete," she nodded.

"Huh?"

"Pete!" she shouted, not at him, just over the noise.

Which it was really noisy, loud, between the plane, and the bullets, and, "Yeah, OK," Joe nodded. "Tell him to hang on."

Julia stared at him.

"Or whatever," Joe waved, realizing how stupid that must have sounded. "He'll call back. Yeah, he'll call back," he nodded, "sure everything's fine. If not, heck, Pete could take care of himself, yeah, he could. Probably even better than me—think you can bring her around again?" he asked, managing all of that including the question before he took a breath.

"Oh, I can take her around until tomorrow," Julia promised. "Just when she's down, she's staying down unless I have a lot of room to run."

"Yeah, well, I can probably handle thirty feet to the ground," Joe nodded, grabbing his walkie-talkie and clipping the harness in place in preparation of a do or die leap. "It's the getting back up that might be a little tricky, even with a line."

"Back up to the down part," Julia requested. "There's thirty of them if there's one."

"Nah," Joe took a quick peek. "Just seems like that."

Even still, he traded in his rifle for one heck of a beautiful cannon, six-hundred seventy-five rounds per minute, and just over thirty-two pounds of power, sheer Herculean in size. And it would take a guy the size of Hercules to keep it under control without the tripod. Good thing Joe was close. If not, he was all he had, and that was close enough. "Ready?"

"Do I have a choice?" Julia stared from his fistful of Yankee ingenuity to him. "You can't be serious, they're our fellows."

"Um, no, actually, they're Jean Paul's," Joe said as she sat there giving him this doe-eyed look kind of like a deer. "And they're not exactly pulling punches with us. Look, what do you want me to do?" he asked. "I've got to get Jeff out of there."

"Oh, yeah?" she countered. "Says who?"

"Says the man with the eagle on his jacket," Joe nodded. "You know, the governor, the Maj, the boss—what?" he barked at the radio and Pete yammering something Joe couldn't quite catch, other than Pete's determination. "What he say?"

"Surrender," Julia nodded.

"Huh?" Joe said.

"Surrender!" she barked, for the same reason as before, the noise. "We're under orders to surrender."

"Surrender?" Joe said. "What's he fucking nuts? There's fifty of them out there. They're firing ... I don't know, they're firing at us, all right? We're under fire. You know, trying to shoot us down?" he snapped at the radio, not that he was snapping at Pete, but in the heat of the moment that kind of thing. "Huh?" he said to Julia sitting there nodding her head.

"From the Maj," she said. "You know, the guv? The boss?"

"Um ..." Joe said, probably making one of the fastest decisions in his life. "Yeah, OK," he pulled on his gloves, ":that's next on the list, this is first. Ready?" he asked, because he was, not bothering with the stirrup or the clip for his harness, his hand poised to hit the release and swing. "Bring her in low and slow as you can ... yeah, low and slow as you can ... I'll swing until I'm sure ... yeah," he nodded, talking it through for himself, "definitely. That'll work ..."

"Joe, you'll be killed!" Julia insisted.

"Don't forget to come back," Joe said. "Once around and then back. I'll have him by then."

"Now, you should know by now," she purred, "I'll always come back for you."

"Yeah, huh?" Joe grinned. "Hold you to that."

So would she, but it didn't matter because it was never going to work. "Joe, it's not a helicopter, it's a plane!"

"Huh?" Joe said.

"Never mind," Julia shook her head. "Hang on, Tarzan," she agreed and cut her ground speed as low as she dared, maybe thirty mph, coming in for a pass forty feet off pay dirt at best, and too slow and low to stall her. Joe hit the release and he was on his way, swinging through the air at probably twice that speed. The line caught a tree though, his trapeze act abruptly halted as he was stopped, yanked back and slammed into the branches but otherwise OK as he let go of the line fast before it tore his arm off. He dropped from there and even with his boots, he felt his ankle twist under him when he hit the ground some three stories down.

"Gotta do better than that, sweetheart!" he thought he'd let her know.

Tell Julia about it, already up and heading out of there, the look on Jeff's face priceless as Joe squared off against Frenchie firing his machine like a madman as he aimed for the trees, screaming, "Stay! Stay!" to Jeff frozen in place.

"The harness!" Joe nodded, trying to wiggle out of it and keep a handle on things at the same time.

"What?" Jeff snapped awake.

"Harness!" Joe nodded. "Put it on. There's a clip, about six feet up the line. She'll reel you in. It's like a pulley, you know, a winch—oh, shit!" he heard what could only be the plane, and Jeff stared up at the swinging vine coming toward them like a steel whip.

"Um …" Joe said. "Yeah, OK, she's right, this is never going to work." And he was on the walkie-talkie screaming for her to pull up before she caught herself on something and hit the dirt like a kite.

"*Not on your life*!" Julia screamed back.

"Will you just shut up and frigging listen?" Joe insisted. "Huh?" he said to Jeff pounding on his shoulder.

"A clearing!" Jeff repeated, shouting kind of loud himself, no idea why, he just was. "There's a clearing. She'll see it."

"*Joe*!" Jewels demanded in his hand.

"He's saying there's a clearing," Joe answered. "We'll meet you. Be there!" He clicked off and Julia pulled up, heading for a new home field. "Hope you can run."

"What?" Jeff blinked.

"Run!" Joe said, and they were up and going. Fifteen minutes later Julia spotted them coming out of the trees on her second swing around and she came in for a dive like the ground wasn't even there. Wheels almost touching as she flew past them like a speeding train, she pulled up briefly and then let her hit, the carriage bending now for sure if it wasn't bent before, bouncing and skidding along the dirt as Joe caught up to her, wrestling to clip his line to ensure he stayed attached, screaming for Jeff to get the lead out as Julia fought to keep the plane from flipping upside down. A moment later they were home free, Joe catching Jeff by the arm and then his belt yanking him inside as they streaked up into the wide blue yonder under a hail of crazed gunfire.

"Yes!" Joe cheered, his fist in the air.

"Quite," Jeff agreed, shaking with the same excitement, Julia in the meantime just doing the easy job of flying the plane. "Can't 'bout believe it. Thought I'd do better if I stuck with the trees—big mistake."

"Nah, I would have done the same thing myself," Joe assured. "Hell, ask Jewels, there must be a hundred of them out there—true or false?" he clapped Julia on the shoulder, ruffling her hair. "Great job, honey, honest. Helluva stunt."

"Thanks," she smiled with a nod back toward Jeff. "He's right. I think we got here just in time."

Jeff would go along with that. "I owe you one," he assured Joe.

"And I'll take it," Joe accepted. "Might have to."

"Count on it," Jeff said, and whether he meant it or not, it didn't change anything. He took the last of his deep breaths to collect himself, reemerge as himself, and that included surprise at seeing Joe. "How'd you come by being here?"

"Yeah, well, you know the usual," Joe said.

"Quite. Well, I guess I haven't been here long enough to know the usual yet," Jeff apologized.

"Yeah," Joe agreed. "Who has?"

"True," Jeff said and smiled. "Think we passed?"

"Um, passed?" Joe said.

"Probation," Jeff nodded and started to laugh.

"Yeah, huh?" Joe grinned, and started to laugh, also. The two of them like two idiots lying there laughing on the floor of the airplane until Joe collected himself, deciding it was enough before the guy, got the wrong idea or something.

"OK, that's enough," Joe sat up, popped up actually as best as he could. Hunched over and looking at a wicked backache by the time he crawled out of there because the plane might be big, in that it could hold four people, two in the seats, and two more on the floor, but, no, it wasn't as if you could walk around.

"What's wrong?" Jeff frowned, wondering, what? If he did something wrong?

"Nah, it's nothing, not you, anyway," Joe flashed his grin. "We've got orders to surrender."

"Surrender?" Jeff repeated.

"Yeah, isn't that the killer?" Joe took the seat next to Jewels, which was probably kind of rude, but, hey, it wasn't like he turned his back on the guy, no, he faced him. "Just got through with this and now we've got to hang our heads."

"I don't understand," Jeff said.

"Who does?" Joe shrugged. "Pete radioed and said those were the orders. To lie down. I don't know," he grinned at Julia. "Maybe they were looking to avoid this?"

"Maybe," she said.

"Yeah, well, too late," Joe laughed. "But that's OK, probably not a bad idea to set the record straight, especially since we've no choice."

“No, we don’t,” Julia agreed.

“I’m warming up to the idea,” Joe nodded. “I’m not warm yet, but I’m getting there. Any idea where you were?” he dug around overhead in the map rack because that’s where the maps were supposed to be. He found them. One anyway. “Think you can figure it out? I mean where you were? And if you don’t already know?”

“Right. Well, I know it was a resort ...” Jeff reached for the map.

“A resort, huh?” Joe said. “That doesn’t sound too bad.”

“Depends on what you call bad,” Jeff said, along with about six other things, a whole paragraph in all, but Joe couldn’t hear him. He could just about hear himself. Christ, the engine was loud.

“Is that normal?” Joe asked Julia, but only because he didn’t remember it being that loud coming out.

“It’s normal,” she nodded.

“Oh,” Joe said. “OK, well,” he shrugged, “you still got to put her down whether she’s working or not, and so I guess ...” he borrowed the map back from Jeff to give it the once over before he stuffed it in his hip pocket. “Yeah, go back, that’s probably the easiest.”

“Back?” Julia looked at him. “Back to Pete, you mean?”

“Um ... no,” Joe said, but only because that was kind of out of the way, and considering the orders to surrender? He opted for the classic double back. “Back to where we were. You said you needed room, well, you’ve got a whole field.”

“I don’t need that much room,” she turned away from him.

Joe grinned. “Maybe not, but we’re still going back.”

“No, we’re not,” she assured.

“Yeah, we are,” he said. “Look, they’re gone, OK? Trust me, we’re gone, they’re gone, that’s how it works.”

“Oh, it does?” Julia said.

“Who the hell knows,” Joe shrugged. “We’ll find out when we get there.”

The French were gone whether or not they would be back once they figured out Jeff and company had returned. The plane hit the ground with a bang, the bent strut folding like it was a matchstick, permanently attached, as in married to the underbelly, through its skin and halfway through the floor. The Maj’s Applecore had seen its day. Put on one hell of a show and died with its boots on.

Great Atlas Mountains
March 18
"Lousy piece of crap," Julia cursed after she checked out the damage that would take more than a welder with a pocket full of rivets to repair.

"Yeah, well, we'll just leave it here," Joe said, practical if he wasn't a realist.

"Here?" Julia said. "They'll pick her clean."

"You mean strip it?" Joe said, digging around for what they wanted to take with them, which after the guns and the water and the map wasn't much.

"Nice piece," Jeff complimented, this coming from a guy carrying a frigging Bren, as Joe slung the strap of his automatic rifle over his shoulder and the ammunition belt for his baby around his neck like a .30 caliber string of beads.

"Yeah, it's a Browning," Joe nodded. "They both are. Little heavy with the tripod, this one," he patted the machine gun, "but it can come in handy." He kept the tripod for the machine gun, but ditched the one for the BAR as something only a sissy would use anyway. "Where's your rifle? Lose it?"

"Yes," Jeff said. "It jammed so I dropped it and grabbed this. Because ... well, honestly, I wouldn't be able to carry both. Should have taken the rifle because I can just about lift this."

"Yeah," Joe wasn't sure how Pete was going to take to him leaving the rifle, but, they'd see. "Well, maybe we can find it. OK? Everybody set? Great." He lit a cigarette, offering Jeff the pack. "Fag? Or, um, cigarette?" he quickly changed it before the guy thought he was insulting him or something. "That's what you guys call them, right?"

"Quite," Jeff said. "Thanks. And, quite," he nodded, "we do. Cigarette, or fag, either will do. Rather like what you fellows call me," he smiled. "Fag, right?"

"Or fairy," Joe shrugged, "queer. It's OK. I'm not prejudiced. To each his own. Know what I mean? Heck, it's a free country, right? When last I looked anyway," he grinned at Julia with a puss on her face a mile long, and so OK, she did not like Jeff right off, probably for the same reason that made everyone else a little uncomfortable.

"Could be a damn military dictatorship by now, who the hell knows." Joe smiled again at Julia worried about the plane falling into the wrong hands. "Say goodbye. Don't worry. They're not going to strip her, trust me they're not. She's fine where she is. Perfect, actually," he nodded around. "Yeah, she is."

"Wouldn't you strip her?" Julia swung her flask over her shoulder like it was a purse, and one she was angry with at that, her rifle she kept handy, just, Joe guessed, in case.

"Well, yeah," Joe said. "But I'm not talking about what I would do. I'm talking about them and they won't. Hell, me ..." he started off walking along the tree line figuring there had to be at least a path around somewhere. "Think the first time I stole a bike I was two ... the first time I got caught I was ten, but by then I had graduated to cars, so, yeah, definitely, I would strip her," he nodded. "Not the whole heap, just, you know the stuff I could sell; so what's this place you and the Sarge were?" he changed the conversation back to Jeff so he wouldn't feel left out. "Something like a governor's palace?"

"Oh, right," Jeff rolled his eyes. "Not quite. Bit of an old run down joint, that's all. Some hut with a barnyard. A few thieves and tarts around. Rather like us," he smiled. "Other than that rather deserted, and, no, come to think of it, I didn't expect that, I guess. Not sure what I expected, other than that wasn't it. But then I also didn't expect Jean Paul to be coloured," he scanned the field, maybe a little nervously as if half-expecting the French to suddenly jump out.

"Yeah," Joe shrugged, watching him, not too closely, just watching. He seemed OK, not like he was going to start crying or anything. The British accent maybe growing a little thicker as he talked. But that was generally normal with most people when they were nervous, and so, yeah, he came across pretty much together, whether or not he actually was, and a lot less fruity than he did back home. Though much of that really was hearsay, Joe having steered pretty much clear of him, where now he was right there walking next to the guy, maybe about a foot apart, and he honestly couldn't tell, he really couldn't. "Yeah, I knew Jean Paul was colored. African, actually, something like half. You didn't know that?"

"No," Jeff shook his head. "No, I did not."

"You?" Joe asked Julia.

"No," she said.

"Yeah, and who cares anyway?" Joe grinned. "I mean, the guy's OK—he's not?" he blinked at Jeff looking back at him, and, yeah, now that Joe was this close to him, if anything about the guy stuck out other than his general lack of size, it was his eyes. His eyes were bright, a real bright blue, maybe a little too bright, almost like he might be on something, or seriously frightened. Yeah, maybe he was just afraid.

"To each his own," Jeff shrugged. "Got this queen for a bitch, you'll see what I mean about her—you sure this is a good idea?"

"Um, you mean this?" Joe gestured around.

"Quite," Jeff said. "I mean this, all of this, the surrender, the guns. Don't get me wrong, I rather like the idea of a well-armed man myself."

"Um ..." Joe said. "Yeah, OK, we'll let that pass. And, no," he admitted. "No, I don't know if it's a good idea. I know we have orders, and I know I don't have a better idea. Why? Do you?"

"No," Jeff sighed. "No, I rather suspect I don't."

"So there's the rub, right?" Joe smiled for real that time, the heck with the falsetto grin starting to make his teeth ache. "I mean we have to surrender to someone, right? Pretty sure Pete meant the French."

"So Pete is here ..." Jeff said, kind of with a tip of his head like he was thinking.

"Oh, yeah," Joe said. "Pete's here. Fred. Hank. The Doc," he said as Jeff stopped thinking to listen. "So, don't sweat it. I mean about finding the place. We'll find it. Heck, it's not like there's a hundred of them out here, or even six. It was a pretty decent size, right? I mean, even if it wasn't *large,* it also wasn't small."

"No, it was reasonable," Jeff imagined from what he had seen. "Wouldn't call it a cottage, more like a hut. Place where maybe the groundskeeper lived. There was a chalet just down from it a piece, but we didn't go there. A rather large one. Looked old and empty, but who knows. Why? You seem to know it?""

"Nah, just from the file," Joe nodded. "So, OK, I think I'm following you. East? West? Any idea which way Nel went when you left? South? You have to have some idea, if only how long it was before he dropped you off?"

"West," Jeff shrugged. "Believe it was west. Nel took a few shortcuts, rather like you, through the trees."

"Caught that, huh?" Joe laughed.

"Rather hard to miss," Jeff assured. "In all it was about an hour, I guess."

"An hour, huh?" Joe considered. "Well, then, it can't be too far—you listening to any of this?" he checked on Julia.

"Heard every word," she assured.

"Good," Joe said, "because aside from a broken back, I'm going to be deaf and hoarse if we keep hanging out together. Man, I can't believe how loud those things are. Like a frigging tin can caught in a wind tunnel. How the hell do you even hear yourself think?"

"Thinking's not the problem," she said.

"No, talking is," Joe assured. "Explains why I'm shouting—am I still shouting?" he checked in with Jeff.

"No really," Jeff said. "Rather suspect I was also, as well."

"Not quite," Joe said. "Actually, I was reading your lips. But now you at least know why I was shouting."

"Figured it out," Jeff promised.

"Yeah, well, let's work on figuring this," Joe suggested. "How far? I mean that resort, honestly, in your best opinion?"

"Oh, right," Jeff said with a glance down for some reason. "That ankle business of yours, noticed that. Bit of a sprain, is it?"

"Huh?" Joe said as Julia paused.

"Ankle?" she said, with a look over him.

"Bent under him when he landed," Jeff nodded. "Never mind you touching down with a bang."

"You noticed that?" Joe said.

"Rather hard to miss," Jeff smiled.

"It was?" Joe looked at Julia, getting all worried now like a girl. Man, she could be a girl when she wanted to be. "Look, knock it off, I'm fine, OK? I'm fine. Yeah, it bent. I felt it bend, and that was the end of it. What, is this some kind of talent of yours?" he asked Jeff. "Or did you just figure, wow, guy jumped out of a plane, had to break something?"

"Talent? No," Jeff said. "Observing, that's all."

"Uh, huh," Joe said. "Yeah, well, that's pretty observant. I mean, guys swinging through the air, bullets flying everywhere, and you notice my ankle twisting like the frigging rudder?"

"Strut," Jeff said.

"Fine," Joe said. "It's fine." He stopped, not to prove it because, yeah, obviously walking would do more to prove it, but to take care of things before he forgot about them. "Let me have it."

"What?" Julia said.

"Your rifle," Joe said. "Let me have it."

"Fine," Julia gave it to him. "You can carry the damn flasks, too."

"No, I ain't carrying anything," Joe assured, "got enough to carry. Just need it for a second ... unless you think it's going to take three-hundred rounds to hit the goddamn gas supply." He took aim and it took one, as in shot, and the plane went off and up like a firecracker, a big one that kept burning.

"OK?" he swung the rifle back to Julia with a grin. "What I said. They're not going to strip her."

"Very funny," she said.

"No wait," Joe stopped her before she ignored him for the next hour or two. "The foot, OK? Check out the foot. It's fine, right? It's not broke, it's not bent, it's ..." he stopped because yeah, he was kind of winging his foot around showing off, like he did with the gun, and something caught his eye. "What's that?" he said.

"What?" Julia said.

"That," Joe assured. "Near the, I don't know what the hell you call it. The sole, near the heel, what's that stuck in the boot? Is that what I think it is?"

"A bullet," Julia nodded, after she looked first, of course. "Quite, it's a bullet. You've a bullet stuck in your foot. It's all right, though."

"Boot," Joe corrected. "Stuck in the boot. And all right compared to what?"

"Well, all right, I suppose to being stuck in your foot," she said, and started to laugh.

"Well, I'm glad you think it's funny."

"No, I don't think it's funny," she shook her head. "I think you're funny. '*Oh, look at the foot. See the foot.*' Quite. I see the foot. See someone damn near shot you in the damn foot. Am I right or wrong?" she asked Jeff.

"Pretty wild," Jeff agreed.

"Looks like a .455," Julia nodded.

"Nah, it's not a .455," Joe assured. "You think someone was out there with a frigging pistol?"

"Well, we'll see," she said, and out came the blade like she was a surgeon or something and he was stupid enough to stand there and let her operate on what would be fifty years from now a DeSapio family heirloom.

"Hey, whoa! Whoa!" Joe danced out of harm's way. "I want that!"

"All right, I'll give it to you," she promised, having more of a personal attachment to his foot than the bullet that almost kissed it.

"No, I mean, I want it just like that," Joe assured. "Leave it alone."

"Leave it alone," Julia considered that. "Joe, there's a bullet in your boot."

"Yeah, I know," Joe said. "And it's staying there. Short for, which would you believe? Someone showing you a boot with a bullet, or someone showing you a boot with a hole and telling you that's where the bullet used to be?"

"Well, there's no saying you couldn't have shot your boot yourself," Julia said, obviously having hung with a pretty strange crowd at some past point in her life.

"No, but you're my witnesses I didn't," Joe said. "So, I'm serious. Put the scalpel away."

"All right," Julia said. "But you're an odd duck, you know that. You really are."

"Yeah, I'm odd," Joe assured. "You get your kicks taking potshots at the laundry, and this one over here's got X-ray eyes."

"Well, I wouldn't go that far," Jeff protested. "I saw you twist your ankle, but I hardly realized you had been shot."

"Which I wasn't," Joe assured, "the boot was. But it's OK," he nodded. "That observant, hell, you ought to be able to find this place with your eyes closed."

"The resort?" Jeff said. "Well, I don't know about with my eyes closed, but, quite, I can find it."

"You can?" Joe said.

"Of course," Jeff laughed. "Never said I couldn't, did I? If you'd not taken the map away I would have showed you then—why did you?" he wondered curiously. "Bit odd, it really was."

It was? "I don't know," Joe shrugged. "Guess I was reading your lips wrong. You seemed to be confused."

"No, I'm not confused," Jeff assured. "May I?"

"Yeah, sure," Joe handed the map over. "Knock your socks off."

"Thank you," Jeff said. "I mean, Nel and I were there. Obviously I know where it is."

"Yeah, OK, obviously," Joe rolled his eyes at Julia. "Was that obvious to you?" Which, apparently it was by the look she gave him. "Yeah, OK," Joe said. "It was obvious to her."

"All without reading my lips," Jeff agreed. "Perhaps I should be amazed."

"Oh, har, har," Joe said. "Look, don't make me have to hit you, OK? I just got through saving your ass. I don't want to have to break it like the rudder."

"Strut," Jeff nodded. "Though, no, I don't know anything about airplanes, other than I agree with you if only because I agree with—Julia, is it?" he smiled at her. "Or Jewels?"

"Either or," she said.

"Well, either or," Jeff agreed, "I agree with you. They would pick her clean, or would have if Joe hadn't blown her sky high. Jean Paul has a plane, at least one. I didn't see it, but I heard it, yes ... so as far as size ..." he scanned the map that didn't tell him much beyond the usual. "Big enough for their purposes, I suppose ..."

Which it was, plenty big enough, and crawling, Joe was talking crawling, with women.

"So who's this Doc?" Jeff asked interested in the moments before they found themselves surrounded. "Don't believe I know him; do I?"

"Just one of the guys," Joe shrugged.

Chapter Forty-Five

Joe wasn't sure what he expected Jean Paul's hangout to be despite Jeff's description of some run-down barn, but it was fair to say he didn't expect the hired help.

"Quite," Jeff nodded in answer to Joe's, "What the?" for the line of well-built killers who seemed to appear from nowhere three hours into their one-hour hike. "Those are Jean Paul's men."

"They aren't men," Julia spoke for Joe.

"Half of them," Jeff shrugged, meaning over-all since none of these were men and there were about thirty of them.

"Well," Julia said to Joe, "at least we found someone to surrender to."

Yeah, Joe believed he noticed, and it was hard to keep the lust off his face. "Damn," he zeroed in on one particularly sexy number with the long naked legs and belt on her shorts cinched tight around her curves, "Pete's going to get a frigging kick out of this."

"Who?" Jeff said.

"Pete," Joe assured.

"Oh, right," Jeff said. "You mentioned something about him being around. I guess I can wait for that," he scoffed, "can't I?"

"Huh?" Joe said after he realized the guy said something.

"I said, I can wait for some ruddy Mick," Jeff nodded.

"I know what you said. And what is it with you? Look, I don't care if you run hot or cold, just pick one and stick with it, and can the rest of the crap, OK? Can it. We're in this together. All of us. In this together, including them."

Jeff eyed him. Joe felt the guy eyeing him before he settled on the tattooed stripes on Joe's upper arm.

"Bit out of line, aren't you, *Private*?" Jeff suggested being he was what? Some kind of lieutenant?

"Um, yeah, maybe," Joe said. "But you're a lot smaller so three guesses who wins?"

"Right," Jeff straightened up, and he kept it pretty much straight after that. "She wants us to give up the guns," he nodded at the number Joe had given the once over and who was now standing smack in front of them with rifle pointed and bayonet fixed. "She's apparently the leader."

"Well, that much I figured out and I can't even read a menu," Joe assured the dreamboat with his smile. "You sure about this, honey? I mean, heck, the two of mine probably weigh more than you do. So what do you say we promise not to use them and that way you're happy, but we're happy, too?"

She was sure. Driving her point home with a prick of her bayonet into the fat of his breast, not hard enough to hurt him, just deep enough to draw blood and Joe was jumping back either way with a startled, "Yo!" in chorus with Julia's, "Joe!"

"No, I'm OK, I'm OK," Joe assured, bleeding but otherwise fine. He eyed the cat.

"Fais-le, *Yankee Doodle,*" she said kind of haltingly.

"Um, Yankee Doodle, huh?" Joe said. "Someone teach you to say that? Because, um ..." he caught Julia's eye. "What?"

"Will you give up the ruddy guns?" she requested exasperated.

"I am," Joe assured, and he was. Both of them, all of them, handed over the whole deal excluding his cigarettes and the map. "Just no more of that, OK?" he scolded the wild one with the hungry claw. "It's not necessary. You following me? Capisce?"

"I don't think she is," Julia said.

"Nah, she's getting it," Joe nodded. "She is." Following his finger as it clicked back and forth in front of her in the international sign for *Naughty, naughty, no, no.* "What?" Joe said as she watched his finger. "Blood? Yeah, blood." There was blood on his finger. "My blood. Could as easily be yours, so cool it, OK? Cool it. We're on the same side."

She licked her lips. Yeah, she did. And while it was kind of sexy, it was also kind of creepy. "Um ..." Joe said. "What's that supposed to do? Scare me? I don't think so. Because let me tell you something, honey, I've seen weird, OK? I've seen weird, and I've been wild."

"Joe ..." Julia said.

"I'm coming," Joe assured, and he was. On the move and being kept in motion and in line by the little jabbing point of her bayonet, not at him, or into him, just kind of at the air. But when she connected again, when she pushed it and caught him again, that time in the shoulder, Joe lost it, almost. Faster maybe even than Pete between the time she hit and he had her by the wrist, and it was her turn to react a little startled, but then what did she think? That he wasn't stronger than her? Like a helluva lot stronger than she was? That those muscles of his were what? For looks?

"Now fucking knock it off," Joe suggested as he held her there in place unless she wanted to go away without her arm. "Next time I won't warn, I'll just do. And not your arm, your neck. Who are you? That fucking nut-jobber on the radio? Is that who you are?"

She spit in his face, dead in his face, and so obviously, she was, though as it turned out, she wasn't. The nut-jobber on the radio looked more like Shirley Temple. This one had the same smoldering style of Julia with a little more fire and a lot more edge. They missed out on the deal of being trussed up to a wooden pole like a Thanksgiving turkey though, and probably not because their group was more compassionate than the ones who had snagged Pete, but probably to do with sheer strength. These were girls, their power in the arsenal they carried, not in the fists they didn't even bother to throw. Even still, they all clearly had their own issues with them. Including Shirley screaming at them like a fish monger's wife about some guy named Henri when they rode in about an hour later to be ordered out of the jeeps they had been ordered into, and led through the jeering crowd, and still Joe did not see a man, not one man among them.

He spotted the chalet, decent enough in size like the rest of the place, set up and back in the pines in what was a gorgeous setting even now. Old and tired as the buildings were, though probably not as old as someone wanted it to appear with the tile roof and big wrap-around porch. Jeff could be right about someone wanting it to look older than it was. Like someone's dead dream, maybe even a hotel, Joe could picture that, back in the 20's when the place was sizzling hot. Not like Cairo that was a urinal and had been for years, dirty and overcrowded, downright filthy like New York on garbage day. Not here though. Here you could breathe the air, clean and fragrant between the cedar and the pine. They locked them up inside a ramshackle old outhouse of some kind complete with a stinking shithole in the middle of it that Pete took a piss in when he finally showed up, mad as nails and stalking back and forth like an angry frantic cat on the verge.

"Whoa!" Joe said too many times for the same day when the door burst open and the rest of their crew tumbled in, Pete and Hank to the floor, Fred and the Doc in a heap up against the wall. "What's with the crucifixion?" he laughed, helping Pete to his feet.

"Just get me the hell out of this thing," Pete suggested, his face red as a beet, and not because he was suffering from some undue strain on his heart from his arms being pinned to his spine. "Because there is a line, that there is." And he drew the line soon as Joe finished picking those knots loose enough for him to wiggle free, grabbed his privates and drew a line of pee about two feet in front of the door before he emptied the rest of his bladder in the stone pool in the middle of the floor. "And that's the damn line! Cross it and you're dead!"

"Think he's serious," Joe grinned at Fred before he turned for Hank.

"Know he's serious," Fred assured with a relieved smile for Julia working to set him free. "Thanks, luv, can take it from here. You all right there yourself, are you?"

"Fine," she said. "Got a cigarette?"

"Pete does," Fred was sure. "Probably the Doc. I'll get you one." He was heading for the Doc anyway to give the thin blond guy (who had to be Jeff he assumed) a hand.

"Thanks," Julia was on her way to Pete, picking up his beret and finding the one or two fags he always kept stashed under the band. One was pretty much beyond hope, but the other she revived, lighting it and passing it on to him.

"Right, thank you," Pete took a healthy drag as if it were laced with something a little more potent than mere tobacco. It wasn't, but he could dream.

"Anytime," Julia shrugged. "Everything else all right?"

"Aye, well that does seem to be the question everyone's asking, now, doesn't it?" Pete looked, not really around and maybe for a moment or two at the pasty-complexioned Jeff, who aside from the height requirement of Justin's, everything else about him still did not make sense. Rather like the Doc who didn't even reach the ruler mark, or whatever it was Justin used to ensure his crew measured up. "Probably most interested in hearing all's well with you. Me, I'm a little mad, that's all. You know how it is."

"I'm fine," Julia assured.

"Right," Pete looked back with a smile. "That I can see, and would be what I wanted to hear. See you managed to get the fellow our boy Justin thought was worth risking your and Joseph's necks for."

"Jeff?" Julia glanced over. "Quite. He's fine, too."

"Right," Pete said. "*Jeff.*" He moved over to introduce himself, check on the Doc while he was at it, clap a little dust off Michael's shoulders, even pat his cheek, and the Doc was mad, he was, quiet at the moment, but still mad.

"It's all right, Doc," Pete cooed, "we'll get you to Gibraltar, dead or alive, we will, count on it." He let the Doc stew about that while he smiled at Jeff who was eyeing Pete's beret with its badge of Irish green.

"Mulrooney," Jeff felt the touch of Pete's eyes. "Lieutenant Jeff Mulrooney. We've met."

"Have," Pete agreed, "and I still don't believe I've ever met a Brit named Mulrooney before you, no more than that little insignia of mine is going to turn itself into the Royal Irish Fusiliers. I don't care how hard you stare at it."

"We'll have to see, won't we? O'Brannigan, is it?" Jeff replied.

"That's right," Pete nodded. "Put the *O* in there, lad. Don't ever forget to and we'll get along fine. You know what a motherfucker is? I mean, apart from the Doc's use of the word that has us all, and everything else a motherfucker, including that piss-pot?" his hand touched Julia's shoulder, but only because her hand touched his. "Sorry about when I came in, luv," he apologized for his unsociable actions that had him urinating on the floor.

"It's all right," she assured.

Pete returned to Jeff. "I mean, do you know?" he asked. "What those coloureds down in Cape Town mean by the use of their word?"

"Sell your brother," Joe nodded, and not because he was taking sides. "Or, yeah, your mother," he grinned. "Heck, even I know that."

"Right," Pete assured Jeff. "So I guess that would make your ol' Nellie a motherfucker not me or mine for leaving you."

"Not necessarily," Jeff replied coolly. "I think you would find quite a few who would disagree with you."

Pete scoffed. "What?" he said to Michael wanting to get in on the conversation, or just have one of his own.

It was the latter. "Gibraltar?" Michael sputtered and Pete sighed.

"You know, Doc," he shook his head, "for a smart man ..."

"I figured it out," Michael cut him off. "I got it." Gibraltar apparently some cover Chuck had come up with for him.

Pete smiled. "Well, now, that's good because if you figured it out you know I am not responsible for this latest delay," he played right along. "I don't care who was or wasn't responsible for the others. So why don't you ask the lieutenant who does know what happened to keep you here longer than your chronicle planned?"

"Happened?" Jeff startled as Michael shot a look at him. "I don't know what you mean, what happened?"

Pierre Forget meant, what happened? That was what he asked when he walked in to introduce himself under protection of a small army, and the tool Pete was quick to grab up was one of the discarded wooden poles. The same as the rest of them did, Joe, Hank, and Fred, leaving Michael the only one of them empty-handed, unless one counted Jewels and Jeff. Pete brandishing the pole like a bat one moment, and slapping it in the open palm of his hand like a copper's baton the next, Pete would, for the rest of his life, carry a baton reminiscent of an oversized Bobby's nightstick. The first whittled from wood, dangling from a cut leather strap on his belt, a scrap of metal nailed around its tip to help drive its point home, quickly painted red to "help hide the blood" as he said. Later covered with leather and weighted with lead, and as quickly replaced by a fiberglass truncheon, as unbreakable and unforgiving as Pete was, as

Justin preferred his army well equipped and modern. Right now though Pete held the prototype of what would become his trademark in his hand, slipping into a relaxed and easy stance with a smiling warning for the well-dressed French lieutenant in uniform who paused, eyeing the line of muscle and men standing in front of him.

"Uh, uh, no, no," Pete shook his head at Forget, "remember that line," and he redrew the line across the dirt with the tip of his hefty wooden pole about two feet in front of them.

Forget's attention moved from the towering young man at the beginning of the line of four tall men with sticks in their hands, to this one identifying himself as O'Brannigan as he had to Cassandra when Forget arrived at their campsite in time to witness the slap she took to her face.

The skinny Lieutenant Mulrooney hung to O'Brannigan's right, a beautiful blonde pressed up against the back of O'Brannigan's shirt. She looked protected, not afraid. Blocked from participation or blocked from the French. Forget snorted. This group should be so considerate of their allies. Pierre Forget had eight dead men, not only the one name Henri, two of them women as the term "men" was generically employed.

A shorter man of average height and muscular size hung to the background at the end of the line his hands in his pockets, an angry look behind his wire-frame glasses. Forget had no idea who the man was, no more than he "got" the tattered white Parisian suit. None of them had any identification or papers with them, though most of them wore what could constitute a uniform, even the one without the shirt, his tattoos as angry looking as the one with the glasses and O'Brannigan whose slight smile did not reach his eyes. He said something, O'Brannigan, as he drew a line in the dirt with his pole. Pierre Forget did not understand what O'Brannigan said, but Forget did not speak English.

Pete did not speak French. Knowing only the French lieutenant said something back, after he identified himself by name and rank. Pete got that much just like Forget got the meaning of the line drawn in the sand.

"Eight," Julia tugged on her earlobe like she was of a mind to start playing charades. "He said something about eight ..."

"Men," Jeff interjected. "He said he has eight dead men."

"Including a couple of girls," Michael shook his head. "Fucking assholes."

"Oh, right," Pete smiled at Michael, Jeff also looking at him. "You also speak French, Doc, that's right, too. So go on," he extended to Michael and Jeff leaving it up to the two of them to do the honors. "Tell him. I ain't got none. No dead. So what's that tell him?"

"It's my position," Jeff answered Pete's directive. "It's what I do. I'm the interpreter."

"Aye, well, now, that's not your only position," Pete assured, "nor only what you do. It's all right, though. Since you've got the means, tell him what I said before the Doc tells him how you want to sleep with him like he did me."

"Oh, yeah?" Joe grinned at Michael. "You said that? Told Frenchie Pete wanted to, you know, make him sing?"

"Not him," Pete cuffed Joe in the side of his missing brains. "That wicked bitch he had with him. That Amazon queen, or whatever the devil she sees herself as."

"Had a wildcat with him," Hank explained to alleviate Joe's confusion. "Right about that. Tall woman. Doc's height."

"Um, thin?" Joe said. "Well, maybe not thin, but you know what I mean, slender?"

"Aye, well, I like a little weight on mine," Hank chuckled, "so right, I'd say a damn rail."

"Think I know who you mean," Joe nodded. "Yeah, saw her, met her. And she's gorgeous, yeah, really a knockout, but definitely, like you said, a little wild. What?" he said to Pete looking at him cross-eyed. "I'm agreeing with you."

"You ain't agreeing with me, lad," Pete assured, "if you think that woman is anything but ugly."

"Nah, she's not ugly," Joe shook his head. "You're nuts. As a matter of fact I haven't seen an ugly one yet even with all their screaming."

"And you got hit in the head or something," Pete assured, "on your way in here."

"Nah," Joe laughed, "but I got shot in the boot. See?" he picked up his foot for Pete to have a look. "So all that big talk about you not suffering any casualties is just because you're lucky. Or rather I am," he shrugged with a wave at Forget yakking about them paying attention, not that Joe could understand him any better than Pete could, or Jewels could for that matter with her high school ability to count to ten. But, yeah, Joe could follow or rather get the gist, of what the guy was saying by his tone that if it were translated, probably went something like, "*Hello*! *Excuse me*! *Remember me*? *I'm talking*!"

"Yeah, we hear you," Joe promised Forget, "we do. And, um ..." he said with a cue for either Jeff or the Doc to start talking, he really didn't give a hoot which one. "Will one of you guys tell him what Pete said? I mean," Joe nodded at who was apparently the boss in Jean Paul's absence, "whoa. Back it up with this frigging dead guy crap. They were trying to shoot us down, OK? They were trying to shoot us down. And I don't give a fuck what his job is," he flipped a nod toward Jeff who the French guy seemed to be focusing on, "I know what mine is. So back it up. I'm serious, knock it off with the whining. What Pete said, you got eight dead guys? Well, we don't have any, and whatever the hell that means, from where I'm standing, and I was there, it wasn't *murder* or *aggression,* it was frigging self-defense. So tell him," he nodded at either the Doc or Jeff. "Do it."

The French guy ignored him to look dead at Jeff who blinked, yeah, he did, at whatever the lieutenant said that had Jeff blinking and the Doc probably on the verge of losing it himself any moment now suddenly concentrating, his brow in a deep scowl.

"What'd he say?" Joe asked Jeff.

"I don't know ..." Jeff said, not meaning he did not know because obviously he knew if he spoke the language. "He thinks I'm responsible."

"Well, yeah, you were there," Joe agreed. "I mean, heck," he scoffed. "Obviously you were there, or what the heck would I be doing there? What are you saying, you didn't fire a shot?"

"Well, no," Jeff said. "I mean, no, I don't know," he shook his head. "Yes, of course, I think I did, I'm sure I did, I must have. I'm sorry," he apologized for not being good at what was not his job. "They were on us, which was why Nel decided to leave me and radio—I thought it was Frank, but it was apparently you," he told Julia. "But it was why Nel decided to radio and go on alone. Really," he assured Forget, "we came here to talk to Jean Paul, and it was Jean Paul who decided he wasn't interested."

"Yeah, OK," Joe waved. "You did or you didn't. I know I did, and I know why I did. That much hasn't changed," he pointed at Forget. "You fire at us, we fire back. Got that? It's not hard to understand."

She walked in just then, some ... woman who clanged when she walked she had so much frigging brass hanging off of her. "Um ..." Joe said.

"Right," Pete nodded. "Tell me again, lad, how lovely she is."

"No, that's not her," Joe assured. "Hell no," he looked at Pete like he was the one who had been hit in the head. "What, are you nuts? My grandmother looks better than her and she's been dead twenty years. The one I'm talking about ..."

"Right." Well, Pete didn't care who or what Joe was talking about. He didn't care what anyone was talking about, what they wanted or what they thought they were going to do, which was nothing. "I've had enough of this that I have."

He took possession of Julia, slung his arm across her shoulders with reassurance to Fred. "That's all right, I've got her. You just watch her back. You, Joseph, get the Doc. Because they either will or they won't, and I'm telling you they won't ... ain't that right?" he tipped his bat in Forget's direction, almost catching him under the chin. "You're not going to stop us, now are you? Dare you to, if you think you have the nerve, and you know damn well you don't because if you did you would have long before now."

And they walked. Pete nodding and talking as they walked. Strolled more or less out the door.

"Cassandra," Forget stopped her from doing anything.

She looked at him, and then took a step toward him. "I told you to stay here," she spit.

And the English would be dead if he had. Forget did not care what she told him, he was telling her. "Put the girls to work. Put them to work," he repeated. "I want to know who he is, the one with the glasses, the one in the suit, the one who doesn't fit." And it wasn't the skinny Lieutenant, the beautiful woman, or the blood-thirsty O'Brannigan, or any of the other three of them, it was the one with the glasses, the one in the suit.

"Who do you think he is?" she snapped.

Forget had no idea. "Put the girls to work," he repeated, and he wasn't going to tell her again. What was their job, after all? What was the point of her whores? "They're no dirtier than the Germans, and we might learn something useful."

"That's right," Pete nodded as he walked, "just walk, luv, keep walking. They aren't going to do anything. I'm telling you they're not." Though he was poised, Joe noticed. Yeah, Pete was prepared for them to do something, and what would he do if Forget decided to unload and nail them right there? Whack the bullets out of the way with that bat of wood he twirled like a drum major's baton?

"You're nuts," Joe grinned. "You've got balls, but you're nuts."

"Walk," Pete said. "Not going far," he reassured Julia. "Just stay with me."

"I'm fine," she assured.

"Know you are," he smiled at her. "Just going to look over that chalet and see what kind of accommodations it has. Hunt down a little food, and those damn cigarettes of mine."

"I think you mean mine," the Doc piped up, either taking Pete at his word no one was going to stop them, or fed up himself, turning on his heel for the door without the slightest bit of hesitation or hint of looking back. The man had a death wish, he did, Pete remained unconvinced the Doc had nerve.

"Share and share alike, Doc," Pete reminded. "In the glory and in the pain. And speaking of pain," he agreed, which they were all bound to be in if they had to spend too much time holed-up in this hovel of whores. "One of you should track down that fanny that had Joseph's tongue wagging like a damn dog's and screw her into cooperation like you know damn well she's going to try and screw a few of you."

"She's gorgeous," Joe assured. "I'm telling you, she's gorgeous."

"And I feel better knowing that," Pete nodded, "worried as I was there for a minute about you."

They were all half-hammered by midnight, relaxing out on the porch in the early spring night with the wintry nip in the air, even Joe had a shirt on as he worked away at resurrecting Christine from a too-early grave, but at least it gave him something to do. Jewels curled up Indian-fashion at the feet of her old man Fred, Jeff lay on his back, his feet dangling over the side, counting the stars in the sky. Pete, the Doc, and Hank, Joe wouldn't necessarily say were more conventional in their choice of comfort between the deck chair, the rail, or the stairs. Particularly since Pete was half-stoned on some Moroccan reefer he managed to come up with, but he still had his wits, as did the Doc though suffering with a bottle of Napoleon brandy, since there wasn't any whiskey, and marijuana was apparently not his style.

"Yo," Michael said to the geek Jeff he recognized from his initial introduction to Justin's freak squad. "I said, hey!" Michael said, "I'm talking to the only thing new and different around here for a week."

"Think he means you," Pete gave Jeff a nudge in the shoulder with his foot.

"Yeah, you," Michael assured Jeff turning his head to give him the eyeball from the ground up. "And what the French guy said was, and I quote, is that you iced some fucking guy for no reason. *That's* what started the fight."

"Now is that what that French fellow said?" Pete stretched with a smile at Joe twisting one of Christine's screws so tight he snapped it right off.

"More or less," Hank yawned from his seat on the steps as he also spoke French, not that anyone had bothered to ask him or Fred.

"Quite," Jeff agreed. "I've been thinking about that myself actually, because frankly, I have no idea what he is talking about. They shot at us first and I shot back at Nel's instruction as he drove us out of there."

"Sounds reasonable," Pete nodded, "because what Joseph said is they were bound and determined to bring the plane down at no spared expense."

"They were," Joe assured.

"So it stands where it stands," Pete said, not worried about it at all. "Self-defense."

"Uh, huh." Michael got up, walked over, and poured the brandy straight down on top of Jeff's head with the suggestion, "Cut your fucking nails first the next time."

"Whoa," Joe blinked in between laughs as Jeff jumped up and the Doc wandered back to the rail. "What the heck was that all about?"

"Oh, he's an arse," Jeff assured, angrily wiping his face with his sleeve, and not about to go one on one with any of them because, quite right, he'd lose. "Isn't that right, Sullivan?" he assured Michael. "Isn't that why Squadron Leader Charles ordered you locked up in a damn room before he apparently ordered you out of town?"

"Sullivan?" Joe looked at Michael. "Who the heck is Sullivan?"

"Gibraltar," Michael assured, and if Pete laughed any harder he'd vomit right there.

"Patience, Doc," he nodded instead, "patience, got more than enough here to keep you occupied in the meantime. You wanted to write about war. You wanted to see it. Well, here are some of the finer points of it."

Until the morning. Come the morning the Lieutenant Forget had them moved out of there to a different ramshackle lodge three hours away until they hit the mountains and three hours turned into ten. They got their gear back though, including their guns, and kept the amenities and home cooked meals.

The Aurès Mountains
March 19,

"Where the hell are we?" Joe asked the important question.

"Hank?" Pete checked with him.

"Best guess?"

"Aye, I'll take it," Pete nodded.

"The Aurès," Hank calculated based on the general direction. "Algeria, still, I would say, not Tunisia. Problem's going to be radio communication with these mountains."

"Problems are more than that," Pete checked his old Mauser and it was fine. "They would have kept the guns."

"Aye. Wonder what it is," Hank looked around. "Vichy or local."

"Is there a difference?" Michael asked.

"Not really," Pete said. "Trouble is trouble, Doc. Dead is dead." He smiled at Julia. "Don't worry, luv. Like I said back at that shithole, they're not going to do anything."

"Bathhouse," Michael said. "It was a fucking old bathhouse. And what makes you so sure?"

"Justin," Pete said. "That lad Dumont would be a fool. He'd be a damn fool."

"Uh, huh," Michael said.

Chapter Forty-Six

The Fezzan
March 18-19, 1942

Reineke was frustrated waiting for the Holy Man's return. Twice a day, for two days, his car shepherded the English woman to and from the children's compound. He saw very little of her, acting only in a supervisory role to ensure her continued safety, otherwise making it a point to avoid her for all the reasons the Holy Man or Diana could propose. Mirabel, when she had arrived at the villa, he had sent her immediately back to the village, suspecting she had been ordered there by Diana, rather than Anne. Soldiers were assigned to deliver the woman's morning and evening meal and whatever else she might decide to need, their appearance timed, and never when he was not present, there in the library, hiding. Reineke felt as if he were hiding, he the one afraid instead of she. He had no idea and no way of knowing what progress, if any, was being made in his plan for her release. After forty-eight hours, on the morning of the third day, he stopped checking his watch for the Holy Man.

Thiele was also late in returning from his excursion to the Kufra. While that threatened to increase Reineke's anxiety of some unknown Allied or French threat, Thiele's absence was a practical excuse for delaying his meeting with his Colonel. Reineke could delay no longer. Schönfeld was insistent with a busy schedule of his own that did not include time for the SS.

Reineke had not been to the children's hospital since leaving for the now long forgotten inventory of waterholes. He went for one reason only today. Adva. She was his favorite, and he was as naturally hers. Diana was there, hidden beneath her unpleasant character Sotma with the face and charm of a mule. She did it deliberately. He knew that. He was awkward around the woman Sotma with her stark reminder of how some charades were more necessary than others. His dialogue stilted and manner stiff, she did not help, speaking to him in their native German when he wished she would compromise and keep to French.

Why? Anna smiled at Reineke from under her ratty mop of long grey hair. Why would he want that? Her precious she called King David and looked upon like some fifth and prodigal son? French was the language of politicians. They were both German and their relationship was personal not political. In another time, another place, another world, they were peers. Both wealthy, established, in many ways, feared. Those of her profession, medicine, and those of his, business and philanthropic, historically reliant on each other, feeding each other's egos and ideas, who could know how one day, they, in their own time and way, would be confronted with the reality of how ruling an empire was very different than attempting to command and conquer a world.

She was better at conquering than he. Her vision narrow and focused. He was scattered, his interests numerous and varied and contradictory as he was. But he had a heart, the German Baron with the arrogant attitude, a conscience that plagued him, a deep one that hurt. A surprising and strong fascination with children, regardless of how he might discard their mothers like last week's fashion or even just yesterday's dessert. The younger the child, the better, the smaller, the weaker, obsessed with some sister Alexia, seeing her fragile, endangered, and everywhere.

His beloved Alexia was probably built like a wrestler. Anna would not know, and shrugged. Dieter not exactly a reliable source of information with half of what he said more what he wanted and wished rather than what was actual and real. But she liked him, her complex little fruitcake with his eccentricities and emotions. He was very strong, in spite of himself, a man, in spite of himself, and so very, very clever. She smiled, enjoying that she could like him. To like him was to remember a time and a world everyone wanted and did not exist any longer. She hated to break that to him, as his mother had hated to tell him there was no *Nikolaus* when the time came.

Oh, that was right. Anna remembered. They did not talk about the mother. It was unclear if she was alive or what had happened to her. The father? Once Dieter mentioned him, but he was drunk, and so she never got the whole story. Dieter drunk had surprised her, he did not seem the type. Drunk was clumsy, falling down when he tried to walk. Drunk was tears, drunk was anger, and what did he have to be so angry about? Nothing at all. A storybook life, a fairy tale castle. Perhaps he wanted to keep them forever and felt they were threatened by that real world he had heard rumors about.

She liked to analyze him. Even though it was not her sphere, it was her sport, competing with her son Abraham, driving him crazy like she drove this one with her matriarch Anna Haas such a know-it-all, such a bitch.

"Adva says she has missed you," Anna explained in her monotone to Reineke's momentary hesitation ... because? Because why? Because he was expecting who to be there instead of she? Marlene Dietrich? Garbo? Why did she believe him when he said he never heard of either of them? Who knew why. She just did.

He ignored her except to take advantage of her Palestinian dialect. "Tell her I've missed her," he instructed, "and apologize ... I do so apologize," he sat down on the bed at Adva's side, his smile tightening when he touched her hot little head. "Indeed, she is burning," he accused. "Why does she still have a fever?"

"Because she still has an infection," Anna replied, the answer simple, obvious, and callous to his ears, like he did not trust her to treat the child equally as she would one of her own.

"Get rid of it," Reineke instructed. "Do your duty, or I will bring someone here who can."

Big talk for someone who could not handle one wayward dentist and one outlaw priest, not that she could do any better, but that was beside the point. She wasn't supposed to do anything better than he. He was the German, she was a Jew. "Eichmann or Himmler?" Anna asked, taking his cigarettes and the field cap he carried for some reason, clutched in his hands like a two year old when he first showed up at the door. She looked it over and it was tailored too small to fit the woman, and so he must have someone else in mind. She wondered who?

"Interesting, because I've tried calling the Ministry of Health, but for some reason they're booked as solid as we are. What?" she said to Reineke looking at her with that tired look of his as transparent as he was. "What's the matter mein Liebchen?" she drawled. "Do you really want a report, or is this a social call?"

"That would depend," Reineke glanced around at the beds, half-empty, half not, as usual. "Are any of them contagious to my men?"

"How would I know?" Anna said. "Pull their medical files and find out. This week's special is measles."

"Measles?" Reineke blinked. "Indeed. What about Adva?"

"Yes, of course," Anna turned the cap around to face him, confront him with the evidence of Mirabel's handiwork and so Mirabel hadn't been sent back to the village quite that fast, or at least not empty-handed, with nothing to do. "I keep forgetting Adva is one of your men. Not exactly a bonnet, but the embroidery's a nice touch. That way when it's lost or laundered they'll know which man to return it to."

"Answer the question," Reineke took the cap back, "before I revoke your privileges and leave their care to the Holy Man."

Now that was silly. "You revoke my privileges?" Anna laughed.

He should have such power, she was right. "Answer the question," Reineke requested. "It is not a hard one."

It never was. "Adva had measles last year," Anna reassured. "She is in no more danger than you."

"Last year?" Reineke smiled at his exotic little princess anxious to try the hat she somehow knew belonged to her. "Last year you had funny little red spots all over you ..." Instead of a dark, purple sore that refused to heal.

"Indeed," he stared at the shortened necrotic stump that had once been a leg only six years old. "You cut it again. Why? When?"

"Why do you think?" Anna asked. "When? Three, four days ago—the day before you sent the woman here."

He had no choice but to send her with the Holy Man gone. "You did not call me," Reineke said.

"You were occupied," Anna shrugged.

"Cut it higher," he said. "Why do you refuse to cut it above the infection?"

"I did," she assured and the result was the same as before, the prognosis negative and inevitable, simply a matter of time.

"Then it will heal," Reineke refused to accept defeat and such a pointless death, reaching to lift Adva carefully onto his lap so she could admire herself in a hand mirror and show off her cap to her audience applauding her with smiles. "May I?"

"A little late to ask, but what else is new?" Anna shrugged again. "Could I stop either of you?"

"No," Reineke smoothed the child's hair, so Asian in color and texture, so unlike his. "She needs to be held. Do you ever just hold them?"

"I try not to," Anna admitted. "It's harder to let go."

"Then do not let go," Reineke smiled at Adva, tickling her hat. "Like mine, see? Me, like you."

"That's one way to win a battle," Anna agreed. "Will it. Dazzle it." She smiled at Adva petitioning her for her opinion of the cap. "Yes, it is very pretty. Anne will be very jealous."

"Indeed. Another way is to treat it properly," Reineke assured, so typical of the parent to blame the doctor for not being God.

"Accidents happen," Anna reminded. "Who knows why?"

"So do miracles," Reineke maintained. "People have lived here for thousands of years, despite the properties of the climate."

"Ja," Anna supposed, "and the life expectancy is somewhere around twenty-seven years, unlike our country where it's triple that depending of course on who you are." She brushed her fingers through Adva's silky Arab hair, finding it somewhat interesting how beyond this compound, they were enemies, too. "She's lived longer than many of her cousins, take comfort in that like I do, and worry about something more practical like the woman," she looked down on Reineke's tipped head. "You're concerned about contamination, what about her?"

"Who?" he said, thinking what? She was the blonde, not him?

"Madame Lee," Anna nodded. "Short, bird-like little thing with a big bandage on her head? You must have noticed her around."

"Mademoiselle Lee," he corrected her for some reason. Who knew why. Did he prefer the idea of a lost daughter to a lost wife? "And I did not mean who. It simply came out."

"No, of course you did not," Anna agreed. "You meant I am not listening. I do not care what you have to say Diana. I am going to do what I feel like doing anyway. This is news? To whom? My first husband was like you, handsome as you, it did not get him any further than it will you. It is all right though," she patted his shoulder, taking his cigarettes again, one for now, and another for later. "Regardless of Lee's marital status, if she is lying and she has not had measles as she claims, she could transmit the disease through your squad, and I would not want to be held accountable for jeopardizing the future of your race, no more than I already am. It is best to leave her here," she snapped the cork tip off and wiped the wet tobacco clinging to her lip. "You really should try the American cigarette. It will kill you just the same but the taste is almost worth it."

"Indeed. Why would she lie?" Reineke frowned.

"Why would she tell the truth?" Anna countered. "I wouldn't. I'm not even sure I knew what the truth was at her age. Did you?" She nodded while he thought about that. "Better question, do you now? Do you yet?"

"No," Reineke said. "No," he refused the offer to make the woman a permanent part of her household instead of his. "This is only a temporary arrangement. She has been terrorized enough."

"Touché," Anna laughed. "Except I do not terrorize, ask anyone. No more than I organize. I comply because I have not the backbone, or the spirit, for that matter, the brains to do otherwise."

"Six guns to my one," Reineke seemed to recall from their last conversation. "What do you call that?"

"The truth," Anna shrugged. "Have I used them? No. Therefore, shall we call a truce, Hauptmann? End the bafouillage? The woman is here, yes, she is here. I do not like it, you do not like it, still there must be something we can work out palatable to both of us—that does not need to involve Pierre, or John ..." She watched him for any sort of reaction. He did not have one. And so it wasn't some idea he was bandying about with the two of them, it was a plan. "In the meantime, I am serious about contamination."

"Apparently," he said. "I do not even see her here."

She should pay more attention herself. "Were you expecting to?" she asked, surprised. "I am sorry am I making you late for your date?"

"Indeed," Reineke rolled his eyes. "Have I ever molested one of your children?"

She thought about that, what he could mean. The answer, no, of course he had not. He had love for children, not lust. The woman however was not a child. "No. What is on your mind? Someone's accusation or your own concern? Funny, you smell like cologne, not wine to me."

"There is nothing on my mind," Reineke assured. Indeed, he had brought a hat for Adva as she could plainly see.

Anna nodded. "The morning has ended, it is noon. If they are not fighting, the woman is having something to eat with Anne. Who will be jealous," she predicted, meaning the hat.

"Anne is always jealous," Reineke set Adva carefully back in bed. "A reason why I love to torment her."

"Who is jealous," Anna assured, "of the woman."

"The woman?" Reineke looked up at her. It was an honest look. "Why?"

"Who knows," Anna waved. "Children. Competition. Preferential treatment. The woman stays at the house."

"There are reasons the woman stays at the house," Reineke assured. "As you well know. Explain it to Anne in the appropriate way. I would do it—except I have to go to town," he rose with a sudden wink and sly smile.

"Of course," Anna said. "Not because you are a coward like all men leaving the talking of sex to women, and the making of it to men."

"No," Reineke said. "Simply a conversation more appropriate for Anne to have with you." He looked around as if expecting something to have changed during the time he had been there.

"What?" Anna said.

"Nothing," Reineke assured. "I am taking the woman with me. Do not ask me why, I have not yet decided why, but I will decide as necessary."

She wasn't going to ask, and would get even for whatever it was he thought he had planned with the Holy Man. He would find that out when he got to town, a warning waiting. Just a warning this time. Next time? Who knew. "Don't forget the milk."

"Very funny," Reineke said. "If you have a list, or a request, give it to me, I will see what I can do. Though you remember we are the supply compound, yes?" he nodded. "Not the town? Whichever, just give it to me. Indeed, I am an hour late and I have not left," he lit a cigarette, like that would somehow help.

"Thiele hasn't returned yet?" Anna turned to scribble a few things down.

"No," Reineke said. "Neither has the Holy Man. It is a good excuse, right? If you need one, use that for my taking the woman with me. I seem to recall saying I will not leave the woman unattended or alone."

Anna wasn't looking for excuses. "Oh, yes, the Holy Man ..." she seemed to recall someone by that name. "Neither has my airplane or my son John returned, a third day now. Curious, I wonder if they are together?"

"Perhaps," he agreed coyly. "Perhaps all three of them are. Pierre, Thiele, and John. Perhaps they have deserted us, leaving us only to each other."

"You should be so lucky," Anna slapped the paper in his hand.

No, she should be. "Caviar?" his look was pained.

Anna shrugged. "It doesn't hurt to ask."

Reineke laughed. "Indeed, no, it does not. I will see what I can do." He stuffed the paper in his pocket and stooped to kiss Adva goodbye on her hot little cheek. "Indeed," he said again. "I will want a report when you have one."

"I have one," Anna assured, only he never got to hear it.

"I!" Joanna announced herself rather loudly when she charged back into the barn following her lunch.

"I!" she gasped, taking a teetering step backwards, and certainly a very flustered step forward to try and stop herself from toppling. All very natural reactions. People really do gasp and stop short when they walk into a room to see the very last thing they probably expect to see. At least people she knew.

"I!" Joanna belched her lunch, really lacking savior-faire.

"You are early," The broad body of Sotma blocked her from bounding any further.

"Early?" Joanna gasped again.

"The Hauptmann is here to take you," Sotma advised with a curt point back at the door. "You will wait for him outside."

Joanna did not know what to say even when she was once again outside. She tried crossing her arms but they insisted on hanging down lifelessly at her side, her hands pulling on her shirttails.

"Fräulein."

He was very tall, and very thin, and he was waving his hand at her—

No, not at her. At who? What? Joanna looked around, finally spotting the car.

"Fräulein, if you please," he directed.

"I didn't see!" Joanna stammered, meaning the car.

"Indeed," he said, his head aiming for the air, hands vanishing behind his back.

"I didn't see the car!" Joanna insisted.

"Do you see it now?" he asked.

She flushed. "Yes."

"Good." His hand reappeared as he walked over to the car, holding the door open, and Joanna tried not to stare but the hand was very long, and very thin—"Get in," he said, and she jumped.

"I beg your pardon?" Joanna whispered, having no idea what he meant.

"Get into the automobile," he said, meaning the automobile whose door he was holding open, and naturally meaning for her to get into it.

"Oh," Joanna said, and you know there is a step to step up into a car. A running board, and after that, the floor, and all the way up onto the seat, if one wanted to be daring. Really, if she wanted to be daring, she could stand on the seat, high in the air, certainly higher than standing on most chairs.

"*Mademoiselle, should look!*" Pierre's voice rang in her head, confiding during one of his speeches. "*Oui, if Mademoiselle should ever have the opportunity to look into mon capitaine's eyes, this is what she should do, and she will see how there is nothing to be afraid of with mon capitaine, no there is not.*" Stand up on a chair and have a look down her nose at him, checking him out but good.

And so Joanna did, directly. Her nose almost touching his as she bent over to stare down into his eyes that were blue, pale, like Pierre had said, but she had seen bluer. His were very nearly grey, slightly crossed for some reason.

"I ..." Joanna said, wondering how well he could see when he did not appear as if he could see anything. She slid down into her seat, his long thin hand coming toward her again holding a hat.

"You will need this," Reineke said, ignoring Diana's stare burning into the back of him. "The sun is high."

Adva. Joanna clearly saw Adva, her arms coiled like a serpent around his long thin neck, hat on her head. "No thank you," she refused, dignified. "I'm perfectly fine." And she was not surprised when they did not stop at the house—correction. They did stop, momentarily. To pick up two motorbikes and another car with a long, thin gun on its back and Joanna knew it was over. The party, as Michael would say, was over.

Silent, oh, so many silent hours away, long past the gate and the terrifying climb up the mountain road, the trees swarming over the house hiding it from sight. a field of sand opened up in front of them, and then finally another road. They moved from their swaying crawl to an energetic flight along the packed dirt. However long it lasted, the trip did not last anywhere near long enough for Joanna's liking. In the distance, she could see the outline of buildings, growing and spreading as towns do, until she was surrounded, the sandy road becoming one of stone linked to others, and she was in the middle of some sort of market. People moving everywhere, dragging carts and massive straw baskets, screaming, shouting, plying their wares.

"You may get out, Fräulein." The Captain alighted from the front seat of the car, his long, thin hand reaching for her door.

Get out? Joanna stared at him, staying precisely where she was, seated in the back. He continued to stand there but eventually it appeared as though she was going to have to get out because his hand was coming toward her, silently snaking through the air when something happened. Something attacking or striking him or something because there suddenly appeared to be something very seriously wrong with him.

I mean! Joanna stared at him, because it certainly couldn't have anything to do with her, whatever it was that gripped him in its claws. Though it was true she was not in any particular hurry to leave her seat, she was leaving it, inching her way slowly toward the door, when suddenly he was there, glaring and snarling at her.

"I!" Joanna gasped, because good heavens he pounced right on top of her foot! Grasped her ankle, twisting it up close to his face so he could have a better look at whatever it was he was trying to see until as quickly as he had attacked, he released her. Flinging her foot back at her in a huff and winding those long, thin fingers around her arm, and Joanna found herself yanked out of the car, crossing the street, tripping and stumbling as he zigzagged through the crowd.

"What are you doing?" Joanna gasped, those long, thin fingers of his hurting, digging into her skin.

He mumbled something and she made the mistake to say, "What?"

"Shoes!" He barked in her face, and flung her into a cart loaded down with leather sandals while he stood there, ripping things out of his pockets, screaming at the greasy looking man standing behind the stacks, and Joanna had herself a pair of—

"Shoes?" Joanna said.

He thrust them sharply at her, declaring how she was to wear them, and he was gone.

"I!" Joanna said. *To market, to market ...*

"I!" Joanna said. Not to be shot? She was holding a pair of sandals, a useful, little pair of leather sandals.

"Oh, but, I!" Joanna said.

"The Hauptmann says ..." A voice behind her spoke and Joanna jumped, almost dropping the shoes right there on the ground. "You may pick anything you like. I have money."

It was the driver of the car, along with the two motorbike fellows, all three of them waiting for her.

"What?" Joanna said.

He seemed a bit put out. "I speak English," he assured, disguising it well, but she got the important part. "The Hauptmann says—"

"Shopping?" Joanna interrupted him. "I'm here to go shopping?"

“Ja,” he nodded. “If this is what you would like.”

Joanna knew she should have worn the hat. She could feel her face starting to itch, tingle, a headache beginning to blossom way in the background. “No, thank you!” Joanna said briskly, stepping for the car—gingerly, because the stones were hot.

Chapter Forty-Seven

Herr Oberst Alfred Schönfeld was an older man as his rank of Colonel might suggest. In his fifties with the usual grey hair and paunch, missing teeth replaced with dentures. He was a busy man, not a stupid one, or someone easily led around. Eric Danzig noted that within the first fifteen minutes of meeting Schönfeld a week ... was it already a week ago? Eric would have to check his calendar to confirm the exact date, an unnecessary waste of time ... March 9th. More than a week ago, Eric nodded, since he had met Schönfeld, or first heard the name Reineke. Hauptmann Dieter Reineke. Now, more than a week later, Eric listened intently, along with Schönfeld, throughout the four-hour discussion Schönfeld had with Hauptmann Reineke. A discussion that reeked of far more than mere dramatics—not to say Hauptmann Reineke wasn't dramatic, because he was. Oh, yes. Eric, rather like Schönfeld, found Hauptmann Reineke to be extraordinarily dramatic in his manner and throughout his speech. Schönfeld apparently always found Reineke to be that way, and usually ignored it. Drama was who Hauptmann Reineke was, as he was most emphatic. Drama combined with emphasis, combined with Reineke's intentions to invoke privileges and take a three-day trip to Tunis equaled a necessary call for help from Schönfeld to Eric prior to the meeting with Hauptmann Reineke.

"You rang?" Help arrived in the form of Hauptmann Eric Danzig just over a week ago early evening on the 9th and again today on the 18th, at about ten minutes to three on a sunny desert afternoon. Eric walked into Schönfeld's office with a beaming smile and uniform similar to Schönfeld's, and, as this was the Afrika Korps, similar to Hauptmann Reineke's. Though Eric's uniform was not custom tailored as Reineke's would soon reveal itself to be, but simply off the rack as were most of the others being worn by the ordinary soldier out there fighting this desert war. Hauptmann Eric Danzig was an ordinary soldier, born an ordinary person, merely gifted with a silver tongue. That tongue could explain Eric's alliance to the Propaganda Ministry if Eric's allegiance happened to be known by these "desert pirates" hijacking Italian supplies. It was not.

No, here Eric was Wehrmacht not SS as being SS was Eric's secret regardless of who else had theirs. No one here knew Eric was SS except for possibly Weiheber and Faust who did not count, and Eric's man, Staff Sergeant Erich stationed in Hauptmann Reineke's compound, as Eric had a man stationed in each of the five compounds. Eric hadn't heard from Erich in over a week, but Eric presumed that had something to do with:

(1) Being busy, which the compounds were, or

(2) Nothing to report, which was possible though unlikely, or

(3) A lot to report, in part already reported by Weiheber to Schönfeld when they met on the 9th . Or the most likely:

(4) Erich had been stupid enough to get caught. In turn, and as would be expected, Erich's moonlighting as an SS informant shut down, shut off. Erich likely dead or soon to be from some freak accident, squashed by an unsecured piling of shells, flattened by a run-away kübelwagen.

It did not matter. Eric was here now and as SS, Hauptmann Eric Danzig would take over where Staff Sergeant Erich had left off.

Similar to how as Wehrmacht, Eric had taken over were Oberleutnant Heinrich Thiele had left off, as aide to Herr Oberst Alfred Schönfeld.

Wehrmacht Hauptmann Eric Danzig was the sixth Hauptmann of Schönfeld's handpicked five. The color of the piping around Eric's shoulder straps, collar patches, and hat, identifying him as Signal Korps, as Schönfeld's colors identified him as Cavalry, and Hauptmann Reineke's identified him as Panzer. The details of why Reineke, a panzer Captain, had been reassigned to Transport and Supply, would be found in his personnel file. Still, for all the information available on Hauptmann Reineke, it was not the same reading it on paper versus experiencing it in person.

Eric's fingers drummed on his desktop in the time before Schönfeld called for help today. His fingers had drummed there many times over the past week, by this time, close to making permanent indentations in the wood. Eric got up for a while to walk back and forth in front of his desk and occasionally to the windows from where the village square was visible only at an awkward angle. His feet cutting the same path they had by now several times, close to wearing the floorboards a little thin.

Eric occupied an ordinary room for his office in a building quite ordinary for the area. Two stories, thick adobe or mud, a slope leading up from the street to the front door that was actually on the side. A small cloistered area to one's left upon entering where a soldier sat in reception, an extensive collection of modern communication equipment piled up behind him in the rear. A slightly larger area on one's right with a disorganized assortment of the usual supplies, and a rickety worn wooden staircase directly in front that led up to Schönfeld's office on the left, and Eric's on the right.

Everything then, save for being SS, about Eric was ordinary, his life, his career, uniform, even his office and desk. To where everything about Hauptmann Reineke was apparently extraordinary.

Eric opened Reineke's personnel file to read it yet again, and Hauptmann Reineke was, on paper:

(1) Slightly taller, and considerably smaller in weight, build and frame than Eric

(2) The product of a once-upon-a-time titled family, which could mean anything in the real world from pauper, to modest income or allowance, to filthy rich

(3) Highly decorated, awarded a Knight's Cross

(4) Accused of murder three times—

"*What*?" Eric naturally had said upon reading it the first time. "*Murder*?" A lot of officers killed their men. It happened all the time and was well within the rights and rules.

As occasionally, men killed their officers resulting in execution if they were unlucky enough to get caught. Many did not.

"*Oh, please*!" was then Eric's natural reaction to the apparent prissy complainant with nothing better to do, quickly drawing a line through *murder,* penciling in what was much closer to the truth "*inclined to be misunderstood*", inserting a period with an emphatic "*There!*" As Eric had a sneaking suspicion as to *why* Hauptmann Reineke had a tendency to find himself the butt of someone's joke.

"*Not another one!*" Eric slammed Reineke's identification photograph down, slamming it back inside the file and slamming the folder closed as despite the poor quality of the black-and-white print, which normally did justice to no one, presented Reineke to be quite fair in feature and face, distinctly femininely so.

That was then, of course and this was now. In the here and now, Schönfeld was calling for help. Eric knew *what* Schönfeld was requesting assistance with, and he knew the *why*, and that was Hauptmann Reineke apparently en route and scheduled to arrive—well, several hours ago, but who was counting?

The *what* was Reineke's proposed changes in the acquisition, transport, and delivery of the munitions slated to be appropriated from the Italians in Tripoli. Details to be found in Reineke's fifty-two page retort disguised as a report that included the events at the compound of March 8th, and the subsequent substantial changes to the plan designed to achieve their objective of:

(1) Hijacking the munitions at the docks prior to the Italians carting them all off—yes, Hauptmann Reineke still had that happening though he had inserted several first-things-first as security measures. None of which were necessary, though, in all fairness, Reineke wouldn't know that. As, of course, Reineke assuming command of the hijacking operation itself at the docks rather than simply participating in the subsequent distribution was thoroughly out of the question.

(2) Relative to the slated distribution, i.e., the exchange of the hijacked goods from the hijackers to Reineke's men along the road to Sebha—Hauptmann Reineke DID NOT have that occurring, not even close, but they would address that. And

(3) Division of the goods on the road to Sebha under the supervision of Sergeant Linke, Reineke's apparent inventory control officer together with the inventory control officer of the second compound whose name was missing and Eric would soon read why.

As an alternative to items number two and three, Reineke

proposed, based on the assumption he had command of the operation in Tripoli:

(a) The original convoy from Tripoli to the Sebha area be split into two convoys, each traveling different routes southwest to a "to be defined" area in the region of Gadames on the Libyan-Algerian border instead of traveling south to the road for the Sebha region of the Fezzan.

(b) Upon reaching said area, both convoys would wait a "to be defined" period of time, again as a security precaution, before moving south along the border and ultimately to Reineke's compound completely eliminating the participation of the second compound.

(c) Upon arrival at Reineke's compound, the munitions would be divided accordingly with Reineke keeping his share, and the remaining share sent on, as planned, to the second compound via a convoy managed by Reineke's men.

In all, about the only thing that remained the same was that Reineke, at least on paper, agreed to ensure the second compound received its share of the hot goods—quite a bit later than initially expected but that had little on the starting end to do with Reineke.

The situation in the Mediterranean was subject to change, and had changed. The finishing line, however, had everything to do with Reineke, and Eric had news for him. Excluding the change in time schedule for securing the munitions from Tripoli, the plan, beginning to end, was not going to change.

"That was easy," Eric smiled shortly before Schönfeld's cry for help, finishing his reading of Reineke's fifty-page summary that had arrived for Schönfeld by special messenger at nine that morning to be promptly preempted by Eric before it got anywhere near Schönfeld's door. Interested only in what Reineke had to say about the planned operation. All the rest of the stuff — the reasons why for the changes, the crying about the SS, including some vague reference to SS prisoners—Eric did not know what wasn't in there and about all he could say to all of it was, "Grow up."

Eric flipped the report closed with a satisfied pat, rising to light a cigarette and glance out the windows wondering if this Hauptmann Reineke was going to show up today, or ever. Eric presumed it would be eventually. As he presumed Schönfeld would at some point call for him—"Oh, what the hell." Eric threw his cigarette out the window for some stupid reason and dove for the report deciding he might as well re-read the piece about prisoners while waiting for Schönfeld's call if only to ensure he had read it correctly. He had.

"Well, what do you know!" Eric whistled in amazement and delight. The brief comments about SS prisoners did not say how many or what kind, but at least spoke in the plural indicating more than one. Weiheber, interestingly enough, had not mentioned anything about prisoners to either Eric or Schönfeld, but had solely argued about the compounds, SS authority, and of course Hauptmann Reineke's, shall one say, unorthodox behavior? As it was apparently Hauptmann Reineke who had punched Herr Major Weiheber in the face, causing the black eye and split lip Eric had observed.

On the other hand, who had said *a lot* about SS prisoners had been the disgusting little Russian Reiss, so long ago now, all the way back in Cairo on the day Reiss had come to see Eric and offer him the moon. Eric had subsequently met Weiheber, and even beforehand, had decided it was all a ruse by the Himmler SS faction to delay the arrival of the Goebbels SS faction with Himmler's boys getting to the compounds first. But, now? Now?

"What *do* you know!" Eric whistled. Were he a different man, for example Hauptmann Reineke, Eric would have possibly hugged the report to his breast, dancing it, *waltzing* it merrily around and around his office in utter and sheer ecstasy and delight.

Eric was not another man, certainly not Hauptmann Reineke. Eric did not hug and dance, he simply planted a great big loving kiss on the report, slapping it back down on his desk, visions of parades and babes and Marks galore greeting him when he returned to Berlin in triumph with an Italian physicist tucked neatly under his arm.

"Hauptmann ..." Schönfeld's call for Eric from his office interrupted Eric's euphoria. and Eric made a face, planted his smile on his face and sashayed on in, in answer.

"You rang?" Eric walked into Schönfeld's office to find Schönfeld absorbed in a Telex that had come in around noon from Hauptmann Reineke. Eric knew nothing about any Telex, immediately concluding the little swine of a reception officer downstairs had bypassed Eric, giving it directly to Schönfeld.

Schönfeld responded somewhat more traditionally to Eric's greeting, wishing Eric good day and inviting him to sit down, indicating a comfortable leather seat suitable for a man of Eric's size, situated in front of the desk where Schönfeld sat. A large desk, wooden and traditional as desks go, reasonably cluttered and organized at the same time. Schönfeld was like his desk, Eric decided. Cluttered and organized with the responsibilities of five compounds. One of which was satisfied, Reineke's. Another scheduled to be satisfied, the second compound, and three that were yelling.

Eric cared only about the Telex from Reineke, wanting it badly so he could race back into his office for the report, erase the doodles over the parts Schönfeld agreed with, add doodles to the parts Schönfeld did not—it was too late. Eric had doodled all over the report because the entire thing was nonsense.

"Sounds serious," Eric folded his long legs, accepting and taking the offer of a seat, though foregoing the opportunity to either seduce or make love to it. Something Eric would soon notice to be a tendency of Hauptmann Reineke's. To seduce things like the chair he sat on, the floor he walked, the air surrounding him. Not literally, of course, simply by virtue of his highly provocative manner, intensely sexual and overheated. Eric wiped the sweat from the back of his neck but only because it was hot in there, as it was hot everywhere.

"This issue with the SS is clearly most serious, Hauptmann," Schönfeld passed the Telex to Eric.

Schönfeld had made a few notes next to Reineke's summary that included Reineke's assurance he would be there sometime before the crack of doom, underscored the seriousness of the SS attempted appropriation of the compound, placing their entire operation in jeopardy.

That was very true if one looked at it from the perspective of the Wehrmacht Afrika Korps operators. From the perspective of the SS, it was nothing to worry about as the SS *had* appropriated Reineke's compound together with the whole of the operation. Weiheber might have intended to do that, tried and failed, but the SS had succeeded. Case in point, Eric was sitting there. This was now an SS operation. Little did the former operators know.

"Oh, yes, very serious," Eric accepted the Telex which included the aforementioned points as well as Reineke's—*requested,* Eric loved that part—three-day pass to Tunis, while advising details relative to all would be found in Reineke's report sent via special messenger this morning. Hauptmann Reineke might be cute but he was apparently not dumb. He knew Schönfeld wouldn't have the time, or take the time to read his forty-pound memo so he sent the one page Telex highlighting the points he wanted Schönfeld to read, buy, believe, and agree with. Call it what one will, it came down to the same thing. A snow job. The SS weren't the only ones interested in appropriating the operation. Out there ... somewhere ... was a towheaded Nordic Prince up to the same game. Reineke's proposed alterations to the scheduled plan gave him absolute authority and complete control at least over the current delivery, the largest thus far. Such absolute authority and control belonged to Schönfeld no one else, and by way of Schönfeld, it belonged to Eric. No one else.

"This three-day trip, however ..." Eric said, while mentioning, "I have the report, by the way. It came in earlier. I took the liberty ..."

"Hardly liberty, Hauptmann," Schönfeld dismissed. "It's why you're here."

"Yes," Eric smiled. It was why he was there, wasn't it? Schönfeld was too busy to deal with the details of five complexes and their respective commanders. Schönfeld dealt with the upper echelon of the scheme, its design and purpose, its goal, and the bottom line of how to achieve it. An extensive and lengthy background in field command explained Schönfeld's current post as field commander of the operation. It also explained his understanding how the achievement of one's goal lay within the details. The commanders of his compounds were a detail. When Schönfeld replaced his invaluable detail-oriented Oberleutnant Heinrich Thiele as his aide, he selected an officer of equal rank to his five Hauptmanns.

"I've been looking over Hauptmann Reineke's report and have made several notes ..." Eric explained.

"Excellent ..." Schönfeld was already moving on to the next item on his desk. "Review them with Hauptmann Reineke and then the three of us will meet. Hauptmann Reineke should be here ..." he frowned slightly at his watch.

"Soon," Eric offered. "Very soon."

"Excellent," Schönfeld said again. "Dismissed."

"Also remarkably easy," Eric agreed upon returning to his office where he drew an unflattering caricature of the twit downstairs, and lit another cigarette that he intended to smoke. Wandering back to his amazingly lopsided windows cut into the thick mud or adobe walls at some point before it dried ... or was it more accurate to say before it cured?

Eric wondered about that briefly, as it was his job to wonder about such things, from his wonderings, create good copy for the propaganda machine by virtue of slogan, press release or script. The explanation as to why Eric doodled versus spent his time earning a Knight's Cross.

Unfortunately, here in this desert paradise there wasn't too much to wonder about except the thickness of adobe walls and how they made those windows that looked like someone had carved through the mud with their hand.

"Ah, ha!" Eric said presently, nothing to do with the windows, but instead everything to do with why he kept sticking his head out of one or both of them. Hauptmann Reineke had arrived.

"I think that's Hauptmann Reineke," Eric frowned. Who else could it be? Up slid two motorbikes that continued past the line of Eric's sight, followed by a staff car that did not continue on, but stopped dead in front of the sloped alley leading up from the street. In it was clearly an Afrika Korps officer who stood up for some reason before stepping out of the opened door to stand on the ground.

"Get out of the way!" Eric muttered at the nobody who had opened the car door and continued to stand there blocking Eric's already obstructed view.

Nevertheless, Eric could at least see the officer was tall. Motionless until he suddenly fell over, toppled head first into the back of his staff car—no, wait a minute, he did not topple, he leaned, quickly, and was in the process of dragging something out.

"Not another memo," Eric groaned, hoping to be spared. He was.

It wasn't something, it was someone, a person—"Oh, my God —" Eric hissed. Hauptmann Reineke had a child with him, ten ... eleven ... perhaps, twelve years old. Eric could not see her very well either what with the oaf still standing there, but he could clearly tell it was a girl by the length of the hair.

"Oh, my God!" Eric almost hammered on the window's frame in his excitement. Hauptmann Reineke had brought the SS prisoner with him.

"He brought the prisoner with him!" Eric sang happily in glee. "He brought the prisoner!" The one and only daughter of some Italian physicist soon to be their physicist.

But where—where the hell was he taking her? Eric could not believe it, staring out the window dumbfounded as Reineke carted her off, dragged her away, not the right way, this way, but the wrong way, that way. There one moment and gone the next, out of Eric's sight.

"What the hell?" Eric gaped. "What the—Oh, Jesus Christ!" Visions of grandeur evaporating, replaced by visions of the idiot selling her to the local slaver, trading her for a couple bottles of beer ...

Eric shot out of his office, down the rickety wooden stairs, out the door, down the sloping alleyway to the street where one of the soldiers who had accompanied the motorcade—which Eric could now see included a small armored car with mounted heavy machine gun—turned to look him over curiously up and down. A soldier, at whom Eric refrained from sneering: *Oh, I suppose, how it would have been so much more acceptable to hang out the window yelling and waving Over here, you idiot! Over here!*

No, Eric did not say that. He simply smiled at the soldier. In a formal and traditional way wished him good day and introduced himself, advising how Schönfeld had noticed their arrival and sent him out to greet them.

The soldier was a little dick. He looked away from Eric, up at the solid blank wall facing the street before leaning forward slightly to look down the alley and up to the windows above. Trapped between witticisms, and wracking his brain to come up with something clever for his tongue to say, Eric was unexpectedly relieved of his moment of embarrassment by the soldier who looked back at Eric, and then past him, over Eric's shoulder in the direction of the street. An act, that prompted Eric to turn around despite his disappointment and heavy heart that knew he was too late. The child was gone. Sold to a slaver for a bottle of beer. Eric's hopes, dreams, and desires, guzzled down, and peed out ...

On the other hand ...

Eric turned to see, watch the approach of the officer who was returning, albeit empty-handed, and was Eric in for one heck of an unexpected treat. Perhaps not of the same illustrious caliber of having nabbed an Italian physicist during his desert holiday, but not half-bad a replacement.

"Hauptmann Reineke?" Eric extolled when he spotted the officer approaching at break-neck speed, hell-bent to sneak off down the alleyway, his tail between his legs for being three hours—count them, three hours late. His pockets and hands empty save for a few drachmas, and beer, unmindful and uncaring of the race for atomic power and weaponry the Allies were perfecting as they stood there.

The officer flew past Eric to stop at the sound of Eric's voice, no less than the sound of his own name, and whirled, yes, *whirled*, up on his toes, around to face Eric, and back down, his heels planted firmly on the ground. His glare presumably at the interruption, burning holes in Eric's skin Eric did not even feel, and if he did, who cared? That was not just some officer standing in the alley, it was a god. Adonis, Apollo. *The* Wagnerian Myth in the flesh, *the* poster child of the Reich come to life. Hauptmann Reineke was gorgeous. In a very feminine way, yes, but also in an enthralling masculine way. The stuff, *the face* of dreams—wet ones, if Eric knew his audience which Eric did, every man, woman, little boy and little child would want or want to be him, whether Reineke sang soprano or not. The Propaganda Ministry would take care of taking care of that.

And since it would ... *Hello*! Eric resisted the urge to circle Reineke. He resisted licking his lips, appreciative whistles, admiring catcalls or provocative looks up and down. He even somehow resisted framing Reineke between his forefingers and thumbs and it was probably a good thing he did. Discounting Hauptmann Reineke's beauty, his aura or charisma, or whatever the hell it was that oozed, Hauptmann Reineke was otherwise a very rude man. As quickly as he whirled to face Eric, he whirled away and whooshed off, down the alley and through the door, Eric on his heels, babbling something like: "*IamhauptmanndanzigandIwishtowelcomeyou ...*"

Reineke was furious. Beyond the anger for the woman not wearing shoes despite what should be a paralyzing fear of losing a leg to a simple scratch, the officer he had briefly noted talking to his man, called his name as Reineke headed up the alley to meet with Schönfeld. There was one conclusion when Reineke turned around to the officer. Schönfeld, after three months, had a new aide. Reineke saw nothing more than that, only his own rage. A simple matter of securing travel passes for Tunis had turned into its own field operation. One he would win, as he won them all.

Reineke burst through the front door and up the stairs after one scalding question for Schönfeld's Leutnant sitting at his desk. "Who is that?"

"Hauptmann Eric Danzig, Adjutant," the Leutnant provided a concise response to what was an expected question whether or not it was issued as a command. Personally, the Leutnant concurred with Reineke's raging demand, but that did not need to be expressed.

"Danke!" Reineke tossed back and was in what should have been Thiele's abandoned office now appropriated by some officer whose name Reineke had already forgotten. It did not matter. Reineke would find the name, together with a sample of the officer's handwriting and signature, and he would find the travel passes in Thiele's former office, rearranged and decorated with trite interests and pictures of fat wives. Seizing the desk chair to cram under the door latch Reineke spotted the office key on the desktop near his report that looked like it had passed through the hands of one of the children at his compound. He grabbed the key, securing the lock.

Ripping through the filing cabinets, Reineke finally found the travel passes, but nothing with the officer's name or writing. "Indeed!" he cleared the ridiculous toys from the top of the filing cabinet with a swipe of his hand, returning to the desk to search again but there was nothing, only more toys that he smashed onto the floor. The officer played, he did not work. Thiele had worked as

Schönfeld's aide-de-camp. This one collected pictures and souvenirs, drawing cartoon pictures, and ridiculous designs on the operation's report—"The report!" It registered as Reineke stood there trying to think. He snatched up the report with all its doodles, ripping through the pages to find writing, which Reineke found, the officer's name, his signature, as he doodled, wasting his time.

"Eric Danzig," Reineke triumphantly held up his prize. There it was scrawled, a dozen times.

"Eric Danzig," Reineke smirked at the door where Eric Danzig was attempting to gain entry by any means, from knocks, to little kisses, and profane mutterings.

"Indeed," Reineke folded the pages of the report with the officer's writing and signature, with a razor-sharp crease, and put them in his jacket pocket. The rest of the report, he threw into the air in celebration of his victory, and waited at the officer's desk to see if *Eric Danzig* was going to attempt to break in the door that opened out, or if he was simply going to ask the Leutnant downstairs for the other key.

Eric banged through the front door in time to see Reineke flying up the stairs, less some cape, to disappear into Eric's office.

"Well, at least he got that much right," Eric had to say as he took a breath, slamming his knuckles down on the reception officer's desk to admonish him lest he thought he got away with his little trick with the Telex earlier. "Do it again you little twit and I'll break every bone in your body!" Following which Eric straightened up and walked up the stairs to greet Hauptmann Reineke waiting for him in his office—

"And another thing," Eric decided to walk back down a few steps first, popping his head around the corner to also advise the little twit, "I wear a gun. Keep it in mind should you decide to tell tales out of school." Particularly since Hauptmann Reineke had not ignored Eric as it may have seemed, but instead, as Eric spoke, was right upstairs waiting in Eric's office for him. "Right upstairs," Eric pointed, "in *my* office." And Eric went up the stairs to his office to find how the door was locked from the inside preventing his entry.

Locked? Eric frowned at the door. It couldn't be locked. It had to be stuck. He had the key ... no, he did not. It was not in his trousers' pocket, and he knew where it was. On his desk, in or about the vicinity of Reineke's report with the doodles on it and the drawn caricature of the twit downstairs. Not a very good first impression for Eric who cared about such things whether or not Hauptmann Reineke cared naught.

"Hauptmann Reineke," Eric knocked politely and quietly for reasons that should not need to be explained. "Hauptmann Reineke," Eric requested amidst sounds of his office being demolished on the other side of the door. There was a momentary pause in the plunder. Not in response to Eric but because Hauptmann Reineke apparently thought he had found what he was looking for, but alas had not, and started looking again even more determined.

"Excuse me, Hauptmann Reineke," Eric petitioned while calculating how he could probably bash the door open with his shoulder, or kick it in with his boot if the damn door opened in. It did not, but Eric gave it a try anyway. "Oh, *garçon*!" Eric rubbed his bruised shoulder with a call for the twit downstairs who had better be prepared to blame it on the wind if he knew what was good for him.

"Yes, Herr Hauptmann?" the head of the twit appeared over the banister in response, less because he spoke French—he did not— but more because Eric had been there a week and he was quickly used to Hauptmann Danzig, his manner and style, about as used as one gets to scorpions and fleas.

"The key," Eric said quietly, almost mouthed. "And say it," he warned as the twit opened his mouth, "and you're dead."

The twit shrugged, disappearing briefly without saying anything. Something to do with having been a member of the squadron for some time and therefore having met Hauptmann Reineke a few times.

"Here you go," the twit reappeared as briefly to toss the key up the stairs, missing intentionally. "Whoops," he said as the key landed three steps down from Eric, but that was the extent of it. No offer to come up and get it and hand it to Eric.

"Thank you," Eric said through gritted teeth.

The twit waved and disappeared for his seat. Eric stepped down, collected the key and unlocked his office door to confront the wind. The wind had wrecked Eric's office and was in a foul, foul mood somewhat unclear as to why. Eric was confused as to why Reineke had intentionally destroyed his office. Things knocked over and shoved out of the way that couldn't have been in anyone's way of anything. But Reineke had knocked them, shoved, pushed, and thrown them, his own report among them, scattered all over the floor in what could be said to be almost a staged appearance of a burglary.

Or a man in a fit of rage, Eric considered. There was no reason for Reineke to stage the burglary he was actually committing. A man, who at the moment Eric unlocked the door and entered, was still standing at Eric's ransacked desk.

A man caught up in a temper tantrum. Eric smiled. Men don't have temper tantrums. And Reineke, at first, second, or third glance was a man regardless of how much like a woman he looked. Could look. Reineke really did not look like a woman. He looked like what he was. An astonishingly handsome artist's conception rather than a portrait of a man. Reineke was a man. An extremely *nasty* man, cream-colored, platinum-haired, and reeking of something that smelled like a bouquet of flowers, too many of them. All right so he wasn't *entirely* a man. Eric smelled of bourbon, cigars, and sweat. *That* was a man. Reineke? Eric remained convinced they would work it out.

"Ah, yes—*choo*," Eric sneezed as the waft of Hauptmann Reineke struck him somewhat more powerfully then it had in the open air, begging Reineke's pardon for his intrusion, and had Reineke not reared in obvious and violent disdain for Eric's attempted invasion, Eric possibly would have volunteered to leave his office before being ordered to do so.

However, since Reineke did rear, and it was Eric's office, Eric did not leave, voluntarily or otherwise, but stayed, admittedly somewhat amused at catching Reineke red-handed, in the process of ransacking his desk.

"Ah, yes," Eric smiled with a wave at his desk, Reineke glaring back at him with hell-fire and brimstone broiling in his large blue-grey eyes ... a little too large, Eric noted. For that matter a little too grey, but balanced nicely with his high pronounced cheekbones and defined, contoured jaw, not quite the preferred and highly coveted three-four ratio but close enough, perfectly symmetrical and therefore perfect, the veritable meaning of the word.

"Perhaps it should have been confirmed how you are meeting with me," Eric nodded, "first, before Alfred, to discuss the particulars of your report—not so fast!" Eric smiled as Reineke bolted dead at him with full intentions of bolting on out the door only to be brought up short by the palm of Eric's hand smacking into the door frame, the length and height of Eric's arm just about level with Reineke's nose. But then Eric was just about level with Reineke. The inch or so difference in height between them easily put down to the heel of one man's boot as opposed to the heels on another's.

In overall girth and proportions, Eric was also twice, if not two-and-a-half times Reineke's size. "Yes," Eric nodded at Reineke, "yes, I am. Twice the size of you." Almost fat by comparison to Reineke who was clearly muscular don't get Eric wrong. Nicely tight and fit under his neatly pressed and open-collar shirt, but he was also at least twenty pounds underweight—not that they couldn't fatten Reineke up a little, because of course they could, and would. Fix what did not work, and keep everything else that did.

"Your key," Reineke retorted, tossed it up in the air where, due to the laws of gravity, it did not stay very long, but dropped to the floor.

Eric glanced at the key, but he did not bend. No, he stayed right where he was, his hand on the door frame blocking Reineke's egress, smiling at Reineke glaring at him, and eventually Eric won the contest. Reineke's head tipped slightly, an almost indiscernible nod of surrender as he stooped to politely retrieve the key.

"No, that's quite all right," Eric reassured as Reineke bent to stoop. "I'll—get it," Eric finished a little late as Reineke bent but did not stoop but instead ducked under Eric's arm, exiting the office, slamming the door closed behind him.

"Hm," Eric remained looking under his arm for few moments before deciding while *bizarre* to say the least, it was also quite all right. "Oh, yes, quite all right, Hauptmann, quite all right," he nodded. "Though be assured, it swings both ways, Hauptmann. Oh, yes, it swings both ways." Not the door, of course, no, the door only swung one way. *Out*, fortunately. Eric was forced to agree that time, otherwise he might have unexpectedly joined his key on the floor had the door instead opened in, knocking him out of the way, knocking him flat.

"Interesting man," Eric collected the pages of the report from the floor, his desk, a nearby chair. "Very interesting man," Eric smiled at the caricature of the twit downstairs he had drawn, and that Reineke had undoubtedly seen, discarding it as he discarded much of his own report. "I wonder what he's up to?" Eric stuffed the caricature in the report, but only to be smart, and went on into Schönfeld's office where Schönfeld and Reineke were already deeply engaged in their conversation, and Reineke's proposed changes to the overall plan for hijacking and distributing the munitions. When it was over, four hours later, and Hauptmann Reineke was gone, Schönfeld asked Eric what he thought.

Chapter Forty-Eight

What did he think? Eric stood looking out of one of Schönfeld's windows, a different view point, the other side of the building where Eric could see nothing of the motorcade where it idled or parked. When Reineke left, Eric could not see the motorbikes or the staff car as they turned around to head off. The armored car with fixed machine gun, yes, because the armored car had to pull up further before it could make the swing around. So what did he think?

Well, in between the few specifics Eric was thinking about, Eric supposed he thought Hauptmann Reineke was serious. Very serious.

He would like to think the shenanigans, the overblown sexuality of Reineke's movements and air, came to an end. Reached some climax or conclusion in all, rather quickly, within the first few minutes ... maybe ten? That Hauptmann Reineke went from being ... well, myth to man. No. The shenanigans, sexuality, myth remained. Interestingly enough however, in amongst all of that, Reineke was focused, intent, determined, a commander.

Eric wouldn't go as far as saying he was brilliant, but he was intelligent. A strategist. His plan well thought out, very elaborate—very good, and would possibly even work. Eric smiled. "Ambitious. I would say Hauptmann Reineke is ambitious."

"Very ambitious," Schönfeld concurred. "Very."

Yes. Eric continued to gaze out the window at what he could not see and in doing so, something occurred to him. Reineke's motorcade when it had arrived, pulled up and parked where the staff car and its occupants could be viewed from Oberleutnant Thiele's office. Or more accurately Thiele's former office. An empty office as far as Hauptmann Reineke would know not having yet met or been introduced to Schönfeld's new adjutant Hauptmann Eric Danzig. In contrast, or comparison, the motorcade and staff car could not be seen from Schönfeld's office. An occupied office. Coincidence? Reineke simply had the motorcade stop and the staff car park in front of the alleyway he would walk to the front door? "I wonder which?" Eric wondered aloud. "I wonder why?"

"Hauptmann?" Schönfeld offered Eric a brandy as he poured one for himself.

"Oh, yes, thank you," Eric accepted with a smile. "Sorry, thinking."

"Yes." Schönfeld likewise extended the offer of one of his trademark cigars.

Tempting. Eric had stuck to cigarettes during the four-hour show provided by Reineke. It gave the appearance of the ordinary man, in this together kind of thing, to where a cigar reeked of a stuffed fat pig. Hauptmann Reineke also smoked cigarettes—chain-smoked like a fiend. He drank black coffee, one cup, and water, one glass. He did not drink brandy, bourbon, or Arabian beer, at least not there. Reineke also stole and accepted credit for Eric's caricature of the twit downstairs, claiming it for his own, as his own. Eric would get him for that, yes, he would.

"Yes," Schönfeld chuckled with a shake of his head. "Weiheber."

"What?" Eric came to attention.

"Weiheber," Schönfeld chuckled again with another shake of his head at the caricature still there on his desk. "Hauptmann Reineke," he said in a manner of not-so-secret appreciation and approval of Reineke including a rendering of the SS Major Weiheber in his report. Eric could not have intentionally placed the drawing in a more apropos place than he had when he slammed it in with the pages he picked up from the floor.

"Oh," Eric said, "yes," with a bite of his tongue, not telling the stupid old goat it looked like Weiheber about as much as he did, while naturally accepting and appreciating the offer and opportunity to share a cigar. "And, yes, thank you, again."

He took the cigar and sat down in the chair he moved slightly off center in front of Schönfeld's desk, ensuring it was close enough for him to set his glass and use the ashtray, while ensuring it was far enough away for him to extend his legs if he wanted to. Reineke had sat dead center, his legs crossed at the knee, the chair much farther back in a position of power, not a bad little boy sitting before his principal awaiting punishment and discipline. Reineke did not need to stretch for the ashtray, he kept one in his hand, using it, moving it as needed, taking it with him, and setting it down when he occasionally stood up to stand or walk. He did a similar thing with his coffee and his water glass, rising and approaching them, picking them up as needed, when wanted, and setting them down again.

He was poised and restless at the same time and did his best to make Eric look like a fool from the beginning to the end.

Earlier

When Eric walked into Schönfeld's office, Reineke was sitting in the chair in front of Schönfeld's desk, leaving Eric the choice of standing, or pulling up an armless side chair that was a stool by comparison, something on which those bad little boys sat, outcasts, off to the side. Reineke ignored Schönfeld's introductions and Eric brought up the side chair, setting in down on the same side of the desk as Schönfeld and sat smiling, watching Reineke from beneath his smile. Eric spoke very little and when he did, it was deliberate, hoping to catch Reineke off guard, break his stride. Eric came close to success once, early on. Reineke was talking first and foremost about the threat the SS represented as a whole, heightened specifically as they had apparently brought Allied prisoners with them to Reineke's top secret munitions compound.

"Yes, that is astounding," Eric interjected in agreement handing Schönfeld Reineke's report with that specific section on top for Schönfeld's convenience, realizing too late the next page peeking out was the drawing of the twit downstairs. Eric ignored it however remaining focused on Reineke, and came damn close to penetrating that armored hide. "Remarkably concerning ... I am a little confused though, Hauptmann," he smiled, "as to why you brought at least one of the same prisoners here. Are you depositing her with us? Making some point? Some other reason?"

Before Eric finished speaking Schönfeld heard "here" registering shock and repeating: "Here?

"Yes," Eric finished what he was saying, smiling at Reineke fixed on him. "Not there," Eric advised Schönfeld who rose from his desk to look out his windows. "You can't see from there—my office," he offered as Reineke stayed fixed on him. "Though she's not there now," he assured as Schönfeld headed out of his office and into Eric's. "No, I believe—"

"That child?" Schönfeld demanded from the other room. "That child, is that it?" he insisted as Eric's brain registered "child". Schönfeld could not have known that unless the girl was there, back in the staff car, and Reineke's lips spread in a slight smile, sitting back, lighting a cigarette while Schönfeld continued insisting "Hauptmann!" in a manner of calling for one of them.

Which one of them? Eric remained fixed on Reineke fixed on him with that sardonic smirk of his and every indication he was going nowhere the son-of-a-bitch. But Schönfeld was insisting "Hauptmann!" and one of them was going to have to respond.

"Fine!" Eric broke, angrily slamming his coffee down on Schönfeld's desk, answering his call.

"Yes, that's her," Eric agreed after a brief look out the window at the child back in the car, who knew why.

Schönfeld did not say anything, heading back into his office.

"Your point, Hauptmann?" Schönfeld demanded.

Reineke shrugged. "If it is inappropriate of me to bring the prisoner here, it was inappropriate of the SS to bring the prisoner to my complex."

"Point made and accepted, Hauptmann," Schönfeld sat back down with an irritated wave of his hand. "Unnecessary completely, but point taken. Weiheber is stupid indubitably. Now get rid of her."

"Indeed," the brow arched as Reineke turned from looking at Eric to Schönfeld.

"You know what I mean, Hauptmann," Schönfeld's hand waved again, irritably. "Let's not get into that. Give her back," he pointed. "Give her back."

"Oh, well, yes, I can certainly see to that ..." Eric offered smiling as Reineke looked back at him.

"Not you, Hauptmann," Schönfeld said, "Hauptmann Reineke. I believe you said you have a plan ..." Schönfeld returned to the report, discovering the caricature on the next page. He eyed it briefly before taking it out and moving on to flipping pages and reading a little more. "The fifth compound, Hauptmann," he made a note without looking up. "The munitions are to be divided between you and the fifth compound, not the second."

"Indeed," Reineke said. "The fifth complex is redundant. It needs to be dissolved."

"Nothing is redundant yet, Hauptmann."

"If the French attack from the south they will attack to the east, Sebha. Not the west, Algeria."

"You're there to make sure they don't."

"Indeed, I know," Reineke assured. "And the fifth complex is a waste of time and men. Supplies and troops I could use."

"Some other time, Hauptmann. A conversation for a later day." Schönfeld found what he was looking for. Reineke's assurance he would return the prisoner to the SS when he went north.

"Yes, that's fine, Hauptmann," Schönfeld accepted, circling the section. "Excellent idea. Let Hauptmann Danzig know where and when and he will make arrangements with the SS, and will be there to supervise the prisoners' remand."

"Indeed ..." Reineke said again, and Eric was really going to have to practice that one for himself, yes, he was.

"That is enough, Hauptmann," Schönfeld stayed any retort or discussion about that as well. "There is to be no further trouble. Our interests are the compounds, and that is where your focus needs to be. I don't care how impudent the SS are, so were you—as is this," he picked up the caricature, displaying it, if not quite waving it at Reineke, "Inappropriate. Thoroughly," he assured, though he gave it the once-over again with a light chuckle and a shake of his head, showing it to Eric. "Weiheber."

"Yes," Eric smiled back.

"Fairly good likeness, Hauptmann," Schönfeld nodded at Reineke, "but nevertheless inappropriate." He set it down on his desk, not in the waste basket Eric noted.

"The SS are not to return to my compound," Reineke replied. "I will kill them if they do."

"They won't," Schönfeld said. "Now, let's begin at the beginning regarding this plan of yours for the convoy ..."

"Well ..." Eric said in response to Schönfeld's inquiry on what he thought. "Hauptmann Reineke has some very valid points."

Schönfeld grunted. Given a choice, he preferred his madman. "That is a concerning thought, Hauptmann."

"Yes," and Eric knew why. He said it diplomatically, however carefully couched. "Absolute power corrupts absolutely."

"It most certainly does," Schönfeld assured. "Appreciating that it is uncertain how much information on the planned transfers of munitions at the docks ..."

Hijacking. Eric corrected silently. *Hijacking of the munitions at the docks.*

"This Sergeant Erich has been able to provide Weiheber and his associates ..." Schönfeld shook his head.

I believe you mean me. Eric smiled to himself, amused and grateful Sergeant Erich remained assumed to be Weiheber's stoolie. Even though Sergeant Erich, at least initially, had to have been as surprised to see Weiheber at the compound as Reineke had ultimately been.

And I believe, Eric smiled to himself, *you mean everything.* Insofar as to what and how much information Staff Sergeant Erich had been able to pass to his SS, and it would be everything over the past several months. Eric knew it all. It was why Reineke's desired changes, at least, for the opening act, were unnecessary. Eric had no intentions of stopping the planned hijacking. To the contrary, Eric had every intention of seeing it through, seeing if it worked, seeing if it could be done, how well and how quickly, and, of course, the return on the effort. What was the return on the guerrilla operation for the overall objective—and Eric meant the overall campaign, North Afrika and Suez—how much, and how valuable. He was there to observe, collect information and not intervene, at least not at this point.

Of course, now that Eric thought about that, he was thinking of something else, someone else. Weiheber. Eric was no threat to the operation, at least not yet. Not so when it came to Weiheber.

"Hm ..." Eric stood there thinking about the pickle they were in, Reineke trickling back into his mind. The intelligent, loyal officer who had something up his sleeve. Eric had an idea he knew what it was—Schönfeld's job. It was written all over Reineke's plan.

It was written all over ... his personnel file.

"I'll be damned," Eric whistled softly. Reineke was going to kill Weiheber. Remove the SS threat permanently and no doubt the Allied should there actually be one.

"I have a question," Eric interrupted whatever Schönfeld was thinking and saying about Reineke wanting to insert himself in the operational plan at the beginning not simply wait on a road north of Sebha for the munitions to come to him. "Sorry," he apologized.

"Not at all," Schönfeld allowed. "Open discussion, Hauptmann, open discussion."

"Yes," Eric said. "And couldn't we *encourage* Sergeant Erich by whatever means necessary to disclose how much information he has been able to pass?"

"I'm quite sure we could. I've no doubt Hauptmann Reineke already has," Schönfeld assured. "However, I think it's reasonable to presume not much."

Eric nodded. "Meaning enter Herr Major Weiheber to obtain said information from Erich."

"Precisely," Schönfeld said.

"After all," Eric rose to help himself to another brandy, forgo the cigar for now and light a cigarette, continuing to mull things over, "it wouldn't be easy for anyone to ... well, pass information to anyone on the outside. No secret love letters, late night telephone calls, notes hidden inside shoes, baked into bread—Brandy?" he offered.

"Yes, thank you," Schönfeld accepted.

"Not at all," Eric assured. "In all it would be very difficult for Sergeant Erich to contact anyone. Instead, his contact would have to come to him."

"Yes," Schönfeld said. "The compounds are isolated and controlled for a reason, Hauptmann."

Yes, they were. No one wanted to get caught, discovered, shut down, by anyone. German, French, or Allied alike. As far as Sergeant Erich, difficult, was not impossible, and would be much easier—or should have been much easier if Erich hadn't been stupid enough to tip his hand by embracing Weiheber. "How much does Sergeant

Erich know?" Eric confirmed. "Specifically about the docks and the men involved in the transfer?"

"A lot," Schönfeld said. "Quite a lot. Not everything," he assured with a smile. "Few know everything, Hauptmann."

"Yes," Eric said, "fortunately. Though, of course," he agreed, "Erich would know enough. After all, he would be a principal player together with Hauptmann Reineke and Oberleutnant Thiele. The man in the field, that sort of thing. The one taking more of the physical chances—expendable, in other words," he smiled. "Or at least more expendable than Hauptmann Reineke and Oberleutnant Thiele."

"Exactly," Schönfeld said.

"Yes," Eric said. "So we're looking at Tripoli or Tunis for Erich's contacts, where he would have shared his information prior to Herr Major's arrival."

"Tripoli," Schönfeld concurred. "Erich would have nothing to do with Tunis."

Eric nodded. "I have another question. Why is Sergeant Erich still among the living now that his betrayal has been revealed?"

"We don't know if he is," Schönfeld chuckled. "But if he is, I would say because Hauptmann Reineke needs him. The hour is practically upon us, Hauptmann."

The *hour* had at least a couple of weeks to go. But that was all right, Eric believed he understood. Kept on a tight leash, controlled, Reineke could make use of what he needed from Erich, such as his contacts, and when it was over, throw him to the lions.

"I propose," Eric nodded, "Hauptmann Reineke is right to make changes to the plan."

"A matter of not taking chances," Schönfeld said.

"Yes. Erich facing obstacles in passing his information on, fine. But there's no saying Erich did not provide Weiheber with the logistics once he arrived at the compound."

"I'm quite sure he did, Hauptmann."

"Yes," Eric said. "So am I. He must have. Of course," he smiled, "there's no saying how much Herr Major Weiheber retained."

"Well, that's to our benefit, Hauptmann," Schönfeld said about that. And that's all he would say. After all, whatever Weiheber was now, those decorations on his breast told a very different story of who he had once been. It wasn't like they just handed them out not even to Göring who also earned his back in the old days.

"Yes," Eric sat down with his smile. "Even so," he said as he sipped his brandy, "shouldn't we be killing Herr Major Weiheber? Shouldn't we have killed Weiheber?" Under that proposal of not taking any chances?"

Schönfeld was quiet and Eric nodded. "Are we killing Herr Major Weiheber?" he asked.

"It's possible," Schönfeld acknowledged. "Perhaps even probable," he agreed. "I wouldn't be surprised, Hauptmann," he extended, "to hear of Weiheber's death, and neither should you. But that would not be a decision of Hauptmann Reineke's."

Amazing, was all Eric had to say about that, and only to himself. Amazing. "And, this ... prisoner business," Eric waved. "This concern about some Allied installation."

"A very serious concern," Schönfeld assured.

"Oh, yes," Eric agreed. "Much more so than even the SS ... after all, at least there we are ultimately on the same side."

"A reason, no doubt," Schönfeld said, "for the delay."

"Delay?" Eric said. "I'm sorry, what delay?"

"Hauptmann Reineke's not maniacal," Schönfeld claimed.

Hauptmann Reineke was maniacal, Eric hated to break the news and so he didn't. Reineke was also, Eric understood, angry and concerned by the recent events. He wanted to control, subdue and end it once and for all. Unfortunately, once and for all included murdering an SS Major. Reineke would have to handle that very carefully, taking care to cover his tracks very well.

"No," Eric agreed. "Hauptmann Reineke is not maniacal. He is angry and concerned."

"Yes," Schönfeld said.

"As obvious in his demonstration with the prisoner," Eric waved, "bringing the child here."

"Oh, that," Schönfeld dismissed.

Yes, that. Eric almost waved back in imitation, but refrained. "Annoying you in demonstration of how annoyed he was."

"Unnecessary," Schönfeld assured. "Unnecessary."

"Yes. But he is returning her."

"Of course," Schönfeld said.

"Makes one wonder why he bothered to take her in the first place," Eric downed his brandy with a smile.

"Spite," Schönfeld imagined.

"One-upmanship," Eric agreed, and he would find out if the towheaded bastard had any idea of that child's true worth or not. "I propose he bring her and whoever else back to us and we take care of that part of the arrangements. I say again, I can take care of it for us, personally, myself, if you like."

"A good idea," Schönfeld supported. "If you can convince Hauptmann Reineke, please feel free."

"Convince him?" Eric said. "In what way?"

"Who knows," Schönfeld shrugged. "Hauptmann Reineke has very strict rules and opinions on the operations of war."

Did he? Eric hadn't heard a rule yet Reineke hadn't broken, smashed to pieces as a matter of fact. As far as opinions? "Opinions?" Eric did not mean to sound as incredulous as he was.

"Regarding the involvement of civilians, Hauptmann," Schönfeld explained.

"Oh," Eric said. "Oh, yes, I understand." One of those. Silent Night. The Christmas Truce and other bedtime stories from the wars.

"It's all nonsense," Schönfeld assured.

It most certainly was. Hauptmann Reineke didn't give two shits about anyone except for Hauptmann Reineke that was very clear to Eric.

"And harmless," Schönfeld promised, what appeared to matter most to him.

And that was also bullshit, Eric would hate to disappoint him. Nothing about the Hauptmann Reineke Eric met appeared harmless.

"Back to what matters," Schönfeld nodded.

"Please," Eric agreed.

"I am not inclined to agree to Hauptmann Reineke involving himself in the organization of the operation at the docks. It's not his place. And let's be honest, Hauptmann, not his privilege."

"Yes," Eric said. "He's one of five, part of a team, not in it on his own."

"Precisely. That being said ..."

Oh, here we go. Exceptions, exceptions, to be made. Hauptmann Reineke was clearly Schönfeld's fair-haired boy. "Tunis," Eric offered.

"I do agree it is within reason to alter the method of exchange," Schönfeld said. "Once secured and en route, I like the idea of passing off the munitions to another group. A different group either on the coast or in the immediate vicinity as Hauptmann Reineke explained ..." Schönfeld was up, walking around, thinking it through. "Exact area, of course, to be determined."

"Tunis," Eric nodded.

"From there, Hauptmann Reineke and this group to transport them to an interim location—again," he pointed. "Still within the same general area, possibly even still the coast or thereabouts."

Not even close. "Tunis," Eric shook his head.

"From there, to a second interim location, much deeper inland, possibly Algeria, we'll leave it to Hauptmann Reineke to decide ... and from there," he said, "if all goes well, and I'm confident it will, south to us." He sat down. "Division to take place at Hauptmann Reineke's compound. All risks, responsibility shouldered by him—I respect that," he nodded. "He feels he is responsible ultimately for the actions of his man Erich, and he is. Completely responsible. I appreciate he is willing to accept that responsibility and shoulder it. I respect it. I respect him."

He ... *him* ... was so full of shit Eric did not know where to begin. That great plan of Reineke's that Eric had decided was great, he now decided was as full of shit as it's orchestrator. Eric had no idea why he decided that, he had no idea where the shit actually lay. He just knew it was there.

"I'm sorry, Hauptmann, did you say something?" Schönfeld asked.

"I?" Eric said. "Oh, yes. Tunis."

"Tunis?" Schönfeld said. "What about Tunis? The docks are in Tripoli, Hauptmann."

Eric's point. "Then why Tunis?"

"In what way, Hauptmann?" Schönfeld asked.

In what way? "I'm sorry ..." Eric said, "perhaps it's me, but I could have sworn Hauptmann Reineke indicated Tunis in his report."

"Oh?" Schönfeld reached for the report.

"Please allow me ..." Eric offered.

"No, I have it. It's in the Telex, Hauptmann," he nodded.

I haven't seen the goddamn Telex. Eric did not say. "Of course," he smiled. "My error. I'm tired."

"Who isn't?" Schönfeld frowned as he read.

Most people, Eric would think at barely nine o'clock in the evening, but for some reason he felt exhausted. "I'm sorry?" he said as Schönfeld frowned, and then suddenly chuckled.

"His whores," Schönfeld tossed the Telex back on his desk.

"Come again?" Eric requested.

"Hauptmann Reineke has a whore house in Tunis, It's just an error. Thinking of his whores. He meant Tripoli."

Of course he did! And, of course he was—who wouldn't be? Eric really, *really* decided at that point that they had covered what they could cover for one day. "Well," he said brightly and stood up, "I'm going to see about having dinner, what about you?"

"Good idea," Schönfeld agreed.

"Excellent!" Eric beamed. "I'm going to freshen up, and I'll meet you outside—and perhaps," he winked, "we'll get lucky without having to go to Tunis."

"Not a bad idea, Hauptmann, let's be honest."

"What isn't?" Eric requested politely. "Going to Tunis for a three-day soirée, or settling for what one can get—as most men do?"

"Well, obviously the former, Hauptmann, however impractical."

"So sayeth you. Hauptmann Reineke apparently an exception to the rule."

"Yes. However, it's not a bad idea, Hauptmann Reineke wanting a whore house here. Can you think of a reason why not?"

"Not offhand," Eric had to say when he stopped choking on his cigar he relit.

"Are you all right?" Schönfeld asked.

"Quite fine," Eric cleared his throat. "Thank you. I'll meet you outside."

He left, exited the office and the building to walk up the sloping alley way, around the bend and into the hovel that was his quarters, his home away from home, otherwise known as a piss-pot. A stinking little shithole made of thick adobe or mud walls, and one small lopsided window facing the twit's quarters across the way.

"Ah! Well, that probably didn't help, did it?" Eric noticed as he dipped his fingers in his washbowl and splashed a little water on his face and neck, checking his teeth and chin in the mirror. His complexion after only two weeks in the desert was ruby red but starting to deepen nicely, promising a healthy bronze tan. The eyes were another story. Eric still wore goggles almost constantly, finding the sun intensely bright even under his brimmed hat. Since he wore the goggles constantly and since his face was otherwise exposed to the sun he had two very large white circles around his eyes where the goggles fit quite nicely.

"Sort of like ..." Eric decided as he examined his face in the mirror. "A raccoon."

He wondered briefly what Hauptmann Reineke might have actually been thinking when he looked at Eric with those large white circles encircling Eric's eyes in his ruddy red face. Eric decided he did not care because men did not care about those sorts of things, they really did not.

Later, after dinner and settling for what he could get, Eric resurrected his office from its battle with the legendary fierce desert wind. It still nagged him what Hauptmann Reineke could have possibly been looking for in the office he thought was Thiele's. Even if Reineke had put two and two together without having been told, realizing the only person Eric could possibly be was perhaps Schönfeld's new aide ...

"It still doesn't explain ..." Eric stood in the middle of his office, hands on his hips, looking around, "what he was looking for ...

"A pass." It came to Eric as he closed and locked his office door. He unlocked it, heading back in, sitting down at his desk lighting the lantern.

"Travel passes," Eric nodded, naturally maintaining a limited supply, as naturally accounted for, and most naturally, two missing. Two complete sets missing. Every piece of paper, permission slip Reineke might need.

"And ..." Eric said, now that that had been solved. "Why, oh why would Hauptmann Reineke throw his report?" Along with everything else in there? Because Eric had doodled on it? Leaving no page unsullied or untouched?

"All sorts of doodles ..." Eric held one sheet up to the lantern, and then another, and another. "From scribbles, to pictures, to curse words, and everything in between ... ah, ha," Eric smiled. There it was. The imprint of his signature on the page he held up from where he had scribbled his name over the page that had been on top.

"*Signed* travel passes," Eric dropped the page down. "No doubt for a three day trip to Tunis."

But why? Hardly to see some whore. Weiheber was the only thing Eric could come up with. The docks were in Tripoli. Perhaps Weiheber was in Tunis? Or Reineke thought he was? Had been told he was by Erich during or after ... Eric shuddered. No reason to think about whatever torturous agonies Erich was put through. Besides, it wasn't Tunis, it was Tripoli, the docks. *Tunis* was not an error, it was deliberate to throw Alfred off the track.

"Why, you little ... little ... *scamp*," Eric scolded. The first set of travel documents were clearly for Reineke himself. The second, the man he was taking with him. Not Oberleutnant Thiele Eric would think. Reineke would never leave his complex completely exposed, even if he wasn't as concerned about the possibility of an Allied installation in the area as he attempted to impress upon Schönfeld. An Allied installation seemed unlikely, as unlikely as a German one being there. They were deep in Italian territory. The complex was safe, at least from the Allies. The French? Who knew. Perhaps Hauptmann Reineke was worried about the French.

Eric decided not to tell Schönfeld about the travel passes. Alfred probably wouldn't care, anyway. He did not seem to care about anything except that the munitions would be where they were supposed to be, when.

"Hauptmann?" Schönfeld appeared in Eric's doorway as if summoned.

"Herr Oberst!" Eric jumped. "Sorry, you startled me. It's rather late, isn't it? Two ... " he glanced at his watch that read not quite two o'clock in the morning.

"It's all right," Schönfeld said, "I've been thinking ... and I think you should meet Hauptmann Reineke at this ... this field hospital he's planning to establish for the transfer of the munitions from the second convoy to the ..."

"Third?" Eric offered. "His trucks," he smiled.

"Yes," Schönfeld said. "Meet him. I'm confident everything will work as planned, but there's no sense taking chances. Hauptmann Reineke's right. Especially with this issue with the SS."

"Meaning Hauptmann Reineke is now taking on—of his own volition—the physical exposure, that is the risk that would have otherwise been Sergeant Erich's, by taking command of the convoy himself."

"Yes," Schönfeld said.

"I'll meet him," Eric smiled. "I'd be delighted. There's nothing quite like hand's on experience."

"No, there isn't," Schönfeld agreed. "We'll schedule a meeting to review the transfer at the docks—however if anyone goes to Tripoli, Hauptmann, it will likely be you."

"Excellent," Eric nodded. "Yes, that's excellent."

"Good night, Hauptmann."

"Good night, Herr Oberst," Eric reciprocated and went to bed. Dreaming about ...

"Italian territory?" Eric sat up. The physicist was Italian according to the Russian Reiss. Herr Major Weiheber was bringing the child to Sebha, planning to bury her literally or figuratively in Sebha. "Clever, Herr Major," Eric agreed. There would be no chance of some Allied raid to spirit her out of there, no more than there would be out of Hauptmann Reineke's compound. Tripoli would be difficult, but not impossible. And certainly Tunis would be a snap for even the French. No wonder Herr Major agreed to go away without the prisoners. They were safely tucked away in the compound. "Either that or Herr Major forgot about them," Eric shrugged and fell happily back to sleep. His future fame and fortune secure.

Chapter Forty-Nine

It was terribly uncomfortable in the car. The seat was hard and the sun was hot. Joanna crossed and uncrossed her legs, her hip sore from sitting for so long, her feet determined to fall asleep, and bladder, as Michael would say, on overload.

"All right, you win!" Joanna wailed before she had an accident she would probably be forced to clean, walloping the driver soundly on the arm, abruptly rousing him. "What does he expect me to do?" she insisted. "Sit here and fry like some egg? You got money? Show me your money. I'll buy everything they have. Move it, Jack!" she belted him again. "Let me out of this tin can!"

Perhaps she should not have done that. The driver had a very queer look on his face.

"I would like to get out of the car now, please," Joanna requested as sweetly as she could make herself sound. "If that's all right."

He sneered, moving his sneer to her feet, dangerously close to her toes. "The Hauptmann says you are to wear shoes."

"They don't fit!" Joanna snapped.

He was not impressed.

"I'll get blisters," she threatened. "Do you know what those are? Horrid, nasty boils. They're poisonous and highly contagious. If you make me get them, I'll step on you, and you'll die!"

His English was not that good.

Joanna tried another approach. "I don't want to!"

That seemed to confuse him. It gave her courage. "Besides," she announced, bravely stretching her foot out the door, "the sun is setting. The rocks are cool—YEOW!" Joanna screamed as her skin touched the hot metal running board, hot enough to iron her pants. "Excuse me!" she said returning her foot to the car to clutch and blow on it.

"Is the Fräulein going shopping?" Was all he wanted to know,

"Soon," Joanna nodded. "Soon" First though, she had some thinking to do. Not about escaping, just about out there, out of the car where she desperately wanted to be even though out there, down there, were some mighty hot rocks. Still, out there, somewhere there had to be something to drink, and maybe even a loo. Maybe only a private alley. She would take anything.

"I'm ready!" Joanna announced, and she was. She was wearing the sandals.

What I did the Spring I was Kidnapped, by Joanna Edwards Lee

One afternoon, I went shopping in an Arab market. Clogged with German tourists and other nasty people pushing and shoving their way. It was gruesome. However, in spite of it all inside of an hour, possibly two, Joanna had practically cleaned the whole damn place out.

"You're out of money?" Joanna stared disbelievingly at the driver. Having been born rich, she could not possibly conceive of such a thing as no money.

"Ja," he nodded, having a tough time with it himself. But that was all right, they were also practically out of room.

"Oh," Joanna said, a touch disappointed because really of all the things she had bought, she really wanted—"These!" she dangled an enticing armful of socks in front of him. "What if you offer him your watch?" she suggested, having seen that once or twice in a film. "They love watches."

"I do not think so," the bastard disagreed, but only because he was a selfish pig.

"But, you said I could go shopping," Joanna protested in a tone that immediately had the two motorbike fellows over there to see what the trouble was. "I only want these last few things."

And she got them, too. Not forgetting to thank the driver for his personal sacrifice as one of his buddies practically tore his watch from his wrist before one of them had to give up one of theirs.

"*Bitte,*" the driver gave Joanna a curt nod, and she was escorted back to the car where she sat for another hot hour or two waiting for the Captain to return from wherever he was.

He did finally. Only Joanna was the one who ended up being miffed not him. *Cheeky devil,* she glared at him. He should have at least had the decency to be angry when he returned to his car to find there was barely enough room left for him to put a foot inside, forget about sitting down.

But, he wasn't angry, no, he was not. Or at least he did not appear to be. He merely glanced at his driver who stared straight ahead leaving the Captain to motion for the two motorbike fellows to come and take temporary possession and responsibility for as many of the trinkets as they could comfortably handle, whether or not they had to wear some of them to get them safely home. A place they left for as soon as Reineke had enough room to sit down.

Bastard. Joanna continued to glare at him, huffing and puffing and half tempted to hit him in the head with one of her baskets and see what he had to say about that.

Bastard! She fussed and fumed. Muttering under her breath, twisting this way and that, really outdoing herself for nothing, all the long way home. This was Pierre's fault, she decided. Really, it was all Pierre's fault, not only for leaving her, but for everything. No one was nice and sweet and considerate as he said. They were not. The crone was grumpy and the little witch really was a little witch. And as far as *this one,* Joanna glared at the Captain. She certainly did not see anything particularly *kind* about him. Nothing so noticeably generous or *sweet.* To the contrary, she was convinced everything Pierre said he made up. Deliberately. Intentionally.

Especially about you. Joanna nodded sharply at the Captain's silent silhouette sitting in front, ignoring his car piled high with sundries no one could ever need. Every item Joanna bought, struck a blow of victory, revenge, and so what? He did not care. He didn't even care enough to be angry about it, and why would he? Who was she? Nobody, that's who. Someone to be dismissed and ordered around. She did not care what Pierre said. She was a prisoner. Make no mistake. For all Pierre kept insisting what he wanted her to see, Joanna could see what she saw, and it was not the truth as Pierre saw it. This was not a car. That *house* of his, not a house. The gardens, not gardens. This was ... well, prison, Joanna insisted, turning around to study the car with the long, thin gun on its back following them.

She might have been shopping, but she would have liked to have tried it on her own, gone it alone. She might pal around with the children, but she was escorted to and from. Some fine and pretty room to call her own? Joanna sniffed, tears starting to burn. Her doors were locked day and night. She knew because she tried them every night and it was infuriating to know she was a prisoner in a place everyone kept trying to pass off as paradise.

There was an exceptional amount of commotion in the rear seat of his car, rapidly approaching unnecessary. The woman was talking to herself, her behavior remarkably similar to that of the Holy Man when he wanted attention.

Reineke paid no attention. She whistled and wished his death upon a star—there were several of them out as the last of the sun faded and the darkness swept in.

She announced she was cold, and it was a lie. It was pleasant tonight, cheery, breezy, brisk.

She began some vulgar dissertation of her treatment, continuing on as he continued to ignore her.

She pinched him. On the arm. A hard, pulling, twisting, painful bite of his flesh between her finger and thumb.

"I just wanted to see if you were real," her nasty voice taunted from somewhere deep inside her pile of garbage as he whirled around. "You know how they say pinch yourself to see if you're dreaming? Well, it's the same sort of thing. Only I know I'm not dreaming, so why pinch myself? It hurts."

It certainly did. Beyond inappropriate.

"Why what's the matter, Captain?" the vicious little elf jeered and sneered barely an inch from his staring, glaring face, his eyes almost crossing to keep her in focus. "Lost your sense of humor? Heaven's, aren't we the pill."

And the pill had three choices. Though the woman attempted to retreat out of his reach, he could easily pull her back and pinch her arm, hard—something Reineke was going to do to his driver if he did not stop laughing.

"Indeed!" Reineke's glare turned briefly on his driver, and the soldier immediately shut up, choking his laughter if he had to choke to death to keep it hidden and Reineke's concentration zeroed back in on the woman who he could easily *yank* back to him, slapping her out of the car—something likely to happen to all of them if his driver did not hurry up and catch the steering wheel as he started to laugh again in spite of his orders.

"Indeed!" Reineke's glare turned back on his driver, and the soldier immediately again attempted to comply and Reineke's concentration zoomed back in on the woman, who he could easily—

"Indeed," Reineke blinked as a ridiculous thought crossed his mind. He decided on a fourth choice and turned back around, ignoring her.

The intent behind Reineke's waiting for the woman to unload herself from the car when they arrived home was a simple one. Revenge. She was frightened of him, and he was going to enjoy making her walk by him.

Only she did not walk. She did not move. She slapped his driver when he reached into the car to encourage her, staying neatly rolled up in a tight ball, her knees tucked under her chin.

Reineke took command. "Get out of the car, Fräulein," he instructed, stiffening at the muffled titter of his driver. He was not about to be ridiculed again.

"Indeed. Get out of the car, Fräulein!" Reineke insisted.

"Hauptmann ..." his driver said, a man who had not laughed that time, but had merely said something, and he said it now, again.

"Sick?" Was Reineke's superior assessment of such a ridiculous suggestion. "Absurd."

It did not seem absurd to the soldier. The woman looked sick to him.

"Indeed," Reineke's attention fastened on Joanna. She looked odd. Pale, yet pink. "Fräulein, are you ill?" he inquired unpleasantly.

"I'm cold," Joanna said.

Lies. He knew it. It was not cold outside. She was pink because—He had no idea, and neither did he care. "Fräulein," he ordered, "you are to get out of the car or I will remove you."

"You just try it, Jack," Joanna promised, "and it won't be a pinch you get."

Reineke would take his chances. The slap she gave his hand when he grabbed her, little more than a bee's sting. The arm he grasped ...

"Indeed," Reineke said. Her arm was sticky, clammy, cold. The woman was ill. Her face, hot, her neck, wet. "Go for the woman Sotma," he ordered his driver. "She is with the children. Fräulein," he returned to Joanna, "you must get out of the car now."

Only Joanna couldn't. She'd vomit. Their bodies were starting to dance around her, sway in and out of focus. Her mouth, watering ...

"Fräulein," Reineke insisted as Joanna tipped over to lay her head down on the seat. "Do as I am telling you."

"But, I ..." Joanna said. "I can't ..."

"Oh, but, Mademoiselle," a familiar voice chuckled, appearing, just like Grandfather had always assured her the Lord would in her final hour. *"Of course you can, of course you can."*

Pierre? Joanna opened her eyes. "Pierre?" she whispered. "Pierre, is that you?"

"Oui, Mademoiselle," he assured. "Of course."

"But you're dead," Joanna said.

"I?" he laughed. "No, not, I, of course not."

"Then I'm dead," Joanna decided.

"No," Pierre held out his hand. "You are not dead either. A little sick and it is nothing. We will take care of it. Come, Mademoiselle, come to Pierre."

"But, I can't," Joanna apologized. "I'm sick."

"Oui, I know. But you do not want to be sick here, do you?"

Here? "Oh, heaven's no!" Joanna gasped. "Please!" Why, she'd die from embarrassment, she would just die.

"So then, come, Mademoiselle," he encouraged. "Come."

"Make them go away," Joanna nodded, "and I will. Tell them to go away."

"Away?" Pierre smiled. "Who? There is no one here. Only you and I, Mademoiselle. Only you and Pierre."

What? Joanna pushed herself up off the seat. He was telling the truth. Everyone was gone, the Captain, and all of the Captain's men.

"Mademoiselle?" Pierre said.

"But ..." Joanna said. "But, where did they go?"

"Into the house, of course," Pierre agreed. "Where we want to be."

"I'm never going to make it," Joanna warned him as she slid towards him.

"Oui, possibly," Pierre nodded. "But we will try. Come, let us try."

"OK," Joanna took his arm, and he smiled, patting her hand.

"You are glad to see Pierre," he said, "this is good. I knew you would be glad to see me."

March 19

Reineke studied the desert night through the glass of the balcony windows. The unrelenting pressure of all of this was getting to him. He never felt relaxed, only caged, guilty and responsible for everything, his emotions as erratic as the woman, disheveled as she looked. He was still standing there when the Holy Man entered from the apartment, startling with the sound of footsteps, breath. He did not turn around but turned to walk briskly for the wine cabinet. "I sent for the woman Sotma," he assured, forgetting it had been more than an hour since their return.

"She will not come," Pierre said, "she knows I am here."

Reineke nodded, pouring the wine. "I had to go to town to see my Colonel to make the arrangements—our arrangements," he reminded Pierre sharply before he could comment. "Diana is well aware—of both," he assured, and stalked for his desk.

"Oui, mon capitaine," Pierre was not accusing. "This is what Mademoiselle tells me."

The woman? Reineke paused. That was ridiculous. "Indeed, the woman? What can the woman know? Do not be absurd."

"About her trip. She tells Pierre how she went to town."

"Oh," Reineke said. He picked up his wine, slamming it down. "Indeed, that is quite correct. *Town.* Not her execution or some *camp*! What happened to her?" he demanded. "Why is she sick again? Hysterical? If she knows, understands the innocence of her trip?"

"Happened? Nothing. The heat, food, excitement. The Arab likes sugar, mon capitaine," Pierre shrugged. "Everything is very sweet. You know this for yourself."

"Food?" Reineke interrupted.

"Oui, food," Pierre said. "You did not feed her?"

Of course he fed her. Not personally, but she was fed. "There is no reason for the woman to be excited," Reineke assured. "Indeed, not about *food* or anything."

"Oui, but she was."

"And it is absurd," Reineke silenced him. "If she chooses to eat herself into a nervous state, that is her responsibility not mine. I did nothing to cause the woman any harm or *excitement*. If she is telling you otherwise, she is lying." He drank his wine. It tasted awful.

"It is one o'clock in the morning," Pierre reminded.

"I know what time it is," Reineke snapped. "What did I do? Break your curfew? The woman in bed by nine o'clock? It was eight before we left the town. If she was that tired, hysterical about her bed or food, she should have eaten wisely and slept in the car—this wine is terrible!" He snatched up his telephone, barking, "Coffee!" when asked to repeat. "Indeed," he said to Pierre, "I also drink coffee at one o'clock in the morning!"

"Mon capitaine," Pierre apologized, "I have no idea what you are talking about."

Neither did Reineke. "I am convinced this woman enjoys collapsing," he assured. "She has done nothing but collapse since she has been here. There is nothing any more wrong with her today than there has been the last three times she has felt faint—or whatever it is she feels that has her collapsing—Come in," he answered his sentry's knock, the coffee tasting much better than the wine when he drank it, feeling alive rather than faint himself. "Indeed, I am the one who has not had food," he said. "I cannot even stomach the thought of it."

"Mon capitaine ..." Pierre shook his head.

"I am not your patient!" Reineke silenced him again. "She is. She is to accept her situation and behave. I will not have any more of this. There is nothing wrong with the woman she has not done to herself—since she has been here," he assured Pierre looking at him. "I am talking about since she has been here. She is fine."

"Oui, she is," Pierre agreed. "And this is good because Pierre is leaving. I will see you tomorrow night, mon capitaine."

Leaving? What did he mean he was leaving? "Wait a minute," Reineke stopped him. "Where are you going? You have only returned."

"To say hello," Pierre nodded. "I am here and I will be back."

"But the woman!" Reineke said. "You cannot leave the woman, she is ill. Call the woman Sotma!"

"She is fine," Pierre assured. "Like mon capitaine said. It is the heat."

Heat? Reineke stared at the apartment door. "Ah, ha!" he turned on Pierre.

"Ah, ha, what mon capitaine?" Pierre sighed.

"The hat," Reineke assured. "Indeed, I gave her a hat—a hat!" he triumphantly sat down at his desk, ordering more coffee. "She refused to wear it."

"I know," Pierre nodded. "Mademoiselle told me this, along with the shoes."

Shoes? Reineke paused.

"Oui, sandals," Pierre smiled. "You purchased sandals for her to wear. That was very generous of you, mon capitaine. Very kind. She enjoyed her shopping outing very much as I can see."

Indeed. He was a devil this priest. The gesture had been neither generous, nor kind, but simply innocent. Necessary. Without a doubt, considering the environment, sound. "She should have seen to wearing the hat," Reineke repeated, ignoring the issue of the footwear and everything else.

"She knows," Pierre promised. "The sandals? Oui, she did. And so while she may have burned her head, she did not burn her feet."

"Enough!" Reineke ended the matter with a wave, he had opened his attaché for a reason. "Indeed," he smiled, suddenly evil himself. "Where are you going? Why are you here?" he asked, "if you are simply leaving again? What is taking now four days that should have only taken two, eh, Holy Man? I have to go to Tunis ..."

"Yes, mon capitaine," Pierre said.

"I know!" Reineke slapped his six-page itinerary down on his desk, the Telex on top. "This is not from me to my Colonel, it is from Diana."

"Oh," Pierre bit his laugh.

"It is not funny," Reineke assured. "You see this? All this about the SS ... and, here, Tunis," he pointed. "Three days to Tunis."

"And it is all true," Pierre agreed.

"I know it is true," Reineke assured. "How is it Diana knows? When did you return?"

"Just now."

"And you did not talk to her?"

"Pierre? No, John is talking to her now."

"But not before?" Reineke said.

"Perhaps oui, once before on the radio," Pierre agreed. "So what does it matter? It is all true."

"Except she could not know that," Reineke said. "It is not a reiteration of something she could not know about. It is her decision, a threat!" He shoved the Telex at Pierre and snapped his attaché closed.

"It is OK," Pierre set the Telex on top of the attaché with a pat. "This is for you. We have a copy."

"Mimeograph?" Reineke scoffed.

"Pardon?" Pierre said.

"Mim-e-o-graph," Reineke assured. "A duplicating machine, next to your Telex. Indeed," he said, "I should have so much petrol to waste."

"Pardon?" Pierre said.

"On the generators!" Reineke shoved his attaché away, rising again for the wine cabinet. "I did not give you the generators to send Telex to my Colonel. I gave you them for the children's hospital!"

"Oui, mon capitaine," Pierre said. "I will tell her."

"Thank you!" Reineke said. He decided against the wine and returned to his desk and his coffee.

"It is just Diana, mon capitaine," Pierre offered. "It has nothing to do with trust—"

"It has everything to do with trust," Reineke assured. "Indeed. In the meantime, it is I who must trust everyone and everything!" He shook his head. "Where are you going now?" he asked.

"Not only I, mon capitaine, You. Pierre will return for you tomorrow night, and then we both go."

"Where?" Reineke said.

"So strong the heat out there today?" Pierre checked. "To Ben, of course. From Ben to Tunis and mon capitaine's whore," he patted the Telex again with a smile. "You have one week to give Ben his money or he will kill you and take his horses back. I have sworn to tell you, but he wishes to tell you himself. For him to see you and for you to see him, and," Pierre said, "the skins of his enemies he keeps, and the saber he has ready to take yours should you try to betray him."

"No," Reineke said.

"Pardon? No? Then mon capitaine does not want his horses," Pierre shrugged.

"I want the horses," Reineke assured. "Linke has orders to begin transport upon arrival—–and it is to be today," he advised. "You have had more than enough time. I have no time for an audience—indeed," he said, "I have no time if he wants his money as quickly as he wants it."

"He does," Pierre assured.

"Then he can show me his enemies' skins some other time," Reineke said, "when I bring it to him. And neither do you have time to waste with any games. The arrangements you need to confirm are with Diana not to attack my caravan. Who is this *John* you spoke of? The dentist? Indeed. I talk with Abraham only, you know this. Why should I trust my life with this John one step out of this compound? I will not."

"Abraham is busy with arrangements, mon capitaine. And from the north to the south, Gadames, or any area, you wish, mon capitaine's caravan is safe. Protected by Diana, oui," Pierre smiled, "and protected by the Free French from the Sahara to the Tell. I have the word of my son, and the sons of Diana. They will kill anyone who tries to stop you."

Indeed. Reineke sat at his desk.

"You are surprised?" Pierre said. You should not be. I am only mon capitaine's messenger. Mon capitaine speaks very loudly for himself."

"Perhaps louder than I realized," Reineke said.

"Oui. To the hearts of the people you are le Metapel, mon capitaine," Pierre assured.

No, he was not. Perhaps for some ragged band of children or some woman barely more than a child herself. *Le Metapel* was some old priest, an old crone maddened by the loss of her only daughter and her children. He was not le Metapel. He was Hauptmann Reineke of the Afrika Korps. "I!" Reineke said, inclined forward, borrowing that strange interjection of the woman and ending it there just like she did.

"What, mon capitaine?" Pierre said. "What?"

Nothing. Reineke straightened up, returning for his wine. "We are not going."

"We are," Pierre said.

"No, we are not," Reineke assured. "I will not leave the woman unattended by both you and I for even a day with only Diana for supervision ... *and* ..." he said as Pierre opened his mouth, "I will not leave my compound unsupervised. Indeed. Diana is not the only one who has some issue with trust. Thiele has not yet returned. I will not leave, until Thiele is here."

"Then we are going," Pierre said, "because your Thiele will be here tomorrow, before noon."

He was the devil incarnate, this priest. Bold.

"Until that time," Pierre reprimanded with his clucking tongue, "mon capitaine is to be careful in what he does to Mademoiselle."

Do to her? *"Do* to her?" Reineke repeated. "I did nothing to her. I told you before you left, I had to see my Colonel. It was an innocent trip to town."

"No town," Pierre shook his head. "No more shoes, no more hats—no Adva," he pointed. "Mon capitaine is to stay away from the children while Mademoiselle is there. That is not your hospital, it is Pierre's. Mademoiselle does not need to know everything. What she knows is enough."

"What are you talking about?" Reineke said. "I did not put the woman with Adva, that was Diana. I sent her to the children that is all—indeed," he said, "I will visit Adva when I choose. I had no idea she was even there."

"You do not go, mon capitaine," Pierre said. "You have your compound to protect, I have my children as Diana has hers. Mademoiselle will be leaving and what she knows is enough."

Now it was enough. Before nothing was enough, the woman allowed to go everywhere, anywhere even his private quarters were not sacred.

"I had no idea the woman was at the hospital," Reineke insisted. "I went to the children's village and she was not there. I went to find Sotma and visit Adva—indeed," his eyes narrowed. "What is wrong with her? Some nervous attack because she saw me with Adva? What did I do?" he waved. "Confused her senses? Contradict what I am supposed to be? Indeed, caught holding some child instead of eating it together with horses? There was nothing wrong with the woman when she left the village. It was the heat—the heat!" he insisted. "That is what made her sick, not me. She refused to wear the hat. I told her to wear the hat! *One thing*!" he assured, "that *I* told her! Because it is not me who *tells* her things, *shows* her things, *promises* whether they are truth or lies. That is you. I merely took her to town for my meeting with my Colonel—which proved useful," he said, "very useful to our cause—*mutual* cause, Holy Man. You could not be the saint you are if I did not allow it!"

"Parading Mademoiselle like some whore before your town," Pierre sniffed, "is not my cause."

The man was insane. "Shoes!" Reineke barked. "Not whore, shoes! They would not have even seen her. It was only an accident they did—some idiot aide with the raccoon eyes," he waved. "And when they did," he assured, "they thought child, not whore. Child! Agreed with the stupidity of the SS bringing Allied here—agreed to her remand at my choosing—which is our plan, Holy Man," he said. "Our plan—I also secured our travel papers," he snatched up his attaché, opening it, and slapping them down.

"Not my travel papers," Pierre shook his head. "John's."

"Abraham's," Reineke corrected. "And mine. They only need to be completed and signed—and I even have a sample of that idiot's handwriting," he assured, "it is only a simple matter of forgery. Any fool could do it." And, so, yes, obviously since he was an architect and artist he would have little difficulty.

"It cannot be Abraham, mon capitaine," Pierre shook his head.

"You have no choice," Reineke assured. "This *John* can take over whatever arrangements that need to be made."

"Abraham has a tattoo in the middle of his forehead, mon capitaine. He cannot go as your officer. It must be John."

"What?" Reineke said. "What?" he almost whined. "What would possess a man to tattoo his head? Why would he do this? Why? A doctor!" he said. "The man is a doctor!"

"And so he can be a doctor here," Pierre shrugged. "We do not care."

"Indeed," Reineke sat down. "Indeed, I am deserting this place," he swore, "if it is the only thing I live to do."

Pierre laughed. "Perhaps one thing you will live to do. You are a young man. You will live to do many things."

Reineke did not feel young. He felt ancient, older than the Holy Man. "You will be late for your meeting," he said. "When you return, if Thiele is here as you say he will be, then we will go."

"With John?" Pierre checked.

"Obviously," Reineke said. "Have Anne bring the particulars to the children's village this morning—nine o'clock when I bring the woman. I will secure a uniform—he is the dentist? Correct? The German?"

"Oui, but Italian, he wants to be, like Abraham."

Reineke sighed. "Abraham was Italian because he could not be believable as German. This dentist John is German—never mind," he surrendered. It was easier that way, less pain. "He can be who he wants to be—he has Abraham's uniform I presume because I do not have one here. Not Italian," he said. "This is a compound, not a tailor's shop."

"They are working on it," Pierre nodded.

Reineke could imagine, but did not really want to. "I will still need the particulars to complete the paperwork."

"I will tell her," Pierre promised.

"Thank you. Now go, please. Go."

Pierre already was, toddling toward the door. "And you will check Mademoiselle at least once this evening for Pierre. I gave her something to help her sleep. So excited she was, oui, so nervous—the heat, of course," he turned around to smile. "You are right. Nothing to do with you. So if you will check for Pierre, once should be fine, just to make sure."

Of what? Reineke regarded him suspiciously. "To make sure of what, Holy Man? What are you not telling me?"

"Nothing. That she is sleeping," Pierre shrugged. "That she is stomach sick, oui."

"Yes, all right," Reineke waved. "If I think of it, if I have the time—if I do not change my mind and just kill her," he rubbed his hot, tired head. "You forget I could always just kill her."

Pierre laughed. "Too late for that, mon capitaine, much too late."

Was it? How? Why? He would still transport his munitions, take the horses, secure the money from Cäcilie to purchase their reigns, and kill the SS. "Go," Reineke requested. "Just go."

"Oui. Good night, and thank you, mon capitaine," Pierre tipped that head of his and left.

Reineke was not checking, not on the woman. He broke radio silence, testing the privileges he did not have to reach their contacts impatiently waiting in Tripoli. It worked. He got through under the name, "Eric Danzig," Reineke repeated to the signal operator, "Hauptmann Eric Danzig," practicing the signature as he waited. An hour later, he was sending a second message, that one to Tunis and Cäcilie, telling her he would be there sometime in the next few days, more than likely evening. He was going to get his money.

He continued not to check on the woman. He stepped in and out of the apartment a few times but it was only to bring the last of the trinkets his soldiers had piled in his office. The woman was definitely sleeping. There was no reason to check anything.

He did not check a third time, about an hour later. The reason was the night. He was in his chambers constructing the travel passes, rehearsing the plan over and over, the cold night air assisting in keeping him awake increasingly cold. He rose to close one of his windows remembering he had opened one of hers. He felt her forehead and it was hot. One chill a night was sufficient, and so he closed and locked the windows to her balcony.

""Pierre?" he heard her whisper, stirred awake by what felt like a hand and then a sound like someone shutting a door.

"Pierre?" she lifted her sleepy head and really who else would she think was in the room?

"Pierre?" Joanna said uncertainly when he did not answer.

"It is Hauptmann Reineke, Mademoiselle," Reineke replied quietly. "The Holy Man has returned to the village." He should not have said *village*, Joanna would not remember.

"What?" she whispered.

"He said you were sleeping," Reineke agreed. "I see you are not. Go back to sleep, Mademoiselle."

That was an impossible request. He reached the basin before she did, but then he knew where it was, away from her. He had moved it to make room for the toys. A mistake. She needed it more.

He got the basin to her in time to catch the first of the vomit and left her half crying, half choking in her tin dish. There was no reason for this. He could not see a reason for any of this to have happened. In one-hundred years, he could be no more convinced of that than anyone could be about him.

Chapter Fifty

March 20

At five minutes to nine Thiele walked in, his disposition not softened by the uneventful exploration of the Kufra and region, or the fact Linke was packing the last of the trucks scheduled to roll. It was instead aggravated by the tale of the Hauptmann's trek to town.

"Town?" Thiele stared at Linke laughing about some soldier who had lost his watch in exchange for a bushel of socks.

"To town?" Sweating, boiling, livid, Thiele bolted through Reineke's office door. "To town?" he hissed, feeling the pressure rising in his head. "You took the prisoner to the town?"

"You are late," Reineke replied, ignoring the fumes and fury of the dripping, dusty man. "You should have been here yesterday. Are we an additional day's travel away? That is good news, if it's true."

"Are you mad?" Thiele insisted. "Are you out of your mind?" Was that the only plausible explanation for the debris Thiele stumbled back to find? "Hauptmann?"

Not yet. Reineke was tolerant yet. He looked up from his desk. "Come to attention, Thiele," he suggested. "What happened at the Kufra?"

"Attention?" Thiele repeated. "Attention to what? See and hear what? You are already in love with your Frenchman, when will it be enough?"

"What?" Reineke said, but Thiele only glared. He glared, and then whirled to glare at the apartment door, attacking it, hammering it with his fists, screaming for the woman to die.

"Thiele!" Reineke was around his desk and on top of Thiele, pulling him away, driving him backwards into the wall, his fingers gripping Thiele's throat, Thiele grasping at his wrist, trying to pull his hand away.

"You are to leave her alone!" Reineke insisted. "Frighten her again and it is you who will die!" he hissed, but his attack brought a harsh smile to Thiele's face, not a look of fear. Reineke's reaction supported the accusation of misplaced sentiment, not proved it false.

"They will find you out," Thiele threatened when Reineke released him to stare at the apartment door. "Like I have.

"What?" Reineke answered. "What will they find out, Thiele? That I choose who I fight against? Indeed."

"They do not return your generosity," Thiele argued. "They only pretend to! Why can't you see that?"

Perhaps he could. Perhaps he did not want to. Perhaps he did not care. Reineke's head went up in the air. "You are wrong, Thiele. This is not a war against old men, women, or children." He returned to his desk, lighting a cigarette, Thiele on his heels.

"It is a war!"

"You are wrong, Thiele," Reineke repeated. "Wrong about everything. It is not their generosity I seek, it is their worship. Indeed, idol worship. Adoration and devotion. I thrive on it as all gods and kings. It is my breath, my blood, my life."

"To seek anything from them," Thiele insisted, "is treason."

Was it? "Really, Thiele?" he looked up again to study the man. "That is an interesting notion when we seek everything they have every day. Their lives, homes, properties, their governments. Indeed, I disagree with you, Thiele," he assured. "It is our duty to seek. Mine. Yours. To seek, win, rule, control."

"And what does that have to do with town?" Thiele was shaking his head, so like the Holy Man whether he wanted to be or not. "You brought that woman to the town. Town!"

"For that precise reason, Thiele," he assured, "your hysteria. It is also interesting to me I am denied this same right when the SS bring the Allied here, but no, it is your right when I do the same thing—to underscore a point, Thiele," he explained to Thiele looking at him. "To make Herr Oberst Schönfeld and you as angry as the SS made me—or at least this is what I have been told, Thiele," he waved, returning to his work. "I really have no idea why I brought the woman to town. I felt like it—and that is another thing, Thiele," he nodded. "It intrigues me how everyone—you, the Holy Man, everyone knows what, how, and why I do something while I seem to know nothing of this myself—so what is the reason I brought the woman to town, eh, Thiele?" he slammed his pen down. "Please tell me!"

"I do not care why," Thiele said. "It is consortion."

"Consortion?" Reineke said. "With her? That ragged little creature in the other room? Consorting with her to do what? Drive you crazy or simply myself?"

"Do not be flippant!" Thiele snapped. "It is consortion, treason, and you know it."

"I do?" Reineke said. "How do I know this? Who brought the woman here, eh, Thiele? What is the difference between the SS bringing the woman here and my deciding to bring her anywhere?"

"The difference is clear," Thiele assured.

"Is it?" Reineke said. "Well, I cannot see it regardless of how clear it is. So tell me the difference, explain it to me. What is the difference between what I do and the SS. Tell me the difference between me and the SS."

"I should not have to," Thiele said.

"And I say you do!" Reineke's fist hit his desk. "I say you will. I say you will listen and obey everything I say and tell you to do, or I will have you shot!"

"What?" Thiele said.

"For treason, Thiele," Reineke smiled. "To question me is treason, Thiele. To challenge, or even doubt. I am the Leader, and the Leader is always right. Eh, Thiele?" he said. "You know your commandments so well why is it you always choose to overlook that one?"

"Hauptmann ..." Thiele said.

"What happened to that woman is a direct violation of the Geneva Convention," Reineke insisted. "An agreement our country signed. The people responsible are guilty of crimes not I. If that woman is a spy, she should have been shot. Not raped, or beaten, shot. That is the rule. What is the matter with you?" he said. "Are you a man, or what are you? I do not need to torment old men, women, or children to prove I am superior. I *am* superior! Indeed, born superior. I do not need some book like you to advise or teach me what is, because it already is. *Is,* Thiele," he assured. "*Is.* It is not a quest, it *is.* It already exists. It is already perfect—*always* perfect. Always right. To dare to suggest otherwise is what is treason, Thiele. If you want to pronounce a verdict of death for treason, pronounce it on yourself, not me." He picked up his water.

"May I speak?" Thiele requested.

"Speak?" Reineke said. "Yes, you may speak, Thiele. You may not rape, beat, or pound on any door, but speak, Thiele? Yes, you may speak. What would you like to say?"

"I meant no disrespect."

"No, of course not," Reineke drank his water. "You meant to advise me, enlighten. Indeed, warn me of the dangers of these people I consort with—except I find it inconceivable, Thiele," he assured, "that a child of her age, an old man and the children of his village to be such a danger to anyone. You will have to excuse me, my naiveté, or ignorance, whichever you prefer."

"Hauptmann," Thiele said, "even if you do not believe they are a danger, you must know you are assuming responsibilities that are not yours to assume."

"Responsibility or guilt?" Reineke looked at him over his glass. "It is all right," he waved when Thiele struggled to find his answer. "Because I have no idea what you mean either way, other than, yes, naturally, it must have something to do with the woman. As everything seems to revolve around this woman as for three months before it revolved around the Holy Man."

"Hauptmann ... " Thiele said.

"What, Thiele?" Reineke sighed. "The men are talking, whispering, gossiping. Clearly, someone is talking, as you know I took the woman to town. So what is it? I am obsessed? Possessed?"

"I doubt if everyone is saying that, Hauptmann," Thiele assured.

"No," Reineke agreed. "No more than everyone is laughing."

"An exaggeration," Thiele admitted.

"Well, Thiele," Reineke said, "exaggeration, or truth, do you think I care what anyone is saying?"

"No," Thiele assured. "I know you do not."

"And you are right," Reineke said. "It is what I am saying that is important ... and I am saying," he inclined forward, "I have heard enough about the woman as I have heard about the Holy Man before. I will listen to no more about the woman as I do not listen about the Holy Man—"

"Yes, Hauptmann ... " Thiele nodded.

"Silence!" Reineke barked and Thiele jumped. "You speak when I am finished and not before! You confuse your position, Thiele, and your authority with mine. If you want to say 'Yes, Herr Hauptmann' to something, say it to that!"

"Yes, Herr Hauptmann," Thiele agreed.

"Much better," Reineke approved. "And I will listen to no more about the woman, Thiele, because she is mine. Her body, mind, and soul, given to me by the right of our superiority, taken by me in my right of superiority. I can do anything with her I please. As I can do anything with all of them," he assured, "the Holy Man, the natives, children and their goats, the men, and even you. I may take them, keep them, forsake, use, or abuse them. I can do any or all that I please in my right as Leader, Lord, God, and King. Now go and find me Erich," he directed, "I need to speak with him. When I am finished, I will need to speak again with you—about war, Thiele," he assured. "While you fret and worry about children and old men, I plan to go to war. To fight it. Win it. Tobruk. Cairo. Suez Canal. Regardless of whom I choose to seduce along the way. Whom I choose to manipulate, or whom I choose to kill."

Such as Sergeant Erich, a machine of the highest caliber, second only to Thiele. A strong background in the field, an excellent strategist on whom Reineke could rely to assist in the operations they planned—or so Reineke had thought. He should have known Erich's skills and training reeked of the elite SS to where Thiele was simply good, merely talented, naturally smart.

"Sergeant," Reineke turned around from staring out his balcony windows to face his desire to murder, destroy this one even more than some SS Major and his fat Leutnant. But then this one mocked him with his betrayal, not simply his actions, with his mouth that was larger than it used to be. Torn by the bottle that tore his face, turning him into what he was, a monster more afraid of himself when he looked in the mirror than he was of the man who destroyed him.

"Hauptmann," Erich replied.

"At ease," Reineke granted, "sit down. There have been some revisions to the operation of which you need to be aware—yes, you are going, Sergeant," he nodded when Erich hesitated. "You are to be remanded to the SS after the munitions are secured."

"The SS," Erich said.

"Yes," Reineke assured. "Those are my orders. Sit down, Sergeant. Do not make me tell you again. No one is interested in what you have told the SS. The plan has been changed. You will cooperate and you will be remanded. You refuse, and you will be shot. What is your choice?"

"Cooperation, Hauptmann," he smiled, and it was disgusting..

"Then sit," Reineke said.

Erich sat and as anticipated embraced the idea of men on horseback, useful as forward scouts or decoys, whichever position may be needed or warranted. The contributing suggestions he offered to the scheme were sound, direct and to the point. There was no banter between them and no argument throughout their talk. There never had been either. The sergeant who upheld the staunch beliefs of Thiele, could also side with the bawdy antics of Reineke. But then this was war. All was fair in war. The idea of whispers circulating about the Hauptmann and his newly acquired toy was treated with a masculine smile sickening to see on that distorted mouth as Erich rose to leave. "Was she really worth all of this Hauptmann?" Erich had to ask at the end.

"Indeed," Reineke said, neither insulted nor appalled simply cold. "You are as disgusting as your face, Sergeant. A question you should perhaps ask yourself. Was it worth all of that?"

Erich shrugged. "I did not do it for a woman, Hauptmann."

"And you think I did?"

Erich looked at him. "No," he assured. "I think some men while more subtle perhaps than others are always recognizable by their brothers. We are two of a kind, Hauptmann. Two of a kind."

"Indeed," Reineke said. Two of a kind? There was only one lion, and this lion was king. He was also a chameleon. Poised to step down from his disdainful throne and transform into a hyena, an animal that laughs at its prey. Reineke broke tradition. He forewarned his enemy, not merely threatened. "Part of my plan is for you to die, Erich," Reineke said and Erich naturally stopped. "You and your men and your SS. My desire for your deaths is my only obsession. I am not content leaving it to chance or by something as impersonal as a firing squad as Herr Oberst Schönfeld suggests. I must take a far more active and personal role. I am going to kill you, Erich," he smiled. "When you are dying, remember how I said I was going to kill you."

Staff Sergeant Erich had no comprehensible answer.

Thiele did. It was ignored.

Reineke collected his attaché with his travel papers and other necessary documents, dismissing whatever argument Thiele was trying to use as a delay, moving from his quarters into the library. "I am leaving, Thiele," he advised. "I will return in a few days. You cannot leave to rendezvous with Linke until then. The responsibility of the woman is yours until my return."

"I take no such responsibility," Thiele assured.

"You do," Reineke nodded, "and you will. I am ordering you. Disobey, and I will have you shot—-you know this, correct, Thiele? You know it is not a joke. When you think how it might be, look again at Erich's face and remember how I do not joke."

"Where are you going?" Thiele insisted. "Why is this necessary?"

"Away, Thiele," Reineke said. "I am going away. Obviously the reason is to ensure Erich's betrayal does not jeopardize the objective—and I would not try to threaten Erich, Thiele. He knows as little as you do, and what he knows, he will not tell."

"Erich will flee the moment he is free of this place."

"As would we all," Reineke agreed. He glanced at the door of the apartment, his attention staying there for a moment or two. "The woman is your responsibility, Thiele," he reiterated. "Refuse, and I will take her with me. Which would you prefer?"

"I do not care about the woman!"

No. But only because he had been told not to care. Reineke turned to leave. "Erich is frightened of me, Thiele," he agreed, "but he will never flee. He is too afraid how that might be the plan. I have told him how I am going to kill him—and I am, Thiele," he assured.

“He is leaving today with Linke and ten soldiers, to be joined shortly by you with ten more. He is afraid I have instructed Linke ... he is afraid, Thiele,” he smiled, “that I may have instructed you. So, no, Thiele,” he shook his head, “Erich will not run until he is ready to run to his SS, whom I am going to kill as well.”

“The SS?” Thiele frowned, ignoring the threats of their deaths. “What does the SS have to do with this?”

“You mean other than Sergeant Erich?” Reineke said. “The woman is to be remanded, naturally. Why? What did you think I was going to do with her?”

Do? Thiele stared at the apartment door. He did not know. He had been trying to think. “You are returning the Allied to the SS?” he said, like it was a thing, an object rather than flesh and bone. “Killing the Allied when you kill Erich and the SS? I do not believe you.”

Reineke shrugged. “Either that or I am plotting her escape. Let me know when you decide which you prefer less.”

He left to meet the Holy Man at the Temple Diana, the priest blessing every rock with smiles as he stepped over the rubble of her lost civilization for Reineke. The glittering white marble washed and faded like the dead bones of the ancients who used to walk in their cooling shadows.

“Mon capitaine,” Pierre greeted him, refusing the hand of assistance Reineke offered. He had come this way many times before, his aging crippled body agile enough even with the weight of his robes and creak of uncertain knees. A boast he would keep all the way to the bottom of the cliffs when he fell, if he fell. He would not. Reineke would not allow it. The heavens would open, raising the Holy Man up on a cloud, and this, Reineke was in no mood to see. His hand became an arm and then another hand until with little effort the Holy Man was beside him on solid ground in front of the kübelwagen. Reineke hesitated, for the first time perhaps.

“It will work, mon capitaine,” Pierre smiled in confidence. “Everything. You will see.”

“I know,” Reineke reached for the door, directing Pierre to get in, even though he had no idea where they were going.

“Algeria, mon capitaine,” Pierre nodded.

"Algeria!" Reineke gasped, missing the clutch and hitting the brake before he hit the trees. "Across the border?"

"Oui, mon capitaine, if we make it there," Pierre righted himself in his seat. "How else to get to Algeria? It cannot come to us."

"Never mind," Reineke wrenched the wagen into reverse. "Of course we are not going to Algeria. You said nothing about Algeria. I cannot go to Algeria ... Tripoli ..."

"Tunis, mon capitaine," Pierre nodded. "You are going to Tunis. The dentist is taking you there after he takes us to Algeria."

"I know it is Tunis," Reineke assured. "I am saying I cannot be flying around the continent. I have told Thiele I would return in two days, not a week!"

"Perhaps four days, mon capitaine," Pierre nodded. "More only if you decide."

"Bring Algeria here," Reineke said. "I will speak with this Ben Akach here. I do not have four days to spend—four days?" he stared at Pierre.

"It depends on the weather," Pierre shrugged.

"The weather," Reineke nodded. "Of course, the weather—I am not going to Algeria," he assured. "Bring it here!"

He went to Algeria, meeting the dentist Haas at the plane at eleven o'clock that night to take him there.

Chapter Fifty-One

John expected a degree of awkwardness, particularly in the beginning. His own and Reineke's whom they all called Dieter in conversation despite the occasional application of the nicknames *David* or *le Metapel* an obscure Hebrew word for caretaker. *Metapel* certainly fit given Reineke's hobbies alongside his military career, but quite honestly, to John, a modern man living in a modern world it sounded fanciful, ominous like the Boogey Man. A deep, throaty nightmare crossed John's mind as the kübelwagen approached announcing. *Le Metapel is coming to get you!*

Le Metapel was definitely not going to work. Rattling his choices around in his head of what to call Reineke, John was most comfortable with his own assessment of the man getting out of the wagen. A Baron, the Baron, regardless of what John would or might call Reineke out loud. The Baron was nervous despite appearances or claims to the contrary, chain-smoking and thin under the broadcloth greatcoat he wore with the comfort and style of a fashion model. If Reineke had an assessment of John, it was that he was one of the broader brothers, tall, but shorter than Abraham like the blond Martin and currently attired in Arab robes not an Italian uniform.

John waited to see what would happen, following Reineke's lead when he walked up, and there was no shaking hands, or even an introduction. The ice-breaker was the plane John stood in front of: a German Storch prized for its short takeoff and landing. The precision aircraft once landing on a patch of grass in Paris to cheers, but that was before the war.

Reineke acknowledged him with a neutral nod, looking up at the plane. "Where is its original pilot?" he asked.

"Abe?" John smiled and Reineke looked at him. No indication in Reineke's look if he thought or wondered if John was being smart mouthed, intentionally misunderstanding the question, or making some joke.

"Abe's coming. Jacob and Hanuk, too," John assured.

"Indeed," Reineke bent his head and lit a cigarette with a heavy silver-colored lighter, even though he had just tossed a cigarette when he got out of his wagen. He turned away from the plane looking around the darkness for a few moments before nodding again, speaking in what was perhaps an attempt to make conversation. "Camouflage netting," he advised John. "You see?" he indicated, pointing out into the distance. "You can see it, even in the dark. The line. A difference in the blackness."

"Yes," John said.

Reineke left it at that, at least with John, speaking to Pierre a slight wryness in his tone, not only his words. "To think I sent Thiele to the Kufra, eh, Holy Man, when all I had to do was send him a few hours south."

"Just a convenient place to park," John offered with a smile.

"Oh, yes," Reineke agreed. He looked around again briefly. "It would be interesting to see what it looks like in the daylight ... you realize I have no idea where I am," he assured John, and so he was trying to talk, strike up some conversation, if only to pass the time, though lighthearted apparently not Reineke's forte. "A simple map and torch for navigation," he said. "Me saying where am I, and the Holy Man with his compass saying drive, I will tell you."

"Yes," John said.

"Intentional," Reineke said, "I assume, yes, and I understand. It is very nice, quite good," he looked around for a third time.

"But not for sale," John couldn't resist a more obvious joke.

"No, oh, no," Reineke agreed without missing a beat. "Neither is my compound."

Touché. John smiled to himself, though refrained from expanding that to 'this could be fun'. He wasn't there for fun. Neither was Reineke. John could see what his mother saw however when she looked at him, at least on the surface, even in the dark. Reineke wasn't a man of his uniform but was a man in uniform. An outfit. Wearing it, moving around in it, enjoying it like Abe moved and enjoyed his robes, even if he was only standing there. What did that actually mean though? Raised in America, his German heritage was foreign to John, finding it steeped in traditions, extremes, and contradictions and therefore dishonest, deceptive. Hospitable and cutthroat at the same time, modern and barbaric, unable to let go of its barbarous roots. Feast followed by bloodbath. Distinctly Roman in that regard. Brutal. Rome mated with the savage Barbarian, and that was some child they had.

Give him New York any day. John settled comfortably into his own superiority, informal and natural as opposed to the unnatural man standing next to him whether Reineke was good or bad.

Who did not speak at all in those first few minutes was Pierre. He was pensive, closed off, his hands tucked in his sleeves, worried. Reineke either noticed and tried to draw Pierre out, into the conversation, or Reineke was just talking. "The Holy Man will not fit comfortably in the Storch," Reineke returned to the topic of the plane, looking at it again.

That was considerate of him, John agreed, to think of the old guy. Though John also noticed it was more of a question of the old guy being comfortable stuffed in the back of the plane, than the young Baron who had enough luggage for two weeks and a reserved seat.

"You're right," John smiled, saved from having to explain as telltale headlights appeared through the darkness. "Here's Abe now," he agreed not too obviously in relief.

Pierre and Reineke were equally clearly thankful, Pierre with his breathy "Oui," the Baron with his quick "Ja", dropping his cigarette, burying it with his boot, and swiftly walking to meet Abe's wagen.

John caught the opening welcoming refrain, most of it, as Jacob pulled up, Abe hopping out to meet Reineke, Hanuk in the back starry-eyed. John did not mean to be cynical as he watched his brothers and nephew, because he wasn't cynical, just not in-step with their trust and comfort level.

His brother Abe and Reineke visibly had a relationship whether or not it was an actual friendship. Hands extended they did not shake, but clasped each other's arms, Abe providing full support clapping his hand to Reineke's shoulder.

"Patient-doctor?" John quipped to Pierre, missing his brother's words, but catching Reineke's reassurance he was well, doing all right as in holding up. You would think he was the victim not Mike's kid.

Pierre was smiling, beaming at the picture in front of him, but not too entranced not to hear John, or to give him one of his snorts. "You could give him your support."

"You mean like Abe?" John grinned, his brother practically hugging the guy to his breast.

"They are close," Pierre said.

"Apparently," John agreed. "I draw the line though at teary eyes."

"I ..." Pierre said.

"It's OK," John assured, "I know. You don't know what I'm talking about." He changed the subject. "You look nervous."

"Of course," Pierre said. "Mon capitaine, too. Terrified."

John would go along as far as nervous. "Worried you're not going to fit?"

"Pardon?" Pierre said.

"In the plane."

"Oh," Pierre said. "No, I am not concerned about that."

"Well, it's a good thing we are," John patted him on the shoulder. "Come on. Let's get this show on the road."

That was fine with Pierre.

"Why so many though?" Pierre questioned as he toddled alongside John. "Hanuk and Jacob?"

That was easy enough to explain. "Jacob is going to come with us. Pierre and the luggage are going with Abe," John took the reins from Abraham when he and Pierre walked up to the group.

"Yes," Reineke agreed, "Abraham was explaining. You are coming."

Well, John was obviously coming, but he knew what Reineke meant. "No offense," he said to Pierre all set to protest—already protesting with his huffing and puffing and thinking going with Abe somehow meant being left behind. "But your friend Ben is a pretty rough character. It doesn't hurt to have a little more power along instead of only the three of us standing there."

"Oh. Oh, oui, yes," Pierre understood. "All of us are going."

"Yes," John smiled at Reineke. "An appearance of power anyway." Since, no, three or six of them against a thousand Arabs wasn't exactly the best odds.

"Indeed," Reineke agreed. "Are you comfortable with this?" he confirmed with Pierre. "This change?"

Solicitous maybe, but who's comfort, really? John wondered. To be honest Reineke did not need to personally involve himself to the extent he had. Making his decision, he could have turned the girl over to them, claiming her death, burning some goat in her stead and scattering the ashes as he had the other one's body. Since he had involved himself, it was a little late now to start having trust issues.

"Oui, fine, mon capitaine," Pierre assured. "I am fine—you?"

"Indeed. Yes," Reineke looked straight at John.

"Then, let's go," John suggested with a smile.

"Yes ..." Reineke said with a bit more breath, turning back to Abraham for the two of them to do the boola-boola bit with the hands and arms, Reineke pausing to shake his head at Abraham's tattooed forehead, and Abe breaking into a laugh. "I have said nothing," Reineke assured. "Nothing ..."

"Oui," Pierre clouted him. "So, stop wasting time, now. We are going—and I am going," he announced, "with mon capitaine and his luggage." He turned on his heel and John hung his head.

"We'll work it out," Abraham promised. "There's some leeway with the weight. You'll be fine."

"I'm talking about space," John assured. "I need to carry fuel."

"And I need to carry three people," Abraham eyed the luggage. "I'm not going to fit that unless you want Hanuk sitting out on the wing."

"I can!" Hanuk perked up.

"Shut up," John shoved him out of the way. "All right. Hold on. We should have kept the damn Caudrun like I told you instead of fixing this."

"The Swordfish is a better plane," Abraham said.

"Yeah, yeah," John said.

They worked it out and it did not include Hanuk sitting out on the wing. It did include Pierre crammed in the back of the Storch with the luggage and as many Jerry cans as John could manage and he was tipping close to the scale of the nine-hundred pounds maximum that was for damn sure. It also included coordinating with Abraham where they would link up since John could not carry the fuel he would need.

"You'll be fine," Abraham promised again and they went their separate ways.

At five hundred miles to the plateaus, John could possibly get by with refueling once. But with three of them aboard? It was going to be close even to his next stop. John kept his airspeed low, periodically checking in with Abe by radio. Just a couple of beeps, rapid and few, times staggered. It was cold, the roar of the wind and propeller loud without a headset. John handed Reineke one as they climbed aboard. He seemed a little perplexed and John assured, "You'll need them".

Reineke put them on with a shrug and slouched down into his seat where he stayed, John cast early in the role of chauffeur. That was set to change though over the next several days beginning about thirty minutes from then and the early unveiling of Dieter from beneath the erect persona of the Baron Hauptmann Reineke that Reineke shed like clothes, a slow striptease, the two people almost unrecognizable when the butterfly finally emerged from its cocoon.

"You cold or just cramped?" John asked presently, personally finding the coolness of his flying tin can refreshing, the dulled whirl of the propeller hypnotic. Reineke did look uncomfortable however wrapped in his greatcoat, staring out the large windows.

"What?" Reineke moved the headset to hear instead of talking into the microphone, and so he apparently did not fly much, at least not in military aircraft.

"Cold," John pointed to the microphone. "There's blankets behind you. Coffee in a Thermos, if you want it."

"I am fine," Reineke said.

"Well, if you get cold," John said, "help yourself."

"I am fine," Reineke assured. "Flying is fine."

Got it. A bell went off in John's head. "You don't like flying?"

Reineke looked at him. "Like this?" he said. "No." He looked away, back out the window, presently remarking, in English, "I speak English if it is easier for you."

John thought about that. "Well, I speak French," he offered, "if it's easier for you."

Reineke laughed. Not loudly, or raucously, but he did laugh.

“That is very good,” he nodded. “Yes, very good. You are the comedian of your brothers, I see.“

Look who’s talking, John could have countered. “You look about as comfortable as my patients,” he agreed.

“I like the cold,” Reineke said.

“But not the plane,” John nodded.

Reineke smiled. “I am accustomed to flying, of course.”

But not something he preferred, John understood. And so, he was mortal after all. His mother would be disappointed. “Just bigger planes,” John offered.

“Much bigger planes,” Reineke assured. “So, no. No, I do not like your small plane, dentist Haas. I am concerned about all of the things you and Abraham are not concerned about.

“John,” John offered, because he might as well. “Please do not call me dentist Haas for the next four days.”

“It is what you are,” Reineke said.

“OK, pedestrian,” John said.

“Pedestrian?” Reineke repeated.

“Someone who prefers to walk,” John assured.

Reineke nodded. “I will think about it.”

“Fair enough,” John agreed. “In the meantime—Baron,” he smiled, “everything is fine. I can make this a little easier for you by going faster. We will need to refuel in a couple of hours, and if I start to run too low before the rendezvous point, I can just put her down and signal Abraham. We can take a short break and let Abe catch up. How’s that? Acceptable?”

“Acceptable,” Reineke nodded. “Why must Abraham ‘catch up’? What is he doing?”

“Oh. Well, driving,” John lied, sort of. To an extent.

“Driving?” Reineke repeated. “Why? He did not mention this. I did not realize this.”

“Why’s a few reasons,” John said. “The plane’s not here.”

“Not here? Where is it?”

“Not far. It needs a longer runway,” John said. “It’s possible to bring it in, but it’s not wise. With the Storch, I can pop in and out with none the wiser.”

“So it is not another Storch,” Reineke said.

"No," John said. "It's a Swordfish."

"Swordfish ..." Reineke frowned.

"British Navy?" John prompted. "Plane that helped sink the Bismarck?"

Reineke groaned. "Why am I sitting here trusting my life to a comedian dentist? Are we taking my Storch to Tunis or your Swordfish?"

"Abe's Swordfish," John said. "He's the Brit. I'm American."

"Indeed. We are taking the Storch," Reineke settled it.

"What?" John said. "No, we are not. It will take twice as long."

"I do not care. I am not comfortable riding in a British war plane. I do not wish to be shot down over occupied territory."

"Like that can't happen in this," John said. "Look, Baron, you say occupied, I remind Free French. We are taking the Swordfish. It has three times the range. You are not the only one who doesn't have a week to spend on this trip."

"Indeed. I will think about it."

"Go right ahead."

Reineke was. "May I smoke?"

John considered that. "One."

"Danke." Reineke looked around for something to use other than the floor.

"Tin can," John said. "Should be one next to you."

There was. Reineke found it and John smiled, wondering how long it would take the Baron to figure out the real purpose for the tin can.

Tassili N'Ajjer, Algeria
March 21

Sheik el Al Abu Ben Akach cut an ugly scar across the desert landscape and he knew it. Anointed and called by the more Christian name Ben, at least by Pierre, there was nothing Christian or Moslem about him but was pagan through and through. An old fat genie drenched in the vivid colors of his awning and brilliant satin pillows, Akach's price probably would have dropped under an offer of a scalp to decorate the sash wrapped tightly around his belly. His eyes brightening with the sight of cousins dressed in their biblical clothes,

Abe and Hanuk confused him. Their faces and scent different, their smell as his nose twitched, checking the air. He knew they weren't him, but he also wasn't sure they were Jews. That meant only one thing to him considering where they were.

"Tuareg," Akach announced with a laugh to thirty or so of his sons. No one disagreed with him, as neither would Abe or Hanuk bother to correct him, or say anything at all. That sealed it. Abe and Hanuk were Tuareg, only John and Jacob the Jewish cousins. Reineke simply twenty-thousand Sterling, following a brief attempt by Akach to raise the agreed price to thirty. Probably something to do with payment for his disappointment the blond beauty was not a girl. It to Reineke's benefit he was not as he never would have made it out of there.

The glint in Akach's eyes for Pierre was different, unfettered recognition, friendship and respect. On Pierre's part that had to be his religion, his place among the murderers, thieves, and otherwise lost souls. On Ben's? Life. Someone's life. A son's. Possibly more than one. Possibly even the heir apparent. There was no other explanation as far as John could see.

They got out of there without having to sleep with anyone despite the offering, Jacob the only one of them who seemed a little disappointed until Abraham reminded him of the odds of his penis swelling up infected and inflamed before he got home. They drank sweet tea in honor of the Tuareg, Reineke leaving several thousand pounds poorer by his oath or throat, with a reliable promise of twenty Arabian horses by Ben's oath less the throat business. It was good enough for John, glad to leave.

They departed the water pools for the high cliffs. Having rested only briefly before meeting with Akach they put down now to rest the planes, sleep, eat, sweating out the high heat of the day in the cool shade of the caves before they took off again early evening—in the Storch. Reineke did not win the argument his luggage did proving the square pegs of steamer trunks did not fit well in the round hole of a Swordfish.

"Haven't you ever heard of a seesack?" John shoved the trunk back inside the Storch.

"Indeed, of course. I do not like them."

"We ever do this again, you will," John muttered.

"Ma's going to be pissed you took the Storch," Jacob helped him pack in the Jerry cans.

"Yeah, well, fortunately, I'm not going to be the one who's going to have to tell her," John gave Abraham the eye.

"Don't worry about it," Abraham said.

John wasn't. "I don't like the idea of you leaving Jacob here."

"Well," Abraham said, "unless Hanuk is going to ride on the wing—don't even start," he preempted him, "there's no choice. I like the idea of there being a point person for you anyway."

"I'm fine," John assured, and he was. He knew the route like the back of his hand—maybe not to Tunis, but certainly into the Atlas or the Aurès—and without Pierre he could fit enough Jerry cans to easily make it to the next drop. The annoying part was, it was going to take longer. John was going to have to rest the plane more often, and refuel more often. They were easily looking at adding a day both ways which meant two days. The upside, the Storch was a safer plane to use, yes, without a doubt. Reineke was right about that.

They went their separate ways. By late evening Pierre was almost home, and John and Reineke were on their way to Tunisia hopscotching along the Algerian-Libyan border, John flying as low and fast as he could for best time, vigilant on the radio as they inched north.

"I can do that," Reineke offered once to spell John with the monitoring.

"I've got it," John assured.

March 22

Come six-thirty in the morning, John had coaxed more than five-hundred miles out of her in twelve hours before he put her down to stay down and cool off. Below her maximum capabilities, she was carrying weight and starting to run hot. She wasn't the only one. Out on the Tamanrasset at 70 degrees in the daytime it had seemed almost cold. Here, no. They were still in the Sahara and it was brutal, the plane quickly a sauna in the sun. John made it across the Erg to the waters scattered between the shallow chotts in Algeria and

Tunisia and that was his goal. You could not drink the water because of the salt, but there was vegetation and the air ran cooler over the surface and rocks.

A breakfast of boiled instant coffee and field rations John was ready to sleep, get up and start the last lap, he was figuring around four o'clock.

"My guess right now is five days, maybe six roundtrip," he advised Reineke. "She just can't do the non-stop distance. We'll see. The trip home will be easier—and shorter."

"Yes," Reineke understood. "Once we cross out of the Sahara, will you signal to let them know who you are?"

"Only as a friend coming through," John smiled.

Reineke nodded. "And what do you use the Storch for, if I may ask?"

"Reconnaissance. What she was built for."

"It was built for pleasure," Reineke said.

"1936? She was built for reconnaissance," John assured. "And she's very good. We use her when we run the convoys."

"Indeed," Reineke said. "Yes, of course. You use it to scout."

"Exactly," John said. "A much more relaxed running. Up for an hour maybe? Down for four. This is putting her through her paces, that's for sure."

Aurès Mountains, Algeria

They crossed into the towering mountain range at just after six, John setting down to refuel about an hour later. It had rained and was already cold and damp. Thirty minutes after takeoff, he was setting down again due to a heavy night fog moving in.

"Where are we?" Reineke asked.

"Just over the border, Tunisia."

"Excellent."

"Not bad," John agreed even though they weren't actually there yet and wouldn't be until the morning all thanks to the weather, so they lost more than half a day. He changed from Arab to Italian as much for warmth as to break in the suit, feel comfortable in it.

"The hair is a little long," was Reineke's only comment.

"The magic of a modern cold permanent," John promised,

slicking his hair back and setting it with bobby pins after he washed it clear, and *violà*! come morning, a headful of tight curls with only a couple of sassy orphans tickling his collar.

Aurès Mountains, Tunisia
March 23
The early rising sun overcast and the air a chilly 45 degrees, John set down on what was clearly someone's mountain property.

"Is everything all right?" Reineke asked startled.

"It's fine," John hopped out to pull open the barn doors and drive out the car. An old car. He really had not noticed or paid that much attention before but today he did as Reineke's eyes swept over it.

"Mind?" John said, seeing as the luggage was Reineke's not his.

"Oh, yes." Reineke assisted in unloading the bags and helped John push the plane into the barn and close the doors. The car though?

"I cannot appear in this," Reineke said. "What is it?"

"I think it's an old Renault," John frowned.

"No," Reineke groaned. "I did not mean *what* is it. I know what it is. I was saying ... never mind, it is unimportant. Do they have a telephone? Is there a telephone? I can call for my car for us."

"Not for here, you won't," John assured.

"No, of course not. I forget," Reineke apologized. "A secret hideaway, like your assortment of airstrips. One for you and the Storch, a different one for Abraham and the other plane. You would not drive me to your actual airstrip, reveal it to me. It was as you said, a convenient place to park while Abraham does then drive to the airstrip after I have left with you. I knew as soon as I saw the camouflage netting. This was a stage. A setting."

"I thought the netting was a nice touch."

"Indeed, very clever," Reineke agreed. "I still cannot ride in that automobile."

"You can ride in it as far as the outskirts." John dumped one of the suitcases into the backseat and left Reineke to take care of the others while he checked the oil and started her up.

The road not much better than the stone pistes of the Hoggar, they drove into town to park and quickly hitch a ride from a sympathetic partisan swallowing the age-old my car broke down story used since the days of the chariots. Coming back, they could just hire a taxi in town to take them to the car.

Chapter Fifty-Two

Tunis, Tunisia

Tunis was an interesting city, European on the outside, Arab within, one John hadn't seen in a while. It was also at best five degrees warmer in town, still grey, overcast with an occasional slap of wind and rain.

"Are you hungry?" Reineke asked as their ride turned onto the boulevard.

"Very," John assured.

"Excellent," Reineke said. "How good is your Italian—you are Italian, remember."

"Yes," John said. "It's right here on my uniform in case I forget … and, I don't know. Good enough to pinch someone on the way in or out."

"No, you do not have to pinch anyone," Reineke said, "only tell him to stop the car. I do not speak Italian. I want to walk."

"Any place special?" John asked handing Reineke his overnight trunks and picking up his knapsack. "You do know that's why we had to take the Storch."

"Yes, Medina," Reineke assured ignoring the comment about his matching luggage. "Where are you?"

"Where am I?" John said. "You mean, where am I staying? The first place I find," he shrugged. "Nothing too luxurious, just in the general vicinity of a bath. But then I'm only a lieutenant," he reminded.

"A public bath?" Reineke said.

"Sure," John said. "Why not?"

"No, I do not use public baths," Reineke shook his head. "You are coming with me. Medina."

"Medina?"

"Of course, Medina. The house."

"Oh ..." John said. "Oh, OK," he smiled. "But I think we should have kept our car. That's quite a stroll."

"No, no car ..." Reineke said, looking around. "Coffee. I need coffee ... I am spinning ..."

"Nervous?" John offered.

"Free," Reineke assured.

"OK, free," John agreed, an interesting thing to say.

"Go this way ..." Reineke decided, heading off to find an acceptable café, not necessarily the first one they saw, but eventually they found one, Reineke preferring to sit outside despite the threat of rain.

It did not matter to John. He was hungry for food and the luxury of a table and chair, Reineke for the refreshing air of civilization and a liquid brunch of water, coffee, and wine, which explained the light weight. John hadn't seen him eat much outside of the field rations except for a handful of olives and some figs. Appreciating Germans carried their stoves into battle the same as they did their guns as field rations were sneered at, there were still times when one had to make do particularly since, let's face it, German food was not exactly gourmet French. When John asked about the continued fasting though since they were now surrounded by food, Reineke disclosed how he had been frightened into starving himself by a recent unsettling encounter with a peach.

"OK ..." John said. "That's a joke, right?" he checked. "Or should I remind you I'm not Abe?"

"No, you are the dentist," Reineke nodded. "Indeed, even the idea is comical, a dentist doing this."

"Oh?" John said. "You don't think there are dentists in the trenches along with everyone else?"

"Trenches?" Reineke frowned. "What trenches?"

"Cancel that," John shook his head. "No trenches, just army. Sorry. It's been twenty years. To where I used to think in German, I don't anymore."

"Really?" Reineke said surprised. "You have been in the army twenty years?"

John smiled. "Actually, technically, I'm in the Resistance. There's no pre-requisite of career. I'm sure you'll find dentists right along with everyone else. Not just me." He waited a moment or two before he inclined forward with another smile, a sly one, sly as the man sitting across from him. "I know I said that right. No, I haven't been in the army twenty years. I'm a dentist."

Reineke shrugged. "Close enough. Your accent is soft, like Thiele's."

"My dialect and accent are Berlinese. Your high German isn't exactly a conversational language."

Reineke's eyes rolled. "Indeed, *high* German. I speak German, not street slang."

With a slight rasp, John noticed, that was probably as much sand as it was smoke. Continue to smoke as heavily as he did and he was practically guaranteeing his lungs would be shot by the time he was fifty.

"Like the plane," Reineke proposed. "In your German—what I can grasp of it," he assured, "I am cold and afraid of airplanes, which I am neither."

Bullshit. In any language he was cold and disliked flying, whether or not he was actually afraid. But that was OK, John was listening.

"Indeed, I prefer the cold," Reineke assured, "to the heat. The snow, to the sand, and the night to the day."

"Sounds like you should be in Russia."

Reineke laughed. He really did, legitimately. "Yes, of course, Russia," he said. "You really are a comedian, dentist Haas. What happened to you? Your Amerika? Do you not know Germans have no sense of humor?"

"John," John reminded. "And I'm a German Jew. Our sense of humor is legendary."

"Yes, of course," Reineke said soberly. "Only lately, there's been little cause for laughter, so I have been told ... " he moved on quickly before John could speak. "I met a German who laughed recently. And while he was laughing, I learned to sign his name."

"Danzig," John said, "if it's the guy on the papers."

"Yes, that is him," Reineke agreed. "Something Danzig."

"Eric," John offered. "And nice try, but back up to what you've been told. You don't believe it?"

"What?" Reineke said. "Stories of persecution and monsters? I have a young woman lying on a bed in my compound. Put there by Germans who also thought they knew how to laugh. Of course I believe stories of persecution and monsters. I have seen them. Just again, as I said, two weeks ago."

"It's different with us," John shook his head.

"How?" Reineke requested.

"Focused intent?" John shrugged. "Organized extinction and annihilation?"

"A trend," Reineke dismissed. "This season's vogue."

"Really?" John said.

"Yes, really. And like all fashions, it will fade—I am not saying it is not serious," he assured John sitting there looking at him. "Or that there are no horrific events that have occurred. I told you, I have a young woman lying on a bed in testament. Yes, there are monsters and maniacs and ignorant people who listen to their marketing campaign. But there are also people who do not—the majority of people," he stressed, "who do not. Who have no idea what they are talking about. And, so, yes," he assured, "the campaign will fade, the fashion change."

"*Wow*," was all John could say.

"Must we really have this conversation?" Reineke asked.

"Yes," John nodded. "I must. I don't give a shit about you."

Reineke eyed him. "You dislike me, distrust me."

"I don't know you from Adam," John assured. "I just know I don't like the idea of my sister dying because of some fashion trend."

"Hannah," Reineke said.

"Hannah," John nodded.

"Indeed," Reineke sat back, pensive. "That is horrific ... I cannot even conceive ..." he trailed off. "My sister?" he thought. "Indeed, my sister?" he could not even say it. "Would I kill? Would I hate? Indeed," he assured John, "you have no idea, dentist Haas."

"I believe I do," John said.

Reineke nodded. "Then kill them. You must. I cannot conceive how you would not. Were we in Poland, I would help you—John

Haas," he leaned forward again. "How can I say this so you understand? This situation has nothing to do with you or me. It has only to do with killing monsters when you see them. Maniacs when you find them. For my sister, yes," he assured, "for yours, and for that young woman lying on the bed. I cannot separate the three. Like the children, the hospital," he waved, "they are all innocent. All victims. Choose one, choose two, it has to be the three—it is the three," he assured. "And I have to ... I *have* to," he said, "believe I am not the only one otherwise I would kill myself. But if I did, who would kill the monsters for the three?"

"Fair enough," John said.

"Thank you," Reineke smiled. He sat back. "Have some more food ... I am hungry myself ..." he called the waiter, aware how John was still looking at him, watching him. "Do not worry," he offered, "I understand you would not help me—Indeed, I understand why," he assured.

John shook himself alert. "Your sister?" he said. "Yes, I would help you with your sister."

"Really?" Reineke said.

"Really," John nodded. He smiled. "What do you want—to eat?" he clarified.

"Oh," Reineke looked up at the waiter. "Fruit ... tell him, different kinds of fruit, and some tomatoes. Whatever he has—a treat," he laughed. "Something other than olives and figs."

"Well, probably something more than fruit," John said. "Not to sound like an Italian mother," he grinned, satisfied to keep the conversation light.

"Italian is a good choice," Reineke nodded. "I understand it for Abraham because he is dark, but I do not understand it for you. Why are you wearing an Italian uniform when you are German?"

"Hannah," John said.

"Hannah?"

"Yes. I'm not wearing the uniform of the bastards who killed her."

Reineke nodded. "Italian is a good choice, as I said. Of course your papers are German, but I am not as experienced with all of this, as you are. Next time, I will ensure I have Italian travel papers ... and

French travel papers," he waved. "Give me a list next time, like your mother does."

"No one will ask," John shook his head.

"How do you know?"

"Gut feeling," John shrugged. "I may be able to pass for Italian, but when's the last time you looked in the mirror? You couldn't be anything but German."

"Oh," Reineke said. "Well, I am German."

"True," John agreed.

"Hm," Reineke nodded. "One hundred years ... I know ..." he stared startled at the bowl of fruit the waiter set down.

"Apricots," John said. "You don't like apricots? They're a Mediterranean mainstay."

"Oh," Reineke said. "No," he shook his head, "I thought it was the peach. I saw peach."

"Oh," John said.

"No, you do not understand ..."

"No, I do," John assured. "I remember. You're afraid of peaches like the plane you're not afraid of."

Reineke looked at him, and John smiled. "You're afraid of flying."

"No," Reineke corrected. "It is not a favorite of mine, but I am not afraid. And, yes, I prefer larger aircraft—I prefer my own."

"You have a plane?" John said.

"Here?" Reineke studied the bowl. "No. My sister—at home. A hobby of hers," he smiled at John, "since she was sixteen."

"Really?" John said. "Your sister is a pilot?"

"A pilot?" Reineke said. "You mean like in the war? No, of course not—" He pushed the bowl away, shaking his head. "I cannot eat that. It looks too much like peaches."

"You're kidding, right?"

"Kidding? No, I am not kidding. The peach killed me. I told you. If I stay away from peaches, I will not die."

"Definitely, a conversation you should be having with Abe," John nodded.

"No. Abraham will tell me to have sex and forget about it ..." Reineke checked his watch.

John laughed. “He’s probably right. You probably should.”

“I am,” Reineke promised with a wink. “Come on,” he stood up throwing about three times the amount of money he needed to at the waiter either because he had no idea or he did not care. It was probably both. “We will have a real feast … a true bath … and you will have the ‘pick of the litter’”, he promised in English with a laugh. “You see, I can do it, if I want to. I simply choose not too … as I choose to walk …” he snatched up his luggage heading off. “No taxi’s John Haas. You are a fat man, you need to walk. You need steam … massage … and you do not need to be concerned,” he assured. “Cäcilie is a nurse, and I am very strict. It is not much, but it is what I can offer you.”

“It’ll do,” John assured.

“Really?” Reineke smiled. “I am glad, because I am very jealous of the exciting life you lead. I have no excitement, I have no quest … I am simply a very boring German,” he teased, “who does not know how to laugh.”

“Are you afraid of airplanes or not?” was what John really wanted to know.

“Terrified,” Reineke laughed. “Indeed, absolutely terrified. I dislike anything I cannot control. But it is not my fault. It my sister’s. She is insane. A death wish with everything she touches. Airplanes,” he waved. “Skis. Parachutes.”

“Parachutes?” John said.

“Trapeze,” Reineke nodded. “She even lives on a cliff. High on a cliff. I should be so lucky to have her life.”

“You’re close to it,” John assured.

“I try,” Reineke agreed. “I do try.”

“I should have known you would keep me waiting,” Cäcilie smiled.

She was the most beautiful sight in all of Afrika. Reineke watched her glide across the floor, her hair and gown gold, and skin so white.

“You’re wet,” she whispered as she touched him, wrapping her arms around his neck, and his mouth found hers.

Chapter Fifty-Three

Reineke smoked his cigarette carefully, allowing Cäcilie room to stir. Her cool, soft shoulder coaxing him he took his time, enjoying the tranquility of her beauty and not wanting to disturb any dream. She was intrigued by his request for money, quite a sizable sum of money, wanting more information. There was none to give. The Holy Man had been fascinating to watch in his dickering with the devil. That was all.

"Welcome back," Cäcilie's hand touched his chest.

Reineke extinguished his cigarette with a smile. "Soon perhaps."

"You are in trouble, aren't you?" Cäcilie surmised with a knowing look.

"No," Reineke denied, "merely a debt waiting to be paid."

"A ransom!" she agreed cryptically with a laugh.

Reineke also laughed, yielding to her straying hand. "For myself!" he whispered. "When you make a bargain with the devil, you should not expect him to be satisfied with only a thank you."

"It sounds dangerous," she said. "Always with you it is something dangerous. Why is that? What is it about life you do not like so much that you are always so willing to give it away?"

"No, it is not dangerous," he kissed her. "Only if you expect the devil to say thank you."

"How much did you say?" she verified.

"Thirty thousand. Do it and you can keep two, less and you get nothing."

"Francs," she said.

"Pounds," Reineke assured. "A considerable sum of money, yes, I know."

"But not impossible," she smiled. "Tomorrow?"

"Today," Reineke stretched for the telephone.

"You're supposed to say tomorrow," she pouted.

"Make your call," Reineke set the phone down on the bed. "If it has to be francs, it can be francs ... but, if," he kissed her cheek, "I have to pay an inflated exchange it is coming out of your two-thousand, not my twenty-eight."

"Fifty percent is an inflated exchange," she picked up the phone. "Ten is a gift. I will probably be able to get it for twenty-five. No one uses pounds here, do not be ridiculous. Here it is francs," she nodded as she dialed. "Lira, if you want to pretend you are loyal to Mussolini, which, of course, we are," she laughed into the telephone at the operator's zestful dialect that Reineke could hear from where he sat.

"You should learn to speak Italian," she interrupted the operator to smile at him. "It is a very romantic language. Passionate."

"No," Reineke said. "I am tired of learning things. Indeed, if I learn anything more I think I shall explode."

"Sounds painful, and possibly fun," she patted his arm while waiting for her connection. "I found a wonderful new bath for you. You will love it. Lemon, salt, and goat's milk. So invigorating to the skin."

It sounded like something invigorating for his food. Reineke was already on his way to concoct his own.

"Nine o'clock." Fifteen minutes later, she joined him, refilling his wine, and lighting her Turkish cigarette exotic in its long, bone holder. The milky water of rose oil and jasmine swirled around her legs like sea foam as she dropped her robe and stepped in, straddling his lap with an offer of his wine and a taste of opium. He refused the opium.

"Put that away," he requested.

"Why?" she blew the smoke lightly in his face, laughing as he winced. "There is nothing wrong with a little recreation."

"Wine is recreation," Reineke assured. "That is for addicts. Put it away!" He snatched the cigarette from the holder almost violently, crushing it out in its little gold dish."

She eyed him. "It sharpens the senses," she promised.

His senses were fine. He pulled her closer in apology. "Nine is too late. Make it six."

"Your suit won't even be ready until seven," she nodded.

"Six," he kissed her. "I had a dream about you. Watched you glide toward me across the floor. It was a party. I remember how beautiful you looked. I remember ..." he touched the gold highlights of her long, blonde hair wet and tickling his chest. The color was wrong. He remembered the dream very clearly, and the hair color was wrong.

"What?" she said, but only because he paused.

Reineke smiled. "Indeed, I remember your hair."

"Well, that's probably because you like my hair."

"I do. I like it very much. Do you ever wear it darker?"

"Darker?" she said. "Why? Are you thinking of changing your mind?"

"No," he assured. "Make it five."

"Five? You said six."

"Then make it six," he said. "Or no two thousand."

She eyed him again. "What could possibly be worth thirty-thousand pounds?"

"A woman, what else?" he reached for his wine with a shrug.

"A woman?" she repeated in an amused, though interested tone.

Reineke laughed. "A distinct exaggeration," he promised. "I would not be concerned."

"I'm not concerned," she assured. "When will you be back?"

"When?" he considered. "I do not know—"

She slapped the wine out of his hand. The glass hitting the cool tiles and breaking.

"Dieter," she protested as he got up.

"Have that cleaned," he nodded, "before you hurt yourself."

"It's fine," she dismissed.

"Indeed, it is not fine!" he corrected harshly before he caught himself. "Have that cleaned," he repeated with a reach for his robe.

"You are in trouble," she continued to eye him.

"No, I am not."

"I'll call them back," she offered. "Tell them to bring the money now—"

"Cäcilie!" he caught her hand, drawing her back to him. "I am not in trouble," he promised.

"I do not believe you."

"Well, you should," he kissed her forehead. "And, actually, I was thinking how perhaps next time you could come to me ..."

"Come to you?" she said. "In the desert?"

"Yes," he kissed her.

"You mean in a tent?" she asked, warming to his caress. "Like a sheik?"

"Field hospital," Reineke nodded.

"Field hospital!" she pushed away from him.

"You are a nurse," he reminded.

"I know I am a nurse. But not in a field hospital—Dieter," she said. "What's wrong? Please tell me. Please?"

He smiled. "Nothing is wrong. I have a job for you."

"In a *field* hospital?" she groaned.

"A man," he assured.

"Man?" she said. "What man? The man you brought with you?"

"What?" Reineke said. "Ha—" he almost said Haas, quickly changing it. "No, not Johann—Johann is Italian," he scolded. "Giovanni. You do not service Italians. You service only Germans, and only one. Me."

She ignored him, except about the man. "Who is the man?"

"Thiele," Reineke smiled. "Heinrich Thiele. Can you remember it?"

"It's not Italian," she agreed.

He laughed, taking her back in his arms. "You service *one*," he said. "Besides, Thiele is married. A lovely wife and a little son. Five years old," he nodded. "A little man. Would you take a father away from a little man?"

"Probably not," she said, that time laughing with him.

"Yes, and probably more to do with the little man than the father. You are so like me, it is uncanny."

"Everything is uncanny to you," she nodded. "What is my job? Where is it?"

"I will let you know," he promised. "But you must be ready to go when I contact you. Immediately. Hire a car so you have one available."

"I have a car."

"Good. You can give John and me a ride to the airport. When I contact you, you are to go south to Tataouine. I will have someone there for you—wear your uniform," he said. "You are a nurse, remember? Do you still have it?"

"Somewhere. I'll find it. How much?"

"Much?" Reineke said.

"Payment," she smiled.

"Oh," Reineke said. "I do not know. How much do you want?"

"Tomorrow?" she kissed him.

He smiled. "Five thousand in addition to your two."

"Tomorrow," she nodded.

"Four thousand," he said and she groaned.

"You are so rude. What am I supposed to do with that?"

Enjoy it, which she did.

His uniform was ready as of five, the money there at ten past seven as promised, an additional five-thousand to help cover expenses and the twenty percent exchange rate. Cäcilie was feeling uncharacteristically generous. He gave her two thousand. She took it with a smile and a question about the other five.

"You will get it when you come," Reineke promised. "You do not come ..." he raised a threatening brow.

"Yes," she smiled. "I do not come and you do not have an alibi for whoever you are killing now."

Reineke groaned. "I have never killed anyone."

"No, of course not," she fixed his tie. "What did this Thiele do to you that you are not killing him, too?"

"Thiele?" Reineke laughed. "Thiele is a very good man, you will see."

"But not service him," she nodded.

"No," he kissed her. "That is reserved for me. Besides, I told you, Thiele is a married man. He is very conservative. Not like you and me—go finish dressing. I will meet you downstairs. You are giving Eric and me a ride, remember?"

"Eric?" she said. "I thought you said his name was John?"

"I lied. You seemed too interested in him and I am very jealous. His name is Eric," he looked off briefly to ensure he remembered it.

"Eric Danzig. Liaison to the Italians in Tripoli."

Cäcilie laughed. "Do you ever tell the truth about anything?"

"No," Reineke assured.

John was in the lobby, rising from his seat impressed Reineke was only an acceptable thirty minutes late. Thiele never would have been so relaxed or patient.

"Right on time," John congratulated him.

Reineke nodded. "I have a ride for us to the airport."

"Airport?" John repeated as Reineke handed him two thousand pounds."

"So you can go back to Tripoli," Reineke assured. "That is for expenses. I changed your name to Eric Danzig, do not ask me why ..."

"Well, perhaps I want to ask you why," John said, which was fine because Reineke was already telling him.

"I cannot believe I almost said your name," Reineke shook his head.

"Well, maybe it has something to do with being high as a kite," John looked him over, annoyed. "What did you take? Why are your eyes red?"

"My eyes? Oh, opium," Reineke said.

"Opium?"

"Not me, Cäcilie," Reineke assured. "I am highly sensitive to the smoke. Something she finds amusing. Indeed, I would strangle her if she was not so beautiful."

"Well, maybe not strangle ..." John said, relieved Reineke was only giddy on oxygen and sex, and certainly much less critical of the questionable practices of some whore.

"No, strangle," Reineke assured, "like you. You are to keep the money. You want it ... the same as I want this," he slapped his suitcase, and suddenly laughed.

"What now?" John said.

"Nothing," Reineke shook his head. "I was thinking of how I have twenty-thousand at my compound. This is to replace it. I was not sure when I would be able to replace it."

"Is that true?" John said, ready to deck him right there if it was.

"Perhaps," Reineke smiled. "As true that I am extremely comfortable in all aircraft."

"Got it," John stopped him. "Don't worry, I won't embarrass you in front of your lady friend—we are going to take a taxi from the airport though, aren't we? At least part way? We are not going to walk again are we?"

"Walk? No, of course not," Reineke turned around to meet Cäcilie coming down the stairs. "Do not be ridiculous—"

"Just checking," John nodded.

"Eric Danzig," Reineke reminded.

"I got it," John promised.

"Good. Because I am not very good at this, I am not you."

Yeah, right. John acknowledged the introduction, and picked up one of Reineke's bags for him so the Baron could walk with his girl. So John had come full circle from chauffeur to partner, confidant to porter—a well-paid porter. John was not complaining.

"What aren't you very good at?" Cäcilie smiled as she tucked her arm through his.

"Saying goodbye," Reineke kissed her hand. "What else?"

The Fezzan
March 23

Thiele kissed the wall with his fist when the second day came and went and Reineke did not return. He would not wait! But he waited. Of course, he waited. Reineke's message finally arrived late the third afternoon while Thiele was on a radio call from a Hauptmann Eric Danzig. A garrulous aide of Herr Oberst Schönfeld's rambling on about the convoy. Thiele nodding, "Yes ... Yes ..." at the appropriate times, flipping his pencil impatiently, with an occasional roll of his eyes at his radio operator.

"*Yes ...*" Eric continued smoothly on his end, moving on to the caravans of horses, special gun mounts even though the bulk of the supplies would be traveling in painted trucks—

"What?" Thiele said into the radio. "Horses?" with a frown at his operator who shrugged.

"*Well, a decoy, is a decoy, Oberleutnant,*" Eric wet his lips with his tongue. "*A deception, a deception, and Hauptmann Reineke clearly excels at both—which is why we like him,"* Eric clarified quickly.

"Yes, I understand," Thiele assured. "You are talking about scouts ... scouts on horses," he looked at the operator who actually thought that sounded like a pretty good idea while not bothering, as Thiele might be, questioning where the hell the horses might be coming from. "What does that have to do with ... painted trucks? You said something about ... painted trucks?"

"*Red crosses, Oberleutnant,*" Eric repeated, joyfully, since he was also a very joyful person, "*Ambulances. The depot will be a hospital—a decoy, obviously.*"

"Oh ..." Thiele said. "Oh?" he considered, intrigued by the idea a little himself.

"*And, then, let me see ...*" Eric drew an *X* next to the *O*, beating himself fairly in tick-tack-toe. "*Ah, yes. Hauptmann Reineke is making arrangements to have the child remanded to the SS—*"

"Child?" Thiele said, and Eric stared at the radio on his end.

Oh, no. Eric groaned. Oh, no, not again. Wherever Reineke had taken her, however briefly, when he had brought her in town—which Eric had decided was something ridiculous like a toilet area—Eric could not imagine where he had taken her now. Certainly not Tripoli. Back to the SS on his own?

"*Oberleutnant ...*" Eric said very carefully. "*You do have a child there?*"

"A child?" Thiele weighed the question.

"*Yes, a child,*" Eric said.

"No," Thiele decided. "I am sorry, what are you talking about?"

"*Nothing,*" Eric sighed. "*Nothing. My apologies, Oberleutnant, apparently I hadn't understood how Hauptmann Reineke had made arrangements to return her to Herr Major Weiheber himself ...*"

Weiheber? Thiele frowned. "Oh," he said, and Eric perked up. "You mean the prisoner?"

"*Yes!*" Eric said. "*And—Well, of course I mean the prisoner,*" he interrupted himself with a curious look at the radio. "*What else could I mean?*"

"I did not understand you," Thiele said. "You ..." Well, truthfully the aide was talking too much for Thiele to easily follow him, extract the points from the jabber. "But I understand now, yes," Thiele assured. "The prisoner is to be remanded to the SS."

"*Excellent*!" Eric beamed. "*As it goes without saying how it is a distinct and unnecessary waste of time ...*"

"Oh?" Thiele said, waiting for the ball to drop because he knew Reineke was not going to remand the woman. He did not know what Reineke was going to do with her, but he knew he was not going to give her back to the SS.

"*Because ... well, the time frame we are looking at ...*" Eric nodded, "*is ... yes, I have it right here ... one to two weeks ...*"

"Weeks?" Thiele complained, making Eric a very happy man when he did.

"*Precisely, Oberleutnant,*" he said. "*Herr Oberst and I have agreed I can take care of this for Hauptmann Reineke ...*"

"Oh ..." Thiele said uncertainly there.

"*Well, I don't understand, Oberleutnant,*" Eric said. "*You and I just agreed how you and Hauptmann Reineke have far more pressing matters to deal with than the SS. Hauptmann Reineke was most articulate ... and, may I say, absolutely correct ... how our primary interest is our supplies. Our anonymity, and hence our circus parade to the front lines ... or almost the front lines,*" Eric agreed, "*near the top, anyway. The SS and some child are naturally last on anyone's list, especially ours.*"

"You will have to speak with Hauptmann Reineke," Thiele refused.

"*Well, I would, Oberleutnant,*" Eric assured, "*if he were there—my apologies, I did not realize he was back.*"

"Back?" Thiele hesitated.

"*From Tripoli, Oberleutnant,*" Eric said. "*I'm sorry, is something unclear again?*"

"Oh," Thiele said. "No. No, it is not unclear."

"*Yes ...*" Eric smiled. "*Though understandable how it could be. My apologies, again, but when Hauptmann Reineke was here, I was under the impression he and you would both be in Tripoli, an obvious misunderstanding on my part since I am talking to you—*"

"Of course he is there," Thiele agreed brusquely. "I will have him contact you when he arrives. I must go now, Hauptmann ..."

"*Danzig,*" Eric assured. "*Hauptmann Eric Danzig. And thank you for the update. In the meantime, in speaking with Tripoli, I have confirmed the area you will be traveling through—Gadames, is it? The region of Gadames? Has been confirmed to be somewhat questionable, hostile even. Herr Oberst accepts the current reports as most accurate considering we torpedoed the hell out of their convoy scheduled to dock at Malta—Oh, wait a minute, wait a minute,"* Eric reread his memo. *"I beg your pardon, Oberleutnant, we should be in the process of torpedoing the hell out of the British convoy. No verdict yet. We'll have to see. Nevertheless, with Churchill, and I don't know who else shouting 'Germany first ... though obviously in a different context than we do, I am positive the Allies, French, et cetera, would not forego the chance to torpedo the hell out of us be it on land, or sea—though obviously, if it is on land, it won't be torpedoes they use. Herr Oberst however is equally confident you will not run into any difficulties you will not be able to handle ... are you?"*

"No," Thiele assured.

"Yes ..." Eric said. *"I'll take that to mean yes, Oberleutnant."*

"Yes, then," Thiele agreed. "However, I cannot release the prisoner to you, Hauptmann. I have no such authority. You must discuss your arrangements with Hauptmann Reineke. I will have Hauptmann Reineke—" He jumped when the Telex started to type, directing the operator to check it. "One moment, Hauptmann," he requested. "We have a message coming now ..."

"Excellent!" Eric said. *"Is it Hauptmann Reineke?"*

"Yes," Thiele nodded. "Yes it is. Anticipated Tuesday. No time. I will have him contact you when he arrives."

"Wonderful! Ciao then as they say in Tripoli, I'll await—"

"Yes, good day," Thiele severed the connection. "Churchill!"

"What?" the operator said.

"I don't know." Thiele was out of his office, heading for the truck yard to ensure the trucks would be ready to roll without any delay.

"Hm," Eric studied the dead radio before he pulled his headset off and threw it on the console.

"I thought you were supposed to be in Tripoli, Herr Hauptmann," the twit behind him mentioned.

"I am," Eric assured, and the twit smiled.

"Herr Oberst requests you contact him," the twit reminded, "when you come in."

"I will," Eric promised, "when I come in—Tuesday," he assured, and headed upstairs to his office.

"I'll tell him," the twit agreed.

"You do, and you're dead!" Eric slammed his door behind him.

Chapter Fifty-Four

The Fezzan
March 25

Reineke returned from Tunis refreshed and confident. No longer afraid of the woman, if he had ever been afraid of her. He had avoided her because there was no reason for him to have contact with her, except for their two brief encounters—his required interview, and the trip to town that work out well, placating his Colonel Schönfeld.

Arguing with the Holy Man about what and where the woman could see and go, he knew the Holy Man was right. Control of the woman's environment was very important because no one could predict what she would say to her people upon her release, other than to tell her story, her interpretation of her experience. The people and acts, the places she had seen and been.

Diana's decision to place her in the hospital had been brilliant. That experience would be in synchrony with the field hospital where she would be brought before her release. It was within reason the conclusion would be she had been in a formal hospital setting—German, in the Vichy controlled colony of Algeria or Tunisia, not Libya, because of the presence of French and Arab constituents.'

Algeria or southern Tunisia most likely Reineke believed because of the location of the field hospital, the desert terrain, and Roman influence in buildings or ruins. The woman transferred from the German hospital to a field hospital because of her obvious injuries and health, and secured by the SS because of her obvious Allied association.

Overall, Reineke felt the plan had been managed and organized very well and he was quite pleased.

The Holy Man left immediately with Abraham and Hanuk to secure the horses upon Reineke's arrival. Initially annoyed to find the horses were not there, Reineke understood the Holy Man's reluctance to leave the woman unattended again. He had already left her twice, disappearing for days, traumatic for her as she had become dependent on his presence. There, too, the Holy Man had worked his magic very well. Whether or not the woman truly trusted the Holy Man or liked him, she was more comfortable with the Holy Man there, despite the distractions of the children and hospital, where she could occupy her time and mind.

In turn, Thiele frustrated by the length of time Reineke was gone, had been appeased by an unanticipated call from some aide of Oberst Schönfeld's who inadvertently provided Reineke with an alibi of having been in Tripoli. Reasonable, as Tripoli was the location of the docks, though Reineke had clearly requested a three-day pass for Tunis. Reineke did not correct the apparent misunderstanding by Schönfeld's or his aide. It was not needed or worth it. Thiele was satisfied and so Reineke was satisfied. He had been in Tripoli.

Sergeant Linke had left with Erich on schedule, though the horses were not yet there. Reineke understood, as had Linke, until the horses were there, they were a gamble and could not interfere or obstruct the operation. Their trailers were ready, however, and would simply be taken by Thiele with his group.

Work on painting Linke's fleet of trucks was completed before he left, and the work on Thiele's convoy continued on schedule. Their hospital colors and crosses to be covered by the usual canvas drapes until their unveiling was required.

Linke had also managed his preliminary reconnaissance very well, and would continue with forward scouts providing Reineke with several alternative locations for the convoy and hospital. Reineke would make his final decision upon his arrival north and assessment of the current climate of the region. There had apparently been a bombing of a British convoy attempting to reach the island Malta off the North African coast. Hundreds of kilometers away, Malta was a principal Allied stronghold in the North Afrikan war, and there would be a pervasive effect through the whole of the region, particularly within the pockets of resistance along the borders. Oberst Schönfeld, if he had questioned the slower pace of the convoy out of Tripoli and the staggered exchange of the supplies, he questioned it no more. A single line of trucks for hundreds of kilometers in the current environment tempted fate. Reineke had never liked the single convoy idea, finding it high risk whether the Allies were sleeping or reeling from an attack on a massive shipment they obviously needed, as Rommel needed his to remove the threat of the Allied held Tobruk that hindered his march into Egypt.

Reineke poured an early apéritif and smiled, hungry for food not field rations. He finally felt more comfortable than he had been at any point in the last two weeks. He was even prepared to terminate his decision to abstain from contact with the woman. If one thing nagged at him, it was how they knew nothing about this woman. Who she was beyond her name, where she came from or who her people were. He shared in the Holy Man's concern of what she would say of her experiences, her environment, the people she met and places she saw. While Reineke could know no more than any of them, what she would say, he wanted to know anyway, and he wanted to know from her. Truth or lies, he was confident he could discern which was which, and possibly learn something of importance or consequence to his operation.

Though he gave the woman time. Four o'clock now, it was after five before he decided to call her in for a second and final interview. She was in the apartment where she had remained all day, not sent to the children's village in the morning by the Holy Man in anticipation of Reineke's return. Factors precluding anyone from pinpointing an exact time of Reineke's arrival, the Holy Man simply waited, and that was his decision.

The Holy Man had also been considerate of the woman's concerns. Reporting to Reineke before he left for Algeria how instead of simply disappearing as he had before causing a near nervous collapse, this time, he advised the woman he had to return to the village to check on a sick child but would return to the villa as quickly as possible. Reineke accepted that and waved Pierre on his way.

"Fräulein ..." At six o'clock precisely, one hour before her scheduled dinner, Reineke gave a swift knock on her door, announcing himself before entering to call her to attention and come out. He did not wait for permission to enter, why would he? His knock announced him, and what he had to say once she appeared as requested to come and sit down for her interview, would not take long.

In considering all he wanted to know, and the reasons why he wanted to know it, Reineke had realized what was most important to him, was her behavior. The manner in which she would conduct herself over the next few days until the Holy Man's return with the horses. Reineke had no time, and certainly no patience for displays of temper, nervous collapse, or hysteria of any kind. The Holy Man had forewarned her of his departure and assured her of his return. She would be brought to the children every day as she had been brought every day now for the past several days as she settled into an recuperative period following the acute stages of her condition the first week.

There would be no alteration to her schedule of meals, morning preparation, evening, and sleep, as there had been none except during the times she saw fit to disrupt them, no one else.

In brief, there were to be no disruptions, and she was to behave. Following those two simple understandings, Reineke was interested in how she felt about her experience and environment. If she felt she needed or wanted something different to help maximize her comfort, he would consider that providing any requests were reasonable and serious. No taunts, no screaming, and above all, no physical assaults. He had not forgotten she had pinched him.

Drugged, unconscious, semi-conscious, hysterical, in the height of the effects of her brain concussion when she had attacked and scratched his face the first day she was there, this was not the first day. It was the third week, and she was now wide-awake, fully conscious when she had pinched him. He did not care how sick she was from the heat and too many sweet Arabian treats. She was well aware of her actions and it was not to happen again, or she would be confined to her room until the Holy Man's return. If she screamed and destroyed the room, he really did not care. He had much too much to do, to care.

The woman was not in the sleeping and studio area of her quarters when he walked in, and so she had to be in her lounge or bath. It understandable she did not see him, as he did not see her, it was impossible she did not hear him, either when he knocked, when he spoke, or when he walked in. The apartment was half the size of his quarters, one-quarter the size of the library. She heard him. She had to hear him. Her brain concussion, to his understanding of the condition, affected her mental processes, not her hearing any more than it had affected her lungs. The responsibility to hear him was hers, not his, and therefore she heard him.

Joanna did not hear him. She really did not. Had she, she would not have come out of the loo, what she called the bath. Certainly not immediately, though possibly eventually once she was certain he had left the room.

As it was, she did not hear him, but saw him instead when she walked into her studio area from the lounge only to stop short in obvious surprise, horror, immediate fear and panic when she saw him standing there in her room.

Fortunately, he did not see her. His back was to her, involved in poking over the assortment of items she had collected during her recent trip to town. Why he was doing that, Joanna did not know, and neither did she care. Her interest and concern was solely in finding him in her room.

Disinterested in the trinkets, poking over them gave Reineke something to do while waiting for her entrance. The assortment and sheer number of them assured him her day of solitary confinement had not been an ordeal. He picked up the hat that had started it all, goading him into wanting to know more about this woman before she left his compound. She should have seen to wearing the hat.

Joanna wished the hat was the only thing she should have seen to wearing. Though her shirt was long, several inches below her knees, longer than any current fashion, the only thing Joanna could think of as she stepped into her room to find him standing there was she wasn't wearing the trousers. Joanna was comfortable in trousers. She hated dresses. She was not Michael's daughter Andrea so beautifully tall and slender like a long, golden, reed. Joanna was short, square, because she was too short to be anything but square, and looked rather like an over-stuffed doll in a dress. Fat, in her opinion, a dress way too much material for her tiny frame leaving her staring in a mirror horrified. Right now, she was wearing something tantamount to a dress, the long cotton shirt like one of Grandfather's nightshirts, hanging practically to her ankles, Joanna would still give anything to be wearing the trousers.

But the trousers were all the way over there on the bed, and she was all the way over here, and even though the Captain was farther away than the bed was to her as he poked over the trinkets, he seemed way too close.

"Well," Joanna announced finally, since apparently he wasn't going anywhere, and she had long forgotten where the doorway was behind her, or even what was behind her as she stood there, "since you're here, would you mind tossing me my slacks?"

Reineke immediately turned around with her voice, and if he had understood what she said, it was lost and confused by the question what was she doing?

What on earth was the woman doing? Reineke stood there puzzled trying to figure out why the woman appeared to be—compressed, was all he could think of. She appeared to be compressed with the side of her dressing bureau, part of it like a wooden figurehead. A random thought crossed his mind wondering if she had actually come out from behind the dressing bureau, or up from under it? And she was glaring at him, tugging and pulling at some shirt she was wearing, trying to hike it up so she would not trip over it he supposed, it was so long. Why was she glaring at him? What was wrong with her? He was not the one crawling around under the furniture popping up in front of her.

"My slacks!" the woman repeated with a jabbing point of her finger as Reineke stood there trying to figure out exactly what he was looking at and why it looked the way it did, the whole of the picture, not only her. "They're right there on the bed next to you! Do you think you could manage to pick them up?"

The bed? *What about the bed*? Reineke looked at the bed. Nothing appeared unusual or out of place. It looked like the bed, and was precisely where the bed should be. Absolutely no difference at all. No scorpions or snakes swirling around it, if that was what she was yelling about, or had been looking for crawling around the floor. In fact, there was nothing on the bed that did not belong there, or could not be there quite innocently. The only thing on the bed other than the pillows and bed clothes, was a pair of uniform trousers. Something yes, he realized, in her caterwauling, she was directing him to pick them up. Why? Reineke looked at the trousers. Was she giving him her laundry? Did she seem to think he was there to collect her laundry? Or was she simply not satisfied? Had she flung them aside in disgust, and was now demanding a new and better pair, because this pair for some reason was unacceptable? Indeed. Few of his soldiers had so many unwanted pairs of trousers they could afford to discount and fling what they had all over the barracks. Uniforms were scarce. Matching sets, a prized possession. They were to be treated with respect. That was a German uniform. Those were German trousers.

"Give me my blasted britches!" the woman screamed.

And that was precisely what he was there to talk to her about. That screaming, that temper, that unrelenting, insistent tendency of hers to make a scene.

"Fräulein," Reineke said, ignoring whatever it was she did not like about the trousers, was screaming about the trousers, "I have come to speak with you."

"Oh, no, you don't!" she bellowed as he took a step. "One more of those and you'll never take another!"

Never take another what? Reineke was not taking anything. There was nothing there for him to take. Not the trinkets. Not the hat even though he held it in his hand, he was not taking it. Not the bed, not the trousers. He was not—

He realized what was wrong. How or why he realized he did not know, possibly it was simply because he was a man. A grown man. As he looked at the young woman screaming, flailing and flinging her arms and entire body like some enraged, terrified cat, her face contorted and blood red. It did not take long for him to realize, nowhere near as long as it might seem, how she did not want or think he was taking the trousers, but that she wanted him to give them to her. She was not wearing any. Though she was wearing some long shirt, a uniform shirt, truly practically reaching the floor, she wanted the trousers. She was embarrassed. She felt undressed, even though she was not undressed. She was not crawling out from behind the dressing bureau, she was trying to hide behind it. Terrified he might see—what? Some young woman practically half his age wearing a uniform shirt three times too large for her, which was what he saw?

It did not matter, once Reineke realized, he also understood. He was a grown man, and she was a very young woman and she was embarrassed, as he had apparently caught her off guard. She had not heard him.

"Indeed," Reineke did not laugh, but he wanted to. Inside, he was laughing, silly with laughter. This was something he was going to definitely have to tell the dentist Haas. Not the Holy Man—definitely not the Holy Man.

But he was going to have to tell the dentist Haas. Particularly since, once realizing, and truly understanding and even being sympathetic, he was also satisfied. Smug and swollen with satisfaction he finally, after almost three weeks, truly had control over her. Control of the situation, the event, the outcome, and the woman who blindly fought so hard for her own control of a situation she could not begin to control, exhausting herself and wreaking havoc with everything and everyone around her.

This moment was better than any talk, more satisfying than any talk with her could give him.

More satisfying than the spanking he had occasionally thought she deserved.

Unfortunately, it was also more of the same. The woman was completely inappropriate from beginning to end. Absolutely no understanding how her behavior also figured into the equation that was her situation. She was not entirely powerless, in fact, she was quite powerful in her ability to take responsibility for herself, regardless of who else took on the responsibility for her, or tried to take the responsibility away from her.

Point offered in evidence: the trousers. Reineke was not embarrassed. He had not even noticed. She was embarrassed. If she knew she was more comfortable wearing trousers, then she should be wearing trousers, not causing herself embarrassment upon being seen not wearing them, in turn, trying to put the responsibility or blame for her embarrassment on to someone else. It did not belong with anyone else, it belonged with her. She was the one not wearing trousers. The one who chose not to wear trousers regardless of the length of the shirt.

Which was another question. Why was she not wearing trousers? It was six o'clock in the evening. Civilized people were properly dressed at six o'clock in the evening. Did she not wear trousers at the children's village?

Did she not wear trousers in the wagen that brought her back to the villa and her dinner?

Six o'clock was an hour that could find anyone coming. It did not have to be him. It could be anyone. Thiele, or some simple soldier for any reason.

A change in her dinner schedule.

An attack on his compound by her Allied cohorts Reineke knew were out there somewhere regardless of what anyone else said.

It could be the Holy Man. In fact, Reineke should be the Holy Man, but for the fact the Holy Man was not there. The Holy Man however would be returning. How did she know when the Holy Man would return? She did not know. Did she feel comfortable walking around half naked simply because the Holy Man was a priest?

Indeed. The Holy Man was a man. Reineke could tell her how much of a man the Holy Man was with some reputed son older than her. He did not care if the Holy Man was a priest, as neither had the Holy Man obviously cared at the time he fathered a son.

Reineke picked up the trousers from the bed.

"Toss them!" the woman screamed.

Reineke did not want to. If he tossed them she would have them and he did not want to give them to her just yet.

If he tossed them, she would not learn her lesson.

If he tossed them she would not have to consider or admit her responsibility for the situation she now found herself in.

If he tossed them his moment of satisfaction would be over. Her stricken expression, fear, and embarrassment, over, past, gone.

"Keep it to yourself!" Joanna warned the sly smile Reineke did not realize he was wearing.

Keep what to himself? The trousers? But she had asked him for them. Since she had now apparently decided he could keep them, Reineke decided he would give them to her, underscoring his point he was the one in control of the situation not her. He tossed them with little effort and great ease, the shield for her modesty floating toward her through the air.

He threw them at her was more like it without any thought at all. The trousers reached the dressing bureau, landing on the floor a good three feet in front of Joanna. "Don't you dare!" Joanna corrected as Reineke made an apologetic reach for them. "Turn around!"

Except Reineke did not want to turn around. If he turned around he would not be able to see what she was so desperate to hide beneath her dressing gown as she stepped from her hiding place to get the trousers, and he wanted to see what it was. He suspected it was her legs despite the length of the shirt. What was there about her legs that was so different than everyone else's legs? Was there something unique about her legs either good or bad? How would she know? They were her legs, her view would be prejudiced. His would be impartial, and he wanted to see those legs to compare them to Cäcilie's he had also recently seen. Not too many hours had passed since Cäcilie had not seen to wearing pants, any more than he had seen to wearing his, though that was irrelevant. Still, he wanted to see those legs.

"Indeed," Reineke said. This woman could not possibly have Cäcilie's legs. If she did, she would simply be a pair of legs with a bandaged head stuck on top of them. She was not long and flowing like Cäcilie, or even politely petite. She was boldly short.

"Indeed," Reineke said, because there was something fascinating about what was transpiring here. Vague memories of the cellar included a recollection of an adequate pair of legs, reasonably shaped and of the appropriate length for her height.

"Indeed," Reineke said, recalling those legs quite clearly, and since he did, this current study was becoming more intriguing by the moment. Vastly important was it now to know if it was the length of a woman's legs, or was it more the leg shape he found himself most frequently attracted to. Cäcilie had both features. This woman, merely one.

"Turn around!" the woman screamed again, stubborn and selfish, as usual putting her interests above his. Hysterically trying to extend the depth and width of her barricade by yanking open the top drawer and succeeding only in blocking herself, hindering her stretch, reach for the trousers ...

What? Reineke glared, *was that?* That ... *foot* starting to creep out, sneak toward the trousers. That was not a foot. "Indeed!" he assured. Never had he seen such a foot. His hand was bigger than that foot with the tiny pink toes, as pink as the flush of her cheeks. So pink one would think they were blushing.

They weren't, but Joanna was. The kind of flushed bright blush someone gets when they're about to cry.

Reineke recognized it. He saw if before. Outside, the other day when she claimed to be sick from too much sun. Typically elfin! There was no sun in here only the beautiful bright light of the desert air. Annoyed, he marched over and scooped the pants up from the floor. It was her own fault for taking so long. Why should he be the one to have to suffer through her crying simply because she refused to be cooperative in his study? Cry away!

Joanna did. Not because he flung the pants at her, but because she yanked her foot back so fast she slammed her ankle into the leg of the dressing bureau. *"OW!"* she yelped, bending over and grabbing her ankle, fortunately, as the shirt was long, informing no one how she was likewise not wearing knickers.

It was a short cry. What a handkerchief those trousers made once she had them in her hands. She blew her nose and wiped her eyes and was a brat once more. "Turn around!" she barked at Reineke frozen in place.

Turn yourself around! Reineke glared back at her in icy silence, unable to believe she did what she did. He was not turning anywhere. If she was so concerned, she could just back herself right back up into the other room.

Except Joanna could not do that. Believe her, she had thought of it. But the door was so many feet behind her and she was too concerned he might see.

"Indeed!" Reineke read her simple little mind with her bourgeois concerns and did she really think he had absolutely any interest in seeing anything belonging to a woman who just blew her nose on a pair of uniform trousers—*German* trousers! So what if he saw? He had a right to see! Those were his legs, not hers. He saved those legs.

Days ago he found those legs in his cellar. She should be grateful and show him those legs at a snap of his fingers. Horrible people had done horrible things to those legs, and he was not one of them.

"Indeed!" Reineke seethed. On the contrary, he was the man who had even stooped to considering them attractive, worthy of respect and fair treatment if for no other reason than his kindness and compassion. Even in the cellar he clearly remembered thinking this. As bruised as they were, dirty, scraped, he nevertheless distinctly recalled noticing how attractive they were. They were short, but she was short, and she would look perfectly ridiculous with long ones.

They were small, but then she was small. Well-formed and nicely shaped, round—

"Indeed!" Reineke came to his senses, turning around. Her naked legs were not all he had seen in the cellar, as they were not all he had seen here when he had helped subdue the screaming naked woman so the Holy Man could give her a needle, putting her back to sleep.

"I'm going into the loo," Joanna informed, keeping a close eye on him as she struggled into the pants. "If you insist on following me, please knock first!"

Reineke stiffened. How dare she. Such a comment was not only uncouth, it was an insult to his character as a human being, not simply a man. "Indeed," he clutched the hat. "Indeed!"

Dodgers. The hat agreed when he grabbed it to twist it, tie it into knots, rip it in half with his bare hands.

"What?" Reineke took sudden notice of the hat he strangled, and the hat read *Dodgers*, in big, bold letters straight across the front of the cap. Black letters. English. Drawn with some fat, greasy pencil.

Blasphemy! Reineke stared at the hat that was a German soldier's field cap, as those had been a German soldier's trousers before she soiled and destroyed them with her fluids. Both given to her out of his concern, goodness, kindness, and look. LOOK! The woman had gone too far. Someone does not scrawl *Dodgers* across a German soldier's field cap.

"Fräulein," Reineke insisted sharply from outside the door to her bath. "Come out of there at once. I wish to speak with you."

"I'm cleaning my teeth," she answered him in some nearly unrecognizable dialect, "it will have to wait until I spit."

Shit? An unearthly sensation spread over Reineke. Hotter and hotter, he could feel the sweat start to drip. The Holy Man had told him, rather amusingly, of her early and unusual fascination with the vulgar tongue as if her command and knowledge of such words infused her with some power other than simply degrading her, as she attempted to degrade her audience.

And though this apparent practice of cursing had subsided quickly with the Holy Man's appropriate handling, it had also apparently not ceased, but it would cease in its entirety as of right now.

"Fräulein!" Reineke barked in reply to her and the inhuman sounds he could hear in her bath, a three inch crack appearing in the wood where his boot struck the door. "That is precisely what I want to speak with you about!"

Spitting? Joanna stopped brushing her teeth with her head half hung over the basin. He wanted to talk to her about spitting? She hadn't spat on anyone. She quickly spit the water she had in her mouth into the basin. Heaven only knew what would happen if he came through the door to find her with water in her mouth. And he did sound as if he was coming through the door, without knocking, at any moment, without opening it first. She opened it, really not able to think of what else to do.

"Yes?" Joanna asked bravely as she finished wiping her mouth and hands dry and he glared at her. "Yes?" she repeated.

"What were you doing?" Reineke asked, bracing himself for the response.

"What ..." Joanna stammered trying to hear the words through his accent.

"What were you doing?" he insisted.

"Brushing my teeth?" she offered quickly and he reacted.

"What?"

"Brushing my teeth?" she said and he glanced inside the bath.

"For dinner?" he frowned.

"Yes.." she said because dinner sounded good though she wasn't quite sure why he was pounding on the bath door to tell her.

"What else?" he waited.

"Tea?" Joanna whispered.

Tea. "Fräulein," he said, "I want to know exactly what you were doing in there, and please do not tell me you were drinking tea."

"Oh ..." Joanna said. "Well ..." she said, likewise looking behind herself into the bath. "Oh ... well ... I ..."

"Fräulein!" he demanded.

"I did not spit on anyone!" her head snapped back as she snapped. "I did not! Who told you I did? That little witch? Because I did not!"

He heard the word correctly that time, and stared at her. She had not cursed, though he had kicked the bathroom door, and it seemed perhaps the inappropriate behavior this time, was his. He walked away.

Chapter Fifty-Five

"Yes?" Joanna said as the Captain turned around and walked away. She hesitated but then followed after him, not too closely, and just to see what he was up to. He did not leave the room, but walked back over near the things she had bought and seemed to be looking out through the opened French windows.

"Spitting?" Reineke heard her whisper behind him. "You wanted to speak with me about spitting?"

No, he did not. He had misunderstood what she said. He could not remember why he had followed her, regardless of why she might have followed him now. But then he did remember and he looked at the hat he still held in his hand. An issue that needed resolve.

"Fräulein," he turned around, showing her artwork to her, offering no explanation as to why he was showing it to her, and awaiting any statement she might care to make.

Joanna studied the hat for a few moments until she offered finally, "Well, they do rather look like a baseball cap. That's who they are. A team, I mean. It's a game," she included and concluded, "though I suspect you don't know much about that considering who you are and all.

"But it's just a game," she shrugged, "with a little ball and stick. You hit the ball with the stick ..." she provided a brief demonstration that he interrupted.

"I am well aware, Fräulein," Reineke assured, "of the sport."

"Really?" Joanna frowned more to herself. He knew about baseball? "How odd," she said. "I mean, it's really quite sophisticated. Terribly modern."

Which he was not apparently. The German to her was someone terrorizing the Roman Empire. A Hun. Indeed. He sought to correct her remarkably inaccurate assessment of not only him, but the whole of world history. "It may be of interest to you, Fräulein," he said, "to know the Rhine was rapidly approaching its height of wealth and civility, while your country remained buried in an avalanche of rats."

"What?" Joanna said.

"Indeed," he said and his head went up in the air.

"I don't like rats!" Joanna snapped.

What? Reineke's head came down.

"Why would I like rats?" she insisted upon knowing.

"Not like them, Fräulein ..." he attempted to explain.

"I don't!" she assured again.

"Indeed, I realize that," he silenced her with a wave, and Joanna quickly stepped back a step or two. "Your country, Fräulein. Your country where you were born was drowning in rats. While my country ..." his head went back up in the air, "embraced a fine glass of wine."

"I don't care how much wine you drink," Joanna assured, and back down came Reineke's head.

"Fräulein," he said, "are you intentionally misunderstanding what I am saying?"

"No," Joanna claimed.

"What are you doing then, if I may ask?" Reineke requested. "I speak English, Fräulein—obviously."

Not really. It was very difficult for Joanna to figure out what he was saying with that biting, harsh accent and it did not help that he was as unnerving as his voice. None of that meant there were rats in her country though. She never saw any rats in her country. If she saw them, she did not know they were rats.

"Fräulein," he said.

"Frogs," Joanna corrected.

"What?" Reineke said. "Frogs?"

"And mice," Joanna shrugged because she remembered there were a lot of mice, but that did not mean they were rats. "Ducks."

She could stop with mice. Reineke did not need a dissertation on the wildlife of Britannia. That was not his point. "Indeed, rats, Fräulein, not mice. One hundred deep in your streets were the victims of the plague drawn from rats, not mice. You wallowed in the stench of their filth."

"I did what?" Joanna stared at him.

"Indeed," he sneered.

"I did no such thing!" she assured. "Who told you that?"

"What?" Reineke said again. "Not you personally, Fräulein—"

"You said me!" Joanna insisted.

Reineke knew what he said. He knew what he meant. So did she despite whatever childish game she was playing. "How old are you, Fräulein?" he demanded.

"How old am I?" Joanna repeated, certainly having no idea why he would ask that. "Why? How old are you?"

Old enough to realize he had possibly made a mistake in his assessment of her recovery and race. He looked at the hat. Baseball was notoriously an American game. Uncivilized. "You are from Amerika?" he said, mastering his struggle with his disdain.

"What?" Joanna said hearing what simply sounded like sounds to her, not words. Something like *zee errrr fum something ka,* which was gibberish. "What?"

"Never mind," Reineke waved irritably knowing she was not. "Fräulein, you are British," he assured. "Whether English or Welsh.

"And!" he advised because she was not a child regardless of her pretense, or the swelling in her brain, "you are aware of the Black Plague. If you are not, you are now. The infection is not spawn from frogs, or mice, but is from rats. Rats!" he said.

"I told you I don't like rats," Joanna said, not that she was too fond of frogs or mice either, certainly not millions of them swarming at a time. "And I've had the measles," she assured as Reineke straightened up unaware he had been bending over. "So I am not getting your dreadful infection."

Infection? Reineke peered at her. "Fräulein, are you ill?"

"What?" Joanna said.

"Are you ill?" he inclined forward. "Fräulein, what is the matter with you?"

"Nothing!" Joanna said.

That was a matter of opinion. "Where are you from?"

Joanna stared at him.

"Where are you from?" Reineke repeated. "What is your land? What is your home? That you know so little of world history?"

"Guess," Joanna challenged.

"No, I am not guessing," he declined. "Do not be absurd. England," he waved, though the English were respectable world historians, he could not resist.

"Guess again," she said.

He called an end to it. "Fräulein, I am not guessing. The British Empire is much too vast, and I could probably recite a thousand colonies, and you would say no to all. Therefore I ask you what is a very simple question, please answer it. Where are you from? Where were you born?"

"The Antipodes," Joanna shrugged.

Reineke blinked. "Indeed. The Antipodes? What do you mean? South Afrika?" That was Diana's territory, the ultimate destination of her people traveling south.

"No, Australia," Joanna said. "But I still want to know why you're asking me."

Why did she think? And, of course it was Australia. Frogs. Mice. He never thought of Australia, the ranks of the Australians in the desert war. This woman had survived in the desert, because her home was a desert. It was a penal colony. Her people iniquitous, criminal, not even uncivilized, the woman's blood thick with the blood of bandits, murderers, and horse thieves.

"Indeed," Reineke said and started to smile. She was the Holy Man, his defrocked Bishop, his fierce and adventurous Anne, her driven and passionate grandmother.

And little Adva. She was innocent little Adva. Just another tiny little creature displaced from her home, bewildered and terrified. Finding herself in a situation she could not possibly comprehend, standing there with the look of refugee in that uniform five-times too large for her.

But in those eyes staring at him and in that temper she displayed, was her country. Fierce, savage, untamed ...

Reineke started to laugh, a light laugh, as much at himself as it was for her. "Indeed!" he threw back his head and laughed, loudly. Chiding himself for chiding her. How could he expect her to act, he questioned his own sanity. Like him? Or Thiele? This sister, child of brothers who painted pictures of kangaroos on their tanks, what did that tell him? He wondered while conveniently forgetting it was the disciplined and civilized German who indulged themselves with painting white circles around their tank guns for every successful strike, similar to notches cut into the stock of a gun.

"Indeed!" Reineke sat down on the bed with apologies for laughing, the little woman so steady in her stance and her glare, her hands planted firmly on her hips. "Forgive me, please," he requested, "but if I have wanted to do anything, I have wanted to do this!"

"Get out of here," Joanna said.

"No, I know, but it is all right," Reineke said. "I realize I frightened you, and even though really," he waved the hat at her, a strange twinkle in his light, almost glassy blue-grey eyes, "this is not something you should do—come here, " he held out his hand. "I want to talk to you—"

"Get out of here!" Joanna retreated rapidly, banging into the dressing bureau.

"Fräulein, please—" Reineke stood up. "I said, it is all right—"

"Don't you touch me! Don't you dare touch me!" she started screaming, her hands thrashing, arms flailing as she seemed trapped again by her dresser, though he was nowhere near her.

"Fräulein!" Reineke insisted. "Come to attention. Control yourself. There is no reason for these hysterical fits."

"Oh, God!" Joanna gasped as she felt him grasp her and start to shake her.

"Fräulein!" Reineke insisted as he shook her, trying to shake her out of it before she had some actual fit. "Listen to me ... listen to what I am saying ..."

"I ... I ... I ..." she just stared up at him with a wild, stammering chatter.

"Yes, I know," Reineke assured. "I am not stupid, Fräulein, and neither are you. Whoever you think I am, I am not who you think I am. You are wrong—"

"Oh, but you are!" Joanna gasped. "You are! I! I remember you ... I remember you ..." she assured, and she did, even though she did not know why, or where, or even when. But she did remember him. His shirt, and his hat ... and those hands. She remembered those hands grasping her as they grasped her now ...

"No, you do not," Reineke said coldly, no longer shaking her, just gripping her to stop her from climbing up his shirt to his face.

"Oh, but I do!" Joanna assured. "I do!" she pulled away from him, wrenched herself away from him, and Reineke let go of her, let her go, stumbling and falling away from him toward the bath.

"Oh, God," Joanna hung on to the washstand trying to catch her breath. "Oh, God!" She did remember him. She knew she did. "I do!" she stared at herself in the mirror. "I really do!"

Reineke stepped out onto the balcony of his library. He loved the balcony, he loved the library. Secrets and answers in the dust of hundreds of books and scrolls and not one of them could tell him what to do. He felt the smoke from his cigarette touch his cheek where she had scratched him with her nails, understanding the time it had taken for them to fade away. What had he expected her to do in a few short weeks?

"Why do I remember you?"

The woman's voice spoke behind him. He turned around. She was inside, having crossed the threshold of his desk, moving as close to the windows as she dared. He stared at her in silence and she eventually turned around walking away to stop before she reached the steps of the landing and turned back.

Her movements seemed to grant him permission to enter, marking what she considered to be a safe distance between them. He understood, but was uncertain as to the actual distance at which she felt safe. She was close to the steps behind her, and he walked slowly back inside, carefully monitoring his steps and the distance between them, concerned if he stepped too far or too fast she might turn and bolt, tumble over backwards. He reached his side of his desk and stopped. She did not move, and so that was the distance. He on his side of the desk, and her near the stairs, six or seven meters away.

"Well?" the woman said, as that was also apparently the extent of her patience.

Reineke's head tipped, in acknowledgement of the question. "I cannot remove my cellar, Fräulein," he said. "But I can, and I will keep you out of it."

"What?" Joanna said after a moment.

Reineke tipped his head again. "I believe you are confused."

Joanna hesitated. "If you speak slowly, I can understand you better."

Reineke understood that. As his command of the English language was perfect and perfectly clear, there was apparently some lingering disturbance to her auditory faculties, probably from the blow to the side of her face.

He was also aware though how he did not help by giving lectures on irrelevant matters, such as the Black Plague. Without her assistance, he could hear his ego in his words, he could hear his egotism. He was an egotistical man, with every reason and right to be as egotistical as he was. She reached his ego, attacked his ego, struck him in it, much harder than she could ever strike his face. His answer now though was prepared.

"It would be my presumption, Fräulein," he said, "what you remember of me is a man in your room—that room," he indicated the apartment with a nod. "I am the man who called for the Monseigneur Pierre Beausoleil ..." he watched her react slightly to the name, perhaps not understanding Roman formality. "Bishop," he clarified. "I am the man who called for the Catholic Bishop, whom you know as Pierre, to assist you.

"I am the man," he said. "who assisted the Bishop Pierre with his helping you. When you were found, you were unconscious. When you awoke, you were in that room where I had asked for you to be placed, and you were understandably confused and frightened.

"I am the man," he said, "who stopped you from falling off the bed on which you had been placed. And, yes," he granted with a another tip of his head, "who held you there, physically held you down so you could not fall and hurt yourself as the Holy Man—Pierre," he confirmed, "could assist you as I requested.

"Apart from that, Fräulein," he said, "I am not any other man whom you may remember in part or in whole. I am Hauptmann Reineke, commander of this outpost at which you are a guest."

"That's what Pierre said," she said quietly.

His head tipped. "And it is true," he agreed, not troubling to question as to why she was asking him who he was when apparently the Holy Man had already explained this to her. He presumed she asked because she wished to hear it from him. "Do you have any other questions, Fräulein?" he asked.

"No," Joanna said. "Not right now."

"Very good," Reineke said. "Please feel free to ask if you do. In the meantime, I do have a few questions to ask you, if that is acceptable to you."

"Maybe," Joanna said.

Maybe was not an answer. He looked at his watch. "It is ten minutes to seven," he said, surprised such little time had passed since he first walked in the apartment to ask her to come out for an interview before her dinner. "Your dinner will be arriving at seven o'clock. What would you like to do? Would you like to eat your dinner as you usually do, at seven o'clock, and we can continue our talk after it—perhaps at eight? Or would you like ..." he asked, calculating how much time he needed for her interview, "me to ask for your dinner to be brought to you instead at seven-thirty?"

"I'm not hungry," Joanna said.

Reineke interpreted that to mean it was acceptable to her to have her dinner later than scheduled. "Very good," he said. "I will call your servant on the telephone ..."

Reineke hung up the telephone and the woman continued to stand there like one of the grave markers in the gardens, marking her space. Finally, he asked her. "Would you care to sit down, Fräulein?"

She smiled slightly. "I was going to ask you ..." she agreed.

"If you may sit," Reineke nodded, understanding.

"If you would sit," she said and he frowned slightly, noticing her hands starting to twitch, her eyes suddenly downcast.

"Of course," Reineke said quickly, interpreting the signs as some impending nervous attack. He sat down and the attack was aborted.

"Thank you," she breathed gratefully. "Because you'd scare even that thing hovering there like that."

That thing she referred to with a fluttering hand was a picture of the Führer. And Reineke was not hovering. He was sitting down, in his chair, at his desk. She sat down as well, walking up to sit down in one of the chairs on the visitor's side of his desk.

She took a breath, either settling herself, or preparing to ask a question. Reineke waited to see which, prepared to intercept any attack. In the meantime, he let the matter of the Führer's portrait slide. She took another breath before disclosing, "You don't scare me though. People might think you do, being what you are and all, but people aren't always right, because you don't."

Reineke incorrectly, though understandably, presumed what she meant was he was German. She did not mean that. She meant he was tall, which she was not. She advised him of this, discussing it in great length and detail in case he had not noticed.

While she rattled on about her lack of height, she elaborated on the inspiring strength one would find she possessed despite her tiny frame, referring to herself as plucky.

"Mind you!" she pointed out to him.

It was nothing to be sneered at.

"Mind you!" she assured.

It was something to reel and rock him.

"After all ..." she reminded how Napoleon was not a tall man, and one would find few people laughing about Napoleon.

Or about her. Reineke was positive. Laughter would hardly be appropriate. There was something wrong with her.

"I've heard about people like you," she nodded.

Indeed. As he had heard about people like her. And there was definitely something very wrong with anyone who thought they were Napoleon.

"I think you are rude," she nodded, "I really do."

"It was time to intercede. "Fräulein ..." Reineke said.

"But that's what I mean," she said. "Why are you calling me Fräulein? I asked Pierre what it meant because I was unsure and perhaps wrong."

"And I am sure the Holy Man explained to you how it is the German equivalent of mademoiselle."

"Yes," she said. "Yes, he did."

And? Reineke struggled to understand what then might be the issue. "Fräulein ..." he said.

"It's Frau, Captain," she corrected him. "I told you that before. Though he's dead," she said sadly, "blown to bits by a fellow like you."

The third person. In his heart, and in his stomach, Reineke knew it was the missing third person the Holy Man had talked about. "My apologies," he extended stiffly, "on the loss of your husband. He must have ..." he did not know what else to say. He only knew this woman was very young. "He must have been very young, " he said, watching her.

"No," she said. "Oh, no. Joe was ..." she said, drifting off for a moment or two. "Oh, my, let me see ... at least ... well, at least as old as you ..." she studied him with her one uncovered eye. "Older, I think. How old are you Captain?" she asked. "I asked you before when you asked me."

His age was irrelevant. As was her husband someone she either made up as some continued taunting of him, or solely a result of her swollen brain. He had to ask.

"Fräulein," he said, "I am sorry, but I do not understand why you are telling me this."

Neither did Joanna. "I don't know," she said. "I guess because you keep calling me Fräulein, and it's Frau."

"I see ..." Reineke said, certainly by his age aware most things were possible regardless of how improbable. Indeed, the idea of some man, any man, certainly one older than she—older than he, if he were to believe her, married to her made his stomach turn. It seemed almost perverse. She was barely more than a child, in her size, certainly, but also in her maturity. He changed the subject. "I extend my condolences, Fräu ... *Frau*," he granted, "on the loss of the members of your party."

"What?" Joanna said. She sat back, her eyes opening wide, her breathing starting to increase. "What do you mean?"

"Nothing, Fräulein," Reineke offered quickly. "I mean nothing of any consequence. You are here alone. When you were found, you were alone. I have no way of knowing how many people were in your party."

"Found?" Joanna said. "What do you mean, found?"

"I mean just that," Reineke said. "I found you, and you were alone."

"Where?" she asked, and she was looking at him very interested, a degree of innocence in her eyes—eye. He kept thinking eyes, but in fact she only had one eye exposed and open. The other one buried beneath a bandage and black eye patch.

"Here, Fräulein," he said. "I found you here ... when I returned from the town you recently visited," he extended. "You had apparently been brought here, and you were alone."

"Oh." She breathed a quiet breath of relief, and Reineke was glad to see her relax. He had not thought the Holy Man had told her of the horrific circumstances under which she had been discovered. He was certain the Holy Man had not. Such would not do anything to speed her recuperation. However, he was also uncertain insofar as what she did or did not know herself, or remember.

"Do you have any other questions about ... that, Fräulein?" he asked.

"No," Joanna shook her head, and breathed another quiet sigh of relief. "I mean, I don't know," she said. "I can't remember. Pierre said I was in an accident."

"Yes," Reineke agreed, perhaps a little too quickly, but she did not seem to notice. "That is my understanding."

"But I don't remember," she said. "Pierre said I may never remember."

"Perhaps," Reineke granted. "Only time will tell."

"Perhaps," she considered, and he noticed her bite her lip. It was seven-twenty-nine. Her dinner would be arriving and Reineke was generally pleased with the progress. He had done very well.

"Perhaps you may wish to continue this later?" he asked before her dinner arrived and he granted entry for its delivery.

"Oh," Joanna said. "Well, yes, I guess so. What did you want to ask me?"

"Nothing that cannot wait," he assured. "It is more important that you eat—I do not wish to be in trouble with the Holy Man—Pierre," he clarified for her again and he smiled. "I call Pierre the Holy Man because that is what he is. A holy man. Like I call you Fräulein, because a Fräulein is a young woman, which is what you are."

"I understand," Joanna said.

"Thank you," Reineke tipped his head. That is your dinner," he explained the knock that had her startling. "Perhaps we can continue this conversation ... tomorrow," he decided.

"Oh," Joanna said. "Oh, well, what about the hospital? Can't I go to the hospital? I didn't go anywhere today, all day."

"To the children's village? Yes. You may. There will be no change in your schedule, Fräulein. Today was unavoidable with the Holy Man having to return to … the town," he extended, "to check on a sick child there, as I understand he explained to you, and I was … negligent," he proposed, "in ordering the car to bring you to the children."

"Oh, you do that," she said.

"I do what?" Reineke requested. "I am sorry, but I do not understand what you mean."

"You call the car?" Joanna said.

"Yes," Reineke said. "I call the car. You may recall I took you to the children's village myself. The other day."

"Last week," she said, "yes. Monday."

If she said so. Reineke did not remember the exact day, only that it was last week … early last week. Monday, yes, probably. The 16th. The morning the Holy Man left after arguing with him all night about his plan for her release. Was it really last week Monday? He had lost track of the time being away. In some ways it was still last week.

It some ways it was still last Monday.

"So I may go to the hospital tomorrow?" Joanna verified.

"Yes," Reineke said. "I will be certain to call for the car."

"I'll have my dinner now," she said.

"I will have it brought to your room," Reineke rose to answer the door. "You may leave, Fräulein, you do not have to wait."

"Oh," she said, but hesitated.

She was uncomfortable getting up and walking away with her back to him, or perhaps it was the soldier without Pierre there to protect her. That was it. She rose as soon as the soldier left. Reineke shut the library door and lit a cigarette, stepping to exit out onto the balcony. If she turned around with the sound of movement, she would see he was far enough away, in fact leaving. She stopped at the door to the apartment and turned back to watch him as he had anticipated she might.

"What's your name?" she asked as he glanced at her, and his glance shifted to a stare.

"Well?" she said when he did not answer.

"Indeed," Reineke said, "I am Hauptmann Reineke, Fräulein, as I have explained to you. I am afraid I do not understand the question."

"Your Christian name," she said. "I mean your Christian name. You do have one, don't you?" she peered at him.

Of course he had one. "Fräulein, I do not consider that to be an appropriate question."

"Why not?" she said.

Because it was not. "Because it is not," he said. "I am Hauptmann Reineke. Good evening, Fräulein," he tipped his head. She hesitated but then went on into her room.

Chapter Fifty-Six

March 26

The second time they spoke they spent an hour or better discussing her American Major Michael. It was not an interesting conversation. It was not a conversation initiated by him. It was fate.

His hand that did not lock the apartment door did not bolt the entrance for a specific reason. It did not want to. This was his choice not to lock it and to pour himself a glass of fine Bordeaux as he waited. Fate would happen by when it was time. It would not let him down. The night was his friend, and it was dark in this desert, so dark, and Reineke was patient, so patient.

"Damn!" In her room, Joanna dropped the nail file, shutting her eyes and holding her breath as it clattered to the floor, but no one came running. She started over. Thinking perhaps she could use the file as a key instead of trying to wedge the bolt, she inserted it into the keyhole of the lock, but the tip was too small and short, and the file itself too wide when she tried to turn it and it got stuck. Jammed in the keyhole, it was minutes before she could work it free and resume concentrating on moving the bolt.

It was simply not going to work. Every time she slipped the bolt, the file slipped and she dropped it on the floor again. She needed a stronger wedge like a dinner knife, or another hand to hold the latch while she worked at the bolt trying to trick the door into opening as soon as the bolt moved the slightest.

"Rot!" Joanna cursed again, because she had neither. No extra hand, and no dinner knife after searching for one for quite some time. She was going to have to wait until tomorrow and try to keep a knife from either breakfast or dinner. Lunch with the children was usually hand food, only a few utensils to share among them. She couldn't take one of their knives that wouldn't be right. She was going to have to wait and she did not want to wait. She had waited long enough.

Joanna studied her door, her first and biggest obstacle. The doors in the library were double-doors and she remembered very clearly how Michael had told her double-doors were twice as easy to pick. She trusted Michael, knowing he was right, because he was always right.

This door however, Joanna glared at it, was not a double door, and had a very thick and stiff bolt if anyone were to ask her—that was not locked.

Oh, my! Joanna stared at the door. When she wrenched the latch in her frustration to show it a thing or two, it turned. She had been standing there over an hour trying to pick a lock that wasn't even locked. The Captain had forgotten to lock it. Well, that figured. What was it he had said yesterday? He had forgotten about her, leaving her locked up in her room all day with absolutely nothing to do. Trying to make up for it by trying to cram her dinner down her throat every twenty minutes when she was trying to ask him questions he said she could ask, and of course, did not listen to her or answer when she did.

Bimbo. Joanna heard Michael, nodding smugly in agreement with her. The Captain was not Pierre. She did not stand a chance with Pierre there. But the Captain? She could probably stroll on out and he would never even notice.

Her stroll was more like a creep, but that was all right. She would save strolling for the road to town, which she remembered very well, paid very close attention to the way the car had turned to get onto the road, once over the mountain. She could find it with her eyes closed, never mind in the dark.

And it was very dark in the library when she turned the latch, opening her door as carefully and quietly as she could to peek out there into the room to ensure it was empty. It was, not a sound, not a soul in the huge, threatening shadows of the bookcases lining the walls, looming in the light of the stars and quarter moon shining through the French windows on the other side of the room. Panic threatened and Joanna wasn't so sure about going out there even though she wanted to and knew the doors to the corridor were down the other end, on the same wall... on the left ... past the bookcases. She only had to follow along, not really even see, the wall guiding her.

"See?" Joanna tiptoed, using the bookcases as her guide, her fingers sliding across the long rows of books. "Just books ... they're only books ... " And heaven knew books could hardly hurt anyone.

"Good evening, Frau." Something out of a book welcomed her with a deep, throaty growl, and once, and for eternity, Joanna was convinced the man was part cat.

"I!" Joanna let out a scream, damn near wetting her pants, flattening herself up against the nearest solid thing.

Reineke did not flick a lash. Painfully graceful he emerged from the shadows of the door to his quarters, gliding for his desk and the waiting crystal glass, lifting it and parading it over to her. "Go on," he invited with a whisper, "take it."

Go on yourself! Joanna stared at the cup, poisoned without a doubt. "Well, go on," she nodded, and did not take it, "shoot me!"

"That would be a terrible waste," the Captain suggested with another deep meow, and Joanna could feel those queer goose bumps come out all over her.

"I don't drink," she shook her head.

"That is a pity," he suggested, dangerously close to her. "It is an exceptional vintage."

So was he. Oh, so was he. Joanna could assure him. Straight out of the queer Victorian novels Claudia loved to read, and Michael threatened to burn if he ever caught her with them. "I!" she said.

"Yes?" he encouraged.

"Never mind," Joanna shook her head. She had a better idea. "You knew about this," she accused him and could feel his smile all over her. "You did it deliberately. Pierre told you how I try the doors."

"Indeed," Reineke agreed, setting her glass to rest on the shelf above her shoulder so he could sip, toast her courage and ingenuity. "That is quite true."

"It might have been a lie," Joanna huffed.

"And I would have been terribly disappointed," he breathed, and

Pierre was right. He smoked far too much. Joanna could practically hear the rattle of his lungs in every word—

Oh, God! She froze, not because of his breathing, or that he suddenly came even closer than he already was, but because he was moving, floating away towards his desk.

Oh, don't turn on the light! Her heart pounded as she prayed. *Dear God, oh, God, please don't turn on the light.* Joanna wasn't sure there wasn't a puddle of urine right there on the floor he had startled her so.

He did not turn on the light. "Come and sit down, Frau," he invited, arranging a chair for her in front of his desk, holding it there, firmly in place to ensure it did not get up and leave.

"Oh, no, that's all right," Joanna declined. "I'm rather tired. I think I'll stand."

"Come and sit down, Frau," he repeated with his purr, releasing the chair to take a gliding walk back towards her.

And, you know, Joanna, my girl, Joanna heard Grandfather's wisdom, perhaps she ought to just go and sit down before he decided not to ask so politely. "Whatever you say, Captain," she nodded brightly, darting over to land in the seat of the chair, her feet tucked up under her, her head inches below the top of its upholstered back.

"And, tell me, Frau," Reineke suggested to the cloud of fire that raced past him, "about you. You do so want to tell me about you."

"Not particularly," Joanna denied from her hiding place, safe and invisible in the womb of the high backed chair.

"But you do ..." he corrected, returning to his desk where Joanna could see his smile, not simply feel it. It wasn't half as dark near the windows as it had been by the book cupboards.

"As I want to know about you," Reineke nodded, taking a moment to top off his glass of wine. "I do so want to know all about you."

"Oh?" Joanna said.

"Yes," Reineke whispered, graciously extending his glass to her. "Would you care for a sip?"

"No," Joanna said. "I still don't drink."

"A beginning," Reineke sat down on the edge of his desk to consider it. "There is more I am certain."

"More?" Joanna moved a little closer to the arm of her chair. "Is this an interrogation?" she asked, sincerely hoping that it was.

Reineke sipped his wine with another smile. "Would you like to be interrogated?"

"Not particularly. I've heard about interrogations. They don't sound very nice."

And she had been interrogated, Reineke had not doubt. "You are probably correct," he agreed. "So then, perhaps we will just talk."

"About?" Joanna glanced down at her feet that she could not find, but only because they were still tucked under her. She settled for picking at her hands. "Talk about what?"

"Whatever you like," Reineke extended. "North Afrika," he proposed with a sip of his wine, savoring the sensation of the glass touching his lips. "Tell me, Frau, how is it you came to be in North Afrika?"

"I was born here," Joanna nodded.

Reineke gave a light laugh. "You were born in Australia where the frogs and mice live," he reminded.

"I lied," Joanna nodded.

"Which time was this?" Reineke smiled. "Now or before?"

"Perhaps both," Joanna shrugged. "Maybe I'm a twin," she looked up at him with a flash of her spirit. "One born here and the other born there."

"And where is here?" he smiled.

"How the devil do I know?" she snapped. "No one will tell me."

"So we will not," Reineke nodded, satisfied as he sipped his wine, preferring her spice to her fear. Conversation, even inane conversation, was an improvement to hysterics. He wondered how long she would banter. Her personality simply inclined to annoy her audience, or if the sass was an involuntary reflex, an injection of her spirit into a situation where she felt overwhelmed. He decided to test it. "But then you were born here, and so really, you should already know, no?"

"No!" she assured.

Reineke watched her over his glass but she was silent. And so she could not banter, not really. She needed to be led. Her spirit provoked. He complied. "No?"

"Well, no," she said again. "I ... well, I wasn't born in this room," she assured.

"Um, hm," Reineke smiled, finding it a perfect moment to take another sip of wine. "Simply North Afrika," he agreed, "and your twin Australia ... tell me, Frau, what is it you or your twin do? What is your occupation?"

"We're spies," she assured and Reineke was glad he only took a sip of wine.

"Indeed," he said.

"You don't believe me."

"Should I?" Reineke smiled. "Tell me why."

"Well ..." she tried to think of something. "I'm not German, I'm Australian. What would I be doing here if I wasn't a spy—and a really good one at that," she assured, "since I am here."

She had a point. If she was a spy, she was a very good one because no one would believe her, as he did not believe her. No one in their right mind would believe her. Still, such a claim whether or not it was a confession called for another sip of wine.

"Indeed," Reineke said, slowly taking steps to not having a right mind. "I thought ..." he was about to say, but had to stop with a look at his empty glass. Strange how few sips of wine a glass held. "I thought ..." he said again with a reach for the bottle, but it too, was empty. "Indeed," he eyed the bottle suspiciously. "Not so good a spy if you got caught."

"Well, that's true," Joanna acknowledged. "My twin's much better than I am."

"Yes!" Reineke laughed, rose for the cabinet and a fresh bottle of wine.

Joanna bristled. "You're laughing."

"Only in appreciation, Fräulein," Reineke reassured. "Sincere appreciation and admiration and ...indeed, intrigue!" he pulled the cork out of the bottle, a few drops splashing, pretty little rubies caught in the starlight, dropping from the air.

"Intrigue?" Joanna's heart started to pound again. "What do you mean?" she asked, aware of the meaning of the word from the books Claudia read.

"Indeed, I mean intrigue," Reineke said, his arms spreading in gesture, the cork waving one way, the bottle another. "Intrigue. You are an intriguing, young woman."

"I am?" Joanna whispered and he paused to look at her.

"You do not think so?" he asked, curious and slightly confused.

"Well ..." Joanna said. "Well, how am I intriguing?" she wanted to know.

"How?" Reineke thought. "You are here," he decided, his arms spreading again. "Here. And, indeed," he assured, "that is most intriguing to me, most curious."

"Oh," Joanna said. "You mean curious," she said, slightly disappointed. "You mean I'm a curiosity," she said thinking of Grandfather's collection of mummies, and all those masks and guns.

"No, I mean intriguing. Most intriguing," Reineke glided back to his desk to refresh his glass. "Most."

"Well," Joanna said, sighed actually. "I hope you've enjoyed it because I will be leaving soon."

Reineke laughed again, he could not help himself. "Indeed, Fräulein," he promised having no idea if she bristled, spit, or what she did when he laughed, "I am enjoying this immensely ... indeed!" he drank his glass of wine down. "I am enjoying this, you have no idea."

Well ... actually Joanna did have some idea because he kept laughing, and it was then she noticed—even though it was not something someone could actually tell. Certainly not in the way he talked. Definitely not in the way he walked, or moved at all. So slowly, so painfully ... gracefully slow.

"Indeed ..." Reineke melted down into his chair. "I am enjoying you."

Oh, my. Joanna bit her lip, noticing the bottle of wine in his hand, but more telling the empty bottle of wine on his desk. *Why, he was drunk. Mashed. Under the table.* Not blotto or soaked as Michael could get, but he was drunk. *Oh, my.* Joanna blinked and stifled a giggle.

"Indeed," Reineke relaxed back in his chair. "Do you know why? Do you want to know why?" he asked without waiting for her response. "Indeed," he said, "because the little Frau does not do anything she is supposed to do. No, she does not," he shook his head.

"Tell me little Frau," he asked, "did she ever? Do you ever do anything you are supposed to do?"

"No," Joanna assured with a confidence she hadn't felt but for some reason was feeling now.

"Indeed," Reineke smiled, feeling like a cat, a provoked and hungry cat, the tip of his tongue grazing the ridge of his teeth. She was bold, very. Brazen, like the Holy Man. So much like the Holy Man. He was pleased. "You should be frightened of me," he proposed, not that he was attempting to frighten her.

"Should I now?" she said.

"Yes," Reineke nodded. "Oh, yes."

"I'll work on it," Joanna promised, knowing she would. Later. When she returned to her room. Oh, yes. Joanna knew that later when she returned to her room she would realize and agree absolutely positively certain she should have been and was frightened of him to death. Right now however?

"Oh, well," Joanna shrugged because she wasn't frightened. No, right now, if she found him anything, she found him a little bit silly. Like Michael. Exactly like Michael. Or one of the books.

She stifled another giggle and unfurled her legs, sitting comfortably in her chair. "My friend Michael is a spy, too," she advised to see what he had to say, not really to keep the conversation alive, because no, she did not want to do that. She just wanted to see what he would say.

Reineke said nothing. He shrugged, disinterested in spies, discussing spies, Michael spies, or any other kind of spy.

"He is," Joanna nodded. "He's a Major," she assured, drawing on the game she and Michael and Grandfather used to play when she was little and was the reason why Michael gave her the dog tags for Christmas with her name and rank on them as she was now in the ATS. Michael was a Major, Grandfather, a General of course, and she a Lieutenant in her brother Justin's army. It was the first time she had thought of Justin beyond that horrible dream she didn't remember having. It did not matter though because she wasn't seriously thinking, or speaking about Justin, but was only thinking and speaking about Michael.

"A real Major," she assured, which was higher in rank than this lowly Captain, even she knew that. "An American spy. One of the best."

"I see," Reineke said with a disinterested sip of his wine.

"You will, because Michael will be coming here," she said, and Reineke wished that was all she said, but it was not. It was a very long, and remarkably boring conversation. But he sat there and he listened, a slave to his duty to ensure the comfort of prisoners of war regardless of how boring they were.

It was a conversation that did little to elevate his regard for the American race or their spies who he knew nothing about and needed to know even less. The American race, whom she clearly held in high regard, had a stock market of which he made use, and ate horses, which he did not.

They were not saviors, as she seemed to think they were with her hushed voice and glistening eyes, rushing to save her as she believed they would. He was the savior, her savior, and she was already saved so there was no reason for them to even come whether they rode in on horses, or like this *Michael*, she kept talking about, rode in on two legs instead of four, galloping frantically like one of his village goats. He did not think so. His palace was a fortress, impenetrable by Americans whether they drank beer, spoke in some dialect *Cagney* he had never heard of, or what they did. They would never cross the Alps. They would never cross the Rhine. What did she think this Michael was going to do? How did she think he was going to get there to rescue her? Swim? Fly? A bottle of beer clenched in his teeth for when he grew thirsty?

"You drink bier?" he interrupted her to accuse, offended she would refuse his offer of wine for some disgusting excrement.

Joanna paused.

"Answer the question," Reineke nodded.

"Well, no ..." Joanna said, not sure why he was asking. "Why? Do you drink beer?"

"No!" Reineke assured. "Why would I drink bier? I drink silk, not acid!" He showed her his wine, moving the glass so it was in line with the side of her head that was not blind. "Why would I drink something so vile when I have this?"

"Oh," Joanna said, frowning, wondering if she had confused the

Germans with ... well, with someone else. It was entirely possible She still wasn't what Michael would call a hundred percent. No, she wasn't there yet, but she was close. "I'm sorry," she apologized quickly before he vomited or something, which he certainly looked like he wanted to do. "I thought you drank beer."

"Well, I do not," Reineke assured. "I am German, not some ... goat," he waved. "And why do you keep telling me your hair is red?" he insisted. "Indeed, I can see your hair is red—I can see it from here!" he loomed forward and Joanna quickly sat back in her chair.

"It is all right," Reineke waved again, not to reassure her he was not trying to frightened her, because he did not notice how he might have frightened her. "It is all right that you have red hair. Indeed," he said, "It is not your fault. I had a dream about a woman with red hair—not you," he assured before she fainted. Screamed and accused him of raping her, or attempted rape, a desire to rape, as she had accused him yesterday.

"Not you," he assured again with emphasis. "Say it," he said. "Say it!" he insisted when she sat there. "Not you!"

"Not you," Joanna barely whispered.

Reineke nodded. It was good enough. She was tired. He could see it in her face. The same as he was tired, very. He downed his wine with a wave of his hand. "It is all right. The color of your hair is fine. You do not have to change it."

"I'm not," Joanna whispered again, really wanting to be back in her room. Yes, now, was definitely the time that she wanted to go back to her room.

"Good," Reineke said. To the dogs with her friend Michael who called her by the color of her hair.

"Indeed," Reineke said. To the dogs was where he would throw her friend Michael if he dared to show up there, which Reineke knew he would not. Men who called women by the color of their hair were frightened, weak, boring, and unimaginative as they were uncouth, disgusting as their beer.

"It has been a very interesting conversation, Frau," Reineke lied, interrupting her monologue about her pet spy with his two legs instead of four. "Indeed," he drained his glass empty of its last drop. "Very interesting."

She did not answer him.

"I said it was interesting, Frau," he assured. "What is wrong with you? Do you not understand what I am saying? That is a lie because you do. My English is perfect. So why are you sitting there pretending it is not?

"Why—" he started, interrupting himself changing the question. "Where?" he insisted as she suddenly got up and started to walk away. "Where are you going?" he insisted. Indeed, where did she think those little feet were going to carry her?

"I'm sorry!" she said, proving she could do one thing correctly as she quickly came to a halt. "I thought it was time to leave."

Oh? Why would she think that? He had not said, dismissed. Usually when someone wanted you to leave they said, dismissed. "Come back here," he pointed at her chair. "Sit down."

"Whatever you say!" she returned, dropping down in her seat.

"Indeed," Reineke observed how quickly she obeyed, and it was upsetting. In a small way, he found it upsetting. Why did she sit down so quickly? Where had her fight gone? Unless … he peered at her. She was tired. Yes, she looked tired. Perhaps in a small way still frightened of him. He should test it and find out. Experiment. See if she would stand up if he said, stand up! Sit down, if he said, sit down! Up, down, up, down. He could do it for an hour and see if she would obey every time.

He would not. No. It was what she would want him to do. What she was waiting for him to do, expected him to do so she could tell all of her English and American friends about the horrible German and the way he treated her. "Indeed," he smiled at her sleepy little head. "I will tell you about the German Captain, instead, Frau. You think he is the one who says, stand up! Sit down! And I could," he nodded. "Indeed, I could. Because I am German. The most significant man in the world today. There is no other even close to me."

He poured the last of the wine from the bottle into his glass, swirling it, the liquid hypnotic. "There is a train … " he began slowly, carefully, gazing off into the distance, into the past. "The Paris, Lyons, Mediterranean railway. Have you ever heard of it?"

"What?" Joanna said. "Oh. Oh, well, yes, actually," she agreed, because actually she had.

“Indeed. Have you ever ridden on it?” Reineke asked.

“Yes,” Joanna said. “Once.”

Indeed. So had he. The last time in 1936. He could see the schedule if he tried hard. “How old were you in 1936, Frau?” he asked.

She sat very still without answering.

“I asked you a question, Frau,” Reineke nodded. “Please answer it.”

“It depends on the month,” she said, and so she had not lost her fight.

“Indeed!” Reineke turned to face her, his interest renewed. “Pick a month,” he offered generously. “Any month you like. The day of your birth, if you like, and tell me how old you were in 1936.”

“Fourteen,” she said.

Fourteen. He had been twenty-seven. Twenty-six the day he rode the train. A ridiculous age. Impetuous, optimistic, arrogant. His wine was warm from his hand heating it, but he sipped it anyway.

“Captain?” she said.

“Yes?” Reineke looked up from his wine.

“Nothing,” she shook her head. “No, nothing. Continue.”

“Thank you,” he said, because he intended to continue. “There is a train,” he smiled. “More than one ...” where from them one could see the Alps.

“Have you ever seen the Alps, Frau?” he asked.

“What?” Joanna said. “Well, yes. I have.” On the day she looked out the window of the train. Michael pointed at them and told her they were the Alps. She remembered because it was such a funny word.

“You are fortunate,” Reineke agreed. “They are very beautiful. Timeless. Ancient.” Weaving its way through valley, mountain, and trees. He was thinking of a river. A very beautiful river. And it was very late, his wine was gone.

“It is very late, Frau,” he nodded. “You should be sleeping.”

“Yes,” Joanna agreed, wholeheartedly.

“Not spending your nights plotting to leave us,” he smiled.

“Oh,” Joanna said. “Oh, well, no, I don’t think I’ll try again.”

“You do not?” Reineke said, distinctly disappointed. “Why is that?”

"Why?" Joanna said. "Oh, well, no reason," she shrugged. "I guess I'm too tired to try again tonight."

"Indeed," Reineke settled back comfortably in his chair. "Then you will try again."

"Oh, yes," Joanna nodded. "Yes, I will definitely try again."

"I salute you," Reineke agreed, and would have toasted her but his glass was empty of wine. "And, of course," he said, "you realize I have the same obligation to stop you."

"Oh, yes," Joanna nodded, "I realize ... but I will leave, Captain," she promised, fully aware what she was saying, and very serious. "I will leave, if I have to jump off the balcony."

"Indeed, the balcony?" Reineke said. "This balcony?" he turned around to have a look at the windows behind him.

"Well, maybe not that one," Joanna said. "The one in my room."

"Indeed," Reineke turned back to her, hearing what she was actually saying. A leap to her death. "The one in your room."

"Well, that one has the porch in the way," Joanna pointed. "There's no porch on my side ..."

She grew quiet again, suddenly. Perhaps considering the finality of her action were she to do that.

Actually, Joanna grew quiet again because she was thinking perhaps how she had said too much.

"No, you will not do that," Reineke shook his head, convincing himself even if she were unconvinced her suicide was not the answer. "Indeed, you would seriously injure yourself," he assured, certain she would not want that. A life of pain? A permanent crippling should she by some miracle survive? No, he was confident she would not want that.

"Well, I might," Joanna said.

"No," Reineke said. "Indeed, what would you do with your spirit trapped in a box? Indeed ..." he turned back around to look over his French windows while Joanna tried to figure out what he meant about some box. "Even I could not do that ... without difficulty," he agreed. "From my quarters, yes, naturally, of course, as you suggest, on the side. But here? Indeed, it would be a little more difficult because of the steps. I would have to run ... yes, run," he considered. Take a running start to clear the balcony rail, the long flight of marble steps below, landing in the courtyard. "And I am not certain ..." he turned back to assess the distance from the library far wall with its book cupboards, "if the distance is sufficient. Possibly it is. We will have to see."

"See?" Joanna repeated.

"See," Reineke nodded. "I will experiment and let you know. Inform you of the outcome."

"Oh," Joanna said, frowned. Unsure why he seemed to think he could do it without killing himself as he insisted she would if she tried. Perhaps he was trying to get her to try it and kill herself, and if that were the case, she wouldn't give him the satisfaction. "Well, we'll see," she said, leaving it at that.

"Indeed," Reineke agreed. "We will. In the meantime though, Frau ..." he rose for the cabinet deciding he might as well have a little more wine before retiring. "There is something else perhaps you should consider while contemplating your escape. There is an organization. The Red Cross. Have you heard of it?"

"Red Cross?" Joanna repeated.

"Yes," Reineke selected a bottle to his liking, uncorking it to let it breathe as he returned to his desk. "The Red Cross. An organization which specializes in assisting people who find themselves separated from their families, such as you have been."

"Oh," Joanna said. "Oh, no, I didn't know that."

"No," Reineke smiled, for some reason he did not think she did. "It is called something else here in North Afrika ... I can't think of what it is but I will find out," he said. "And provide you with the information ... for you to do with as you wish, of course," he extended with a nod aware of how she was watching him suspiciously. "Whatever you wish. But that is the name of the organization. *Red Cross*," he emphasized. "You may even recognize it, if you were to see them. They have big red crosses on their trucks ... like le Christ," he drew a cross in the air. "Not an *X*. But the cross of le Christ."

"Oh," Joanna said. "Well, I'll see."

"Yes," Reineke nodded. "I believe you will. But now you really should be sleeping, Fräulein. It is very late. Two?" he imagined, "Perhaps three, or one o'clock in the morning?" Reineke did not know himself, and when he looked at his watch to check, all he could do was smile, thinking of his soldier's watch she took in payment to the Arab vendor for all her trinkets.

"Yes," Joanna agreed, though sat there.

"You may go," Reineke nodded. "Indeed, you may leave."

"Yes," Joanna agreed, but sat there.

He was uncertain why she continued to sit there and he looked from her to his glass of wine, wondering perhaps if he should offer her one to help her sleep. "You do not have to be afraid, Fräulein. It is very true what the Holy Man has said. There is nothing here for you to be afraid of. Not the Holy Man, not the children, and not me."

Joanna wasn't afraid, she was ... checking. Yes, checking. "You won't forget to bolt the door?" she verified.

"Pardon?" Reineke said inadvertently in the Holy Man's French.

"The door," she nodded and Reineke looked over at the door, wondering if she meant her apartment.

"I mean, so I won't escape or anything?" Joanna said, finding it rather unnerving the way he was looking at the door.

"No," Reineke shook his head. "No, I will not forget."

"You're sure?" Joanna bit her lip.

"Yes," Reineke nodded. "Yes, I am sure."

"Positive?" she pressed and he looked back at her. "I mean, so I won't escape?"

"Indeed, Fräulein," he smiled, "Are you inviting me to stay?"

"Certainly not!" Joanna almost killed herself jumping out of the chair, tripping over her pant legs as she struggled to stand upright brave and respectable.

She looked like Anne with her chin jutting forward, the size of Anne with the strength and innocence of Adva. "Indeed," Reineke smiled. "Then stop—*wittering on* and go to sleep."

Wittering on? Joanna flared. She did not witter on. Old women and creaking old men went wittering on.

"Sleep," Reineke whispered before she could curse him with her quivering mouth. "Go to sleep."

"Whatever you say, Captain," she clamped her lips closed with a snap, turning on her heels.

A cutting remark. No two people should go their way on such a cutting remark. "My name is Dieter," Reineke replied quietly, and he thought for a moment she might have heard him because she seemed to take a little time opening the apartment latch. But, no, he knew she had not heard him because she disappeared into the apartment without the slightest indication of looking back.

He waited awhile before locking the door and then relaxed, enjoying his evening wine, eyeing the distance between the library far wall and the balcony rail with the courtyard at least the equivalence of three stories below. "I could do that," he dismissed. "Indeed, of course I could do that."

"Oh, my!" Long after she heard the Captain bolt the door, Joanna still sat very still on the bed, her arms wrapped across her knees. "Oh, my," was all she could say. "Oh, my!"

Chapter Fifty-Seven

The Tell, Algeria
March 24

Justin's third message inviting Jean Paul to Cairo for a talk was less chatty than his first two that were brief and to the point. The third put it a little more emphatically.

"*What the hell is going on*?" Jean Paul read the transcript handed him by his radio operator. "Yes, that is pretty straightforward," he agreed. Justin wanted to know what was going on that had several of his top men tied up for a week in a house with a bunch of French whores.

"Not quite a week," Pierre Forget offered facetiously.

"No," Jean Paul crumpled the message, flipping it up into the air and smacking it away with his hand. "But then we aren't sure we have all of them."

"Pretty sure," Forget said.

"Except for Frank," Jean Paul nodded, Justin's invisible and invaluable surveillance boss. Reynolds was with Claude, so they also had him, just in a different way.

"The Black Watch is always out there," Forget shrugged, not concerned. Frank's sweep was too broad to be any true threat.

"Well, it's a little narrower for the time being," Jean Paul said. Frank currently hovered in the general vicinity of the resort, except when he had to go to the can or refuel or something. Jean Paul was aware Justin had a small airstrip in the Aurès somewhere, but that seemed a waste of fuel to jockey between there and here. So there had to be another airstrip, one closer. "But, so what. They are going nowhere. We'll release them when it's over."

"Over, mon caporal?" Louis asked, having one of his better days.

Jean Paul did not know what he would have done if he had left Louis behind to drive the lead jeep, with Louis killed instead of Henri. He probably would have gone to Cairo himself and killed Justin, returning to be honored by Cassie with laurel leaves. This was backwards. Jean Paul could not help but think that. This was all backwards. The entire situation, backwards.

But perhaps that would change when it was over. Jean Paul had spoken with his lieutenant Pierre Forget and Cassandra about assisting his father. Both of them concerned, Pierre in favor, Cassandra, vehemently opposed. Not satisfied the miraculous recovery of the girl Lee might relieve them of Justin's scrutiny, at least for now. She wanted to kill them. Kill them all. And that would relieve them of everything.

Pierre Forget only wanted to kill the skinny one and Reynolds. So did Jean Paul. They murdered Henri in cold blood, responding to a warning shot with lethal, deadly force, looking to kill everyone in the jeep, not only the driver who by chance happened to be Henri. Pierre Forget, Jean Paul's top lieutenant was in that jeep. Jean Paul would use that in his argument he was preparing for Justin. Wondering how Justin would like it if one of his top men were killed by accident or chance.

"Anything else on that other one with them?" Jean Paul asked before he answered Louis's question. "What is he? Have the girls managed to get anything?"

"He is the foreign correspondent mentioned in the English transmission." Forget said.

"I don't believe it," Jean Paul replied and wished he could speak with Abraham who knew Justin's men. "Why would Justin tell one truth in amongst ..." he almost said lies. Justin did not lie. Justin said he had men en route, and he did. They came.

Justin said a foreign correspondent was with them, continuing with his assignment following the loss of his convoy. Jean Paul's people were the ones who read into Justin's message what they wanted to read, and they were right. Reynolds was coming, and Reynolds arrived.

Abraham was right. O'Brannigan was out there, assisting with the transport of the correspondent through Algeria and so forth.

"Does any of this sound right to you?" Jean Paul asked Forget.

"It is possible," Forget said.

"I am not convinced. He is an American. Why is Justin involved with an American correspondent?" Jean Paul gave up though, tired of trying to read tea leaves instead of sticking to the facts.

"We are going to rescue and return Justin's sister to him," he explained to Louis. "We are going to assist le Metapel in killing the SS who brought her to Eden."

"We are?" Louis stared wide-eyed.

"Yes," Jean Paul said. "Cassie is concerned about her supply depots. I cannot blame her for that. The SS are here ... or rather there," he granted. "She cannot risk it. Neither can we—neither can I," he added for the benefit of Cassandra standing there silently. "If they find Cassie, they find my father, the hell with le Metapel."

"Mon caporal," Louis warned him not to speak with such blasphemy. "We are sworn to le Metapel."

"No, you are sworn to le Metapel," Jean Paul corrected. "I am sworn to the people. And of course," he agreed, understanding how he was fiercely outnumbered by the fans including his radio operator sitting there listening to every word, "I uphold the people's ..." he almost said belief like a pagan worship of some god. He changed it. "I uphold the people's commitment as I am also of the people," he assured. "We are all committed."

"That is beautiful, mon caporal," Louis breathed.

"Yes, Louis, thank you. Please don't hug me," Jean Paul shrugged free, patting him on the shoulder with a smile. "It's not necessary. I am Algerian, remember?"

"Mon caporal, you are French," Louis assured.

"True," Jean Paul said. And French or Algerian there were a few things he could not help but question. No one knew why, or even seemed to be asking, why the SS had brought the girl from Siwa to Eden however far away it was, and it was very far, certainly from the Siwa Oasis in Egypt. Jean Paul continued to prefer not to know the specifics of his father's home. Giving the arrangements however it seemed likely it was in Algeria. Southern Algeria perhaps but who knew? It could be French West Africa, the Equatorial Region, Libya. The French and Germans, and the Italians were throughout there.

"Mon caporal?" Forget inquired into his pensive expression.

"No, it's nothing," Jean Paul said. "Something is nagging at me that's all."

"Suicide," Cassandra spoke up. "To go to Cairo, is suicide. In hours, the Germans will know you are there. It is what the Germans have wanted, for you to emerge, and now you freely give it to them?"

"There is a risk," Forget supported, "but not only from the Germans."

"No, from this Justin, too, as the Jew says," Cassandra assured. "To find this woman Lee alive will mean death to us all. The Germans would not let her live."

"The woman is with the Germans," Jean Paul reminded, "and she is alive. Justin will have to accept that."

"Never!" Cassandra said.

"Well," Jean Paul shrugged, "that is up to Justin. I am going to Cairo to tell Justin about Henri. I don't care what he wants, I don't care how mad he is about his men. I am mad about Henri—and my other men killed."

"Six," Forget said.

"Make sure we have their names," Jean Paul directed. "This is madness. Utter insanity. I have eight dead men. We are allied with the British."

"Perhaps we should think about that," Forget said.

"I am thinking about it," Jean Paul assured. "I have one le Metapel, I don't need two. Someone else who does what the hell he feels like doing, the hell with everyone else."

"The people are very angry," Forget assured.

"Hm," Jean Paul grunted. "Because of Henri or some threat to le Metapel?" He turned on the radio operator. "Keep in mind, he took France. He is not going to give it back. You want to scream victory and revenge, scream *Vive la France!* Not le Metapel. I know Justin, I trust Justin, and I am pissed off," he assured her, "at Justin, not his fight. But then I am Jean Paul Dumont, not Pierre Beausoleil who puts one man before the cause. And *that* Justin will realize before I finish opening my mouth! I am not for sale, not for anyone."

Cassandra saw that for herself in the moonlight when he kissed her goodbye.

"You betray more than your father if you do not come back," she wished him luck in her own way.

"I will be back," Jean Paul promised. "And Justin will have to listen to what I am saying from the depots to his own sister once he has her. Victory is in our hands."

"No," she said. "No, I know these people, Jean Paul, these English. These French. The Germans. They will kill you. I saw it in John Haas's hand. Many deaths surround him. Few will survive."

"He is a Jew. You saw the deaths of Jews in John's eyes," Jean Paul corrected, "screw his hand. The same as you see what I see. Idol worship. And the idol will stand until it falls, yes." That was something he was beginning to realize.

"Find out more about this ... reporter," he requested. "Keep yourself occupied. I will be back. I have work to do. There is still a real war," he smiled. "The one I am interested in fighting."

"I see darkness," Cassandra insisted.

"What else is new?" Jean Paul kissed her again and climbed aboard with his Lieutenant Pierre Forget.

Jean Paul's flight to Cairo would take him south, down through the interior of Algeria and across, risking the skies of French West and Equatorial Africa, and then eastern Libya, until finally into Egypt. His reliable Caudrun had reasonable endurance and a greater range than Cassie's Swordfish and being French, was a safer plane to fly through the occupied colonies. Presumed Vichy, it could also be Luftwaffe. His choice of the deep south though would extend his journey to four days. Four days to ruminate about his father and the possibility of other arrangements with the Germans not as agreeable as the one the Monseigneur claimed. He did not care about Cassie's claims.

"Three sides," he said talking to himself as he stared out the window of his plane. "A triangle, not a round table. Which is less believable, which is more? The German, the French, or the Jew?"

"It depends on the side, mon caporal," Forget shrugged. "They are all telling the truth for their own side. I do believe what your father claims. Simple unity. Not collaboration."

"Shut up and drive," Jean Paul replied, meaning pilot of course. "It is the same thing."

“Is it?” Forget said. “You are united with the British, are you collaborating with them?”

“In the instance of war, yes,” Jean Paul assured. “The same as I am collaborating with you, my father’s French. Algeria does not belong to Vichy. But it also does not belong to France. It belongs to us. The Nationalist. The Muslim. Arab. Berber.”

“And that is the same thing, mon caporal,” Forget assured. “They are not doing anything you are not doing—that we are not doing. It is simply a different war they are fighting together than the one they fight on different sides. It is true what your father says. Not three sides, two wars.”

“You should be with my father,” Jean Paul rolled his eyes.

“I choose to be with his son,” Forget shrugged again.

“Why?” Jean Paul said. “I shouldn’t even know you. But for this war, I wouldn’t know you.”

“Except there is this war, mon caporal,” Forget said. “It is my war you are fighting, so I fight with you, not against. I have no understanding of the Algerian situation, I simply know, like you, it has to wait.”

“I think that is my point,” Jean Paul said. “Cassie, my father, do not wait to fight their war. But are you telling me le Metapel does? That he does not know beyond Cairo is the Suez? Arabia. *Palestine,*” he stressed. “So he protects them, so what? Three months? Six? A year? What does that mean? Le Metapel has them believing in pipe dreams. The concentration camps will be full again in Libya. Merely erected in the name of Italy *and* Germany this time. Arab side by side with the Jew. Who is le Metapel going to pretend to be then? Omar al Mukhtar? I don’t think so.”

“We are all united in pipe dreams, mon caporal,” Forget reminded. “That is what Resistance is. The preservation of pipe dreams. Your father and the Jew simply resist differently than you and I. But they do resist.”

“And I fight myself,” Jean Paul agreed dully, staring out the window of his airplane. “You and my father. Politicians. I am not, and I am not profound. I am a soldier.”

“You cannot tell this Major Charles anything,” Forget was worried about that. “Cassandra is right.”

"Cassandra wants everyone dead, including you," Jean Paul assured. "But don't worry, I am not telling Justin anything except about Henri and the other six—you have their names, correct?" he checked, a little late now. "I don't want to have to make something up. They deserve the honor of a mention, and recognition."

"It is actually ten, mon caporal," Forget said. "I am sorry, but when you said men, it is six men, and then yes, four of the girls. I have their names, all of them."

"Ten," Jean Paul stared out the window. "I could kill all of Justin's men, including the one who is a girl, and it would still not equal ten. Maybe you and Cassandra should run the outfit. I'm not sure I have the stomach for this. I kill enemies not friends."

Forget laughed. "We do not have your charisma, mon caporal. Cassandra is also right when she tells you, you lack confidence in the face of the British. Keep that in mind when you are talking with this Charles. It is his only real weapon against us. His attention and interest makes sense from Cairo to Benghazi, Benghazi to Gadames to Algiers, and beyond, and so what? He wants to work with you, he works with you. He does not want to, he does not work with you. That is his decision and his problem, not yours. We are not going to stop fighting the war because of some Major Charles."

"You are so French, But, no, I agree," Jean Paul agreed. "I just don't see Justin accepting a minor role in anything."

"Again, his problem," Forget shrugged. "Sometimes the only role is minor."

"Yes," Jean Paul said, something else to keep in mind during his discussion. He closed his eyes until they set down and after resting the plane and eating, it would be his turn to relieve Forget so he could close his. Occasionally he wished his plane would be shot from the sky. It wasn't. He read through the names of his men so he had them correct and memorized. It was the least he could do for them. He also read through the names of Justin's men to ensure he had them right. One caught his eye.

"Is this a joke?" Jean Paul stuffed the list in front of Pierre, his finger pointing.

"A joke?" Forget glanced. "No, that is the correspondent."

"Michael," Jean Paul said. "*Michael* is the name of the foreign correspondent?"

"Yes," Forget said. "That is the name we have."

"My father asked about a man named Michael," Jean Paul assured. "Some friend of this girl, Justin's sister."

"All right ..." Forget said. "There can be ..."

"I know there can be more than one Michael in the world," Jean Paul snapped. "I don't like coincidences. A week ago I am asked about a man Michael and now I am looking at the name *Michael* on a piece of paper. That name came from my father on behalf of the sister. That man is sitting with Justin's men. What did you say happened to him? His convoy was also attacked? Bullshit," he assured. "That's one coincidence too many."

"Ask him," Forget shrugged. "Ask Charles."

Jean Paul intended to. "Tell me about him. Tell me everything we know about him."

The Fezzan

March 27

It was eleven a.m. and Reineke, far away from Jean Paul's plane approaching the Kufra, picked his face up off the floor, and it was a struggle all the way.

"Indeed," Reineke said. Would he never learn not to sit on the floor? What demon was it that possessed him to sit on the floor whenever he decided it was time to have a drunk—drink.

"Indeed." Reineke glared at the sides of his nose, managing to force his pupils back where they belonged. He had no head. Not even a sensation of a head. No mind. And therefore no memory.

But, he had something. Little bits and pieces of something floating around where his head should be, and whatever they were, they succeeded in making him laugh, loudly.

Carelessly. Reineke found his head. Not in a usual way, but in an effective way when he picked it up and slammed it into something that was not soft.

He would have preferred another way.

The demon thoroughly enjoyed this one. So much so it wanted a drink.

Of coffee.

Ice cold.

Reineke spat the coffee back into the cup, wondering what his Korporal must have thought when he found the Hauptmann asleep aside the bed, under the chair, instead of atop the bed, next to the chair—

"Indeed," Reineke blinked. One piece connected to another, the two together starting to form a puzzle.

A possibly frightening puzzle.

With cautious bravery, Reineke chanced a look around, sweeping a dozen or so times over the linens of his bed, attempting to deduce whether a different little thing had been subject to the same demon as he, by he, through he—

"Indeed," Reineke closed his bloodshot eyes in relief. If the woman had, she had straightened the bed sheets militarily neat, and so she could not have been angry.

Which, of course she had not been because she had never been there. Reineke laughed another laugh, a good one, the vile little demon haunting him fading away. The pressure of the swelling in his groin he felt had nothing to do with anything other than unwanted wine.

Much too much wine. He should learn not to drink so much delicious red wine, and then he would not have to worry, or struggle to remember if one bed was one bed, one chair a different chair sitting in another room. It had all taken place in the neutral zone. Whatever it was that had taken place had been confined to the neutral zone of his library.

"Indeed," With a haughty shrug he stood up to relieve himself of the stagnant wine, carefully, lest he should topple over into the commode and drown. A distinct possibility. But it was only eleven o'clock in the morning and not even he would expect anything different after two—

Reineke frowned. He seemed to recall two particularly enchanting bottles of wine and a third tried and cast aside, less satisfying for some reason. "Indeed."

Long about two o'clock when he picked himself up off his bed from where he had flung himself, the three, two, or more bottles of wine, were history, fragments of memory as well. He remembered nothing. His favorite postscript to a night spent inappropriately. In daylight, he retained the right not to remember anything. It was, after all, the Holy Man's fault.

Deserted. Reineke had been deserted by the Holy Man in this, possibly one of his most desperate hours. Abandoned. He could not be held accountable for anything he did, wanted to do, or thought he had. After all, had anyone told him where they were going?

Yes.

Had anyone even bothered to mention they were going anywhere?

Yes.

And Thiele. Thiele, as well. What right did Thiele have to take it upon himself and obey? Thiele should learn to refuse to do what he was told to do and not leave his Hauptmann alone.

"Indeed," Reineke eyed the fresh cup of coffee he did not remember ordering. But there it was. Hot, steaming, blacker than black and tasting like perfect sewer water.

It was the best thing.

It was his favorite thing.

It was the only thing available to hold off the thoughts of the one person who had not seen to leaving him alone. The woman.

He was back to thinking about the woman. And there she was, sitting in front of his coffee. Pert, wide awake, her face shining brighter than the midday sun.

Reineke stifled a frown. It was she, not he, who should find last night unforgivable. How serious was her brain injury that she did not find a drunken man unforgiveable, untenable, morally depraved?

Where were this woman's principles? Her sense of self dignity? Had nothing been left intact, undamaged by the Americans? She should be outraged. Horrified. Insulted.

Wipe that stupid smile off your face! Reineke threatened Joanna's blank look. What right did she have to be sitting there popping up and down in her seat like some insufferable child's toy making his headache worse?

"Indeed!" What right did she have to be the first human he saw? She had no right, none. But there she was.

Of course, it could not be considered important how it would have been difficult for Joanna not to be the first person Reineke saw as he was standing in her room having walked in there from his.

And Joanna was not sitting in her seat popping up and down. She merely got off the chair she was sitting on when he appeared in her doorway, and naturally she was wide-awake. It would have been peculiar for her to be otherwise midafternoon.

Maybe she did try to smile, perhaps a small one. But only because he told her she could go and spend time with the children and not worry about being back for her dinner at six o'clock. Her dinner would be later. Perhaps seven or so. Depending upon what he deemed appropriate. It went without saying that to upset his soldier to drive her all the way to the children, only to turn around and go back and get her to drive her back, was ridiculous.

Therefore.

The time of tonight's dinner, he would let her know.

"Indeed," Reineke nodded sharply to Joanna, "I will see you at eight o'clock!"

And where in there, truthfully, could she possibly find a reason for the funny flick of her lashes as she looked at him? None. There was none. Yet she did it again when she walked by him.

Joanna did nothing of the sort. Honestly, she did nothing of the sort. At least she didn't think she did. Really, she would have known if she had, wouldn't she?

Chapter Fifty-Eight

Cairo
March 28-29

Late morning Saturday, Jean Paul's plane touched down in Cairo, around the time Nellie was steadily making his way back up through Algeria and east. Two hours after touchdown Jean Paul was in Justin's office with Pierre Forget on his right, facing Bobby Roberts on Justin's left. It was a candid discussion that started out poorly and got worse.

Justin studied the upstart Dumont whose feet barely touched the floor when he sat down. The intense black eyes watching him in return shone integrity, intelligence, and arrogance. They also showed something else. Dishonesty. Jean Paul blinked less than he should and occasionally looked away when speaking. He was lying about something, though Justin couldn't put a finger on it. Not yet.

Jean Paul offered no reason for his delay in responding to Justin's wire, or any reason why he showed up in Cairo unannounced. Showing up in Cairo was about the only thing Jean Paul got right even if the visit had been unexpected. Justin wanted Jean Paul in Cairo to discuss a few things that could not be discussed over the radio unless they did not care about the whole damn world tuning in on it.

"Yes, well, it is a bit unexpected," Justin acknowledged as Jean Paul settled in his office after being detained downstairs by the fellows who rang Bobby to advise a couple of French were asking for him.

Bobby was with Justin when Jean Paul walked in with his lieutenant Pierre Forget, the twin without the glazed look in his eyes. Justin remembered him. Forget, unlike his last trip to Cairo, this go round was dressed in Western civilian clothes rather like Jean Paul, though Justin doubted it meant Forget had given up the ghost of his rank.

"Found the place all right then," Justin said, his words open to interpretation, including deadpan sarcasm.

Jean Paul did not care what Justin meant by his words, he was there only to talk about the situation that had occurred, deny his people had in anyway provoked Reynolds and Mulrooney.

Yes, well, if that was true, it was a wasted trip because Justin did not care about the situation as Jean Paul called it. He cared about some of his top men being shut down for more than a week before Jean Paul started out from his hovel for the pyramids.

"Gone on long enough, hasn't it?" Justin said as much to Jean Paul right off when he parked himself at Justin's desk. It did not go over well, and Justin cared little about that.

"I know where it is," Jean Paul ignored him to answer the notice he had found the place, leaving his words open to interpretation for a change.

Justin wouldn't go as far as 'for a change'. To the contrary, much of Jean Paul seemed opened to interpretation lately. As far as Jean Paul's words, they were about the only thing that was clear, certainly supported by his actions. Jean Paul would get around to answering Justin's wires when he got around to it, whether he showed up in Cairo to answer, or what he did.

"Yes, well, good," Justin said. "Down to business then ..." He lit his pipe, pulling a couple of folders over and opening them.

"Yes," Jean Paul pulled what looked like stenographer's-paper out of his shirt pocket as Justin looked up under his brow. Unfolding the paper, Jean Paul leaned forward, placing it on Justin's desk for his consideration. "I have ten dead men."

"Yes, well, what the devil is this?" Justin gave a nod at the paper.

Jean Paul looked at him. "Ten dead men," he said again.

Justin ogled him and then flicked his head at Bobby who picked up the paper, refolding it and stuffing it in his shirt pocket.

"Back to business then," Justin's attention returned to the folders in front of him. "You have zero-time and zero-options to letting Pete and the lot of them off their leash. It's to be done now.

You can make the call from here after we're done. Bobby will take you down."

Jean Paul looked at Forget and then back at Justin. "Out of the question."

"Oh?" Justin looked up, leaving it at that.

"Yes," Jean Paul assured.

Justin ogled him again and closed the files, sitting back in his chair. "Why are you here?" he asked.

"Ten dead men," Jean Paul said.

"Got that," Justin assured. "What about it?"

"What about it?" Jean Paul repeated. "What do you think?"

Justin thought nothing. Out of patience for something in which he had no interest. He did not dismiss it with a wave of his hand, but he might as well have. He leaned forward, opening the folders. "Yes, well, if that's what you're here about, it's a waste of time."

"What?" Jean Paul said. "Of course it's what I'm here about!'

"Then it's a ruddy waste of time," Justin slammed the folders closed that time. His owl-eyed stare narrowed into an angry glare. "Damn situation's resolved—was resolved," he assured, "five minutes into it more than a week ago. So what's your point? I didn't call you to Cairo for a chat. I called you to discuss business—and the first order of business," he assured again, "is you're to let my damn men out on the double. And quite," he said, "we'll talk about it. Beginning with who the hell do you think you are?"

"Henri was murdered in cold blood," Jean Paul insisted.

"Who?" Justin said and Jean Paul stared at him before he snapped his fingers at Forget who unfolded and handed him another piece of stenographer's-paper that Jean Paul slapped down on Justin's desk.

"Yes, well, how the devil many of these do you have?" Justin at least bent to pick that one up and give it a look over.

"Two. And that's who I think I am. I have ten men killed by your men. So, yes," Jean Paul assured, "your men stay exactly where they are until I get some answers and satisfaction—if I have to take it," he promised, "by an eye for an eye and a tooth for a tooth."

Justin's owl-eyes fixed on Jean Paul as Bobby bristled next to him. "Is that a threat?" Justin asked, because aside from the fact Jean

Paul or his lieutenant would never make it out of the office as Justin just blew their heads off their shoulders, Justin really wanted to know.

"It is ten dead men who are hardly a waste of time to me. Pierre was in that jeep," Jean Paul's head flicked at Forget. "Henri its driver but for the fact Louis was with me. They knew Pierre was in that jeep. We fired a warning shot over their heads and they fired—that skinny bastard Mulrooney fired back to kill," he cursed bitterly with a spit, a thin cold smile touching his lips, his eyes flicking to Bobby. "So, yes, excuse me while I blow his head off, and then we'll talk about how much of a waste of time that is to you and who in this 'situation' is really threatening whom.

"Because, quite frankly, Justin," he said as a slight movement from Justin's hand stopped Bobby from doing anything more than stay bristling in his meat, "to hell with who I think I am, who the hell do you think you are?"

Who Justin thought he was, was not on the table. Jean Paul however had caught his attention with the idea Mulrooney had shot to kill. That differed from the account Justin had received from Joe in the one message had been able to get out. There was one way to resolve it and it would be without the hysterics.

"Yes, well," Justin said, started to, "apart from Nel isn't available to tell his side of the story—"

"Story?" Jean Paul did not bother to look at Forget that time, any more than Justin bothered to look at Bobby. "Well, Justin," he said, "the story goes like this. You either tell me what the hell is going on, or this association is over, and those men you are so concerned about will be turned over to the people—on the double," he promised. "Give me a break. Why the hell do you think they are 'shut down' and with me? They want their throats that's why. The people want their throats, and I wash my hands of it, I do." He rose to take his leave with a parting shot. "And as far as you, good luck trying to do anything about it. Because I don't think so. I really do not."

He stalked out with Forget.

"Let him go," Justin stopped Bobby from picking up the phone. He lit his pipe and sat back thinking.

"Aye," Bobby agreed. "Money where his mouth is as they say."

If by money Bobby meant men, Jean Paul had them, quite a lot of them. The same as Justin's few were quite a few miles from home. As far as the mouth, yes, well, Jean Paul clearly had that.

"Yes, well," Justin said, "he'll be back."

"Think so?"

"Quite," Justin assured, among other reasons rather doubting Jean Paul came all the way to Cairo just to deliver his ultimatum. "Rather can't tell him what the devil is going on unless he's here."

"Aye, well, maybe he doesn't want to hear it."

"Yes, well," Justin said, "that's rather covered under the first reason why he'll be back. He didn't come all the way to Cairo about some fellow Henri."

"Ten fellows Henri," Bobby snorted. "If you believe him."

"Yes, well, either way, he's gone off to cool off."

"For how long?"

"As long as he needs," Justin supposed. "Or at least as long until I want him back." He got up to eye his maps.

"Aye, a little sightseeing," Bobby snorted.

"Tea," Justin said without having to check his watch. A bit surprised Bobby hadn't thought of that. "They're a bit hemmed in," he noted insofar as Jean Paul's Algerian lair where Jean Paul had Pete and the rest of them. The girls' house up in the Aurès. It was a devil to get to and radio communication wasn't the best.

"Aye." Bobby agreed. "Face it, lad, you're not going to get in there unless you're invited." He was starting to get fidgety again. Justin could hear it in his voice. Wanting the order for Jean Paul to be followed issued so they could bring him back.

Picking up Jean Paul's trail, Justin wasn't concerned about whether they gave Jean Paul a two or ten-minute head start. Bobby could also use a little cooling off period, as could Justin, personally. As far as getting into Jean Paul's territory, to Justin's understanding he had a standing invitation aside from the fact he'd get in there without a problem ... if he had an army to spare, which he did not. Justin turned away from his maps, lighting his pipe.

"What?" he asked Bobby.

"What do you think, lad?" Bobby huffed.

"Yes, well," Justin moved to his desk, "rather hard to miss a small coloured fellow walking down the street with a damn French flag at his side."

"If he were wearing his French flag, lad," Bobby agreed, "you'd be right."

"Oh, right," Justin recalled another reason he believed Jean Paul intended to stay around at least long enough to talk before heading back. Forget wasn't in uniform translating into time on the street if only for food, possibly an overnight stay. Unlike the security measures of Jean Paul's first trip to Cairo, which was all very hush-hush. Plane to covered car and back to plane once contract negotiations were completed. "Make the ruddy call then," he agreed with Bobby's anxiety. "Get a tail on him."

"Could have said that ten minutes ago," Bobby picked up the telephone to order a squad.

"Eight minutes," Justin sat down to consider his options rather than stand there and stare at the lack of them on a map. "Don't think a squad's needed. He's on foot, I rather suspect. It'll take him a few minutes at least to clear the colour bar. That and he's the size of a twelve year old, so he shouldn't be too hard to find."

"Aye, if he were looking for a three-course meal," Bobby agreed with the notion of taking a while to find a place to even let him in, never mind opening the back door. "And you've got a few thousand twelve year olds out there black, white, and brown."

"Just find him," Justin suggested.

"We'll find him," Bobby assured, meaning Keith would, who Bobby had hanging on the line waiting for a description rather than a lot a blather.

"And then what?" Bobby asked after he hung up.

"Find him already?" Justin asked.

"Give them a moment to get out the door and they will."

"Yes, well, as long as they do."

"And you might have to consider compromising when you do," Bobby outlined the options available to them. "Trying to call his bluff is no damn good when he knows you're bluffing."

"Yes, well," Justin said, "compromise and calling Jean Paul's bluff are both out of the question because of Mike."

"You're the one who put the Doc out there, lad, instead of shipping him home."

"Yes, well, neither is second-guessing much help. It's still the best place for Mike right now. What's Frank's latest word?"

"The same as before," Bobby shrugged. "He's not been able to get a word into them and they apparently can't get one out. Jean Paul's lot might have busted Christine if they didn't take her away."

"Well that would have Joe in a foul mood," Justin agreed.

"Aye," Bobby said, "and the devil with Joseph. He's not the one Jean Paul's up in arms about. So any time you are ready to stop playing games, you can get down to the options that are available to you. What's the harm in listening to him, hearing what he has to say?"

"I heard him," Justin assured. "And it's not Joe I want, it's Pete."

"Pete?" Bobby said. "Pete wasn't there, no more than Joseph was. They've no damn idea what happened with Nel and Mulrooney. Hearsay the two of them."

"Quite," Justin got up, tossing him a two-way and keeping one for himself. "So let's go find Jean Paul and get ahold of Pete."

"Right. Well, I'll leave you to explain it, because I sure as hell don't understand what you're doing," Bobby assured as they walked out, Bobby with his weighty waddle and Justin with his relaxed stroll, also rather a sight for sore eyes themselves, never mind anyone else.

""The truth," Justin assured, not to suggest Joe was lying.

"Come again?" Bobby said since it certainly could be interpreted he was suggesting that.

"Impartial truth, I should say," Justin said. "Something Joe isn't."

"Oh, right," Bobby scoffed. "Might want to try that again. A Mick impartial about one of you. A Nancy boy and lieutenant, to boot."

"Fine," Justin said. "In the meantime, ignoring the window dressing, good or bad, Pete would know what he's looking at, if he's looking at anything at all. How's that?"

"Reasonable," Bobby considered. "Still, should know right away, shouldn't he, if there were anything to look at? For that matter," he scoffed again, "if he were all that good at seeing it in the first place."

"Yes, well, now you know why I don't want Joe's opinion," Justin grunted. "Prejudiced bastard."

“Or mine,” Bobby understood. “Got it, lad. Following you. No need to be coy.”

“As far as Pete,” Justin said, “Pete could be looking dead at it right now and there’s nothing he can do about it because he can’t get the word out. I also never said Pete wasn’t necessarily above needing a little prompting to look. Because, yes,” he said, “Pete would know what he was looking at it, if he were looking, rather than ignoring it as he did here. Got that?”

“No,” Bobby assured. “But I’ll leave you to explain it, as I said.”

Yes, well, Justin wasn’t explaining anything. That was someone else’s job.

Keith found Jean Paul in about thirty minutes. He had not gone far. Perched up against a jeep with his lunch when Keith’s group spotted him, and so Jean Paul had either given up early or did not bother to try and cross the color barrier on the Yank side of the street. Justin gave Jean Paul another ten minutes before he rolled up with Bobby blocking him in. Jean Paul looked, but did not budge. Opened a bottle of fizzy pop to wash down his lunch as Justin got out of his jeep to settle on the bonnet of Jean Paul’s, tapping his pipe against the fender to loosen some of the soot.

“You can always tell when the Yanks are in town,” Justin agreed with a reference to the fizzy drink.

“Funny, I would have presumed an offer of something stronger,” Jean Paul looked off nowhere in particular as he drank his pop.

“Is that what you want?” Justin asked.

Jean Paul looked at him. “Why don’t you tell me what you want?”

“Pete,” Justin said. “O’Brannigan,” he clarified.

“I know who Pete is, And, no. Out of the question.”

“Just on the radio,” Justin said. “I can’t give you those answers you want if I don’t know what they are.”

Jean Paul’s head snapped back to him. “I gave you the answers. What the hell is O’Brannigan going to say?”

“I don’t know,” Justin agreed. “What’s the harm in finding out?”

“Well, maybe, Justin,” Jean Paul nodded, “the harm is I told you what happened. I believe my man—Forget,” he indicated the establishment where Forget had apparently gone inside while his caporal ate off a plate standing in the street. "It would be nice when I tell you something I am given the same respect without the need for a solicitor."

"Yes, well, I suppose in a perfect world you have that right," Justin agreed.

"But it's not a perfect world," Jean Paul understood.

"No," Justin said, and got off the bonnet. "Let's go."

"I am waiting for Forget," Jean Paul refused.

"Been taken care of," Justin more or less gave a nod when he bent his head to light his pipe and a couple of his fellows moved in to get Forget.

"Of course," Jean Paul said. "That's how it is."

"That's how it is," Justin agreed. "Unless, you don't mind Forget coming out and thinking you've been arrested."

"For what?"

"How the devil do I know?" Justin gave a nod at the jeep. "Where did you get the jeep, or was it just some place to sit?"

"Up the street," Jean Paul shrugged. "Couple of blocks. Why should I walk?"

"No reason," Justin agreed. "It's all right. We'll take mine. You can leave that one here. They'll find it. They probably think they forgot where they parked." He glanced over as Forget came out. "So what's the verdict? There's beer at my place, and quite," he indicated the half-eaten lunch Jean Paul tossed in the front seat. "Something better than that probably."

"Fine," Jean Paul said. "On the radio only." He stalked the few steps for Justin's jeep, Forget joining him in the backseat. "And I am there to witness. Forget, too."

"Fair enough," Justin said, but only because the behemoth was a lot harder to put out of service than Joe's Christine.

Down in the dungeon and Justin's war room between the behemoth radio setup and Jean Paul's seventy-foot antenna out on the Tell, it wasn't long before Pete was on the line, almost as clear as a telephone so Justin didn't know what the problem was with Frank unless the problem had been fixed. Including the niceties, it lasted a little longer than Justin would have preferred but it was worth it.

"*Hello, luv,*" Pete sounded well, pleased, and ready to leave a week ago regardless of the female company, curious how long it would be. "*How's the weather? Rang just in time. 'Bout ready to fold, but you'd be pleased to know I'd be the last.*"

"Yes, well, would think JB would be the last," Justin lit his pipe, and meaning Julia being the last to uncross her legs for the pleasure of a whore.

Pete laughed. "*Right as usual. What's up?*"

"Got a fellow here who thinks things were deliberate rather than accidental. Any thoughts on that?"

"*Rumor going around and, well, if I were to take a poll ...*" Pete considered.

"Don't want a poll. Just a simple probable, possible, or not on your life. What's your gut say?"

"*Aye, well, anything's possible,*" Pete reminded. "*And not to say I've considered it, but I will. It is funny though you should mention my gut, because I'd have to say what's obvious isn't quite so obvious. Whatever that means. Other than like I told you, I'd be last.*"

"Got it," Justin said.

"*Anytime. Any idea on that weather?*"

"Couple of days," Justin suspected.

"*I'll keep my legs crossed long as I can. And I'll be sure and get back to you on the possible.*"

"Do that," Justin signed off and got up for Joe's cache of beer to check the selection. "Want one?"

"Yes, all right fine," Jean Paul said.

"What about Forget?" Justin asked.

"Just give me the goddamn beer," Jean Paul requested. "My girls are not working your men. That's bullshit."

"Yes, well, your girls are working my fellows," Justin assured, "and the fellows are working the girls. It's the way it works, even among friends. So let's cut the bullshit is right. After all," he said as he handed out the libations, "think most of us can last a week."

"You don't know my girls."

"True," Justin agreed. "But I'll wager you didn't know I had one out there, too. So touché. You're a little stuck with that."

"'JB'", Jean Paul nodded. "Julia ..."

"Barnes," Justin offered.

"Yes, I have two lists with their names on them as well," Jean Paul assured as he opened a beer, handing it to Forget, keeping the better one for himself, Justin noted. "I think names are important."

"Henri," Justin understood. "Sorry about that."

"So what's obvious and not so obvious?" Jean Paul asked.

"Experience," Justin lied. "Or rather lack of experience. Mulrooney's inexperienced in the field. That's not saying he's not a loose cannon, which I believe is your point. Pete's going to check it out. Provoke him, see what happens—which, I wouldn't suggest you recommend to the girls. Leave it to Pete, per chance Mulrooney is a problem.

"Right now the only thing that has occurred to Pete as being obvious with Mulrooney," Justin lied again, "is he has taken to his situation somewhat better than one might think, given his inexperience—but then he is a ruddy lieutenant," Justin took a swig of his beer. "Inexperienced or not. You ought to be able to understand that," he directed that point to Forget, in French, since Forget did not speak English.

"Oui," Forget agreed. "As I understand O'Brannigan said, anything is possible."

"Well, it is, actually," Justin said. "It could have been deliberate or Mulrooney could have panicked. It could have also been a damn accident. Fate. Not too easy to shoot from a moving jeep, terrain's pretty rough, isn't it? So you tell me, Lieutenant, since you were there. Which do you really think it was?"

"Deliberate. And I am not inexperienced in the field."

Justin nodded. "It's why I'm asking. All right, I'll take care of it. Hope you don't mind if I wait for confirmation from Pete. Might find this a little hard to believe, but I also need to know if I've a loose cannon out there."

"So that's it?" Jean Paul said.

"Yes, well, what would you suggest?" Justin said. "Cut him loose now. Frank can bring him back here. Could be why Nel cut him loose."

"We can talk about 'Nel'," Jean Paul assured.

"Yes," Justin said, "we can. In the meantime, what do you want to do? You're welcome to think about it for a little while. We can check with Pete in the morning, see if he's come up with anything else interesting about our Mulrooney—"

"Your Mulrooney," Jean Paul corrected.

"Ours," Justin assured. "He's in your camp at the moment. That makes it our problem."

"I'm thinking," Jean Paul looked at Forget.

"As I said," Justin said, "take your time. You're also welcome to bunk here if you like rather than sleep in a doorway. Some of the big boys are out right now," he added dryly, "there's more than enough room."

"Let's just talk business," Jean Paul suggested. "I'll decide later where I sleep, if I sleep."

"Fair enough," Justin rose to return to the comfort of his office. "Dinner's on me."

Later, Justin talked to Bobby about a lot of things. But right now he was rather looking forward to that dinner, and not because it meant a night on the town.

Chapter Fifty-Nine

"What the devil was that all about?" Bobby grumbled while Justin tried to get some work done in between politicking.

"Jean Paul?" Justin shifted his pipe to the other side of his mouth.

"Pete," Bobby assured. "You two ever consider that Cockney slang? Be a bit easier on the rest of us."

"Yes, well, not very good at it," Justin acknowledged. "That's something more Mike's expertise. But, no. Nothing too mysterious. There is talk Mulrooney killed the Henri fellow deliberately. Other than that, think about Mulrooney, and think about what Pete said. Mulrooney's a dandy whether or not he's a Nancy boy, which I rather suspect if he's a mole, he's not. In the meantime, he's not acting like a dandy at the moment, and he's not a Nancy boy, at least not behaving like one. He's been with the whores. So, interesting notice. Jeff there is a different Jeff than the Jeff here."

"Covering for himself," Bobby sniffed. "He's afraid. He's got Nel here to protect him. Doesn't have Nel there."

"Yes, well," Justin wasn't going to get into all of that.

Neither was Bobby. "Aye, well, if it's a night out on the town with this Jean Paul," Bobby nodded, "you can count me out."

"Yes, well, I didn't say it was a night on the town. Fairly certain it's not. Said it occurred to me there could be another reason Forget left his uniform at home such as a night on the town. After all, France did not fall yesterday. It fell two ruddy years ago. Hasn't taken it off in two years, what's so special about now?"

"He'd be out of his mind to call attention to himself appearing with a ruddy bodyguard," Bobby scoffed.

"Jean Paul doing the appearing, I take it," Justin said. "With Forget the bodyguard. And more a potential for attention rather than a given. But, quite, Jean Paul would be out of his mind to take such a chance. Daylight's one thing, but night's quite another. Be a bit of an ironic end to Jean Paul, knifed in an alley just for being coloured by some drunken sot who didn't know who it was he killed, regardless of how much I don't know the real Jean Paul Dumont, representative of the people or whatever the devil he is."

"Aye, well, some of that arrogance you have to let go, lad," Bobby suggested. "Some of it's his damn age. Not all that experienced himself. Can't be, he's too young. As far as that uniform of his French friend, you don't know if he really wears one or not. Could have been to show off the day he wore it here back in January or whenever the devil it was.

"For that matter," he said, "when he did wear it, it could have been on account of his damn twin brother, rather than confuse the fellow. He's the one who probably doesn't know enough to take his off. Probably still thinks he's in France. You know how that goes."

"Probably," Justin agreed. "What do you think about Jeff?" he asked since they were on the subject of probabilities. "Think it's possible he could have taken deliberate aim to kill? That's quite a shot if he did. Not sure I could do it from a speeding jeep even on the best terrain."

"Well, apart from these guns nowadays do half the job for you," Bobby said as such was his expertise, "it's two different things isn't it? Taking deliberate aim and making the shot? Aye, he could have taken deliberate aim, if that was his intention. No saying he'd have made it though. Same as there's no saying it couldn't have been a lucky shot. An accident, in other words nothing deliberate about it."

"Yes, well, an unlucky shot from Jean Paul's perspective," Justin said. "And, quite. Different as night and day. Rather the same if he turns out to be a crack shot, that is definitely not in his file."

"No, it isn't," Bobby assured. "Admit it will be interesting to hear what Pete has to say—if he has anything to say. Provoking Jeff into showing his colors as a killer is one thing. But how the devil is Pete going to calculate some shooting ability is a good guess—and nothing but a guess, I don't care how he does it. I wouldn't base anything on it. And you can be damn certain if they took their damn radios, they took their guns."

"Yes, well, obviously, they did not take their radios. There must have been a problem with Christine Joe has fixed, or Frank was the one having a problem and did not realize it. As far as Pete? I don't know. Friendly game of ball? Should have told Pete to set up target practice for sport."

"Aye, well, a game of football's all right, I suppose. It will get the blood up. Might work if Jeff's really a case."

"Catch," Justin said. "Motor skill. Eye-hand coordination that sort of thing—like you do."

"Oh," Bobby said. "Aye, well, that's not bad, either, though I wouldn't base anything on it. Want to see him with a gun in his hand. Not whether he can rub his stomach and pat his damn head at the same time. And don't forget he could always fake it. If he's clever, he's clever. Not to be underestimated.

"It's only to get an idea," Justin said. "Not looking to re-write the rule book."

"No, and it would be easier all 'round," Bobby could not resist, "if Pete could tell you what he's looking at beyond the fellow not minding getting his hands dirty, since Pete knows so well."

"Pete does," Justin said.

Bobby ignored him. "Not sure what you're going to do with the information, or what help it will be. That was a stroke of genius you had to offer to have Frank take Jeff out of there. Innocent or guilty, there's one of them ... only six to go," he counted off on his fingers to make sure he had them all.

"Yes, well, glad there's one thing I did that's up to someone's snuff," Justin grunted.

"You can't kill a man because he thinks you're a prick, lad."

Yes, well, Justin could, actually, but no, Bobby was right. "Bit interesting Jean Paul didn't say yes right off to removing Jeff."

"Because he thinks you're up to something," Bobby assured. "No mystery in that. If the two of them weren't in the damn showers getting ready for their night out you might have a little more information—Joseph's going to have to work on that when he comes back," he shook his head. "Can't hear a damn thing in there—and you know they did it deliberately too, unless you were planning on following them in."

"Yes, well, no," Justin said, but that did bring Pete's point back to mind. "What's a damn sodomite doing with a whore?"

"The same as you or I. Working her."

"About?" Justin said.

"About what? He's working her about whatever he can get, same as the rest of them—" he scoffed, "Pete probably gave a class on how best to. Jeff can't be that inexperienced. If he is, he could take notes. You do what you need to do, in other words, lad," he assured. "You know that."

"Within reason."

"All right, within reason," Bobby said. "But just because he's safe with the French does not make it smart to show your true colors especially when you're outnumbered by your own fellows."

"Yes, well, that much is true," Justin returned to work.

"You can have the lieutenant Mulrooney," Jean Paul advised when he came in with Pierre Forget, the two of them looking a little cleaner but wearing the same clothes. So they had at least stopped their consultation to take advantage of a shower. Justin did not care about the consultation, certain any grand scheme had been hatched and rehearsed on the plane ride to Cairo, not waiting until they arrived to complain about 'Henri' and losses under unfriendly friendly fire.

"And the girl Julia," Justin answered.

"Fine," Jean Paul agreed without checking with Forget and Justin was immediately suspicious. 'Girls' were not only good for collecting information, they were also good for passing it. Justin right now was incommunicado with his men. He had no idea what was going on, and he wanted Julia for the information the 'guys' would pass to her, what he couldn't necessarily trust getting from Jeff, at least not now, if at all.

So Jean Paul failed his A-level in espionage and Forget should have stepped in wanting to know what was being discussed rather than waiting until later to find out. What the devil was going on was right. Either these two men were incompetent, or something was afoot. Justin studied Jean Paul. Had Jean Paul manufactured the situation with Jeff and Nel as an excuse to encircle Justin's men and shut them down? Had it backfired, or at least taken an unexpected turn with the death of this Henri fellow whom Jean Paul apparently cherished and was Jean Paul also manufacturing that? Jeff a convenient whipping boy, firing back in panic, fear, and getting off a lucky shot that killed this Henri?

Justin wasn't sure himself why Nel had abandoned Jeff, but presumed Nel would tell him and it would be a good reason. It could be Nel wouldn't want or need a man with him who could not stand up under fire without panic regardless of his inexperience. That wouldn't just hinder Nel, it would put him in danger. He would abandon Jeff under those circumstances definitely, as was Jeff actually lucky Nel did not kill him, never mind anyone killing the French. Nel did not carry wounded men with him, whether wounded in mind, spirit, or body. He would kill them like a horse with a broken leg, moving on. He possibly did not kill Jeff because he knew Frank was in the area and could pick up Jeff and take him out of there if the French didn't get to him first.

That was uncharacteristic of Nel to be so generous, but Nel, as Justin had noticed had some sort of relationship with Jeff whether or not Jeff could also do what he needed to do, as Bobby had put it, and work a whore. Justin made a note to himself Jeff's influence over Nel extended to the field. Jeff could not stop Nel from doing what he was there to do, but he did appear to have the ability to extract a response from Nel few could.

Justin was the only one who had that level of influence over Nel, and even Justin wouldn't rush to gamble Nel would carry him along, or abandon him to his own fate, were Justin in some way wounded, rather than put a bullet in him. Though, in the case of Justin, Nel would probably do it out of the idea of doing Justin a favor, rather than getting rid of the baggage holding him back.

"Thank you," Justin said to Jean Paul's agreement to also release Julia.

"It's all right," Jean Paul dismissed. "This is not a challenge, Justin—"

"Yes, it is," Justin assured, "and I am admittedly damn curious as to why. I'd also like to know what you think happened ... or may have happened to set Jeff or Nel off before the shooting started. Nel wasn't there to shoot up your camp whether Jeff's a loose cannon or what he is. Nel did not go off half-cocked on his own. Something had to trigger him."

"Except I do not know," Jean Paul assured. "I know they wanted to leave, not wait. I said we would leave with them in the morning with an escort—"

"Escort?" Justin interjected.

"To verify the coordinates," Jean Paul nodded. "Reynolds reported they had been in the foothills several days attempting to examine the area of one of these reported depots to locate evidence it had been there ... or evidence of movement," he said, "without success. I reiterated I did not find the reports credible as I have already told you, whether they are supposedly depots, or transfer stations, or whatever you choose to call them. I am satisfied if there was something there—"

"Yes, well, there is something there," Justin assured, "or there was."

"Another group?" Jean Paul offered. "A splinter faction? Ambitious farmers ... Justin, we have been through all of this. It could be any number of things other than German or Italian depots."

"Then there should be evidence of something," Justin lit his pipe, " if only movement."

"Precisely. I proposed to Reynolds perhaps the problem lay within the reported coordinates. Either they were wrong, or perhaps he was wrong about the location. In short, I offered the assistance you seem to be looking for otherwise why was Reynolds there? Why did he come to me?"

"To let you know he was there," Justin shrugged.

"Fine," Jean Paul said. "I disagree with that, and we'll get to that, but right now it has nothing to do with shooting up my camp. I told Reynolds I would organize an escort to retrace his steps *with him,*" he stressed. "Examine the area he had been in *with him* and go from there, assessing the coordinates, and so forth. Your Mulrooney agreed with that. He did not *like it,*" he assured, "but he agreed. I told Reynolds we would leave in the morning—a few hours from then that's all. I left with Louis to organize the squad, all very routine, and the next thing I know Pierre is on the radio screaming something about Henri. So you tell me what happened."

"Yes, well," Justin said, "offhand I would say Nel wanted to leave. He did not want to wait."

"And that's a problem," Jean Paul said. "That is a problem if you are going to send men into my area who are incapable of rational thinking, incapable of lucid and balanced process or action that is a very big problem."

"Yes, well," Justin said, "I'm not sure what you mean. If you mean compromise, what it sounds like you're talking about, then no. Nel has orders, and he follows his orders, no deviation."

"To the point that he—" Jean Paul's excitement rose.

"No," Justin stopped him. "Not to the point he shoots up your camp unless he's told to. Nel did not shoot up your camp though. Mulrooney did according to you."

"Yes," Jean Paul said.

Justin nodded. "Just so the record is clear and straight. Do you want that dinner now? If you want to go out, we can continue this later. Or if you want to stay here, we can continue now. What do you want to do?"

"Well, here, of course," Jean Paul appeared caught off guard. "Here, yes, naturally. I am not here to wander the streets of Cairo. I am here to talk."

"Good," Justin sat back to relight his pipe with a nod at Bobby. "Want to take care of that?"

"For your record to keep it straight," Justin offered Jean Paul while Bobby ordered enough food for a small army, "I am not here to cause some international incident by aggravating the French cause."

"Well, this is certainly aggravating, Justin," Jean Paul said.

"Yes," Justin said. "And before we have another incident neither of us wants, you have that foreign correspondent with you?"

"Oh, yes," Jean Paul said, and perhaps that's when the eyes started to move, or the blinking decrease. "What is all that about?"

"Explain," Justin requested.

"Explain?" Jean Paul said. "Why do I have a foreign news correspondent sitting in my camp? How is that?"

"Yes, well, you put him there," Justin said. "You're keeping him there."

"Who is he?" Jean Paul came out and asked.

"The devil if I know. Some ruddy reporter. With that envoy who's convoy was attacked. A bunch of Yanks. Diplomats," Justin threw in.

"Really," Jean Paul said. "Here in Cairo?"

"Originally, from what I gather. But, no, Siwa," Justin nodded. "They were on their way to Tobruk is my understanding. A story for the correspondent, photograph opportunity for them. Politics as usual. Not my cup of tea. Nor my interest."

"No," Jean Paul agreed. "No, of course not. But then what does it have to do with you?" he asked. "Why are they ... or he," he said, "with O'Brannigan?"

"Oh," Justin said. "Yes, well, we were asked to escort him. My sister was with the envoy as driver—you got the broadcast," he said.

"Oh, yes," Jean Paul said. "Yes, of course. I'm sorry. I haven't even mentioned ..."

"It's all right," Justin assured.

"No, sincerely," Jean Paul said. "You have my sympathy, sincerely."

"Yes, well, thank you," Justin said, "but it's all right. Nothing that could have been foreseen ... or quite, even prevented," he grunted. "Just one of those things. She was picked out of the motor pool to be the driver. She was with the ATS—that's one of our Auxiliary services. Civilians, mostly. That sort of thing."

"Yes," Jean Paul said, "you do what you can do."

"Yes," Justin said, waiting a respectable moment, before continuing. "The extent of my doing however, is giving the fellow a hand in getting on his way to his next stop, Algiers, Morocco, or wherever the devil they were going. Find his story and some new lot of diplomats anxious for their photograph opportunity for the folks back home. There is no story in me or my sister that's for sure, nor can there be. Fellow's neither wanted or needed underfoot."

"Well," Jean Paul said, "at least he's got a story ... perhaps not the one he expected, but things happen as you said."

"Quite," Justin said, waiting another respectable moment before continuing along about the time the food showed up, the fellows pulling up Justin's poker table so they'd have something to eat off instead of their laps. "Read about it in the morning chronicle though and we will be having another little chat."

Jean Paul laughed. "Yes, I was just thinking that."

But that was all he said, at least about Michael. Could be because the food showed up. Could be because he was pondering his options with playing with fire with the Yanks whom the French were keen to embrace above the English.

"Reynolds mentioned your sister," Jean Paul said as he sat down. "I forgot about that. He confused me. I thought perhaps I had read something wrong in your wire."

"Wrong?" Justin said.

"Your sister living versus dead," Jean Paul nodded. "Sorry to be so blunt."

"Oh," Justin said.

"Who can I expect for this Mulrooney and the girl Julia?" Jean Paul moved on as he dug in. "Frank?"

"Yes," Justin said.

"All right. When we contact O'Brannigan, I'll tell Cassandra, and you can call Frank in. They'll be ready to go when he gets there."

"Fair enough," Justin said. "There will be a call though once Frank's off."

"Is that your idea of trust?" Jean Paul asked.

"No," Justin said, "that's my idea of a guarantee."

"You'll get your call from Frank," Jean Paul promised.

"No," Justin said again. "You'll get your call from Cassandra."

"What?" Jean Paul's teeth sunk into the meat he was eating.

"Sorry," Justin said, "but no one here is going anywhere until I know Frank's off the ground with Mulrooney and Julia."

"You're joking," Jean Paul said.

"No," Justin assured.

"Now, you see, this is what I'm talking about, Justin," Jean Paul threw his dinner down. "Holding me and Forget hostage is not the way to address these issues."

"Just following your lead," Justin kept on eating.

Jean Paul looked at him. "You want them all."

"Of course I want them all," Justin said. "Told you when you came in, on the double. Zero-options, zero-time."

“So what the hell was all of this?” Jean Paul waved.

“Listening to what you had to say,” Justin shrugged, “as you asked. And you have a point. I’ll take care of Mulrooney. Next time, however, just call.”

“Next time,” Jean Paul said.

“Yes, next time. Should there be a next time, get on the damn blower and ask me what the hell is going on, instead of taking it into your own hands. I told them to stand down to avoid escalation. Had I known that instead of resolving whatever the devil happened, you would aggravate it with this kind of nonsense I’d have told them to blow your goddamn place off the map.”

“I won’t do it,” Jean Paul said. “Screw you.”

“You will do it if you want to see Algeria again before the end of the war,” Justin assured.

“Why would I even believe you?”

“Why the devil would I keep you here?”

“Oh, I’m sure you’d think of something,” Jean Paul shook his head. “Cassandra told me not to come,” he reminded Forget, explaining things to him.

“Yes, well, she was right,” Justin said, “if all you came to do is throw your weight around. What the devil makes you think any of this is worth my time?”

“Fine,” Jean Paul dismissed. “Fine, you can have them.”

“That’s more like it. Where are the planes?”

“We have one. A Swordfish,” Jean Paul agreed. “It is my understanding another plane was destroyed.”

“By whom?” Justin said.

“I have no idea. Maybe by the girls? Maybe by O’Brannigan.”

“I’ll confirm it with Pete when we call him—in the morning,” Justin said. “Either way you owe me a plane for the inconvenience. Pick of the litter available. Julia gets to choose. You’re also to give them back their guns, their equipment, and whatever else you took. I’ll confirm with Pete there’s to be no shoot-outs. So don’t try to start anything and blame it on them.”

“Of course,” Jean Paul said. “I made this whole thing up about Mulrooney. That is exactly why Pierre and I are here. To waste your time.”

"I'm telling you," Justin said, "Pete follows orders, like Nel. No deviation—unless provoked."

"Well, then it must have been Mulrooney who provoked Reynolds," Jean Paul said, "because we didn't."

That was probably the most important thing he had said. "Yes, well," Justin said as he paused in his Roman feast to smoke his pipe and enjoy his beer, "once my lot are clear, you and Forget can leave."

"Oh, right," Jean Paul said.

"In the meantime," Justin extended, "you are welcome to stay here rather than sleep in a doorway."

"Oh, right!" Jean Paul said.

"Either way," Justin said, "I wouldn't try the same route as Nel. There would be no doubt the first shot fired would be to kill and hit its mark cleanly."

"That," Jean Paul assured, "is the only thing I believe is true."

Justin shrugged. It was probably the only thing he should believe as true except that he and Forget were going nowhere until Justin's lot were clear.

"He's going to run, lad. Try," Bobby predicted after Jean Paul left with Forget to sleep in some doorway and eat in some other stolen jeep.

"No, he isn't. He knows if he does, it's over."

"It's not over?" Bobby looked at him.

"Oh, it's over," Justin assured. "Not saying I'm not curious as to why, and that it's not too bad, because it is. It's all right though, we can still make use of him—good use of him," he promised. He ogled Bobby. "What are you standing there for? Get Keith and the fellows on him and a guard on that plane."

"Aye," Bobby waddled to the phone, "just to be sure."

"Quite," Justin said. "After mine are out, I don't care what the devil Jean Paul does."

"Oh, right," Bobby said, almost incredulously as Jean Paul had.

"Figure of speech," Justin assured. "Be interesting to see what he does do."

"Aye, well, he could go after them as soon as he is out of here, is what he could do," Bobby said after he rattled off the orders to Keith.

"Yes, well, he could," Justin settled into finishing his dinner. "But that would rather confirm he is playing the other side."

"Which he could be," Bobby sat down to join him.

"Of course he could be. But if that is the case—"

"I know," Bobby waved, "you need our fellows out there, not here."

"And I need to make use of him," Justin said. "Find out what the devil is going on with those depots."

"What about the Doc?" Bobby wiped his mouth.

"Mike will be fine. Still the best place right now regardless. Jean Paul doesn't know who Mike is, that's for damn sure—" he cracked a smile.

"What?" Bobby said.

"Thinking what Jean Paul said about the reporter getting a story he didn't expect. Touché, Mike. If you can't take the heat, you should stay out of the kitchen."

"You could lose a ruddy physicist," Bobby said. "Not to some Jerry, but some damn French bullet."

"No," Justin said. "I could lose a man who is a physicist. Is a bit of a difference. Doesn't matter. Mike's another Pete. He'd have made that shot without difficulty. Forget wouldn't be standing here complaining about some fellow Henri that's for damn sure."

"Is that sober or drunk, lad?" Bobby asked.

"Sober," Justin agreed, and made a note to check with Julia once home how that part was going with Mike. "Who I do want out is Julia and Mulrooney. Julia can spell Frank on the way in, but also help with ensuring there's no problem with Mulrooney—if there is a problem with Mulrooney." Justin rather suspected there was. "Make sure she's well armed."

Bobby waved. "My girl could kill him before he knew it."

"If he is what he is on paper," Justin agreed. "I'm talking about if he's not."

Jean Paul did not try Nel's route, and made the requested call in the morning. Frank came in and took Mulrooney and Julia out. Julia left the plane picking business to Frank for when he got back. Right now, she took two jeeps for her fellows so they could easily move around.

Pete reported the landing gear of the Albacore damaged beyond repair and Joe had blown the plane to prevent it from being stripped. He advised Mulrooney had no interest in playing ball or any other sport. He mentioned Joe's Christine had been the only casualty with Joe managing to patch her up pretty good for now. There was no mention on how Christine's injuries came about.

Pete promised to signal once they were settled in Frank's safe house deep in the Atlas. Justin looked forward to talking to Julia when she arrived. Pulling Mulrooney out was put down to his lack of experience in the field, giving him high marks for his brief outing and recommending him again for the next appropriate excursion.

Jean Paul was understandably cold and sullen, when Justin gave him a lift to the airport. Jean Paul gave his parting shot, assuring he would continue to check the reported coordinates, and reexamine the areas. Justin wished Jean Paul good luck with that and had only one new point for Bobby's consideration before they launched into fretting through the possibilities and probabilities of what might be going on.

"Need that damn second gun," Justin reminded as he watched Jean Paul's plane until it disappeared. "Get cracking on that sooner rather than later. Pete will need a replacement at some point with that eye of his. This sun could prove the end of it."

"On the list, lad," Bobby assured, "on the list. Never been off it."

March 29-April 1

Jean Paul had one question for Forget after they boarded their plane and Jean Paul took off heading for Gadames to take charge of the operation. He could shortened his return trip to three days if he went by way of the Kufra Oasis, and then heading west. "What do you think about the story of the reporter and the diplomatic envoy? What do you really think he is? Justin wanted him out, he claimed to send him on his way, but not back in Cairo."

"Some kind of specialist?" Pierre shrugged.

"Like the rest of them," Jean Paul nodded. "That's what I think, yes. It's all right, we'll find out."

By the point they reached the Kufra, Jean Paul had softened his hardened stance on Justin's actions. Flying relaxed him. It always did. A passenger, no. But, piloting, yes. "Well, at least Justin took that

Mulrooney out. At least he did that. That's one worry off our backs. No interpreter with some trigger-happy finger.

"He understands," he assured Forget, "Justin does understand the situation out here. His methods though, are not conducive to partnerships. Not even close.

"But," he shrugged, "we'll see how it goes. Justin needs us even if he doesn't want to admit it. I'm satisfied," he smiled at Forget. "You? We put on a good show. Independence, arrogance, anger, compromise, even surrender."

"Oui, mon caporal," Forget assured. "I am satisfied. The bastard will have to eat crow when his sister shows up alive, inadvertently rescued by the clumsy foot soldiers of the Free French."

"Yes," Jean Paul said. "I wish it was a little farther away from us, deeper into Libya."

"It's far enough." Forget agreed with the plan. "How much farther could it be? Who would be finding her in the middle of Libya? Not us."

"True," Jean Paul said. But when it came to the story of the sister that made sense as Justin presented it, Jean Paul continued to wonder why the SS would have brought her from the Siwa to Eden. Clearly the interest of the SS extended beyond some American diplomats directly to Justin.

"Perhaps they don't know where this Major Charles is?" Forget suggested.

"A good point," Jean Paul agreed. "I will have to talk to Justin about that after this is over and we're talking about the sister. He has a problem with the SS apparently, and he should know about it."

Forget shrugged.

"He should," Jean Paul assured. "I like us in the role of heroes, not villains. Saving his sister is much better than killing his men. Jesus Christ, Cassie," he still shook his head over that. "You know Justin owes us one—a big one," he assured. "It didn't have to be us who took his men, can you imagine if it were Cassie? They'd be dead. No in between."

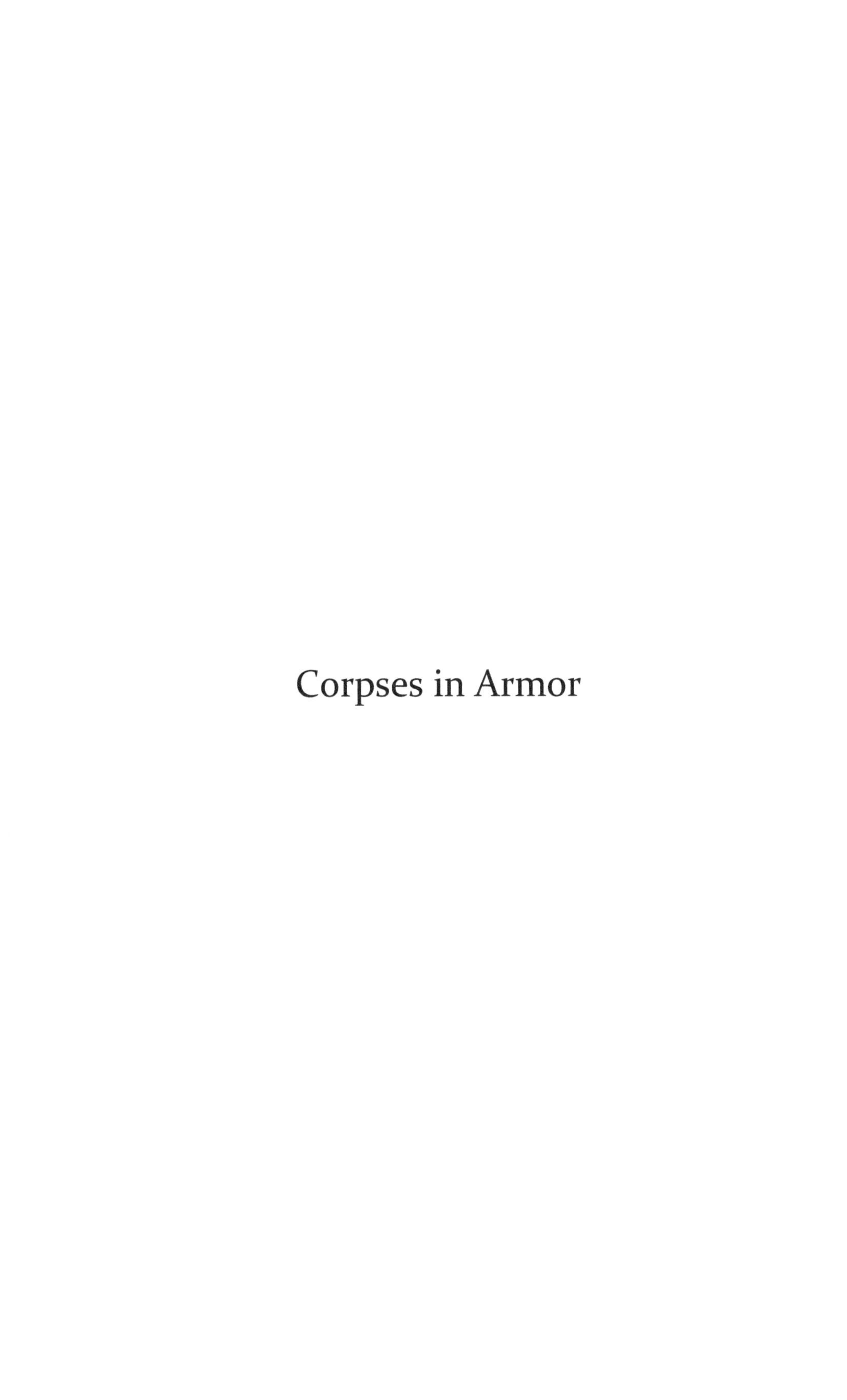

Corpses in Armor

Chapter Sixty

The Fezzan
March 29

It was eleven a.m. Sunday. Joanna stood inside her room at her windows watching the Captain race around the courtyard atop a black stallion. She had been outside on her balcony only a few minutes before, attempting to study the distance between where she stood and the ground below. She was doing that in some ways out of spite. The Captain had discounted, laughed at her ideas of escape, and for the second day in a row, had left her locked up in her room. Yesterday it was three o'clock before he considered allowing her to go to the children's village, and today it looked like it was going to be the same thing.

Whether or not she would risk jumping from the balcony, Joanna hadn't decided. It really was very far to the ground and wasn't as soft as it looked. She confirmed that yesterday evening, walking around on it without her sandals while the Captain chatted with Pierre who had finally returned, the powder-soft sand was littered with tiny pebbles and shallow as Pierre had said, with rocks hard as cement underneath.

"*What are you doing*?" the Captain had caught her, realizing she had left the front porch and found her wandering along the side, ordering her back onto the porch.

Reineke shook his head at Pierre and glanced up at the balcony above, but shook his head again. She could not possibly be considering jumping.

Couldn't she? Lifting her eye patch to see if that changed anything there was very little difference other than Joanna could see much better out of her eye. Pierre had finally removed the bandage last night but told her she had to continue wearing the patch for a few more days because of the sun. The sun seemed fine, and the ground was definitely far below her when she leaned over the balcony rail.

Joanna settled on studying the outside wall, remembering how Michael had told her there was no such thing as a smooth wall. There was always some crack, some crevice, some toe, or finger hold. These walls looked very smooth though. Cracks and crevices in the marble blocks, deeper in some places than the length of her fingernail, were also very smooth, narrow like a line. She couldn't get her finger or toe in there. Even the discrepancies between the blocks themselves were very narrow, at least along her outside walls. Joanna thought about the sheets, and long linen draperies, about tying them together and tying them around the balcony rail like a rope. She was still thinking about the sheets and draperies when the Captain made an unexpected appearance in the courtyard below, streaking across the marble sand atop a racing black horse.

Joanna rapidly retreated, back into her room, behind the draperies where she could see him, but he could not see her watching him. First on one black horse, and then another, twenty minutes, and two horses and Joanna still couldn't figure out what he was doing racing around, back and forth.

"Funny, but you know," Anna did not seem to have any problem figuring out what Dieter was doing as she watched, standing with her eldest, Abraham, and her second eldest John, Justin's sister visible in between the glare of the sunlight as she stood in her windows.

"Even this distance ..." Anna adjusted her binoculars. "Through the trees ..."

"Ma," John said.

"What?" she snapped.

"Don't worry about it," Abraham turned away with a wave of his hand, "it's harmless."

"Which explains why you're divorced, because that just worked about as well with me as it ever did with your wife."

"I agree," John said.

"With him or me?"

"Freud?" John said and Abraham laughed.

"Eh, heh," Anna did not. "Too funny, the two of you. But, that's all right," she gave John a whack on his back that would have killed a smaller man. "I agree with you. All men do marry their mothers."

Something that definitely explained why Abe was divorced. John straightened up once he was able and turned to follow his mother following Abraham hell bent on getting out of there.

"Did you hear what I said?" Anna announced to Abraham. "I agree with John."

"And I agree with Abe," John assured.

"That's not what you said," Anna said.

"I'm saying it now. Don't worry about it."

Anna nodded. "I wish I had a penis like you two. I'd be so much smarter like you two."

"Ma," Abraham turned around, older than John, taller, and much better looking until he decided he was Picasso with an embroidery needle.

"What?" Anna said.

"Dieter is exercising the horses. Selecting the one he wants."

Anna frowned. "Why am I thinking of Chiron?"

"I have no idea," Abraham assured while John said, "Who the hell is Chiron?"

"An American education," Anna nodded to Abraham. "I told you. Instead of a doctor, he's a dentist. Instead of a doctor, the other one's a lawyer.

"Instead of a doctor, the other one's a dropout." She turned to the Holy Man Pierre standing there not having too much to say about Prince Charming showing off for Cinderella. "He better be exercising only his horses." She walked off to wait in the wagen.

Abraham shook his head. "It's fine," he reassured Pierre.

"Oui, I know. You do not have to tell me."

"It's just ..."

"Guys?" John offered.

"Yes," Abraham said. "And it's almost over, almost history."

"Oui, I know," Pierre smiled, Anna calling for them to hurry up. Reineke wiped down the horses, passing them to one of his sergeants he was considering as a replacement for Erich. Behind schedule, he gave permission to Thiele to leave with the remaining trucks, and the responsibilities of the horse trailers to the sergeant and squad of men who would act as rear scouts leaving as well in the next few hours.

Thiele was glad to go now, ideally be in position early, ready for the word when it came, and the convoys from Tripoli. Rear scouts were a good idea. They had a challenging journey in front of them. There could not be too many precautions.

By one o'clock the last of the trucks were climbing the road along the mountainous quarry wall. Reineke thought about the woman, but wanted to relax. He called for his car, speeding away to gather up as many children who would fit and take them all for a swim in the shallow pool at the Temple Diana. The Holy Man was back, and the woman safe in the villa. Reineke presumed the Holy Man was with her. He had no idea Pierre was not there, but had gone to the other side to settle the arrangements with Diana.

"When are you leaving?" Anna set down a lunch of couscous and dates, some olives and wine in one of the lower Roman apartments to relieve Pierre of the climb to hers. No roof, it had a little terrace and was nice considering.

"A few days?" Pierre guessed. "As soon as my son confirms the site. I have heard nothing yet."

"Tonight," Anna shook her head.

"Tonight? Mon capitaine is not going to leave tonight without knowing where he is going," Pierre assured. "We will have Mademoiselle with us."

"No, you will have the girl with you," Anna corrected. "Dieter can leave once he knows where he is going. You are leaving tonight with the girl ... and," she eyed her sons, particularly the tattooed one who would work very well this time. "All right, you," she told Abraham. "Dieter's men will definitely think you are from the town, simply assisting the Holy Man with the girl. And you," she nodded at Jacob, "and you," she assured Martin. "You are closest to Thiele's size and that hair of yours is perfect."

"Thiele? What are you talking about?" Martin sputtered and the brothers laughed, picturing him in his little suit like an organ grinder's monkey. "It will be too short."

"You can wear puttees."

"The jacket," Martin said. "The arms, sleeves—"

"All right, all right," Anna silenced him. "Oberleutnant Thiele," she instructed Pierre. "Get one of his uniforms. We will need his patches. And then get another uniform that will fit Martin. Mirabella and Anne will go with you to collect the laundry. Martin will be the representative from Dieter's town ...What is that officer's name Dieter used?" she asked anyone who could stop laughing long enough to answer her.

"Danzig," John offered.

"Him," Anna assured Pierre. "Martin will be his representative in charge of the horses."

"They're gone," Abraham corrected.

"Gone? What do you mean they are gone?" Anna said. "They just got here."

"Well, they're going, except for ours. They have to get north. Those carriers are loaded. It will take a little longer. As it is, Thiele will have to wait at least a few hours for them to catch up."

"Well, they're not going to catch up," Anna assured. "Thiele can go and meet up with this ... " she waved again.

"Linke," Abraham said. "Sergeant Linke. He will camp and wait for Thiele, yes. That is the plan."

"At this interim location," Anna said. "Until Dieter knows where he's going."

"Yes," Abraham said. "Linke has the ambulances ... as does Thiele to set up the field hospital. Dieter will have one or two for his convoy."

"We're talking about Linke," Anna said.

"I know," Abraham said. "Linke will camp, set up a few of the tents and wait for Thiele. Linke is ahead because ..."

"I understand," Anna stopped him. "He's reconnaissance. Dieter still needs his reconnaissance. The men would wonder why there are no forward scouts."

"Yes," Abraham said. "Dieter's not supposed to know where he is going."

"And mon capitaine does not," Pierre assured.

"Specifically where he is going," Anna corrected him. "He has a general idea. I understand that part, too. Thiele will have the orders by that time for the actual location—presuming Jean Paul radios. We presume he will."

"He will," Pierre nodded.

"So, see, I was listening," Anna assured Abraham.

"Yes," Abraham said. "Thiele will confirm orders after he reviews Linke's reconnaissance—there will be no problems for Linke to report, guaranteed. Thiele will then proceed to the actual location and set up the hospital. Linke will wait for Dieter—and us with the girl. We will then proceed with the squad of horses to Thiele and the hospital, Dieter behind us with Linke and the other ambulances. It's really rather simple."

"Yes," Anna nodded. "yes, it is. Just not as pretty as Dieter wanted because the horses are late."

"Well ..." Abraham said, because, yes, the staging was going to be somewhat more stark than Dieter had envisioned. "Linke has to settle for hospital tents instead of an Arab encampment because the horses are late. But, really, the delivery of the girl to the hospital by Arabs is more important for the local show. Linke was only staging, a place to hold the horses until Dieter arrived. Now the horses will be following after Thiele. That's why Dieter is sending them on now. To get them there."

"Well," Anna said, "the Arabs would have to come from somewhere so it was a bit more than a corral. People who see, notice, also look. As they talk. A few who saw an Arab camp, not only horses, does not hurt."

"Perhaps," Abraham said. "But I really don't think Dieter cares. He just wants it to work."

"Well, I do care," Anna assured, "and I also want it to work. So we are going to give Dieter his pretty Arab camp. To hell with the locals, that girl is going to remember an Arab camp not only her Roman palace. Where are the tents?"

"Here. Why carry what you're not going to use?"

"Very good." Anna turned back to Pierre. "Uniforms. Two of them. One of Thiele's and another to fit Martin. Hanuk will be at the children's village. Give them to him along with the set of papers from this Danzig identifying Martin—I assume Dieter secured more than one set? Something without an Italian name on them? So they can be used again?"

"Mon capitaine's men do not carry their papers," Pierre shook his head.

"Martin is from the town, and I am not having my son shot because no one knows who he is. He can destroy the papers after they pass him—you will make sure they pass him because he will be with you and the girl in Dieter's car—not as the driver. The driver, Dieter can choose whomever he wants. Abraham and Jacob will be in the lead truck with the tents. Whatever Dieter has. All of it. Behind them, the two trucks with your horses—Where are the camels?"

"Mon capitaine did not want the camels," Pierre shook his head.

"Get them back, now, today. He's getting camels. You will need them for the sand sea."

"We are not going to the sea," Pierre shook his head, "only a little bit. Mademoiselle will see, oui, five of the six horses with Abraham, John, Hanuk—"

"No," Anna said.

"Jacob and Martin," Pierre assured, "oui, as mon capitaine's own forward scouts, and she will see the dunes."

"The girl will see dunes from here to Gadames," Anna assured. "John is taking Hanuk north next week by plane in time to greet the SS. I am not losing all my sons because something does not work. John and Hanuk go only when I know everything is precisely on schedule, precisely as planned. Abraham, Martin, and Jacob will be with you. Dieter can take care of himself with his convoy on Sunday, or Monday, whatever day he leaves. *You* are going to the sea tonight with the girl—how long are you thinking for Dieter on the roads?" she confirmed with Abraham.

"The usual? Four days?" Abraham said. "It depends. Linke took one of the guns—"

"Yes," Anna nodded. "I saw that."

"Yes. So, Dieter's traveling empty if you're sending everything with the girl. There is still that area of the sea they have to cross with no road. The trucks could get stuck, cause a delay."

"Dieter will not allow his trucks to get stuck," Anna dismissed.

"I have been with him three times and they have never gotten stuck ... as he would make it in three days if he could ... All right," she said to Pierre. "Four, five days. Two, three more days on the sea for you with the girl before you move back to the roads. You may still get there ahead of Dieter depending when he leaves, but that is all right. You will all go to the hospital as planned on the horses. John and Hanuk will be there by that time. Dieter can come in behind you with the ambulances as he is planning to anyway with this Linke."

"No," Pierre said. "Mon capitaine will not agree."

"He has no choice. They are my sons."

"And that is his Mademoiselle until he says she is not," Pierre reminded. "He does not have to let her go. He can keep her here forever, and Pierre will take care of her," he folded his arms.

"Oh, really," Anna said. "Forever in this ... *paradise* you love," she waved around her camp of broken stone and rocks. "Graveyards for gardens. Sand, the only rain that ever falls here. A world that has nothing for her. No life. No future. You would really do that to that young woman? After all of this? You will do that?"

"It does not matter," Pierre shrugged. "Mon capitaine will not agree to Mademoiselle on the sea for three days. He is hysterical at the idea of one. Convinced she will die and it will be his fault—when it will be yours."

"Perhaps I am not making myself clear," Anna turned back to Abraham.

"Ma," he said, "it does not matter. Yes, the Arab encampment was a good idea, but it does not have to happen—it can't happen. The horses are gone—going," he assured, "in a few hours. Pierre is right, why provoke Dieter with any of this now?"

"Because you are my sons!" she insisted. "I am thinking of you—and you," she assured Pierre, "your children, *and* Dieter, who is not thinking at all. That girl is not to remember anything, or know anything, except here. A hospital with children, a *beautiful* Arab camp and a field hospital—and that is it!" she spit. "Nothing more. She is not to have any idea where she was—"

"She doesn't," Abraham assured.

"And I mean, *any* idea," Anna ignored him for Pierre, "not where, or how long to the coast, or anywhere, by car, horse, camel, or truck! She is to be drugged. Here, when she leaves, to wake up in her Arab camp for her three day adventure on the sea with camels and horses only. No trucks! Martin will order the trucks to release the horses with Dieter's Arab riders and their tents for her pretty stage. You will have the camels there, waiting.

"After the three days," she said, "you will rendezvous with Martin and the horses' trucks and continue along the road as planned—*and,*" she assured, "where she is to be drugged again for the trip, waking up in a field hospital with you there to console her. Three days on the sea is not very long or very far. She will be fine even if she gets sick from the sun. That girl survived Siwa to here. Do not talk to me about three days—though, no," she could compromise a little bit. "We do not have to provoke Dieter with the business about the drugs—except for here," she told Pierre. "Dieter will know and he will agree the girl is to be drugged here for her ride to the Arab camp where she will travel for three days on the sea.

"After you talk to him, if they have left," she said, "Dieter will radio his caravan of horses and tell them of the change in plan, and where to stop so you can rendezvous with them—*and,*" she pointed, "he will also tell them the representative from his town will be there to ride with the trucks—Martin. That will ensure Martin's passing without any difficulty. I don't care what reason Dieter gives his men for the change. Blame it on this Danzig, blame it on whatever he wants—he *feels* like it should be good enough. He is the Hauptmann. They will listen.

"Find Mirabella and get Pierre back to the house so he can talk to Dieter and secure the uniforms and papers," she waved at her sons, not caring which one. "And kiss Mademoiselle goodbye, because she is leaving tonight—midnight or so," she shrugged. "But that is the plan, or you might as well radio that girl's people now and give them the address, never mind the SS, because they will track her to here and it will be over for all of us."

"It's a good idea," John spoke up.

Pierre looked at him.

"Dieter will agree," John believed. "He might argue—he will argue probably, but he'll agree. He knows Ma's right. He knows it without Ma telling him—so do you," he assured Pierre. "The girl can know nothing except what she already knows. An Arab encampment, a few days on the sea, will confuse her, yes, but more importantly, it will confuse her people. Ensure that they have no idea where she was when she talks to them. I can help speak with Dieter, if you like."

"I can take care of that," Abraham said. "You're right. Ma's right."

"No," Pierre shook his head. "I will speak with mon capitaine. Because it is ... " he eyed Anna. "Oui, yes, a very good idea. I will tell him it is my idea, and then I know he will agree."

"You do whatever you need to do, Holy Man," Anna nodded. "Just do it."

"Oui," Pierre said. "That is something Pierre does very well."

Joanna was bored. She waited at her windows for a while to see if the Captain would reappear with another horse, but he did not. Neither did her lunch. Not at noon, not at one o'clock, not even by two o'clock when she was not only bored, but now hungry, starting to starve by two-thirty. She wandered back to her windows to see if he was outside in the courtyard, and she had missed him returning.

She had missed him, or could not see him and she ventured out onto her balcony where the sun streamed down and she still could not see the front. She retreated to watch and wait behind her draperies. Ten minutes, twenty, by three o'clock Joanna had figured out what was going on. He was tempting her, taunting her, trying to trick her into escaping again. He had intentionally not fed her because he knew she would be hungry and take it upon herself to try to find some food. She knew it.

Joanna knew, if she walked over to her door right now though locked all morning and practically the whole of the afternoon, the bolt to her door would be unlocked.

She knew as soon as she opened her door, her lunch would be sitting out there, and he would be out there, sitting at his desk, greeting her with a satisfied, smug smile.

Fine. Joanna was hungry, she wanted food and the door to her room was not unlocked. She stared at it, trying again, but the knob did not turn when she grasped it, twisting it, the bolt neatly tucked in place.

You bastard! Joanna could not believe it. He had left. He had actually gone off, leaving her with no food, locked up in her room.

"Why, you bastard!" she kicked the door much to the dismay of her toes, but she did not care. Hopping around until the pain subsided she searched for something, anything, enormous and huge to have ready to heave off the balcony, down on top of his head, killing him the moment he returned.

Unfortunately most of the breakables that weren't too heavy for her to lift she had already broken, thrown out the windows, or Pierre had removed them long ago.

"You absolute bastard!" Joanna seized the stupid nail file she tried on the door the other night, ready to drill holes in her pillows when she suddenly realized she was holding the stupid nail file she had tried on the door the other night.

"Yes!" Joanna said, even though the file had not worked, she wasn't sure why she hadn't thought of—

"Two files!" Joanna snapped her fingers. There had to be a second nail file somewhere. Two of something was always better than one, and if she could find the second file ...

There was only one file. If there had ever been another one, someone had lost it before she came there and never bothered to replace it.

"Rot!" Joanna cursed the lazy sot too lazy to bother replacing the file they lost. What did they think she was going to do with one file? She had already tried one file for hours and it did not work then and it did not work now.

Joanna hammered and jammed file in and out of the latch until drenched with exhaustion she dropped against the door. What did they think? She had all the time in the world to escape? Spend more worthless hours trying to escape?

No, they did not think that. What they thought of was a knife. A much stronger, flat wedge to easily slip the bolt. And it came delivered on a tray.

Footsteps sounded outside her door in the library, quick ones, hard ones, unknown to Joanna made by a soldier who obeyed the cook bringing the prisoner food even though none had been ordered, and was presumed to be an oversight. The Hauptmann had kept an erratic schedule with the woman's meals, as he kept with his own. It was safer to feed the woman than risk a reprimand from the Hauptmann for not feeding her when a missing order for her food was clearly in error.

At the sound of the footsteps, Joanna jumped up to race over to sit in the seat by the windows. The bland soldier who knocked before entering, set down a tray of food and left without comment, a butter knife provided for her meat. Joanna had probably an hour before the soldier returned and it took less than five minutes to slip the bolt with the knife and open the door.

She was in the library, the room silent and empty. She tucked the knife in her belt to use for the lock on the library doors, and took a bite of the piece of meat she rolled up in her bread, proceeding carefully, quietly, along the shelves of books. Fat ones, skinny ones, her hand glided over them. All of them unreadable when she stopped to open a couple and have a look, filled with funny wiggly lines or spindly writing in a language she could not read. How odd. She continued to look over them for a few minutes while she finished her sandwich before chiding herself for wasting time and left them alone, studying the library doors at the end of the line wondering what she would do if the knife did not work. Steps from freedom, it would be awful if the knife did not work.

"It'll work," Joanna reassured herself and darted back into her room to get her sandals and the rest of her lunch for the trip over the mountain. She closed the door quietly behind her when she left, wishing she could lock it so it would take them longer to realized she was not there, but she only had a knife, not a key ...

"A key ..." Joanna stared over at the Captain's desk lonely as the room. It was really quite a nice looking desk with absolutely nothing interesting sitting on top of it when she ran up the steps to see if by chance there was a key, not only for her door, but for the library's.

"Drat." Joanna looked under the blotter, and the lamp, moving the ashtray and the funny looking glass ball, but there was no key.

"The drawers!" she pulled the knife out of her belt to pry them open but it was unnecessary. Unlocked, the center drawer slid open when she crammed in the knife. It too, though, had nothing interesting. Some pencils, paper, and Turkish cigarettes, but no key.

The top right-hand drawer was the same, more papers and an odd looking packet of small books bound with a rubber band. Twenty-four of them Joanna counted, and then another one by itself. She picked up the single one, opening it. It was the Captain's ... or at least it had a picture of the Captain with a few pages of things that looked like dates ... and names of some kind, with stamped seals one might see on a passport, and then a number of pages had more lists of what again looked like dates.

"What is this?" Joanna wondered, wishing she had paid as much attention to learning German as she had when learning French. She sat down in the chair as she looked through the Captain's book, trying to find something that might look familiar other than his picture, but she couldn't, the writing so bizarre.

"Rot." Joanna threw the book down on the desk with the rest of them and returned to looking though the drawers for a key but there was none.

"Oh, well." She scooped up the books to bind them back up in their rubber band and put them away neatly so no one would ever know when she heard the creak of the library door.

Oh, my God! Joanna reeled in terror. Dropping the books, she snatched them back up to dump them inside the opened drawer and slam it closed as she ducked down under the desk, whacking her forehead on the edge as she did so.

It was Pierre. Joanna peered over the top of the desk at Pierre in the doorway peering back at her and she breathed a deep sigh of relief.

Chapter Sixty-One

Oh, God, dear God, thank God. Joanna near died where she was until she saw it was Pierre. "Oh, God," she stood up, her knees knocking. "It's you."

"Oui, Mademoiselle," Pierre said, his eyes and face unfriendly and frozen. "So this is how you repay kindness?"

"What?" Joanna paused in thanking her lucky stars.

"She steals," Pierre accused.

"What?" Joanna said.

"Trust!" Pierre assured and Joanna blushed embarrassed.

"Oh," she said. "Well, no, I wasn't stealing. I was ... Well, I was looking for something, that's all," she tossed her head. "Really," she said, as Pierre came closer, "Stealing what? There's hardly anything here worth stealing. Besides," she said, "I mean, I ..." she hardly knew what he meant about stealing trust. "I ..." she said because Pierre did not look as happy to see her, as she was to see him.

"What are you doing?" she asked as he hoisted himself up the steps and stopped in front of the desk glaring at the few booklets she hadn't managed to stuff back in the drawer in her haste to hide.

"Mademoiselle speaks German?" he accused.

"What?" Joanna said. "Well, no. I mean ... Well, perhaps a little I do. Though hardly ..." she sneered at the booklets, "anything there interesting."

"That is unfortunate," Pierre agreed.

He was telling her. Joanna struggled to keep her stiff lips from quivering. She looked down on the desk.

"That Mademoiselle speaks German," Pierre snatched up the booklets to put them away.

"Oh. Well, I can do that," Joanna offered, but he glared at her and she stepped back, moved out of his way so he could slam them inside the drawer and slam it closed and glare at her again. “Well, fine,” she said. “Shoot me.”

“If Pierre had a gun, Mademoiselle,” he assured, “it is exactly what I would do.”

“You would?” Joanna blinked.

“Yes,” Pierre said.

“Oh. Well, I don’t think so,” Joanna said. “Really, I’d like to see you—don’t you touch me!” she screamed as he attacked, grabbing her wrist and clamping his cruel crooked hand over her mouth.

“Now, you listen to me, Mademoiselle,” he told her as Joanna stared back at him terrified, “and you listen very closely. Pierre and mon capitaine have not been anything but kind to you. Good. You are an extremely fortunate young woman, how fortunate you will never know. But what you do not seem to realize, Mademoiselle, for all the good that has been given to you, for all Pierre likes you, he likes le capitaine even better. No harm is to come to him. I will not allow any harm to come to him. I will kill anyone who attempts to harm him.”

“I’m not ...” Joanna tried to say under his hand.

“Then why are you doing this?” Pierre insisted. “Why? What is in those books you need to know? What lies are you going to tell about mon capitaine? Because it is lies, all lies. I don’t care what those books say!”

“But I’m not!” Joanna started to cry, grabbing his hand to pull it off her mouth. “I’m not trying to hurt anyone. I was hungry, and I was looking for the key!”

“What?” Pierre said.

“My lunch!” Joanna cried. “And then they brought me my lunch, and I had the knife, but I was afraid to use the knife—and I can’t!” she wailed as Pierre tried to calm her down. “Don’t you understand, I can’t. I want to go home. I just want to go home!” she sank down on the floor sobbing.

“Oui, Mademoiselle,” Pierre said.

“I’m sorry,” Joanna tried to catch her breath. “I’m really sorry.”

“Oui, Mademoiselle. It is all right. Come on,” he encouraged.

“No. No, I don’t want to go,” Joanna said. “I don’t want to go anywhere except out that door.”

"And that is where we are going, Mademoiselle," Pierre assured. "Oui, out that door to mon capitaine."

"The Captain?" Joanna pulled back from him.

"Not for punishment, Mademoiselle," Pierre swore, "please. I want you to see him ..." he stared at the desk drawers. "Oui, I simply want you to see mon capitaine."

Joanna saw him swimming. Before Pierre could take her to where the Captain was swimming, he had to bring her to the children's village and the handsome brother of the little witch who drove them in one of the Captain's cars through the oasis to the gardens that were far, far away on the other side.

"I!" Joanna said as she stood in the stone ruins of a massive building, a giant towering woman of marble looming above her.

"I!" Joanna said as she looked around. Huge columns, some standing, but most laying torn in half on the ground, uprooted from their pedestals, crushed by enormous stone blocks and toppled walls of the buildings, all of it dazzling and blinding in the sunlight.

"Oh, but where?" she said. "Where am I?"

"The village, Mademoiselle. A city that is no more."

"Village?" Joanna said. "Where you were? Where you went?"

"Oui. This is where many of mon capitaine's guests live, many of his friends."

"Friends?" Joanna looked around again, and there was no one.

"Oui," Pierre said. "They are there. Behind the rocks, behind the walls. Do not be afraid, they will not hurt you. To the simple ones, the nomad, you are what you call, a curiosity. To the others, they know only mon capitaine chose for you to stay at the house instead of here with them. They do not question his decisions."

"Oh," Joanna said.

"Are you all right?" Pierre asked.

"Yes," Joanna said. "It's ... it's all so big."

"Oui," Pierre smiled. "And very beautiful because here, in this garden, the flowers are its people. Diana welcomes all travelers."

"Diana?" Joanna stared up at the stone statue of the woman who's head tipped and hand was reaching to the sky as if she was looking for something, her other hand reaching down.

"Oui. Diana. This is the Temple of the goddess Diana. That is her statue. Do you know Mademoiselle it has been said how the most beautiful statue of the goddess Venus ever found was in Libya not Rome? I believe this, because this is the most beautiful statue of Diana I have ever seen. This is a most magnificent country where you are Mademoiselle, and this a most beautiful oasis. It is," he assured, "a garden of Eden, as mon capitaine calls it."

"What is she doing?" Joanna asked.

"Doing?" Pierre said. "Oh. Well, she is holding a bow, only it has been broken. If you walk around, you will see where some of it is still there across her back. And this hand, oui, touching an animal. If you climb up to her pedestal, you can see the feet, and part of the hind leg where it once was."

Joanna nodded. "What happened? Why is it broken? Why is so much broken?"

"Perhaps age? Perhaps an earthquake Mon capitaine thinks is possible. To strike one side of the oasis, but spare another? I do not know. Come. I want you to see mon capitaine. The man who saved your life, the man to whom you owe your life, and has asked for nothing except for you to live as he and Pierre have helped you."

He was swimming. Beyond the tall statue was a marble pool of water reflecting the blue sky, crushed by a toppled pillar at the far end, water bubbling up around it.

"Mon capitaine's bright side," Pierre nodded. "This is his swimming pool where he likes to take the children. The water is from the springs. This is the area where all of the water of the oasis originates. All of this ... " he pointed towards a bridge-like structure, "was part of the viaduct that brought the water from the springs into the town and the Emperor's villa. It is no more, but the springs are there as I have told you. Above the ground here, feeding Diana's pool. Under the ground for the plumbing of the villa, and the forests of dates and fig and olive gardens."

"Oh," Joanna said. The Captain was out toward the center of his shallow pool, a small mob of wet children crowded around him. All of them splashing and laughing. "He knows about this." It came to her as she stood there, watching them. "Why, he would have to know all about this. Everything. The children's village, the hospital," she turned to Pierre.

"Does it matter, Mademoiselle?" Pierre asked.

"Yes," Joanna nodded. "Yes, I think it does," she said, thinking of other broken buildings, air raids and sirens, spending the night with Michael in the tube, clutching him, the shaking and pounding of the bombardment, explosions, and smell of fire. "I'm not sure this is right," she shook her head. "I'm not sure it is."

"Mademoiselle," Pierre said.

"No," Joanna turned away from him to stare at the children playing. "No, they don't know who he is. He's lying to them."

"That is who he is, Mademoiselle," Pierre said. "That is mon capitaine."

"Is it?" Joanna whispered.

"Oui," Pierre said, and called out to him.

The Captain looked up from laughing and wrestling with the children trying to pull him down into the water. He pushed his dripping wet hair out of his face and with three great strides was out of the pool, reaching and picking up his abandoned shirt, heading straight for them, the little witch girl Anne quickly at his side.

"I!" Joanna said as the Captain said something to the witch and the girl turned away, barking orders to a few of the older children to assume the role of monitor for the younger ones still in the water.

"I!" Joanna said, uncomfortable watching the Captain stride towards them, wiping his face and arms with his shirt, draping it over his shoulders like a towel, the sleeves hanging down in front.

"I!" Joanna said, watching the soggy, barefooted, bare-chested man hike towards her, a brilliant gold chain and ornate gold cross dangling and dancing in the sunlight as it hung from his neck, down his naked chest, framed by the wet sleeves of his shirt.

"Mon capitaine," Pierre greeted Reineke. "Mademoiselle, has asked so many times to see these other gardens that today Pierre thought it would be a wonderful idea."

What the Captain thought of the wonderful idea, he did not say, though Joanna had a feeling he might be in agreement with her. It was not so wonderful.

"Indeed," Reineke briefly studied the world over Joanna's

shoulder, and then he called for his boots. The little witch girl responded, rushing them over, cramming them into his hand, along with his cigarettes and lighter.

Reineke lit a cigarette, exhaling with a glance down at his chest and then at Joanna.

Joanna flushed. She had not been staring at his chest! She was staring at the idea of a cross hanging there, a large cross with some sort of design instead of a figure of Christ. Even if she had been staring at his chest, it certainly wasn't her fault. His chest was her eye level, and she would certainly get a crook in her neck if she tried to look anywhere else for too long.

"Do you swim, Fräulein?" Reineke asked.

She must have heard him wrong. "What?" Joanna said.

"If you swim, Fräulein," he said, "you may go into the water. If you do not, you are to stay on the banks with the babies."

And he was gone. Boots and cigarettes, chest and cross, wet clothes and hair, gone. Nothing left behind except a puddle on the ground where he had been standing.

"Stay here, Mademoiselle," Pierre instructed Joanna, not that she heard him, and he was gone, too.

"Mon capitaine!" Pierre made his way after the fleeing giant.

Reineke ignored him. Not bothering to sit down and strap on his boots, he stalked his way through the native camp, hoping to lose Pierre in the maze of rocks.

Pierre kept pace with the gallop, showing no signs of slowing. "Mon capitaine!" he assured gleefully on Reineke's heels, "there is no reason to hurry. Oui, there is still plenty of time."

Reineke continued to ignore him for several meters until he grew tired of sidestepping the hot sharp rocks, and stopped, flinging his boots on the ground.

"Mon capitaine." Pierre toddled up as Reineke dropped down next to his boots, slamming his bare feet into them and lacing them up tightly.

"Oh, but what is the matter, mon capitaine?" Pierre chuckled. "You should not worry, no. Mademoiselle is very clever, oui, but there was not enough time, no, to make certain she uses her clever mind correctly. So it was wise, mon capitaine, oui, for Pierre to show her the other side."

Reineke was not going to argue. If he argued, he would only lose, and so he mentioned only the issue of time.

"Indeed," he hissed, "you could have chosen a more convenient time!"

"Oh, but, no, mon capitaine, there could be no other time. Non. The time is now, oui, it is. Mademoiselle is to leave us tonight."

"What?" Reineke stopped his attempt to wipe away the desert clinging to his wet pants. "Tonight?" he repeated. "What are you talking about? The woman is not leaving tonight."

"Oui, she is," Pierre nodded. "You will see when you get back to your office what she has done to it."

"What?" Reineke said.

"She was looking for the key," Pierre explained. "To escape. She took all your books out— your soldiers' books out—you need locks for your desk, mon capitaine," he clucked, "I have told you this before. It is not good enough to lock the library door. You are a soldier. You should have locks on your desk. Make it difficult for people like Mademoiselle to get into it," he nodded as Reineke stared at him. "What is the matter, mon capitaine? You look upset."

"Upset?" Reineke said.

Pierre shrugged. "She meant no harm. She wants to go home. So, we send her tonight."

Reineke silenced him. "Do not be ridiculous, the woman is not leaving tonight."

"Oui, she is," Pierre nodded.

"No, she is not!" Reineke snapped. "Indeed, I am not prepared for the woman to leave tonight."

"Oh, mon capitaine, of course you are," Pierre assured. "What is the difference of a few hours—"

"Hours?" Reineke said.

"Days," Pierre agreed. "You are still prepared."

"I am not!" Reineke assured. "That is it, the answer is no!" He stalked off.

"But, mon capitaine!" Pierre hurried as fast as he could after him.

"I said, no!" Reineke shouted back. "Indeed!" he sputtered and halted, waiting for Pierre to catch up.

"Thank you, mon capitaine!" Pierre puffed up to him.

"It is all right," Reineke dismissed. "But you must understand, I cannot leave until I know where I am going. I cannot simply take the woman into the desert and have no idea where I am bringing her. Are you mad?"

"Mon capitaine, you know where you are going."

"And you know what I mean," Reineke assured. "I do not have the final location yet until I see Linke. I am not bringing the woman to Sergeant Linke."

"But you are bringing the woman to your Sergeant Linke—"

"You know what I mean!" Reineke barked.

"Oui, I do," Pierre agreed. "You are not prepared."

"Indeed," Reineke said. "I am not prepared."

"And it is all right," Pierre said, "because it will not be you, it will be me."

"What?" Reineke said.

"Come," Pierre took his arm. "Come back to your office and we will talk. You have to call your horses, anyway ..."

"What?" Reineke shook himself free.

"Just come, mon capitaine," Pierre requested, "please. We cannot talk here—especially if you are shouting, too many ears."

"I am not shouting," Reineke assured.

"No, you are not prepared," Pierre understood.

"I am not!"

"I know," Pierre agreed. "Of course you are, but that is not the point—"

"It is the point!" Reineke insisted.

"Mon capitaine, please. Mademoiselle attacked your office, you will see when you get there."

"But ..." Reineke could not understand what he was saying.

"Because she wanted the key," Pierre said. "The key to her room. I did not know. I was not there."

"What? Why were you not there? Where were you? I thought you were there!"

"I thought you were there," Pierre agreed. "Where were you?"

Reineke had no idea. He did not even know when this attack occurred. He could have been anywhere. With the horses, with the trucks, perhaps already swimming with the children. "All right," Reineke said. "All right! We will talk, come—but that has nothing to do with the woman leaving tonight," he assured and walked off for his car. "The woman is not leaving tonight!"

"Oui, she is," Pierre said, and toddled after him.

Chapter Sixty-Two

Reineke smoked his cigarette, gazing out the French windows of his library. "It is a good idea," he acknowledged Pierre's plan to reinstate the Arab encampment at Linke's camp for the woman to remember.

Pierre smiled in his seat at the front of the desk. "Thank you, mon capitaine, I had to think of something."

Indeed. The woman attacking his office was an exaggeration. Meat packaged in a napkin on his desk, and yes, the paybooks of his soldiers currently out of the compound. It was the pathos of the packaged meat that affected him. Field rations for her journey. Reineke turned around, picking up the packet to drop it back down. "What was she thinking?" he asked. "A packet of meat for a twelve-hundred kilometer trip?"

"She is thinking, mon capitaine," Pierre underscored his point.

"Yes, yes," Reineke understood. The natural evolution of her plight as her mind continued to clear and her strength continued to return and screams turned to curses and threats, and then into thoughts, and now into action.

"She will continue, mon capitaine," Pierre said. "Her thinking becoming more logical, her assessments and realizations and plans, more refined."

"This is desperation not logic," Reineke waved the paybooks before tossing them into the drawer. "Indeed," he said, "this is our fault. We are doing this to her. Yes, prisoners evolve—or decline," he agree as that was more in line with the reality. Little by little until their spirit was broken, turning supermen into gelatin.

"She is not a prisoner," Pierre said.

"My point," Reineke assured. "We are doing this to her. On one hand we are encouraging her to think, to regain her strength, and then we lock her in a room where what is she going to think? Except how to get out? What she will need to get out, what she will need once she is out?" He picked up the meat again, dropping it back down. "How does she know how long her journey is, if it is fifteen-hundred kilometers, or down the street."

He sat down with another wave of his hand, clearing the air like a medicine man, wiping away the evil spirits and negative tension. "It is all right. I am not upset, I am disappointed. Indeed, I am disappointed in us," he assured. "Someone needs to talk to her, not play games, enticing her with this, confusing her with that.

"It is all right," he said again, "I am disappointed. I thought we were reaching her, not only her reaching us." He paused. "I tried," he said. "Indeed. I thought it was ... reasonable," he considered, thinking of the conversations. "Not too bad for the first time, not quite so afraid."

Pierre frowned. "Pardon?"

"Talked to her," Reineke waved, massaging his stressed forehead and mind. "I talked to her. I ..." he looked up at the Holy Man looking at him with a look Reineke was not certain of, its meaning or intent.

"Indeed, I talked to her," Reineke said. "You do not seem to understand the difference between when you are here and when you are not. No one is in there with her when you are not here. Talking to her at her breakfast or dinner, fixing her head or there to answer some cry in the middle of the night. She is alone and I do not have the time or interest in answering every thrown statue—or escape attempts with packages of meat." He pushed it away. "I must be able to trust she thinks when she thinks, before she acts or does.

"And so I talked to her, yes," he assured Pierre, "about that very thing. I thought I was reaching her," he considered the conversations again. "Indeed. I thought she was understanding. She seemed to understand, perhaps not all, but enough."

"That was a very good idea, mon capitaine," Pierre agreed.

It seemed like a good idea perhaps. Sounded like one. But there are ideas and then there is actual. Results.

"Diana is not going to agree with this," Reineke shook his head.

"I will tell Diana it is your idea," Pierre proposed with a shrug. "She will have to agree. She will," he smiled, "have no choice."

"That is true," Reineke said. "Yes. But I do not wish to provoke Diana. Indeed," he rose for the windows and the outside world. "I have enough things to think about and do without provoking Diana."

"She will understand," Pierre shook his head with a promise. "Diana knows Mademoiselle's world, what she sees, what she knows, has been very controlled. Confusing, perhaps, oui, of course, a little," he agreed, "but not to confuse her as much to protect her."

"And us," Reineke nodded. "Protect us. I am thinking of us," he assured. "Indeed, of all of us. Myself, Diana, and you, the children."

"I will tell her that," Pierre assured.

"I know." Reineke turned around. "I wanted the encampment for this very same reason, a façade for the onlooker out there, any onlooker out there. The same as it is here in camp. Arabs. That is what you see. Arabs."

"Oui, mon capitaine," Pierre said. "An excellent idea.

"We still have it," Reineke considered, "perhaps not the stage, but the horses. Arabs together with the French will be sufficient to seduce my Colonel or anyone else. The woman seen with Arabs. The SS killed by French. There will be no questions. No," he said. "No, I have to think about this. I am not prepared."

"Mon capitaine ..." Pierre said.

"I said I have to think!" Reineke snapped.

"Oui, mon capitaine."

"Thank you." Reineke sat down to crush his cigarette, rub his forehead again. "What time were you thinking of leaving with the woman?"

"Late?" Pierre said. "Perhaps midnight? It is up to you."

"No, night is good," Reineke nodded. "Yes, very good ..." he checked his watch. "Who will stay with the children if you were to leave tonight?"

"Hanuk," Pierre shrugged.

"No, Hanuk is going," Reineke shook his head.

"Hanuk has always been going, mon capitaine."

"Now," Reineke said. "Hanuk is going now."

"That might be difficult, mon capitaine," Pierre said thinking and watching as he thought. "I was thinking Abraham ..."

"Yes," Reineke nodded.

"And Martin ..." Pierre said. "For the driver of the trucks with the tents ..."

Reineke understood what trucks. "Martin?" he said. "The lawyer? Why not the dentist? No, I would prefer the dentist Haas. John."

"The uniform, mon capitaine," Pierre explained. "I was trying to think. Martin would be closer to your lieutenant's size."

"Oh," Reineke frowned. "Diana has no uniforms?"

"Pieces perhaps," Pierre imagined. "Different kinds. For clothes though, mon capitaine, not disguise. Disguise is Arab, nomad, Berber. Like here."

"Diana should have uniforms," Reineke nodded. "That has been one of the biggest inconveniences. Even the horses were easier than the clothes."

"Oui, mon capitaine."

"All right, and Hanuk," Reineke agreed. "You are right. John has no uniform to fit ... I cannot think of one ..." he shook his head, trying to.

"And I was thinking Jacob ..." Pierre said.

"Jacob?" Reineke reared. "To protect the woman?"

"But you are right," Pierre quickly agreed. "It should be Hanuk. John can bring Jacob when he leaves. Until then, Jacob can stay with the children."

"Indeed," Reineke said, "you will be on the sea with twenty men for three days. It is Abraham and Hanuk. And, yes, the lawyer Martin."

"Oui, mon capitaine," Pierre nodded. "And on the road for four."

"I am talking about the sea!" Reineke assured.

"Oui, mon capitaine," Pierre sighed.

"The woman is not going to survive on the sea three days, it is to be shorter!" Reineke snatched open his left-hand top drawer, pulling out his keys and the maps. Had the woman looked in it she would have had found her way out, at least the library until stopped by one of the sentries at the door.

At least by the patrol if she happened to make it to the outside. Though who knew, the Holy Man came and went as he pleased. The cook downstairs who sent the woman her lunch causing all of this, had clearly forgotten no one did anything unless so ordered.

"Mon capitaine ..." Pierre shook his head again at the unsecured drawer.

"No one looks on the left," Reineke assured.

"Oui, mon capitaine."

"Yes, oui," Reineke looked through his keys. "I will be right back with Sergeant Erich's uniforms after I radio the convoy and tell them where to halt—"

"Sergeant Erich?" Pierre said.

"He will not be needing them," Reineke assured.

"Oui, I know. I was thinking though of mon capitaine's Lieutenant Thiele."

"Thiele?" Reineke said. "The lawyer Haas will not fit Thiele's uniform. It will be too short for him."

"I was thinking for the patches? His rank?"

"An officer," Reineke said. "Indeed, yes," he liked that. "A very good idea. I will bring you one of Thiele's."

"Thank you, mon capitaine. And then the papers for Martin?"

"Yes, yes, the papers," Reineke said. "I will take care of the papers—and then I have to go," he tapped on his watch. "You see the time? It will be dark by the time I am back from the temple with the woman. I cannot send my car to the other side, I have to do it."

"She could come back with Anne," Pierre shrugged, "and the other little children you left there."

"And who is going to tell her?" Reineke said. "You think that is something she is going to think of herself? A woman who wraps meat in a napkin for a two-thousand kilometer stroll?"

A stroll that got longer the longer they spoke. "Radio Diana," Pierre suggested. "Tell her there are children at the temple ... if she does not already know," he said. "They cannot stay either. They cannot come down the rocks."

"I am not concerned about the children," Reineke wrestled with his keys. "They at least know the way."

"Pardon?" Pierre said.

"You know what I mean," Reineke said.

"No," Pierre assured. "No, mon capitaine. I do not. You are bringing my children back whom you have abandoned on the rocks!"

"Of course I am getting the children!" Reineke gave up on the keys and grabbed up the ring of them. "Go to the children's camp and send Hanuk for them now while I am calling the convoy. I will get the woman—she will not go with him anyway," he shook his head, knowing that. "I will get her after I am finished with all of this—if she is even still there!" he slammed out of his library.

"Not bad," Pierre was satisfied, confident Diana would agree to the change from Jacob to Hanuk. Jacob did not have the experience of Hanuk should they encounter unanticipated problems on the sea or the road for the next week or so.

He rose to head for the children's camp and have Hanuk secure the children stranded on the rocks, wondering if the woman would ask or demand to leave with them, and if not, why not.

"It will work, mon capitaine," Pierre promised as he gathered up the uniforms and papers for Martin Reineke brought when he returned.

"Yes." Reineke was back to looking out the French windows where he could see the Holy Man's reflection in the glass. "That is all right, I will take them."

"I am fine," Pierre assured, "I am going to give them to Anne. Mirabella is waiting to fix them."

"I will bring them to Diana for Mirabella. I have to get the woman, anyway ..." Reineke turned around. "You see? I told you. One hour until sunset and soon dark—black as night on the rocks."

"The moon is almost full and it is always dark at night, mon capitaine," Pierre smiled.

"No jokes," Reineke requested. "I will take them. I want to talk to Diana—indeed, there is no time to panic," he assured.

"I am not panicking," Pierre shook his head.

"Or argue," Reineke silenced him.

"Oui," Pierre said.

"I am confident Diana will listen. I will explain your plan and how I agree with it."

"Oui," Pierre said.

"Then what is wrong with you?" Reineke asked irritably. "Why are you standing there?"

"Nothing, mon capitaine. I need to also get something from

Diana ... but it is all right," he said. "We can go together. You can take me to Diana, and go get the woman and come back for me."

"What?" Reineke said.

"You can still explain your plan, mon capitaine," he assured. "Do not worry. I will not tell her. I will leave that to you."

"I cannot bring the woman to Diana!"

"Oh," Pierre said. "Well, yes, that is true."

"Indeed," Reineke took the uniforms away from him. "One would think it was you who is not prepared."

"You are prepared, mon capitaine."

"For the woman to leave in the middle of the night to die on the sea?" Reineke said. "You have a different idea of prepared than I."

"It will be fine. She will be with me, and, oui, Abraham. A doctor himself."

"What is this you need from Diana?"

"It can wait. Do not worry."

"You will not be here."

"Oh," Pierre said. "That is true. All right, Martin can bring it when he comes."

"Martin will be with the trucks. He is not coming here, he is going to the yard. Holy Man!" Reineke warned because it was not too difficult to figure out the priest was up to something, withholding something. "What do you want from Diana?"

"A little something to help Mademoiselle sleep?"

"What?" Reineke said. "No. Drugs?" he said. "No."

"Mon capitaine ..."

"No!" Reineke threw down the uniforms and stupid papers, heading for the wine cabinet.

"Oui, that is an excellent idea," Pierre agreed. "A toast. We should toast to the beginning and to success, and then toast at the end to the end and success."

"Indeed," Reineke should just ignore him, pretend he did not hear him and not bring two glasses, but he did not. He brought two, banging them down on the desk, watching the Holy Man as he uncorked the wine. "Think of something else."

"Such as?" Pierre said.

How did Reineke know? He had no experience with any of this.

"Are you thinking of this woman's comfort at all? And you wonder why she is packing lunches and threatening to jump off the balcony?"

Pierre gasped "Threatened to jump off the balcony?"

"Answer the question!" Reineke insisted.

"Oui, of course I am thinking of it," Pierre assured. "I am thinking, mon capitaine, it might be easier for her to be asleep than to carry her screaming from the house and away in a car, having no idea where she is going and being terrified—"

"All right," Reineke said.

"And no matter what you say—" Pierre shook his head.

"I said all right!" Reineke said. He poured the wine.

"Thank you, mon capitaine," Pierre accepted his glass. "Did Mademoiselle really threaten to jump off the balcony?"

"No," Reineke said. "She talked about it, yes, but no, she did not threaten."

"Oh, oui," Pierre agreed. "She has talked about it before. But I do not think she would do it."

"No, of course she would not do it," Reineke assured. "Indeed, I do not wish to talk about the woman anymore."

"No, I know," Pierre understood. "You have a headache."

He did, and he should be glad it was leaving.

"To what do we toast, mon capitaine?" Pierre asked, happily.

"To the children," Reineke said. "Indeed, it is for the children."

"I know," Pierre smiled. "To the children then, mon capitaine," he held out his glass.

"Indeed," Reineke said, and their glasses clinked.

"Liar!" Pierre laughed as Reineke took his drink his teeth striking the rim of his crystal glass at the Holy Man's taunt. "Mon capitaine is such a liar," Pierre clucked. "But that is all right, because he is also a very good man."

Reineke drove to Diana's town, rehearsing what he would say to her. There was not much time to argue if the woman was to leave tonight with sufficient time to reach the sea before the intense heat that would settle in by mid-morning.

"Ma," Jacob, her youngest called for Anna's attention as Reineke's car pulled in down below at the rocks before the narrow climb to her terraced marble shell.

"I will take care of it," she stopped Martin. "Get the chairs and table ready. And, you," she told Jacob, "go get some wine."

"Is that really necessary?" John asked, so full of questions he had never asked before. So in the foreground he had shunned.

"Yes," Anna assured, "it is called diplomacy. Come on," she took Abraham and John with her since Dieter had apparently decided to adopt two of her sons as brothers, not just the one, Abraham.

Dieter was carrying the uniforms, a good sign, as he climbed the rocks, looking up slightly startled to see her standing there, and that was just typical. Of course, she would be standing there. Of course someone had seen the headlights coming even if it hadn't been her.

"What's all this?" she smiled as Reineke stepped up. "A little late for a visit, isn't it? What's wrong? Is something wrong?"

"No," Reineke assured. "I want to speak to you. I have made a few necessary adjustments to the plan."

"Oh," Anna said. "All right. Have you heard from your reconnaissance? Because the Holy Man's son has not yet radioed—do you want to sit?" she asked. "Have some wine? Of course you do," she agreed before he answered, calling for Martin to bring chairs and Jacob to bring her the wine she had up there. "And a glass for Dieter," she assured, "in case he changes his mind."

He changed his mind, having a glass of wine, and though he sat, he walked mostly as he usually did, smoking, talking, still thinking it through himself.

"Indeed," he said as he sat down, a signal he was finished, had made his decision, "I had to think of something. The woman rifled my office. She rifled my desk."

"Yes," Anna had to agree how that was not the best news. "And it will get worse. She is half-prisoner, half-guest. Neither wants to stay. Not good. It does not work that way. One is either a slave, or one is free. Keep it in mind," she smiled, "for the next time."

"Indeed," Reineke said. "I will shoot myself next time."

"Who won't?" Anna laughed. "May I?"

"Yes, of course," he handed her the uniforms and papers.

"Infantry," she approved, looking it over, and it was not too worn and not too new. Perfect. "Very nice. Very common, nothing exotic ... is this one of Thiele's?" she asked noting the rank.

"Yes," he said. "A sergeant, of course, would suffice, but I prefer an officer. The uniform is for size, fit. You can promote it to Thiele's rank."

"Yes," Anna nodded. "Yes ... but still I don't know. Who are you thinking of for the squad leader? John? I am not sure this is going to fit John ... but maybe ..."

"No, Martin," he stopped her, probably good because John did not look like he wanted to play.

"Oh," Anna said. "Well, yes, definitely then. It will work ... who else?" she asked with a smile. "I mean other than Abraham. No question Abraham would be a village assistant to the Holy Man. Jacob?"

"Hanuk," Reineke assured.

"Really ..." Anna said, pretty sure John enjoyed that, if he wasn't enjoying too much else. "Why Hanuk instead of Jacob, or does it matter?"

"Experience," Reineke said. "They will be on the sea three days and the roads another four."

"Experience ..." Anna opened her mouth and closed it, thinking about that. "That's actually very true."

"Then are we in agreement?" Reineke asked.

"Now?" Anna said. "You want an answer now? Can I think?"

"Indeed, quickly, if it is to happen tonight," Reineke said.

"All right ... all right." Anna chose to gaze at Abraham, count the number of pinholes in his forehead, and decide when she got to the end. It would be about the right amount of time without appearing too anxious. Dieter such an impatient man. Taking hours to decide something himself but giving the other person ten minutes. She wondered what her reaction would have been if this were his plan instead of her own being recited back to her.

"Have you radioed the convoy with the horses?" she asked, deciding to make Dieter sweat a little longer. After all, she did not want to set a precedent of having him expect the same immediate response the next time he came and asked her something ludicrous.

"Yes," he said, and so there was at least one honest crumb

between the two of them, except for, of course, that it was a lovely evening to sit out and drink wine with a handsome young man.

Anna nodded about contacting the convoy. "Reasonable. I could say yes, and it not too difficult to call them back if I change my mind and say no?"

Abraham shifted his feet, a cue she was starting to push it.

"All right," she turned back to Reineke. "I guess, what I want to know is, are you comfortable with your plan, Dieter? It is a very good idea. Best for all of us, I believe. But are you comfortable, Dieter?" she asked. "If you are, I say yes, and leave it up to you."

He looked off for a moment or two before his eyes turned back, and she noticed how he did not say the word 'Yes', though he was apparently in agreement with the plan. "Have Martin go up the road and come back down through the north," he instructed.

Anna nodded. "That makes sense. You will pass him? You have notified your men?"

"Of course," Reineke dismissed.

"Of course," Anna smiled. "A silly question, but what can I say? I am a mother. Anything else? When do you want them? It's going to be what ... an hour to fix the uniform, maybe ninety minutes?". Hanuk is at the children's village ... if not, we'll find him and make sure he is there at the villa—do not worry. He is young. He'll be there in time. Abraham, should also leave now to ensure he is ready when you are—what about the Holy Man?" she interjected, realizing she had not asked, and that was probably not good. More himself, Dieter would have noticed. He wasn't himself. He was quiet. Looked tired. Perhaps his conscience was hurting a little more than he had anticipated. It is never easy to betray your own, regardless.

"Indeed," Reineke sighed, and rolled his eyes, downing his wine, as he rose, checking his watch. Now that was more like him except for the wine. Dieter sipped wine he did not guzzle it. "The Holy Man thinks the woman will fling herself from the balcony if she stays another day."

"Eh ..." Anna considered, "It is what girls do ... but, no," she assured as Reineke blinked. "I do not think so. No one is hurting her, we just ... well ... we confuse her," she rose. "It would probably be less confusing to her if someone did hurt her as she anticipates—

anticipation," she eyed John, "is the true stressor ... do you want Abraham to go with you now? He might as well."

"No, I still have to secure the woman," Reineke explained.

"Oh ... all right," Anna did not know what he meant, but why would she? Why would she be thinking of swimming pools? "Wait a minute, though, I'll get you something ..." she called again to Jacob, asking him to bring down her bag.

"I was working on the inventory for the hospital," she explained as Reineke stared at the black satchel handed to him. "That's all right, you can take it. Give it to the Holy Man. He will secure it after he takes what he needs for her trip."

"Indeed," Reineke said. "Should you give me what he needs? The woman is to sleep for the trip to the sea, not the rest of her life."

So the Holy Man had chosen not risk telling him the woman would be sleeping a lot. "Me?" Anna said. "How could I tell him?"

"How could you?" Reineke repeated.

He's starting to get nervous ... Anna could feel Abraham trying to communicate through the third eye in the middle of his forehead. "Because, Dieter, I don't know what he needs," she said. "The Holy Man should know that. Did she eat today? When did she eat? How much did she eat?"

"Oh," Reineke said. "Indeed, I have no idea what the woman ate today, if she ate anything. Her meat she had packaged for her trip."

"Well, I would tell the Holy Man that," Anna suggested, "and give him the bag. Do not be concerned. He knows what to do."

"All right," Reineke said. "Yes, all right. I have to go—Indeed," he assured as he thanked her for the wine, "the woman will kill herself on the rocks in the dark if she has not already done so."

He took the bag and left, down the narrow path for his car leaving Anna to mull that over.

"Kill herself on the rocks ..." Anna poured herself another glass of wine with a wave at Abraham. "Go before he forgets he's taking you."

Abraham left, fast enough to catch Dieter as Anna sipped her wine. "Kill herself on the rocks ..." she shook her head with a call to Martin to come get his uniform and get it to the girls to fix for him, quickly, if it took three of them. Martin came down to collect it and by that time, Abraham was climbing back up.

"OK ..." Anna said because from where she sat, Abraham should have caught Dieter. "I give up," she surrendered. "I have no idea."

"The girl's at the pool," Abraham nodded. "Dieter has gone to collect her."

"Pool?" Anna frowned.

"Diana's Temple. I'll meet him at the compound. I just came back for my cigarettes."

"Oh," Anna said.

"It's fine," Abraham assured "Everything is fine."

"Oh, I know," Anna agreed. "But, you know, you are going to have to walk because Martin needs the wagen and the other one is with Hanuk at the children's village—that's the one without my big statue," she confirmed for him in case he was unsure he went there so infrequently. "Eight kilometers."

"I can walk," Abraham gave her a kiss in retaliation. "I am not the Holy Man yet." He collected his cigarettes and jumped down the path, off on a fast trot for the compound.

John was still there as Anna sipped her wine. "It's a little early for a midnight swim," she mentioned.

He did not answer her and so she guessed he was really mad for some reason. She waited him out. It did not take long.

"Did you really have to do that?" he asked.

"Do what? Please," Anna scoffed. "Dieter told as many lies as me. It's not his idea it's mine. I am sitting there listening to my own idea. But, what are you going to do," she shrugged. "It's how it is. The way it works."

John did not answer her again and she was admittedly curious.

"Besides," she said, "since when have you been considerate of Germans?"

She was sorry as soon as she said it. It was cruel, to her son, herself, and certainly her daughter for invoking her memory.

"At least Dieter is sincere," John said. "He did not know it was your idea, he thought it was Pierre's. At least he came here to speak with you about it. He did not send Pierre as his mouthpiece—like you did for yours."

"All right, all right, all right," Anna waved. "But it was still the

Holy Man's idea as far as Dieter knew and he did not say that, he said it was his—all right!" she said before John countered with something else. "I'm sorry. I should not have said that, invoking Hannah. Yes, Dieter is sincere. He is very sincere. A very sincere, fascinating, and intriguing man ... and it is still a little early for a midnight swim!" she insisted.

"Well, that ..." John said.

"Yes, that," Anna nodded. "That."

"Well, that's just boredom," John said.

"Boredom?" Anna said. "Boredom?" she almost choked to death on her cigarette.

"All right, Ma," John said. "Please. Put it to bed. She's kind of young for him, don't you think?"

"She is way too young for him or anyone—including Hanuk," Anna assured. "But, fine. You're right. The girl is leaving—not too soon," she pointed at him, "But, yes, you are right. I am not concerned. I trust Dieter. I like Dieter. I like him very much. I do.

"And, yes," she said, "when it has to happen, I will miss him. I will. Life is shit," she shook her head as John walked away. "It is shit."

He was not a liar. It was for the children. Reineke did not have to convince anyone, not even himself as he stood there looking at the woman. An interesting and unexpected distraction. Temporary. Pretty. How strange it was to notice that now. Ridiculous, since she was leaving. She should have seen to being pretty on the day she came. He would have been much more comfortable if she had seen to being pretty then, instead of waiting until now.

"Indeed," Reineke dallied where he did not need to be. He should have told Hanuk to bring the woman back if he had to carry her, even if she screamed. "No," he knew that. She would have frightened the children. Upset Anne.

He could have radioed Diana and told her the Holy Man had brought the woman to the pool and to please have someone bring her back. It did not have to be him. It should not be him. He was still trapped in the aroma of Cäcilie, and it was unwise.

"Indeed," Reineke said. It was dark out there, across the fractured and broken footprints of the oasis to the other side, the air chilly, the half-moon bright, shining milky white light. He could not see the woman's bruises from where he stood, or where her hair grew in funny red bristles covering the wounded side of her head. He could only see a very small woman standing on a patch of ground staring up into the night sky, and he never should have drunk the wine.

"Indeed," Reineke whispered and took a step forward, the woman's head coming down from staring at the stars to gaze at him.

Why *NOW* was he angry at her? Joanna blinked at the Captain's contorted expression. She had been out there for hours. Alone out there for hours as one by one people came to take the children and babies away until the witch's handsome brother came and took the last of them, never asking if she might want to go with him.

Not that Joanna wanted to go with him, or any of them, because she certainly did not. She wanted only Pierre. Something she told that horrible ugly Anne who was the last one to leave with her handsome brother. Casually mentioning to Anne, "Is Pierre ever coming back? Where?" she asked, though not to suggest she was afraid to stay out there. "Where is Pierre? When will he return?"

Anne shrugged. "If the Holy Man has said he will return, he will."

"Before dark?" Joanna sought a few specifics.

It would soon be dark was Anne's disheartening reply before she left reiterating that if Pierre had said he would return, he would return, though probably not before dark.

"Oh," Joanna said. It was at least an hour into dark before Pierre returned, and it was not Pierre at all, but the Captain, angry about something, she suspected the bit about her escape and his desk.

Joanna wrapped her arms around herself, hugging her shirt very tightly as he crept up to her. "It's cold out here?" she suggested as a reason for something, anything, including his frozen stare.

He said nothing.

"It's nice though," she nodded in case his opinion differed from hers. "Oh, yes, I think it's quite nice. Though, I do think it is rather cold out here."

It sounded like he mumbled something but a breeze came by and took his words away, and so Joanna wasn't sure. He was at least twenty-feet away from her, though coming closer with each step.

He was only about six-feet away from her when she saw him

raise his arm, his hand reaching out and she gasped because certainly he wasn't thinking of striking her because she said it was cold. "Maybe it isn't cold!" Joanna nodded wildly. "I mean, perhaps it's not cold at all.

"And just because it's cold," she nodded, "doesn't mean it's not pretty. Because it is really very pretty out here. Oh, yes, I think it's quite pretty out here," she assured, "not frightening at all."

So did Reineke think it was very pretty out there. It was more than pretty out there. And if the woman was going to make him walk the entire distance for her instead of starting to meet him half way, she was going to find out just how pretty it was out there. There was a strange yellow grass that grew on the far side of the pool. The ground was soft, and he was beginning to feel pleased he had drunk the wine.

"Indeed," Reineke said. It was delightfully cool out there, and he could think of several interesting ways of keeping warm. She was such a pretty, little woman whose name was not Cäcilie.

"Indeed," Reineke whispered, no breeze happening by to whisk that word away. Joanna heard him very clearly, and there were a hundred different words, a hundred different thoughts, suggestions, all wrapped up in that one word that did not sound angry. He was three feet away from her and then only two.

He was at best six inches away from her and his hand coming toward her no longer looked like it was going to strike her. This man was not angry with her, not in the least.

"Come here," the Captain whispered, murmured, actually.

Only Joanna could not do that because if she did, as close as he was to her, she'd be right on top of him. Pressed up tight against him, with a little luck clean through to the other side of him.

"I!" Joanna stammered.

"Come here," he said, and she knew his hand was going to touch her shoulder, or perhaps her elbow, or maybe her hair.

"Oh, my," Joanna swallowed. "Oh, my!" she said, frozen, staring up at him because his head was coming down, those strange blue eyes were starting to close—this man was going to kiss her!

"Oh, my God!" Joanna closed her eyes and stood there thinking all kinds of things, some of them rather embarrassing including what might it be like to kiss such a handsome man back. She felt him grasp her elbow and she heard him say rather impatiently, “Indeed, if you are cold, Fräulein, why are you continuing to stand there?”

“What?” Joanna opened her eyes.

“Indeed,” he said. “It is extremely late.”

And he did not release her arm until he brought her across the rocks to his car. He ordered her into the front seat, pulled a jacket from the back, insisting she put it on. They rode the entire bumpy ride not talking, and he was five steps ahead of her as she followed him up the stairs.

Chapter Sixty-Three

Joanna was as nervous as any cat. The Captain kept pushing up his sleeve, glaring at his watch, up and down out of his chair like some confused Jack-in-the-box, hands in his pockets, walking back and forth from the desk to the balcony. Finally, he stayed down, drumming his fingers on his desktop, announcing she would have a glass of wine.

Joanna did not want a glass of wine. Wine gave her a headache. She sat there holding her cup filled with syrupy red fluid that smelled like cough medicine to her.

"Indeed, drink your wine, Fräulein," Reineke said roughly. "It will help you to sleep."

Now that sounded like a wonderful idea, except for the part about the wine. "But I don't like wine," she said.

"Drink it!" Reineke insisted. "Before you are sick with cold or fever."

"Fine." Joanna grimaced once more at the cup, squinted her eyes shut and swallowed the whole thing down in a series of gulps. It tasted horrible.

"Indeed," Reineke blinked wondering if perhaps they should have only used the wine.

"There," Joanna set the glass down on the desk. "May I go to bed now, please?"

"In a little while," Reineke said, "you must relax."

"Why?" she asked with perhaps a slight slur, or perhaps it was his imagination. The woman had drunk an entire glass of wine like a man dying of thirst would drink water. He watched her closely, but she seemed fine.

"Why am I sitting here?" Joanna asked.

"We are waiting for the Holy Man," Reineke checked his watch.

"Oh," Joanna said. "Oh, all right." Her words definitely not slurred. He poured another glass of wine, and Joanna groaned.

"No, I don't want it," she said.

"Indeed, you are to do what the Holy Man has asked," Reineke extended the glass to her, "and drink it properly this time before you upset your digestion. Wine is sipped. You are supposed to enjoy wine."

"But I don't enjoy it," Joanna took it, drinking it slower as he asked, and it still tasted terrible, even worse. She couldn't possibly finish it. "I can't finish this," she set the glass down on the desk. "I'm sorry, but I can't. But you're right, I don't feel right."

"Indeed," Reineke stood up.

"No, it's all right," Joanna shook her head and she probably should not have done that because when she did she suddenly felt dizzy. "I think ..." she said and realized she was looking down on his feet which made no sense unless he had come around. "Captain?" she tried to look up, and yes, he was there.

"Relax," she heard him say.

"What?" Joanna said.

"Indeed, relax, Johanna," he said.

What? Joanna tried to say, but couldn't. When she tried to get up because it did seem like something was very wrong, she could not do that either. "Cap ..." she managed, felt her head tip back and then nothing, just nothing.

Reineke caught her before she toppled out of the chair onto the floor and she was perched safely on the edge of his desk, her body limp. He laid her down so he could button her up inside her jacket. The Holy Man came in from the shadows, but he was not speaking to the Holy Man. It had taken too long. The woman was confused. Her face, frightened. She knew something was wrong.

"Indeed," Reineke seethed, "your sedatives are stale. It should not have taken this long."

"No," Pierre shook his head. "Sometimes when a person is excited it can take a moment or two longer. You did not need—"

"Go and get a long coat!" Reineke snapped, finished with talking with him except to tell him that. The ends of the woman's hair were wet, her blouse damp. He discovered this as he tried to bind her up inside her jacket, unbuttoning what he had just buttoned to tuck her hair inside and start again. Little wonder she had complained so loudly how she was cold. Who would splash around in a puddle in the middle of a desert night, and not expect to be cold?

"Oui, mon capitaine," Pierre toddled away to find a greatcoat.

"And where are her things?" Reineke demanded as he wrapped her up in the coat, the collar pulled up around her ears, trying to smooth the stubborn strands of her hair clinging to her face. It was reminiscent of the cellar and he stopped.

"Well?" he said.

"Right here, mon capitaine," Pierre held out the light canvas bag.

"All right, go," Reineke nodded.

"Oui," Pierre trotted to the door.

Reineke carefully picked her up, carrying her from the villa, his driver obligingly stepping out, and opening the rear door of the car when he appeared on the outside steps. Pierre climbed in and Reineke laid the woman to rest at his side.

"It is cold," Reineke reminded in an order to the Holy Man straightening her coat to leave the buttons alone.

"Oui. Mademoiselle is fortunate she will not feel this."

"You are to ride all night and into the dawn, only," Reineke nodded. "It you have not made your rendezvous with the convoy you are to stop and pitch. The other horses will come to you—"

"And, camels, oui," Pierre nodded. "yes."

"Camels?" Reineke said.

"To cross the sea, mon capitaine," he smiled. "It will be easier for Mademoiselle on the camel—"

"Easier?" Reineke said. "A woman whose feet do not touch the floor? Easier to ride on a camel than a horse?"

"No one's feet touch the floor on a camel, mon Capitaine. It will be easier for her, yes. The men are stronger, they can steer the horse through the sand. She cannot do that."

"Enough," Reineke ended it. "You are to pitch, and the horses—and camels," he assured, "will come to you. The Oberleutnant Dönitz will contact the convoy who is waiting for his orders—has he left?" he confirmed with his driver.

"Yes, Hauptmann," he pointed at the wall.

"Yes, all right," Reineke could occasionally see the bouncing headlights of the trucks as they climbed the road. "And your assistants?" he said to Pierre. "Where are your assistants?"

"Right here," Pierre clapped his hands, and the two nomads from the village came in from the dark near the porch. The driver startled at the sight of Abraham, but Reineke reassured him of their trusted association with the Holy Man, and while not particularly comfortable when Abraham climbed into the front seat, he obeyed. Hanuk jumped up to ride on the back so not to disturb the girl.

"She is your responsibility," Reineke reinforced one final time before he let them go. "Indeed, I hold you to this responsibility. There may be trouble. Attacks have been renewed on Malta."

"Malta, mon capitaine?" Pierre said.

"Yes!" Reineke assured.

Pierre nodded. "Mademoiselle will be all right. Do not worry."

"Indeed," Reineke was not as certain as the Holy Man. He was testing more than his authority more than a thousand kilometers from there. "I will see you Sunday," he said, aware of how Sunday was seven days from then.

"Or Monday," Pierre agreed, "oui. As will Mademoiselle."

"Indeed," Reineke assured, as would the SS and Erich and the others.

He withdrew from beneath the canvas top of his staff car, and waved his driver on. Diana came down from her throne to sit and talk with him a few hours later at the foot of her Temple.

"I am insane," Reineke admitted. "Quite, quite, insane."

"Intoxicated a little perhaps," Anna helped herself to his offering of grapes.

"Indeed, insane," Reineke shook his head, dangling her sedative in front of her. "Magic sleep."

Anna shrugged and took it away from him to ensure no accidents. "I told him to give her a needle—"

"You told him?" Reineke interjected, and Anna nodded. He was not that intoxicated. Very close to being himself, back to being himself. That was a good sign.

"Always," she assured. "I have always told Pierre that. It would have been instantaneous. I am not surprised he did not listen."

"No. No, I did not want needles," Reineke shook his head. "I do not like needles. Indeed," he said, "the woman had needle marks up one arm and down the other when she came there. She looked like a pin cushion."

"Sodium thiopental?" Anna considered. "That is advanced—and ineffective after a minute or two unless you know what you're doing," she assured. "I use it myself—or I should," she downed her wine. "It must be the German in me. I prefer to torment them."

Reineke laughed, refilling her wine. "You are a sick woman," he assured. "Indeed, as sick as me."

"Salute," Anna's glass clinked his.

The Fezzan
March 30-April 2
Joanna slept for more than twelve hours, waking up with her head in her lap. It was beastly hot.

"Oh, but no, Mademoiselle," Pierre stopped her from pulling off the queer black scarf wrapped around her face. "We will be leaving soon. You must keep the keffiyeh with you. The sun is very hot."

She had to do what? Joanna sat up with a start, much too quickly for her stomach, but that was nothing. She wasn't in her room, or even the library, or any place else she had seen before, but was inside, underneath actually something that looked like a very large kite. The world around her as she looked around looked like scorched egg meringue. "Why, where am I?" she gasped.. "Where on earth am I?"

"North Africa," Pierre smiled. "This is your awning while we wait."

Joanna did not know what to question first. "Wait?" she said.

"Oui," Pierre nodded. "While they take down the tents ... see?" he pointed off. "See the pretty tents? That is where you were. But now you are here waiting, comfortable in the shade, until they are done."

Comfortable? Joanna was dying. Roasting. She could feel the heat inside cooking her.

"No, no, no," Pierre slapped her hands away from pulling at the scarf suffocating her. “You must keep it on. The jacket, too, oui. Until you put on your robe, and then you can take the jacket off and you will see how much cooler the robe is with the air floating around you inside. Until then, I know it is not comfortable, but the sun will burn you right through your shirt. Your skin is much too light for this. Even with your tan, it is much too light.”

“The wine,” Joanna mumbled.

“Pardon?” Pierre cocked an ear.

“The wine,” Joanna pulled the scarf away from her mouth. “He drugged the wine!”

“Mon capitaine?” Pierre said. “No. Pierre did.”

“You?” Joanna stared at him. “But, why?”

Pierre shrugged. “So you would not be frightened. So you would sleep—you slept very well, Mademoiselle,” he nodded. “Pierre is very pleased. A nice long rest, exactly what you needed.”

What she needed? “You drugged me!” Joanna said and could feel tears in her eyes before they quickly started to dry.

“Oh, Mademoiselle,” Pierre said as she bent her head, “do not cry. It is fine.”

“I’m not crying,” Joanna slapped his hands away. “I have a headache. My eyes always tear.”

“Oui,” he said sympathetically, “and you may have one for a while. But it will get better, especially when it starts to cool, you will see. It will cool so quickly you will forget you were hot ...” he laughed, “and then, yes, the sun will rise again like Phoenix and you will forget what it feels like to be cool.”

Joanna did not care about any of that. “Where am I—” she said.

“Here, North Africa,” Pierre said, before she even finished her question, “as I told you. The Sahara.”

“Going!” Joanna finished. “Where am I going?” she said.

“Oh,” Pierre said. “To a new home,” he shrugged. “Oui, a very nice one. So come,” he rose, and held out his hand. “I want you to stand and see how you feel and then we will put on your robe and you will take your jacket off.”

“Wait a minute!” Joanna pushed his hands away from her again. “I can get up myself. I just want to know—”

“Where is the house?” he smiled before she asked. “Many miles behind you, Mademoiselle. As we have many miles to go."

"Go?" Joanna said.

"Oui, Mademoiselle," he nodded. "To your new home."

"Oh," Joanna said. "Well, when am I—"

He did not interrupt her that time and he could have because she did not say it. She did not have to ask when she was going back. She could see the answer in his eyes peering back at her through the funny-looking black mask he was wearing.

"Burnoose!" he pulled back his brown hood to show her the black one he wore underneath. "To protect Pierre from the sun, just like you."

"Let's just go," Joanna got to her feet.

"Mademoiselle ..." he said.

"I'm fine," Joanna assured. "I'm hot. Where's that robe you were talking about?"

"Right here." He produced it proudly though only heaven knew why. It was only a robe. Cooler, Joanna supposed than the jacket when she put it on or maybe not. It was long, and very wide. Almost as if she were a kite that if she were to spread her arms she could fly.

"And, you will see," Pierre promised as he helped her hike the robe up with a sash so she would not trip, "the very special transportation Pierre has arranged for you to cross the dunes.

He could say that again because when Joanna walked out from underneath her awning that was not a car parked waiting it was a camel. A beast quite unlike its pictures and was positively huge, licking and smacking its slobbering jaw.

"I am not getting on that thing!" Joanna gasped.

"Oh, but you are, Mademoiselle," Pierre assured. "And so is Pierre!"

"I'll get sick," Joanna knew she would.

"Oui," Pierre agreed, "possibly. But the camel will not care."

Bully for the damn thing. "I am not," Joanna refused, "getting up there."

"Oh, but you are, Mademoiselle. You see all those men?" his arm swept around.

Of course Joanna saw them—now. A line of robed men waiting.

"They are your escort, Mademoiselle, the camel, your carriage.

A gift from Pierre to you!"

"I'll walk," Joanna said.

Pierre laughed. "Oui. To the camel. Because it you do not ... you see the tall man with the tattoos on his face? He will carry you."

"Fine," Joanna marched to the camel not quite able to look the beast in its eyes, but only because she could stand under its belly.

"I have a step for you!" Pierre assured, patting the little red footstool when what she needed was a ladder. "Come on, up. Up!" he encouraged, snapping his fingers for a few of the men to help her.

"Don't touch me!" Joanna's hands connected with one of them lifting her into the air, his brilliantly colored face rubbing off on her hand. "Paint," she stared.

"Oui, of course!" Pierre was hoisted up behind her, wrapping his arms around her waist. "The pagan paints their face, Mademoiselle, did Pierre never tell you this?"

Joanna did not care. Only that it would be interesting to spit in his face to see if his color ran, too.

Joanna stopped marking time on her second day. It was confusing, similar to how it had been early on at the house. She was sick, and Pierre was right, no one cared. Some of the men were sick themselves, Pierre explaining again how it was the heat, though proudly in admiration of them. "Not too many men can do this, Mademoiselle," he advised, "no. It is amazing."

Who cared? Let them try it on a camel, and then they'd see how great they were. The swaying plod of her prehistoric steed rolled like a boat in dock. Joanna was down off the thing vomiting as often as she was on it. The warm, giddy feeling of nausea ever-present and constant, the heat rose from the sand like the opened door of an oven, the sun so bright she was convinced she would go blind. Even in her tent as she lay inside it, a pair of tight goggles strapped around her head the nausea lingered, the camel still swaying.

"No, I can't," Joanna refused the potato pudding stodge Pierre kept trying to force her to eat. "I can't."

On the third day one of the horses fell and had to be shot. She remembered it clearly, the explosion from the gun, but then maybe she didn't. Maybe it was a dream. The camel had picked up speed and was no longer swaying but bouncing her painfully up and down, the seat hard and uncomfortable. The night was wonderful though. Cool and comfortable as she stretched out wanting to stay there but the camel bounced again so hard she was awake, Pierre still sitting there with his bowl of black mush.

"Oh," Joanna said when she realized it was he. "I thought it was the camel."

Pierre chuckled. "The camel? No, it is Pierre. You fell asleep."

"Yes," Joanna said. "I was dreaming ..." she sat up, too fast for the damn nausea, but who cared, she was so thirsty. "Where is the water?" she asked.

"Right here," Pierre handed her a cup. "But not too fast, Mademoiselle, remember you have been sick.

She remembered. "It's still night," she nodded as she drank the water.

"Night?" Pierre said.

Dawn then. Early dawn or early night ... grey ... or dark, actually, not really grey. Joanna shook herself awake. It was the tent. She was in the tent and it wasn't grey or dark. Tightly closed, she could see the shadow of the sun through it and the ropes along the sides like pulls for its heavy cloth draperies. She frowned.

"Mademoiselle?" Pierre said.

"What happened to the tent?" Joanna asked.

"Tent? Oh, no, Mademoiselle," he said, "you are in the truck."

"Truck?" Joanna said.

"Oui. I am sorry, Mademoiselle," he said, "you were sleeping. So tired from the camel, I did not want to wake you."

"Oh," Joanna said.

"Yes," Pierre smiled. "You can go back to sleep if you like. It is still very early."

"All right," Joanna settled back down and Pierre breathed a sigh of relief at Abraham who wasn't concerned.

"Don't worry about it," he shook his head.

"You are sure?" Pierre said.

Yes, Abraham was sure. "She needs food not that stuff. Ma will never know, and if Grandma's boy over here," he flicked his head at Hanuk who grinned, "says anything we will tell Dieter how long he lasted on the back until he made the girl give up her seat."

And that had been once up on the road after climbing the quarry wall. Hanuk slipped down into the backseat, the girl propped up between him and Pierre, her head resting in Hanuk's lap.

"Good," Pierre agreed.

"I knew you would like that," Abraham slid over to check her once he was sure she was back to sleep and she was fine. A little dehydrated, but who wasn't? "It will be a couple of days before she's back to herself," he advised. "And what's she going to see except us? She's in a truck."

"She will want to look out the flap to see what's out there."

"Another truck," Abraham assured.

"That is the point though, isn't it?" Pierre said. "Not to see?"

"Time," Abraham said. "Time is the point and it will be as confused stuffed up inside a truck as it was on the sea. Why? What's the matter?" he asked. "Do you want to sedate her?"

"No," Pierre assured. "I do not want there to be any problems. Not for her, and not for us. As Diana and mon capitaine keep saying they are thinking of all of us. So is Pierre."

"It will be fine," Abraham promised. "She could remember everything but she still has no idea where she is or where she was. Besides," he said, "you should know Ma by now. She will take what she can get. Sedated a couple of days, sick another couple is good enough." He slid back to have a cigarette, something he really wanted after four days pretending to be an Arab.

"And I am not kidding," he assured Hanuk. "Keep it to yourself, or it won't only be Dieter who knows you took her seat, it will be Ma who finds out who took the old guy and the girl over to the Temple. It wasn't Dieter. He was already there with the kids. So I wonder who it was?"

Hanuk shrugged. He was no snitch, he was having fun.

"That's my boy," Abraham patted his nephew's knee. "It's great, isn't it? Some life. I love it. I could do this forever, stay here forever."

"Think we'll make it in time?" Hanuk asked.

"Of course we'll make it," Abraham said. "It can't happen without us. That's the star attraction right over there. We might even make it by Saturday, if the roads stay like this," he agreed, but again, it was not something that concerned him. There were a lot of pieces that needed to come together. Chances were someone was going to arrive early, and another late. But it would come together. None of them were amateurs however much they might fuss, fume, or fret. Not them, Dieter's group, Jean Paul's, and certainly not the SS.

"We'll make it," Abraham promised.

"Good," Hanuk said. "It's fun."

"Especially when you win," Abraham laughed.

Chapter Sixty-Four

The Fezzan, Libya
March 30–April 2

Reineke had two field hospitals planned. One of them as much a blind for the French as it was for the SS. That was the one where the woman would be brought for remand, and a convoy of ambulances would sit and wait. Enough trucks to pacify Thiele expecting the convoys from Tripoli after the business with the SS.

Except the convoys would not come there, but proceed to a different location to be received by Linke. Reineke was not jeopardizing their objective of securing and transporting the munitions from Tripoli because someone in the crowd of the Holy Man's French decided to expand his mission to include Reineke's camp.

Sergeant Linke was the only person apart from Reineke who knew anything about the actual transfer station where the truck convoys would bring the munitions to be unloaded and reloaded onto Linke's convoy of ambulances.

Reineke trusted Thiele and Linke explicitly. It was not a question of trust that prompted Reineke's decision to also temporarily blind Thiele to the full plan. It was merely that above all Reineke trusted Sergeant Linke to simply obey. Linke would not ask questions. He would do what he was told to do and get it done presuming the reasons why he was doing something had been decided by the Hauptmann and Linke did not need to know the reasons. That was not Linke's position.

As First Officer, it was Thiele's position to an extent. As was Thiele, a man who asked questions when he did not quite understand something. Thiele had asked a lot of questions lately.

Troubled by the SS, concerned by the Holy Man's close involvement with the prisoner, and the overall preferential treatment Thiele believed she was receiving from Reineke. Thiele did not want to have those concerns. He wanted to focus on their objective of building their compounds.

Thiele needed to focus only on their objective and cease involving himself in concerns that were not his. Reineke chose to live a schizophrenic existence with his conflicting relationships with the Holy Man Pierre and Diana the doctor Anna Haas. He was not asking Thiele to live the same life. He was asking Thiele to be First Officer of his munitions compound. Thiele had to stop seeking confirmation of his concerns or worse fears, asking questions and then complain about the answers he received. If Thiele did not like the answer, he should not have asked the question. Thiele was an intelligent man. He knew without Reineke telling him his concerns or fears were valid. They were however, also irrelevant. Reineke owed Thiele no explanation. Thiele owed him obedience. Blind obedience.

The expected call from the Holy Man's Algerian connections came early Monday, March 30, providing Reineke with five possible locations for the hospital, and one clear recommendation. Prepared despite claims to the contrary, Reineke left within hours of receiving the awaited communiqué with the remaining ambulances, working during his trek to reach his decision as to where to establish the two hospitals.

German reconnaissance, whether it came from Linke, the German-held garrison town outside his compound, Schönfeld in Algiers, or directly from their contacts in Tripoli, confirmed a sliding scale in the region's stability currently somewhat more unstable than it had been a couple of weeks earlier. Some of the reported increase in hostilities had been intentionally planted by the Holy Man's French as requested, however not all of it. There were distinct pockets either confirmed highly volatile or in their own state of flux.

French reconnaissance positioned Reineke's options around the legitimate areas of concern as best it could, and current reports from Linke, as well as Thiele en route, advised no problems to date. All was quiet, and ultimately Reineke's decision was governed by simple logistics. The transfer station would be established in the area that provided easiest access to the Holy Man's roads south, and the woman's hospital at the site recommended by the Holy Man's French. They were approximately fifty kilometers apart, the woman's hospital slightly less stable than the area of the transfer station. However, her area had been recommended because the Holy Man's French claimed it to be completely under their control, The other four were not.

Reineke was not concerned. Along with his parade of horses, camels, and veiled men, he carried ambulances and two big guns, one of them with Linke. The other behind him at the end of his convoy. He had a dream the second night out about tracks in the sand. He considered it prophetic and made his decision to use the French recommendation for the field hospital.

Consulting his maps, he would keep Linke's interim site for the transfer station for the munitions, fifty kilometers southeast of the hospital, and establish the originally planned Arab camp closer to the field hospital at approximately twenty kilometers due south. The collection of colorful tents covering vehicles and one of the big guns, a squad of ten heavily armed men in uniform, not flowing Arab robes to hinder their movements, would be ready immediately should there be an issue at the hospital.

Linke would keep the bulk of Reineke's forces, and the second big gun with him at the transfer station as planned.

April 1

Reineke contacted Tripoli from the field and gave the order, telling the waiting convoys where to go. They left immediately to begin their trek to the transfer station, with an anticipated arrival late Saturday or early Sunday April 4-April 5.

He contacted Thiele and told him where to establish the hospital, and he contacted the garrison town outside his compound telling them the munitions were expected to arrive late Saturday or early Sunday at the location that was the woman's hospital. He did that to assist in keeping attention solely on the hospital location.

Finally, Reineke sent a message to Algiers and Oberst Schönfeld, notifying him a camp would be established to remand the prisoner to the SS. The date and place not yet forthcoming but would be confirmed in the next few days. Schönfeld assumed it was based on completing the munitions transfer before involving the SS. He had no argument with that.

Hauptmann Eric Danzig assumed the same when apprised by Schönfeld and likewise had no argument.

Algiers, Algeria

"Take care of it." Schönfeld left it in Eric's hands eager to accept, with Eric immediately dispatching two messages to Major Weiheber in Tripoli. One message from Wehrmacht Hauptmann Eric Danzig advising confirmation of the date and place of the prisoner's remand would shortly be forthcoming, and requesting the presence of Weiheber and his squad to secure the prisoner.

The second, from SS Hauptmann Eric Danzig reminding Weiheber of their acquaintance and agreement not to interfere with one another and requesting an opportunity to chat, offering to accompany him from the hospital location back to Tripoli after securing the prisoner from Hauptmann Reineke.

Eric then left Algiers, flying into the Tataouine region of Tunisia to wait himself for confirmation of the camp location.

Tripoli, Libya

April 2

Weiheber sat at his desk in front of the broad windows of his office, the city of Tripoli behind him. He chuckled as he read the wire inviting him to secure his prisoner from Hauptmann Reineke after four long weeks, a Hauptmann Danzig en route to ensure the prisoner's remand.

"Faust," he clicked his intercom calling for his Leutnant Faust, chuckling even harder as he read the second wire he had received from the Propaganda Ministry's representative Hauptmann Danzig, requesting the opportunity to negotiate.

"We have prevailed, Faust," he returned his Leutnant's salute, handing Faust the wire confirming the prisoner's remand. "We have prevailed."

"Excellent, Herr Major!" Faust exclaimed in delight as he read the wire.

"And this," Weiheber waved the second wire, "is even better."

"But what could be better, Herr Major?" Faust beamed, "than securing the physicist's daughter to help pursue our quest in securing him ... Particularly, since," he sneered, "this Oberleutnant Reiss has proved so useless."

"Eh?" Weiheber said. "Who?"

"Of no concern, Herr Major," Faust assured, "little consequence. Merely a useless Russian operant."

"Oh, they are like that," Weiheber nodded, "they are like that. You will find that out, Faust, you will."

"So what is this other good news?" Faust requested.

"Simply this, Faust," Weiheber handed him the second wire.

"Negotiations?" Faust read as Weiheber had read. "For what purpose? For what reasons?"

"Why do you think, eh, Faust?" Weiheber said.

"About ...?" Faust needed a little more information. "This?" he offered the wire.

"The compounds, Faust," Weiheber nodded. "The compounds."

"Of course," Faust agreed. "And it is ridiculous, Herr Major, you are quite right." He handed him back the wire. "You have no obligation to negotiate with this—*Danzig*," he sneered. "I remember him. A fool."

"The Commanding Officer of the compounds?" Weiheber blinked. "Do not be ridiculous, Faust, of course, I do."

"I beg your pardon, Herr Major?" Faust paused. "Is Herr Oberst Schönfeld no longer Commanding Officer? And even still ..."

"Perhaps not negotiate," Weiheber agreed, "but to meet, Faust? To—chat," he snapped the wire, "as Hauptmann Danzig proposes? How will we know about the compounds? How will we secure the information we seek?"

"We know about the compounds, Herr Major," Faust replied. "We have the information."

"Are you so sure, Faust?" Weiheber teased. "Are you?"

Yes, Faust was, but he nodded in agreement as required. "Yes, naturally, Herr Major," he apologized. "What was I thinking?"

"Never mind," Weiheber waved. "You are dismissed."

"Thank you. I will prepare our trip immediately," Faust assured.

"Eh?" Weiheber looked up from reading the wire. "Trip?"

"To secure the prisoner, Herr Major?" Faust said.

"Oh, that," Weiheber waved. "You do not need me for that, Faust. Take a squad and bring her back once you know where and when."

"Excellent, Herr Major," Faust beamed at the privilege and left. "Thank you!"

"Not at all. But this," Weiheber said. "This," he waved the second wire with another laugh. "This I cannot wait to pursue, eh, Faust? The SS Danzig is worried about something, Faust. Concerned. Of what, Faust?" he wondered. "What do you think, Faust? Faust?" he looked around, settling on the closed door, nodding. "Of course, Faust," he said, "Of course," and sighed.

The Fezzan
April 1-2
Sergent Claude L'Heureaux with the Irish sergeant Nellie Reynolds and their band of renegades crossed over into Libya from Algeria days ahead of schedule, marking two-hundred and fifty kilometers south of where the hospital was to be established. Forward scouts reporting a convoy of ambulances north on the same path, they were going to run right up the convoy's ass unless Claude could detour Nellie.

Presuming the convoy to be rear scouts of le Metapel keeping an eye on the road, Claude attempted to raise Jean Paul to alert him to the situation. Increased traffic as they moved north though, he could not raise a clear channel, and Claude turned back to the maps. The Sahara at their feet, the convoy would shortly cross out of the sparsely populated lower altitude, into Tuareg territory along the ancient caravan route. A hundred kilometers north, the path branched off into a spider web of small roads down which the convoy could disappear if only to use the dunes for their cloak, but not here. Here, the convoy had to continue on course or plow its way through the sand. There was no place along the spotty wastelands to hide a convoy, or a small band of Free French. Claude had to either turn his troop into the sand themselves or turn back to get back over into Algeria and quickly.

It was not going to be easy. The Irish sergent moved with the flow of the land and the stars for his compass, his progression steady and natural. He would sense the shift in the land know it was rising even if it did not initially rise high. Land shifts, meant land possibly, a break in the dunes. An oasis, large or small, people and their structures, current or past and abandoned. It meant there might be a road.

Claude should kill the sergent. He had orders to do that if needed. That, too, though was not going to be easy. Jean Paul's men varied in their loyalty to le Metapel from the accepting to the fierce. Claude's staunch and uncompromising loyalty was reserved only for Jean Paul. For the time being Claude hit upon the idea that perhaps it would not be so bad if they stumbled onto the convoy. They would follow it. See where it was going. They wanted to get to the same area anyway, so why not follow the convoy in? It was the same thing as stumbling onto the site as the plan already called for them to do. Did it really matter how Reynolds was led to the site, as long as he was led?

Claude wished he could trust Reynolds would see the logic of tracking the convoy for a few days to confirm what it was and where it was going, but he was not so sure Reynolds would be content with only watching for the next several days. There was also the Germans to consider. Too close and the Germans could spot them. It did not have to be them catching sight of the German convoy. Le Metapel's men did not know they were traveling north in a plot to kill the SS. They would not know the small group of French was friend, not foe.

Claude attempted to raise Jean Paul again but the channels remained congested, traffic out of Tripoli to the north contributing to disrupting the lower bands. He knew he would reach Jean Paul eventually, possibly in the evening when radio communications naturally improved. In the meantime, Claude encouraged they shift back west. Continue their move north through Algeria where the elevation was slightly higher and the dunes broke more frequently against the shores of small oases, the population not quite so sparse or non-existent. People could tell them things, not the sand. What could the sand tell? If it failed there was also the possibility they would not spot the convoy because of the dunes. Such was the desert.

It could pass right by them and they could never see it, not at night and not during the day.

They saw it. Reynolds taking a piss, standing on the top of a dune as if it was a mountain, noticed the line of ants. His eyes were unnatural Claude decided when he heard the call, "Boy," and Claude knew what it was. He had seen it earlier himself, an hour ago as he worked to move them deeper into the dunes, claiming it was a better advantage. It should have been worse, blinding them. It wasn't.

"Where?" Claude looked down on what could be anything kilometers away. A column of men, an impression in the sand, simply the sun. Jean Paul's second Lieutenant Jacques Renault joined him. The two of them stretched out next to Nellie with their binoculars. Urban, from Algiers, Jacques spoke English, and was included in the group so it wasn't only Claude communicating with the sergent.

"That is something," Jacques nodded in agreement, his English halting. "Very good, sergent. Congratulations. We should watch, no?" he checked with Claude. "For a little while? It could be Arabs, it could not."

"Watch," Claude assured, "definitely".

"Aye. Going to have to camp soon," Nellie added, feeling the sun on his back.

"Arabs?" Claude chuckled. "No, sergent. Us, yes. Don't worry. They are much slower than we are. They will be there—if there is anything to be there ..." he pulled the map forward so the sergent could check with him.

"Need to get a little closer before camp," Nellie said.

"We will," Claude promised. "We will."

They did. The convoy broke for camp earlier than Claude would have hoped. They were conservative, concerned with overheating.

Come late afternoon, Claude and his men broke camp at five o'clock, preparing for the night run. The sergent Reynolds sat on his dune with his binoculars. "That's motorized."

"Maybe ..." Claude nodded with a call for Jacques looking at the map. "What do you think?"

"Who knows," Jacques shrugged. "It's probably not."

"Aye, well, let's find out," Nellie picked up his rifle and fired.

"Sergent!" Claude pulled at Nellie's arm, attempting to pull it down. "Are you crazy? You could give away our position!"

Nellie chuckled. "Just making a little noise. Not going to do anything at this distance. Let's see what they do with a little noise."

Thiele and his men heard it, their heads snapping up at a muffled sound, unsure where it came from other than in the distance. Thiele's eyes searched the horizon around them, the lowering sun creating its mirages of water. It appeared pretty flat in their immediate vicinity before the dunes, but who knew. He ordered the men to pick up the pace so they could move, hopefully into an area of high dunes to help protect them before they vanished into the night.

"They're moving," Nellie was up, climbing for his jeep. "Let's go."

"Sergent," Claude caught up with him. "Of course, they are moving. For a couple more hours if they are Arab. The Arab moves from dawn to dusk, sleeping at night. I doubt if they heard the shot. You are right, we need to watch them while we can," he agreed as Nellie eyed him with those marble eyes. "But we will proceed carefully. We don't know who that is, or even what that is yet. We must also think of the men. There are only twenty of us."

"Then let's go," Nellie said, not sure what all the talking was about or why the fellow suddenly seemed a little tame. His marble green eyes narrowed. "Nellie's not losing them in the dark, boy."

And he did not lose them. In a couple of hours, the sun setting, they were practically on top of them. Nellie sat on a dune watching the convoy stop and figures slowly start moving around. There did not seem to be that many of them. Nellie couldn't count much higher than ten but it looked about the same amount of bodies they had, maybe a few less.

"Those are ambulances," Jacques said beside him.

"Is that what that is?" Nellie replied.

"I think so, yes," Jacques said. "It looks like it to me.

"That is ambulances, definitely," Claude assured. "They must be out of Sebha."

"I can't think of anything else," Jacques agreed. "For Tripoli, probably. I'm not sure why they are stopping. Perhaps a flat tire?"

"How so?" Nellie said.

"How so, what?" Jacques said. "Where else would they be going, sergent? You tell me."

"That's Jerry," Nellie assured.

"German patients possibly, sergent, along with Italian," Claude agreed. "But that is International Red Cross. Neutrals. They must be bringing them to the hospital ship."

"Then they won't mind saying hello before they leave," Nellie opened up with his rifle.

The men of the convoy below them heard the gunfire and scattered, diving for the ground and behind the ambulances, as Jacques and Claude screamed at Nellie.

"I told you!" Claude said, Jacques confined to "Jesus Christ! Jesus Christ! You stupid idiot!"

"Just want to see what they're going to do," Nellie chuckled.

"What the hell do you think they're going to do—shit!" Claude ducked as the bullets came flying and he screamed at his men to drop back. 'That is what they are going to do!"

They fell back, out of range except for a determined shot or two from any man who had the better rifle.

"Get aboard, sergent," Claude told Nellie. "Because they are coming up that ridge, you better believe it!"

"That didn't sound much like neutrals to Nellie."

"Go!" Claude ordered the jeeps. "And don't stop until I tell you."

They stopped about twenty kilometers north. Checking his maps again, it seemed to Claude they may be farther away from the site then he had thought they were initially, but he did not care about that. "We need to get back into Algeria," he told Jacques.

"We need to get ahold of Jean Paul!" Jacques assured.

"Yes," Claude agreed, and finally he got a clear channel, the sergent Reynolds asking him what he was doing.

"Seeing if we can get some information on those people. What the hell do you think I am doing, sergent?" he snapped. "That is International Red Cross. Someone out there knows something."

"Those aren't ambulances," Nellie shook his head.

"Those are ambulances, sergent," he assured. "You hear any big guns? No, you heard what we heard. Rifles! They dove under the ambulances, sergent. You think they did that if they had anything in them—except patients, possibly?" he accused. "Transfer to hospital in Tripoli? There could be prisoners in those trucks for all we know. English, Arab—or French!" he assured. "If you think I am letting you kill the French you are as crazy as you are stupid!"

He finished typing his message for Jean Paul, requesting immediate assistance and direction.

The Tell, Algeria
April 2
"*The situation is critical ...*" Cassandra read Claude's communiqué to Jean Paul advising the sighting of a southern convoy and Reynolds's attack. "*Danger to both imminent. Arrival still several days. No heavy equipment. Advise.*"

"Check Claude's coordinates!" she snapped to the men crowding around grabbing for the maps, Louis Forget standing by looking frightened. "Get ahold of the Jew," she directed Janelle. "Ask who this is so deep in the south. See if they know."

"The one John should be here tomorrow," she was told.

"Radio him now!" Cassandra insisted, "and check on the status of Jean Paul." She grabbed the maps to look them over for herself with a shout for Yvette, pushing her way through the stream of men on the ladder to get to the radio platform.

"Claude needs to turn west, into the sand," Yvette advised. "That will slow them down. What is he doing in Libya now?"

"He thinks Libya," Cassandra said, "and he can't. He'll be deeper into the dunes. That will slow them down too much. With jeeps? They'll never make it. They will be late."

"No, here, here," Yvette showed her on the other map where the road in Algeria moved to the Libyan border. "This is where he needs to be. Another forty kilometers north if his coordinates are correct. He should be able to cross over and then continue north until he needs to cross back at Gadames."

"You'll tell him?" Cassandra said.

"I'll tell him," Yvette assured and shoved Janelle aside. "I have this. Wait for the Jew on the other set —and get these men out of here before they collapse the platform. What the hell is the matter with you?" she snatched up the headset to talk Claude out of his predicament.

"You heard her," Cassandra insisted to the group of them, ":get off here! The ladder, too. What?" she snapped at Janelle jumping up for her seat.

"I have the Jew," Janelle nodded. "He says ... rear ... guard. Knock it off," she read from her paper.

"What?" Cassandra said.

"Rear guard knock it off," Janelle shrugged.

"Le Metapel", Cassandra assumed. "Scouts," she rolled her eyes at Yvette tapping her watch. "Tell Claude."

Yvette would. "We might have to wait until *Lili Marléne* is over."

"Keep trying," Cassandra insisted. "You, too," she told Janelle. "Reach Jean Paul."

"I'm trying, I'm trying," Janelle nodded.

"The message has been received," Jacques advised Claude and the sergent Reynolds. "We should know something soon."

"And we are quiet until we know," Claude assured Nellie.

Nellie was quiet. Stayed quiet as they moved along, tracking the convoy ahead of them hoping to disappear into the dunes.

"He's getting nervous," Claude noted to Jacques as they approached the hour mark and the sergent started playing with the radio. "What the hell is taking them so long?"

"*Lili Marléne,"* Jacques said. "She's on now."

"Jesus Christ," Claude said. "How the hell did we even end up in this situation? No one said anything about a rear guard, if that's what it is."

"He saw it," Jacques shrugged. "Whatever it is. You told him Arabs sleep at night so who else can it be? Germans or Italians?"

"Berber," Claude waved. "And some Arabs sleep—sergent!" he barked as the strains of *Lili Marléne* filled the air.

"There's your song, boys," Nellie chuckled. "There she is."

Claude looked at Jacques. "I am going to kill this man simply because I do not like him."

Jacques nodded. "You should probably start asking permission."

"Yes," Claude agreed. "Yes, I should." But first, he pulled his jeep ahead to Nellie's and told him to shut that goddamn thing off.

Nellie did, but found another way to occupy himself when the dunes thinned again. Claude ordered the men to kill the headlights and fall back a little to ensure the convoy did not see them. The leader was undoubtedly keeping a close eye on his surroundings as they moved on, likely a few men posted on top of the trucks.

If there were men posted atop the trucks, it was a bumpy ride. Nellie considered the situation from his perspective. That convoy was moving as fast as it could. Nellie did not know what was in the trucks, but whatever it was, it was not heavy. Nellie decided he wanted to know, and came up with a way without risk to any patients or French or Arab prisoners or whatever the fellows he rode with seemed so concerned about.

"What the hell?" Claude said as Nellie suddenly spun out of line aiming across the sand at high speed straight in the direction of the convoy before the dunes closed around. "Shit!" Claude took off after the sergent with a scream for his men to stay back with no lights. "No lights!" he barked as he headed after Nellie.

Claude could forget about catching him though. Nellie whirled his steering wheel around, keeping the jeep under control. His elbow coming up and knocking the complaining French fellow with him out of the jeep into the sand as it caught him under the chin. It was a wonder it did not take his head off, never mind not break his neck.

Before he stopped, Nellie was reaching in the back and pulling up the French rocket launcher. Up on his feet when the jeep did stop, he aimed and let it go, straight at the open kübelwagen bringing up the rear. And it was a glorious sight to watch those four fellows in their jeep go up like acetylene torches, bright lights in the night sky.

Pity though. It was a pity the fellows never knew what hit them. Nellie liked to hear them scream. And scream the others down there with them did, flew into an absolute panic until they got themselves under control.

"Howl, laddies," Nellie chuckled, standing there with the rocket launcher casually hanging at his side. "That's it, come to ol' Nellie. Now let's see what you have down there for a fight."

Thiele had nothing. What he had he could not use less risk revealing there might be a reason they were out there other than a parade of ambulances. His head whipped around with the deafening explosion in the rear, in time to see the black outlines of the four corpses engulfed in their wave of fire, one of them standing up.

They got themselves under control, quickly. The retaliation nothing to speak of, as well as being a little late because by that time, the attackers were gone.

"Better get back," Nellie suggested to the slack-jawed Claude and the other one, Jacques, parked at his side in shock. "Even though you could be right. That could be ambulances. Have to wait and see what those friends of yours have to say—and don't forget that other fellow out there in the sand," he mentioned, in case they were wondering what had happened to his passenger. "That one who seemed to want to stop Nellie ... don't ever try to stop Nellie," his green eyes smiled at Claude. "Not a smart thing to do."

"Kill him," Claude ordered Jacques as Nellie took off. "Kill him!" he snatched the rifle out of Jacques's hand and took aim. "Let them find his body and mount it on their walls—shit!" he ducked as the bullets rained down.

Claude dropped back into his seat to get the hell out of there, too, headlights bouncing as the jeep bounced, swerving out of the way as the lights caught the figure of his soldier, trying to get to his feet, the man dazed, with a mouthful of blood from his shattered teeth and fractured jaw. They got him aboard and plunged into the dunes.

Claude careened to a halt at a shout from Jacques in the back with the radio.

"I have something ..." Jacques assured as these others stopped and waited for him to work it out. "Confirmed ..." he nodded. "Scheduled transport ... patients," he stared at Nellie. "International Red Cross. Possible prisoners aboard. Do not engage."

“Thank you,” Claude took the communiqué from him and walked up to the sergent Reynolds sitting in his jeep.

“Aye, there you have it,” Nellie agreed with a smile as Claude walked up. “Ambulances.”

“Not just ambulances, sergent, “Claude assured. “Neutrals. International Red Cross as I told you. You could see the flag.”

“Boy,” Nellie told him. “I do not care. They could fly the flag of Éire, I do not care.” Fellows who could not shoot back half straight did not mean anything to Nellie. “They’re just playing with you, boy. Nellie has a feeling, and Nellie does not play.”

The Jacques one stepped up, and he was a little bit small for the size of his jaw. Starting to remind Nellie of someone named Jean Paul even though Jacques was taller. “Neither do we play,” he assured Nellie. “And you put your finger on one more trigger, and I will blow your damn head right off your shoulders.”

“Well, now,” Nellie digested that bit of interesting news. “Will you, boy? And what will you laddies, do?” he looked around. And wouldn’t you know how they backed up this Jacques Renault who suddenly wanted everything done his way.

“And what way is that?” Nellie verified with his smile.

“They also have information of a small convoy approaching from the northeast,” Jacques handed Nellie the wire.”

“Well, come,” Nellie agreed. “Come right on in.”

“And we will know,” Jacques assured, “the nature of that convoy before any action is taken. We do not attack hospitals and neutrals, sergent. Is that clear? Feel free,” he offered, “to contact your Major Charles and ask him any time you like.”

Nellie’s eyes narrowed. “Call Charlie and ask him what? You know something Nellie doesn’t?”

“I know what you know, sergent,” Jacques assured. “You found the convoy, not me. This next one, we are going to find together. Attacks have been renewed against Malta you seem to be forgetting this. It is possible the Italians are preparing for a British retaliatory strike against them.”

“Here?” Nellie said. “Italians, you don’t say.”

“Or Germans!” Jacques snapped. “I am sorry, sergent, are you here to find installations or have your own war? We are not going to have Italians or Germans, pouring down onto our necks over something as stupid as a hospital!"

He walked away, leaving Nellie to sit there and muse over the situation while he reported to Jean Paul: *Situation unstable. Proceeding but unlikely to hold.*

"Well, what are we waiting for?" Nellie asked Claude. "Let's go find those other half-moons."

"Crescent moons, sergent," Claude assured. "Islam. As I told you, and will tell you again, International Red Cross. Neutrals. There are few hospital facilities in North Africa. The Italians and Germans apparently don't see the need. But the people do and so do the soldiers when they scream."

"You say, boy," Nellie agreed. "But Nellie has a feeling, like Nellie told you."

Jean Paul responded with orders to kill once the package was secured. It was only a couple more days and Pierre Forget and another squad of twenty were on their way.

Great Atlas Mountains, Algeria
April 1-2
Hank found himself relieved of his boredom for a short while, taking to the skies as Justin's aerial surveillance substituting for Frank transporting Julia and Mulrooney. Busy combing the area for any sign of the Irish woodsman Nellie Reynolds, Hank caught fragments of a transmission requesting information on scheduled transport of patients to a hospital in Tripoli shortly before he was ready to put down for the night. Hank had no idea what it meant other than someone was asking questions. He continued along his route, but in the morning before takeoff for his first round, he asked Joe, curious if he had picked up on anything.

"Bored already?" Joe moved his headset off an ear so he could hear him.

Hank laughed back. "You?"

"Nah, it's great. Can't wait to come back," Joe assured.

"Got to leave first," Hank rubbed a little salt into the wound.

"Watch out for pigeons," Joe clapped back.

"Patients," Hank got down to business. "Pick up on a voice

message last night six, seven o'clock? Anything on patients, hospital, Tripoli?"

"Um ..." Joe said. "Actually, yeah, that sounds kinda familiar. Hang on ..." He rifled through his trove of paper scraps. "Had a couple of voice messages last night. Bits and pieces. Had the Doc listen, see if he could figure it out ..."

"Quick, lad, quick," Hank encouraged.

"Yeah, I am. Doc ..." Joe called over to him. "Patients. Last night. Tripoli. Remember that?"

"Gadames," Michael answered over the rim of his coffee cup.

"Huh?"

"Gadames, lad," Pete came out to bounce a ball off the wall above Michael's head. "Why?"

"Hank was asking."

"Aye, and it's fine," Hank assured Pete. "Caught part of it myself. Patient transport to Tripoli."

"Aye, Italians have a boat there," Pete nodded. "That it?"

"Yeah, Armistice," Joe assured. "We're going home."

"By the light of the silvery moon," Pete stopped annoying the Doc to bounce his ball off the top of Joe's head.

Chapter Sixty-Five

Region of Gadames, Libya
April 3

Thiele's convoy pounded into Linke's interim camp at dawn, less one kübelwagen and four men. Situated along a narrow plateau, Linke's site had the Libyan Sahara at its front door and a rocky glade of harsh grass at its back before dissolving into the sands of the Grand Erg Oriental spreading into Algeria. Few abandoned structures, and fewer straggling palm or fruit trees, Linke had more protection there than Reineke would have on the open caravan route, and so if they needed to make a stand, they could.

Thiele leapt from the lead ambulance, Sergeant Linke there to greet, clipboard and pencil in hand and knowing immediately by Thiele's expression something was wrong.

"How bad?" Linke asked.

"How bad?" Thiele pulled a canvas bag out of the cab of the truck and threw it on the ground. "That is what is left of four men!"

"What?" Linke said. "What is that?"

"Nothing!" Thiele assured. "There is nothing left of them. Their bodies are in the back. You will need a detail." He jogged off for the radio tent, Linke blowing his whistle.

"Did you receive your orders?" Linke yanked them off his clipboard as he caught up with Thiele.

"No." Thiele barked at the radio dispatcher to contact Reineke, snatching the communiqué from Linke. "I know approximately where to establish camp, but I have been unable to reach the Hauptmann to advise him of the attacks. They are jamming the signals, and this is the only way to come, so they will be coming this way. ... Let me see your map," he snapped his fingers as he scanned Reineke's directive even though Thiele knew before he checked it was too close.

"It is too close," he folded the map up, thrusting it at Linke, checking with the dispatcher. "Anything?"

"Nothing yet," the soldier reported.

"You see?" Thiele pointed at Linke.

Linke did. "You know who it is?"

"Well, I do not think it is the Tuareg ," Thiele said, "with signal jammers and rocket launchers. It is the French. Free French."

"Or the Italians," Linke frowned.

"No, it is not the Italians," Thiele said. "These people hit and pulled back into the dunes. The Italians would not be doing that. They would simply attack. It is the French. How has it been here?"

"Sporadic sightings of Arabs," Linke shrugged. "Nothing unusual. No attempts to breach the perimeter, and nothing at all for the last day."

Thiele nodded bitterly. "Moving south to harass us. You are too well armed. They are not Arabs, they are French. French scouts."

"Come, I can show you the reports," Linke said. "It's been very quiet. I have another group returning within an hour, if you want to wait before moving on."

"Reports," Thiele scoffed. He did not care about the reports. He believed the four men put in the ground. He went to the latrine to empty his bladder wishing he could do the same with his anger.

When he came back, Linke had his reports ready, and the reconnaissance was arriving, two soldiers on motorbikes coming up through the glade, another skidding into camp from the direction of the road. "What happened to your horses?" Thiele asked sarcastically.

"They have not arrived yet," Linke said with a sharp nod at the third motorbike, "That is not reconnaissance." He dashed for the messenger, Thiele behind him and then in front, the reports scattered in the wind, soldiers running to collect them.

The message was from Reineke still at least a day south. An official charge of treason levied against Erich, the Staff Sergeant to be arrested and remanded at the time of the prisoner's remanding to the SS on April 5 for transportation to Tripoli for trial and execution. It was submitted by Reineke and the other four Hauptmanns, signed and bearing the seal of Herr Oberst Alfred Schönfeld.

"Not bad," Linke read over Thiele's shoulder. "That should make the men happy."

Thiele looked at him. "Sergeant Erich is not responsible for the French attack."

"You don't know that," Linke assured.

Perhaps not, but Thiele did know the charge was signed two weeks ago by Schönfeld, not a day. His finger jammed down on the date for Linke's consideration.

Linke still shrugged. "Anything else?" he asked the messenger.

"Report, please," the messenger pulled out his notebook with a point of his pencil at the radio tent as a reminder. "Please also report your arrival Oberleutnant. I will make a note."

"I have been attempting to contact the Hauptmann since the first French attack, thirty-six hours ago," Thiele assured.

"First? How many?" the messenger wrote down.

"Two," Thiele said.

"Injuries?"

"Four dead," Thiele assured.

The messenger nodded. "Excuse me, Herr Oberleutnant." He headed for the radio tent to try for himself to no avail.

"I will make a note, Herr Oberleutnant," he promised.

"Yes," Thiele said. "Are you telling me you came up from Herr Hauptmann's convoy with no difficulty?"

"I am not from Herr Hauptmann's convoy, Herr Oberleutnant," he explained. "I am from Herr Oberleutnant Dönitz's convoy, approximately sixty kilometers south? And we have had no difficulty except for some sand on the road."

"Who?" Thiele said.

"Herr Oberleutnant Dönitz. Herr Hauptmann Danzig's envoy."

"Oh," Thiele said. "Yes, all right. Is Herr Hauptmann Danzig here, too?"

"Not with my convoy, no. If I may make a recommendation, Herr Oberleutnant?" he requested permission.

"What?" Thiele said.

"If the dead are not buried, you should consider wrapping them and transporting them to the hospital camp as patients. It will help to authenticate its purpose if there are French observing us."

"Attacking," Thiele corrected, "and I'll think about it."

"Of course, Herr Oberleutnant."

"And I want that report dispatched to Herr Hauptmann, not some Oberleutnant Dönitz."

"Of course, Herr Oberleutnant," he assured. "His messenger is waiting. He was dispatched to us, I was dispatched to you—"

"I understand," Thiele silenced him. "When is Herr Hauptmann expected?"

"Tomorrow?" the messenger guessed. "It depends on the sand."

It always depended on the sand. "Danke," Thiele said, and let the man go.

"Let me have the maps again," Thiele stood there thinking. "And get me some coffee," he asked the scout standing there with Linke. "And wait a minute," he stopped the scout before he left. "I'll take those reports, yes. Danke."

Fifty kilometers north was either better or worse than fifty kilometers south. They would find out. Thiele walked to the lead ambulance to mark the location on his map.

"It is set back from the road. You will know it by small rock formations," Linke outlined should the coordinates be wrong and they always were to some extent. A compass was almost worthless out here and reading the dunes was something born to the Arab, not the German. "And a small abandoned Arab settlement. It is very well protected from the west."

"Yes, yes," Thiele was confident he would find it. He thrusted the map at Linke.

"Yes, Herr Oberleutnant." Linke blew his whistle and waved, and an ambulance rolled up.

"I do not need the ambulance," Thiele said. "The kübelwagen was lost."

"It has your equipment," Linke said.

"Equipment? What equipment?"

"Medical, Herr Oberleutnant. Stretchers, bandages, flags."

"Flags?" Thiele said.

"Red Crescent Society, Herr Oberleutnant. Neutrals. You are setting up a field hospital. It needs to look like one."

"Where did we get flags?" Thiele demanded.

"Tripoli?" Linke imagined.

Yes, of course. "Never mind," Thiele said. "Fine. Field hospital."

Linke nodded. "And I would consider the soldier's suggestion, Herr Oberleutnant, of wrapping the dead. Transporting in patients could only help to detour any French you think are out there. It is unlikely they will attack a hospital."

French Thiele *knew* were out there. "I will take four men in replacement," Thiele replied. "They can wrap themselves and each other. You are to bury the bodies. It is difficult for the dead to fight the French."

"Right away, Herr Hauptmann," Linke blew his whistle.

Yes. *Man*! Thiele wanted to say to Linke when he left. *Can you really not see what is going on around you*?

Thiele didn't, and he walked right by Nellie when he arrived at the designated area some three hours later.

Chapter Sixty-Six

Region of Gadames, Libya
April 4

Reineke pulled into Linke's station late morning earlier than expected despite the poor quality of the road, Martin's convoy already there. Their heads high above their carriers the disinterested camels were quiet, Abraham and Hanuk out tending to the horses. That left the Holy Man with the woman inside the truck, Reineke presumed, where Martin stood smoking. Reineke and he did not acknowledge one another. His efficient Sergeant Linke greeting him, Linke reported no problems at the camp or north where Thiele had set up the field hospital the day before.

"Indeed, no problems except for Thiele," Reineke sourly agreed. "How many dead?" he verified.

"Four," Linke confirmed. "Rocket launcher."

"That is French," Reineke assured. "Show me. Come."

They walked back to Reineke's car to review the maps, the first attack approximately one-hundred-fifty kilometers south, and then the fatal attack at approximately one hundred kilometers.

Reineke frowned, noting how it was on the line of the area supposedly under complete control of the Holy Man's French. "So Thiele was in the sand for both attacks."

"Trapped in the sand for both attacks," Linke assured. "He is not carrying any weight except for the men. It was deep. I struggled some myself with the empty trucks and I was not being chased."

"Yes, it was," Reineke nodded. "And you are right. Interesting. They attacked twice in fifty kilometers, pursued Thiele in the sand but as he approached the road they did not continue. I do not know. Thiele was clearly an ambulance convoy. It sounds more like Tuareg than French pursuing uncertain until Thiele is out of their territory, but not with this 'rocket launcher' as you are saying."

"Thiele said they were shelled," Linke said. "The kübelwagen destroyed, the men incinerated. They were," he assured.

"Indeed," Reineke said. "That is French acting like Tuareg. Checking to see what Thiele had with him, hoping to have him reveal it. When he did not, they left. All right. Did the Oberleutnant ..." he snapped his fingers to recall the name.

"Dönitz," Linke extended. "Oberleutnant Dönitz. Aide to the Adjutant Hauptmann Danzig."

"Danke. Did Oberleutnant Dönitz report any issue?"

"No. And I did not mention Oberleutnant Thiele."

"No, naturally not. Get the Oberleutnant. I will do the talking. You are to nod. I do not care about some Adjutant, but I do not wish to raise any alarm with Herr Oberst for something I believe was probably random."

"I think so, yes," Linke agreed. "Oberleutnant Thiele disagrees. He thinks they are still out there."

"And Thiele may be right," Reineke assured. "We will not take chances. Have the Oberleutnant bring his maps."

"Herr Hauptmann," Martin said when he walked up, maps in hand.

"Oberleutnant," Reineke tipped his head in reply. "Put your maps up here, I want to show you something. Oberleutnant Thiele reports two attacks on his convoy here, and here," Reineke circled the areas when Martin spread his map out on the hood of the staff car. "Resulting in the deaths of four men."

"What?" Martin was already challenging the claim. "Attacks?"

"Indeed. Yes," Reineke noted the flash of temper in the eyes and voice. The lawyer was his mother. "I am speaking, Oberleutnant."

So was Martin. "Reconnaissance should have confirmed all areas clear of any scattered factions," he assured."

"That includes you, Oberleutnant," Reineke replied, "since you were part of the reconnaissance. Did you experience any difficulty?"

Martin eyed him. "No. We came in from the sea. Above this first area here, and perhaps ten kilometers south of the second position. Did you come under attack when you came through the sand?"

"No, I did not, Oberleutnant. Neither did Sergeant Linke. And so I am convinced the attack on Oberleutnant Thiele was random. Possibly Tuareg. Nevertheless, we will take precautions. Twenty kilometers south of the field hospital is another site proposed as an option for the hospital camp. That is where you and I will set up the Arab camp we intended to establish here. The new location is much closer to the hospital and will provide additional protection. Sergeant Linke and his men will remain here as rear guard, maintaining watch should these hostile forces reemerge."

"Excellent idea," Martin rolled up his map without waiting for permission. "Hauptmann Danzig will want a full report."

"Indeed. I will want a full report, Oberleutnant," Reineke assured, and he would get one from Abraham and the Holy Man. "Is Erich ready?" he confirmed with Linke.

"Yes, Hauptmann."

"Good," Reineke said. "Ten minutes, put Erich with my trucks. You are dismissed, Oberleutnant. When those men are finished checking the horses, have them check the ones I have brought. I will be right there to confer with the Holy Man on the status of the prisoner. I am also not losing her and having to answer for it. Let the SS lose her."

"What is going on?" Abraham wandered over when Martin walked back.

"I don't know," Martin dumped his maps back in the front seat. "Dieter's saying Thiele was attacked. Four dead men."

"What?" Abraham said in disbelief.

"You sound like me," Martin agreed. "Laying it on a little thick, isn't he with this *quote* instability of the area?"

"No," Abraham said. "No, he wouldn't be doing that. Thiele would never go along with claims of dead men."

"Maybe he's telling Linke it's Thiele and telling Thiele it's Linke," Martin shrugged.

"No," Abraham assured.

"Well, we'll see," Martin said. "He'll be over to check on the girl in a few minutes you can ask him then. In the meantime, he's going to establish the Arab camp about ten miles from the hospital."

"All right, well, there is something to the story then. Get on the radio and tell John Thiele's been spooked. Stay put—"

"Stay put?" Martin argued. "He and Jacob are out there alone—on frigging horses for Christ's sake!"

"Those horses can out run the jeeps without breaking a sweat," Abraham assured.

"These horses maybe," Martin said. "You don't know what fucking piece of crap Jean Paul gave them. Probably some fucking plow horse."

"Tell John to stay put and stay alert. Will advise." Abraham rapped on the side of the truck for Pierre.

"Mon capitaine?" Pierre's head popped out between the drapes.

"On his way. You can leave that open to let in a little air. How is the girl?"

"Still sleeping," Pierre nodded.

"Yes. She has another few hours before it wears off." Abraham nodded at Martin giving him a head's up. "That's our cue. Look smart—and innocent," he assured, "because you better be."

"Pardon?" Pierre said.

Reineke stood to the side of the truck to ensure the woman did not see him. "How is the woman?" he lit a cigarette.

"Oui, fine. She is sleeping," Pierre assured.

Reineke almost nodded. "Sleeping?" he checked his watch. "Drugged?"

"Sleeping powder only," Abraham answered. "She's had a couple of rough nights. Last night one of them. Nothing too bad, but she needed to get some sleep. She did very well on the sea, but she does not like the truck."

"Indeed, of course not. Why would she? Reminiscent of her ordeal."

"Possibly," Abraham agreed.

"Definitely," Reineke assured. "She has to get on a horse. How long will she sleep? She must be there before evening."

"A few more hours?" Abraham calculated. "Do not worry. I will take her."

"That is fine," Reineke said. "In the meantime you and Hanuk can help set up my Arab camp," he smiled, but only briefly. "Did he tell you?" he flicked his head at Martin. "Thiele was attacked. I have four dead men."

"Mon capitaine!" Pierre breathed sharply.

"It is all right," Reineke reassured him. "I know it is not you. But I will want a full report and explanation."

"So will I," Abraham assured. "Where was this?"

"One-hundred, one-hundred-fifty kilometers south. Twice he was attacked. The second time with shells, rockets, as he has called them."

"That should have been clear," Abraham's said. "This doesn't make sense."

"No," Pierre supported. "Mon capitaine, something is wrong."

"Some random faction," Reineke reassured him again. "I had no difficulty, neither did you ... or Linke. But I must respond. Linke and his convoy will remain here to ensure a safe perimeter but this is too far to protect the hospital should this faction reemerge and decide to pursue. We are moving to a site twenty kilometers from the hospital. There we will establish the Arab camp providing sufficient coverage for the trucks and gun."

"Yes," Abraham was nodding. "Yes, absolutely."

"I knew you would agree. We will take your full convoy and my carriers, and the gun, yes. The other gun will remain here with Linke. We do not need my trucks, that is too many. A squad should suffice to maintain the camp. There are twenty men with Thiele. I do not want to make it too difficult for us. Too many eyes. The point is to protect, not hinder."

"Yes," Abraham agreed.

"Good," Reineke said. "Radio John. Give him the information on the new camp and tell him to come in now. He will be there before us but that is fine. I will radio Thiele and advise I am recalling the two forward scouts to relieve them with a half squad to maintain the perimeter—in fact I will do that now to ensure no risk of engagement. Danke," he accepted the radio from Martin. "We have been talking too long. Take Hanuk and check my horses and then I want to leave."

"Five minutes," Abraham promised.

Reineke eyed Pierre. "What do you think of the situation?"

"Mon capitaine," Pierre shook his head, "I do not like it, no. Abraham is correct. That area should have been clear of Tuareg or French."

"I think it will be fine," Reineke nodded. "It is why I am creating the Arab camp closer and bringing one of the guns with me to ensure everything will be all right. How was the woman really on the sea?"

"Sick," Pierre acknowledged. "Not too bad. She did not like the camel."

"I told you. Next time you will listen to me." He hesitated. "How angry is she?"

"Angry?" Pierre said. "She is not angry, only with Pierre."

"No, she wants to leave," Reineke understood. "And she will."

Thiele was not impressed by the use of forward scouts dressed as Arabs but he nodded, "Ja, ja," to Reineke's notice. He reported no further issues and Reineke was pleased to hear that.

"You need to speak to him," Reineke paused to mention to Abraham checking the horses as requested.

"What? Who?" Abraham turned around. "The Holy Man?"

"Your lawyer. Five minutes," Reineke said. "We are leaving."

"What did you do?" Abraham accused Martin.

"Me?" Martin said. "Nothing. Why?"

"Dieter said I had to talk to you."

"Oh," Martin said. "Fine. You talked. Let him eat cake."

"What?" Abraham said.

"I forgot my kid gloves," Martin groaned. "All right? Sorry. He got me riled up with this assault claim and I took it out on him."

"You're hopeless."

"Never send a boy to do a man's job," Hanuk laughed when Abraham walked away shaking his head.

"Shut up," Martin suggested.

John was suspicious. First they got a message of trouble from Martin with instructions to stay put. Ten minutes later they got a second message to proceed twenty kilometers south of the camp and wait.

"What's going on?" Jacob asked.

John did not know, only that it was unlike Abraham to jump the gun. "I guess we'll know when we get there."

There was a broad, largely open area off the road, four times the size of the hospital camp without its protections. John could see why Reineke had not chosen it for the field hospital. Why was he choosing it now for their parking lot? Perhaps because it was closer? Closer wasn't necessarily better. Right now it was neutral when he and Jacob arrived. Empty. The whole place to themselves until the troops showed up with the horses and tents and one of the big guns. Reineke was definitely not taking any chances. Once John found out from Abraham what was going on, about the attack on Thiele's convoy, John understood why.

"What the hell?" he said to Abraham.

"I don't know," Abraham said. "Pierre doesn't like it either. So far Dieter's on the alert but calm. It could have been Tuareg. I wasn't there. I don't know."

"What about Martin?" John turned around to eye his brother.

"What about him? He'll be fine. He's looking for a fight, any fight."

"Who isn't?" John said.

"True," Abraham agreed.

Joanna stirred, thought she heard Pierre say something about a horse before the handsome brother of the witch lifted her up into his arms, but she was too groggy to fight or complain.

"Shit!" Abraham clouted Hanuk when the girl pulled at his litham scarf wrapped around his face. "Keep that damn thing tight if you have to nail it!"

"She didn't see me," Hanuk promised.

"No," Abraham assured, "and she won't, because you've just graduated to the back of the line."

Reineke was in the front of the seven Arabs on horseback.

"You look like a bandit," Abraham swung up on his horse.

"I am a bandit," Reineke assured.

"Yes." Abraham took the girl passed to him by Hanuk without further incident. "Where do you want us?"

"Third," Reineke decided. "Make sure she is comfortable and can be seen if we do have an audience."

"Comfortable ..." Abraham said, even though it was no more possible for her to be comfortable now than it had been over the past month. "All right ..." he shifted a little to make it look good. "Hanuk is at the end, is that all right?"

"No," Reineke said. "Martin should be at the end flanking the disguised scouts like I am leading them in the front. That is what the men and Thiele would expect. Put Hanuk second, behind me."

Abraham knew Hanuk stuck his tongue out underneath that litham of his but that was OK, so did he.

Nellie kept silent watch with Claude and Jacques, tucked in the small hills above the hospital set up in the front of the deserted settlement. The Jerries had some litters with them, carried out of the trucks, and into their new homes. It looked like a full squad to Nellie and that seemed like a lot of soldiers for so few patients.

Anticipating the patients would not reappear for a while, to Nellie's interest most of the soldiers also did not reemerge from their tents, only about three of them. One of them the feisty fellow from yesterday who had crossed right in front of Nellie though apparently the fellow had not realized it.

"Medics," the Jacques one said after watching a while yesterday and he said it now again. "They are medics, sergent. Here to take care of the patients not sit around in the sun. Medics."

"Shut up, boy," Nellie suggested. "And tell Nellie if you think that's the same fellows we were following the other day. Nellie doesn't think it is. Seems to be more ambulances than there were."

"Well, I would have to agree with you," the Jacques one claimed, his English continuing to improve over the last two days. "No, sergent, I think that convoy probably kept right on going to Tripoli."

"That's what Nellie would do," Nellie agreed.

"I mean, apart from there are ten ambulances here instead of only six," Jacques said. "But you are right. Who's counting?"

Nellie was focused on the feisty one. "Nice, meaty piece of a mother's son that one is, isn't he?"

"If you say," Jacques looked at Claude.

Nellie did say. “Going to remember you, boy,” Nellie made himself a promise. “Aye, Nellie is going to remember you,” he rolled a match stick around in his lips compressed with glee.

“Sergent,” Claude reminded, “you are talking too much.”

“Shut up, boy,” Nellie suggested to him, too, “and tell Nellie, what’s a fellow’s First Officer doing all the way out here, and wearing his Sunday best at that?”

“How do I know? Perhaps accompanying his wounded officer?”

Nellie scoffed. “That boy is accompanying no one. His officer wounded, he’d be out there doing his duty for him, whatever that duty might be instead of walking around here telling everyone else what to do.

“That isn’t any medic,” he assured the two of them, “that’s Infantry.” A marksman’s emblem on his jacket, Nellie could see it fine. And that had Nellie thinking back to the first convoy of ambulances they had shadowed. It had him thinking about how there had seemed to be a few bullets falling only inches short of contact like a fellow taking careful aim but was too far away.

“That is no hospital,” Nellie decided around four-thirty or so in the afternoon. “Ain’t no one down there wounded. You better hope some other litters start showing up, because there is going to be a need. Aye,” he assured. “There is going to be.”

“Claude,” the Jacques one gave the other one an alert a couple of hours later, no more than that.

“Aye,” Nellie whistled in agreement. Horses were coming, Arabs. The feisty one walking up to meet them.

“Think that is the boss of them?” Nellie asked as the first Arab jumped down to gesture at the Jerry and back at his little line of sheiks.

“I don’t know. What is he doing?” the Jacques one asked.

“Shut up and watch,” Nellie proposed.

“Bartering for something perhaps?” Claude moved up to them. “Food or water?”

“Said shut up,” Nellie warned, “or Nellie will snap your neck in two. That a girl they giving him?”

“Where?” the Jacques one asked.

“Right there,” Nellie said.

“Oh. Maybe,” the Jacques one nodded. “It could be. It looks like a child. Perhaps he is sick or injured.”

“That’s a girl,” Nellie assured as another Arab got off his horse to help a fat one down, the rest of them turning off, to keep traveling like they were passing by and saw the place.

“Maybe that’s the mother?” the Jacques one wondered. “The fat one?”

“That’s no mother, boy,” Nellie assured. “That’s a white girl. That fat one’s brown as mud.”

Nellie watched them, the second Arab taking the girl and carrying her off into a tent, the fat one following, the first Arab walking with the feisty one into another tent.

“Now, that is interesting,” Nellie nodded, not sure what he was watching, but it was interesting. “Need to get down there, boy,” he told Claude. “Need to get down there and see exactly what that is. Nellie’s not leaving some white girl in there. Want to know why she’s there.”

“It is a hospital, sergent, but, yes, all right, all right,” Claude agreed. “Nightfall.”

Nellie would go along with that, as long as it was early. “Nellie wants to see, boy,” he replied. “He wants to see.”

“You will,” Claude promised, and they did.

At eight o’clock, forty of Jean Paul’s fifty men slipped down over the mountain to see what they could see. They saw it all by nine o’clock, and thirty-two of them died watching.

Chapter Sixty-Seven

Joanna felt the sway of the camel, her stomach more hungry than sick, and tried to rouse herself from what was a dream. She could see the tent, feel the cushion of the pillows, her breath hot in their comfortable pocket, though the air around her seemed cool. She turned over and tried to lift her head but Pierre's hand pushed her back down into the pillows. She could see him sitting, swaying with his smile, watching as he always did, scolding her when she tried to pick her head up again, his voice gruff and loud.

Joanna frowned. Something was odd, but she drifted off before she could figure out what it was.

Sleep remained uneasy and uncomfortable, shadows in the distance whispering secrets she was too frightened to listen to.

"You drugged me again," Joanna accused Pierre sitting with his bowl of black stodge when she snapped awake.

"No, Mademoiselle," he smiled with his denial. "It is the heat. The excitement."

That was a lie. Joanna was not hot, she was freezing cold. "Where is my blanket?" she felt around her bed.

"Right here, Mademoiselle," Pierre tucked it around her.

"Not that one," Joanna pushed the rough, scratchy sheet away, sitting up, rubbing her eyes. "Who was that man?" she asked.

"What man?" Pierre said.

Joanna did not know. "The one with the dirt on his face. The one screaming at the door."

"A nightmare," Pierre assured. "It does not matter. It is behind you. Let it go. Let it all go. Everything is behind you."

It would be another hour, past six o'clock when Joanna woke up and realized she was in a tent. An unpleasant looking tent in a dull lifeless color with a cruel harsh pitch like a witch's hat. The cot she lay on stiff and uncomfortable, Pierre sat watching her from an equally uncomfortable looking wooden chair.

"Oh, my God ..." Joanna whispered as she looked around. "Oh, my God ..."

"It is all right, Mademoiselle," Pierre reassured, the bowl of black mush in hand. "You will see. Have something to eat now, and some water. You must be very thirsty. Remember you have to keep up your strength."

For what? Joanna wondered. She couldn't imagine for what. But the stodge tasted good, the water better, and he even let her have a cup of sweet tea.

Joanna lay back on her cot. She could not believe it when Pierre told her it was seven o'clock, an entire hour gone so fast. He brought her a jacket reminding her she was cold and should put it on. Joanna was no longer cold. Awake, the air felt wonderful, the tent breathing in a light breeze, sand blowing against it.

She looked up. "Rain," Pierre agreed. "Oui, I think rain, Mademoiselle."

Rain? "Rain?" Joanna said.

"It rains in the desert, Mademoiselle," he said. "Not too often, but occasionally, and never very long."

"Oh, but it can't be rain!" Joanna jumped up as the drops hitting the tent fell faster. "It can't be rain!" Rain would be too wonderful. It had been so long since she had seen rain.

"Mademoiselle!" Pierre protested as Joanna darted to the funny wooden door trying to see outside through its worn and dirty window streaked with rain.

"I want to see the rain," she said. "I want to see the rain!"

"All right, all right ..." Pierre toddled over quickly. "But put on the coat ... put on the coat ..." he waved a long coat at her. "And one quick look only."

"Fine!" Joanna crawled into the greatcoat large enough for six of her as Pierre turned the wooden latch, and she stepped outside where the sky was one great cloud. A solitary, light grey cloud covering what was left of the sun. It was all over much too soon only lasting another minute, the sun returning before it would set. Joanna looked down at the tiny rivers of water running through the packed sand, and the rainbow puddle where the water mixed with the oil spilled from one of the Captain's wagens. "Oh," she stared at the wagen and the tents forming a drab, sad circus around her.

"Oui, Mademoiselle," Pierre said with only a slight nod to Reineke safely in the distance. "Come back inside. I will be right back with your dinner."

"Yes, of course," Joanna returned to lie on her cot trying not to wipe the rain off her cheeks with the sleeve of the coat.

"Mademoiselle," Pierre said presently and Joanna groaned. Was he now going to tell her it was eight o'clock?

No. It was only a minute or two past seven-thirty. Joanna noticed there was a clock hanging on the wall of the tent near a writing desk with another hard folding chair. Pierre was wet. She had forgotten he had come outside with her and then left for her dinner.

"Mademoiselle," he said as she waited for him to hand her something, even a piece of bread. "Mon capitaine is here. He wants to speak with you."

"What?" Joanna said.

"I would recommend it," Pierre said.

"Oh," Joanna said. "Oh, all right." She got up.

"And not the greatcoat, of course," Pierre smiled. "But your jacket, yes. It is cold, and there is again a light rain."

He stepped back outside with her. The clouds darker, swollen, and close together as they moved rapidly across the sky. A lantern lit a halo in the distance with a funny, blinking amber light. Pierre had told the truth about the light rain as Joanna looked down the path through the small village of tents where the Captain stood with his back to her at the end of the runway of his camp, but then as if by a sixth sense, he turned around.

"*Fräulein*." Joanna could not hear him, but imagined that was what he said when he stepped down from his pile of rubble with a tip of his head. Joanna noticed he was wearing a long, thin, broad coat similar to the one she had on earlier.

"Go with him, Mademoiselle," Pierre encouraged her softly.

Go with him? Whatever did the funny priest mean? As soon as the Captain turned around to her, he turned back to walk away and was already very nearly out of sight.

"Go with him?" Joanna repeated. "But it's dark," she said. Moment by moment the sky was turning darker. "No," she said. "I can't."

The Captain stopped and turned back around waiting for her at the corner of a wall someone once called home.

"I!" Joanna swallowed with a look at Pierre, but she was alone. Pierre was gone, back inside the tent.

"I!" Joanna said, the sky so black it was almost blue again, a deep, regal navy blue.

"Wait!" Joanna said, not because the Captain was leaving, but because he was heading back for her.

"Wait!" she pleaded, and he waited, as she waited before she started to walk, slowly, in the dark, one foot forward, and then the other, until she caught up to him.

"Oh, well, now," Nellie whistled softly in his cradle of sandy rock. "Now if that isn't the smallest soldier ol' Nellie did ever see."

"That is a girl, sergent," Claude quietly agreed with him. "I wonder where they are going?"

"This way," Nellie hoped. "This way," he prayed to the patron saints of Eire even though he was a Protestant boy.

And they did. Slowly, but they did, and Nellie proved how quiet ... silent ... and still he could be, like part of the sand, the shadow of a ragged rock formation in the sand.

"That's right," Nellie encouraged the silhouette of a tall man, moving slowly with the little girl he had next to him. Near tall as Charlie he was and about as thin. Nellie hadn't seen him before, no idea where he came from, but he was seeing him now.

"That's right," Nellie encouraged. "A little closer, come on, boy, you've still got a ways to go ..." before he was out of the cloister of his hospital tents, and the row of parked ambulances, deeper into the haunted mud buildings, away from the amber lights.

"Pick a nice deserted spot," Nellie coaxed, pleased to see the fellow did. Moved through the buildings to the sand and rocks on the other side.

Claude could feel the tension rising in the giant next him. "After lights out," he agreed, "we will go in and take her out."

Nellie did not hear him, wasn't listening if he did. "Watch out for Nellie," he nodded to the Frenchie. "If ol' Nellie makes it down there, give him a couple of minutes, and if he ain't out, ol' Nellie would appreciate it if you came and got him."

"No," Claude's hand clamped down on his arm. "Later. Not now. No."

Nellie smiled. "Why, that is what Nellie is going to go down there and tell that fellow!" And he was up, and gone, moving down, fast, with the speed and stealth of a mountain cat before Claude could say another word.

Claude did not bother. The rippling murmurs of concern behind him said it for him as Nellie shrugged out from under his hand and was gone. "Drop back," Claude whispered his order that was passed on. "Quietly, and keep your fingers crossed. It is always possible he won't come back and our job will be done for us."

"Well," Joanna announced bravely to the Captain as she walked up. "Here I am."

"Indeed, I would like to speak to you, Fräulein," Reineke quietly reaffirmed what he presumed the Holy Man had already told her.

"Out here?" Joanna questioned to cover her shiver. "It's dark out here."

It was one minute into night out there. "Are you afraid of the dark, Fräulein?" Reineke asked.

"No," Joanna assured.

"Neither am I," he disclosed.

Good for you, Joanna was inclined to say except he took her by the arm and they were walking.

"Where are we going?" she did ask that. "Where are you taking me? Are we going for a ride?"

"No," Reineke said. "Would you like to go for a ride?"

Joanna was already on a ride, a Ferris wheel, roller coaster, or maybe a carousel on a hot Sunday afternoon after too much candy. She took a deep breath trying not to sweat, vomit, or faint. She stopped walking and asked again, because she had a right to know.

"Where am I going? Where are you taking me? What?" she swallowed, her mouth so dry. "What do you want from me?"

His head went up, on guard. "Indeed. What do you mean?"

"I don't know," Joanna shook her head. "I'm asking you. Why won't you answer me?"

"I apologize," Reineke inclined his head. "I have not meant to alarm you."

"Which time?" Joanna scoffed.

He gave what sounded like a small laugh or cough. The light flickering there was his lighter as he lit a cigarette, offering it to her."

"No, thank you," Joanna refused. "I don't smoke either."

That time he did laugh lightly, whether he had laughed before or not. "You are very wise," was his amused reply. "The glamour can leave a distinctly unpleasant taste in the mouth."

"If you say."

He chose not to say anything, reaching to take her arm again, but she moved away, his eyes round as they looked over her. "I am not going to hurt you, Fräulein," he assured. "I simply wish to speak with you."

"You said that before," Joanna reminded, "when you gave me the wine."

That was definitely a light cough when he cleared his throat. "Indeed."

"Yes," Joanna said. "Pierre said it was him. But, Pierre ..." she felt the first tears she held back start to irritate her eyes, and she looked down because it was easier than looking up. "Pierre has never lied to me," she said, believing that even if he had. "I know that. I know he's never lied to me unless you told him to."

"Indeed," Reineke said. "As I have already apologized."

"True," Joanna said. "May I go now, please?"

"No," he said.

Joanna guessed she should have expected that but it still would have been nice to hear him tell her she could leave. She moistened her lips, focused on her hands trying their best not to shake.

"Fräulein," Reineke said with his own look down to the ground before he looked back up at her. "I am asking you to understand I apologize for anything that has brought you any concern."

She did not answer him and he wondered what she was thinking. He wondered if she knew herself.

"Tomorrow …" he said, and paused.

"Yes?" Joanna looked up quickly, perhaps thinking of that.

"Tomorrow," Reineke said, "you are to be sent with a group of soldiers you may know as SS. No harm will come to you. I apologize you are troubled by the inconvenience. It was not my intention."

"Oh," Joanna said.

"That is all?" Reineke asked after a moment. "Johanna, do you know who the SS are?"

Joanna looked up at him. "May I go, please?"

"No," Reineke said. "No, I want to talk to you."

"But I want to go," Joanna shook her head. "I don't want to stay here. I want to go. I can't …" she said, and she couldn't, not even get it out as the tears came pouring out and she hid her face in her hands.

"Johanna!" Reineke said as she started to sob. "Please …" he crouched down so he would not be towering over her but eye-level like Pierre. "Listen to me, please listen to me," he pleaded as she wept so deeply she did not have the strength to lash back at him.

"What is going to happen to me?" Joanna sobbed. "Oh, what is going to happen to me?"

"Nothing," Reineke promised. "Nothing," he swore. "Johanna, listen, please …" he tried to encourage her to look up, take her hands away from her face. "I want you to believe me. I want you to trust me. I know you have no reason to, but I want you to try.

"Johanna," he said, "if I could change whatever has happened to you, I would. I cannot, but I want you to try to believe no one is ever going to hurt you again. They are not. I swear to you …I swear to you," he smiled as her hands slowly came down away from her face and she watched him. "All right?" he wiped her wet cheeks and nose with his handkerchief. "And we do not have to stay here. We do not. I will take you back to the Holy Man—"

"Why are you calling me Johanna?" she interrupted him.

"What?" Reineke paused.

"You are calling me Johanna," Joanna nodded. "Why?"

Reineke did not think he was aware he had. "I do not know," he smiled. "Perhaps because it is your name?"

"Oh," Joanna said.

"So, is it all right?" Reineke asked. "You are all right? We can go back now to the Holy Man?" he offered before something happened. Joanna had no idea what happened, other than he seemed to be holding her arms one moment before he suddenly let her go as something like a gust of wind came from nowhere, and the Captain was face flat on the ground in front of her, the barrel of a rifle, jammed in the back of his head.

"Well, now, there'll be no more reason for you to be doing that, boy," Nellie chuckled as Joanna clapped her hands over her mouth with a gasp.

"And no more reason for you to be crying either, little lady," his head turned to Joanna, "Ol' Nellie, he's here to rescue you.

"Ain't that right?" he turned back, verifying with the Captain. "I say, are you listening to Nellie, superboy?" he prodded the back of the Captain's head with his gun, and Joanna shut her eyes, burying her face in her hands.

"Now, little lady," the man who seemed to be calling himself Nellie chuckled for her again. "Don't you worry about anything, Nellie's not going to make any loud noises with his gun.

"No, he's not going to do that," he promised, "because Jerry here ... why, Jerry here," he nodded at Reineke, "he's not going to scare anyone either. No, he's going to roll over and he's going to sit up nice and quiet and politely for Nellie. His hands clasped on the top of his head ...

"That's right," Nellie approved as the Captain did what he was told to do. "You got that right ... maybe you've been through this before?

"I said, boy," he chuckled, tipping Reineke's chin up and back and back with the barrel of his gun, "has superboy been through this before?"

"Indeed," Reineke said, more for the sheer size and astounding appearance of the man than anything he might be saying, or doing.

"Now, Nellie is going to take your gun," Nellie said. "And you are going to keep your hands right where they are because we do not want to upset Nellie. Nellie's gun might go off, and we do not want to frighten the little lady more than she already is ...

"Now, little lady ..." it was Joanna's turn again and Nellie was calling for her complete attention. "Nellie is going to give you this," he eased the Captain's pistol out of its holster. "Nellie is going to give it to you, and you are going to take it and stay right with Nellie ..." he nodded. "Do you think you can say something, little lady to let Nellie know you understand? Do you understand?"

"Yes!" Joanna hoarsely whispered.

"Well, then, do it, little lady!" his bark was quiet and coarse like the man in her dream. "Come on, here you go. Take it."

Joanna did, and she had the Captain's gun in her hands.

"Now, get behind, Nellie," Nellie instructed her. "And you stay right there. Do not move."

Joanna did. Got behind him and did not move.

"And, superboy, here," Nellie eased back to rest on his heels, "he is going to stand up nice and slowly, keeping his hands right where they are, where Nellie can see them, and then the two of us are going to take a walk ...

"Just you," Nellie whispered at Reineke, "just Nellie. Ain't that so?"

God only knew. The Captain did something, though what he did, Joanna did not know, only that he did it fast. One moment he was sitting there starting to rise, and then he was suddenly up, off the ground, his foot stretched out catching the man in his chest. Joanna watched Reineke catch the man square with his foot, almost dead center in his chest, but the man did not fall down. He moved. Joanna watched him sway, but he did not fall down.

"Shouldn't have done that, superboy," Nellie chuckled as Reineke replanted his feet firmly on the ground.

"Should not have done that," Nellie smiled, and Reineke went flying backwards ten feet with one shove of Nellie's giant hand.

Oh, God! Joanna gripped the gun and shut her eyes but she could still hear them fighting.

God! She jumped because someone was near her feet, but she kept her eyes closed and her hand on the gun as tightly as she could.

Stop it! She wanted to scream, but she couldn't get it out, afraid if she screamed she would bring the soldiers and she did not want to do that.

Stop it! She gritted her teeth, biting back the words, listening to the man talk and talk as he talked all the while.

"Stop it!" she managed hoarsely and opened her eyes, but neither of them heard her. She could barely hear herself.

"Stop it!" she tried again even though she knew they were not going to stop anything. The Captain was back down on the ground, she could see him lying flat with the man's knee on his chest and hands around the Captain's throat as he kept talking, and talking ...

The man was still talking, and Joanna heard him say something that did not make any sense at all.

"This one's for Charlie!" Nellie nodded.

Like he was giving something to someone, and Joanna saw him reach down. She watched his hand slide down, and the man had a knife in his boot.

Oh, my God. Joanna stood there. She could see herself standing there, and she knew she should tell the man he did not have to do that. There was no reason for him to do that. He could have just come and taken her away. Why, oh, why, didn't he just come and take her away like he said he was there to do?

"Don't," Joanna whispered, and she could feel her hand loosen its grip on the gun.

"Don't!" she insisted, but she knew he wasn't listening to her.

The knife came out, his hand came up, the Captain clutching desperately at the man's wrist, trying to keep the knife away, and Joanna turned the gun around, gripping the barrel tightly in both her hands. "Please!" she begged one last time as her hands swung back, and then forward like one of Michael's bats hitting a ball, "don't!"

The man looked so funny. It hadn't occurred to her he might look funny as her hands swung and she caught him flat on the side of his face at the temple with the hilt of the gun and he dropped, dropped where he was and lay there very still.

"I ..." Joanna said to Reineke staring at her.

"I!" she said. "Well, I just couldn't," she whispered, wishing he would please stop staring at her.

"H ... h ... how could I?" she stammered. "He was ... he was ... Oh, no, don't!" she jumped back as Reineke moved. "Please don't do that. Please don't!"

Reineke did not. Crouched on the ground, he stayed, but Joanna was shaking anyway. She was starting to shake and she was shaking so hard, anyway.

"Give me the gun," Reineke said quietly, carefully holding out his hand.

"No," Joanna said. "No!" she refused, quickly turning it around in her hands and pointing it at him. Though it did not make her stop shaking, no, it did not do that.

"Johanna," Reineke said softly, "Give me the gun, hm? Please?"

But Joanna could not do that. If she gave it to him he would have it, and she did not want him to have it, she wanted it. "I!" she said. "You'll call the soldiers."

"No," Reineke shook his head.

"Yes, you will," Joanna nodded. "You'll take the gun and call the soldiers."

"I will not," Reineke promised. "Johanna, I will not."

"No," Joanna refused, but he was starting to stand up, anyway.

"Don't," she warned him, and he hesitated, but then moved again.

"I said, don't!" Joanna jumped back another step. "No! Why aren't you listening to me?"

She could not figure out why he was not listening to her when all he had to do was look. Look right over there at the man lying there who hadn't listened to her either and look what she had done to him.

"Johanna," Reineke said firmly, "give me the gun."

Joanna did. It went off. She was standing there, holding it so tightly, shaking so hard, and the gun went off.

Instinctively Reineke dove, but Joanna missed him, and with no less of an instinct, the soldiers came running.

Thiele was at the forward end of the camp when he heard the shot and he turned and flew, screaming for the alarm as he ran. Pierre was waiting in the tent, and in an instant, he was outside.

They came from every direction, running in the same direction as the sound of the shot.

Joanna stood there paralyzed, a siren wailing in her ear. She could hear boots coming across the rocks and stones of the broken buildings and so she ran, too. Dropped the gun and ran.

"Johanna!" Reineke jumped to his feet with a horrified shout. "Johanna!" he screamed. "No!"

The soldier crashing over a low wall had a rifle in his hands, up and aiming.

"No!" Reineke barked, and the soldier stopped so quickly he fell.

"No!" Reineke shouted again, screaming for his soldiers to stop, and somewhere in the confusion, he had his gun. In an instant, he had his gun and he was off, running in the same direction Joanna had run, racing after her, screaming her name, shouting for his men to stop when hell vomited up from the grave.

The soldier who fell was in the process of picking himself up when he dropped again, a bullet lodged in his brain. There was a blinding flash, a building behind Reineke erupting into flames. His men scattered. Through the smoke Reineke could see the woman huddled in a corner, near a wall. But she saw him, and she was off, running again, away from the houses, and out into the open.

"Johanna!" Reineke screamed in terror for her, and there was a second flash. A noise so loud, it knocked him to the ground.

The woman was on the ground. Reineke lifted his head and saw her lying on the ground so many dozen feet away.

"Johanna!" He was next to her in an instant, lifting her up.

Joanna gasped and choked, sputtering and spitting dust from her teeth, and then screaming when she realized the hands clutching at her belonged to the Captain, and they were fighting. She slapped his face, and if her hand still held the gun, Reineke would be as quiet as the man she had struck before.

"No!" Joanna screamed all arms and legs when Reineke tried to pick her up.

"No!" she screamed, teeth and nails when he let her go.

And there was no time for this! Bullets streaked passed them. Another building and another bursting into flames, the woman screaming, "I didn't mean to! I didn't mean to!"

Over and over.

"I didn't!" Joanna gasped. "I didn't! Oh, please! I really didn't mean to!"

Neither did Reineke. It was instead of slapping her. She was hysterical, and he did it only to keep from slapping her. He grabbed her hair, grasped her shoulder, and the last thing he remembered was bringing her mouth up to meet his.

Something popped inside his head, and Reineke could no longer hear the noise. The woman's hands were two hard knobs buried in his chest. "Johanna ..." he whispered, his lips leaving hers to slip across her cheek, his hand leaving her hair to touch her chin, his fingers pressing lightly into the flesh of her throat. She was ramrod rigid as his arms went around her, cradling her head against his chest, his hand smoothing her hair.

But there was no time for this. The noise came banging back and Reineke was up, Joanna in his arms. The corner of a room more outside than in was the best he could find. He did not dare leave her in a building, and so he stuffed her in the makeshift foxhole near the ruins of a wall, instructing her to stay down. He pulled off his greatcoat, draping it over her and telling her to leave it there, like a cover over her, and he gave her back his gun.

He did not ask her if she knew how to shoot, he told her to shoot. She was to shoot anyone who came near her, German or not. He would be back, and he inched away.

"Dieter?" Joanna whispered.

Reineke turned around. It was a mistake for her to say his name. Why did she pick now to say his name? He could not stay, and he wanted to. He did indeed want to. "Arms over your head like this," he said softly, crossing his in demonstration. "Keep your head down. I will be back!" he promised, and the night took him.

Chapter Sixty-Eight

Reineke darted through the camp, searching for Thiele. The guns were quiet, but only for the moment. They would be back, and he was glad because he wanted them all.

As they wanted his trucks, only they did not know where they were. They wanted his munitions, and so they blew the buildings, trying to find them, only they did not know they were not there.

His boots carried him to home plate where he found Thiele. "Rockets, eh, Thiele?" he whispered excited to Thiele's sullen face.

At least two. Had the Hauptmann thought to pack a tank?

No. Reineke had something better. He had men. Primed and kept dangling, three months without a fight. He had horses and camels and soldiers dressed as Arabs. Two rocket launchers? One was low, but the other was high. He gave away his position when the houses nearer the center hit the sky in flames, and Reineke was going to silence them both.

Reineke had a big gun already on its way from the Arab camp only twenty kilometers south.

Ten! The desert reported. The vicious rubber treads ripping through the packed sand, pounding along the caravan route, heading for the field hospital. Reineke was going to put a hole through the center of the enemy's fortification the size of the Almighty's fist!

"Eh, Thiele?" he said.

And he had Pierre. Every unmarked, untouched tent bearing witness, they knew the Holy Man was there.

And he had the woman. "Indeed!" Reineke threw back his head and laughed. The tiny, little Johanna perhaps the most unexpected weapon of them all. He was back in France, a sight Thiele had not been there to see. As he ravaged that French village, he was going to ravage this mountain, there were no children here.

"Vive la France, Thiele!" he teased, stealing a clip for his weapon from Thiele's pocket, his eyes blazing with a fire so hot it was cold.

And they would see how hot he was, how cold he could be. They would all see. "Indeed!"

And they did.

Jean Paul's sergent Claude L'Heureaux was critically injured, disfigured, and blinded by shrapnel tearing through his right eye. Lieutenants Pierre Forget and Jacques Renault were unharmed.

Reineke lost six of his own men and two of the horses. He was particularly sorry for the horses. Le capitaine loved horses.

"I should have you stuffed and hung upon a wall." Reineke was back in Libya, his love affair with steel and powerful weapons, over. He reviewed the carcass of the mastodon Johanna had brought down for him, poking it with his foot to see if it was alive and still breathing. It was.

"Das ist eine Nellie!" he laughed to Thiele walking up. "And I am Hauptmann Reineke," he assured the giant. "The finest superman you will ever see."

But did the woman see the same?

Would she, could she, ever see the same?

Was she even alive to see?

Reineke looked at Thiele, only he was not looking at Thiele, and Thiele knew that. The Hauptmann stared across what was now nearly a parking lot of rubble and left in a hurry.

It was strikingly cold tonight. A defiant chilly wind kissed Thiele's hot cheeks as he stood there taking an eon to decide what to do, a soldier waiting patiently with him.

And what did you see? Thiele challenged the footman with a silent, suspicious glare. But the soldier did not answer him, as Thiele had not asked, and it did not matter because Thiele knew what he saw. "Go with the Hauptmann," he nodded tersely at the soldier, "he is unarmed."

The soldier glanced down at the automatic weapon Reineke had let drop to the ground, and moved on as requested to escort the Hauptmann who was already gone. "*Run!*" Thiele hissed under his breath after the fool who walked, and Reineke had run.

"*Run*!" Thiele muttered. "*Run*!"

Thiele had run with the sound of the first shot, faster and faster each step he took, in time to see the ring of mud houses shake from the first blast.

"The Hauptmann?" Thiele had screamed above the roaring flames to the soldier he hugged, but the soldier was dead, and Thiele threw the warm cadaver back down in the rubble. A second blast and Thiele was picking his way through more soot and smoke in time to see Reineke rise up from the dirt and rocks, his boots take flight, and Thiele heard the Hauptmann scream, "*Johanna*!" terror in his voice, a moment later the woman in his arms.

Thiele retreated from the scene to take temporary command of the men. Right now, Thiele stood for another long moment before he went for the Hauptmann. He called a few soldiers wandering around with nothing to do and assigned them the duty of guarding the monster littering the ground until the Hauptmann had the time to decide what he would like to do with it, other than add it to his growing collection of freaks.

Thiele walked. Each step he took slower than the last. He met the three of them, the Hauptmann, the woman, and the sentry returning far enough away from the groggy eyes of Nellie coming 'round, his brain not quite clear enough yet to be able to see and comprehend as he lifted his heavy head off the ground. He'd have to see it again to know what it was that was trying to catch his attention. And don't you know he would? Oh, so many months from now, don't you know he would?

Joanna saw nothing except the inside of a very large coat. The bright lights and deafening thunder, came and went, but she kept her eyes shut, counting like she did in the underground tube below London until they sounded the All Clear.

The All Clear here was quiet. For what must have been a half hour, Joanna heard only an occasional muffled noise. It was a while longer though before she dared to poked her head out from under the Captain's coat.

The woman was a funny little lump blending in with the bricks of the wall behind her, another rock strewn in the corner, with fiery red grass growing on top of it. And would she never learn not to look up at him the way she did? Why, oh, why, did she tilt her head and open her eyes the way she did? She was the innocence of Adva and steel of Anne, packaged together, and set down in front of him and somehow he was supposed to resist. Did someone somewhere know a magical spell to help him resist?

Reineke removed his hat from his head, holding it in his hands as he watched her. Joanna looked up from under the coat into the silence that included the Captain standing there. She climbed to her feet, her back touching the wall behind her.

"I came back," Reineke offered, quietly, his fingers toying with the chinstrap around his hat. And it was such a ridiculous thing for him to say.

"Yes," Joanna nodded, "I see."

Did she?

"Do you?" Reineke whispered, and where was the magic to stop him from doing the wrong thing?

She did not stiffen, even move, but he could tell she was frightened. He could see in her eyes how frightened she was of him.

"Don't hurt me," Joanna whispered, not really wanting to say anything, but the Captain was an inch away from her and drawing closer.

"Hurt you?" Reineke murmured. "I could never hurt you."

She did not believe him. He could see in those wild, brown eyes she did not believe him, and he wanted her to. He really did not know what to do. Why was there never anyone to tell him what to do?

His lips touched hers lightly, then again, slowly. He would have stopped. He swears he would have stopped. By the third soft kiss, he knows it would have ended except he felt her lips part, her mouth move against his, and she was kissing him back.

They were on the grass. The odd yellow grass around the desert's puddle he loved to call a pool.

They were on the mattress of the sturdy wooden bed in the miniature Roman suite he called the Apartment, and later would call her room.

They rolled in the sensuous sheets of his bed in his room of his royal manor where from the balcony he could see the river Rhine instead of limestone ruins.

They were on gravel of broken rocks and hardened mud and he wanted her, anyway. He wanted her so badly, to touch her, and for her to touch him.

"Touch me," he begged, "Do that to me."

And he had her on the table, her nails shredding his back until the blood mingled with the wine.

She was the woman in the dream. The woman he did not know, but now did.

Reineke slid out from under the spell of his fantasy back into reality where he had not kissed her, but was holding his hat as he stood in front of her, her back against the broken wall.

"Do you like peaches?" his head tipped curiously.

"Peaches?" Joanna whispered. "Yes."

"Indeed," Reineke said, and possibly would have kissed her after all except the magic to stop him announced its arrival.

"Hauptmann."

His soldier was embarrassed. He gave a short acknowledging nod to the woman and respectful salute to his Captain, and there was no reason for him to be embarrassed. Say, or do anything out of the ordinary. His Hauptmann had done nothing inappropriate, it was all entirely innocent. The erotic fantasy was a memory, gone like the French.

And besides, Reineke was not the one touching anyone, not even their shirt. That was the woman who had her hands on him. She blushed when he looked at her after he looked down at his shirt. He enjoyed the blush, liked it, even though yes, perhaps, the only reason for her hands touching his shirt was entirely his fault. He was standing extremely close to her. He should learn not to stand so close to her, and for a moment, he was very glad it was dark.

The soldier explained how Thiele had sent him, something Reineke did not need to hear. It only supported his belief how this little woman was Adva, Anne, and Pierre, and Diana, combined as one. His eyes left hers for a moment to focus on the eagle watching him from the peak of his hat he held in his hand.

"It appears," he suggested wryly to Joanna, "you are the only one who does not believe it is I who should be frightened of you, instead of you so frightened of me.

"Unless, I am in error," he looked back into her eyes, and her hands came down from touching his shirt, "and you knew when you came you were meant to be my death."

Joanna did not answer him. She bloody well did not know what she would have said it she tried to. It was such an odd thing for him to say. Almost as odd as him asking her if she liked peaches for some reason.

Though nowhere near as odd, oh, no, nowhere near as odd as *Touch me*!

Whatever had he meant? If Joanna had the nerve she would ask him with the wickedest hope of hearing him say it again.

"Come," Reineke picked up his greatcoat, holding it up for her, encouraging her to put it on, "as you have said, it is cold out here."

It was, and Joanna gratefully slipped into it regardless of its overwhelming size, pulling her hair out from under its collar as he set it up on her shoulders. She straightened the front, buttoning the top two buttons so it had a better chance of staying on, instead of falling off, straightened her hair and turned around announcing she was ready. "OK," Joanna nodded.

He looked uncertain.

"Dieter?" she said.

And so it had not all been fantasy. Reineke's mouth was dry. He recalled asking to be touched. But then again somewhere before he left she had called his name and somewhere before that he had kissed her while bullets shot through the sky.

He smiled. "We will discuss it later, Johanna," he said, and put his hat on her head completing her outfit.

An unromantic Thiele picked up his plod towards the trio on their leisurely stroll down through the burned shells of the Libyan backdrop.

"He is awake!" was the contents of Thiele's greeting.

And this meant what? Reineke should resume being the Hauptmann? Assume his role of commander complete with uniform and take back his greatcoat hanging off the shoulders of the woman, its hem dragging across the ground as she walked and his hat two sizes too large for her head? Reineke would not do either. His soldier, unlike Thiele, would never admit under torture he saw a coat or a hat, and Reineke liked that. He liked Thiele's crossed eyes even more. So the woman got to keep his coat and his hat, at least while he left her side to resume his survey of the captured prize.

"I am Hauptmann Reineke," Reineke advised in English to this soldier of the enemy ringed on three sides by his men. "You are Nellie? Nellie, what? Name and rank, Allied, if you please. I care little about your identification numbers."

The man lifted the top of his lip in a sneer, "Now, ask me, how I knew you'd be asking me that, boy?"

His accent was South African ... or Irish ... possibly a mixture of both. His tone and manner, even his words vulgar as his appearance. Reineke was distinctly pleased and satisfied to meet such a disgusting example of the Allied after having been confronted with so many of his own.

"Indeed, you are not in uniform," he gloated. "A soldier not in uniform could be shot as a spy."

The man gave a throaty chuckle, wiping his hand across his chin as he spat saliva tinged with blood onto the ground. Reineke laughed delightfully, turning away to admire the tiny woman who had toppled a man the size of this massive creature who had to weigh one-hundred-thirty kilograms and stand more than two meters tall. Reineke was in awe of her and her strength dealing the blackening welt forming on the side of the man's face where she had struck him with the gun with such force.

Reineke walked back to Joanna to ask her politely, "Do you know him?"

"No," Joanna shook her head.

"He appears to know you," Reineke offered gently.

"He does?" Joanna stared at the gigantic man.

"No, that is all right," Reineke turned Joanna back to him. "I should clarify by his actions, his words, he suggests he may know you," he smiled.

"Oh," Joanna said.

"What about a Charlie?" Reineke asked. "Do you know a Charlie? The name the man mentioned?"

"Like he was giving something to someone," Joanna nodded.

"Yes ..." Reineke said because that was exactly how the man had sounded. "Do you know a Charlie?"

"No ..." Joanna frowned. "No, not offhand. No, I don't think I do. I know a Michael," she offered.

"Yes, of course," Reineke said. How could he forget?

"But that's not Michael," she said.

"No, of course, it is not," he assured, disappointed. He had been hoping perhaps that it was her friend Major Michael. He took a breath, not wanting to push her too far. He smiled. "Thank you. Do you mind if I ask you one more question to help me? Do you know what he is? His nationality," he offered before she said something like 'big' or 'ugly'. "I am unfamiliar with the name Nellie and his accent."

"Oh," Joanna said. "Well, he's Irish ... I think," she frowned. "He sounds something like Grandfather's man."

"Yes," Reineke smiled. "Me, too. I think he is Irish." And in thinking of that, he thought of perhaps a mercenary. A hired soldier. "Thank you. I will need my hat now, do you mind?"

"Oh, no," Joanna said.

"I have it," Reineke lifted it from her head. "Take her to my tent," he requested with a nod to his soldier. And she was gone.

"Indeed," Reineke watched his coat drag away.

"Where are the trucks?" A voice on the verge of its own hysteria insisted from behind him. Ah, ever Thiele. Reineke turned around.

"They are not here, Thiele, clearly," Reineke said. "You should be pleased."

Thiele was not pleased.

"The trucks are safe, Thiele," he assured. "The ambulances ..." He critically eyed his parking lot. They had only three of them left. That was all right. It completed the picture beautifully. He would have to remember to thank the Holy Man's French for their efforts.

"Hauptmann ..." Thiele was requesting a little attention.

"We have a guest, Thiele," Reineke reminded, drawing the chin-strap tightly across the band of his hat. "Do you think it is appropriate to air our differences in front of a guest?"

Thiele would air them anywhere. "She is your whore, not mine!" he hissed. "Where are the trucks?"

The chinstrap snapped in two. "Indeed," Reineke chose to speak rather than embrace a dangerous silence. "You are fortunate you will be alive to see them in the morning, unlike so many others." He whirled on his guards, barking for them to take the enemy away. They did.

"They are laughing at you," Thiele resurrected a stale defense. "Behind your back, they are laughing at you."

"Let them," Reineke watched the enemy, annoyed it was not the American Michael. "They, like you, will be over it in the morning when she leaves."

"And will you?" Thiele insisted.

"Indeed." How shrewd Thiele could be at times. "No, Thiele," he said, "I will not." He turned back to face him. "I will also not tolerate crude, coarse, or violent behavior reminiscent of animals. This is not a war against women or children or old men. Sergeant Erich will die for his participation in the crimes perpetrated against the woman, if that is what you are actually asking me. So will all others involved, including the SS. I see you have figured out my scheme. I do not know if I am impressed or surprised it took you so long."

"Hauptmann?" Thiele startled.

Reineke ignored him, more interested in watching the enemy soldier as two more of his men stepped in to open the tent flaps. They were taking no chances with the man's size.

"I was not expecting him, Thiele," he acknowledged. "Foolish. Johanna mentioned angels waiting in the wings."

"What?" Thiele said with a quick look after the man himself. "Angels?"

"Archangels," Reineke shrugged. He believed Johanna when she said she did not know him. That did not mean he believed the man had not come from her friends. "Michael!" he shouted after the creature, loud enough for the man to hear.

The man looked. He moved his large head, turned it, and looked.

"No," Reineke said. "No, I do not think that is a messenger from the angels for Johanna. I think ..." he reached in his pocket for his cigarettes, "Indeed, I think, Thiele," he said, in reconsideration, "I may have made a mistake."

There had been more than one. Thiele was silent, recovered from Reineke's confession of his intent to murder. It was nonsense.

"I advise against pursuing any talk of the woman," Reineke warned him. "Johanna is not a subject for discussion." He walked away.

Chapter Sixty-Nine

She could have sat in one of the folding chairs. Reineke looked at the woman propped up against one of the tent's support poles, her hands lost in the pockets of his coat. How incredibly small she was. He would never be comfortable with this woman's size.

"Are you still cold?" he asked lightly.

Joanna shook her head.

He thought not. She should be perspiring as he was. With exaggerated indifference, he removed his uniform jacket, tossing it over the back of one of the folding chairs, making his way to the table set up as his desk.

"Sit down," he invited her.

She did. And he did. On his side.

How absurd. They could play as if they were in his library. Have the most entertaining conversation before he tossed her to the SS. Reineke took off his hat, ran his fingers through his glistening white-blond hair, rested his elbows on the table and folded his hands. "Johanna ..." he said.

"I don't want to die," she interrupted him.

He made the funniest movement with his chin, his eyes sort of wrinkling before they slid to the side, to the cot neatly laid out, the bedding rolled down. Johanna frowned, wondering why he was looking out of the corner of his eye over there when she was trying to explain to him she was very frightened and wanted to know more about the soldiers he had mentioned.

It came to her as she frowned why he might be looking over there. This was her tent, or at least the tent she had been in with Pierre. There was the writing table, there were the chairs, the clock hanging on one of the sides, and the cot she had slept on. Or was it her tent?

Joanna closed her eyes. Maybe it was the way he walked in, maybe it was the way he sat, maybe she could not explain why there might be a writing desk in her tent even though there had been a writing desk in her room. "Is this your tent?" she asked.

It was unnecessary for her to defend her concern. They were not in the library. Reineke should pretend he did not know what she meant about not wanting to die because for a moment he had not known. He did now however, and since he did ...

He cleared his throat, starting again gently. "Yes, it is my tent, Johanna. However, you are not going to die—"

Absolute terror. Her brown eyes were wide with absolute blind terror. Reineke frowned. He should be insulted, and he was. He should also propose how this was now the third time, she, not he, had brought up the topic of her being forced to lie down in his bed. He said she was not going to die. Did she really think his next sentence was going to be, however you must have sex with me?

Indeed. From the expression on her face, it appeared she would much prefer to die. He almost snarled how she could be assured she would not be subjected to having sex with him. However, if he said that he would be insulting himself without any further assistance from her. Women were hardly subjected to his sexual prowess.

"I'm sorry," she said before he even spoke, obviously realizing her smear.

"Indeed, you do not have to apologize, Johanna," he said. "But it concerns me you would continue to have this idea I may be interested in *commanding,"* he chose as his alternative to subjected, "you to have sex with me. I am not in the habit of ordering women to lie down with me." He finished haltingly. He was embarrassed.

Joanna wasn't. She was shocked. She had absolutely no idea what he was talking about. "What?"

He sighed. "Johanna, I am attempting to relieve any concerns you may continue to have—"

"I'm not concerned," Joanna shook her head.

"Indeed," Reineke said. "Good."

"I don't want to have sex with you either," she shook her head.

"Thank you," Reineke said, because no matter what he said, it was not going to come out in his favor, "for that information."

"You're welcome," Joanna nodded. "Could we please talk about something else?" she requested because obviously she would be horribly embarrassed to have such a conversation, even though she had no idea how she even started having such a conversation. She did know she wanted it to stop.

So did he, thank God.

"Of course," he said. "What would you like to talk about?"

Joanna didn't know that either. She was too busy not having sex if only in conversation. Once she was finished, she presumed whatever she had wanted to talk about would come back to her. "I don't know," she shook her head. "What do you want to talk about?"

Reineke had no idea. This little drama had not been planned. It simply happened. And since it happened, he wanted to talk. Not particularly about it. Not particularly about anything at all. Just talk. He found he had a desire ...

He was going to say he enjoyed talking with her, but that would be incorrect. He had not known her long enough to know if he enjoyed talking with her or not. They had actually been in each other's company so few times, even when they were, one could not say he had ever actually talked to her.

He never actually talked to anyone. He did not enjoy talking.

Except perhaps to Pierre.

Diana.

Abraham and John Haas.

Hanuk.

Anne.

"Indeed," Reineke found his cigarettes. He apparently talked to more people than he realized. It did not matter. None of them were there, and even those who were there, were not here in the tent.

Regarding the woman who was here, he found he had a desire to talk with her, he did not know the reason why. Aside from finding her attractive, he found her to be ...

What did he find her to be? Reineke searched his brain for the answer. Fascinating? Yes. Fascinating. That was sufficient. He found her fascinating and he had a desire to talk with her even though he did not know why.

"Johanna ..." he said.

“You kissed me,” Joanna interrupted.

So he had. His mouth set. Was she going to ask him why? Indeed. Because he wanted to. He wanted to again.

“Indeed,” Reineke said. Kissing her was something he had actually done. It was something he could truthfully say he enjoyed. He enjoyed it tremendously. He would enjoy it again. He should tell her this. Better still show her. Simply stand up and walk around the end of the table, lift her up out of her chair and kiss her. He studied those lips he recently held against his own, and they were quite capable of kissing him back. He looked at the small hands lost in his greatcoat and they were quite capable of taking it further. With a little encouragement, a great deal further, all the way to the cot.

Willingly.

Reineke smiled. A magic word. “You ran,” he suggested lightly, rising from his seat to round the table and rest against the edge of it.

Joanna looked at him. “I was frightened,” she said.

Reineke shrugged. “It was a thank you for saving my life.”

And she sat there.

He stood there.

“You couldn’t have shaken my hand?” Joanna asked, and Reineke laughed.

“Indeed, yes,” he agreed. He supposed he could have done that. He supposed he could sit down, and he did, folded his long legs, sitting Indian fashion on the ground in front of her.

Joanna eyed him from her seat on the chair. Not sure what he was doing down there. “What are you doing?”

“Sitting,” Reineke nodded. “You are very small, very petite. I find the difference between our two heights disconcerting. And this way,” he extended, “sitting here, I am smaller than you. Shorter in height.”

“Oh,” Joanna said.

“Is that all right?” he asked.

“Yes,” Joanna shrugged, who was she to say otherwise? If he wanted to sit there on the floor that was up to him.

“Good. But now I have to get up because my cigarettes are on the table, and I cannot reach my cabinet of wine.”

“You have a cabinet of wine?” Joanna asked as he rose and she wondered how she had noticed the clock and missed the wine cabinet. "Oh," she said as he opened the footlocker, which, yes, she guessed she had noticed that.

"No, no," he stopped her before she said something unflattering about his wine cabinet. "This is not a footlocker, it is a cabinet of wine. If you are to know anything about me, you are to know that. It is a wine cabinet, if I say it is. Nothing else matters ... but that is how all man are, correct?" he smiled as he uncorked the wine to let it breathe. "Not only German soldiers?"

"I ..." Joanna said.

"You do not know this?" Reineke sat down at his desk again, at least briefly. "Of course you do. That is something women learn about men when they are two years old. Think about the men in your life and tell me if that is not true—and, actually," he said, "before you do that. What would you like to drink? You have to drink something and you have to eat. I know you do not want the wine—or do you?" he checked.

"No," Joanna shook her head.

"What would you like then?" he asked, sounding like Pierre. "Some water? Perhaps coffee, or tea, or juice? I will tell you what," he said, "we will make it simpler. I will request all of that and food for two. That way," he nodded as he picked up his telephone, "you will have a choice, and they will think we are having a party to which they have not been invited."

He ordered their party and hung up the phone, picking up his wine with a smile. "What were we talking about?" he asked.

"Men," Joanna nodded.

"Yes," Reineke said. "So you tell me Johanna Lee, of all the men in your life, whether father, brother, friend, husband, or lover, do not all men want to have it their way? Must have it their way?"

"I don't have any lovers," Joanna shook her head.

That was not the question, but he commented on her answer anyway. "Well, you are not supposed to have lovers. You are nineteen. You are supposed to have romance, not cots," he waved at the cot, watching her startle. He smiled, set down his wine, and folded his arms, leaning on the table. "You are concerned about being in a situation in which you would not be comfortable?"

She looked back at him blankly.

"Sex," Reineke said. "I am talking about sex."

"Oh," Joanna said. "Well, I just ... well, I guess I don't understand what you said before. Why you said," she nodded, "what you said before about not having sex."

He understood. He thought he did. "Because that is what you were asking me? No?"

Joanna blinked. "No. Well, no," she said.

Reineke nodded. "I am confused. What if you ask me again?"

"Oh," Joanna said. "Well, I guess ..." she frowned. "Well, I don't think I was going to ask you anything. I thought you were going to ask me why I was sleeping in your bed ..." she flushed vividly. "I mean, because I was. I didn't know it ..." she frowned again. "I'm not sure why I was there ..."

Reineke stopped her. "Johanna, you were sleeping on the cot because you were asleep when you came and I instructed the Holy Man to put you on the cot, because your tent was not ready."

That was a lie, because she had no tent, but she did not need to know that. This was her tent. His tent. The Holy Man would be leaving and Reineke was not leaving her alone in a tent to try some ridiculous escape attempt into the desert.

"Oh," Joanna said.

"So then we are clear?" Reineke asked. "We do not have to continue to talk about it?"

"No, please," Joanna took a breath.

"Good. So answer the question," Reineke smiled. "Are not all the men in your life, regardless of who they are, the same? It is their way, or it is no way."

"I don't know," Joanna said. "I really haven't paid any attention."

Reineke laughed. "And that," he assured, "is what men learn about women when they are two years old."

He rose to sit back down on the floor Indian fashion, facing her, remembering to bring his wine and cigarettes.

"You're kind of funny," she said.

"Am I?" Reineke dipped his head. "Indeed. I would think I am serious because I am serious," he said. "I am a very serious man."

"Oh," Joanna said. "Are you being serious now?"

"Yes," Reineke nodded.

"What about?" Joanna asked.

"Well, let me see ..." Reineke looked up at the pitch of the tent as he thought. "I am seriously thinking how to ask you a question I really want to ask."

"Oh ..." Joanna said.

He heard the hesitation in there. "Not about sex," he assured. "No, much worse. Much more serious."

"Oh?" Joanna said.

"Perhaps I should simply ask the question," Reineke offered.

"Well ..."Joanna said.

"I will ask it," Reineke decided. "Does it trouble you," he asked, "does it concern you to sit here speaking with Dieter more or less than it would if you were speaking to a German soldier? Because I am Dieter, and I am a German soldier. We are not two different things. We are one and the same. Dieter ..." his hand drew through the air like a title or a headline, "the German soldier."

She had no idea what he was talking about.

"You do not understand," Reineke shook his head. "I will try again ..."

"No ..." Joanna said.

"Indeed, you do understand?" Reineke said.

"No," Joanna said, but she was trying to.

"I will make it simpler. Johanna, are you afraid of me?"

"Yes," Joanna said, unequivocally and very quickly.

"Indeed," Reineke said. "Why are you afraid of me? Are you afraid of me because I am a German soldier, or because I am ... a tall man," he tossed out what she had once said.

"Could we talk about something else?" Joanna requested.

"No," Reineke said, but it would have to wait for a moment because two of his soldiers were knocking at the door requesting entrance.

Reineke granted entry, rising and picking up his wine and cigarettes. "No, here," he stopped the soldiers from setting the party out on the desk, pointing to the floor. "We are having a picnic. One moment, I have to get the table."

He borrowed the blanket from the cot, spreading it out, thanking the soldiers for setting the table with food and drinks before they saluted and left.

"Come on," Reineke encouraged Joanna up out of her seat. "You have to eat, and to eat you must sit for our picnic."

"All right," she shrugged, rose as he pulled out her chair, and sat down on the floor for the picnic.

"So have you decided why you are frightened of me?" Reineke asked when he sat down.

"Yes," Joanna sipped her water. "I know why I'm frightened of you."

"Because I am a German soldier," Reineke calculated to be the answer even though he was also tall and she was not.

"I haven't met very many German soldiers," Joanna said, "but yes."

She was, and had been surrounded by German soldiers for a month, and who knew how much longer than that during her time with the SS, but she was also correct. She had not met them, only he. "Any other reason?" he asked.

"Yes," Joanna said. "You are very handsome."

"That is true," Reineke agreed. "I am an extremely handsome man. I am Dieter," he drew his title through the air again with his hand, "the extremely handsome German soldier."

"You're teasing me," Joanna said.

"Perhaps a little," he smiled. "But, no, I also am serious. You be serious, too. Indeed, I am not frightening because I am a handsome man."

"Oh, yes, you are," Joanna corrected. "Oh, yes, you are."

"Really?" Reineke said. "Why? Because I am older? I would not be concerned about that. Indeed," he said, "you should be concerned if I were younger."

"Like the witch's brother," Joanna nodded. "Anne," she said as he paused in eating ... well, whatever it was they were eating. It could be horses for all she cared, it was delicious she was so hungry. "Her brother. He is very handsome like you."

"Indeed You think Anne is a little witch?" Reineke said, the only point worth pursuing because while Hanuk might be a handsome young man, Hanuk was hardly as handsome as he. That was ridiculous.

"Yes," Joanna assured. "What is his name?"

"Who?" Reineke said. "Anne's brother? I cannot tell you that," he shook his head, unaware she had met Hanuk. "But I am glad you asked. Johanna, you understand there is a war. And in the war situation you and I are enemies."

"Yes," Joanna nodded.

"Good," he said. "Because you should not ask your enemies questions like that, *and*," he said, "you should not talk about your friends. For example, your friend Michael," he offered, even though right now, he could be eating Michael and he would not care, it was that delicious, and he was very hungry. "Speaking to me is one thing, but you should not speak even to me about too many things. I am still Hauptmann Reineke even if I am also Dieter."

"I know," Joanna nodded.

"You do?" Reineke said.

"Yes," she said. "Was it Dieter or Hauptmann Reineke who asked me who the man was?"

He smiled. "Dieter. I do not want to harm your friends."

"That is not my friend," she assured.

"No," he said, "I would not think he is. But I wanted to confirm."

"Thank you," Joanna said. "May I ask you a question now?"

"Of course."

"Why did you kiss me?"

Reineke decided it was probably a better idea not to speculate why she was asking her question again. He smiled as he bit into his meat. "Because you saved my life. Why? Do you not believe that?"

"No," Joanna sighed. "No, I believe you. I just wanted to confirm."

"Indeed," Reineke said. "You sound disappointed."

"No," Joanna sighed again. "I knew it had to be something like that. I'm not very pretty."

Reineke stopped eating. "What are you talking about? Of course you are."

"I am?" Joanna said.

"Yes, of course. You are very young," Reineke agreed. "But you are extremely pretty. Indeed," he said. "When you are older, you will see, you will be beautiful."

"Really …" Joanna thought about that.

"Yes," Reineke assured, and could not resist but only because he was sly, "I would also recommend if you are going to think about men kissing you, you think about men somewhat younger than I, and somewhat older than Anne's brother … who is, I believe … fourteen?" he lied.

"Fourteen?" Joanna said. "Really?"

"Well, he is tall," Reineke shrugged. "Anne is tall. Indeed, I was tall at fourteen. I was this tall."

"At fourteen?" Joanna said.

"Almost," Reineke said. "Indeed, almost. Very close."

"Oh," Joanna said. "Well, I was almost this short at nine."

Reineke laughed. "You are a unique woman, Johanna Lee," he assured. "Quite unique."

"Is that good or bad?"

"Very good," Reineke promised. "Quite good."

"Oh," Joanna said. "May I ask you another question?"

"Well, I do not know," Reineke smiled, "if you are going to ask me again why I kissed you, I might have to kiss you again."

"Oh, no, you don't have to do that!" Joanna quickly assured.

He did not think so. "I am teasing you," he nodded, lighting a cigarette. "Go ahead, ask me your question."

"I am frightened about going with the soldiers—I know you don't want me to be," she also quickly assured him of that. "But I am. Is that all right?"

"It is understandable," Reineke agreed. "But you truly do not need to be frightened. No harm is going to come to you. Everything will be all right."

"Do I really have to go with them?" she asked.

"Yes," Reineke said. "You do. Not for very long," he assured as her eyes dropped down. "And again, everything will be fine. You will see. Trust me, Johanna, please. Try to."

"Why?" she looked up.

"Also a very good question," Reineke considered. "Because I am asking you to?

"No, that is not a very good reason," he shook his head as she watched him. "Because you have every reason to," he said. "That is the truth, even if you do not understand or believe it is the truth. I can tell you this," he said. "Something I told someone else not long ago. I have a sister … Indeed, a younger sister," he said, "the same age as you. And if my sister were to find herself in your Australian camp—"

"English," Joanna said.

"Indeed," Reineke said. "What happened to Australia? Did you and your twin move?"

"No," Joanna said. "I live in England."

"I see," Reineke said. "Well, then you should be very frightened of German soldiers," he sipped his wine, "that is very true."

"Yes," Joanna said. "What were you saying about your sister?"

"Well, let me see … I was saying," Reineke said, "if my sister were to find herself in your—*English* camp," he granted, "I would want her to be treated with the respect she is due. I cannot ask for that and treat another man's sister differently if she were to end up in mine."

"Oh," Joanna said.

"Does that make sense to you?" he asked.

"I think so," Joanna said. "I'm still frightened, but yes, it makes sense."

"Then why are you frightened?" he asked.

"Because they are not you?" she said simply.

"True," he agreed after a pause. "But then that is where the point of trust comes in." He smiled. "We should probably not continue to talk about this. I do not want you to be upset."

Well, Joanna didn't want to leave with soldiers in the morning, so she guessed they were even. But she did not say that. She wasn't sure why. She yawned.

"You are tired," Reineke said.

"No," Joanna shook her head.

Yes, she was. He could see she was. Her pretty little face was drawn. Her mane of red hair covering most of her prickly mowed patches of scalp not as vibrant as it been earlier. He stole a glance at his watch. It was eleven-forty. He would have to leave soon if he wished to speak with the Holy Man.

"Would you like to go to your tent and speak with the Holy Man for a little while perhaps?" he offered.

“Would you mind?” Joanna said.

“Not at all,” Reineke assured and rose. “I will find him for us. It may be a few minutes. But do not be concerned. This is not the library, but it is like the library, no one enters—or leaves,” he pointed at her. “Without permission.”

“I won’t leave,” Joanna said.

“Good,” Reineke downed his wine, put on his jacket and hat with a smile as she watched him. “Yes,” he said. “Now I am Hauptmann Reineke again. Dieter has gone to sleep. In the meantime, finish your picnic. I will be right back.” He would not, but perhaps she would be asleep soon and not realize it. If not, and she was still awake when he returned, he would explain to her the Holy Man would be there shortly, and continue talking to her until she fell asleep.

Joanna was asleep within fifteen minutes after he left.

Chapter Seventy

"You are late," Reineke told Pierre when the Holy Man joined him on the sandy slopes of the dunes not far from the body of his encampment.

"No," Pierre denied, "not I."

Reineke moved a few feet further away from him before he sat down. He could smell the acidic aroma of victory, loss, and retreat. See the pitch of the tents in the distance, the cast of lights as his men continued collecting the dead, patrolling, and searching the enemy's field. Bored sentries would be alert tonight, the moon brighter than Reineke had hoped with the earlier clouds. It would not be easy for the Holy Man to slip away from the camp.

"Nothing has changed," he assured the Holy Man. "I will order Martin to assume command of the forward scouts. This will allow him to leave as planned."

"Oui, mon capitaine," Pierre said.

"I will also order him," Reineke advised, "to escort you up the hills so you may pray for the dead before he leaves. This will enable you and he to leave together through the sand. Sentries will be advised you are not to be disturbed and will return at your own pleasure when you are finished. This will naturally happen after my soldiers have cleared the dead. This will have you both leaving later than planned but you should be able to be in position by morning."

"Oui, mon capitaine," Pierre assured. "The horses will get us there. A good idea. This will enable Pierre to bless the hillside and spit on the betrayers releasing them to le Christ to forgive them as I cannot." He spit now into the sand, cursing them.

"Indeed." Reineke's thoughts move to Abraham and Hanuk and the other brothers, assuming they were in position for the morning. The SS approach was under close monitoring by the Holy Man's

French as the SS moved through Libya. Anticipated arrival, early morning, a small squad, only ten. Reineke had been pleased when he received the report forwarded to him by Abraham only minutes before the battle. It was why he had chosen to speak with Johanna when he did. To give her enough time as he could for her to absorb the information, and not too much time for confusion and concern to erupt into panic.

There had been no panic attacks on the sea or during her trip, only a few disturbed nights, and an expected stubbornness and resistance. Reineke was hesitant in considering it a good sign because she had remained with Pierre throughout her journey. Tomorrow she would be alone.

Reineke pushed the thought of the woman being alone away. Her journey was almost over. She would be back with her people and whatever happened after had nothing to do with him.

"How is Mademoiselle?" the Holy Man intruded.

Reineke lit another cigarette. "In the tent," he assured, "my tent. Sitting." Or perhaps sleeping. Reineke presumed she was sleeping by this time. "I have no plans to touch her, if that is your concern."

"No, of course not," Pierre agreed, surprise in his voice. "Mon capitaine is a good man."

Le capitaine was going to have to work on his reputation. Suddenly, he could be trusted with spending the night alone with a woman sleeping in his bed. Suddenly, according to Thiele, only whores would find him attractive.

Suddenly, nineteen year old women found him second choice to seventeen year old sheiks.

Reineke ignored Pierre to think about Diana. Abraham and the others gone, Martin was there and Martin fought. Reineke saw him with his soldiers. A gun in his hand, defending the camp. The sons of Diana knew nothing of the impending altercation or the attack on Thiele's convoy. Diana was not the betrayer.

Reineke looked back over his camp where the stench of betrayal was also heavy in the air. "Very believable, Holy Man. I salute your friends for their efforts on my behalf."

"This did not come from Pierre's friends," Pierre assured. "Betrayers, oui, possibly, but they are not friends, they are enemies."

"A separate faction, perhaps," Reineke said, not inclined to persecute the ancient priest for something he knew he had not done. "But why was the area not cleared? I do not understand. These have to be the same group that attacked Thiele. What do you think has happened? Where are your friends? Indeed," he said, "I have taken the caravan route three times without incident."

"Cleared at the time, oui," Pierre said. "But after you have left? Hundreds of kilometers from the oasis? One cannot wash the desert clean, mon capitaine. Not I, or you, or Ben Akach. It would be your scouts responsibility to issue an alert. Thiele. You. Me with Martin and that sergent of yours. I have no idea where these people have come from, who they are. Only that something is wrong—it is very wrong, mon capitaine," he nodded. "Very wrong."

"Indeed," Reineke said. Recoilless guns did not have to be Free French. They could be Allied. "Do you think your friends are lost to them as well?"

"You did not lose the fight, mon capitaine. And, oui, I am as confident my friends are safe. I suspect like Abraham, they are in position waiting for the SS. Believing as we believed everything here is fine. But that man ..." he hesitated.

"Atlas come down from his mountains," Reineke nodded. "Yes. Indeed. I have decided he is a mercenary. It matters little if he is Irish or South African, or what he is. Johanna's people are English, and those bodies are French not Allied."

"Decided?" Pierre said.

"Yes, decided," Reineke said impatiently. "Indeed, decided. Please, Holy Man, no lectures. Be assured whatever you are going to say, I have already thought about it. I have already considered ... indeed, decided," he assured.

"Oui, mon capitaine," Pierre said.

"Thank you. Our plan will work. We are to proceed if your friends are here, in position, lost, or regrouping, attempting to clear the area of this unexpected faction. The SS are to be killed. If you wish to be concerned about something, be concerned with Johanna being alone with those SS for hours. You saw what they did to her ... you know what they did to her. You will not be riding with her. Not Abraham or John or any of them. She will be alone."

He rose and walked away to think.

"Mon capitaine," Pierre followed him.

"It does not take three hours to rape and kill a woman," Reineke argued. It could take ten minutes for all he knew. "Johanna will be alone, by herself for three hours with those men—and that man," he assured. "That creature." The one he knew came from her people, even if she did not. Johanna had not survived the SS unless they wanted her to survive for some reason other than as a toy to play with until it broke and died. The Holy Man was right. A woman always belonged to someone. And, indeed that woman did if there were mercenaries employed to find her. There were probably hundreds of them out there. Mercenaries, soldiers. Who knew.

"The creature is what I wish to speak with you about, mon capitaine," Pierre nodded.

Good. "That creature is not to be killed," Reineke instructed. "He is from Johanna's people. I will not kill her people."

"Pardon?" Pierre said.

Reineke groaned. "He is from her people. Of course he is. We are fortunate Thiele was engaged hundreds of kilometers from the oasis. They will not find us in the Sahara. Once they have her there will be no need. With the SS, they will assume SS. This is a field hospital. Thiele's a convoy of ambulances like here. The creature will not harm her. Indeed," he said, "he is her only protection while she is with the SS."

"Mon capitaine," Pierre said, "the man is very large, this is true, but he is not bulletproof."

"I said he is not to be killed! If someone kills that man, I will kill them without need of any of this charade," Reineke assured, "but immediately, where he stands!"

"All right," Pierre shrugged. "Kill, do not kill the ugly one. It does not matter. I have a plan. We will bring her back. Oui, back," he smiled. "To you, to Pierre. What do you think?"

Think? Reineke thought he was lying dead on the battlefield from the second rocket blast, Johanna as dead up ahead of him. "No," he said.

Pierre scoffed. "What do you mean no? You do not want her to leave, mon capitaine. I know you do not. So? Why leave?"

"You are talking nonsense," Reineke turned to walk back to his camp.

"No, I am not."

"Of course you are!" Reineke turned on him. "Indeed, do not be ridiculous. Bring Johanna back to do what? Play with the children? Cook and clean perhaps?"

"Mon capitaine, you like her," Pierre said.

Like her? Reineke stared at him. He did not *like* her, he was bored. The woman happened upon a time when he was bored, and stayed long enough for him to stop being bored. "Indeed, Holy Man," he assured, "I am bored."

Pierre laughed. "Mon capitaine, you are in love."

"That is enough!" Reineke snapped, in no mood to banter or play. "This is a desert. I am in a desert. Imprisoned in a desert fifteen-hundred kilometers from civilization. Where it is hot," he reminded. "Where it is quiet ... indeed, eternally quiet. Any infatuation I may have with that woman, if I have any, is a natural extension of war—"

"Mon capitaine ..." Pierre said.

"It is a war," Reineke insisted. "This is a war!" Was that not what they were always telling him? "I am a prisoner of war. Dead on a battlefield in France, if I am not lying dead here. Johanna is to leave, the SS are to be killed, and that creature is not. Disobey and I will kill everyone. Do not doubt that I will not!

"Indeed!" he wrestled with his cigarettes. "Bring the woman back for you and I? And do what, eh, Holy Man? What would be her role with me? I have Cäcilie if I am that bored. Johanna is leaving!"

"OK," Pierre surrendered.

"Thank you!" Reineke said.

"But you are a stupid man, mon capitaine," Pierre clucked his tongue, and shook his head. "Oui, a very stupid one ... But," he said, accepted. "It is all right because you are also a very good one. Oui!"

Reineke never should have gotten out of bed. On the day the call to arms came, Reineke knew he should have gone back to sleep and let them fight their war without him. "I will see you after it is over. We will rendezvous here, and ride to the sand and the southern road. I am ordering the camps disbanded now to erase their existence. They have served their purpose."

"Good," Pierre nodded. "The horses will be fine for us. We will need supplies."

"I will ensure we have supplies—including a radio," Reineke assured.

Pierre laughed. "Should we need to cry for help. A good idea. It will be fine, mon capitaine. I feel the trouble right now is over. I am glad these people are dead. It is not only you, or I, or Martin they could have killed, they could have killed Mademoiselle. This is how I know they are not her people. The same as they are not mine or Diana's or yours. I will advise my son of all of this. There may be something he knows, or can find out for us that I do not know."

Reineke did not wish to discuss it any further. "I have to return to Johanna before she escapes into the desert, sets fire to or destroys my tent."

"Mademoiselle will not do that," Pierre shook his head.

"Indeed. You are wrong. Holy Man. Johanna captured the creature, not I, the soldiers, or Martin. She struck him in the head with my pistol ... of course, she then shot me," Reineke said, "but it was unintentional."

"Oh?" Pierre said.

"She missed, obviously. That is not the point."

"No, I understand the point, mon capitaine," Pierre nodded.

So did Reineke. "She saved my life. I owe her, hers. And it is not here. Give her this when it is over," he handed Pierre her chain with its charms. "It is also not mine."

And he was off, running, but not so fast, nowhere near fast enough not to hear the French voice cackling behind him, in his ear.

"And what would this be, eh, mon capitaine?" Pierre called gleefully after him, dangling the silver chain with the Prince's Cross strung in place of one of the little silver dog tags, its ancient gold shimmering in the moonlight. "If there was no war? What would this be?"

Hers. Not his. Merely placed in his care by his grandfather for his courage in the face of his father, at age fourteen.

"After which, I remember going to play ball with Alexia." Reineke looked down on the petite young woman fast asleep when he returned to his tent, her head on her hands for her pillow, resting on the wooden table set up for his desk. In love? The Holy Man was French. Though he did like her, mysteriously fascinated by her for some reason. Perhaps due to her plight? er age, diminutive size, or perhaps simply due to his moods.

No. Perhaps in the beginning. Now, Reineke knew it was her strength, her courage, her will that fascinated him. He had collapsed in France faced with the carnage of war. But she did not for all her fits of rage, temper, and hysteria Abraham jokingly diagnosed as spoiled when Reineke complained about her behavior, wondering if she was as deranged as she seemed. She was not spoiled. He was spoiled. She was strong.

"Indeed," Reineke knelt down at the side of her chair to see if she was sleeping, or pretending. She was asleep. He picked her up and carried her to the cot. Pulling her picnic blanket up over her, he sat down on the ground next to the cot, smoking his cigarette, drinking what was left of his wine in the cup that made it taste like tin, watching her breathe.

April 5

Reineke woke up quickly when his cigarette burned down and burnt his fingers. It was four-thirty. The woman was still asleep, and he was again outside, walking to see if Sergeant Linke had arrived. He had, with two ambulances from the Arab camp and his report. Reineke's principal concern the munitions, they had safely reached Linke's camp six hours ago.

"Excellent," Reineke said. "You have brought Erich with you from the Arab camp?"

"Yes," Linke indicated the second ambulance. "This one has your requested supplies for the scouts."

"Yes," Reineke said. "Come."

They went for a walk with the candidate for Staff Sergeant to discuss the current status and plan, including the gruesome sight laid out on the desert floor. Ten soldiers dead was the final report, six during the altercation there and the four previously from Thiele's convoy. Another six were wounded. The enemy count of French or French Nationals dead was confirmed at thirty-two, some young, some old, the extent of their identification, and no one cared about that.

"Oberleutnant Dönitz," Linke noted when Reineke handed him the list of dead for his records.

"Yes," Reineke nodded his head at a canvas bag of remains set with the covered bodies of his men. "I had ordered him to take charge of the rear scouts, but that is now not possible. I will take command. A nurse and medics have been dispatched from Tataouine to assess the injured and will be arriving in the next few hours. A medical tent is to be set up at the Arab camp for that purpose. Oberleutnant Thiele is among the injured, but not seriously. He should be ready to leave to join you in a few hours after the Allied prisoners are remanded—there is another one, yes," Reineke nodded to Linke's surprised look. "English or Irish, possibly a mercenary, taken alive when he attempted to breach the perimeter. And so the SS have someone to interrogate as to his connections with Allied forces," he shrugged. "Our interest is the area remains extremely unstable."

"That is a large group," Linke agreed. "I would not trust that there are not more of them."

"It is possible," Reineke said. "The Arab encampment remains clear, so this group had to come in from the north, not the south. It matters not. I am not in the mood for guesses. This group is large, yes, and reasonably organized. They were clearly looking for something, if only harassment. An example must be made, as it will be made of our own traitors. Since you are here, you will stay for the executions, of course. There will be two," he confirmed, "the third traitor is dead. His body is over there. You will take the three of them and burn them with the French. Scatter their ashes in the wind and dust of the trucks. I will not have them insult this ground."

"Understood. Do you have enough ambulances left to transport the bodies?" Linke turned to look.

"Why? Are there others available?" Reineke said disappointed to learn that.

Linke smiled. "I have none and will need what I can take from the Arab camp to finish packing the munitions."

"Excellent," Reineke said. "Indeed. That is better than I had hoped."

"It is," Linke agreed, "not bad."

"Take what you need," Reineke nodded. "Including the two you brought. The supplies can be put in my tent, and Erich with the Allied prisoner. The Arab camp must be dismantled now, a grave dug for the French bodies. If you will make the order before returning to your station."

"Yes, Herr Hauptmann."

"Danke."

Reineke left to return to the woman in his tent. A cup of black coffee in his hand as a greeting. She was awake.

Chapter Seventy-One

Reineke was unable to tell if the woman was more afraid or less than she had been earlier. She appeared clinical in her manner after her initial response when she sat up on the cot to regard him and the coffee. "Where is Pierre?" she naturally inquired.

"Preparing for services," Reineke replied. However untrue, it was also a natural comment to make. He wondered what he would have said to her if he did not have six dead men outside.

"Services?" Joanna said. She frowned. "Is it Sunday?"

Yes. Easter Sunday. Reineke had forgotten, but perhaps he would have remembered and said something to the effect of the Holy Man holding services after all.

"Burial services," Reineke said, even though he did not want to talk about death.

"Oh," Joanna said. "Yes, of course."

"Would you like the coffee?" Reineke attempted to change the subject. "I apologize, but I will need to leave again to see to duties. It has been a busy evening."

"Yes," Joanna said again. "Yes, of course." She took the coffee and he agreed how it was bitter when she winced.

"Pierre is all right then," Joanna said.

"Of course. He is—"

"Busy," Joanna nodded. "How long do I have?"

Reineke presumed she meant until the soldiers came rather than preparing to attend some military tribunal. He was thinking of the executions, not the burial, what to say. "You will hear shots. Only a few. Do not let them alarm you. It is a salute to the men."

Joanna nodded. "How long do I have?" she asked again.

Reineke looked at the clock, wondering if she had spent time studying it. "Perhaps an hour? Perhaps two after services?" he said.

"Thank you for the coffee," Joanna said.

"Johanna ..." Reineke said at that point.

"I don't want to die, Captain," she reminded him, and she was cold, not clinical, icy cold, angry. He should probably encourage that, not for him, for her. If she could hold onto her anger, it might help her with her fear, at least for a little while.

"You are not going to die, Johanna," he assured.

"Yes, I am," she nodded.

"No, you are not," he said somewhat impatiently. Neither was he. Or why he was looking at the floor instead of at her. He looked up. "A soldier will be here to take you when it is time. It would please me if you were to see to accompanying him quietly."

"Would it," Joanna said.

"Yes," Reineke said. "I would also ask that when the soldiers come, you remember when you address a German officer who holds your British rank of Captain, you refer to him as Hauptmann. Herr Hauptmann. I am Herr Hauptmann Reineke."

"Perhaps I will miss you, Herr Hauptmann," she said.

Miss him? That was not only absurd it was a pathetic attempt at feminine wiles. "Miss me?" he heard himself say. "I am asking you to trust me, Fräulein that is all." And he was through the tent flap and gone, a sentry stepping in to stand guard. Sometime later, a second soldier appeared with a length of rope to tie her hands behind her back while she waited, and that did rather settle that.

Thiele woke up from an unexpected nap to stumble out of his tent blinking in dawn's breaking light at the graves dug near where a few stubborn mud walls continued to stand beyond the shells of the burned ambulances. Everything the same and expected as it had been before he found himself suddenly asleep, except for the sunlight and Sergeant Linke in the background with a small group of men stacking bodies of French into an ambulance.

"Good morning, Thiele," Reineke rose from his perch against one of the tent ropes, a small loaf of bread in his hand that he cut with a Bowie knife, offering Thiele the slice. "You are early. I will need to speak with the Holy Man. He guaranteed me five hours, and his powders have lasted not too long past four."

Thiele frowned slightly at the knife before knocking the slice of bread from Reineke's hand with an angry swipe. "Where are the trucks?" he insisted. "What have you done with the trucks?"

"Calm yourself, Thiele," Reineke suggested, inviting him to step back inside his tent. "They are out there, of course."

"Where?" Thiele stomped in after him.

"There," Reineke waved with the knife as he cut Thiele a fresh piece of bread. "Out there. Safe. I have decided to break camp as a precaution. You may leave with Linke if you wish after the executions," he offered Thiele the bread. "Linke is preparing for the transport of some of the equipment from the Arab camp with the first group of men."

"He is stacking the French into a truck!" Thiele snatched the bread, biting into it hungrily. "And what *men*? We have twelve men. The rest are dead!"

"We have forty men, Thiele," Reineke assured, "as you are well aware, only ten are dead, as we have twenty others, seventeen horses, and three camels."

"Yes, all right, all right," Thiele waved. "I forgot about your Arabs and horses. And I meant here," he assured. "Twelve men here. Where are the trucks?" his fists hit his desk Reineke borrowed to cut the bread. "And what execution? You are executing the mercenary? Why? He should be remanded to the SS with—the woman," he said, catching himself before he said something else. It was a struggle, but he did. Reineke wondered what Thiele had been about the say before he caught himself.

"Indeed, you believe the Irish is a mercenary, Thiele?" Reineke asked.

"Of course," Thiele scoffed. "And I would not recommend his execution. There may be valuable information he can provide on his association with the Allied."

Reineke smiled. "Good, because I am not executing him, Thiele," he agreed. "He is being remanded to the SS along with Johanna."

"Oh," Thiele frowned. "Then what are you talking about?"

"Executions," Reineke said. "I said executions, Thiele. I am executing Erich's men after the burial service. Two are alive. One is already dead from the fight. They are an example to the men, as they are to you. I will not tolerate betrayal. Their bodies will be burned with the French—at the Arab encampment, Thiele," he said, "where the munitions also are not. They are not here, they are not there. These are both blinds to ensure if this happened, it happened here, not at the transfer station where the munitions were brought. Linke's camp. Fifty kilometers south."

"What?" Thiele said.

"You seem impressed," Reineke noticed.

"I am impressed," Thiele assured. "I do not understand. Why would you tell Sergeant Linke and not tell me this?"

"Because you prefer to worry about women and Holy men, Thiele, to where Sergeant Linke does not."

"That is unfair."

"No, it is true," Reineke assured. "You are First Officer of my munitions complex, Thiele, not guardian of my conscience. This hospital is also a trap for the SS, whom I am going to kill, as I have told you. It is my alibi for Herr Oberst Schönfeld. The SS will also be killed by the French, two hours after they leave this camp. Their executioners are waiting for them now, assembling into position. Fifty of them against a squad of ten SS. Which side do you think will win that fight, eh, Thiele? It will not be the German SS. The French would have been here to annoy us, nothing major, only minor, to underscore the area's instability. Except they were also disrupted by this unexpected faction, as we all were, as were you earlier. They are working to clear them now—as I believe they will succeed, Thiele," he assured, "because I believe the Holy Man."

"What?" Thiele said.

"What, what?" Reineke snapped. "Why is it you feign stupidity at the answers yet find your questions so smart? I am killing the SS, Thiele, with the assistance of the Holy Man and his French. Johanna will not be remanded to Tripoli, she will be secured by the French and returned to her people, whoever they are, wherever they are, and we will take our munitions and return home to my complex where you are my First Officer. So you tell me what part of that answer to your questions should you find relevant to your interests? Your concerns, your position as First Officer to Hauptmann Reineke of the Afrika Korps. Johanna, the Holy Man, or the munitions for our bins?"

"I am simply asking why," Thiele said.

"Choices, Thiele," Reineke shook his head. "No more questions. Choices. There are three. You may choose the one that suits you best. One, Thiele!" he flipped the knife holding it, pointing it at Thiele for his perusal while he considered his options. "You may leave with intentions to betray me to Linke, the SS, or Schönfeld, knowing I will shoot you where you stand before you have a chance to open your mouth.

"Indeed, Thiele," he said, "should you doubt, remember your predecessor Oberleutnant Goetz. He did not understand how this is not a war against women and children or old men. He thought it would be interesting to rape some girl with a knife. I killed him and I killed her to provide her with relief because there was nothing I could do for her. I did not have the Holy Man then, but I do now and so this one did not die, nor will she."

"That is not in the report of the incident with Oberleutnant Goetz," Thiele studied the knife.

"Of course it is not in the report, Thiele," Reineke snapped, "because no one cares. It is irrelevant what Goetz did, as it is irrelevant what I did. I killed him because I did not like him. He was insubordinate. Threatened the operation with his disobedience. Do I have the report correctly?"

"Yes," Thiele said.

"Your second choice, Thiele," Reineke assured. "You may go with the SS, to assist them, protect them, defend them, and die with them. Or, Thiele," he said, "you may leave with Linke for the transfer station and assume your role as First Officer. Ensuring the continued safe transport of the munitions to my complex for division and subsequent transport to the second compound."

"I will go with Linke," Thiele assured.

"Good!" Reineke slashed him across the upper right arm with the knife, its blade slicing through Thiele's jacket, shirt, and powerful muscles, deeply.

"You are insane!" Thiele grasped his arm, blood running and seeping through his clutching fingers.

"Thorough, Thiele," Reineke calmly wiped the knife with the napkin from the bread. "I am thorough. In the weeks to come, should questions arise as to why I did not consider providing the SS with an additional escort in light of the area's instability—for example, you, as First Officer with a squad," he nodded. "It will be clear how I could not as you were wounded."

"What about the squad?" Thiele said.

Reineke shrugged. "I am not sending my men to their deaths, so I suggest you think of something creative."

"We have lost ten of twenty-two men," Thiele was already thinking. "What squad would we send? The other men are at the transfer station securing the convoy, our first priority," he assured Reineke. "Of which the SS know nothing about, and Herr Oberst Schönfeld will certainly support. If the SS chose to continue with only their squad after being apprised of the situation here, it was their choice."

"Excellent, Thiele," Reineke said impressed. "Who apprised them?"

"I did."

"Also, excellent," Reineke agreed. "Let me see your arm," he rounded the table. "Burial service is at six o'clock. I can delay it. There is a nurse arriving at the Arab camp ... as part of my authentic charade," he smiled. "She will provide you with exquisite care. But, you need something now ... indeed," he nodded as he helped Thiele off with his jacket, tearing his shirt sleeve to expose the wound. "That is deep. You need a tourniquet and some pressure. I will get you a medical pack, but we will use this now," he pulled off his jacket to use his shirt. "It is a powerful knife."

"It is a Bowie knife," Thiele nodded.

"What is that?" Reineke asked.

"Jim Bowie," Thiele said. "An American frontiersman. He carried a distinctive knife. That knife," he nodded. "It is called a Bowie after him."

Reineke eyed him. "Indeed. How do you even know these things, Thiele?"

"I just do," Thiele shrugged.

"Well, it is fascinating," Reineke agreed. "The officer with Johanna was American. Are you thinking they are connected?"

Thiele frowned. "What American?" And Reineke smiled.

Herr Doktor Danzig, Schönfeld's private physician, was an officer Reineke did not know and would forgo their introduction when advised by Linke of the doctor's arrival, referring him to Thiele.

"Ah," Eric smiled when Linke returned to hand him back his paper and grant him entry, advising Oberleutnant Thiele would be with him in a moment.

Eric understood because they were busy, clearly, as there were not very many of them, and the ... well, *set*, Eric supposed as he wandered in, was large and quite authentic for the hospital theme, particularly the burned ambulances, bested only by the truckload of dead bodies. "Something go a little awry or amuck?" he wondered, not that anyone was listening. "Or did you also bring your own morgue?"

"Excuse me," a defiant voice answered, but it was nice to hear one. It was the indomitable Oberleutnant Thiele who looked like a wrestler in glasses. Eric recognized him from the photograph in his file when Eric turned around.

"Not at all," Eric assured, and stepped aside out of the way.

Thiele looked at him. "Excuse me," he repeated. "I am Oberleutnant Thiele. You are, Hauptmann?"

"Oh. Sorry," Eric apologized, "I thought you wanted me to move. Yes, thank you, Oberleutnant," he smiled at Thiele, handing him his papers. "As I advised your Sergeant Linke, I was to arrive yesterday, but was unfortunately delayed ... hopefully, not too late," Eric looked around again, particularly at the burned ambulances, of which apparently only three had survived. "I am Herr Doktor—"

"Doktor?" Thiele took the papers. "Yes, of course," he said, now that he was paying attention to the man and his uniform. "You came with the ambulance. Excellent. The wounded are in the truck. I was bringing them to the medical camp."

"Ah ... no, I came in a car," Eric said. "And, I'm sorry, but did you say wounded? They're dead."

Thiele looked at him again.

"Oh, you mean another truck," Eric said. "A different truck. The one with the...ah, wounded." Eric looked at the one parked next to him with the bodies dangling from its interior.

"Yes," Thiele said. "Excuse me."

"Not at all," Eric waited.

Thiele looked at him for a third time. "Herr Doktor, they are attempting to get through. Please move your car."

"Make up your mind," Eric said. "First you want me to stand, and then you want me to move, and now you want me to ... move again ..." his attention briefly wandered back to the truck.

"Yes," Thiele said. "Herr Doktor ..."

"Danzig," Eric tapped his papers. "Read them, Oberleutnant, while I go move my car."

Eric left to move his staff car, and shortly thereafter, the body-laden truck, under Thiele's expert guidance, completed its three-point turn so it could pull up to the exit and stop with the sharp blow of Thiele's whistle.

"Oberleutnant," Linke leaned out the driver's window to alert Thiele to their guest standing by his staff car.

"Yes, yes," Thiele waved the papers. "I have it. I will confirm with the Hauptmann."

"Who is he?" Linke asked curiously not having looked at the papers himself.

"The Adjutant Hauptmann Danzig," Thiele scoffed, recalling him from their bizarre radio conversation, and not surprised by the equally bizarre demeanor. He walked away with a shake of his head, muttering, "Are we moving them? No, we are keeping them, you idiot. Yes, we are moving them!"

Reineke turned to Thiele with his approach. "Thank you," he thanked Thiele for moving the bodies out of the camp before the arrival of the SS. It was not something he wanted Johanna to see.

There was no reason to thank him. "The SS have confirmed arrival in thirty minutes," Thiele said. "And there is an officer here from Herr Oberst to confirm remand. Linke advised you?"

"Yes," Reineke said. "Herr Oberst's aide. Some Hauptmann. Did you confirm the instability of the area with the SS?"

"Yes. With Leutnant Faust when he radioed. Do you want to release Oberleutnant Dönitz to the Adjutant now?"

"Indeed," Reineke looked over at the canvas bag, amused by the lawyer Martin's gruesome joke. "A good idea. Then call assembly."

"Understood." Thiele collected the canvas bag of French bones and Martin's disguise bringing it to the idiot Danzig.

"Ah ..." Eric said as Thiele set a canvas bag in the back of his car, pushing a clipboard under his nose, requesting signature.

"Herr Hauptmann," Thiele repeated, "please sign."

"I think not," Eric smiled. "After all, surely you are joking, Oberleutnant."

"Joking?" Thiele said. "Of course I am not joking. Please sign, Hauptmann," he thrust the clipboard at Eric, "so I may release it."

"It?" Eric said. "Yes, 'it' does cover it, Oberleutnant, doesn't it? However, you will excuse me, appreciating we cannot always guarantee final tonnage—"

"What are you talking about?" Thiele sputtered. "Hauptmann, I must insist you sign the release for Oberleutnant Dönitz's remains. And then please come, we are ready for assembly."

"Remains," Eric stared at the bag. "Oh, yes, of course," he took the clipboard. "Oberleutnant Dönitz," he said, trying to recall the officer whose name was certainly familiar. "Really."

"Yes," Thiele said.

"Very unfortunate," Eric handed him back the signed release. "Then I take it ... Some of this is real."

"What?" Thiele said. "Of course it is real. We have lost ten men."

Eric nodded. "And the trucks—with all due respect to our losses," he assured Thiele quickly. "However, where are the munitions, Oberleutnant? Was anything salvageable?"

"The munitions are secure at the transfer station, Hauptmann," Thiele assured. "Now, please, assembly."

"Oh, yes, of course," Eric said. "I am honored. But I'm afraid I do not understand, Oberleutnant," he pressed, accompanying Thiele. "This is the transfer station."

"No," Thiele said, "this is the field hospital. We are fortunate Hauptmann Reineke was not satisfied with the reports even though Sergeant Linke's early reconnaissance supported *yours*," he emphasized. "It seemed unlikely any one particular area could be truly stable. That was proven by an earlier attack on one of our forward convoys."

"Really," Eric said. "Whose?"

"Mine," Thiele assured.

"The arm," Eric nodded.

"No," Thiele said. "Four of the ten men dead. My arm is a shrapnel wound from last night's fiasco. It is all right though," he assured, "the SS traitors are both secured. The third was killed last night in the altercation with the French faction—the last of the bodies," Thiele indicated the truck.

"Yes," Eric said. "My apologies for blocking you earlier."

"Yes," Thiele said, and sounded the call for assembly with their arrival in the body of the camp.

Eric watched the execution of two of Sergeant Erich's henchmen in silence. Each killed by a single shot to the back of the head, the honor of performing the executions given to some candidate for Staff Sergeant, their bodies picked up and thrown into the truck with the French. Eric watched the truck leave, Sergeant Linke driving.

"I will want to speak with you, Oberleutnant," Eric mentioned quietly to Thiele as the men reassembled for the burial ceremony.

"We will be leaving after the prisoners are remanded to the SS," Thiele replied. "That is why you are here, correct?"

"Yes," Eric smiled. "And I am not talking about the munitions, Oberleutnant—" he paused. "Prisoners? There are more than one?"

"There is a second, yes. A mercenary apprehended when he attempted to breach the perimeter last evening prior to the French attack. He is English ... or Irish," Thiele granted. "He is also being remanded to the SS for appropriate handling. What did you want to ask me?"

"Oh," Eric said. "Simply confirming the remand of the prisoner remains on schedule—given the circumstances," he nodded at the camp.

"Yes," Thiele assured. "I spoke personally with Leutnant Faust."

"Excellent," Eric smiled.

Chapter Seventy-Two

Herr SS Major Hanse Weiheber was not there, not in the staff car with his Leutnant, or in the kübelwagen behind the truck in the middle of the small convoy of three vehicles. Reineke stared at the truck. Weiheber could not be in the truck.

"He is not here," Reineke voiced aloud from Eric's right.

"Herr Major? Apparently not. As apparently," Eric said to Thiele on his left, "they read the same erroneous reconnaissance reports as we did. Foolish though to send a small squad given the instability of the area, moronic ... yes," he nodded as the staff car halted at the entrance. "Excuse me, gentlemen, that's my cue."

"Indeed," Reineke looked at him. "This is my camp."

"*Our* camp, Hauptmann," Eric smiled broadly. "However, if you are concerned with the SS being granted entry to our camp, be assured, they will not step one foot over that dividing line. In the meantime ... Read." He took out his papers for the third time, extending them to Reineke, who, as expected, ignored them. Though Eric did have Reineke's attention, burning holes in Eric with those blue Siamese eyes of his and that was also expected.

"Fine," Eric stuffed his papers at Thiele. "You read them to him, especially the part about Commanding Officer." He left to walk up to the SS halted by the sentries.

"I do not understand, Thiele," Reineke looked over the convoy again. "Where is he?"

"Perhaps there were issues in other areas?" Thiele suggested. "Hauptmann Danzig was also late, expected arrival yesterday."

"Indeed," Reineke said. "Possibly, yes."

"Do you want these?" Thiele offered Danzig's papers.

"No," Reineke said. "Schönfeld is Commanding Officer. That is an idiot."

"Yes," Thiele agreed. "I will see what I can confirm about Herr Major's arrival."

"Danke."

"Leutnant," Eric returned Faust's salute with a smile. "Where is your Major? Has he lost his way?"

"Hardly. Oberleutnant," Faust assured with a nod in greeting for Thiele also walking up.

"Oberleutnant?" Eric repeated. "I believe you mean Hauptmann, Leutnant. We've met. I am Hauptmann Eric Danzig, Adjutant to Herr Oberst Alfred Schönfeld. The uniform," he explained his jacket with its medical badges, "is borrowed. We had some trouble, as you can see."

"Yes ..." Faust could. "Is that why the delay, Oberleutnant?"

"Oberleutnant? It's Hauptmann," Eric said testily. "Really, Leutnant—"

"No delay, Leutnant," Thiele assured from nearby Eric's ear and Eric jumped with the unexpected voice of the bullfrog behind him.

"Oh, *you*, Oberleutnant," Eric said and Thiele looked at him and, yes, if Thiele was going to continue to look at him with that look of his, Eric was going to snatch those glasses off Thiele's face, throw them on the ground, and crush them. He smiled at Thiele.

"Yes," Eric said. "Oberleutnant Thiele is quite correct. There is no delay. So where is Herr Major, if I may be so bold to ask—*again*," Eric turned back to Faust. "Taking some necessary ... *sojourn*." he put it delicately, the attempt at tact flying over Faust's head like one of their Stuka's.

"What?" Faust said.

"Fine. Where is he, Leutnant?" Eric asked. "Urinating on some bush? Peeing behind a palm tree? Time is a' wasting, and you're not the only one who wants to get out of here."

"Hardly, Hauptmann," Faust's plum-shaped face shriveled into a prune. "This is a simple matter. It does not require the attention of Herr Major. He is in Tripoli naturally."

"Ah," Eric refrained from asking alive or dead as that was another unresolved matter waiting. Even though Eric had recently confirmed Hauptmann Reineke had *not traveled* to Tripoli, as everyone thought he had, but merely *radioed* Tripoli passing himself off as one Hauptmann Eric Danzig instead of who he was. A pain in the ass.

A gilded pain in the ass. One apparently as disinterested in any of this as Herr Major since neither was Hauptmann Reineke making any move to join them.

"Yes," Eric smiled at Faust. "That explains why he would send you to handle this meaningless business." And *that* Eric noted generated a brief, glimmer of approval over Oberleutnant Thiele's otherwise constipated expression. There was hope for Thiele yet.

"As does Hauptmann Reineke wholeheartedly concur. Neither does he have the time for this trivial matter," Eric assured Faust.

"Which is why," Thiele advised, "Hauptmann Danzig is here to see to it."

But then again, perhaps hope and Thiele was also a pipe dream. "Yes," Eric smiled. "After this I am returning to guard the latrine."

"Excellent," Thiele gave a curt nod. "One moment, please."

He left to apprise Reineke while Eric considered heaving a rock after the retreating head but pursued the issue of security with Faust instead.

"Nevertheless, Leutnant," Eric said, "I am amazed Herr Major chose to send only a small squad under the circumstances."

"What circumstances?" Faust asked.

He was joking, of course. "Did Oberleutnant Thiele not advise you on the situation here?" Eric asked.

"Oh," Faust said. "Yes, of course, of course. Something about instability ... Hauptmann," he assured, "we are in control of Libya. These petty nuisances are to be expected."

"Most of Libya," Eric concurred. "Certainly here. However, Leutnant, I believe you and your Major are not fully appreciating the situation. I have ten dead men, and, yes," he said, "in the time I have been here, I have personally witnessed the deaths of two more.

"One of my officers is over there in a canvas bag in the backseat of my staff car," he pointed. "Oberleutnant Thiele himself has been injured, you may have noticed, and, let me see ... " Eric wondered, how long it was going to take Faust to start or stop peeing in his pants. "Need I go on?"

"No," Faust said. "That is not necessary."

"Yes," Eric thought as much. "So what is the verdict, Leutnant? Are you staying or going and we'll see you another day?" he smiled, because after all, if Eric could get out of another arduous trip and have the prisoner remanded to him that would work out very well.

"Oh. Well, I must secure the prisoner, Hauptmann ..." Faust looked around.

"It's your funeral," Eric shrugged. "Up to you. Solely up to you."

"Well, I must return to Tripoli, anyway, Herr Hauptmann," Faust said. "Why would I not take the prisoner since I am here? Why would I leave without them?"

"Oh," Eric said, though it had been worth a try. "I am not talking about the prisoner, Leutnant," he assured. "I am speaking of the size of your squad. I have no men to give you. Certainly, I am not going with you."

"You are not?" Faust startled.

"No, Leutnant," Eric said. "Do I look like an idiot to you, apart from my responsibilities here to my men in this situation?"

"Oh," Faust said. "Well, what about him?"

"Who?" Eric said.

"The prisoners are being brought out," the voice of the bullfrog Thiele croaked behind Eric.

"Tempting," Eric settled back into his skin with a smile for Thiele. "But, no, sorry, Leutnant, also out of the question."

"What is?" Thiele asked.

"You, Oberleutnant," Eric assured. "I was explaining to Leutnant Faust I have no men to give him under the present circumstances ... or anytime," he assured Faust. "This is not our issue, it is yours. If Herr Major wishes to speak with someone about that, he is welcome to contact me. Even though, obviously, Leutnant," he said, "as already noted, your Major is not interested or concerned as he chose not to accompany you. Now, if you will excuse Oberleutnant Thiele and me for a moment, the prisoners will be with you forthwith ... in the meantime," he nodded sharply, as he turned away with Thiele, "don't even think of putting your toe over that line into my camp, because you'll get more than a black eye."

"Disinterested my foot," Eric lit a cigarette with assurance to Thiele. "Gutless ... and, not stupid," he concurred. "No, not stupid. So, where are they, Oberleutnant? Where are the prisoners? Let's get going ... Oberleutnant?" Eric said, when there was no reply. The wrestler had walked away, returning to his handler's side.

"Hm. Someone's not as disinterested as they would like others to believe," Eric observed the team of Reineke and his Oberleutnant Thiele conferring. "And all I have to say to that is ... whatever you are up to, mein Herr those munitions had better be there."

"Status?" Reineke requested from Thiele.

"Faust's requests for additional men has been denied."

"Indeed. By whom?"

"Hauptmann Danzig."

"Indeed," Reineke eyed the court jester Danzig debating about entertaining the king. "Under what authority? He is an aide, nothing more."

"What are your orders?" Thiele asked.

"Have the prisoners brought out," Reineke agreed. "We have business to attend to."

"Understood." Thiele nodded to the waiting candidate.

"Who, in turn, nodded on down the line," Eric loved their inefficient efficiency.

"Erich remains in irons?" Reineke confirmed.

"Yes," Thiele said

"And the Allied?"

"Ropes," Thiele shrugged. "Do you want irons?"

"No. The irons are only to complete Erich's humiliation ... yes?" Reineke asked his candidate waiting at a respectful distance.

"The order has been issued, Herr Hauptmann."

"Thank you," Reineke nodded. "Wait here. Hauptmann Danzig may need your assistance in his escort of the Allied—you have advised Hauptmann Danzig of the additional prisoner?" he asked Thiele.

"Yes, Herr Hauptmann."

"Good. And the woman? Is she also secured?"

"No. I did not think it was necessary. Do you want her secured?"

“No,” Reineke shook his head, watching the jester Danzig who had arrived at his decision, daring to approach. “That is fine.”

“Excuse me, Hauptmann ...” his sergeant said.

“Yes, I see him,” Reineke assured as Eric stepped up.

“Yes,” Eric smiled, “rather difficult not to see me. How are you, Hauptmann Reineke?” he saluted and extended his hand because that was what they had taught him in school.

Reineke had apparently been schooled by wolves, ignoring the hand, not bothering with the salute. “Yes?” he abandoned Eric for his candidate still waiting. “What is it?”

“Yes, excuse me, Herr Hauptmann,” the sergeant said. “The woman has been secured as with the Allied. I did think it was appropriate.”

“What?” Reineke said, aware of Thiele’s bristle and the quiet, cautioning, “Hauptmann ...” Thiele spoke in his ear.

“Is something wrong?” the court jester Danzig added.

“Under what authority?” Reineke stared at the sergeant.

“My apologies, Herr Hauptmann,” he paused, uncertainly.

“Indeed,” Reineke said.

“Well, small matter,” Eric beamed before they had another execution on their hands. “No sense making mountains ...” Eric noticed there appeared to be a mountain approaching now. “Out of molehills ... What the hell is that?” Eric stared at the prisoner roughly the size of the Sphinx.

“A molehill,” Reineke replied.

“Ah, ha, yes ...” Eric agreed. “So, I see. Excuse me.”

Eric pardoned himself to have a better look because unless he was mistaken that was none other than the rather large, rather hairy man the Russian Reiss had identified as Reynolds. Something Reynolds. It was in the notebook back in Algiers. “Amazing,” Eric whistled. “Absolutely amazing.”

“What is?” Thiele asked.

“You jest,” Eric grinned at the muscular Thiele who had shrunk rather quickly from a bullfrog down to a toad in the face of the giant. Faust had probably fainted or run for the hills. The other two prisoners were also out. Sergeant Erich bound in chains, and the little girl in ropes. A bit overdone for the two of them, Eric concurred though could nevertheless understand the sergeant's position, as he was also someone for protocol. However, Eric was not there to make friends with sergeants. He was there to make friends with Reineke. He lit a cigarette. "Your Hauptmann is right, Sergeant. What threat again were you in fear of from that child?"

"Indeed," Reineke said to Thiele. "Erich is to be put in the staff car with his friends."

"Understood." Thiele reprimanded the candidate. "In the future, you are to remember it is the Hauptmann who gives the orders."

"Yes, Herr Oberleutnant," he said.

"Very good. Bring Hauptmann Danzig's car. You will escort the SS until they are out of the immediate area, and then proceed to the hospital ...We can spare one man," Thiele assured Danzig clearing his throat. "They need assistance obviously."

"No, I understand," Eric agreed. "And, yes, they do. They need the assistance of more than one, and probably beyond the immediate area. But the gesture is considerate of you, Oberleutnant," he smiled. "It is appreciated. You wear your rank well."

Thiele rolled his eyes. "If you please, Hauptmann," he gestured for Eric to get on with remanding the prisoners to Faust.

"Yes, of course. They're all mine ... or should I say ours?" he teased.

"No, they are the SS's," Thiele assured with a brief glance at Reineke who did not say anything, and Thiele shrugged. He did not like the candidate anyway, and they did not need another Staff Sergeant who did not understand the chain of command.

"Thiele," Reineke called him as Thiele turned away.

"Yes, Hauptmann?" Thiele turned to him.

"Oberleutnant Dönitz is in the jester's staff car."

"Oh," Thiele said. "Yes, thank you. I will secure him."

"Thank you," Reineke glanced at his watch. It was nine-twenty-five.

Thiele returned in a few minutes with Eric carrying the canvas bag. The SS were gone. "Is everything ready?" Reineke confirmed.

"Yes," Thiele said.

"Proceed then," Reineke gave the order.

Eric watched as men appeared in response to Thiele's sharp whistle, to climb into the first ambulance and aboard the gun. The wounded in the back of the second ambulance, where Eric decided to set Dönitz, were not injured except for the usual bumps and bruises one might expect from an evening dancing with the French, and were busy removing their bandages.

Oberleutnant Thiele however was injured. His arm bleeding through his jacket, Eric noticed, as Thiele climbed into the cab of the second ambulance with a call for Eric. "You will ride with me, Hauptmann."

"Oh," Eric said. "Isn't Hauptmann Reineke coming?"

"Hauptmann Reineke is staying to ensure the area between the hospital and station remains clear until the convoys are en route."

"Alone?" Eric said, not to discredit the man's abilities, but the gilded Hauptmann Reineke did look lonely standing there, his camp clearing around him.

"Alone?" Thiele said. "No, not alone. We have forward scouts. They have been recalled to join him."

"Ah!" Eric said.

"Yes. Please, Hauptmann?"

"Yes, of course," Eric climbed in. "Elaborate, Oberleutnant," he agreed. "Quite elaborate, I must say, and certainly authentic." He smiled at the gun and all that it represented from the power to the glory and everything in between. "Are there usually guns at field hospitals?" he wondered out of simple curiosity.

"I would think yes," Thiele maneuvered the truck around with the hands of an expert, and they were heading out. "Why? Do you want to ride on the gun instead?"

"No," Eric declined. "Why? Do you want to ride on the gun?"

"No," Thiele assured. "I asked because some soldiers think it's fun."

"Ah, ha, another good one, Oberleutnant. However, perhaps you and I should get something clear between us."

"Yes," Thiele said, "perhaps we should. You are aide to Herr Oberst Schönfeld. I was aide to Herr Oberst. I am aware of the duties and responsibilities of the post."

"It's changed slightly," Eric offered, "as you can see."

"Yes," Thiele could see.

"And that's it?" Eric said. "No comment?"

"Comment?" Thiele said.

"On the changes. Make it opinion, Oberleutnant. What is your opinion of the changes?"

"Good luck with that," Thiele shrugged.

"True," Eric smiled, "and thank you. In return, and certainly not to belie your skill with handling a truck, I can drive, if you like."

"No, why?"

"Your arm is bleeding," Eric advised.

"Oh," Thiele glanced at it. "It's fine. There is a nurse at the hospital."

"Well, there's a doctor sitting next to you. But let's not carry the charade quite that far."

"No, there is a nurse at the hospital," Thiele said. "I will have it taken care of there."

"Oh," Eric said. "You mean an actual nurse."

"Yes," Thiele said. "Hauptmann Reineke felt there should be medical personnel available—though, no," he said, "we were not expecting the degree of difficulties we encountered.

"No, obviously not," Eric said, trying to stay out of the way of the blood starting to drip onto the seat. "Perhaps the one point Leutnant Faust had. We are in the control of this area, and obviously we're not doing that good of a job ... Oberleutnant, I really must insist ..."

"What?" Thiele looked at the seat. "Oh. All right, all right. It's my arm, Hauptmann," he assured after he pulled the drape and advised the men they were stopping for a change in drivers, not because the French were ahead.

"Well, it's my ass," Eric said.

"I understand." Thiele slammed out of the cab to pull off his jacket, and slam back in on the passenger side. "Go ahead."

"Thank you." Eric put the truck back in gear, missed the clutch, and got it right the second time under Thiele's guidance.

"Anytime you're ready."

"Yes, thank you. And, no, I don't drive like a girl, Oberleutnant, and I don't faint at the sight of blood, if that is what you're thinking."

"I am not thinking anything," Thiele wrapped his handkerchief around his arm, maneuvered it into a knot, pulling it tight with his teeth. In all, very masculine, Eric agreed, surprisingly nimble for a left-handed man.

"I simply prefer not to be bled on, if it can be at all helped," Eric said.

"I don't like the sight of blood either," Thiele pulled his jacket on, "especially when it's mine. Who does?"

"Few," Eric smiled. "A few. Is it all right?"

"Yes, of course," Thiele said. "It needs a bandage change."

"Well, we'll be there shortly," Eric promised. "However, speaking of skill ... your skill," he said when Thiele turned that look on him. "Are you a truck driver by trade, Oberleutnant?"

"School teacher," Thiele assured.

"Really?" Eric said. "Explains the discipline."

"Perhaps," Thiele shrugged. "Haven't you read my file?"

"Oh, well, there are a lot of you, Oberleutnant," Eric reminded, "between five compounds. Some files larger than others, and I've only been here a few weeks."

"Well, my file is not large," Thiele said.

"Perhaps not," Eric agreed. "But by that marksmen badge it does appear that it will be interesting."

"I have a skill," Thiele shrugged. "So what."

"More than one," Eric assured. "Your Hauptmann Reineke is a full-time job himself." And the look Thiele shot him that time was the one Eric had been waiting for. Eric lit a cigarette.

"Calm yourself, Oberleutnant," he suggested. "I meant no disrespect to Hauptmann Reineke."

"Hauptmann Reineke is an exceptional officer," Thiele replied. "Decorated with an Iron Cross, not a marksmen's badge. He is a Panzer Captain."

Yes, an exceptional commander et cetera. Eric was aware. "I am merely doing my job."

"And what exactly is your job, Hauptmann?" Thiele asked.

"To know the men under me, of course," Eric smiled. "That includes you. After all," he said, "we recently had a situation where a high level sergeant thought it was his job to jeopardize our operation."

"Sergeant Erich was an arrogant asshole. A fool, and a traitor," Thiele denounced.

All of that, Eric noted, crossing Thiele off his list as a potential replacement for Erich as his SS stool pigeon. "And you are not Sergeant Erich. Good," Eric nodded "We are in this together, Oberleutnant. I want to make that point perfectly clear."

"We are all in this together," Thiele corrected. "Not only you and me. All of us."

"Oh," Eric said. "Well, I am not a school teacher by trade, Oberleutnant," he smiled. "Any more than I am a truck driver. You will have to excuse me."

"Yes," Thiele could tell. "What are you?"

"A car salesman," Eric grinned. "Used cars."

"Yes," Thiele considered. "Yes, I can see that."

"Ah!" Eric breathed in the aroma of sulphur and beautiful girls. "Nurse?" he leered at the latter. "Are you the nurse?"

Yes, she was. She was Cäcilie, with a specific assignment. Thiele.

"You are Heinrich Thiele?" Cäcilie smiled pleasantly, bypassing Eric for Thiele. "Dieter has told me about you. I am very pleased to meet you"

"Thank you," Thiele said. "I am pleased to meet you. I need assistance with my arm."

"So, I see. Let's have a look."

"Shrapnel," Thiele said when her smile paused after cutting away his bandage, unsure whom he was protecting, the Hauptmann, or this girl. She was very beautiful, and very German, and Thiele was very surprised.

"Yes," she brightened. "Shrapnel."

"You are Cäcilie, then?" he verified.

"Yes," she smiled. "And is Cäcilie," she wondered, perhaps a little clever herself, "really that much of a surprise to you, Oberleutnant?"

"You are very beautiful," Thiele said in explanation. She was not his to hurt.

"And you are a gentleman," she graciously accepted the lie.

And the Hauptmann was a fool.

Chapter Seventy-Three

Joanna heard the gun shots the Captain had mentioned she would. The loud noise did not penetrate really though as she sat there quietly waiting for whatever was to happen. At nine-twenty by the clock hanging on the side of the tent, a different soldier opened the door and the one who had watched her led her out in response.

Joanna could see a group of men and vehicles at one end of the camp. The Captain among them, he never moved or looked in her direction.

When Joanna looked away, there was the large man with the long orange curls from the night before, his hands tied like hers. Smiling in his smiling voice when he said, "Hello, little lady. Now, don't you worry, little lady, don't you fret," before the soldiers with him pushed him on a few steps ahead.

There was another tall man. A soldier in chains with a distorted face. "Oh, my," Joanna stepped back from him because he seemed to be looking at her and he did not look very nice. She did not have much time to think about it though, because they all moved on, led by a group of soldiers, one of them the man with glasses who had been talking to the Captain last night.

Joanna's heart did not really start to pound until they picked her up and put her in the truck, the drapes pulled closed by a fat, ugly man, shutting out the light. That she did not like. It was terrifying and her stomach went cold and nauseous. A soldier with a gun inside the truck took her by the arm, moved her away from the drapes, and sat her down on the wooden floor.

The big man with the long orange hair was also in there. Joanna noticed his eyes, and they were green and very bright, seeming to shine in the darkness as they looked at her, and they did not look friendly. That was fine because Joanna did not like him either.

The soldier in the chains was not in the truck and Joanna eventually forgot about him as the truck started to move with a bang. She set her jaw and stared into her dim surroundings. Her eyes growing accustomed to the limited light, she could see it looked like the truck she had been in with Pierre. Moved like the truck she had been in with Pierre.

Oh, God! Joanna caught her breath because there was no Pierre sitting there with his bowl of black mush.

"You all right there, little lady?" the man with the green eyes asked.

Joanna did not answer him. Of course, she was all right. For an hour, if not more, as the truck moved along, Joanna could hear the Captain's voice asking her to trust him, telling her everything would be all right. It did not seem all right, and as the time grew longer, the Captain's voice seemed to fade. Joanna practiced trying to say the words to herself, but even that seemed ridiculous after a while. Everything was not all right. It had never been all right. Not in the beginning, and not at the end.

"Oh, God!" Joanna could not catch her breath that time and a sob slipped out, and she heard the man with the green eye say, "Here, now, little lady," a pasty smile on his face when Joanna looked at him.

"Sure you're all right there, little lady?" Nellie inquired with only half the heart he had last night because there was something about the little lady that did not seem quite right. Nellie did not know what it was. Did not have the faintest idea. It was just something about the little lady that seemed to want to confuse him, and Nellie would be damned if he knew what.

"So, here, now, little lady," Nellie started to remind her not to fret, when one of the wheels must have hit a rock, because a pebble hit the drapes with a dull slap.

"Spooked you, didn't it?" Nellie chuckled as Joanna jumped, and the soldier leapt to his feet. "Spooked you. It did."

It had. But not as much as the next one that hit and rolled inside.

"Now, easy, boy," Nellie said slowly to the soldier standing there wary and alert, the boy's eyes moving from the pebble to the drapes.

"Easy," Nellie purred, his eyes finely tuned, focused on watching the boy's grip on his gun as he moved a few steps away from them to study the curtain, looking like he might want to take a cautious look outside.

"Now, little lady," Nellie started to say softly in a whisper to Joanna.

"Shut up!" the soldier turned his gun on Nellie, ordering in his language Nellie did not understand, but got the boy's message just fine, and ignored it just the same.

"Don't you move, little lady," Nellie cautioned Joanna, under his breath.

"I said, shut up!" the soldier insisted, still trying to decide what to do about the drape.

"Don't scare that boy, don't do that," Nellie finished what he had to say, whether that boy would ever make up his mind or not, which Nellie knew he would. And when he did, when the boy was foolish enough to take those last few steps, part the drape, and poke his head outside, rope or no rope lashing his hands behind his back, Nellie was going to make that boy sorry he ever thought to point his gun.

The soldier decided, ready when the third pebble hit the truck, and the poor stupid Arab swinging through the drape got the bayonet right in his belly before Nellie had time to push his body to his feet. There was a second Arab right behind him though, and it was the soldier going down.

"Turn around!" the Arab instructed in a guttural and foreign voice muffled by the yard of fabric wrapped around his face. "Turn!" he insisted as Nellie hesitated and Joanna was frozen where she stood.

"Sergent!" the Arab yanked his scarf free and Nellie could see it was the Jacques one. Nellie spun around, the ropes around his wrist, slashed loose by two whacks from Jacques's knife, and Nellie had Joanna and the dead boy's gun, while Jacques grabbed the other one, the three of them on their way through the drapes of the truck already slowing down.

"Down, little lady!" Nellie flung Joanna to her knees, using his gun like a bat to slam the bastard trying to climb out of the cab.

They never had a chance. Eleven soldiers against an army of ants who came up from the ground, from nowhere on horses, in jeeps, and on foot.

"Oh, God!" Joanna watched as the soldiers dropped in front of her, one by one, SS Leutnant Faust tumbling from the staff car, blood gushing from a bullet hole in his throat.

"Oh, my God!" Joanna screamed, struggling to get to her feet, up off her knees, because no one had stopped to cut her ropes. No one had stopped to set her free—

"Oh, no!" Joanna gasped as she saw the large soldier with the horribly distorted face no more than six feet away from her, no longer bound by chains.

"No," Joanna shook her head because he seemed to be focused straight on her with his face and his eyes she could not begin to describe and he had a gun.

"No!" Joanna said. "No!" she screamed as she stood there and the man suddenly pitched forward, face down in the sand, a knife sticking out of his back.

The Arab who threw it was six feet away from him, paused for a moment standing there, but then he jumped, two jumps and he was on top of the soldier, pulling the knife out from between his shoulder blades.

No! Joanna had no more voice to beg him to stop as she watched him wipe the blade and start to come towards her.

No! She had no legs to run and only stumbled when she tried to back away.

"No!" Joanna cried when he caught her by the shoulder and she was being forced face down back on the ground, listening to him exclaim in her ear, "Mademoiselle, it is I. It is me. It is Pierre!"

Joanna choked in the sand suffocating her, feeling the ropes cut away from her wrists, and something being pushed into her hands. It was her dog tags.

"Oh, no," Joanna whispered, staring from them to Pierre helping her to her feet, his face hidden under his funny hood, but she knew he was smiling.

"No," Joanna shook her head, the chain slipping from her hand, dropping into the sand. There was only one tag. One was missing. The Captain's brilliant gold cross strung in its place.

"Oui," Pierre rescued the chain for her as Joanna gasped and bent to pick it up. "From mon capitaine with kind regards," Pierre pressed it back into her hands, grabbed her chin, planting a quick kiss on her cheek. "God go with you, Mademoiselle. You are free!"

"What?" Joanna stared at him. What did he mean she was free? She had never been a prisoner, isn't that what he had always said to her?

"Free?" Joanna whispered, her lips starting to tremble, her hands starting to shake, suddenly seeing Adva and Anne and the others.

"Free?" Joanna said, watching the Captain toss his head back, his hands running through his wet blond hair as she stared at the gold cross dangling from around his neck and she heard the Captain say, "*You are not going to die, Johanna. Trust me.*"

"Wait!" Joanna called after Pierre.

"*Oh, but we have many teas here, Mademoiselle*!" she heard his voice interrupting the Captain's. "*India. Russia. Even your England. Mon capitaine does love tea*!"

"Wait!" Joanna shouted after Pierre.

"*Many coffees here, Mademoiselle,*" Pierre continued with his babble, ignoring her plea for water. "*France. Jamaica. Afrika. Mon capitaine loves coffee, even better than tea, I think.*"

"Oh, but, wait!" Joanna cried, but she was too late. Pierre was gone, and tears ran, running down her cheeks like the day the water was poured over her head.

"Oh, please, wait," Joanna stood there sobbing. "Please, please wait. Wait!" she screamed. "Don't go!"

"It is all right, Mademoiselle!" an anxious voice interrupted behind her, and Joanna jumped, quickly wrapping the chain tightly into her fist so she wouldn't lose it again. It wasn't Pierre, but he was French, and there were others all around her.

"Who?" Joanna gasped. "Who are you?"

Jacques smiled at the young woman terrified and confused. "I am Jacques Renault," he introduced himself. "I was once a lieutenant in the French army. Now I am a lieutenant in the army of the Free French. Are you English, Mademoiselle? You sound English."

"What?" the young woman stared at him. "What?"

"This man is Irish," Jacques nodded at the sergent Reynolds standing there and looking rather well except for a bruised face. "His

English is better than mine. He can tell you how we were with him before he was taken by the Germans."

"The Germans?" the young woman was looking again, wildly around, and Jacques stopped her.

"No, it is all right, Mademoiselle, there are no Germans. You do not have to look anywhere except at me. It is over. We are here to help you. Sergent Reynolds saw the Arabs bring you into the camp."

"Camp?" Joanna whispered. "The hospital?"

Jacques smiled. "Oui, Mademoiselle, the hospital."

"Oh," Joanna said. "Are you taking me back to the hospital?"

"No, Mademoiselle," he assured. "But we can, if you like, try to assist you in taking you home."

"Home?" Joanna whispered.

"Oui. Do you live here in Libya?"

"What?" Joanna said.

"I will take that as a no," Jacques agreed. "It is all right. We will continue, Mademoiselle, but now, I must tell you how we have to leave."

"You're leaving me?" Joanna gasped.

"No, no, of course not," Jacques reassured. "But, yes, we must leave this area to somewhere more safe. It will not be very far. Only a few hours by the jeeps. We will talk as we go and we will see how we can help you. Would you like to do that?"

"Oh," Joanna said. "That man, too?"

She stared at the Sergeant Reynolds and she did not look too pleased. Jacques could not fault her, assuming it was his size and appearance, which was freakish, yes. Something out of a circus.

"Sergent Reynolds?" he said. "Yes. But in a different jeep. Do not be alarmed. So may we go now? Come," he encouraged when she hesitated. "We will go now."

"Pick her up and carry her, boy," Nellie rose from his perch against the staff car, cleaning his fingernails with one of the Arabs' knives as he waited, watching, taking it all in.

"Ignore him," Jacques advised Joanna. "Come. Look at me. Talk to me. Let's talk more about how we may be able to help you ..."

But Joanna couldn't. She couldn't, not even move. She knew what the man was going to do by the way he was holding the knife.

By the way he kept looking at the men lying on the ground. She knew, even if they did not, and she waited for him to do it, and she was right, because he did, not one of them able to move fast enough to stop him. Nellie bent down, grabbed the hair of the man lying face down on the ground, and off came the head of SS Leutnant Günther Faust. Impaling it on the bayonet of a rifle, Nellie jammed the butt inside the steering wheel to hold it straight.

"Mon Dieu!" Lieutenant Jacques Renault gasped as a thousand hands surrounded Joanna pulling her away, but she had already shut her eyes.

"Sergent!" Jacques was upon Nellie in horror. "She is a woman! What the hell is the matter with you?"

"Aw, he can't hurt her," Nellie dusted his hands off, quite unperturbed, wiped the blade of the knife off on his pants, debating about keeping it as a souvenir. "Little lady should know by now ain't nobody here going to hurt her."

Free? Joanna Lee was numb.

"My son!" Pierre clasped Jean Paul's hand. "Thank you. He will repay you. So many times, I swear!"

"Ten times?" Jean Paul said. "I believe this is what you say?"

"Not I," Pierre shook his head. "No, not I. But, yes, it is true. At least ten times, you will see."

Jean Paul nodded, and like most things, he would believe it when he saw it.

"Mon caporal?" his Lieutenant Pierre Forget walked up.

"I have to go," Jean Paul smiled at his father. "Be there to hear the unexpected news with the rest of them."

"Until next time," Pierre agreed.

Next time. Jean Paul studied the wrinkled old man with the robes blowing gently around him. "I could be you," he admitted, thinking of his own. "In these, I am the image of you. Is that what you see?"

"Perhaps," Pierre smiled. "But in the image of yourself. You are too dark to be me. Like your mother, so dark."

"Yes," Jean Paul agreed with a grin at John Haas pulling at his robes. "Are you all right?"

"Hot as hell," John assured. "But I'll get used to it. I wanted to say to you before you left, I'm glad I lost the coin toss to be the first one in the truck, but I am very sorry for ... Roget, was it?"

"Roget, yes, Forget reported to me," Jean Paul said. "Thank you."

"It's OK," John said. "Thank you. Heck of a rollercoaster ride, but anytime. I'm serious ... and, as far as you," he said to Pierre. "Ready to go there, Holy Man? Your stallion awaits. We've got a hot date to keep ourselves before le capitaine becomes impatient and burns down the place himself, leaving us in his dust."

"Mon capitaine will not leave us," Pierre assured, "unless he wants to walk to his trucks. I hid his horse."

"Oh, yeah?" John said as he and Abe gave the old guy a boost up into the saddle. "Where?"

"Right here," Pierre laughed with a pat of the Arabian beauty. "He is nice, isn't he? He is very nice."

"Are you satisfied, mon caporal?" Forget asked as Jean Paul watched his father ride away with his band of Arab bandits every one of them a Jew.

"As far as the rescue of the girl?" Jean Paul said. "Oh, yes. Very. As far as the SS? Reasonably. We did not get them all, but then we never do," he smiled at Forget.

"And with the Major Charles?" Pierre asked.

"Justin?" Jean Paul said. "I don't know. We will have to see. I am optimistic. Even though I know Justin will find fault with something. Something that does not set right with him. But then I have begun thinking perhaps nothing ever does. That is the nature of his life."

"But there is nothing here for him not to like."

"That is I think our saving grace," Jean Paul agreed. "There is nothing here for Justin not to like."

Epilogue

Algeria
April 5

"Any of you boys know Johnnie?" Nellie wondered while they waited for the little lady to stop vomiting up her guts.

"I presume you mean Jean, sergent?" Jacques replied. "Take your pick. There are probably a few Jeans here."

"That so?" Nellie looked over the group, noticing a few familiar faces other than the Jacques one who had been with him, but none was the Jean he wanted. "Not there."

Jacques shrugged. "Sorry to disappoint you."

Nellie wasn't disappointed. He was thinking. "That wasn't any hospital, boy."

"Yes," Jacques said, "it was. I agreed to investigate, not to attack them, sergent. That young woman could have been killed, never mind how many others who probably were."

"Don't care about Jerry, boy," Nellie assured. "Surprised you do."

"I am talking about the patients!" Jacques snapped. "We do not attack and kill hospital patients!"

"Nellie didn't see any patients."

The dim-witted English remained difficult to persuade. "Oh?" Jacques indicated the young woman with her raggedy red hair and wounded head. "What the hell do you call that? She looks like a hospital patient to me."

"Stop chattering, boy." Nellie was starting to lose his patience. "Nellie wants that radio of yours so he can file a report with Charlie about that depot before it leaves."

"Hospital, sergent," Jacques nodded, "hospital. It was a hospital, not a munitions depot. We are almost to Claude's safe area, I am told, where there is a radio, I am confident, most definitely. Believe me, if we had a radio here, with us, we would gladly give it to you. But we don't. The one we had, what's left of it, is back there – at the hospital!" he stressed. "Now, if you will excuse me ..." He walked away to assist the young woman who appeared ready to try riding in the jeep again.

"I'm sorry," Joanna apologized after she finished trying to cover her tracks in the sand like an embarrassed cat.

"It is all right," Jacques smiled at her. "If you need to stop again, tell me."

Joanna nodded. He helped her wrap her scarf around her face and neck, and put her hat back on her head. Joanna climbed into the jeep and they started moving again in a rolling, bumping, bounce, the sun filling the sky, beating down.

"Mademoiselle?" Jacques asked, concerned.

"I'm fine," Joanna lied. "It's just...I'm hot. I'm so hot..." she tried breathing slowly, deeply to keep the vomit quiet. "Are we really almost there?"

"Soon," Jacques promised. "We are in Algeria. Have been for a while."

Algeria? Pierre had talked about Algeria as if it was a different place. Joanna looked around, but there was only sand, nothing but sand everywhere. She couldn't see past the sand. "It looks the same."

"The same, Mademoiselle?"

Yes. The same as where she had been. Just larger. The walls of sand closer, great mounds sweeping up and all around her. No tents. None of the Captain's men...and no Pierre telling her she must climb up and get on the camel even if she didn't want to do it.

Joanna breathed. If she could think beyond her roiling stomach, she would probably be horribly frightened. She couldn't think. The sun was too bright and she was so hot. "Yes, the same. Everything looks the same to me."

Jacques laughed. "Yes, it does. But don't worry. We know where we are. Are you ready to tell me your name now?"

"I'm thinking," Joanna nodded. "I'm trying to think."

Joanna was still thinking when they brought her into a village not at all like the Captain's. It was very small. A few mud buildings, all of them empty. They continued to be very nice, gave her some water out of a cup and Joanna was finally sitting in a chair that wasn't moving, inside a room where the sun wasn't so bright.

"Better?"

Jacques stayed with her. The nasty big man with the bright green eyes was also still there. Standing in the corner, slouched against the wall.

"He is leaving soon, Mademoiselle," Jacques assured. "He needs to use the radio...you see the radio?"

He pointed over at the table where another man sat doing something with a radio. There wasn't anyone else in there and Joanna suddenly realized there didn't seem to be very many of them at all, to where there had been so many of them before.

"Why, where are the people?" she blinked. "Where did they go?"

"People, Mademoiselle?" Jacques paused. "I do not know. I have never been here before."

"But the ones who were with us..." Joanna started to panic, look wildly around. "I don't understand..."

Jacques reacted quickly, calming her, reassuring her. "Relax, Mademoiselle," he coaxed. "Do not be afraid. I think the people you are talking about were friends. The friends who helped us ..." Jacques fixed a glare on Nellie who he blamed for the deaths of his men, and would always blame him.

"Most of our own people were not available," Jacques explained to Joanna. "So we had to find others to help us, and now they are gone, too. Back to their homes."

"Oh," Joanna sipped the fresh water he poured into her cup. "And he's going too. That horrible man is really going?"

"Oh, yes." Jacques considered what they would do if the sergent Nellie Reynolds did leave them. It would be all right, he decided. Reynolds was still a witness. It would have been his decision to abandon the girl with the French at their safe area. The girl could testify if there were questions. Still, it would be better if the sergent remained there because it gave the Holy Man and his people enough time to get out of the area. Jacques did not trust the sergent would not attempt to go back to the encampment. He was amazed the Germans had not killed him if only because of his size. Why did they keep that man, of all men, alive? Jacques could not answer that, and he did not like it. It made no sense.

"We do not like him either, Mademoiselle," Jacques smiled. "He is very big, and he is not very nice. But you really do not have to be afraid of him. He is the man who wanted to save you. Take you away from the Arabs."

"Arabs?" Joanna did not know what he meant.

"The men who brought you into the hospital camp?" Jacques reminded. "You do not remember them?"

"Because they weren't Arabs, boy," Nellie assured.

Jacques sighed. "They were Arabs, sergent. The same as it was a hospital camp."

"No, it wasn't," Nellie maintained.

"Yes," Jacques assured, "it was. But, it does not matter, because we are not going to talk about any of that, are we?"

His smile returned to Joanna. "No. Mademoiselle is only going to talk and think about nice things. Her family, her friends ... Do you want to tell me anything about your friends now, Mademoiselle? Perhaps we can use the radio after the sergent and try to reach someone who may be able to help you?"

"And that boy of yours better hurry up with that radio, too," Nellie nodded.

"Sergent ..." Jacques said.

"Shut up, boy," Nellie advised. "Nellie knows how long it takes and how long it does not. And, as far as you, little lady," he told Joanna. "You tell that Jacques one what he needs to know. You should know by now ol' Nellie isn't going to hurt you. No reason for you to be afraid."

"Ignore him, Mademoiselle," Jacques shook his head at Joanna. "If you want to tell me anything, it is up to you."

"To help me," Joanna said.

"To certainly try," Jacques swore.

Joanna nodded, thinking about the Captain, and what he had said about trusting him. About the Captain's chain Pierre had given her, and she had wrapped up tightly in her trouser pocket. "Joanna," she said. "My name is Joanna Lee."

Finally. Jacques hung his head. Despite his apprehension with the Holy Man's elaborate plot to return this young woman to her English, in his own way, a small way, Jacques was intrigued. It might work. This part, anyway. The young woman's unwitting role in her own salvation, it might work. The rest? Convincing the English of some miraculous survival, discovery, and rescue? Who knew. Jacques would never believe it. Why should they? But that was their problem. Jacques proceeded slowly, less to alarm Joanna, but more not to press his luck with the cagey sergent Reynolds.

"Joanna," Jacques repeated. "A very pretty name. It is from the bible."

"Is it?" Joanna said.

"Yes," Jacques nodded. "It means 'God is gracious'." He hoped he remembered correctly. It probably did not matter. She probably did not know. She was young and frightened, almost childlike in her demeanor. He wasn't sure what that meant other than she was understandably overwhelmed, some of the reasons probably to do with her background. Upper English classes. They were always so fragile. "May I write it down, Mademoiselle Lee?"

"Joanna," Joanna requested. "Please call me Joanna. I haven't heard it for so long."

Jacques frowned, curious what she meant. "You have not heard your name?"

"No," Joanna shook her head. "No, I haven't."

"Oh. Well, then of course I will call you Joanna." Jacques wrote it down, waiting, hoping, but there was no particular reaction from the sergent. That figured. When he wanted the sergent's attention, he did not get it. He tried again, showing Joanna what he had written. "Did I spell it right? I tried ... *Joanna*. In English."

"Yes," Joanna beamed, excited. "Yes, that's it!"

"I have something ..." Jacques's man at the radio, announced.

"Sergent," Jacques waved, but Nellie had already tossed away his matchstick and straightened up, aiming for the table, interpreting the nodding head even if he could not understand the fellow's words.

"About time." Nellie snatched the headset from the boy to listen for himself and give his approval. "Aye. Think your boy's got something ... think he does. Tell him to get it in a little clearer and give it a try." He tossed the headset back to the fellow and sat down right there next to him, popping a fresh matchstick in his mouth as he leaned back in his chair waiting.

"And friends, Joanna?" Jacques pursued his agenda. "Are you ready to tell me about a friend? Perhaps give me a name? Someone in your family? Your mother, father ..."

"They're dead," Joanna said.

"I am sorry," Jacques extended kindly. "Very sorry."

"Thank you," Joanna nodded. "But there is Grandfather, what about him? Will he do?"

"Grandfather ... " Jacques wrote down. "That is a good one. We do not like to use names when we try to call over the radio. We try to give them something the person will recognize without telling them your name. Do you understand me?"

"I'm not sure."

"All right, let me see ... " Jacques thought it over. "I am Jacques, my friends call me Jack. What do your friends call you?"

"Red," Joanna said.

"Really?" Jacques frowned. "Why is that? I do not understand."

"Well, because of my hair," Joanna said, not sure what was so confusing. Her hair was red, they called her Red.

"Oh," Jacques said. "Yes, of course. The color."

"Yes," Joanna said. "It's red."

"I understand," Jacques smiled. "All right. Let me see ... " he scribbled a few more things down on his piece of paper, crossing some of them out before he nodded. "Yes. If I said something like, 'Hello Grandfather, from Red'. Do you think that might be something your friends understand?"

"Oh, yes!" Joanna agreed, excited. "Michael will definitely understand that!"

"Michael ..." Jacques wrote it down, too, the sergent sitting up straight in his chair, a coincidence perhaps or perhaps not.

"My friend," Joanna assured. "Michael is my friend!"

"That is good ... " Jacques agreed. "Very good. What do you call your friend *Michael*?" he stressed the name and the sergent's attention wasn't a coincidence. Jacques could feel those cold green eyes on his back. "What is the color of his hair?"

"What?" Joanna said. "Oh. Well, blond. But, no, I call Michael, Michael."

Jacques nodded. "Anyone else? Is there anyone else? A sister perhaps? Brother ... "

Joanna frowned, thinking hard. "Well, there's Justin. But he's not my brother. He's my stepbrother."

"Well, that is like a brother," Jacques agreed. "So, we will write down your stepbrother Justin, too ... all right. Let me make sure I have this right ..." He read aloud, to be sure the sergent behind him heard should he be listening; he was definitely listening. Jacques could feel his tension, not only his eyes. He could hear him breathe. "There is your stepbrother Justin, Michael who is your friend, and then there is Grandfather. Do I have all of them right?"

"Yes," Joanna nodded. "Yes, you do!"

"Very good." Jacques waited for something more from the sergent Reynolds, but nothing seemed to be coming.

But that was because Nellie was listening, not because he wasn't. He heard the name *Michael* and it caught his attention away from the boy at the radio. The Jerry Captain had called Nellie *Michael* out there in that hospital of his, and Nellie knew a *Michael* he did at that. He did not like him, but knew him just the same.

But then the little lady said something about a fellow named *Justin* and that had Nellie a little confused. He knew a Justin. He did not call him that, but he knew him, too.

"And their other names ..." the Jacques one was asking, pencil in his hand.

"Other names?" the little lady said.

"Like Lee ... " the Jacques one asked with his smile. "Is your stepbrother Justin Lee?"

"Oh," the little lady said. "No, Charles. My stepbrother is Justin Charles."

And Nellie almost killed the French boy sitting at the radio, and it would have been an accident. He grabbed the headset so fast the fellow fell right out of his chair.

"What the hell!" the Jacques one reacted, as of course the rest of them did, suddenly appearing and rushing in from outside. Nellie never met so many people who jumped at the slightest noise.

"Sergent!" Jacques insisted.

"Shut up, boy," Nellie said, "and get that information from the little lady," sitting there staring at Nellie as she was. He leaned forward with his massive face and cold green eyes. "And you tell that boy, little lady," he told Joanna. "You tell that Jacques one exactly what he wants to know, and you do it now ..."

And as far as the fellow sitting there on the ground, Nellie should not have to tell him what to do, but apparently, he did.

"Get up in your seat and get that signal in clear now, boy," Nellie directed, leaving the Jacques one to explain it to him, while he looked back at the little lady still staring at him. "You Charlie's little sister?" Nellie asked her. "Nellie wants to know. Are you Charlie's little sister, little lady? The one who was lost in the car?"

She didn't answer him, but it didn't matter what she did. That was Charlie's little sister sitting right there. Nellie knew it, he did.

"Charlie ..." the Jacques one was looking at his paper. "Do they call your brother Charlie, Joanna?"

"What?" Joanna said.

"Do you know what the sergent is talking about?" Jacques asked her. "Were you lost in the desert in a car?"

"A car?" Joanna repeated. "Well, yes, I was in a car ..."

"That's her," Nellie nodded. "It is. Aye." He didn't care if the Jacques one was unsure, he was positive. "What you call your brother, little lady?" he asked her, his head tipped, and thick lips spread in a sickening smile. "Called him Justin. Do you call him anything else?"

"Do you?" Jacques asked when Joanna stared at him. "Joanna, try to think, try to relax. This is important, very important, if the sergent is right ..."

"Oh, but he can't ..." Joanna shook her head. "That man can't be from Michael ..." Or even Justin, she knew that. She did. "Why, he tried ... he tried ..." Joanna closed her eyes and felt herself sway, watching the horrible man try to kill the Captain with his knife ...

"Mademoiselle!"

Jacques caught her before she fell off the chair, and he really sounded so much like Pierre. Everyone in there sounded so much like Pierre. "Justin ..." Joanna nodded. "I call my brother Justin ..."

"And your friend Michael?" Nellie crooned. "You talking about the Doc Michael, little lady? The fellow with the eyeglasses and the suit?"

"What?" Joanna whispered.

"That's him," Nellie nodded at the Jacques one. "Aye, it is."

"Is it?" Jacques asked Joanna. "Is your friend Michael a doctor?"

"And your brother?" Nellie smiled. "Do they call your brother, little lady, Squadron Leader Justin Charles?"

And Joanna passed out.

"Start with Grandfather," Jacques instructed Nellie.

"Nellie knows what to do," Nellie assured. "You just take care of the little lady and make sure nothing else happens to her. Because it better not."

"It hasn't so far has it?" Jacques thought he'd remind who was interested in the young woman's comfort and safety right from the start, and it was not Nellie.

"It hasn't?" Nellie said. "You looking at the same little lady Nellie is? The one you were calling a patient?"

"She is obviously a patient," Jacques assured.

"Aye, and she'll be dead before Nellie starts out, so it looks like Charlie's going to have to come to him."

"It is the heat, sergent," Jacques assured. "The young woman is overwhelmed."

"Don't care what it is," Nellie said. "You take care of her."

And Nellie sat there watching him, keeping an eye on her while the fellow played with his radio to get the signal in clear. And Nellie was thinking about things, from before he got to the hospital with the French fellows, and after he was there.

Now I ask you, little lady, I ask you, Nellie didn't ask anyone but himself, *why is it Nellie keeps thinking about his face and how he handed you a gun?*

Why is it, Nellie keeps thinking about that Jerry Captain calling ol' Nellie 'Michael' out there in the middle of that hospital of his? Can you answer me that?

Charlie was not going to like this. No, Charlie was not. Charlie was going to think like Nellie did, it was all just a little too pat.

Atlas Mountains, Algeria
April 5
There was nothing unusual or different about the night Joe got the call. At first, he did not pay much attention to it. They were still at Frank's safe house. Hank back with them, sitting there playing solitaire, Frank back up somewhere in the sky.

The Doc stretched out on the porch, Pete bounced his ball on the wall up over the Doc's head, Fred out taking evening first watch.

"Going to have to kill something soon," Pete mentioned earlier, licking his lips at the Doc who came back with his usual about Pete's juices being stopped up. Joe got mad, thinking the Doc was making a crack about Julia who did not return from Cairo but stayed there with the Maj giving Bobby and him a hand with whatever was going on with Jeff.

Hank ignored them and Fred continued walking around like the cat who'd swallowed the canary approaching his thirty-day anniversary with the girl everyone wanted and occasionally had, but not when she was married. No, Jewels was a saint when she was married. Might still swish, might still tease, invoke a few memories but it did not go any farther than that.

"I'm not doing Jack-shit today," the Doc announced around ten o'clock, about an hour after everyone calmed down from their fight.

"Damn ten o'clock at night, Doc," Pete banged the ball on the wall up over the Doc's head. "Think everybody's figured that out by now."

Pete walked away after he said that because he wasn't in the mood to start something up again, wandering over to Joe playing with his radio on the steps of the porch.

"Reception any better?" Pete asked interested or not.

"Yeah, actually. Right here's pretty good. Surprised I didn't think of it before."

"Aye, well, it would have come to you," Pete said, "like it did now. No ... eventually, lad ..." he tossed his ball in the air, "it would have come to you after you wore out everyplace else."

"I haven't worn it out," Joe assured. "And don't call me lad."

"Said lad, not boy. What's that, a new rule?"

"And don't hit me in the head with the ball," Joe reminded.

"Aye, well, now you are getting carried away, Joseph. Peter's got to have something to do."

"Yeah, well, here," Joe handed him his stack of notes he made of what was going on out there. "Knock your socks off."

"Not wearing any," Pete took them. "This it? Quiet night."

"So far, yeah," Joe agreed.

"Too quiet," Pete flipped through them. "Time to make some noise ... see Jean Paul's still keying you, trying to see if you're around."

"Oh, yeah, like clockwork," Joe assured.

"Aye, well, could have been to Gibraltar and back by now, if we were to have gone," Pete supposed. "Want to go to Gibraltar, Doc?" he asked. "It will give us something to do."

"Tomorrow," Michael answered.

"Oh, right, sorry, forgot," Pete said. "You're not doing anything today ..." he chuckled at the note he had in his hand. "What the devil is this?"

"Um ...." Joe said. "Well, let me see it. The Armistice?"

"That was last week," Pete nodded. "You're starting to become redundant. No, this one ..." he held it out, "Your secret love letter to me. Stumped me on this one, have to give you that."

"Um ..." Joe took it. "No, that's legitimate."

"Oh?" Pete took it back. "Is that so. Anything else to it?"

"No," Joe said. "That's all I got."

"How many times?"

"Um ..." Joe said. "I don't know. It's on there, isn't it? Maybe a couple?"

"I see it," Pete nodded. "Have to work on your writing, Joseph. Peter's not ready for glasses ... unlike some other folks I know."

"Yeah, well, I'm not ready to jack off in a sock yet," Michael said, "so we're even."

Pete laughed. Not long, but he did, with a shake of his head at Joe. "That man is insane. Yes, he is."

"Yeah, he's a pistol," Joe grinned. "He's OK."

"To each his own," Pete handed him back his notes. "All right. That's someone keying someone for sure. Keep an ear out. Haven't heard that one before."

"Uh, duh ...." Joe said. "What does this look like?"

"You know what I mean." Pete hit him in the head with the ball, catching it as it bounced off before Joe could knock it away. "Anybody here a grandfather?" he asked not serious about it as he walked back to bounce his ball above the Doc's head. "Joseph's got a message for you if you are. 'Message to Grandfather'," Pete banged the ball on the wall. "'with love Red'."

Michael did not know what he did, other than he was lying there one moment, and the next he was up on his feet. "Fuck!" Michael jumped up with a bark, blind until he got to Joe at the radio not twenty feet away.

"Whoa, whoa, whoa!" Joe yelled, Pete in there somewhere, too. Even Hank stopped playing solitaire.

"That's her!" Michael hollered, riffling through the goddamn notes Michael could write better with his foot, finding the one he wanted, and wrenching the headset off from around Joe's neck.

"Do not touch the radio!" that was definitely Pete.

"Fuck you—get it back!" Michael barked at Joe. "Get it back! That's the kid. That's Red!" He felt himself swoon, and he did not have the time. He yanked off his hat, fanning himself, wiping the sweat from his forehead.

'Think he's serious," Joe said to Pete.

"Aye." Pete caught the Doc by the arm before he fell over, even though Pete was pretty sure the Doc would not.

Michael wrenched his arm free, standing there heaving and breathing like a bull. "That's the kid," Michael pointed at the radio. "That's my kid. Get back on that goddamn radio and get her back."

"Wait a minute," Pete stopped Joe before Joe did anything. "What kid, Doc?"

"What do you mean, what kid?" Michael snarled. "My kid. Joanna. Fucking Chuck's sister!" he barked.

"I've got it," Pete assured. "That's not possible, Doc."

"What do you fucking mean it's not possible?" Michael said. "That's her!"

"About her, maybe," Pete accepted. "Could be definitely about her, and it is no doubt a lure for you. Joseph is checking ..." he gave a nod at Joe who clapped his headset on his ears with his usual "Right!" as he set to working his magic regardless of who else was trying to spin a little web of intrigue out there.

"He is checking, Doc," Pete assured, "keying them back."

"Key this!" Michael said, "that's my kid!"

"And Joseph will find them," Pete assured. "How did this come in, Joseph? Voice?"

"Um ..." Joe said. "No. Code. Old code. Ours."

"Aye, well, Frank just brought us back the new one."

"Yeah, that's what I'm saying. It was old."

"Aye, well, that's a bit unusual. Get something like it again, let me know right away."

"Yeah, OK, OK," Joe said, trying to listen to him, the Doc, the radio, and type at the same time. "Could be a thousand miles away, Doc. OK? A thousand—Whoa!" he said as the static suddenly cleared and Pete stared at him, the Doc diving for the radio again yelling how it was her.

Pete snapping back to attention and grabbed Michael for keeps. With the help of Hank, the Doc was in his bracelets hugging the porch rail where he could yell all he wanted to without causing harm.

"All right," Pete said to Joe scribbling down the information he was given by whoever answered his callback ten seconds after he placed it. "What do you have—and don't tell me it's the girl, Joseph," he warned, "because that is bullshit."

"Um ..." Joe said. "OK. That was Jean Paul."

"Jean Paul?" Pete said. "You don't say."

"Yeah," Joe said. "Put that frigging antenna of his up finally, I guess, so the static's clear. And, yeah ..." he said, trying to be careful in how he said it so the Doc didn't die right there. "Yeah, they've got somebody who they think might be the girl. You know, the Maj's sister."

Pete just looked at him.

"Think," Joe repeated. "You know. *Think* might be the girl."

"I got it," Pete assured. "All right," he said, thinking himself. "Identify. Got it? Identify. I don't want anything else."

"Got it!" Joe got to it.

"Good," Pete lit a cigarette and nodded at Michael. "You're right here, Doc, don't worry, nobody's leaving you out. Joseph will tell us everything they say, and you will be able to tell us if it is true, or it is false. Understand?"

"Fuck you!"

"He understands," Pete assured Joe. "Anything yet?"

"Not yet," Joe shook his head.

"You did the one word, right?"

"Oh, yeah," Joe said, "Oh, yeah." And a minute or two later, he had Jean Paul again.

"OK," Joe reported as he worked on the code. "Wow. It's Nel who's got her," he looked at Pete.

"That's interesting," Pete agreed. "Anything else? That's not an identification, lad. We know who Nel is."

"I'm working on it. He's got like six different versions of the code here."

"Well, for something like he would. Trying to be careful himself with who he's talking to. Someone find that girl alive ... that's unusual," Pete kept it as neutral as possible for the Doc.

"Oh, yeah," Joe said. "To say the least. He didn't find her at the local bar that's for sure," he grinned at the Doc before he made his day. "JL, Doc. Are those her initials?"

"No, they're mine," Michael said, calmer for some reason, not so anxious to reach into the radio and pull her out through the wires. "And about as fucking good as them. They'd have all this shit if they tortured her. That could be anybody there with 'Nel'!"

"Now, you're catching on," Pete agreed. "Looking for something wrong, Doc, same as we're looking for what's right. Nobody's going to be perfect."

"Except me," Michael assured. "You need something she would know, and they would have never thought to ask. Tell her Mikey's got the tickets to Arizona. What's the name of the boat?"

"Um ..." Joe looked at Pete. "What do you think?"

"Just fucking do it!" Michael said.

"It's the name, Doc," Pete shook his head. "Rather not include you in this."

"Screw my name. I know my name, they know my name. Fucking do it, exactly the way I said it!"

"Go ahead," Pete gave the nod to Joe, and Joe sent it out.

"OK, so what are we waiting for Doc?" Joe asked as they waited. "Pearl Harbor? The date?"

"No," Michael said. "We're waiting for the name of the boat. The *Lusitania.* I promised the kid I'd take her to Arizona to see the *Lusitania* when I got back from New York. Trust me, she'll remember. She fucking bugged me about it enough."

"OK ..." Joe said to Pete. "What am I missing?"

"Do not ask me," Pete shook his head with a quizzical look at Hank who shrugged, not having the faintest idea either. "Is that some kind of joke, Doc, between the two of you?" Pete asked.

"No," Michael said. "The kid wants to go to Arizona to see the *Lusitania.* So if it comes back with *Lusitania*—or something equally as nuts," he said, because it was possible she might not remember the name of the boat she wanted to see, "that's my kid," he assured, and he said it rather proudly.

It came back with *Lusitania.* Joe twisted the paper so Pete could see before he said it aloud for the Doc.

"I'll be damned," Pete shook his head. "I will be damned."

"Well?" Michael insisted. "Well?"

"It's your boat, Doc," Joe said, and Michael hung his head for a moment.

"So ... um ..." Joe looked at Pete smoking his cigarette. "You satisfied?"

"Aye," Pete said.

"You sure?" Joe said. "Because ... well, I mean if she wanted to go that bad, and he had promised her, she couldn't have said something like that to them? I mean, I know it's nuts, but it could be a code."

Pete looked at him. "Joseph, you ever hear the expression beating a dead horse?"

"You really think it's her?"

"Aye," Pete knew it was. The same as he knew Nel did. The same as he knew Justin would. "Somebody got too close to something," he assured Joe. "I don't know if it's the Doc. I don't know if it's Justin. I don't know what it is. But somebody got too close to something, and they let the little girl go .... Now, you go," he took the headset from him. "Get everything set, ready to get the devil out of here. I need to get ahold of Justin, make his day, and get some orders ... early as it is," he checked his watch. It was two o'clock in the morning Algerian time. April 6.

Cairo
April 6
Justin worked all sorts of crazy hours so Pete was not concerned. To ensure he could get through, he went for the jugular, Mediterranean straight to Cairo, after they patched him through. That was as much for Bobby as it was for Justin because Pete was not repeating himself, arguing his way through to get to Justin, and he was not playing with code but would risk a little chatter.

It worked for the most part. Bobby answered the behemoth, which meant Julia had broken something and was upstairs playing secretary to work it off, or she was asleep. Bobby fussed a little wanting something for his services, but Pete told him he wanted Justin, and he only had to say it twice.

"What?" Justin answered Bobby's call from downstairs. Julia was there helping with the paperwork, but not because she had broken anything. With Joe not there to keep it reasonably organized, Justin's office was in a particularly unreasonable mess.

"*Got Pete on, Mediterranean,*" Bobby said. "*Said he's not talking to anybody but you and wants me to get upstairs. Wants Julia there, too.*"

"Well, Julia's here," Justin said. "Anything else?"

"*Aye. Said he wouldn't be the man who killed me if I didn't. It would be you.*"

"Yes, well," Justin motioned for Julia to come over, "better put him through in case I would, and get upstairs."

"*On my way.*" Bobby signed off, put Pete through, and headed up having an idea what it might be about, and that would be the Doc.

"*That you?*" Pete's voice came over Justin's phone.

"Yes," Justin said, "and this better not be another fight with the French, because if it is, you can all go to hell."

"*And you better be sitting down,*" Pete said. "*Bobby there yet?*"

"Yes," Justin lied, wanting to hear what he knew he was going to hear about Michael, the same as Pete knew Bobby wasn't there. Justin took his pipe out of his mouth. "Get to the bottom line. When and where did it happen?"

"*Now, don't start guessing,*" Pete said, "*because that is not the way this is going to work. The Doc is fine. It's hot, and so is this radio ... about ready to burn a tube. I'm going to tell you what I have, a few particulars, no specifics. You'll get those later. I'm going to tell you what I think, and then you're going to tell me ... Bobby there yet?*"

"No," Justin said, pencil and paper ready, Julia breathing on his neck, trying to hear, "but Julia is. Go."

"*All right,*" Pete said. "*Nel has your sister. Alive in a remote location. Border, my side, staring at the sand.*"

"Really," Justin said, and Pete let those kinds of comments slide.

"*Some locals with him, had more, but there were problems. Fellows have limited ability only, and the area's very hot.*"

"Yes, well, you can stop right there," Justin said, "how hot?"

"*Simple Simon.*" Pete assured, and Justin wrote *SS* on his paper for Julia but she had heard Pete, and Bobby was coming in the door.

"*JP's working to help,*" Pete advised him about Jean Paul.

"Stop," Justin said. "Who called JP?"

"*Nel.*"

"Got it. Go," Justin nodded.

"*Can get in, but prefer over ground, the same with coming out, at least for a little while to put some distance behind them.*"

"Yes, well, if that's the case," Justin said, "any idea why Nel can't bring her out and meet the plane? Or is that covered under specifics?"

"*In general,*" Pete said, "*I would say it's covered under location, limited ability, area hot, and your sister's alive, status questionable.*"

"Yes, all right," Justin said, "got it. Rescuing distressed damsels is not Nel's forte. Anything else?"

"*Only what I think, and then you.*"

"Go," Justin said.

"*Think it's legitimate, identification is confirmed, but I do not want to walk into a trap. I prefer ground, if practical, given where it is, definitely need some distance between where she is and where we'd like her to be. Think coordinating with Jean is mandatory, and I'd like to take the Doc. Not needing to be said what he would prefer. Your turn.*"

"No, not needing," Justin agreed, "but let's leave that until the end. The Doc is a doctor, if he needs to be, has a degree. Identity confirmed by who and method how?"

"*The Doc,*" Pete said. "*Joey picked up on a key from JP. A good one. Doc knew what it was. 'Message for Grandfather, love Red'.*"

"Yes, the Doc certainly would know, and therefore is a little concerning," Justin agreed. "Meant for the Doc, could have come from her, could not have. Definitely being coached if it's her, and not by Nel. How confirmed?"

"*Message only, She was there. Sent Doc's question, got back right answer. Ready*?"

"Go," Justin said.

"*Question,*" Pete said. "*Mikey has tickets to Arizona. What's the name of the boat*? *Answer,*" Pete said, "*Lusitania.*"

"Yes, well," Justin said, "not sure I want to understand what that's about, but we'll leave it as confirmed. Last question. What's the status of these locals?"

"*Took her and Nel out,*" Pete said.

"Really," Justin said. "Nel was in? Should have started with that. Want specifics immediately. Status Simple Simon involved?"

"*Dead,*" Pete said.

"All right," Justin said, "that's hot. Ready?"

"*Go,*" Pete said.

"Leave for JP's now and contact me when you get there with specifics. The three of us will coordinate. Presume areas to be very hot, and locals know what they're doing. It's reasonable they don't want to move beyond their own safety net. Prepare for distance and ground to be decided. Want confirmation from you it is Nel. Want a voice if possible, whenever I can get it. Nel is not to move or do until I say. Doc's a go, speaks all necessary lingo." Justin paused.

"*Anything else*?" Pete asked.

"Yes," Justin said. "Bring my sister home."

"Got it," Pete said and signed off.

Justin hung up, lit his pipe and got up to eye his wall of maps. Neither Bobby or Julia said anything, but waited for him. Julia was still translating his notes into legible writing that would eventually turn into a report and filed.

"Nel found Joanna," Justin said.

"Aye," Bobby was also writing, taking his own notes.

"Area hot with SS. Currently on the Algerian side ... looking at the sand ..."Justin nodded. "She's in the Erg, crossed over from Gadames region. We'll get specifics in a few hours, but that's it."

"Sounds like Tripoli," Bobby offered.

"Yes," Justin agreed, "it does."

"Anything else?" Bobby said.

"Yes," Justin ripped his maps off the walls. Stood there a few seconds after he did, then lit his pipe and sat back down.

"Nel and Joanna were apparently both in wherever Joanna was and both got out alive."

"Impossible," Bobby said. "Nel in, aye. Can happen to the best. But out alive? Never. They'd have killed him, lad. You know that."

"Yes, well," Justin said, "I know they should have killed him before he got in. It's a set-up. Reeks."

"Got too close to something," Bobby nodded. "Aye, you did. Too close. They didn't have the Doc, so they let her go. You know why, don't you?"

"Yes," Justin assured. "They'll try again. They need to get the two of them together. Her to get to him."

"Pete could be walking into a trap."

"Pete knows that. But it's all right," Justin lit his pipe. "He's taking Jean Paul with him."

"Also heard something about taking the Doc. Sure you want to do that?"

"Yes," Justin said. "The window is small, but we've got one. Something went wrong on Jerry's end. Locals who got them out killed the SS. That's not just hot, that's a wrinkle. Doesn't fit."

"Fits as a wrinkle. What do you want to do?"

"Get Evelyn on the line. About time I asked him if he's any idea where his granddaughter might be."

"New York, course," Bobby scoffed. "With the Doc."

"Yes, well," Justin said, "now she's with me. Mike and Joanna could use a holiday, anyway ... get Evelyn on now."

"On it," Bobby waddled out the door.

Justin waited until Bobby left and even a few more minutes before he said anything to Julia who had started picking up the maps.

"Might want to talk to you later about a few things," he said.

"No, I understand," Julia said. "Pete give you any specifics on her situation?"

"Alive and uncertain," Justin said. "Take it from there."

CPSIA information can be obtained
at www.ICGtesting.com
Printed in the USA
LVHW102052171022
730905LV00013B/488/J